Tallchief and Una Fearghus
(5 children, including Liam)

Liam and Elizabeth Tallchief
(3 children, including Jake)

Jake and LaBelle Tallchief
(2 children, including Matthew)

Matthew and Pauline Tallchief

Duncan	Calum	Birk	Elspeth	Fiona
m.	m.	m.	m.	m.
Sybil White	Talia Petrovna	Lacey MacCandliss	Alek Petrovna	Joel Palladin

Legends of the Tallchiefs

Duncan—The woman who brings the cradle to a man of Fearghus blood will fill it with his babies.

Calum—When a man of Fearghus blood places the ring upon the right woman's finger, he'll capture his true love forever.

Elspeth—When the Marrying Moon is high, a scarred warrior will rise from the mists to claim his lady huntress. He will wrap her in the shawl and carry her to the Bridal Tepee and his heart. Their song will last longer than the stars.

Birk—The maiden who rocks upon the chair and sings a lullaby will claim the man of Fearghus blood who stands closest to her. She will be his heart and he will be her love.

Fiona—To finish the circle, an unlikely love of the battlemaiden will come calling, bearing his angry dragon on one arm and the chest to win her heart. Then the magic circle will be as true as their love.

The Tallchief Saga

And don't forget to look for more exciting stories in Cait London's wonderful Freedom Valley series!

GABRIEL'S GIFT

will be available from Silhouette Desire in April 2001.

CONTENTS

Dear Reader,

Thank you for your wonderful reception of the Tallchiefs, a family who has struggled against fate, stayed united and found happiness. I love combining legends and history and weaving them into contemporary women's fiction. And for this series I created a genealogy chart with ancestral romances. I am humbled by your loving letters and e-mail, and am thrilled by your excited and continuing response to the Tallchiefs.

Enjoy!

Cait London

THE COWBOY AND THE CRADLE

To Isabel, Lucia
and my special editor, Melissa Senate.

*The woman who brings the cradle
to a man of Fearghus blood
will fill it with his babies.*

Prologue

"**W**ipe your nose, Fiona," eighteen-year-old Duncan, the eldest Tallchief, told his ten-year-old sister. October layered fire-colored leaves over the graves of their parents, buried that day on Tallchief Mountain. "Nothing is going to separate us. We'll be just the same, only Mom and Dad won't be here."

Duncan fought the pain inside him. And the guilt. The day their parents were murdered, he'd argued bitterly with his father.

"I'm scared," Fiona stated, clutching Duncan closer, her long legs dangling down him as he held her on his hip. "Why did that bad man have to shoot Mom and Dad?"

Duncan adjusted the blanket around her, the one she had been fighting and crying into during her nightmares. Inexperienced in taking the place of his comforting, calm mother, he'd swept Fiona up in his arms, shielding her from the storm's mist and the night. He'd taken her to his special place overlooking the lake. He'd done his share of crying apart from the rest, not wanting them to see him in pain and fear. Could he hold them together? Could he protect the four younger ones?

Duncan straightened his shoulders. He would do his best and better.

Wyoming's cold autumn winds whipped around Tallchief Mountain, sweeping through Duncan's mourning heart. The wind lashed whitecaps on the small, icy lake. The jutting rocks and lush meadows had reminded their great-great-grandmother, Una Fearghus, of her home in Scotland.

When the convenience-store robbery occurred, two customers had just dropped in. Pauline and Matt Tallchief had decided to bring their hungry brood home a treat: enormous pizzas with every topping possible. They had been traveling, buying a new, long-horned hairy sheep. The Scottish ram was for their small herd; cattle and wild, proud children were the Tallchiefs' main crops.

Now they were gone, and Duncan held his frightened baby sister. Calum, the second eldest at seventeen, swooped out from behind a pine branch and glared at Duncan through the night. "So you've got her. You should have left a note."

Then Birk, the third son, pushed through the bushes, wrapped in his quilt. He glared at Elspeth, who was just behind him. "See? I told you Duncan would take care of her. Stop nagging."

Duncan held Fiona closer; he'd known his brothers would find them. Matthew Tallchief had been a top tracker, equaled by few in his lifetime. His sons and daughters were almost as skilled.

Duncan rocked his sister, needing her against him for comfort as much as she needed him. Calum, Birk and Elspeth moved as one, keeping very close in the storm.

The three brothers had immediately taken to the mountain after the killer; Elspeth had taken care of Fiona. When they returned, three sets of gray, determined eyes had leveled at the sheriff. "Here's your man. No one is separating us," Duncan had stated flatly.

"We're staying together," Calum had added in his too-soft, precise tone.

"On Tallchief Mountain." Birk, usually laughing and boisterous, had nodded curtly. He looked as grim and determined as the other two Tallchiefs.

They had tracked the killer throughout the night, going places the sheriff would not have taken his men until full light. At dawn, while the sheriff's men were still checking their riding gear, the three grim Tallchief sons had ridden into Amen Flats, the killer in tow, made to walk every step. They'd left their boyhoods behind.

When the sheriff had heard the Tallchief clan was on the killer's trail, he'd deliberately dragged his feet. No one could track in the night like the Tallchiefs, and once they set their minds to a task they did it. They were bred from a Sioux chieftain who had once hunted the lawless.

Duncan pushed away his grief. He had a big job in front of him. He had to unite his family so that no one could tear them apart. The Tallchiefs were born to challenges. He turned to his brothers and sisters, raising his right hand. "Hold up your thumbs."

"Aye, sir!" The Tallchiefs immediately obeyed his command, right thumbs shoved skyward.

"See that scar? The tiny one that Mom blistered our backsides for cutting. We've sworn to hold one another safe, and we will. Do you swear it?"

"Aye!" The Tallchief cry carried in the wind, sailing over the rocky mountain and the white crests of the deep waves.

"No one is separating us. We'll live here just as before. Calum?"

"Aye, Duncan the defender." Calum stepped up to Duncan and waited for his orders. As children they'd followed Duncan into scrapes and perilous adventures, shouting the Scottish "Aye!" But this was more than skinny-dipping in the icy lake, or waylaying bullies, or stealing their mother's freshly baked pies cooling on the windowsill, or finding a renegade bear and calling him out. Calum recognized what Duncan meant to do, to reassure his family on scant crumbs.

"Calum the cool." Duncan used their childhood names. Heritage ran deep in the Tallchiefs, their blood a blend of a Scottish bondwoman and the Sioux chieftain who had captured her. "You are now in full charge of accounts and payments. Check with the vet to see if there was anything Dad was planning to do with the cattle that we didn't know about. Check the hay baler and machinery and see what is owed. Do your damnedest."

He shot a look at Elspeth, who was just parting her lips. At fourteen, Elspeth disdained almost everything about her brothers. According to her, they were savages with endlessly empty bellies. She and Calum possessed the calm genes of the Tallchiefs. Elspeth had a quiet strength and nurturing that would be tested. He ached for her and the burden she would carry. "I know. I am disgusting and crude and you love me. I'll watch the swaggering, the bullying and the bad language.... Elspeth the elegant, you list what needs to be done in the house. We're 'reconfiguring' as Calum says. From now on, no one leaves a dirty dish or tosses their clothes everywhere. Clean out the bathroom when you're done, etc., etc. Or Elspeth will have your backside scrubbing floors. Mine, too. Got it?"

"Aye," she said, crossing her arms.

Like Fiona, she wore long, black braids. But for the gray

of her eyes, she could have been an Indian princess. When it came to a good fight, Elspeth would be inventive. "I will and the pigs will be punished. Duncan, I'd love to see you scrub a floor, so watch it."

"You make lists, Elspeth. We'll all help. Birk the rogue?" Duncan looked at the third eldest Tallchief.

"Correction. That's Birk the beloved," he returned, preening a bit in the night and lifting an arm to flex and study. "Girls like me."

"Lacey MacCandliss doesn't. She hates your guts. You're disgusting," Elspeth shot back.

"And me?" Fiona asked Duncan, brushing the tears from her eyes.

The pain in her tone matched the pain he felt, but he would never show it.

"What about me, Duncan? What do I do?"

His eyes softened when he looked at her, this last child of his parents. "Why, Fiona the fiery, you make us happy. You mind your grades and always remember to call me your king."

Duncan touched her nose with his finger, a gesture she knew meant he was very serious.

"No more fights on the school ground for causes that aren't yours. No more pranks. We're walking a tight line, Fiona. Do you understand?"

She nodded sheepishly and fluttered her lashes. "I will be Miss Goody Two-Shoes, my king."

Duncan didn't believe her innocent look, but he knew she'd try. Her siblings hooted, then Fiona threw Duncan a punch of her own. "Will you sleep next to me tonight, Duncan?"

He didn't hesitate. "Aye. I'll always be here when you need me."

"Me, too," Calum stated loudly, straightening.

"Me, three," Birk shouted to the cold October wind.

Elspeth jabbed him lightly in the arm. She cuddled close to Fiona. "Fiona, I'll sleep with you every night," she whispered. "Duncan, are we really safe?"

"We'll put some glue in it, as Dad used to say. We'll make it." He was scrambling now, fighting the realistic fear that the children's agencies would come calling…or perhaps the bank. They'd have a hard fight of it. He reached into the storm and latched on to a bit of glue—a whimsical murmuring of his mother swirled around him. He ached and mourned for a heartbeat, then stepped into the role he must play to keep the family safe. "In Una's journals she mentions her dowry, which was sold to keep Tallchief Mountain. I think…"

He glanced into the shadows, and found his brothers and sisters leaning forward, latching on to what he said. A tall, rawboned clan, they had the same raven hair as their Sioux great-great-grandfather and the steady, gray eyes of their Scottish great-great-grandmother. They were a tough brood, all rugged angles and tempers and stubborn, bred from Wyoming stock. They'd need that steel to get through this one. "I think that each of us should pledge to return Una's dowry to the Tallchief family. We can do it if we try." *Could they keep together? Could they?*

"Aye! To Una's dowry!" the Tallchief siblings yelled, strong together.

Calum, always sensible, quietly asked, "What about college for you, Duncan? You were to start in January. If Dad hadn't had heart trouble, you would have already been gone."

"You'll go, when the time comes. And the rest of you. I'd rather be here with my family, but I'll work on my education. Dad and Mom are going to be proud of each one of us," Duncan said, quieting the fears of the others.

At eighteen, and with the support of good family friends, Duncan just might pull off the difficult task of keeping his family together. "Each of you better bring home A's and mind your P's and Q's, because we'll pay hard if you don't. Now, lift your thumbs and swear that you'll do your best to try…just try."

The Tallchiefs shot their thumbs high into the stormy sky and cried in unison, "Aye! We are the Tallchiefs and we will make it through!"

One

Duncan Tallchief uncoiled his six-foot-four-inch, lean body from the bar at Maddy's Hot Spot. Shielded interest flickered in Birk's and Calum's expressions, as they sat, feet propped up on the tavern's scarred table.

Jack Smith, belligerent and drunk, had just come calling for Duncan...with four of his drinking buddies. With reddened eyes Jack glared at the man keeping him from his battered wife. Jack, a powerful bricklayer, needed his wife at home. He knew how to deal with a complaining, runaway wife. The one man barring him from Wyonna stood with deceptive ease, a tough breed of Wyoming cowboy who drew women's eyes by just walking. The Tallchief men were all like that, Jack thought. But Duncan protected Jack's wife, and the bully's pride had been cut. "I want my wife," Jack demanded again. "It's time she came home."

This time Jack planned to bog her down with brats; then she'd stay put.

Duncan's gray eyes flashed. "Wyonna has finally realized she's not to blame for your hard times. She's made her choice."

Maddy, the bartender, glanced uneasily at his new mirror sprawling behind the bar. A veteran of the tavern business, he knew that a night like this could brew a brawl.

October made the Tallchiefs restless, stirred their emotions. Years ago on this day they had buried their parents and fought the world to stay together. The bartender eyed Jack Smith. The man was a fool to seek out the Tallchiefs on a night like this.

Especially Duncan. Packed with muscle from ranch work, he was heavier and more broadly built than his brothers. While he looked too solid to move quickly, Maddy had seen Duncan easily vault over a rodeo fence to save a little girl. Maddy pushed his cigar to the other side of his mouth, chewing it. Duncan was a hard man who set his own rules.

Liquor and four of his buddies gave Jack Smith the backbone he needed to walk into the tavern, calling out Duncan Tallchief. "You've messed in my life for the last time, Tallchief," Jack sneered as Duncan faced him.

Duncan's careless stance belied the anger Jack had pricked. He slowly drew on the leather working gloves tucked into his belt, pushing aside the need to color Jack's face the way Wyonna's had been, swollen and bruised, three days ago. He'd found her huddled in a battered pickup near his ranch, and now she was safe.

It was then that Duncan had decided what to do with the small house he owned in town. Lucky, an old cowpuncher, had willed his house to Duncan for good use. Women and children needed protection from men like Jack; the house would do nicely.

Duncan's isolated, mountain "castle," the remodeled Tallchief house, wasn't the place for Wyonna; she needed a woman's care and no gossip. Lacey MacCandliss had tucked Wyonna safely under her wing. A sane man would think twice before facing Lacey over an issue of abuse.

"Let it go, Jack. You're drunk."

"I'm in the mood for a good one, Duncan," Birk offered easily.

Calum tipped his chair back against the wall, glanced at the picture of a nearly naked woman above him and braced his beer on his flat stomach. "There's only five of them. Hardly enough to break Duncan's sweat."

"I think Jack and I can settle this without your help," Duncan drawled in a tone more commonly used for discussing the weather.

Maddy glanced uneasily at the brothers, aware of them sizing up Jack and his gang. "Mind the mirror," he muttered, and dialed Elspeth for help.

Duncan shot Maddy a disgusted glance, his hard jaw contracting. The tavern owner kept Elspeth's number near the phone; Duncan recognized Maddy's frown and said, "Elspeth will spoil the fun."

"I'll teach you a lesson, Tallchief. You tell me where my woman is." Jack threw a punch that Duncan easily sidestepped.

Duncan smiled coolly, showing a row of white teeth against dark skin covered with black stubble. The wind whipped through the open door, catching his longish black hair and lifting it away from his face. Whoever had entered the tavern didn't distract Jack from his next punch. It slashed through the air near Duncan's cheek. The five men were upon Duncan like a pack of wolves.

Sybil stood in the shadows near the tavern door. The large, wood-lined room, studded with pictures of cattle drives and nearly naked women, exploded in the sound of grunts, labored breathing and body slams. She breathed quietly, furious with the man who was outnumbered and clearly enjoying the brawl.

Music for a fast-moving two-step slid from the jukebox, background music for primitive male grunts.

Duncan—she recognized the jutting angles of his face and the slashing, black brows—grinned almost boyishly as he ducked a punch. The grin died, replaced by a dark anger, as another punch connected against his flat stomach. He had the ruthless, cold look of Satan about him then, not fitting his code name ''Mother.''

To rescue her daughter she'd need a man who could find his way through cities and mountains alike…a man known to the law as ''Mother.'' She had studied her choices and the best man was Duncan Tallchief. As a top researcher, she was rarely mistaken. ''Mother'' was the operative name for a man skilled at manhunting in the mountains or in the cities, and Duncan was especially gentle and loved by the children he rescued. Now, immersed in a brawl, he looked nothing like the tender, compassionate man in the children's reports.

Sybil closed her eyes as Duncan's tongue flicked out to taste the trickle of blood beside his hard mouth. His torn shirt exposed a hair-flecked, tanned chest, and every ounce of his lean body, which was packed into the standard cowboy outfit, surged with power. His rakish grin, showing a lurking dimple, could disarm a woman. He was a tough man, bred of the Wyoming elements, and just what she needed…when he wasn't having a good time brawling. He was massive and smart. She deplored the knowledge that this was the man who could rescue her child.

A chair skidded across the floor to her. She glanced at the men leisurely observing and commenting on the technical aspects of the fight. She recognized them from her research photographs. Duncan's brothers had the same sleek, black hair inherited from their Native American ancestor and gray eyes from their great-great-grandmother. The three of them could power-devastate most women. Sybil wasn't most women. She was clinical and cool and had hardened her heart against love. She glanced at the men lounging at the table. There was Birk, a race-car driver, rodeo star and builder. Calum, a professional hit man for businesses with problems, had the only neatly trimmed haircut. Fiona and Elspeth, the Tallchief sisters, weren't in sight.

In the pictures of the three brothers, Duncan had appeared the hardest, his expression like a closed door. The eldest brother and the major owner and manager of Tallchief Cattle Ranch should have been wearing spurs on his boots and low-slung Colt pistols on his hips. The younger brothers sheltered that dark and dangerous look, but Duncan wore it like a cloak.

A patrol car slid by the window and a search beam shot into the melee, outlining Duncan's head above the others. The stark, primitive power in a brawling male horrified Sybil. Maddy waved the car away and caught a liquor bottle on its way to his mirror.

Oh, fine. Here she was in Amen Flats, no more than a wide spot in the road, faced with settling a fight Tallchief clearly enjoyed. Sybil straightened her shoulders. She couldn't let Duncan Tallchief be beaten to a pulp; she didn't have the time for him to recover from broken bones.

Sybil stepped over one chair and another, making her way to the brothers. "Hello."

Two sets of masculine, gray eyes drifted over her expensive sweater and slacks. The Tallchiefs shared a look before returning their eyes to her.

"Well, hello."

Birk's deep voice held sensual interest that caused Sybil to stiffen. She didn't like to be peered at; she preferred to research and examine. Calum, a methodical man, studied her dark-red hair, pulled up and away from her face in a tight, neat knot. His gaze touched her large glasses, penetrating them to find her light-brown eyes and the slant of her cheekbones. Sybil knew her features ran more to plain than beautiful; she had been told the same often. She shifted restlessly and glanced at Duncan, who had just pushed a man away to get at a beefier man, Jack. Jack was raving about Duncan stealing his wife.

Sybil closed her eyes and lamented inwardly. Oh, fine. Oh, fine, oh, fine.... She had chosen a womanizer as her daughter's white knight.

Aware that the Tallchief brothers' sweeping study had taken in her tall, slender, long-legged body, Sybil turned to them. She detested the male interest. She wasted no time; because two men had grabbed Duncan's arms, supporting him for Jack's fists. Duncan's expression should have been fearful; it wasn't. He lifted his bruised lips for a kiss thrown in Jack's direction.

"He's outnumbered. I really think that you should help him," she stated in her best cool and logical voice.

"Nah. Duncan has them overmatched. I'm Birk. This is Calum. Sit down and enjoy the view."

"He's your brother," Sybil insisted, striving to remain calm and contain her rapidly growing anger. Here was the man she hoped would help her...the man her research had shown to be most proficient at the kind of work she needed done. Duncan Tallchief could be disabled or, worse, killed, and there wasn't another man her research had shown would be as effective.

"How do you know he's our brother?" Calum asked quietly, always the cool, dissective mind.

Sybil dismissed the question. The Tallchief brothers looked as though they were cut from the same arrogant mold, though Duncan looked fiercer. Of course, he was brawling and they hadn't lifted a finger to help him. Sybil pushed away a dram of sympathy for the massive man battling away at the bar. "I've come for Duncan. I want you to help him before he's disabled."

Birk's and Calum's matching frowns deepened. "Tell us more," Birk invited.

She dismissed his humor. "I don't have time for this. Duncan could be hurt. Are you going to help him or not?" Sybil demanded, pushing away a shiver of dark anger. When the brothers didn't move and the man, Jack, sank a ham-sized fist into Duncan's middle, Sybil shot Birk and Calum a look of sheer disgust. "Very well. I'll take care of it myself."

Both brothers stood instantly, looming over her. Each took an arm, their hold firm, yet gentle. "You could get hurt."

Sybil's research had shown that the brothers were too protective of women. They towered over her now like guardian angels. "Do something," she ordered, politely gripping their wrists and pushing lightly. She disliked being touched.

Calum and Birk released her and glanced at the fight. Birk nodded thoughtfully. "He's doing okay. Duncan doesn't usually like interference."

"Oh, he doesn't, does he?" Sybil closed her eyes, counted to ten and began to step over a chair on her way to help Duncan. A big hand latched on to the back of her sweater and began to reel her to safety. Because she had learned the hard way that women should protect themselves, Sybil unleashed her best martial-arts kick—tempering it a bit because the brothers meant well.

Birk grunted satisfactorily as she continued making her way to Duncan. She brushed back the long, curling mass of hair that had come unwound and now flew around her shoulders. She paused a moment thoughtfully, then tugged away her glasses and tossed them to Calum, who was grinning widely.

"I detest what I am about to do," she muttered grimly.

Duncan ducked another punch and caught sight of the tall woman making her way to him. She was glorious; long, red hair flying as she moved toward him. Her eyes flashed murderously, reminding him of topaz lit by fire.

He deliberately took a punch, reeling with it. The red-haired woman gracefully hopped over a chair. A Tallchief trait was playing to the audience and Duncan took another light punch and sagged, carefully watching the woman come to his rescue. Birk and Calum were standing, noting her progress. One wrong move from the men toward her and they would haul her back to safety. The woman continued mumbling darkly to herself. "You're hurting him," she said very properly. "I insist that you stop."

The five men paused, glanced her way and frowned, then leaped at Duncan.

"Very well. If you insist on violence..."

One of her kicks sent Lyle Maddox curling to the floor. A neat clip of her hand caught Bobby Law on the neck. She elbowed Henry's beer belly and sent a hand flying into Paul's face, bloodying his nose. She looked at her palm, grimaced and quickly dunked a napkin in a glass of water. She scrubbed her hand thoroughly and returned to her mission, all in a matter of seconds. Birk let out a guffaw just as she caught the flaccid muscle in Jack's shoulder and brought him to his knees.

She glared up at Duncan, who was observing her through one good eye and a slightly swollen one. He found himself grinning at her. "My heroine," he murmured, and watched fire ignite in her eyes.

They were light brown, he decided. Lit by flames of her temper.

She grabbed his torn shirt. He watched her hands tremble upon him, and was fascinated by her pale skin against his chest, exposed by the torn cloth. Her lips worked for a heartbeat before sound came.

"I detest violence. *You are to come with me, Duncan Tallchief.*"

Shivering in her temper, her freckles dancing across her skin and her lips tight with anger, the woman continued to glare up at him. He decided she was trying to shake him.

"Oh, fine," she muttered.

Her fingers fluttered over his face, checking the damage. Her expression lay between disgust and grim concern. He gave himself to those elegant fingers, as they gently touched his swollen eye and lip. She dabbed a napkin at the trickle of blood and leveled a dark look up at him.

"Shame on you."

He pushed a kiss at her fingertips and wanted to carry her off as his prize. As if he were her little boy, she tugged his torn shirt together, did up the remaining buttons and smoothed the cloth on his shoulder.

Duncan stood absolutely still, dazed by the idea that she was fussing over him.

God, she was lovely, her furious topaz eyes filling her face, the russet strands of her hair fiery against her pale skin. Duncan watched the rapidly beating pulse in her throat and saw the passion course through her slender body. Dressed in pale green, she reminded him of a cool fern— a delicate, lacy frond, quivering in a summer breeze. Then the tigress shifted within her, the image changing to a passionate huntress locked on to something she wanted badly.

Duncan went light-headed. He was the prize she sought. Heat skimmed across him, enveloped him as he stared at the curve of her mouth, untouched by color. Creams, reds, pinks, subtle golds danced and flashed around her, heightened by the cool green of her loose sweater and slacks.

Duncan struggled against Jack's well-placed last punch and wondered how her lips would taste beneath his.

There was little he could do but wrap her against him and kiss her.

With one hand, he cupped the back of her head, fitting her to the kiss. He dived into the scent of her hair, which flowed around him, catching on the stubble of his cheek. Spice and flowers enveloped him. He pushed closer to the fire, the heat within. Against his body, hers was slender, strong and pliant. The nudge of her breasts against him sailed right into his desire, heavy needs that he hadn't allowed to escape for years....

Her mouth parted beneath his, a tender flower to be treated gently. He lifted his head and found softness lurking in her stunned gaze...before the fury came ripping back.

"How dare you..." she demanded.

She was livid with anger, and trembling with an urge Duncan recognized—the woman wanted to hurl herself at him and make him pay. He'd seen Fiona's temper often enough, and Elspeth's, too. Other women didn't fly at him; there was no reason they should.

"Thank you for rescuing me," he murmured, enchanted by the hot color rising up her cheeks. For her, he pushed the muscles around his lips into a rusty smile. He wondered if tigresses kissed bruised lips.

"Let me go," she whispered between her teeth.

He wondered how they would feel beneath his tongue.

Slowly, reluctantly, he released her. Because fear moved within the woman, shrouded her, reaching out to chill him after her first dazed reaction. He saw the fern again, quivering, hoarding pain. Dew glistened like tears on the fragile, lacy frond.

He mourned losing the soft movement of her lips against his, a kiss lost before it was truly given. The woman had known the worst of fear and was untutored in lovemaking...even now she wrapped her fury around her like a protective cloak. What had made her come to him, fight her way through a low-class tavern brawl, when clearly she was well-bred? He lingered on the question and enjoyed her simmering anger. He guessed it was a bit of the boy in him, rising to the surface after a brawl.

Birk hooted and Calum lifted his beer mug in a toast. "She's come for you, older brother."

"Is there somewhere we can talk?" the woman asked tautly, catching and donning the huge glasses Calum tossed to her.

Duncan mourned the shielding of her eyes, with their curious slant and reddish brown lashes. He realized she fought now to draw a colorless cloak around her, to return to the shadows and safeguard the vibrant woman within. Unwilling to release what he had touched a heartbeat ago, Duncan eased a willful russet strand of hair behind a well-formed ear devoid of jewelry.

Her eyes darted away. Clearly she was a woman unused to tenderness. Fear—worse, panic and desperation—rode her more than the need to be enclosed by shields and shadows. What had driven her to leave them?

She had spoken like a mother—"Shame on you."

Tenderness lurched within him, replacing the passion sweeping through him a moment ago. He carefully put his hand around her trembling one, sensing that she needed reassurance. She tensed, hesitating, weighing, then finally allowed him to hold her hand. Her cold hand was smooth, the slender, ringless fingers strong. The woman worked with her mind—he traced her fingertips lightly, just once, and found slight calluses. In those shadowy brown eyes was a desperation he'd seen before—when parents came to him, asking for help.

"What is it?" he asked quietly, placing a firm boot on the back of Jack's head as the man started to rise. "Take a note, Jack. I'm busy.'' Jack groaned and sank back onto the floor.

A very private woman, he decided, as she quickly glanced around the room. One who kept her pain to herself, but now must leave that safe shroud to expose herself to another—

"I'm going to my ranch now." It was an offer, quietly put, so as not to frighten her. "We can talk there." Would she come, or would fear anchor her?

When someone agreed too quickly to his terms, he knew the matter was not light.

She nodded. "I'll wait outside for you. I'll follow you in my car."

Duncan watched her move elegantly toward the door and close it softly behind her. No questions, no conditions. The woman was more desperate than he thought.

He steered his pickup slowly toward the mountains, keeping sight of her headlights in his mirror. The woman drove an expensive car, unsuited to the rugged road leading to his isolated ranch house. She drove skillfully, returning his flashing lights to signal she was all right. They circled the wind-tossed lake that had reminded his great-great-grandmother of Scotland, just as the jutting mountains had. Meadows and rich grazing land lay upon Tallchief Mountain like sprawling jewels among the rocks and pines. Duncan's small flock of sheep, a hairy Scottish breed, had adapted well to the mountains.

His rock-and-wood addition to the Tallchief house was new, built by him and his brothers. The spacious home nestled in the pines and jutted into the night sky. Elspeth's woven goods softened the wood interior with a few Native American artifacts. His great-great-grandfather's peace pipe lay on the roughly hewn mantel. The Tallchief's first branding iron lay beside it, the pattern of a stick man seared in barn wood. The dull red of a Sioux shield, decorated by feathers and porcupine quills, hung in the shadows.

Blood tied him to this raw, beautiful land. He was bred here, loved it. The woman would look fragile and pale inside his home. Duncan knew gossip would flame immediately, because more than a few women wanted to claim him. He'd been a celibate man since his divorce, yet none of them had stirred him like the woman tonight.

The woman who needed him, a woman of fire and shadows....

He left the front door ajar for her, then went to coax the wood furnace into life. He rarely used the comfort, but the woman needed warmth and a bit of care. Despite her well-groomed, expensive exterior, she seemed very lonely, as though untouched by concerned loved ones.

''They call you 'Mother.' ''

When she referred to his code name, he understood why she was so desperate. Framed against the huge windows skimmed by the light, falling snow, she was too thin. Used to tracking with his senses, Duncan prowled through what he knew of her and what he felt. She was probably missing a child—

Duncan continued to prod the hearth's fire. The woman's knowledge was not shared by the townspeople. Duncan, too, had his secrets; he preferred not to expose them or to lose his effective shield. Keeping the newspapers at bay wasn't easy after the rescue of a wealthy child.

''We haven't been properly introduced,'' she said, confirming her good breeding. ''I'm Sybil White. You're Duncan Tallchief and I need you…ah…that is…my daughter, Emily, has been kidnapped. We live in Seattle. I've traced her to this area. I'm…I'm pretty certain my ex-husband has her…at least the flight attendant's description fitted him.''

Straight to the point. Sybil hadn't glanced at his house,

searching out bits of his privacy. Desperation left little space for idle curiosity.

Duncan rose slowly to his feet and realized that Jack's punch had bruised a rib. He rubbed his side, and behind the large glasses, Sybil's eyes darkened with a flash of impatience. Her eyes skipped down to his chest, lingered briefly on the whorls of hair, then moved away into the night. Across the room, she looked drained, shadows beneath her eyes. "Let's talk in the kitchen," Duncan said, allowing her to follow him. "I'm in the mood for a snack."

She could do with food and rest. He began to heat stew laced with barley and vegetables. She stood very rigid, clasping a leather file holder to her as if nothing could tear it away. He saw in her a mother's fierce love and despair.

He saw in her a woman who could claim his heart.

The thought shook him to his boots. He'd had close relationships, but a woman like this one—wounded, vulnerable, holding pain within her—raised his protective instincts. That was his problem with women, Duncan brooded—his need to protect. Too often women misinterpreted that care for something else.

He preferred to keep to himself after he discovered how some women were drawn to him and he to them.

Marriage wasn't a dream he'd try again.

Duncan tugged a refrigerator magnet away and let it snap back. When it came to wounded women, he didn't have a callus to protect himself.

Duncan ran his hand over his jaw. But he hadn't known how vulnerable she was when she'd come like a tigress for him. Maybe he'd been flexing his muscles even as he saw her walk in, all cool and style, to the tavern. If that tigress appeared again, there would be a duel, because she touched sparks within him—a bit of boyish show-off and a deeper, primitive need.

Tension ran through him now, simmering and lodging heavily in his lower body.

That damned Tallchief kiss. He'd known he needed the fire of her mouth beneath his the moment she'd hopped over that chair....

Duncan used the excuse of a shower to take him to the privacy he required. Moments later, dressed in a worn, flannel shirt and jeans, Duncan padded on bare feet to where she ladled the stew into bowls. "So you're domesticated. That's a nice addition to martial-arts skills," he taunted her gently, aware of his own uncertainty.

She shot him a dark, moody look, dismissing his nudge to reveal something about her life. "You could have gotten hurt. Emily...we need you. If you think I liked my first debut into—"

She hesitated and some past horror wrapped itself around her. What was it? Duncan wondered.

She looked away and rubbed her hands as if they were chilled to the bone. "I detest physical violence."

He wanted to wrap his arms around her and tell her he would take care of her—that he would rescue her daughter. She pushed away her food and resented his insistent spooning of it into her mouth. For her, submission wasn't easy, but she wanted his help desperately and made the small concession.

Duncan's lower body hardened each time the spoon slid into her mouth.

"Any amount of money—" she began, only to be stopped by another rich spoonful.

Elspeth wasn't long in calling. After answering the phone impatiently because he didn't want to be distracted from the woman, Duncan scowled. He should take a dip in dignity, Elspeth advised tartly, and shot through a quick account gained from Birk and Calum.

"You've never taken a woman to your house, Duncan.

You were showing off at Maddy's. Think of what people will say. If she needs a place to stay—''

"You'll be picking at whys and whats," he finished, used to Elspeth's caring tongue. "Maybe I want her here without your advice," he added to rile his sister's temper. "She stays with me."

"Poor woman. She hasn't a clue. Exactly what are you doing with her now?" Elspeth demanded, not to be put off.

"Why, I'm feeding her, dear sister. She's eating out of my hand," he returned in a drawl that always brought her temper soaring. He spooned another bite into Sybil's parted mouth, and patted the softness with a napkin. "Leave me alone with my rescuer, will you?" he asked before replacing the receiver in the cradle, none too gently.

He smiled grimly. Sybil reminded him of Elspeth, tall and elegant, with fire and steel running beneath. He thought of the woman coming to his rescue, the pampering and the petting, her fragile fingers smoothing his torn shirt. He was unused to that tenderness; it would do for a start....

"Show me what you've got," Duncan urged gently. "By the way, you realize that we are alone here and the situation could be..."

Again that flick of impatience, a woman with one goal in sight: the safe reclaiming of her daughter.

"I've investigated you. I'm a researcher, Mr. Tall-chief—''

"'Duncan' to you," he interrupted, disliking the formality she placed between them. He wanted to rip it away, but thought better of it.

"Duncan. Very well. I'm a researcher and you are the best. Can you help me?"

He tilted his head and crossed his arms. To be investigated was a novelty. "So you've tapped into information only granted to lawmen. Interesting. You must be very skilled and desperate enough to play illegal games. What do you know about me?''

She preferred not to look directly at him, but studied her long, pale hands, instead. The sight of her slender fingers splayed open caused his heart to thud more quickly.

''Thirty-five. A cattle rancher with an interest in Scottish sheep and replenishing buffalo on the lower plains. You've lived here all your life. Lost your parents when you were eighteen and kept your younger brothers and sisters together. It couldn't have been easy. You're respected and active in community affairs. You could have a degree with all the courses you've taken—animal husbandry, environmental impact, wildlife—but you don't. You found a child when no one else could, and your wife left you shortly after. The court papers stated irreconcilable differences, I believe. Law officials call you 'Mother.'''

''That's enough.'' Duncan didn't like anyone prowling through his private life, a marriage gone sour. He'd been filled with dreams when he walked into his marriage. He'd given his all to that marriage, but it hadn't been enough for Lauren. He'd hated the ugliness within him then, the desperation as the dreams died. Lauren had wanted to sell Tallchief Mountain for her share of the divorce and shouldn't have backed him into that corner. Protecting his family's heritage, he hadn't been nice. The divorce had been messy and had strangled a good amount of trusting women out of him. They were still friends, he and his ex-wife. He realized later that he'd wanted more than she could give; he'd wanted the deep love his parents had shared. He'd wanted a houseful of children, and it wasn't meant to be. At times the memory of what he'd wanted, his dreams, was too fresh—

The Tallchiefs were said to have their backbones forged in steel....

''I'll help you.'' Duncan knew that whenever a child was

taken, he would help if he could. He examined Sybil's files, forgetting her momentarily as he immersed himself in facts, dates, the suspect.

They were in his office now, studded with books, files and computers and overlooking the Wyoming night. Her scent caught him unawares just as he was prowling through the background material on her ex-husband. He slipped a disk into his computer and ran through more information. "I like your perfume," he said truthfully. "But you distract me."

"I do?" Her reaction was shocked, honest, a woman unaccustomed to male attention. "I'm not wearing perfume."

This time he was impatient. Sweeping her body with his eyes, he spared her nothing of his desire. "A woman's body has a scent of its own. I haven't been near a woman in a long time. There's enough tension in me to— Look, you can't be completely naive. Didn't anyone warn you about following men to isolated places?"

"But I..." She didn't finish, cut short by his dark look.

The flush rising from her throat caught him in the gut, turning it wickedly. A hard surge of desire ran through him, even as he recognized her pain. His tigress had scars all her own. "Tell me about yourself. Everything."

"I'm not interesting," she protested, that flag of anger rising in her topaz eyes. "Emily—"

"Take off your glasses," he ordered. "You're near-sighted. You only use them for distances anyway. I want everything you know and nothing shielding it."

"You are a demanding man."

Reluctantly, daintily, she removed her glasses. He admired her courage as she plopped them into their case. She placed them in a functional bag. Everything about her was neat and classic and expensive, from her large bag to her clothing. Despite her travel, she barely looked rumpled.

"Something isn't here," he said carefully as she sat by his side, examining the scrolling lines on his computer screen. He studied her face—the high, elegant forehead and the slight lines around her eyes; lines of fatigue were etched around the generous curve of her mouth. He studied her slightly squarish jaw and watched it tense; she didn't like his surveillance as he said, "Early thirties. Evidently with money and breeding. One child. Emily is how old? Thirteen? Your marriage to...Frank, wasn't it? Lasted six years? Who is Emily's father?" he asked, and watched Sybil pale instantly.

She shivered and looked out into the night. "I don't know the exact identity of Emily's father."

Duncan waited. She was too untouched, too fiercely protective of her body, to have given it easily or often. He was good at ferreting out gaps, but he sensed he wouldn't like this one. "I need everything, Sybil," he told her. "Or I can't help. Details leave a trail."

She closed her eyes, struggling to force the past from her. "I was raped. Emily's father could be any one of four boys...men now, I suppose."

Duncan reeled with that punch, more severe than the physical ones of the brawl. He saw a frightened young girl attacked by a gang, and with professional determination blocked the scene from his mind. He wanted to hold her against him, to soothe her— Instead he asked, "And your ex-husband? What was his relationship to Emily?"

"Strained. I...I am actually Emily's only parent. Her only relative. She's always depended entirely on me. She must be terrified now." Sybil's voice was low, haunted by fear and a little guilt. "It was three days before I got the note. Today is the fourth day. I spent time researching, locating the flight...finding you, a man called 'Mother.'"

"We'll locate her. It's just a matter of time." The circles beneath her eyes said she hadn't slept in days.

"You'll help me, then...to get Emily?" She needed his reassurance, her shadowed eyes begging him.

Duncan doubted that Sybil asked very much of the world; he would try his best to help her.

"Yes. Now, leave me alone," he said too gruffly, covering the tenderness he felt for this woman. Experience told him that every moment lost was dangerous to the girl. "Get some sleep. You can use one of the bedrooms upstairs."

"I'll stay here," she returned firmly. "You might need me. I've already tried researching the sources available."

"On the couch, then, and you don't have my resources. And by the way, Miss Light-fingers...keep your nose out of my private business," Duncan ordered, admitting a reluctance to let her leave him. He wanted to hold her against him, protect her and tell her her child would be safe. But he'd found two children who hadn't lived, and he wasn't offering false hopes.

She shivered, crossing her arms and digging her fingers into the knit sweater. "I am sorry. I realize the value of privacy."

He felt as if he'd slapped her, and she looked as if she'd already been battered. Duncan cursed himself silently. "You did what you had to do. Lie down on the couch. It's comfortable." The thought of her sleeping in one of his beds nettled him. Unused to the fierce tug of desire, Duncan began working quickly, tapping keys, finding sources, tracking....

Two

Sybil dozed, cuddling warm softness closer to her...her baby was her sunshine, her world. Emily was a special part of her, the best part, renewing Sybil's faith in family love. From the first moment she'd discovered her pregnancy, she'd loved Emily desperately. When Emily was placed into her arms, the pain within Sybil had settled....

Wrapped in a half sleep, she found Duncan's eyes at a level with her own. In the lamplight, his face was all rugged angles and harsh lines. Textures of tanned and weathered skin blended with blue-black hair. Light glistened on the raven stubble covering his unrelenting jaw. She looked away from the shadowy heat in his eyes, the pulse beating slowly in his well-muscled throat. Duncan Tallchief was a very physical man, just the sort of man she avoided...not safe relationship material at all.

The huge dog at his side watched her with unblinking white eyes. "This is Thorn. Part malamute, part wolf and the rest mean yellow dog."

"Thorn." Sybil held very still. The dog appeared the perfect match for a man like Duncan, fierce and savage. Then the animal lowered his head to nudge her hand.

Duncan's expression was sheer disgust. "He wants you to pet him. Elspeth and Fiona have spoiled him rotten. He thinks all women should cater to him."

Sybil scratched the dog's ears and he preened, turning to let her rub his throat. Master and dog were more well suited than Duncan knew.

She caught a fresh, grassy scent wrapped in smoke. Duncan's eyes revealed little as he jerked his head to smoke rising from a large, flat dish with Native American designs. "I meditate sometimes."

She studied his angular face, his lean cheeks and shadowy eyes. There was more to the man than the hunter.

"I uncovered a lead," he said quietly.

"What is it?" Then she caught the fresh scent of soap, wood smoke and leather on him. He was no dream—but a grim hunter. She came fully awake. "You're going after her now, aren't you?"

He nodded, the lamplight flickering across his straight, black lashes. His bruised eye was only slightly swollen now. She realized that during the night, he had placed a heavy blanket over her and had removed her shoes.

Emily! She flung back the blanket and jammed her feet into her shoes. "I'm going with you."

"Frank left a trail of credit-card expenditures, including renting a car from the airport. He purchased camping gear and rented horses for trail riding. That was in Ridge Point, ten miles from here. He asked directions for a line cabin up in the mountains. He had a young girl with him and said she was his daughter. The girl didn't talk. He's probably threatened her."

Sybil stared at Duncan. "I couldn't get any information from the car-rental people. How did you find out?"

He drew on a heavy shearling coat over his black sweater. He looked lethal, his face hard and his gray eyes wintry. An anger ran beneath his cold expression, an anger that would serve to track Emily. In another time, he would have frightened Sybil. But she knew instinctively that Duncan was determined to find her child. She could trust him, as she had trusted few people in her lifetime.

"I have friends. I'll bring her back. Four days, maybe five. The sheriff knows what's happening and who to look for. They've given me five days' head start. The sheriff will be waiting for word of Emily. His number is near the phone. Keep in touch with him."

Fifteen minutes later he was closing the pickup door after her. Within the shield of his hat brim and his turned-up collar, his eyes were narrowed into slits and definitely unwelcoming. "Women" was all he said as Sybil, dressed in his jacket, had piled into the pickup. Two horses waited in the trailer behind the truck.

Between them on the bench seat, the dog turned white eyes from master to her. She hugged the dog, needing the reassuring warmth. Duncan glanced at her before turning the key. "Show them to me."

"What?" This man was not the happy brawler of the previous night, or the gentle one who had awakened her. With his coat collar tucked up around his jaw, his face shadowed and taut beneath the low brim of his western hat, he could have been a killer. A man to be feared.

But she didn't fear him. He would help her. She knew it.

His eyes flashed, the color of winter light on steel. "The damned long johns, that's what. You're not going without them."

She forced a tight, triumphant smile and unbuttoned her shirt to show the silky, thermal underwear. He nodded and looked meaningfully at her jeans. Without hesitation, Sybil jerked open the snap and slid down her zipper.

For an instant, she was horrified by her reaction—her opening her clothing for his inspection. But they were bound together, this man and her, to find Emily. Little else mattered. What he wanted, needed, to know she would give him. Anything to help her daughter. *Emily....*

"Good." Duncan reached for her ankle, wrapped his fingers around her boot and drew it onto the steering wheel. Thorn watched with interest as Duncan tugged back her jeans leg. He found the top of her boot and probed inside to her heavy stockings. "Italian boots on a Wyoming mountain.... But you put on my stockings. They're silk and good insulation."

Sybil dismissed the slight trembling, even as the fear of being touched rose within her. She'd chosen the right man.

Hours later, Duncan rode his horse ahead of her, glancing back through the mountain's morning mist to seek her. Wrapped in his coat, his scents, Sybil admitted needing his strength.

A loner, she rarely made friends, and this man had taken her lips as though placing a claim on her. She'd had most of her life laid out for her by people with claims. She preferred loneliness.

Draining hours later, the dog rested his muzzle across her legs and she stroked his ears. She prayed for Emily and hated Frank. Freezing mist settled on the knit hat she wore and penetrated her clothing to chill her. She was unused to riding a horse, and her muscles protested.

"How do you know this is where Frank took her?" Sybil asked, the fatigue draining her. *Emily...please be safe. I love you, honey.*

Duncan glanced over his shoulder, then scowled. He crouched beside the campfire, cooking their meal. The campfire lit his face, all angles and planes, glistening on his beard and on the sleek black of his hair. Sybil saw the warrior in him, the fierce line of his cheekbones gleaned from his chieftain ancestor. Beneath slashing brows, his eyes flickered over her as she sprawled on the sleeping bag, too tired to remove her boots. Duncan stripped them away. The dog stood, shook himself and moved to curl up on a saddle blanket.

A woman used to living alone with her daughter, Sybil resented Duncan's care. She was always the strong one, the one in charge. His efficiency both nettled and soothed her. Duncan left no doubt that he was disgusted by taking her, yet he wouldn't deny her the smallest comfort.

She hadn't asked him for anything but her daughter's safe return. Schooled at covering her emotions, Sybil avoided Duncan's level, too-astute gaze. He began to rub her legs, which now felt like logs after a day in the saddle. Here he was, strong in his element, while she was helpless. She knew books and computer files, not the touch of a man. Frustration and fatigue tore at her as she jerked her leg away from his strong, massaging hands. She'd been held down and—

Duncan quickly retrieved her ankle and circled it loosely with his fingers. None too gently, he yanked her legs across his and began massaging them. "Do you know that I've never allowed any woman to bully me?" he demanded between his teeth. "Look at you. You're undernourished, half dead with lack of sleep. You'll eat every drop in your bowl, understood?"

"I haven't complained, have I? I've followed every order you've shoved down my throat, haven't I? I'll keep up. I'm stronger than I appear." She hated the arrogant way he tossed out orders, expecting her to obey.

He loosened her single, long braid, then ran his fingers through it. "Right." He didn't sound as if he believed her. "You're really up for camping, aren't you? You're wearing

Italian boots with thin soles on Wyoming rocks, lady. Why didn't you ask your family for help?''

"They wouldn't give it," she answered truthfully, feeling empty. She'd begged them once to love her daughter. They couldn't be bothered with a child spawned during a rape...rather, the tawdry affair they'd thought she'd had. They hadn't believed her tale of the well-bred boys attacking her that night. She was lying, they'd insisted. The old-money society families couldn't possibly allow her lies, her mother had said in a quiet, cold way.

No...she wouldn't give her baby away....

Duncan, looking more like an outlaw than a rescuer, brought their bowls to the sleeping bag. They ate quietly and Duncan insisted Sybil clean her plate. He ignored the angry flick of her eyes. "We'll find Emily. There is only one place on the mountain that Frank will go. From the camping gear he bought, he isn't skilled at roughing it."

He placed his arm around her shoulders, and for once Sybil accepted the comfort. "She's all right," he reassured her.

"You don't know Frank. He delights in tormenting the helpless." Sybil fought the tears rising in her eyes, burning her lids. She never cried, not since... Then Duncan was lifting her, placing her on his lap and shoving her face into the warmth of his throat. She struggled for an instant, then sank into the shelter he offered. Few people had given her a safe harbor, nor had she asked them to. Now, raw with worry and fatigue, she desperately needed the refuge. She clung to him, digging her fingers into his coat. "I'm so scared," she whispered, shocked that she was crying against his skin, letting him hold her like a child.

"What about your family? Where are they?" Duncan asked gently, stroking her hair. She listened to the steady beat of his heart and wondered why she let him hold her....

Alone on the mountain, nestled against a man she barely

knew, Sybil found herself voicing a raw pain that had torn at her for years. "They...they can't accept Emily. She doesn't exist for them...."

"We'll find her," Duncan repeated slowly, rocking her.

She fell asleep to the sound of his heart, each beat bringing her closer to Emily.

Frank's capture and the recovery of Emily were easier than Duncan had believed. Frank, an inexperienced woodsman, had lit a roaring fire in the old cabin. The smoke brought Duncan and Sybil to him. Frank had known he was no match for Duncan and submitted easily. He'd begged them not to set Thorn on him; the dog had been baring his fangs and growling, his hackles raised.

All cool grace, Sybil had walked over to Frank. His sneer dropped as Sybil looked at him. He shouldn't have laughed in her face, Duncan decided. She had leveled Frank to a groveling ball curled on the frozen earth. When their offspring were threatened, mothers could be very effective in their rage. Later they were usually shocked—Duncan knew that Sybil had probably never used her knee so effectively as she had against Frank.

Duncan had tucked the girl against him and leaned back against a tree. "Princess, your mother is choosing a method of therapy she'll probably regret. But maybe we'd better let her get it out of her system. A release sort of thing."

The girl had huddled against him. "I knew she'd find me," Emily whispered. "My mother is special."

Duncan believed it. Sybil had shaken herself and stepped back, contemptuous of the fallen man. Clearly embarrassed, she'd straightened her clothing with shaking hands. "Emily, dear. I'm sorry for that. I detest violence."

To the girl's credit, she'd managed a shaky grin. "No television for you tonight, Mom."

Duncan laughed outright and tapped Sybil's nose. The

tigress flashed in her before it was concealed; she steamed magnificently.

"You!" she muttered, as if he'd caused her to release her revenge.

Duncan bent to brush his lips across hers, needing the taste of her to satisfy him that she was safe. He wanted her to know that they'd found her child and now all bets were off. The flames leaped within her at the caress of his lips over hers; a hurricane brewed—sultry, hot and unpredictable—before she jerked away.

Emily began to giggle, out of nervousness at first and then with growing humor. "Mom, you look—"

"I think she's cute," Duncan murmured, watching Sybil steam, the color rising in her throat.

"My mom?" Emily asked, shocked, her eyes wide.

Elspeth had claimed Sybil and Emily the moment Duncan brought them into Amen Flats.

She'd taken the White females under her wing, showing them Amen Flats, and Duncan resented Elspeth's interference. He was driven to tossing pebbles at Sybil's window after five days and nights of Elspeth's hoarding of them.

There wasn't a moment of those five days when Duncan wasn't damning himself for wanting to see Sybil White again. For wanting to hold her....

She had scars written all over her and he'd had his share of hard times, a broken heart. He was a fool for thinking twice about her.

Sybil appeared at the window, scanning the night, and Duncan stepped from the shadows of the pines. "Come down," he whispered, not happy about his need to see her.

He'd watched her sleep in his arms, and she wasn't aware of him as a man. That irked him.

"I'll see you tomorrow," she whispered back, framed by

the open window. Her hair caught the moonlight, the chilling wind lifting it around her pale face.

"Like hell," Duncan told her, not to be put off by a woman who intrigued him. Few women had set terms for him. Sybil White was far too cool. "Get down here—now."

"I'm done following your orders, Duncan Tallchief. You're arrogant—"

Sybil threw a book at him and he caught it, smirking into the night. The moonlight lit Sybil's shocked expression, her hand covering her mouth. He leaned against an old shed and stared at the moon, mocking himself and his need to see her again.

Sybil, dressed in a black sweater and slacks, her magnificent mane of hair catching the moonlight, marched toward him. He admired the length of her stride, the square set of her shoulders. She hit his chest with a mass of his borrowed clothing. "There. I suppose you came for these. Though I don't know why you couldn't show up at a reasonable hour. Your sister is so caring I don't want to disturb her. We've already caused her so much inconvenience."

He placed a fingertip on her nose, entranced by her snit. This is how he wanted her: with the cool, perfect shroud torn away. "She loves mother-henning…. But what if I came for you?" he asked.

"Emily and I are very well," she said politely, although his drawl had widened her eyes. She shifted restlessly and shoved back a swath of willful hair. "Thank you."

"Did you miss me?" Duncan wanted to draw her into his arms, to take that sassy mouth beneath his and make her pay for his wild emotions. He moved to block the chilling wind from her and to better let the moonlight stroke her face.

Her eyebrows lifted. He saw her prowl through the

proper returns before she said very carefully, "I am grateful to you."

He strolled a fingertip down her cheek and tapped her bottom lip gently. "It's not your gratitude I want."

She frowned, then shook her head. "Oh...oh, yes, of course. I should write you a check. I've been so busy with Emily. Frank is very good at demeaning. This time with Elspeth is helping. She's very good at making us feel special."

"Yes." Duncan remembered Frank's ravings before the tape had sealed his mouth shut. Emily, a quiet, well-mannered child, had been stunned by Duncan's quick dealing with Frank. She had giggled softly as Duncan swooped her up in his arms and tossed her lightly on his horse. The girl was too fragile, nothing more than white skin covering angular bones, and Duncan had fallen under her spell immediately. Perhaps it was because Emily had her mother's intelligence and her shyness. Or maybe it was because he was a sucker for children who looked as though they had taken too many of life's subtle punches.

The mother had also taken more than her share. But fire danced between Duncan and her, like a sword quickly lifted at a word, a look. His instincts told him that in the end, he would fight to have her, and not in a brotherly relationship, either.

Anger wrenched Duncan's gut. Sybil had roused him from his privacy and dared to tempt him. Now she wanted to pay him off and send him on his way. A Tallchief didn't walk away from something he wanted...not just yet. "A check," he repeated flatly. He chose to switch the raw subject. "How's Emily?"

"Wonderful. You're her hero. Birk and Calum dropped by, and between the three of you calling her 'Princess,' she's half in love. She's calling you and your brothers her three Black Knights." Sybil tossed back the strand of hair the wind had whipped across her lips.

"She is special. But so is her mother." Unable to wait longer, Duncan leaned down to brush a kiss across her mouth, startling her.

She was unused to tender touches. Her fingers hovered across her mouth, and then she shook her head. "Thank you again for Emily," she whispered, before running back into the house.

Duncan slammed his open hand against the fence. He'd frightened her.

The next morning Elspeth called to say that Sybil and Emily had gone.

By kidnapping Emily, Frank had sought a hefty ransom. Instead he received a trial and was sentenced to prison. At the trial Sybil avoided Duncan, and though irritated, he let the matter go. She needed healing…for the moment. The tracker's instinct within him told him that there would be another time.

Christmas passed and Duncan traced Sybil to Seattle. He investigated the basic elements of her life—where she lived and her work—and disliked himself for doing it. He had to know she was safe.

Elspeth didn't look up from her notes as the kitchen door slammed and a blast of January wind lifted the lace at her throat. "Shut the door, Duncan. I can't afford to heat the world."

"She sent me a thank-you note and a fat check." He tossed his snow-frosted hat to a chair and ripped away his heavy winter coat. Duncan sprawled on a chair and glared at Elspeth. Here in her soothing home filled with delicious aromas and calming colors, she looked too much at peace to suit him. "A damned note."

"I presume you are brooding about Sybil." Elspeth arranged the drawings she had been making from Una Fearghus's descriptions. The journals of the Tallchiefs' great-great-grandmother told of the loss of her Scottish dowry; as children the Tallchiefs had pledged to find Una's treasures. Elspeth pushed the drawing of a handmade cradle at Duncan, a circular Celtic design carved in the wood. Elspeth smiled, used to the quick moods of her family. "Una said that the woman who brought the cradle to a man of Fearghus blood would fill it with his babies."

"Prod one of the others, will you? I've been around that bend. It didn't work." Duncan stared sightlessly at the drawing. Thoughts of the cradle no longer brought the pain they once had after his divorce. His dreams had died slowly, futilely gasping for life during that time. The quest for the cradle belonged to the past, back when the Tallchief children were struggling against fate.

Duncan glanced around Elspeth's home, at her weaving studio looming off the kitchen. Mourning their parents and fighting the world, the Tallchief clan had plotted to return Una's dowry to the family. The ink in her journals was blurred when she described how the dowry had been sold to keep Tallchief Mountain and the ranch safe. The mountains were enough to remind her of Scotland, she wrote…her dowry was nothing compared with her love for the chieftain who had captured her. And whom she had tamed to a loving husband. So the dowry was sold in bad times and Una had cried.

Calum the cool was to retrieve Una's garnet ring, a gift from her grandmother. Birk the rogue was to find the rocking chair; its dainty wooden design was Una's inheritance from her brother, who was also an indentured servant in the new land. Elspeth the elegant tended Una's journals, and had begun creating designs from Una's detailed descriptions. Elspeth had pledged to retrieve the fine woolen paisley shawl, and Fiona the fiery, the youngest Tallchief, was to find Una's sewing chest filled with crochet hooks and baby shawls.

Duncan traced the circular Celtic design of the cradle. He'd tried to recover the heirloom and had failed. "I'm not in the mood for legends. The original one she brought to this country was burned for firewood by the people holding her papers. Tallchief carved another cradle from Una's drawings."

"She still considered it a part of her dowry. Tallchief recognized that she would not come to him without it. He carved another and arranged for his father to give it to her. Eat another cookie and tell me about Wyonna. Does she like her new life, her new job?"

"She's happy. She's gotten a grant and is studying abuse situations while she works. When the women's shelter is done, she'll be ready to help others." Without Jack's unkind attention, Wyonna was blossoming; her strength grew each day. Duncan had tucked her away and found her a job she liked. But Wyonna had grown up in Amen Flats and she wanted to return. If she did, she'd have to face Jack, and it would be with Duncan's protection.

Duncan frowned, remembering Frank's futile threats to Sybil. Frank had said he knew things—a kidnapper searching out the possibility of blackmail. From the stiff way she'd looked at him, head high and topaz eyes glowing in her pale face, Sybil no longer cared and Frank had known it. He'd pushed too hard and lost.

"Thanks to you. You're very good at defending the helpless, Duncan. And a disaster as a gentleman. I'm afraid my brothers inherited a bit of our great-great-grandfather's wild temper. And Fiona, too." Elspeth shoved a freshly baked cookie into his mouth. "For sweetness. You gave Sybil the Tallchief kiss the first moment you met her. Latched your lips to hers and took. There you were, brawling at Maddy's and loving it…. Tossing pebbles at my windows. You break one of them while you're woman hunting and I'll make you pay and replace it. You frightened her, Duncan. Sybil's life hasn't included moonlight trysts or Black Knights or warriors capturing her.''

She leveled a look at him. ''I'm afraid you have inherited your share of our great-great-grandfather's attitudes toward women.''

Duncan munched on the cookie and ran the back of his hand across his mouth. That kiss had haunted him, caused him nights of lost sleep. During the trip up the mountain, he'd thought only of the child's safety and prayed. But Sybil's kiss had lingered, stirring him, and his brotherly notions had fallen at his boots.

He wondered how she could have married a man like Frank. How had he hurt her? There were other scars left by an unforgiving family, and Duncan shook his head. He had his share of pain and had decided to leave marriage to those who were braver than himself. Tangling once with a woman he loved desperately could last him a lifetime. Once, he'd wanted a family to wrap around him; had wanted the loving that the Tallchiefs shared. Duncan and Lauren had been two separate halves that should have grown together. But when the white-hot heat of youth began to cool, they were still separate.

Looking back, Duncan could see the ill-match that had lasted only a year. Lauren had needed a gentler man, and she found one, having two children in short order.

Duncan toyed with the woven place mat in front of him, circling the Celtic design. Pride kept him from going after Sybil, waylaying her and kissing her with the hunger that lurched each time he thought of her. To protect himself from Elspeth's sharp intuition about his need of Sybil, he asked absently, ''How's Fiona?''

''She's in Arizona, and you know very well she's fight-

ing land sale con-men. You're mooning for Sybil, Duncan.
Admit it,'' Elspeth prodded, jotting down another note, this
time a recipe. "She's got you. There you were, a lonesome
old wolf, tried and failed at marriage, settling in that mountain castle like a hermit—''

"Lay off,'' Duncan ordered lightly. "My social life is
none of your concern.''

Elspeth ran an elegant hand up to smooth her sleek, black
chignon and Duncan thought of Sybil's wild, red hair as
she'd leaped across the barroom chair. He studied Elspeth
beneath his lashes and watched her knowing smile. Elspeth
placed her thumb against his, tiny scar to scar. "I could
leave you alone to mold. But I won't. As the eldest sister,
it's my right to torment you and see you safely tucked
under the care of another woman. I'm doomed until then.''

Duncan leveled a glare at Elspeth. "You're sticking up
for her, aren't you?''

Elspeth met his hard eyes with her softer ones and
grinned. "She hasn't a clue about you. She doesn't know
how beastly you can be. I do. I've seen you at your worst.
You've bullied me my entire life. Only because I've let
you. You can't just sweep down off your mountain and
expect her to be glad—imagine, tossing pebbles at my windows. Now, eat another cookie and go pick on someone
else. I've got a loom that needs feeding.''

Sybil tucked the shelving paper into place and began
stacking dishes in the cabinet. She'd had to leave Seattle;
she'd felt too vulnerable there after the kidnapping. She'd
wanted a new beginning for herself and for Emily. Because
she could think of no place safer, and because she had
nowhere else to go, she'd come back to Amen Flats and to
Elspeth's gentle friendship. Emily, her red hair tied in a
ponytail and a fresh batch of freckles dancing across her
nose, grinned up at her mother. "I'm going to love going

to public school in Wyoming. Do you think we can go to the rodeos this summer? Maybe I could compete? Huh, Mom? Maybe barrel-race?''

''We'll see. You'll have to learn how to ride first.''

''Duncan will teach me. I know he will. Elspeth says that all the Tallchiefs can ride like demons. She said that only the Tallchief men could have ridden after their parents' killer. She said that she thinks Tallchief men might have a touch of the devil in them. She said that right in front of Birk and told him not to snarl about Lacey, her friend.''

Emily shifted gears, her expression delighted. ''Or maybe Birk or Calum will teach me to ride. I've never been a part of a family before, Mom. But if Birk and Calum and Duncan are too old to be my brothers, then they can be my uncles, huh? They call me 'Princess' and sometimes I really think I am special—when they say it. I'm hoping that since I've never called anyone 'Dad' that Duncan might—''

She grinned hopefully when her mother seemed to be mustering a protest. She'd plagued Sybil about Duncan's light kiss after the rescue and innocently lit her mother's smoldering temper. Emily had never seen her mother truly angry except with Frank on the mountain. Yet the mere name Duncan Tallchief set her mother off nicely. Emily loved to tease Sybil about the man who looked like a desperado and had the gentle touch of one who cared. All thin arms and long legs, Emily ran out the screen door. Her laughter flowed after her, curling around Sybil. ''Gotcha, Mom!''

Sybil smiled; her daughter had completely forgotten the few days of Frank's mental abuse and was flowering nicely. The move to Amen Flats was exactly what she'd needed. Computers, overnight delivery and facsimile machines allowed Sybil to research wherever she lived; her work ran to genealogy and investigation of antiques, the location of desired articles. If she had to travel to her sources, Elspeth was ready to watch Emily.

The two cool, precise women had quickly become friends. Through the eldest Tallchief sister, Sybil had grown to like Birk and Calum and Fiona. Elspeth was nothing like her volatile, arrogant and playful brothers and the two women had corresponded since Emily's recovery. Elspeth's quiet, nurturing friendship filled an emptiness within Sybil and she had decided to move to the town that Elspeth had grown up in and loved so much. Sybil decided to wrap Emily in the close-knit community, something she'd never had. Sybil's fingers trembled on the dainty teacup. She released the china, pushing away her family's coldness. She desperately wanted Emily to have the warmth she'd discovered in the small town.

The homey, sunlit kitchen was perfect, gleaming and airy, nothing like the sterile ones at the mansion and her uptown, high-security apartments. The small house had a yard and space for a garden. Sybil had never lived in a real house and this one had a spacious front porch and a screened back one. Emily was already planning to plant flowers, and adopt a kitten and a puppy, her first pets. The rooms were plain and the bedroom she'd converted into an office was open and light. The house soothed Sybil, with its spreading shade trees and calming view of the mountains.

Warm, tender hearts resided in Amen Flats and half of them had welcomed her. Elliot Pinkman had mowed her yard and turned up the old flower bed. Lisa Brown and her friends had popped in with plant starts and cookies and casseroles. Children played on the sidewalk, shooting curious glances at Emily, who now wore a constant grin and acted as though every day were Christmas.

Duncan was another matter. He ignited Sybil's mild temper—she'd actually thrown a book at him—and the memory that she had slept in his arms on the trail disturbed her. Duncan could be tender and playful with children, but running beneath his quiet looks were steel and a brooding darkness she didn't understand.

He'd touched her as a brother on their way up the mountain, comforting, holding her.

After the brawl at Maddy's, he'd touched her as a man, kissed her. Wrapped her to his hard, warm length and placed his lips upon hers as though staking his claim. She'd thought of that kiss constantly, the brush of his lips across hers, seeking. The scents of his body tormented her; the texture of his unshaven chin snagged on her memories. Despite the brevity, the light possession, there was nothing cool about the kiss. Rather, it spoke of summer heat and male demands—

She'd had her share of male demands—much too rough, the hurting and the taking.

She'd had time to think, to remember how solitary Duncan's home was, softened only by patches of Elspeth's loom work and bits of Native American crafts and artifacts. He'd swept through the shadowy interior like a warlock, a dangerous male at home in his lair. He'd been hurt—she'd seen it in his eyes when she'd recalled his divorce. Then a steel door had slid closed, barring her from his secrets.

Despite his seemingly open life, Duncan was a man of secrets, hoarding them.

A woman would have to be a fighter to meet Duncan on a fair plane. Sybil had done all the fighting she wanted, from her cradle to the last cool, well-barbed argument about her leaving Seattle for the wilds of Wyoming. The Whites' eldest daughter had been marred; she'd ignored her duty to dispense with the illegitimate baby.

Sybil shivered just once, placing Duncan's storms and heat and her family's chill aside as she arranged her teacups in the cupboard. The screen door crashed behind her, and with a reprimand for Emily on her lips, Sybil glanced over her shoulder.

Duncan leaned against the kitchen counter, appearing just as dangerous as when she'd last seen him.

He was everything she'd never wanted in her life. Everything she didn't understand. Storms and lightning and tingles. Just looking at him, she knew the arrogant stance dried her mouth and lifted her temper. Or was it her temperature?

He raised a black eyebrow as she stared at him. "So you're back."

There was the dark, rough tone, accusation running through it. His gray eyes flickered down her loose, brown sweater and slacks.

"Duncan, how nice to see you..." she began, and stopped when he walked slowly to her, looming over her.

Suddenly the spacious, sunlit kitchen was too small. Dressed in a low-fitting western hat, a battered shirt and dirty, worn jeans and boots, Duncan looked as he had when they'd returned from the mountain. The muscle in his jaw rhythmically contracted and released, his day-old stubble gleaming. A spear of black hair shot across his forehead as he whipped off his hat and tossed it to the counter. "Miss me?" he demanded.

The low, dangerous purr of his voice lifted the hair on her nape.

Sex. Everything about Duncan Tallchief said he wanted her, from his sultry expression to the heat of his body. She'd been forced into sex and found it ugly.

"I...I...it is nice to see you." Sybil's hand went to her throat, shielding the fast-beating pulse. With Duncan she felt she needed shields and swords.

Duncan's eyes flicked to the movement and his hard mouth tightened. "So much for etiquette. I didn't like the check. Or your note."

"Wasn't it enough? According to my bank statement, the check hasn't been cashed. I'll write another one...." Sybil began to move around Duncan, but he placed his hands on the counter beside her hips.

"I tore it up. Rude of me, wasn't it?"

He was too close, and her breath came in gasps. Amusement glimmered in his eyes and curled on his lips. He was taunting her with something she didn't understand, yet feared. His thumbs stroked the curve of her hips; his flickering look dared her to toss away her manners.

Sybil inhaled and straightened. She did not like to be the butt of anyone's amusement. "Step back, please," she whispered as he continued studying her, from the tight knot on the top of her head down to the pounding pulse in her throat. She tried to breathe and failed, forced to tilt her head back to look up at him. She told him with her eyes how much she disliked his scrutiny.

"So you've moved to town," he drawled, inspecting her mouth. "*My* town." He might as well have said "My kingdom." "Now, let's see just how cool you really are."

Sybil found her lips were moving; she wished her brain would start turning again. Duncan's searing look had stopped it. She heard herself say, "Elspeth has been so kind. There were others...after we got back. I couldn't believe it. Emily never stopped talking about the people here—"

Emily had never stopped talking about *Duncan,* idolizing him. Sybil glanced over his shoulder to find Birk grinning at her.

"Duncan. Elspeth sent me. She's afraid you'll frighten our Miss Muffett away," Birk drawled. "Hello, Syb. I'm glad you've moved here. When you feel like playing tourist, give me a call. I'm in the book."

"Get out," Duncan returned easily, without unlocking

his stare from hers. "Sybil-belle was about to tell me how much she missed me."

Feeling slightly guilty, fearing that Birk could sense the sensual tension hurtling off his brother, Sybil stood on tiptoe to look around Duncan's shoulder. "Stay and have cake."

Birk sniffed the air. "Chocolate with chocolate frosting? Don't mind if I do."

"I taught you how to drive, remember? How to shave and pitch a knuckleball," Duncan murmured, pulling rank. "Don't you have a building to level or a race to run?" Duncan said slowly before turning to his brother. He glanced at the white paint in Birk's hair and smirked. His brother had always had problems with one female. "Tangling with Lacey MacCandliss again?"

"Lacey hasn't learned that I'm her better. I've come to welcome Sybil to Amen Flats," Birk returned, the proud angle of his jaw matching his brother's.

Inches beneath the brothers' warring gray eyes, Sybil blinked as if she didn't believe the scene.

"Dibs."

The word curled from Duncan's mouth, softly and firmly. Sybil frowned, not understanding. She frowned again, and slowly remembered that "dibs" meant Duncan had claimed her...claimed her as his. *His? His what?*

"Yours?" Birk asked lightly with a grin. "How interesting. I thought you had rusted away up in your castle. Guess I'll be going, then." He tipped his hat to Sybil and winked at Duncan, who scowled back.

"Dibs? I hope that doesn't mean what I think it does," Sybil said when she could speak. She wanted to throw the chocolate cake at him.

Duncan slid his hands into his back pockets and tilted his head. His rangy, broad shoulders shifted, straightened. "You kissed me back. I'd say that said something."

It took Sybil a full two heartbeats to understand that Duncan had placed his claim upon her. *From the moment they'd met!* She fought the slow curling of heat up her throat and the press of her fists against her thighs. "No."

Temper flickered through Duncan's stormy eyes and was gone. "Don't write another check, Sybil-belle, or we'll tangle. You might not like the result."

She went very still, panicked by his dark, intimate look. "Please don't call me pet names. I really don't like it and I always pay my debts."

She fought the next words and lost. They leaped out of her like a hungry trout going for bait. "Especially to a muscled show-off who swaggers and enjoys brawling. By the way, I do not appreciate the research you did after I returned to Seattle. I'm not the only one with light fingers. You—Mr. Tallchief—apparently are quite the computer 'hacker'—you had a nice little stroll through my computer, didn't you?"

Anger lurched and flamed before Duncan shielded his gray eyes from her. His smile was cold, matching his eyes. "That would be Calum. And no, we're not in cahoots. Calum likes all the pieces to fit and yours don't. He's got the notion that Frank isn't done with you, especially after your testimony at his trial. You have an upscale clientele who request repeat performances, meaning you must be good. You're underpaid at times, proving you are a ten-derhearted romantic after all."

While she fumbled with an accusation gone wrong, he nabbed a word and tossed it to her. "Swagger?"

"I'll deal with your brother later." Her temper flared. She'd learned a hard lesson and rarely met men in danger-ous situations. Duncan was a dangerous man, yet she didn't fear him. She preferred to take him down a notch. "You saunter, Duncan. Swagger. Strolling in tight jeans as if you owned the world. That loose-legged walk with your shoulders—"

Duncan latched on to that, his beautiful mouth curving and the dimple in his cheek appearing.

"So you noticed my backside. Things are looking up. Yours is nice, too. A little more rounded than the last time I saw you." His gaze leisurely drifted down her body, warming it.

"Leave me out of your dreams, cowboy." Sybil's retort surprised her, but she held her ground as Duncan glared down at her. No one, but no one, had ever commented on her backside.

The morning air sizzled with heat as each refused to look away. Sybil broke the stare when a knock sounded on her screen door.

Calum nodded at her. "'Morning."

Sybil's eyes locked with Duncan's. "Come in, Calum. How nice to see you. We were just chatting about your investigative techniques."

"Always useful in a dangerous situation. I understand you're quite good, too," he stated without apology. Calum stepped into the kitchen, sniffed appreciatively and held out a basket of herb starts to her. Lemon balm and fennel added a bite to the sweet wood scents, tarragon and thyme. "Elspeth says to plant these on the shady side of the house."

"I hope they were obtained legally." Sybil bent to nuzzle the lemon balm scents, and found Duncan's stark desire when she looked up. "Thank you, Calum," she managed unsteadily, rocked by the uncertainty and the answering tinge within her. "How nice of you to bring them. I'll call Elspeth later."

"I like chocolate cake," he returned, eyeing Duncan, who was staring at Sybil through narrowed lids. "Birk said you had dibs, older brother. From the look of things, you're not doing too well."

"What is this, a party? I don't suppose you would leave," Duncan said softly.

Despite Duncan's ill mood, Sybil wondered how it would have been to grow up in this close-knit family.

"No. I can't leave. Sybil wants to feed me." Calum sprawled in a chair and winked at Sybil. The second Tallchief son, he had fought Duncan's bullying the longest. "I want my slice of cake."

Sybil tried to muffle the laughter bubbling out of her as Calum innocently met Duncan's dark stare.

The screen door banged again and Emily launched herself into Duncan's arms. He picked her up off the floor and grinned at her, his dark mood quickly past.

"I missed you," Emily said, giggling as he tossed her once in the air and placed her on her feet. She patted his stubble-covered jaw playfully and Duncan nipped at her fingers, causing her to laugh again. "You don't look like what Mom said—a desperado. You look like a movie star. Sort of cute."

She smoothed the hair flowing into his collar. "And shaggy."

"Desperado?" Duncan lifted an eyebrow at Sybil. "Is that why women throw themselves at me? I thought it was for my sweet nature."

Calum hooted. Duncan tugged her ponytail and Emily beamed. "I missed you. I told Mom every day that I wish I had a dad like you—"

"Emily!" Sybil shook her head slightly and Emily blushed, gazing up at Duncan with adoring eyes.

"He's not that great," Calum muttered, and held out his arm to flex a muscle and study it theatrically. "He's old and worn-out. I've got more desperado appeal. I'm great uncle material."

Duncan's disbelieving snort caused Emily to giggle again. She hugged him and Sybil remembered how badly she wanted her daughter to have a father. Frank hadn't cared and Emily had remained unshared. Emily had been Sybil's alone for so long that the thought was frightening—

Just as frightening as the light touch of Duncan's finger as it trailed down her cheek.

His eyes said there would be another time…when they were alone, and then he was gone, with Emily skipping after him. The screen door crashed and Sybil pressed her lips together. Wherever Duncan passed there was noise and storms and motion. Even when he was still, energy snapped around him. A flash of steel-gray eyes, a movement of his hand, a tensing of his jaw—nothing about Duncan was calm. He strode rather than walked, a long-legged western man who always knew his path. She preferred quiet. And safety. Where he was concerned, Duncan offered none of that commodity to her.

Sybil crossed her arms over her chest and watched Duncan swing Emily up on his horse. He held the reins and began walking down the street with her. Emily trusted the brothers; they could lead her anywhere. For a moment, a sadness went zipping through Sybil. Her baby was no longer hers alone. "That man…" she finally muttered, and turned to find Calum dipping his finger in the chocolate frosting.

He had such a guilty, boyish look when she caught him that Sybil couldn't help laughing. Apparently all the Tallchief men were rogues and full of themselves.

Three

Duncan stared at the neat handwriting on the new check in his hand. Every letter was slanted perfectly, the curves exactly riding the lines. Sybil was like that—exact, cool, remote, with a deep, carefully shielded stubborn streak.

Calum and Birk pulled their attention from Emily, who was earnestly trying to milk a cow in the barn. After two weeks in Amen Flats, Emily had blossomed. She looked like any other country girl her age as she scolded the cow for not holding still. It was Calum's day to play uncle and he was looking forward to another slice of Sybil's cake before he left for Denver. He peered at the check and frowned. "Taking money from Sybil?"

Duncan folded the check and tucked it into his pocket. "I am trying to be sweet."

Birk grinned. "Right. Syb is the first female not to fall for your brooding 'desperado' act. You'll have to dust off your manners to catch her."

"Lay off," Duncan returned easily. "Or I'll tell Elspeth that you'll wear a kilt if she'll make you one."

"Now, that's a serious threat," Birk stated. "She's been threatening us with that since…since we all decided we'd reclaim Una's dowry and Elspeth found notes on the plaid."

Emily stood up and grinned, lifting her bucket of milk. "What now?" she asked the brothers, beaming at them.

"We take it home to your mother," Duncan said.

"Really? We can have it?"

Duncan winked, cherishing the thought of Sybil's carefully concealed temper rising to the bait. "She can make me pudding and chocolate-buttermilk cake and butter for fresh-baked bread."

Birk stuck his finger in the cream-rich milk and sucked it. "Cow's milk. You're pitiful, older brother. I'd have brought chocolates and a good year of champagne."

"Or flowers with a good video movie. Maybe with take-out Chinese food," Calum added with a disgusted tone. "You're ruining our reputation, Duncan."

"Huh?" Emily asked, looking curiously at each one.

"Since he's old and rusty, I'll help older brother out. After this, he's on his own." Then Calum invited Emily to ride out into the pasture with him to see the horses.

Emily glanced back at Duncan and grinned.

Wrapped in her research, Sybil dismissed the light knock on the kitchen door. She continued working in her office, tracing the heritage of a San Francisco matron. Marcella Portway was determined to include Spanish royalty in her family tree. She wouldn't settle for less, and if royalty lurked in Marcella's blue blood, Sybil would find it. She'd worked from early morning on the project, not changing from her nightshirt. "Come in," Sybil called when another knock sounded.

"Honey, I'm in my office," she said, studying the file on her computer screen. "I'll be done in a minute."

A moment later, a teasing finger prowled up her nape and probed the loose knot of hair on top of her head. Sybil stiffened. She instantly recognized Duncan's scent and turned to him. "You should have knocked."

Dressed in a battered work shirt and worn jeans, he lifted an eyebrow, mocking her. "I did. Twice for good measure. Come riding with me."

She stared at him. Just like that. Duncan Tallchief entered her home, looked at her as though he knew something she didn't and asked her to go riding with him. Asked? Duncan Tallchief?

Sybil tried to keep her fingers steady as she tapped the keys, shutting down her research file to keep it from harm. The way Duncan made her feel, trembling and uncertain with a bit of temper tossed in, she didn't want to lose weeks of hard work. She jammed her glasses over her nose. "I'm busy, Duncan."

"You can't see any better close up with those." He plucked them from her and she refused to ask for their return. She would not ask anything of Duncan.

He looked around her office and picked up a picture of her holding Emily as a baby. "She's a terrific kid."

Sybil reached for the picture. She didn't want Duncan too near what was precious to her, though Emily clearly adored him. Duncan resisted her for a moment, then relented. His gaze slowly took in her nightshirt with the sunflower on her chest.

"Been working all day?"

She refused to answer him and wondered if her rapidly beating heart lifted the material over it.

Duncan surveyed her cold coffee and the portion of a bagel. "I'll feed you," he offered. "If you'll come with me."

"Bribery," she shot back, wondering where she could fly for cover. "You'd want to pick at my past—"

Duncan's eyes, the color of shaded steel, pinned her. "Did you love Frank? Ever?"

Sybil rose unsteadily. The dishes clattered as she collected them. She refused to run from him. From the look of him, he'd catch her easily. Duncan was unrelenting when he latched on to something he wanted. She'd seen that during Emily's rescue. He probably deserved answers about Frank. She'd give them to him and he'd be on his way. "I tried. I'd hoped to provide Emily with a balanced home. Now I know that sometimes a single parent is better than two."

"You've done well alone," he insisted, pushing her into corners she didn't like.

Sybil tried not to shiver. Duncan knew how to hunt inside people, trapping them. "Leave me alone. I don't like nosy people."

"Cowboys who swagger?" he offered, recalling her opinion of him. The muscle running from his cheek to his jaw momentarily contracted. He planted a big boot on the chair beside her, effectively blocking her escape.

Sybil saw his lips lower to hers slowly; the dishes left her hand. Duncan placed them on the counter and settled his hands on her waist.

"I brought you Emily's harvest—cow's milk."

Her thoughts weren't on her daughter as she asked, "Emily milked a cow?"

Duncan nuzzled her nose with his. He sniffed at her hair, shampooed when her eyes had gotten too tired and she'd needed a break. "She did and she's proud of it. I'd like to give her a calf, if you approve."

"We don't have a place to keep one and I..." His heat reached out to tangle her usually clear thinking—

Duncan kissed her cheek, rubbing it with his, the slight

abrasion causing her fingers to curl at her thighs. "She can keep it at the ranch. She's safe here now, Sybil. Give her a chance to grow and spread her wings. Give yourself a chance."

Her bare feet were rooted to the sunlit, warmed rug, her body leaning toward his.

Duncan eased her hand upon his chest, spreading her fingers and stroking the back of her hand. His heart beat heavily beneath her palm and Sybil felt her knees weaken.

He drew her free hand to his lips, kissing the center and placing it over his heart. The light from the window ran across his lashes, tipping the black sheen with blue and creating shadows to soften his cheeks. Nothing could soften what she read in his eyes: the need of a man for a woman.

"Go get dressed and come with me. It's too pretty to stay inside."

Duncan looked dangerous, almost desperate, and she sensed the tension running through him. Why would he be restless or nervous?

In her lifetime, Sybil hadn't played hooky or games with too-dangerous men. "I've got work to do. I...uh...I'll pay you for the calf—"

The hand paused. "The calf is a gift. From me to Emily. Every child in the county will be entering the fair. I'd like to see Tallchief Cattle represented in the children's division."

"So you're giving her one for selfish, business and promotional reasons?" Sybil asked as his heartbeat quickened beneath her hand. She hadn't touched a man who was affected by her. The idea intrigued her. She moved her fingertips slightly and steel-hard muscle rippled beneath the cloth.

"I like her." His muscles leaped beneath her smoothing fingertips. "Come with me. Out into the sunlight."

Away from shadows and privacy and beds still rumpled.... He wanted more than to pry her from her work, Sybil realized. He wanted more....

Her fingertips rustled the paper in his pocket and Duncan tensed. "It's your check, sweetheart. I can't be bought."

"I owe you for Emily's rescue," she persisted as his large hands circled and locked onto her waist.

Duncan watched her hair, a lock spilling down to her chest to cover the sunflower, russet on gold. He traced the lock, tugging it, until his touch circled her breast.

She stopped breathing, denying the need to arch up into his kiss, denying the fires flowing through her.

"You owe me nothing, but this...."

Duncan's whisper ensnared her with magic promises; his eyes were tender as his mouth found hers.

Her lids slowly closed as she gave herself to the taste of him. Peace. Quiet. Comfort. Those emotions swirled around her. Then she found the darker elements, the fire and the hunger, as Duncan wrapped his arms around her, gathering her closer to his hard body, his scents. He moved so gently that she thought she was floating....

Then he was lifting her, holding her against him, his mouth moving magically, sweetly, over hers.

Duncan's heat and trembling surprised Sybil as he nibbled at her lips, nudging them slightly open. She tasted his tongue as it flicked over her bottom lip, the tempting kisses at the corners of her mouth seducing her.

Why was she standing still? Why hadn't she leveled him to the floor? Where were all her hours of self-defense classes?

Wasted. Her mouth curved slightly beneath his light, teasing kisses. She was dreaming. Duncan would take a more than average amount of leveling.

He challenged her on another plane, taunting her with gentle, tormenting kisses. She'd never been played with or kissed like this: as though they had all the time in the world.

Sybil, fascinated by this strong man tempering his touch, moved closer, and his dark, hungry groan swept through her hair. He crushed the strands in his fingers, bringing them to his face.

She didn't understand the dark-red color moving up his tanned cheeks, or the trembling of his denim-covered thighs against her bare ones....

"You're standing on my boots, sweetheart," Duncan murmured huskily against her hot cheek. "I've just come from work. They're not exactly clean. You might have a bit of dirt on you if you tangle with me. That and maybe sweat, too," he added, humor and something else lighting his eyes.

Sybil realized that she'd locked her arms around his shoulders, holding that safe, broad anchor while her hands caught his hair, keeping his mouth on hers.

His eyes were tender, watching the blush sweep through her. She realized that he had caressed the curve of her bottom luxuriously and that her breasts lay nestled against his chest. "Uh...I...you..." she began.

"Come with me."

Come with me. Just like that. He'd said that when he'd first come; now he demanded again. When he wanted something enough to hunt it, Duncan could be relentless. She refused to be his trophy—

Sybil shook her head and inched away, her body shaking. She realized unsteadily that she'd never had to step off a man's boot before. She clasped files to her chest, protecting herself against what he offered. What she'd never experienced. "You'd better go."

Duncan eased himself away from the wall, and with horror, Sybil realized that she had pressed him to it. He'd taken her weight upon him. He slowly pulled the check from his pocket, tore it and tossed it in her wastebasket.

"Duncan, I owe you. We can't leave it at that," she said shakily. She moved without ties of any kind except Emily.

His smile wasn't nice. "*That* hasn't got anything to do with *this*." Then he bent to kiss her before she could move away.

Sybil found herself staring, dry mouthed, at Duncan's backside as he walked out the door. The sound of her heartbeat covered the sound of the door closing quietly behind him.

Fifteen minutes later, Sybil dug her fingers into her arms and strode the length of the kitchen. Duncan was tormenting her. Elspeth said he was a champion tormentor once he'd decided upon it. Sybil shook her head. She'd actually stepped onto his boots to reach his mouth.

He could kiss the devil out of her and swagger away, could he?

She studied her trembling fingers, the ones that had locked into his straight, black, gleaming hair and the ones that had smoothed the hair on his chest. "Ahhh!" Sybil screamed quietly, releasing the tension riding her.

When she could, she'd pay him back—both for Emily's rescue and for tormenting her. Here she was, minding her own business, earning a living in her own house, and he'd pounced on her and demanded that she come with him. She promised herself that the next time they met she would be fully dressed, her defenses intact.

Then she saw the wildflower bouquet nestling near the gallon of rich milk layered with cream. Sybil stroked the delicate flowers, her anger toward Duncan flying away, out into the sunlight. She'd never had a wildflower bouquet— nor had she ever experienced the tempest that Duncan caused within her. She lifted the flowers to her face, the rich fragrances enfolding her. Duncan was too dangerous to ignore.... Every feminine instinct she possessed told her

that he wanted her, that he'd inherited his chieftain ancestor's tendencies to claim the woman he wanted.

The flowers trembled around her face. *She was that
woman.*

Emily came bursting into the kitchen, cuddling a kitten.
"Can I have her, Mom? Can I? She's from Duncan's barn
cat, but Birk said she'd do fine in town."

The way Emily held the kitten reminded Sybil of how
Duncan had held her at first. As though afraid he'd frighten
her....

"Birk said we should skim off the cream and put it in a
fruit jar with a little salt. If I shake it, we can have butter.
Real butter from a real cow that I milked. Can I have the
kitten, can I, Mom?" Emily pleaded.

The phone rang and Sybil picked it up. Her mother was
acting hurt. Memories came slashing back at Sybil, chilling
her to the bone and made worse by the warmth of the Tallchief family. Emily slumped into a chair and fiddled with
a flower while Sybil tried to deal pleasantly with her
mother's usual unpleasant forays. Sybil noted the small
ferns tucked into the bouquet. "Yes, it's a small, one-horse
town. No, there is not an airport nearby and no, I am not
moving back to Seattle soon."

She glanced at Emily and winked at her. "*Emily* is doing
just fine. She's looking forward to public school this fall.
She's going to get a kitten, a puppy, and she's raising a
calf to show at the fair. Yes, business is good and I think
we're getting along nicely."

Emily leaped to her feet and turned a circle, clapping her
hands quietly.

Her mother's cutting words caused Sybil to frown. "My
daughter is my business. You've made that quite clear
enough. Take care of yourself. And Father.... Boarding
school for Emily? No. Goodbye, Mother."

Emily hugged Sybil when she stood bracing her hands

against the counter. Her parents weren't easy, hadn't been even before she'd told them of the rape and the coming baby. Sybil had always loved them, and the basic conflict was a war, hurting....

Because she had inherited her grandmother's share of family stock, she had threatened them to protect her child.

"It hurts, doesn't it, Mom?" Emily asked in a tone wise beyond her years. She'd understood from a young age that Sybil loved her desperately...and that her grandparents weren't warm family. The polite distance between mother and grandmother was obvious. Perhaps it hurt more than Sybil's own pain as a daughter. Sybil had gone to great lengths to reassure Emily that she wanted her, that she wasn't the reason for the family dissension. It had existed long before Emily was born.

"Yes...it does hurt," Sybil admitted, and wondered who was becoming the nurturer and who was being tended.

Elspeth served tea. Evening shadows settled over her front porch as the two women watched Emily frolic with her new puppy. Sybil, dressed in a comfortable, light-gray cotton sweater and slacks, sipped an herbal tea while Elspeth continued, "The problem with growing up in a house filled with brothers and one rebel tomboy is that hot tea, served properly, isn't appreciated. I tried it once and my reward was hoots and slurps. When I cried, Duncan made everyone sit down and drink the stuff. Birk was certain he was drinking grass. I really enjoy having a proper pot of afternoon tea, nicely served...especially with you, Sybil."

"I enjoy your company, too." She'd lost a sister— Norma had always aligned herself to The Family's Reputation. Elspeth came close to being the warm sister missing in Sybil's life.

Elspeth lifted her eyebrows. "You've got Duncan in a snit, you know."

Surprised, Sybil turned to her. "What do you mean?"

"Women usually come clawing at his doorstep. He looms up there in his castle, the addition he built on to the old house. He plays big brother often enough. But as to what lies deep in his heart, he's kept to himself. And to us, his family. You're resisting his mysterious charm. My brothers aren't used to resistance. If you only knew the midnight calls I've gotten from girls wanting them. My brothers are too attractive and too cocky."

Since Sybil had moved to Amen Flats, she'd gotten a midnight call of the worst kind. With heavy breathing and coarse language, the unidentified man told her what explicit sexual acts he wanted from her. She'd handled threats before, in another time. Then there was Duncan, who was a threat to any woman wanting a measure of peace.

"Duncan is arrogant and rude and—" Sybil shot back, then relented, because she did like Elspeth and knew how much she loved her family. "He tore up my check for the rescue. I don't like owing anyone. Especially him."

"Yes, he would do that. They say we got our pride from our great-great-grandfather, a full chieftain. Una tamed him, of course. While he was swaggering and ordering his captive around, she snagged him well and good. They had a happy life, despite Una selling her dowry to keep the land safe. We've all sworn to recover pieces of it. Duncan came up with that idea just after our parents' funeral. We had regular family meetings to pick over Una's journals and pry out information about her losses."

Elspeth gracefully poured another cup of tea. "Later, Duncan told me how frightened he was—we were all frightened—and the quests were the only thing he could think of to prod us on. We lived through disasters with the lure of Una's dowry ahead of us. And the threat of separation behind us. We've recovered a few things, like the loom Tallchief built for Una, but so far not one of us has gotten what we set out to recover. I thought Calum would be the first. He likes tidy endings. But his career and marriage waylaid him, and then his wife died in an accident. They had just quarreled bitterly. He'll find Una's garnet ring soon, I'm certain.''

''What was Duncan to recover?''

''A cradle. He tried, and then there was a kidnapping and his divorce, another kidnapping and then running the ranch. I believe he was deeply wounded when his ex-wife told him she didn't want Tallchief children. He'd wanted them so desperately until then. The cradle would be a painful reminder. He's put away dreams in his lifetime. I'm certain that raising us cost him dearly. But he didn't complain. Not once.''

Elspeth studied the tea leaves in the bottom of her cup. ''If Duncan wanted the cradle enough, he would have it. He's like that, getting what he goes after. My guess is he had plans for the cradle, and the scars went deep when his marriage failed. Sometimes the pieces never go back together again. I'd hate to see that in Duncan.''

Elspeth's fingertip traced the flowers on the teacup. ''Duncan says little about that time in his life. He's a survivor. We all are—he told me that when I thought I couldn't go on.''

Pain quivered in the air between the two women as they shared a look, survivor to survivor. ''Our parents would have been proud of the way he's built Tallchief Cattle. I remember listening to him and Birk and Calum working over bills and adding rodeo winnings they hadn't yet earned. They saved the serious discussions until they thought Fiona and I were asleep. They're like that. Protective and maddening.''

Sybil thought of an eighteen-year-old boy, grieving for his parents and trying to hold his family together. Elspeth wiped a tear from her eye. ''Those were tough times, but good ones, too. Duncan never let the rest of us know how frightened he was that he would fail. When his marriage shattered, he blamed himself. I didn't. Lauren wasn't the right woman for him. She never should have tried to sell Tallchief Mountain. Until then, she didn't really know Duncan.''

"Tell me about the cradle. Where would I start looking?'' Sybil didn't want to prowl through Duncan's marriage. The sudden, savage jealousy within her had shocked her. She forced it away.

Elspeth showed Sybil the drawings she'd made from Una's journals. "See? That's a Celtic design for good luck. Before he stopped hunting it, Duncan traced the cradle Tallchief carved to Chicago. He probably thinks the quests served their purpose, gluing us together, and we survived. So the actual object didn't really matter. It was the bond between us to get us through. Why are you interested?''

"I'd love to pay him back. Retrieving the cradle might be the way to do it. I've hunted for family treasures before. I usually don't like doing it because often the item is less than what was remembered. The client can be disappointed.''

Elspeth petted the cat, which had just leaped up on her lap. "Duncan wouldn't be. He treasures everything he's given. He's got other ideas for you.''

"I know. I don't share his plans. I'm not in the mood for an easy affair.''

"Easy? With Duncan?'' Elspeth lifted her eyebrows in disbelief, then sipped her tea. She thoughtfully traced the delicate rose pattern of her cup. "All the things we've pledged to find have legends attached to them. It's said that the woman who brings the cradle to a man of Fearghus blood will fill it with his babies.''

Sybil flushed at the quick memory of Duncan's hard body thrusting against hers. "Well. With it in his posses-

sion, he'll have a better chance of finding someone to produce his babies, won't he?'' she asked a bit too tartly.

Elspeth laughed, a pleasant musical sound that blended
with the tinkling wind chimes.

A hummingbird zipped by on its way to morning-glory
flowers. Emily jumped onto the porch, cradling her barking
puppy. "Mom, did you know that all the Tallchiefs cut
their thumbs when they were kids? They made a blood
promise to take care of one another."

Elspeth handed a cookie to the girl. "We got a tongue-
lashing for it. Duncan paid the price because it was his idea.
Rather, it might have been mine because I loved reading
Una's stories and the blood-brother idea came from something my great-great-grandfather did. Duncan took my pun-
ishment," she added. "This is a recipe of my great-great-
grandmother's. She said she trapped her husband with her
baked goods. It's said that Tallchief men are suckers for a
woman who can bake."

Emily giggled. "That's why Birk and Calum and Duncan keep dropping by. They sniff to see what Mom is baking. I think Calum likes her brownies better. He snuck two
when she wasn't watching. But I think Duncan would
rather have Mom's kisses. He looks at her the way Birk
looks at her chocolate cake."

"Emily!" Sybil placed her teacup in its saucer before
she spilled the tea. It was true, however. At any time she
could sense Duncan looking at her, his eyes glittering. The
taut set of his body told her things she didn't want to know.
More than once, his hot stare had shot down, then up her
body, leaving her trembling, while he continued any light
conversation at hand.

Emily munched on her cookie and gave a bit of it to the
puppy. "Calum and Birk say he can't run as fast as he used
to. They tease about strange things…like Duncan forgetting
how to plant the Tallchief kiss properly and net him a long,

cool maverick and having to work on his pucker. But they really love each other. It's warm around them, and Elspeth, too," Emily stated clinically, and Sybil mourned the coolness her daughter had known. "They say Fiona would cause grown men to shake. She's got a temper, but they say that if you're in a snit, watch out. They think you're a witch. That you know stuff from Tallchief's mother, a shaman, and stuff from Una's mother, who was a seer."

Elspeth's smile was smug. "I tell them that to keep them on their toes. My brothers seem to have taken you into their confidence."

"We're buddies. I even know that Calum has been married. He's what's called a 'widower.' I'm supposed to consider them my uncles, and if any boys want to walk or talk with me, the Black Knights want to know it immediately," Emily continued.

"They're protective." Elspeth tossed the puppy a cookie crumb. "Especially of girls and women. It was a hard cross to bear when Fiona and I were growing up. Having three tall, tough, grim brothers check out our dates and lay down rules wasn't easy. They'd wait there on the porch when Fiona and I came home with our dates. The three of them would stand, legs apart and arms crossed, and glower at our dates."

"They like me. I'm 'Little Sis.' Or they call me 'Princess.'" Emily stated the fact proudly, as if she were wearing a badge.

Sybil laughed outright. The image of the three Black Knights led by Emily-Princess flew by her. "They've latched on to you for certain."

Emily beamed, her freckles shining on her pale skin. "I've got a big family now, huh, Mom?"

Before Sybil could answer, Elspeth said, "I think you're just the partner in crime that I need. I've been trying for years to get my brothers to wear the family plaid—it's

Una's Fearghus design with a Tallchief stripe. The wool is from the descendants of sheep Una brought to Wyoming. Duncan retrieved them. I've woven enough now that I could dress us all. I haven't found a way to get my brothers to cooperate.''

"Tell me more about the cradle, Elspeth. I may be able to help.''

"You'll have to ask Duncan. He managed to get a trail. The cradle seemed too personal with him and I've never interfered with his quest.''

Duncan walked across the top of the building's beam, two stories high. The new roof on the shelter house would add space. In the heat of the day, he worked without a shirt. He needed the hard, physical labor to relieve the unexpected tension skimming through his body. He should have given Sybil the flowers; he should have conversed pleasantly. Instead he had frightened her.

It wasn't his fault. He'd always been a sucker for sunflowers and long-legged women with flame-colored hair and huge honey-soft eyes that a man could fall into. He glanced down just then and found Sybil gazing up at him, shading her eyes.

Against the lush alfalfa field behind the shelter, her cream-colored cotton sweater and slacks caused her to look very slender and feminine. Far too cool for the fire running beneath her lips.

Duncan wiped away a trail of sweat that had escaped the bandanna tied around his head. No woman should look so cool and inviting. Just the sight of her made him want to carry her away.

Or kiss her. He thought about her cool lips moving beneath his, thought about the fire simmering beneath—

Her eyes widened and slowly he realized the direction

of her stare—straight to his bare chest. Her gaze shifted, tracing his shoulders, his chest and down his stomach.

His stomach lurched and Duncan sucked in air, surprised at the need surging through him.

Duncan realized he was flexing his arm, pounding the nail too deep. But from this height, he could see Sybil's eyes widen, her mouth part. He wanted to fascinate her, to rip away the cool facade and meet her as a man meets a woman. He'd have to walk carefully, Duncan thought grimly, placing the hammer aside.

On the ground, he poured a dipper of water over his head and shook his hair. "What do you want?" he asked rudely, aware that his sleepless nights, his restless emotions were pushing him.

"Out of your debt. I want to know what you know of the Fearghus cradle. I'm returning it to you and then—"

Duncan stepped closer. He had no intention of anyone entering his quest. But if talk of it gained him time with Sybil, he'd talk. "And then?"

Awareness leaped in her eyes and a quiet happiness flowed through him. She'd been as enthralled with the kiss as he had been, searching out the tender depths, tracing the hunger. He shrugged, pushing away his need to kiss her. Her eyes skimmed his shoulders, and pushing his case, Duncan flexed his arm. Sybil's eyes widened to satisfy him. So she was interested— "Since you've come to me, let me show you around."

A willowy woman with luminous brown eyes came to his side and Duncan nodded. "Wyonna, this is Sybil. She's Emily's mother."

Sybil forced herself not to look at Duncan, not to feel the brief rage surging through her. Obviously from the way Wyonna looked at Duncan, the tenderness in her expressive eyes, Duncan had one woman. Why did he want another?

"I'm glad to meet you," Sybil managed stiffly. Just managed, her fury whipping through her.

"Come with me," Duncan said curtly, taking her hand and tugging her along after him.

By the time Sybil had caught her breath, they were standing in a small, unfinished room and Duncan had her pressed against a wall, his hands on either side of her hair. He toyed with a strand while she fought her dark mood and the need to physically attack him. He knocked lightly on her head. "You're easy to read. Your eyes ignite like sunlight glinting off topaz. Now, what's going on in there?"

"You're having an affair with her and you kissed me." She exploded with the accusation, shoving both hands at his hard, bare stomach.

He blinked, not understanding. She shoved reality under his broken, arrogant nose. "You kissed me. Came into my home and kissed me. You touched me *and* you kissed me, Duncan."

He shook his head as if clearing it. "So? I like it. You come unglued magnificently. I have great expectations where you're concerned."

"Ohh!" Sybil ducked under his arm, only to have him grab her sweater from behind and draw her back to him. "What's that supposed to mean?"

"Let me go. I was the karate class's top student." She forced her eyes away from his wide chest, from the sweat glistening on the hair running down the center of his stomach. His flat nipples gleamed and Sybil subdued the urge to trace and explore them.

Duncan's smile wasn't nice. He stood there, all dangerous male, gorgeous in his tanned skin and his rakish sweatband. His jaw clenched dangerously, the damp hair on his nape as untamed as the man. The color of night smoke, his eyes challenged her. "Try it. Take me down."

A gentleman would have apologized; Sybil didn't expect Duncan to do anything but stand there, challenging her.

She tried not to notice the pale strip of flesh beneath his navel, where his jeans waistband had slipped. She wanted to lick the drop of water trailing down his temple and nip the one on his bottom lip.

Sybil pushed back the curls that had escaped her tight chignon. Duncan could dishevel her too easily and she resented him. He could bring her down to his elemental level within seconds.

"I am not involved with Wyonna," he stated very carefully. He was unused to explaining his life, and his smoky eyes flickered. A hunter, he spoke too softly, wrapping his deep, husky tones around her with an intimacy like silk. "But it's nice to know you care. Next time bring lunch. Cook me something sweet and tasty, just like you. But with enough tart to make the taste exciting."

She recognized his challenge—since another woman wasn't occupying him, he wanted her in his bed. "You are positively beyond belief. If you think for one moment that I actually would wait on you, serve you— Take a flying leap, Duncan Tallchief."

Duncan shook his head, mocking her. He was playing with her. "Harsh words for a woman who came to see me."

Anger balled her fists. Sybil tried to remember that she had a reputation for being a cool, methodical, unemotional woman.

Duncan's fingers strolled around her lace collar. He studied the fragile cloth, tracing his finger to her throat. His fingertip meandered at her racing pulse. "Very prim and proper. Almost a virginal look."

She shifted slightly as he said, "If you take the day off and come riding with me, I'll tell you what I know of the cradle. But you won't find it. I lost the trail in Chicago."

"I am very good." She paused, shocked with her bold statement. His arrogance had washed off onto her.

Duncan bent to brush a devastating kiss across her lips. He nibbled her bottom lip before she could gasp and move away. For a big man, he moved very, very quickly, and she didn't trust him. Not for a moment. "We'll see. I've always wanted to taste 'good.'"

"Nothing can happen between us," she asserted shakily, drawing an unseen line between them. Duncan, clearly experienced with sensual play, couldn't possibly know how inexperienced she was with men. She wanted to keep it that way. Safe. Neat. Without Duncan smashing the reserve that had kept her safe. "I won't let it."

Duncan smoothed her hair, lifting the russet strands to the sunlight and studied the glistening shades. "There're two of us in this, sweetheart. Two. You and me. I think you know that our time is coming—"

Her eyes widened as she stepped back. She wasn't having any of what Duncan proposed. "No."

"Dress for riding a horse and wait for me if you want to know about the cradle. If you aren't a coward. Are you, sweetheart?" he taunted in a low, soft voice. It caused her to tremble.

At suppertime, Birk was treating Emily to a hamburger at the local hangout and Sybil sat alone at her kitchen table shredding wildflowers. Dressed in a bronze sweater and matching slacks, she dropped the petals into a plate and set about ripping apart another flower.

Duncan could see her through the screen door, and from the look on her face, he knew he was only a heartbeat behind the shredded wildflowers. She turned to his knock, and in that moment, he caught the blaze of her eyes—the woman who would like to stake him out on an anthill. She'd be worth it, all fire and shadows. In his mind, he glimpsed the image of the tigress stalking from the cool fern.

"Manners, Duncan. You need them. I've waited for hours. Riding horses at night can be dangerous," she informed him as she sailed past him to the waiting animals.

He watched the sway of her hips and found himself hardening, his boots riveted to the porch. He forced his legs to move, following her grimly.

Wyonna had been threatened and Duncan had returned the favor to Jack. He didn't want to tell Sybil how long he'd taken to preen and make himself acceptable to her. Nettled that she hadn't noticed, Duncan swung into his saddle and watched her struggle up into hers. The loose slacks tightened, defining the long length of her legs. She had a very nice backside, softened by the slight weight she had gained.

He locked his fist onto his saddle horn and wondered how the shape of her would feel beneath him.

Four

"This is what I wanted you to see," Duncan said, sliding from his horse. *What was he doing? He'd already been burned, and here he was, asking for a second helping. He wouldn't be good for her; she deserved a solid man, a gentle one with breeding who followed the rules. As a Tallchief, he made his own rules....*

Yet his gut instincts told him to capture her and make her his...his what?

Love as he'd known it could be sheer agony. He had no plan to fall beneath her spell. None at all.

The sun was setting on Tallchief Mountain and he'd brought her to the lake rippled by the mountain winds and glinting gold in the sunset.

Entranced by the red, jutting rocks and the stately timber studding the mountain, Sybil never noticed that Duncan had helped her from her horse. "It's beautiful," she whispered in an awed tone.

That's how he felt every time he stood there, wrapped in the scents of pine and fresh, clean sky. "Look—" He pointed to the deer grazing in the meadow studded with daisies. The Scottish sheep peered at them, then returned to grazing, the lambs frisking with one another.

"You have no intention of giving me information about the cradle, do you? What do you want from me?"

Direct, to the point. He liked that. Duncan noted the lift of her head. With the dying sunlight tangling in her hair, the shadows kept her expression from him. He read the rigid stance of her body. She distrusted men, the set of her shoulders was defensive.

Her scent clung to the breeze...erotic, distinctly feminine and uniquely— Unique. Too fragile. Wounded. Hardened. Frightened. That was Sybil. He could hurt her too easily, with just a look, a word. Unused to the uncertainty within him, Duncan inhaled sharply, catching the scents of pine and earth and woman. He was driven to touch her one day, his basic instincts simmering each time he caught her fragrance. He pushed away his protective instincts concerning her. He wanted to touch her on a deeper level, the way a man touches a woman. There, deep inside her, held by the flowering bud, he'd know if she'd accept him on every level. He was torn between pulling her in his arms to console her and the heady need to kiss her.

More. To take her, to make her a part of him. To claim her. To sink so deeply within her softness that she would remember him forever and he would replace any man she'd known before—Duncan didn't want to think of Sybil's male relationships.

"I like your family, Duncan. But you've got to stop pushing me. You've got to stop giving people the wrong impression."

"Wrong impression?" He intended to ferret out her opinion of him.

She crossed her arms and looked out onto the lake. "You may like playing games with women. It isn't my intention to be a passing toy for you. I'd like what information you have on the cradle and then that will be it."

The finality in her tone cut him. He wasn't done with her, nor was she untouched by him.

"Now that we've had our ride—" She started toward the horses, dismissing him.

He caught her instantly, lifting her up into his arms. Sybil glared at him, refusing to push back her hair, which had begun spilling from its confinement. Disgusted with the tumbling russet curls, she ripped away the band holding them. He liked watching her unravel, fighting the temper nipping at her cool reserve.

"Put me down," she ordered, breathing hard.

He tossed her lightly, and watched her eyes flash with anger. "Can't."

"You're perverse. Tormenting. Disgusting. I dislike this physical—*primitive* showing of strength, for a better description. You know very well how I feel about you and yet you—"

"So you've fallen for my charms?" he offered.

"Why do you persist?" she asked harshly when she'd had time to circle that tidbit. "Don't you have other toys?"

"Sit with me and watch the sunset." He saw her eyes close as he planted a quick kiss on her nose.

They jerked open, lashing at him. "I've never been a fan of swashbucklers, Duncan. And you're one. A cross between boyish charm, a swaggering cowboy and—"

She found him studying her and pressed her lips together before going on. "You're a throwback, you know. All tall and proud and arrogant like your chieftain ancestor. You actually want me to continue owing you. I refuse. What is it with you, a power thing?"

He cuddled her closer, his thumb smoothing her thigh.

Just holding her like this settled the deep ache within him. She'd laugh if she knew. Or think him mad. "You owe me nothing."

Sybil gazed at her hands, neatly folded in her lap. He wanted them on him, latched to his hair or floating lightly over him, taming the lonely darkness within him. Instead he carried her to his favorite spot and settled with her upon his lap.

"I'm not a child," she mumbled, sitting very straight. "And you're not that soft."

There in that hour with the red sunlight enfolding them, Duncan found his peace. Sybil gradually eased back, resting against him. He kissed her temple and nuzzled her hair, letting her softness, her scent soothe him. He feared she'd run from him; but she stayed.

She sighed once, caught by the beauty around them. "Duncan, this is beautiful."

"Aye," he whispered, wrapping the moment around him.

"Aye," she repeated more quietly, in a tone tinged with amusement. "'Aye, sir'—isn't that what you made Elspeth say as a child?"

He shrugged. "Arrogance and size won back then. She's been torturing me ever since."

Sybil turned to look up at him. "You still want life to fall your way. I can't afford your games, Duncan."

"Maybe it's not a game," he said lightly, testing. "I like you. We could be friends." Friendship wasn't what he wanted; she gave him peace and he wanted more.

"You wouldn't stop at that. I doubt that you ever stop until it suits you. You want too much. Find someone else."

"And let you off the hook?" he teased, rocking her. He moved her carefully so that she rested upon the sun-warmed flat rock. He read the set of her jaw and changed the subject. "We went skinny-dipping here as kids. I can almost hear Fiona's war whoop."

Sybil lay quietly, her eyes drifting over the lake, her mind flowing away from him.

But Duncan's mind wasn't on the past. It was on the woman in his arms. "Right is right," he said, more to himself than to her.

Her look—the dark, closed expression of a woman torn by pain—set him off. "I won't hurt you," he whispered against her lips, brushing them with his.

She lay so still he feared he frightened her. That the past had locked around her, freezing her, keeping her from him. "I've never been a physical person," she murmured, gazing out onto the black lake, with the gray sky hovering over the mountains. She shot him a rebellious look. "I'm not apologizing. Don't think you've lost it—whatever the Tallchief men are famed for. I have never been a sensual woman and you—you are too dynamic, you want too much."

He decided not to tell her that her fingertips, prowling across his chest, were raising his temperature. "We could be friends," he suggested again, and realized they already were.

She dismissed that with the curve of her lips. "Oil and water."

He kissed the soft hand that stroked his cheek. Sybil's eyes met his and clung. "You shaved."

"I'm trimming my desperado image." He smoothed the strands of her hair against the rock, the silk curling around his hand. He didn't want to harm her in any way; his beard would mar her fine skin. But there were other ways to harm this fragile woman—

"This is easy for you, isn't it?"

"No. I'm out of practice." He nipped her lips and heard her gasp.

She laughed then, the sound warming him. Her kiss, freely given, was worth waiting for. He held himself very still, braced against the tender, sweet tasting as she explored his lips. Sybil raised herself to her side, looking down at him. He waited, his heart racing. Would she fly away from him? Would the past grip her so painfully that the future had no chance?

She traced the shape of his lips with her fingertip and his body quaked. He pressed down the urge to wrap her closely against him. The nudge of her breast against his side caused him to groan slightly, he closed his eyes to treasure the moment. She traced his lashes and his ears. "Why me?"

Duncan lifted one eyelid to mock her. "Didn't your parents tell you about the birds and the bees?"

She flushed; he could feel her heat, even though the night was fully upon them. "Actually, no. I found out the essential details in an unpleasant way."

He damned himself for bringing her rape into the present. And he ached for the girl torn by pain, her parents' rejection. "It's not always like that."

"Like this?" she asked, bending to brush her lips over his.

"Very much like this."

She lifted to mock him with a smile. She'd seen the worst of men, the beast within them. "That's all you want? Just kisses?"

"Do you want me to lie?" he asked, smoothing her back. His tone was dry, laced with humor.

"You're a physical man, Duncan. You frighten me."

"No more than you frighten me." Duncan sucked in his breath as her hand hovered, then rested lightly upon his stomach. "You're a savage when you're aroused."

She glanced up at him, surprised. "No."

The night owl hooted and Duncan eased his hand into

her hair, finding the shape of her head and bringing her down to him. "This time, don't hold your breath. I like the sweep of it across my cheek, warming me."

He folded her carefully closer, drowning in the scent of her, exotic and very fragile. She shivered and he forced his mouth away to ask, "Are you cold?"

"No." She squirmed a bit, getting comfortable. "You know that I'm lying on top of you? Doesn't that threaten something deep and masculine within you?"

He found honest interest beneath her teasing tone. "If you're so curious, we could try this in reverse," he offered lightly.

"No, I don't think so. You'd crush me." She lowered her head to his shoulder. "The lake is peaceful, when only a short time ago the wind was tossing the waves."

Crush her? He'd be so careful with her— Duncan rummaged through that thought. Sybil had no idea how light a big man could be, a caring man. He frowned slightly, sensing how virginal she was, though no longer a girl. He prayed that he could control himself when they made love…and they would. Every nerve in his body told him that they would taste each other.

"How long has it been since someone has held you? Cared for you?" He ached for her, wanted to take away the past. Yet he couldn't. All he could do was give her peace now. He hoped she'd come back for more, wounded kitten that she was.

She shook her head. "If you feel sorry for me now, I'll kill you. I don't want to talk about it. We should go."

Duncan bit her finger. "So you are a savage after all. I knew it the moment I saw you coming to rescue me."

"I would prefer to forget that momentary lapse. There you were, my only hope to save Emily, living the macho cowboy-chieftain image to the hilt. Though you wore jeans, I was certain a loincloth was under them and that any min-

ute you'd dab war paint on your face. You were outnumbered and too high on the warpath to know it. What was I
supposed to do?''

''Loincloths have their advantages.'' When his lips
found the pulse in her throat, Sybil inhaled. Duncan's body
arched slightly, nudging her softness intimately. His jeans
were definitely too constricting. He agonized as Sybil's hips
lowered delicately, finding him. Her expression told him
she was curious, told him what he wanted to know. She
trusted him enough to reveal this side of herself to him. He
held very still as she lifted her hips slowly and lowered
them again, her teeth biting her bottom lip as she concentrated on the tormenting movement.

In another minute, he'd grab those curved hips and—
Duncan, though frustrated, caught the look of the sleeping
tigress, newly awakened. ''You can ignite now,'' he whispered, sliding his kiss lower.

''Mmm?''

''Ignite.'' Dressed in her nightshirt, Sybil punched her
computer keys with a vengeance. She had lain upon Duncan's very prime, very hard body and kissed him desperately. She had rhythmically nudged his very full and hard
masculinity and dampened at the contact. Little had kept
her from exploring the amazing, heavy evidence of his desire.

He hadn't lifted a finger to stop her. She remembered
the hard surge of his body to hers and the way she had
melted instinctively, achingly, responding to him. He'd
tethered her to his beautiful body with a mere touch of his
lips.

Duncan was very experienced. He'd known how to draw
out her reaction and he'd been successful. She had fitted
her mouth to his and slid her tongue against his. He'd
gently enticed her into his warmth, the rhythmic suckling

echoed in the gentle arching of his long body. He'd tutored her until she'd matched his strokes— Sybil slapped the stack of research papers on her desk. "Ohhh!"

She'd never experienced an intimate, tender, playful kiss. She'd fallen like bricks—or flower petals struck by spring rain—under the light pressure of his mouth. He'd kept her on him, teasing her, enticing her, and she'd let him. When his hands had gently curved around her waist, following her hips to her bottom, she'd wanted— Sybil didn't know what she'd wanted, except those skillful large warm hands fitting to her, cupping her. Gently, so gently, his hand had curved lower, smoothing her intimately.

She was certain he could feel her damp warmth through her clothing. The butterfly-light caresses had tormented her until she'd pressed her hips against him, seeking more.... He'd murmured something about her scent—luscious and sweet, it told him of her heat; of how she waited, tight and shy and tender; of how he would press so deeply in her that their bodies would be like one. How her tender petals would enfold him— The husky, unsteady words had pleasured her—

Of course she wasn't waiting for Duncan Tallchief. Not one heartbeat.

The horror of what she had done, locking herself to him and taking, grinding her hips and breasts against him, had shocked her throughout the night. By four o'clock in the morning, she had to admit that Duncan had dropped the swashbuckler image and had been assaulted by her. Her breasts had ached painfully for his caress, for his mouth. Yet he had not— If he had wanted to prove that she had one molecule of primitive sexual needs, he'd succeeded.

Only his control had tempered her need to rip away his shirt and taste that beautiful chest he'd flaunted at the shelter.

She closed her lids and saw Duncan lying, rumpled and

desirable, beneath her. The tenderness in his expression had frightened her worse than the trembling needs heating her.

"Kissing," she muttered now to her kitchen clock, then sipped fresh, hot coffee without tasting it. Five o'clock had not found her in a better mood. Duncan had not given her any information about the cradle. He was keeping that to himself and had lured her into kissing him. And flattening him on that sun-warmed stone. He'd been so noble to sacrifice himself, tethering her there with those devastatingly tender kisses.

"It's his fault." There he had lain, stretched out, keeping his hands to himself except for the exquisite stroking of her back. And the tormenting, light touches between her legs. A woman could get very warm next to Duncan.

"Oh, fine," she mumbled, prowling through a list of antique dealers in Chicago. She created labels for the dealers, and would send them a picture of the cradle. She'd pay him off and walk away.

Sybil gripped her arms across her aching chest. There was no reason she should be tempted by Duncan Tallchief. None at all. He was exactly what she did not want in her life—hard, arrogant, boyish at times…and devastating.

And tender. She'd have to watch out for Duncan's tenderness and his compassion. And his deep love of his family.

The composite man was too dangerous.

She glanced up at the pickup headlights, saw them die and hurled herself out of her chair. She met Duncan on the porch, the dawn outlining his tall, long-legged body. She'd know that walk anywhere, the broad-shouldered, confident, swaggering male, strolling into her world. He could take his confidence somewhere else. She wasn't buying. "Go away. Just go away and do not come back."

He looked up the steps to where she stood dressed in her

long nightshirt. "You've got nice legs. Interesting knee-caps."

Kneecaps interesting? Sybil dealt with that tidbit while Duncan sniffed the early-morning air, tinged with the fragrance of herbs and freshly cut grass. His eyes locked on her.

"No kissing," Sybil stated unsteadily as he walked up the steps toward her.

Duncan tipped his western hat back on his head and locked his thumbs in his belt. The rakish cowboy stance weakened her slightly. She excused herself. She was only human. There he stood, rangy, tough and looking kissable. She'd had his temperature rising last night— The thought knocked her sideways; Duncan had trembled and heated. His deep, unsteady groan had been steeped in frustration.

She had actually...actually gotten to him. The evidence had pressed intimately against her lower body.

For a moment Sybil basked in the knowledge that as a woman she could tempt a highly desirable man. That insight shot to her senses, curling her toes.

"No kisses," she repeated, trying to deny the hunger within her.

"I'd settle for coffee."

His wistful expression rocked her. Early morning was never a good time for her, Sybil decided. She was too weak, her defenses low. She needed all her walls with Duncan. Every last one. "Okay, I'll give you coffee. Then you'll go— Why are you here this early?"

He followed her into the kitchen. Duncan's tone was too sexy as he drawled, "Couldn't sleep."

He took the cup of coffee and sniffed it appreciatively. Sybil jerked a raincoat from the rack and jammed her arms into it. She tied the sash firmly. Duncan's amused expression taunted her. She could have killed him. "I don't have a robe. I don't usually have visitors this early."

"Uh-huh." Duncan leaned against her kitchen counter as though the scene happened every day. "Lacey left a message on my machine last night. Jack Smith and his buddies know you're in town. You've bruised their feelings. They may want to return the favor."

Her hand trembled slightly. She fought the old fear and almost lost. She wouldn't let Duncan see her shadows, not now. Duncan carefully placed his coffee cup aside. "If you feel up to it, there are women here who need to talk with someone like you."

"Me?"

"You're a survivor. They need to see that. You're a strong woman, Sybil. No matter what happened before. You've built a life for you and your daughter."

"I...I'd rather not." Exposing herself could only bring more pain.

He nodded and flipped open the knot she had tied around her raincoat. "Think about it. And watch out for Jack."

Duncan's hands slid inside to rest on her waist. His thumbs stroked her stomach. "Be careful, Sybil. Or you'll find me glued to you for protection. I take up a lot of space and a certain lady recently told me that I'm not that sweet. You might not be up to the taming."

Entranced, she watched his expression change—darken as he drew her to him. "I'm not what you need."

She found her fingers had latched on to his western belt, anchoring him. He wasn't taking that hot, dark, dangerous look anywhere but in her kitchen. "I know."

He rubbed his cheek, freshly shaven, against hers and groaned. The deep, hot male sound hovered in the air and shot for her lower stomach, weakening her legs. "Lay off," he whispered rawly. "Stop looking at me like that."

Morning would be a wonderful time to make love.

Make love? Sybil had never indulged, had never been

tempted— Duncan was easing her from the raincoat. It fell to the floor with her last thoughts to run....

He dropped kisses softly on her parted lips and her re-sistance wilted with each one. She leaned against him, sighed as his hands warmed her skin, sliding beneath the nightshirt. His touch eased upward toward her breasts, smoothed the sensitive outer perimeters. His thumbs stroked her nipples, just once, very lightly, and she tensed, jolted from his dreamy, sweet kisses.

When his hands slowly enclosed her breasts, gently hold-ing them, Sybil barely breathed. She stood very still, the tender pressure making her want more.

Duncan eased her nightshirt away and she realized that he'd drawn her to a shadowy corner. Sybil crossed her arms, fearing what he would say as he looked at her.

Duncan's expression hardened. "You're a beautiful woman, sweetheart. Will this help?"

He moved too quickly, startling her. His mouth brushed her breast and her heart stopped. She knew she should move away, even as he took her breast into his mouth.

The heat and gentle suckling took her breath away. Her legs gave out and Duncan supported her, gently treasuring her breasts, the tip of one nipple, the underside, and then her other breast, already hardened, aching. She cried out then, latched her fingers in his hair and held him to her.

With an unsteady groan, Duncan trembled, his hand slid-ing downward to her stomach.

His hand curled around her softness, pressing gently. Something within Sybil waited, pleaded for his touch and tightened as his long fingers smoothed her.

When he touched her intimately, Sybil bolted, pushing him away. She covered herself with her hands, shaking with need.

Duncan loomed over her, the heat and tension pouring

off him. She saw the hunger shimmer in his gray eyes, the hardening of his slightly swollen lips.

She'd nipped him.

Sybil blinked as horror spread into her. She'd tugged open his shirt. His stomach contracted sharply and released as if he'd been holding his breath too tightly.

She feared looking lower, yet could not help herself. Duncan's arousal thrust at his clothing and he made no move to shield it.

She waited for the fear to chill her, but it never came. Only the savage beating of her heart, the hunger of her body throbbing for his.

"Come here," Duncan said too quietly. "I won't hurt you."

Why did she trust him? Why did she need him? Sybil thought as she moved into the safe harbor of his arms. "Frank never touched me. I couldn't bear it," she found herself whispering desperately against his throat. "He changed immediately after the wedding."

"He's not here now." Duncan rocked her against him and Frank slunk back into the past. "You set me off. You're too sexy."

She let that soak in as she nestled against him. She shouldn't trust him, but she did. "No. I've never been that."

His lips curved against her temple. "No? Then why am I in this condition?"

She was horrified, her gaze drawn to the firm outline above his thighs. Her body ached, but she knew that a man— "Oh! Oh! I am so sorry."

Instinctively she reached out to soothe him, and Duncan tensed, edging back from her. "Don't. Just don't touch me. I...I could use a cup of hot coffee."

Looking devastating, his hair rumpled and his shirt open, exposing his chest, Duncan scowled down at her.

"Duncan. This is not my fault," she began, and took a step backward. He slowly drew his hands away from her body, closed his eyes and groaned.

"That is no way to leave a lady," Sybil stated unsteadily after Duncan shook his head as if to clear it and walked out the door, banging it behind him.

A nifty little thought zipped by her and she replayed it, savoring it. Duncan had been clearly aroused. *She* had ignited him. Sybil eased into her nightshirt; if Duncan wanted to play games, she just might challenge him.

She found herself humming.

"I have to check the hems," Elspeth stated coolly as she faced her three brothers. They weren't easy men to deal with alone; united they were almost a war. She'd fed them a huge meal, baked them their favorite apple dumplings soaked in buttery sauce, and yet they sprawled in her kitchen, defying her.

Calum leaned back against the counter, his glasses glinting at her like round mirrors. Just returned from a business trip, he'd stopped by Elspeth's to check on her before going to his contemporary home. Birk, fresh from a new battle with Lacey, had dived into Elspeth's beef-and-potatoes meal as though he hadn't eaten for a year. Duncan—looking as untamed as ever, his hair shaggy down to his collar—sat, boots propped on another chair, leveling a dark Tallchief frown at her.

She leveled one back, careless of her brothers' set expressions. "I cooked a meat-and-potato dinner, not my usual fare, dear brothers. I prefer pasta and salad. But oh, no. I'm only here to serve my family. I suggest you cooperate or our family dinners are going to have a very leafy, green look to them."

"Fodder," Birk said, disgusted by the thought of salad without a hefty beef menu.

"What's right is right," Elspeth stated airily as Calum began to clean away the table. "As the sister who bothers to sew on your missing buttons and make chicken soup for you when you have the sniffles, I demand that you submit."

"Submit," Duncan repeated, glowering at her. "She gets ornery when she uses that word."

"I never asked for your chicken soup when I had pneumonia," Birk mumbled.

Calum came through with a thought that jerked the brothers' heads to him. "Winds. Cold ones, right up our backsides. We'd have to sit with our legs crossed and check the weather report before going anywhere."

Elspeth was desperate. If she didn't corner them now, they'd get out of her clutches and be prepared for her next volley. She was circling her next attack, when Sybil knocked on the door and Emily called merrily, "Ho, Black Knights of the Tallchief clan!"

"Aye!" the three brothers' deep voices returned.

Birk opened the door for Sybil and Emily. With a gallant, courtly sweep of his hand across his stomach, he invited them into Elspeth's home.

Sybil handed Elspeth a freshly baked cherry pie sprinkled with sugar, and Calum zipped it to the table. "I'll just take that."

"Behave," Elspeth muttered, crossing her arms.

Birk was just slicing into the pie as if he hadn't eaten two apple dumplings. Elspeth's cool, crisp voice slashed across the room. "Cut that pie now and you'll never have another one of mine."

While Calum and Birk sulked, Duncan studied Sybil. She had a happy, secretive look about her. The cool, ferny green of her blouse and slacks set off her fair coloring; her hair gleamed like polished copper, in the knot at the back of her head. She would taste better than the apple dumplings and the cherry pie.

Sybil glanced at the Tallchief family, studying their expressions. "Did I interrupt?"

"Not a thing," Duncan murmured, enchanted by her quick blush and glance away from him. He nudged her shoe with his boot and those furious tigress eyes whipped back to him. He smiled and moved his lips in a kiss that the others missed.

Sybil ignited nicely, color rising in her cheeks.

"She wants us to wear kilts." Birk's tone labeled Elspeth's idea as something she'd pulled out of a child's toy box.

Calum made a restless move toward the pie and Elspeth tugged his ear. "Our tartan plaid. Pie after kilts."

"Once Elspeth makes up her mind, we're goners." Birk's stage whisper to Emily caused her to giggle.

"Emily, I would be so grateful if you help me with this…little matter of persuading my brothers to try on their kilts."

"Oh, fine. Women of all ages bonding, forming ranks," Calum muttered.

Duncan shrugged. The brothers had always stood together against Elspeth's feminine whims concerning them…. Except when she really needed them. Duncan did not see this as a dire time. "Looks like we're not buying, Elspeth."

Sybil smiled at Calum, and waded through an appeal to his logic. "Elspeth has worked so hard to duplicate the design—the sett—of the Fearghus tartan, adding the streak of Tallchief vermilion. She's spent hours studying the design alone, let alone all those hours at the loom and sewing."

Her eyes strolled down Birk's six-foot-three body. "I think you'd be marvelous in a kilt. Rugged, masculine, dashing…"

"He's got knobby knees. Football cleat scars all over

them.'' Calum bent to sniff the cherry pie and dip his finger in it. "How do you know they'll fit?"

Elspeth eyed him. "I've seen enough of your backsides to know the width. You remember those shorts of yours I borrowed for a pattern? I adjusted from them."

Duncan and Birk glowered at Calum, the traitor. "That's low, Elspeth," he muttered.

Sybil began to cut the cherry pie and Duncan's heart stopped. The graceful flow of her pale fingers entranced him.

"I baked this for the celebration. Elspeth invited me to see the grand display of her brothers in their clan's first tartan. You'd be so handsome, Calum. Personally, I've always loved men in kilts. They seem so brave. Mmm...cherry pie with ice cream later. I can't wait to see you all decked out."

Duncan cherished the smile playing around the corner of her lips. Elspeth placed her hands on Emily's thin shoulders and bent to ask her, "What do you think, Emily? After all, you're the Black Knights' princess, aren't you? I'm sure they would like your opinion."

Emily played to the question, walking around each of the brothers and studying them. "I will have no one say that the Black Knights are cowards. Unless...they won't try on the kilts."

"Emily!" Betrayed by their princess, the three men roared in unison.

Duncan picked through the mutters and groans and Elspeth's ushering of her brothers to the living room, where she had hung the kilts. Sybil had just laughed. The sound was like a tinkling of a wind chime, or summer rain falling upon a still pond, a flute rippling through a sweet chorus.

He locked on to her hand and tugged her onto his lap. She glared at him, refusing to rise to his bait.

"I'm a desperate man. I'll wear that skirt for a dance."

He brought her hand to his mouth and kissed her palm. "Is it a deal?"

"Ohh! You are so maddening. It's a kilt, not a skirt. She's worked so hard for this and you are all acting like—" Sybil inhaled unsteadily, obviously warring with her need to fight with him. She shook her head as if to clear it. "I didn't come here to bargain with you, Duncan. I came to work with Elspeth on the—"

She glanced toward the living room, where Birk had just hooted and Calum was mumbling darkly.

"Your turn, Birk. Step into the closet," Elspeth commanded firmly. "Lacey said you were a chicken-heart and that you'd never do it. I said you would."

"Oh, she said that, did she?" Birk muttered, and a door slammed as he stepped into the closet.

Emily peered around the corner, to find her mother sitting on Duncan's lap. "Your mother has agreed to go dancing with me if I try on Elspeth's nightmare," Duncan told her.

"Dancing? You said 'a dance,'" Sybil protested, sliding out of his lap and smoothing her hair.

Duncan stood and bent to kiss her nose, dodging her swat. "Technicalities."

Five

The three Tallchief brothers, dressed in tartan plaid and white dress shirts with ruffles, loomed in Elspeth's living room. The sashes draped over their shoulders broadened them even more, and their scowls filled the room with a dark, brooding aura. Elspeth smoothed and patted and adjusted the plaids and kilts as though she were lining up boys for church services. They crossed their arms and stood stoically, as if they'd been through this routine before—though never wearing kilts.

With the air of a sister, Elspeth bent to tug up Birk's white socks. He kept his eyes locked to the ceiling with an air of resignation as she said, ''Hose and brogues. I'll have to work on that.''

''Boots,'' he shot back, stormy eyes locking with placid ones.

''Mmm. We'll see.'' Elspeth knew her brothers well. She had to pick her wars and with whom. Given a chance, they'd join forces against her.

"Our sheep probably caught cold over this," Calum muttered.

Duncan, looking miffed, enchanted Sybil. After his exit from the closet, Birk and Calum had whistled and smirked.

"Don't let them go anywhere," Elspeth whispered to Sybil and Emily. She looked at the three, tall cowboys dressed in tartans and socks. "They're very good at leaping out of windows."

"I heard that," Calum muttered. "We're not going anywhere with our clothes locked in the closet, sister dear."

Elspeth raced up the stairs and returned a moment later wearing a matching outfit. "Oh, great. The unisex look," Birk groaned, and flopped into a chair.

"Sit with your knees together, dearie," Calum offered with a grin. "Better work on your tan. If the sun can get through the hair."

"Likewise," Birk shot back, coming to his feet.

Elspeth pivoted around her brothers, clearly happy. "Let's stand together. I want Sybil to see us all together, dressed for the first time in our family plaid. The Fearghus-Tallchief tartan."

She wrapped a length of the tartan around Emily's shoulders and secured it with a safety pin. "I thought we would design a crest for the broach. The Fergusson original badge was a small sunflower—Una thought the Fearghus family was related to them. Maybe ours could be a peace pipe with a feather crossing it. Or two sunflowers for Una and Tallchief. Or five feathers for the five of us. I rather like the five feathers. We'll see. For now, this will have to do."

"Gee…all dressed up and nowhere to go," Birk mumbled, picking at the plaid pleats covering his thighs.

"Wind. Straight up the backside." Calum pitched that volley at the Tallchiefs and it dropped to the floor like a fresh cowpile.

Ominous, dead silence lay over the room until Sybil decided to support Elspeth against her brothers, who were looking as receptive as a brick wall. They stood together and glowered at their sister, very much resembling their Sioux ancestor preparing for a warpath. She lifted the tartan plaid at Calum's chest. "Such lovely work, Elspeth. Every stripe is measured and repeated exactly right. The vermilion is perfect against the green and black. What shade of green is that?"

"I call it 'Dragon Green.' A little extra touch of goldenrod in the dye. I've changed the sett a bit, broadening the vermilion in lieu of dark red."

"Elspeth, this thing doesn't have a place for a belt." Calum hooked his thumbs into the kilt's waistband. "I will not—repeat, not—wear that hairy purse thing."

Elspeth waved her hand airily. "Details. It's called a 'sporran.' Stockings would set it off—knee-length hose...." She pressed her brooding brothers into line, stepped beside Duncan and said to Sybil, "Oh, I wish Fiona were here.... What do you think, Sybil?"

Sybil tapped her finger to her lips, admiring the fine display of tall, adorably nettled men in front of her. Clearly the brothers adored their sister, and Elspeth loved them, beaming up at them. Though Birk and Calum were gorgeous, Duncan's dark frustration intrigued her. In her lifetime, she hadn't indulged in revenge—other than Frank— but Duncan caused her to forget the past and the moment was too tempting. There he stood, all broad shoulders and narrow hips and long legs, dressed in tartan plaid and looking like a disgusted masculine bonbon. She tried for a serious expression and failed. "From loincloths to kilts.... You're beautiful, Duncan."

Staring coolly down at her from his lofty height, Duncan lifted a thick, sleek, black brow. "You'll pay for that, Sybil-belle."

She batted her lashes innocently. Teasing Duncan was a

sport that she could feed upon nicely. "I will? Really? Tell me more."

Before she could move, Duncan hauled her to him, bent her over his arm and kissed her. Enclosed in his scents, the ruffled wall of his chest hard against her and his arms holding her firmly, Sybil gasped. Duncan instantly took his advantage, deepening the kiss. Before Sybil could jerk up her defenses, she dived into the kiss, fed upon it, searched for more. She found sunlight and flowers and heat so burning it swept to the very center of her. She was strong now, taking, giving, slanting her mouth against his, nipping his lips as hungrily as he tasted hers. The hot wind washed over her, melding his hard body to hers. The kilt, lighter and less confining than his jeans, allowed his desire to lurch and press heavily against her.

When her knees buckled, she found herself released too suddenly, Duncan's dark hungry stare locking onto her. "You're not up to it," he said finally, when all she could hear was the drumming of her heart.

To her satisfaction, Duncan wasn't unaffected; he was breathing deeply, dragging air into his lungs.

He lowered her toes to the floor; she'd thought she was floating. She realized then that his hair was rumpled by her grasping hands, that she had locked herself to him and had taken as much as he, draining and feeding what lay within her. Yet she couldn't let him leave it at that and foraged for a proper sword to his challenge. Duncan was a taker...if she let him reel her in.

The satisfied smirk riding his lips raised her thorns. Sybil shook loose of the fever gripping her. She had to keep the play even. "That's one," she said, stepping up to Birk. She'd never played a bold woman, but to shock Duncan, she would. He deserved a nip at his confidence. "For your bravery, Birk Tallchief—"

Birk's kiss was playful and light. Calum's was sweet and

brotherly. They both winked at Duncan, who didn't change his grim expression.

Emily giggled. "That's the first time I've ever seen my mom give kisses like candy."

"I'll candy you," Duncan threatened with a grin, and tugged Emily to him for a kiss on her cheek. She beamed up at him, her eyes glowing.

Elspeth looped her arms through Duncan's and Birk's and Calum stepped behind her. There they stood, tall and fierce—the brothers proud of Elspeth's handicraft, her intelligence in creating the new Tallchief tartans. And she was proud of them. Together, they seemed to grow and luminate, overpowering Sybil with the love shared among them.

Duncan raised his hand and yelled, "Aye!"

"Aye!" returned the others, lifting their thumbs.

"One more time," Duncan ordered. "This time with Emily, our princess."

That "Aye!" went straight to Sybil's heart. Emily's "Aye!" trembled with joy; it spilled from her bright eyes and grin.

Sybil wrapped her arms around Emily and looked at the Tallchiefs. Tears she hadn't shed in a lifetime burned at her lids, emotion swirling around her. This was what a family was, a gentle circle of teasing and giving and love. They'd managed bad times and now as adults they stood just as close.

Sybil turned to Duncan. Rumpled and fierce, he glowered at her from his height. She noted his fists at his sides, and the first step he took toward her she knew he wanted to carry her out into the night. She'd give her heart then and she couldn't afford the loss. Not to Duncan Tallchief. He would want everything.

She met his wintry-gray eyes and caught the set of his mouth and jaw. He was angry now; his moods ran as fast and deep as the wind-tossed mountain lake, not suiting her. He bore rugged, untamed male edges with as much pride as the family tartan. He wasn't an easy man, and linking herself to him would be a disaster. Survivors avoided disasters—if they were smart—and that was exactly what she intended to do.

"Cherry pie on me," she offered lightly. She managed to walk stiffly to the kitchen without collapsing.

Last week, when they'd tried on the tartans, Duncan had caught the pain in Sybil's expression, the tears shimmering in her eyes, and ached for her. He stroked his jaw and listened to the coarse sound of his stubble meeting his calloused hand.

July hovered in the clover field, the bumblebees droning over the meadows. Tallchief Mountain caught the heat of the day quickly and just as quickly tossed it away into the night shadows. Cattle grazed in the fields leading up to the mountain and deer kept to the higher pastures. Duncan, freshly showered from chopping wood, allowed the night air to sweep over him.

He'd needed the exercise to ease the tight need Sybil had ignited. Duncan ran his hand across his chest, rubbing the hair. He wasn't a boy, allowing his body and moods to rule him; yet Sybil raised something dark and hot that cried out for her cool touch…and her heat.

The breeze causing his unopened shirt to flutter was scented with a coming storm, hot and furious, that would lash at the mountain. A softer scent, one bringing memories, settled in the air—his mother's scarlet climbing roses and an ache he didn't want to name. He preferred the safe reality of thunder and lightning, the fierce elements of wind and earth and sky, to the uncertain emotions running within him.

He'd forgotten his dreams and closed his heart in a

closet. He pushed the cradle away from his mind; he didn't want to ache for children to fill his heart, his home.

Then there was the driving, fierce, elemental need of a man for a woman. A woman who suited him. More than once he'd found himself thinking of Sybil's soft breasts, the sweet sigh of release running through her, her hunger as she'd lain upon him—

Duncan's raw emotions caught at him, matching the still, heavy heat of the approaching summer storm. He'd been away for days. This time he'd found a runaway child, frightened of her parents and turning to a street gang for comfort. He'd circled the family and found an aunt with the backbone to take and protect the girl.

Sybil had enticed him away from the shadows, stirred the old dreams.

For her sake and her wounded past, he'd be very careful.

He reached for the telephone after the second ring, unwilling to stop prowling through his thoughts. Elspeth was worried about Sybil, who had just dropped Emily off for safekeeping. Elspeth had watched Sybil's car race toward Tallchief Mountain. "There's a storm brewing, Duncan. She has no idea of summer storms—the washouts or the trees that can fall when struck by lightning. Watch for her, will you? She was driving too fast, not like her at all."

Duncan caught the flash of headlamps in his windows, and from the darkened open door, he watched the car wind up the mountain toward the house. "I'll take care of your baby."

There was a pause, before Elspeth countered, "Don't use that sneer with me, Duncan Tallchief. You can be nasty tempered when you're prickly as a wounded bear. Sybil isn't in that stable a mood, either."

"I'm fairly quivering with fear," he drawled.

There was a fierce, angry pause before Elspeth shot a

dose of the truth at him. "The two of you are a fiery mix and you know it. Take care of her."

Duncan hung up the phone and watched Sybil lurch her expensive car to a stop. She pushed free of it and went to snap open the trunk, fighting a bundle that appeared to be heavy. He lodged his shoulder against a post, tethering himself to the porch. Because if he caught Sybil in the night with her temper riding her, he couldn't trust himself. Elspeth had been right—they were a fiery mix.

"So, you've come after me." He shielded the lifting of his heart with a drawl as Sybil struggled up the porch steps, lugging a huge, paper-wrapped object. Her hair had escaped its moorings and moonlight caught the waves flowing down her business jacket to her slacks sheathing her long legs. Raindrops sparkled on her gray suit jacket, marring the perfect cloth.

"You could help me with this, Duncan. It's heavy," she snapped, and the raindrops glittered like sequins. Simmering in her temper and fresh from the night wind, Sybil looked as elemental as Duncan felt with the storm hovering around Tallchief Mountain.

Her stare locked onto him and the jolt hit Duncan like lightning. This was how he'd wanted her, the ice cracked.

"Ask nicely," he ordered, on edge with his emotions and the woman whom he wanted desperately. She had nerve turning up tonight of all nights, when his own storms threatened to shatter his control. Yet he took her burden and nodded toward the door, following her through it.

She stood in the dark shadows, and God, she was fierce, legs spread, the material taut across her thighs. Her arms were folded over her chest, her head held high. He couldn't resist nettling whatever control she might have. It wasn't fair for her to raise his temperature just with a look. He placed the heavy object on his scarred coffee table—the boards were from Una's first kitchen table.

He leaned back against the wall and watched her simmer, an entertainment he had learned to relish. "Are you going to explode?"

She took a full minute to draw herself together; he looked on, entranced. She pushed her hair back with both hands and he noted the expensive cut of her pristine, white blouse. A pearl button had come undone with her efforts. Rather than act the gentleman, he preferred to cherish the line of her breasts rising and falling sharply within the suit's jacket. He envied the bit of lace that bound them snugly away from him.

"You are just as beastly as Elspeth says you were as a child," she stated finally.

"Your friend Elspeth is a tattletale. She told me you were coming."

"Yes, that's like her. She's a caring person. She loves you and I don't know why." Sybil jerked off her coat and bent to tear away the wrappings of the bundle. Paper and cord flew everywhere.

Duncan enjoyed the passion of her movements. "Are you like this at Christmas, tearing through the gifts?"

She paused to glare at him. "You could have come to the car and helped me. This is heavy."

"I could have, but I really enjoyed the sight of you lugging something to me. I found myself wondering if you sweat...or if nothing ever warms or wrinkles you." He reached to trace a crease across her blouse, pressing the softness beneath. His fingertips lingered on the bit of lace exposed by the freed button. "Could it be a peacemaking gift?"

"Ha! Why in the world would I want to make peace with you?" she demanded as another length of wrapping paper flew his way.

"I'm sweet. Elspeth says so. A real charmer."

"Ha! I feel sorry for any woman near you, Duncan Tall-chief. You make promises you don't keep and you—"

He caught her upper arm, whirling her against him. "Explain that."

Enfolded in his arms, Sybil struggled slightly. "Oh, fine," she muttered after blowing a strand of hair from her face. "Just what one could expect from you. Brute force."

He released her so quickly she leaned against the back of the sofa. "What do you mean?" he asked quietly, tethering his emotions.

She dashed the back of her hand against her eyes and tears shimmered in her eyes. "What do you mean?" he asked more softly, and watched her expression close.

Smoke and topaz, the color of their eyes, locked and held.

She shifted instantly, hurrying to drag the wood cradle from the last of the wrappings. "There. That is the Tallchief cradle. It's the one that Una's chieftain husband made for her dowry. She wouldn't marry him without it. The cradle held their five babies. Her husband had to learn to live an entirely new life, but he did. He learned how to farm and carve presents for her. He was shunned by white settlers and by his own people and Una salved him with a clan all their own. But he never looked back. Neither did she. They loved each other. I think he must have enjoyed nettling her and they fought horribly."

"Really?" Duncan asked without surprise. "The Tallchiefs were known for their passion and honor. So Elspeth has been spreading our family history before you," Duncan murmured, watching the silvery tears flow slowly down her cheeks.

He cursed silently; he'd wounded her.

She shook her head, pushed back her hair and tried to swallow her tears. Duncan eased her into his arms, stroked the back of her head and hoped she'd let him comfort her.

''What's this about? What promise did I make that I haven't kept?'' he asked unevenly as Sybil clutched him, burrowing into the curve of his throat and shoulder. Whatever edge drove her, she clung to him, her fingers digging into him. Duncan fought the fear clawing at him—had she been hurt? Had Jack had his revenge while Duncan was away? Had Frank's tentacles reached from prison?

''You rat,'' she muttered, jerking herself away.

The fury within him settled; he enjoyed having her passion directed at him.

She pointed at the cradle. ''My debt is paid to you. It's a lovely old thing. I found it in the basement of a woman who had just passed away. There's a little carved feather under the Celtic design. I suppose that is the mark of Tallchief. It's no wonder that Una mourned having to sell it.''

Her fingers trembled, then drifted, lingering across the curved headboard of the cradle. ''I'm tired. I've got to go home. Emily is at Elspeth's.''

''It's too late to collect her now.'' *Stay where I can see you. Let me hold you.*

She wavered, wary of him. Moonlight slid into the house, wedging a silver square between them. Thunder rolled and a cloud covered the moon. Duncan heard his heart beat, his need to hold her warring with his need to kiss her as a man who needs the other part of him held close and tight. ''Stay and tell me about the cradle.''

''The woman who brings the cradle to a man of Fearghus blood will fill it with his babies....'' Duncan reeled with the legend, the thought that Sybil could take him within her and create a life—

Too late. He'd given up long ago, his dreams shattered. Yet his pulses hummed with the urge to make love to her. His instincts told him that one taste wouldn't be enough.

''I detest owing anyone, anything, especially someone as arrogant as you. Even now, when I've gone to all that work to ferret out something you should have already found easily, you *demand* that I stay. *Demand,* Duncan. I'm not one of your siblings to be ordered around. I doubt that there is a 'please' in you.''

Duncan found himself smiling. Sybil wasn't giving an inch. He touched her nose and she eased back a step. He took another toward her. ''I'm despicable, of course.''

''True.''

Before she could move toward the door, leaving him alone, Duncan lit an old kerosene lamp. The light spread over Sybil's skin like honey. She tasted like that beneath his mouth, like warm, flowing honey. ''Storm coming. Sometimes it knocks out the electricity. Will you…please look at the cradle with me?'' Because of her accusation, he was very careful in phrasing the question.

She'd foraged and harvested for him, lugged and struggled and brought him the cradle. Unused to having others take care of his needs, Duncan weighed the thought. A gift from Sybil was worth the wait; she had pleased something dark and just as fierce as his great-great-grandfather's pride. She had brought the cradle to him, rather than let another bring it for her. Her passion to rid herself of him was too contradictory to be true. Duncan salved himself with the thought and prayed she'd linger close to him.

He placed the lamp on the coffee table that had also been Una's. The cradle's rich, old wood glowed in the soft light and he crouched beside it. It was almost a yard long, but light enough for a woman to carry. Tallchief had taken great care to keep the wood thin, yet sturdy. Duncan ran his fingers across the smooth wild cherry wood, tracing the intertwined Celtic design on the headboard. The arced bottom allowed for rocking. ''The Tallchief cradle,'' he murmured.

Sybil couldn't know how fiercely his emotions caught

him—a woman of passion sharing his Tallchief heritage. His woman. The primitive thought struck him, winded him.

She touched the tiny, aged carvings running down the sides of the cradle. "There's the intricate Celtic circle.... The cradle is carved from a solid piece of wood. If you clean it properly, you'll probably find good-luck symbols."

The images depicted a warrior on a horse, claiming a woman who fought him; the tepee and then the five babies, carved at each birth. A man and a woman stood together, a happy marriage. Duncan traced her finger, then slid to the circle of tiny marks. "Teething babies."

She smiled tenderly in the lamplight and circled the marks with her fingertip, which lay next to his on the gleaming wood. Duncan's emotions shifted as her low, husky voice curled around him. "Mmm. Probably a Tallchief brother or a sister playing on the floor, peering at the new baby in the cradle."

"Probably." Did she know how she lightened the shadows within him?

"It couldn't have been easy—Tallchief and Una coming from different worlds and loving each other." Sybil's tone held reverence and disbelief that matched his own feelings.

Lightning flashed outside, violence striking the tentative sharing between them and breaking the mood. Sybil gently moved her hand away. "I have to go."

"What promise did I make that I didn't keep?" he asked, watching her. Her lashes fluttered and she looked away. "I'd rather forget I said anything of the kind."

He traced the carved symbols and prayed she'd believe him. "I always keep my promises, Sybil. Always."

Clearly she gnawed on a private bone that he had picked. "Yes, well. I've got to go," she stated briskly, rising to her feet.

He rose slowly. "I've hurt you and I don't know how."

Her tone sliced him, as brittle as glass shards. "Think again. I don't wound easily. Not anymore."

"Then why did you cry?"

"Duncan…"

Her unsteady whisper curled around him; he clung to the notion that it held longing, that she'd come to him…for him.

She looked down at the glass lamp, blue with age. "Is it a family heirloom, too?"

"Changing the subject?" He kissed her cheek and breathed in her fresh, feminine scent, finding it akin to his mother's roses.

"I love heirlooms, especially those that are cherished and have stories behind them."

"Una thought her heart would break when the things were sold to keep their land. I can understand. No doubt her husband ached just as much, his pride nicked."

Sybil smiled, her hand drifting back to the old cradle. "Probably. He made more cradles, you know, and got a good price for them. But this is the one, the one with the Sioux symbols, that held their children."

"You've been reading Una's journals, too." It pleased him that she wanted to know more about the Tallchiefs than what she'd learned to recover the cradle.

"Theirs is a love story, a romance that will endure forever. A fairy tale, really."

"Don't you believe what she wrote?" Duncan barely breathed.

"A woman in love writes with her heart."

"She was in love with him until death. And he with her. He adored her."

"You would take up his side. Tallchief captured an indentured bondwoman who was deserted by the people holding her papers. He took advantage of her, Duncan. He ran her down and jerked her up on his horse and made her his woman. She had little choice but to survive.''

He shrugged. ''True. And he had the devil to pay for capturing her. He had a few scars from it. She had very sharp teeth and dumped food over his head when he got too arrogant. In the end, she got what she wanted, a proper wedding and a well-trained groom.''

Sybil closed her eyes and shook her head. ''Men. I say she had the worst of it with your great-great-grandfather. You're probably just like him—cocky, arrogant, showing off—''

If her glance hadn't locked to his bare chest, Duncan might have let her go. Might have.

He found her face with his hands, cupped it, treasured the delicate bones and smooth skin. He took her startled gasp into his mouth and tasted the moist texture of her lips, once...twice....

''Duncan...'' His name was a spell, coming soft and sweet to snare him.

Her lashes feathered against his cheek, her mouth slanted, moved curiously against his, tasting....

Duncan responded instinctively, sweeping her up against his chest and carrying her up the stairs to his bedroom. Lightning flashed beyond the window and thunder rattled the panes. The sound was no more than his heart as he lay her down on the rumpled sheets.

''Thank you for the cradle.'' Duncan opened the buttons to her blouse, one by one. He caressed her skin with his fingertips and found her arching up to him, all silk and heat and softness. Her scent swirled around him, a deeper, feminine fragrance beckoning to him.

The bit of lace covering her breasts floated from his hand. Her breast was so soft, so sweet to hold, her heart racing in his hand. Her hips moved restlessly and Duncan slid his fingers beneath her waistband to where she was moist and warm and fragrant. Her slacks came away easily; long, smooth legs freed to his touch.

She continued kissing him, moving like the wind, the warm ebb and flow of silk beneath his hand. He traced her hips, curving his hand lightly over them to edge away the last scrap of lace.

The wind crashed open a window shutter and Sybil's eyes filled her pale face. Her hair tossed around them, twining across his head and drawing him closer to her. Duncan carefully lowered himself to her, easing away his shirt.

Did she know that her fingers dug into his shoulders? Did she know how sweet she was, trembling beneath him, a mixture of heat and fear?

"You're...very warm...hot, in fact," Sybil whispered, then bit her lips and shivered.

"Are you cold?" The wind filled the room, elemental and fierce as his need for her.

She laughed unsteadily. "Hardly.... You've got the longest lashes."

He fluttered them against her throat and nipped her ear. He found the tender whorls of her ear and traced them with his tongue. Sybil went rigid, shivering in his arms. "I've got to go."

Duncan forced himself to lie still, his body raging with the need to fill hers— "Yes, you should. That, or stay the night. Because once we've begun, once I've tasted you, the ending will take forever."

Sybil scrambled into her clothing, forgetting the bits of lace on the floor. She was gone then, running from him into the night. He watched her car lunge into life and soar down the curving mountain road. He picked up the telephone and prayed that Elspeth could be reached.

She sounded sleepy and then worried. "Yes, I'll watch for her. Right. I'll allow for the storm. I'll call you back if she doesn't drive by here in forty minutes."

* * *

Without her glasses, Sybil fought to see the road; she'd
forgotten them at Duncan's house. The rain slashed across
the car's windshield, the wipers ineffective. The wind
whipped the trees and small branches, and pine needles
caught in the wipers. Sybil pulled over to one side and
leaned her forehead against the wheel. She shook, fighting
the violence of the storm beyond the car and the shattering
need within her body.

She was furious. With herself and with Duncan.

What was she doing? Battling a war by herself? Duncan
was responsible for her undoing and here she was handling
the matter by herself.

"Marcella, I am truly sorry that I left your Spanish gene
in the lurch. That your claim to royalty had to wait while
I freed myself from one Duncan Tallchief. I promise I'll
find your royal gene and document it thoroughly. But right
now, I have to hold my own." Sybil jammed the car into
reverse, backed into a turnaround and soared toward Duncan's lair. She threw open her car door and ignored the rain
pounding at her.

Duncan swooped her up in his arms. He ran with her
through the gray sheet of rain. She was out of breath as he
carried her into the house and kicked the door shut behind
them.

"So you're back," he said, none too sweetly as she
struggled out of his arms. He shook his head and the water
sprayed around him. "You packed up and left and now
you're back."

"Everything is black and white with you, isn't it? What
do you mean, 'once you've tasted me'? That statement is
so typically you—one hundred percent male arrogance."

"Okay. You could taste me."

"In a pig's eye." She caught his stare, which was locked
to her breasts. The rain had soaked through her blouse,

plastering it to her skin, her bra— "Where are my under-clothes, Duncan?" she demanded, furious that he had pos-session of something so intimate.

"Those bits of fascinating lace?" he drawled, and sent her over the edge.

Her body should have been chilled; it wasn't. Every fiber flamed with the need to launch herself at him. "Never pick me up again," she finally managed, out of breath again.

"No? That sounds like a threat."

"You're oversized, Duncan Tallchief. And arrogant. And…" She felt herself warming to it now, the need to level him. "And what right do you have, hiding up here, keeping your secrets while rummaging through mine?"

He shifted slightly, but she caught the tension humming through him, a panther about to spring. Good. She'd snagged his confidence and she planned to peel back his edges. He'd taunted her and this was the price. "You know everything about me, Duncan. Everything. And yet, you keep your secrets to yourself."

"Like…?" he prodded.

His easy stance as he leaned a naked shoulder against a wall and crossed his arms over that magnificent, broad chest didn't distract her. Almost didn't. She took a second look at the rain clinging to the hair on his chest and trailing down his tanned, gleaming skin to his opened jeans waist-band. It sagged slightly as he bent to whip off his muddied socks. Then straightened. Without thinking, Sybil snapped closed his jeans waistband.

Duncan's smile was not nice. "Are you getting on with whatever snit you're building to explode or…?"

"I will not have sex with you, Duncan. You're out for notches on your bedpost and you've got women waiting for you when you finally do decide to…to fulfill your needs. Count me out." She flung out a hand in a gesture of frus-tration, then jammed her fingers into her wet hair, pushing it back. "It's your fault Marcella doesn't have her Spanish gene and my clients are clamoring for results. And your fault that I'm soaked. You just took off for a few days, just like that, without a word. You come, you go and suddenly here you are. I like a planned schedule. All the pieces in place. You have no rules but your own," she finished as she ran out of breath.

He reached to brush away the wet hair clinging to her cheek. She fought the draw of his tender expression. "Where were you?" she demanded finally, and hated herself for caring.

"Denver. How did you get the cradle?" A question for a question, no quarter given.

"I went after it. It was lying under years of dust in a Chicago matron's basement. I will ask the questions here."

"What did you pay for it? I'll write you a check."

"Ohh! I'm paying you back, you jerk. I hired you to rescue Emily, and you did. Why were you in Denver?"

She held her breath. She shouldn't be interested in what he did. Shouldn't. Her fingers curled into a fist. If Duncan had been with another woman...held another woman... She fought the pain surging through her, tearing her heart. She stood her ground, calling him out. Would he care enough to explain?

"Someone needed me. A runaway girl."

Diverted from her tirade, Sybil hesitated. "Is she all right?"

"A bit shaken, but she'll be fine."

Sybil inhaled sharply, her nails biting her palms. Duncan infuriated her; he made her drag details from him like a miner digging for gold. "You could have told me, but you just left. Just like that, you jerk. You packed up and just left me without a word. I worried about you. You can't kiss a woman like that and then leave with no word, Duncan, no matter how important your mission. Those may be your rules, but they aren't mine.'' She rounded on him, jabbing a finger in his chest and allowing her hand to be captured and brought to his lips. She paused, distracted. ''Since I'm behaving absolutely like a madwoman, I might as well get everything out.''

She took a deep breath and crossed her arms, walking away from him to the fire. ''You know what you're doing, Duncan. I don't. That seems a little unfair to me. But it seems like you. You just…'' She struggled to define Duncan and her feelings about him. ''You just swoop. I have the feeling that any minute, at any time, you'll pluck me up, toss me over your shoulder and make away with me. Somehow I think there's a step missing in that technique.''

She swallowed and started walking back and forth in front of the fire. Periodically she leveled a stare at him. ''I'm usually very cool and logical. How do you think I've survived? I don't just leap into emotion as though it were a heated, luscious swimming pool filled with jasmine petals and floating, perfumed candles.… Stay where you are. One kiss and I'll toss that cradle at you.''

''May I sit down?'' he asked too properly, and sprawled on the couch. ''Keeping up with you could drive a man to his old age.''

She closed her eyes against the beckoning of his body to hers, the magnificent line of angles and cords and textures and colors. ''You have no idea how to behave. Not a clue. You've had your way far too long.''

His smile mocked her. ''With women, you mean?''

''What happened to you, Duncan?''

He ignored her question, and infuriated her more. ''I'll tell you myself. There you were, an eighteen-year-old boy saddled with a houseful of younger children. What were your feelings? Did you know you're still hiding them? Do you know how maddening that is? It's like this wall.'' She slapped the dark, rich paneling. "Do you know anything at all about fair play?"

He rose slowly to his feet and stood legs apart, hands at his side. Clearly she had struck something sensitive within him. "You give, but you don't know how to take. Isn't that it? You move by your rules.... Make a note, Duncan. I've been through a lifetime of overbearing parents. I'm not about to add one more. While I appreciate you and your family's warmth toward Emily, I am not entering a relationship in which I do not hold an equal vote."

"Are you finished?"

Duncan's dark look said she'd better think about winding up her tirade. He wasn't used to being told about his particular P's and Q's.

"Not by far." She wasn't quitting now, just when she'd nicked that fine veneer. "Back off."

His disbelieving snort set her off again. "Ohh!" Sybil pressed her finger against his chest, winding up for another round.

He watched her pale finger against his dark skin and hair, then lifted cool, gray eyes to hers. "Go along home, little girl," he murmured. "Come back to play when you've calmed down. Better yet, I'll drive you home. You're in no mood to be behind a wheel."

"Are you laying out the rules again and expecting me to follow them?" She floundered, and knew she was acting like an idiot. Duncan did that to her. She tossed all caution away and lifted her chin. "I've decided that..."

"That?" he prodded while she circled the wide abyss she had created. That Duncan Tallchief had pushed her into.

"I've decided that I am ready for a sexual relationship. Oh, not with you. But I'm certain there will be some-one—"

Duncan jerked her to him, holding her tightly. His expression was the fiercest she'd ever seen. She reveled in the knowledge that she alone had reached inside him.

His voice was too soft when it finally came. "Try that game and you're in for it."

"Threats?" she asked again, this time sweetly. "You see, lover—"

Lover. The name suited Duncan. With a sense of the gambler she'd never been, Sybil decided to have her due and take her first walk on the wild side.

"Not yet. I am not yet your lover," he corrected between his teeth, his eyes flashing like steel at her.

"Hmm. You're very good pointing out technicalities, aren't you?" she returned thoughtfully, smoothing out the peaks his fingers had created in his black, glossy hair. She'd gotten to him quite nicely and she'd decided to run him down and have him...on her terms. "You know about my sexual life...there isn't one. There's never been one because I thought I was damaged. I was terrified whenever a man touched me. But I'm not anymore, apparently—since my underwear is in your possession. And you know everything about me, yet I don't know anything about you. Is that really fair, Duncan? I think I'd like to go home now. You may drive me if you like."

His eyebrows jammed together. "May?" he repeated, sturdy outrage rimming his tone. "There's more to this than—"

She looked into his eyes, meeting his frown with her own. "Than what? We're far from being friends, Duncan. You've written 'claimed' all over me. So far, I haven't had any say in our relationship. In a way, you remind me of Una's Tallchief...an arrogant male who swaggers and thinks women will come running when he crooks his little finger.... Well, crook, Duncan-lover. Go ahead. See what it gets you."

Sybil paused, rummaged through her list of complaints and decided to settle for glaring up at him.

He slowly released her and stepped back as though uncertain of his control.

Pride, newly recognized, shot through her. She'd never taken off her gloves and gone toe-to-toe with anyone—except for her brief brawl at the tavern—also caused by Duncan—and later, the kneeing incident with Frank. She studied the new Sybil and reveled in the feeling of being alive. She felt glorious, in charge of herself and thoroughly empowered. She lifted her hair and let it spill slowly from her fingers.

Through narrowed lids, Duncan traced the fall, then let his eyes drop lower to her breasts, taut and tilted upward against the wet material. Desire shot through his eyes before he shielded his expression. Sybil reveled in his need, that she—cool, generic Sybil White—had pried him from his shadows. She lifted her chin. Duncan would have to hold his own with what he had released.

"It's not like that," he said very carefully, studying her.

"What is it, then?" she pressed, hoping for the world, the sunlight and the storms. Praying against odds that beneath Duncan's fierce scowl, she had touched the man....

"It's like this...."

His tender, seeking kiss almost melted her resistance. Almost.

When she forced herself away from what he offered—because she knew she'd only won half a prize—Sybil patted Duncan's rough, lean cheek. "Call me. We'll chat. Hmm. I'm feeling much calmer. It must have been the storm. I'm ready to drive home now."

Six

"In comparison to Birk, Calum and Duncan are pussycats. I'll take a dull, predictable man anytime. If I wanted one." Lacey MacCandliss plopped her heavy work boots on the tavern's table.

The middle of July lay hot and sultry outside Maddy's Hot Spot. Inside, air-conditioning hummed, blending with friendly conversation. Ladies' Night, Lacey's idea, included lemonade, nonalcoholic drinks for those who preferred them and draft beer at half price. The paintings of naked ladies were shrouded for the evening and the jukebox was dead. Maddy had plopped jars of flowers everywhere and had sprayed the smoky interior with air freshener. In honor of the ladies, Maddy wore a T-shirt with no holes and an elastic tuxedo bow tie. Patty Jo Black was playing the old piano, a mix of soft rock, rock-and-roll and country music. A farm wife with rusty tones dipped in rhythm and style belted out the tunes like a nightclub professional.

"Duncan is not predictable or a pussycat. One minute he's flashing this boyish charm with Emily. The next, especially with me, he's all caveman." Sybil traced her lemonade glass's rim and remembered how happy Emily was to go on the camp-out with Duncan. At thirteen, Emily was blossoming, and thrilled to be his helper with the younger children from the shelter. Her feet never left the ground, once her mother gave permission to go.

Emily was growing up and no longer hers alone. While she loved the thought of her daughter adapting to the small, busy community and friends she'd never had, the mother within Sybil ached. She mourned her baby growing up too quickly. Sybil ignored the prick of jealousy when she thought of how Emily had taken to Duncan, claiming him. Placing Duncan at a distance was not easy with Emily constantly spouting his name and his all-magnificent wonders.

Sybil had intimately experienced a bit of Duncan's magnificence.

Lacey glanced around the bar. "You've got him going and he's afraid he'll tumble off his shelf— If he does, he'll grab you and run."

"I do not—repeat, not—have Duncan going or falling anywhere."

"Ha. Anyone can see it's a war between you two. Under all that warrior beef, he's delicate, you know. Treat him gently or you'll have to deal with me. I couldn't bear to see him go through that pain again...." Lacey scanned the room. "Ladies' Night was a great idea. Seemed only fair, since all the men hang out here."

Elspeth shook her head and her sleek, black hair gleamed in the light. "You were making a point with Birk. And you dragged me and every other woman who could manage to get away into it. Because I took your side about equality in Amen Flats, I have to come down here every Tuesday night…whether I have work to do or not. I'm doing a huge order of throws for a gift shop and here I am. With you."

"So? What's your point?" Lacey, petite with a mop of curly, black hair around her elfin face, didn't back down. She tapped her fingers to the music's beat and swayed her boyishly trim body.

"Thank you for helping card the wool, Lacey," Elspeth said very properly in a manner that Sybil recognized as dry humor.

Dressed in a black "muscle" shirt with a Harley-Davidson logo and worn, paint-stained jeans, Lacey propped her beer mug on her flat stomach. She shoved her motorcycle helmet aside with a paint-splattered boot. "We should get a male stripper— And I would have done anything to see Birk in a skirt. It was worth every minute of those hours of carding all that wool. Sybil, how about a brewski?"

"Do not say the word 'skirt' around my brothers, dear Lacey, or…" Elspeth's tone implied dire threat.

Sybil decided that anyone in Lacey's near vicinity could do nothing but adore her. As graceful as a dancer and only five foot three, Lacey was in constant motion, tossing off energetic sparks to anyone around her. At any minute, Sybil expected Lacey to leap onto the tavern's table, dancing Cossack-style. She owned a small remodeling and construction business and the men working for her could barely keep up with her whirlwind pace.

"A brewski," Elspeth muttered delicately. "The last time you talked like that, Birk carried you out of here on his shoulder. You were sick everywhere."

Lacey leveled a look at Elspeth. "He's *your* brother. He challenged me to outdrink him. Anyone knows you don't carry a person with an upset stomach over rock-hard shoulders. Besides, that was years ago."

"So I'm responsible, right?" Elspeth shook her head. "It

was only two years ago and you frightened Birk badly. You're almost family, Lacey. You should know when he's tormenting you.''

Lacey frowned. ''I've been putting up with him for years. Just because you Tallchiefs have one black sheep doesn't mean you're all bad.''

Lacey looked at Sybil. ''Duncan almost raised me. Tucked me into their brood when no one was watching. Matt and Pauline Tallchief were probably the only parents I ever knew. I sat at their table like one of their own.'' Her expression darkened with memories of the past. ''Those were the only meals where I had enough to eat and there was enough love around the table to spare—even when they were arguing, if you can call it that. My earliest memories are of my parents brawling. Then at school, while I had my fights, no one messed with the Tallchief family. Duncan, Calum and okay…Birk, too, pulled me out of more scraps than you can imagine.''

''You and Fiona drew trouble like a magnet,'' Elspeth said with a grin, and hugged Lacey, who obviously enjoyed the gesture.

''We had our times,'' Lacey said smugly with an impish grin. ''She wrote me. She's trying to jerk the rug out from under a crooked developer in Arizona.''

Elspeth shook her head. ''That's Fiona. If there's a cause, she'll go for it.''

Sybil wished for a moment that she'd been as tough as Lacey, that she'd fought instead of endured. Duncan brought out thorns she hadn't realized she possessed.

''Duncan cut my thumb and his, too. Stuck me with his penknife after…well, after something unpleasant happened with my parents. He said I was to come to him or any of the Tallchiefs when I needed them—for anything. And I did. I knew someone cared for me. That I was part of a family. Pauline Tallchief was the sweetest woman I know and she never backed down from a fight. With the Tall-chiefs around me, I survived. Just like you, Sybil White, Miss Long Cool One who has Duncan Tallchief on her mind.''

"I do not."

"Shoot." Lacey's snort denied Sybil's claim. She leaned closer to Sybil, her gaze too sharp. "You found it, didn't you? Whatever Duncan is holding too close."

"What do you mean?" Elspeth asked sharply, sensitive to any problems within her well-tended brood.

Her expression serious, Lacey nodded to Sybil. "You have to be a hoarder to recognize another one. And Duncan has been hoarding since your parents passed away. Sybil has peeled back something in him that he's kept hidden and he doesn't like her prodding through his ashes. He's used to setting terms and having everyone follow them."

Elspeth frowned lightly. "He was shattered by our parents' deaths. And then his marriage."

Lacey's fine, black brows lifted. "He never cried or complained, Elspeth. He did what was expected of him. That left little time for understanding of himself. Then his brood flew the coop."

"He grieved. I'd find him staring off into space or at the graves. He looked so lonely."

"He's not like Calum or Birk. Calum is methodical and cool—ah, therefore Calum the cool, right? And Birk is disgusting—he actually salivates around women. But Duncan's still waters run deep and swift and this lady here has set him off. The air sizzles when he looks at her and she's like a high-strung filly around him. I saw it down at the center."

"Oh, good grief," Sybil muttered, and shook her head. "We're talking farm animals, right?"

"Okay, okay, so it's a dark and…hot night. But you've got him netted, Sybil. And he doesn't like you calling the terms,'' Lacey returned with a impish grin, and leaped to her feet. She arched and flexed gracefully, like a dancer before a performance. ''Sitting isn't for me. I get restless. Tomorrow I start another remodeling project and the lady has already changed her mind five times about one wall. Since I snapped that contract from under Birk's nose with a low bid, I guess I'm doomed. How about line dancing a few?''

''Make 'em eat dirt.'' Lacey's order echoed in Sybil's ears as she bent, bottom in the air, placing her hands on Duncan's lawn. Duncan, in the same pose opposite Sybil, blocked everything from her vision. She tried not to look at his shoulders, flexing and gleaming and broad.

Emily played cheerleader on the sideline and children screamed for their parents.

Sybil hadn't played touch football before. Ever. Her self-protection classes had been her only athletic adventures. Lacey had been firm; she wasn't losing another year to Birk's team and with Sybil she believed she had a ''killer edge.''

The afternoon game preceded a bonfire wiener roast that evening, hosted by Duncan. It was his first party, Lacey had said, and he was showing off his fangs for Sybil. With Duncan distracted by ''edge,'' Lacey felt the football game lay in her small fist.

The summer wind, scented of pines and sunshine, swept across the spacious lawn. Duncan faced Sybil. ''You'll have to go some to catch me.''

Sybil caught Duncan's smirk and instantly her competitive instincts lurched to life. ''You think you'll win, don't you?''

''Always do.'' The boyish grin on a man wearing afternoon stubble could devastate Sleeping Beauty—while she was sleeping....

"Not this time, Mr. Tallchief. And don't wait for me to do any running after you." She tried not to glance at his shoulders, and failed. A muscle rippled and she almost jumped. Duncan flexed his arm again and she glared at him.

"What's the bet?" His glance settled on her lips, then rose to the neon-pink shorts covering her bottom, high in the air. "That's up too high. Good form, though."

Sybil wanted to take him to the ground and demolish him. Her family's admonition to "act like a lady" didn't apply with Duncan Tallchief. She flexed her muscles, loosening up. "Get ready to lose."

Lacey yelled impatiently, "Okay, okay. Cut the chatter. Birk, you are dead meat."

Sybil inhaled and watched Duncan's eyes cut down to her Harley-Davidson muscle shirt, a gift from Lacey. "If you please," she snapped at Duncan.

Sybil glanced down the line of opposing players. There was Calum on her team, bent to pass the ball through his legs to Lacey. Birk, facing Calum, had just blown a kiss to Lacey, and grinned when she ignited.

The five-man teams were balanced and Lacey was out for blood. In the huddle she had ordered, "Do what you have to do. Just be there when I toss the ball to you. They think I'll pass to Calum, but I won't." Lacey had wiped the sweat from her face and whispered to Sybil, "Tallchief men never hurt women. Fake pain, flutter your lashes, say something outrageous. Just get him off-balance. In games, Duncan is a wild card, not predictable at all. You just think you've got him pegged and he throws a curve. Toss something at him that will shake him."

She had glanced at Duncan. "He's got great eyes. Expressive, you know? Watch him. He's a pushover. I'm going right over the top of Calum—got that, Calum? Give me a lift, okay? Calculate the amount of thrust for around one hundred pounds. I can somersault over Birk before he knows what's happening.''

Calum had snorted. ''You don't weigh a hundred soaking wet.''

''I make up for it.'' Lacey's eyes had darted to Sybil. ''I'll act like I've twisted my ankle, and while their big, strong, slow male brains deal with that, I'll toss the ball to Sybil, who is just low-down nasty enough—no offense, Elspeth, but you don't have a mean bone in your body. When it comes to Duncan, Sybil is all thorns. I'm counting on you, Syb. *I want this game*,'' she had demanded.

''Lacey is up to no good.'' Duncan, across from Sybil, frowned at Lacey. ''She's got murder written on her face. She knows she hasn't a chance without Fiona.''

Sybil looked at the wide set of his shoulders and the teasing, you'll-never-win, arrogant gleam in his eyes and knew how Lacey felt. ''Don't be so sure, big guy,'' Sybil murmured, and fluttered her lashes. She hiked up her bottom and his eyes jerked upward.

She hadn't done much smirking inwardly, but Duncan was definitely susceptible. Lacey was right.

Duncan blinked, then frowned. To add just the right touch, Sybil formed a kiss with her lips and blew it at him.

''I'm going to enjoy this,'' Duncan threatened warily.

''Try, why don't you?'' Sybil asked, feeling very empowered as he struggled to get a fix on her behavior.

The count sounded, Calum passed the ball through his legs and tossed Lacey into the air. She somersaulted, stepped on Birk's back and came down like a feather. She hesitated, then let out a cry and began to fold slowly.

Instantly Birk and Duncan stopped—Duncan was standing, blocking Sybil's path. She dived around him and ran before Lacey tossed the ball. It landed just right; she tucked it to her body and leaped over the player Calum had just downed. Lacey was cheering wildly behind her—Birk was yelling for her to get off his back.

The goal tree was only yards from her, when Duncan scooped Sybil up, tossed her over his shoulder and ran into the woods with her.

Upside-down, Sybil dropped the ball and braced her hands on his waist. She yelled, actually forgot everything and cursed Duncan Tallchief into the earth.

"Our point, our point! We won!" Lacey yelled.

"My, my, Sybil-belle. Such language," he taunted before leaping into the air.

For a moment all Sybil saw was air and space and Duncan. The next moment she found that the water in Tallchief Lake was colder than it looked. She came gasping to the surface and met Duncan's boyish grin. In the next second, bodies hurtled through space and the air was filled with shouting and laughter. Birk surfaced near Duncan and pushed him under. Calum splashed Lacey, Wyonna and the rest.

Emily swam to her mother and snagged an arm around Duncan. "This is the most fun I've ever had. A family picnic. I always wondered what they were like."

Calum floated nearby. He methodically spurted water into the air, the exact amount every time.

Lacey was crowing that Duncan had carried the ball over the goal line and that her team had won. "You did it, Syb!"

Duncan's eyes cut to Sybil. "Did what?"

She fluttered her lashes innocently. "I have absolutely no idea what she means."

Duncan blew into the water and it splashed on her nose.

"You have a nasty tendency to swoop and carry me off, Duncan Tallchief. You're not a fair man at all."

"Sorry." His tone lacked sincerity. "When you're all heated up, I can't help myself."

Emily surfaced near Duncan and held on to his shoulder.

"Mom? Are you swimming with your clothes on, too? Isn't this great?" Then she was gone, heading toward an inner tube in the lake.

"What if I decided to return the favor?" Getting Duncan under her fingertips enticed her. The lighthearted mood had shifted and Duncan was studying her closely. His thighs bumped hers gently as they treaded water, and his hands smoothed her bottom.

"I'll try to survive." He eased her closer, his bare thigh between hers, nudging her as he treaded water, supporting them both.

Birk and Lacey were racing to a floating log. Lacey beat Birk, but he leaped up onto the log and began rolling it. "I'm for that," Calum stated, beginning to swim toward the log.

"Mad at me?" Underwater, Duncan pulled Sybil even closer to him. She allowed her hands to rest on his shoulders.

She shot him a hot stare. "What do you think?"

"You might not want to know." He grinned wickedly and Sybil found herself feeling very young and certain. Duncan gently eased her hair away from her cheek and his look lingered and warmed her despite the cold water.

The rest of the evening passed in an outdoor barbecue and stories from the Tallchiefs' childhood. Sybil sat with Emily on a blanket and watched the fire toss sparks into the night sky. Legs crossed, Duncan sat beside her. He took up a huge portion of the blanket. He eyed her lazily. "You could toast a marshmallow for me."

Her snort sounded like Lacey's and surprised Sybil. She turned to the faces around the fire. Love circled the fire, the Tallchief family tethered by the past and the future. They'd included others in their love. Emily was tired, but she floated in happiness. Voices were hushed now, the children sleeping on the blankets close to their parents. It was a time Sybil would hug close to her. She found Duncan's large hand had claimed hers, and the gesture warmed her heart.

She forgot for a time that she didn't belong. The Tallchiefs loved and cherished each other. Sybil had never known that warmth, or how to nurture it. Compared to the Tallchiefs', her family traditions and relationships were that of icy stones. It would be dreaming to think that she would fit into this happiness, and more pain if she tried. She stroked Emily's head upon her lap and knew that she couldn't afford any of it.

Emily reached sleepily toward Duncan and his hand enfolded hers. "Thanks, Duncan. This is the best day I ever had."

"There'll be more, Princess." But his eyes were locked on Sybil's.

Then his kiss came softly to her lips. For that heartbeat, she gave herself to promises that could not be.

The first week of August lay hot over the fields, and the streets of Amen Flats baked in the sun. In the cool mornings, Duncan chopped wood. The exercise trimmed the need steadily humming through his body—the need for Sybil. According to Emily, she'd flown to England to research a potter's mark on the bottom of porcelain vases. Her client wanted to collect the distinctive pottery; he believed that the royal family commissioning the work was an ancestor. Emily stayed with Elspeth, soaking up how to gather mosses and herbs at their peak. Beneath the shady trees in Elspeth's backyard, lengths of dyed wool hung on a huge rack. On her screened porch, bundles of drying herbs scented the air. Emily had a small loom of her own, next to Elspeth's huge, ancient one, which she believed was Una's.

Duncan watched them walk together in the meadow, a

tall, willowy woman and the girl, each wearing long, cool shifts and tattered straw hats. Elspeth had her shadows—a baby who had never drawn breath. "I don't want to talk about it," she had said firmly. She'd been studying in Europe, and when she'd come back, Duncan knew she'd seen too much of life's darkness. She preferred her dyes and wools and her family, except for the rare business trips to various weavers' fairs or to city buyers.

Sybil. Cool. Elegant, with shadows running just as deep as Elspeth's. Duncan narrowed his eyes, refusing to admit he waited like a love-starved teenager for the sight of her.

At one o'clock in the morning, Sybil entered her darkened kitchen. The crates of pottery were being shipped to the client; Sybil was exhausted after hurrying to return to Emily. She rubbed her back, the long hours of work and travel weighting her muscles. She'd fall into bed and surprise Emily with her gift in the morning—

She caught a movement and Duncan's scent, then found his arms enclosing her. Her breasts collided with his chest; his shadow loomed over her, his body like a wall against hers. His hands splayed over her back to stroke her. *Were they trembling? Why?*

She should have shaken free—he held her loosely enough. Instead she arched into his warmth and strength, careless of her draining fatigue. *Duncan.*

She didn't wonder why or how he was there waiting for her. She just took, fitting herself to his length. *Duncan....*

His mouth moved hungrily upon hers at first, biting gently, brushing to her cheek, his arms lifting her higher. "I missed you," he whispered roughly against her cheek. "Too much, damn you."

Then he lowered her toes to the floor and pushed himself away. He thrust his hands in the back of his jeans pockets and glared at her. Dressed in a cotton, short-sleeved shirt and jeans, his hair mussed and at angles, Duncan fairly bristled. He jerked a hand from his pocket and rammed his fingers through his hair, leaving more peaks. His look said she was the cause of his bad mood.

The space between them filled with tension, Duncan's raw emotions almost tangible.

She clamped one hand to the kitchen counter and with the other straightened her steamed glasses. Duncan, in full force, had gone straight to her head, making her slightly dizzy. Or was it elation? Did he care so much? Could she believe it? He'd been worrying, had he?

"Did you get what you went after?" he demanded rawly, his eyes blazing in the shadows.

"I generally do." She was too glad to see him, shocking herself. She, who had kept the corners of her life cool and unattached. Yet here was Duncan and her challenge.

"Sorry about grabbing you."

The apology lacked sincerity. He was a taker. Perhaps she was, too. Perhaps. Sybil plowed through the past—years ago someone should have been waiting, concerned about her. No one had been there for her. Duncan would always be there for those who needed him.

But he had caught her when she was drained, her defenses down. Sybil placed her hand on his cheek, wondering how a man so fierce could be so caring.

"I've cooked dinner. Would you like me to heat it for you?"

Her body heated just looking at him. The room seemed to shrink, the air too light to breathe. His jean-covered thigh brushed up and down on the inside of her legs. "Tired?"

Not really. Not now, the voice inside her stated as every nerve in her body latched on to the way Duncan looked intently at her. Like a hungry man who needed her desperately. There was something else in his dark eyes, a challenge that set her pulses racing.

His knee moved higher, and liquid warmth pulsed through her. "More," she murmured across dry lips.

He lifted a mocking eyebrow. "Whatever do you mean, Ms. White?"

"Do it," she commanded recklessly.

"This?"

Duncan unfastened her skirt and Sybil forced herself to breathe. She'd forgotten to in the last heartbeats. The business skirt pooled to the floor, leaving her in panty hose. One of Duncan's hands caressed her waist, while the other supported her head gently. This time his kiss was slow and filled with enticing promises.

Sybil breathed roughly, her hands locked to his shoulders. "Open your mouth," she whispered desperately as he removed her glasses.

"Mmm."

He didn't hurry, his firm mouth heating hers.

She bit him lightly. Someone had to take charge of her desperation and she decided that Duncan would linger too long. Was she on a schedule, at the mercy of a stopwatch?

Yes. The ache within her budded and flowered and she almost wept for his touch. *And he was moving too darn slow. Trust Duncan Tallchief to be obstinate at a time like this.*

"You're shaking. And so hot. So hot...." Duncan's warm breath swept across her breasts, now covered only with lace. She tried hard to think then and felt the jolt shoot through her when his lips ran lightly over the tops of her breasts.

"Duncannnn...." She heard a desperate woman cry out frantically.

His hand curved slowly, firmly, over her femininity, his

fingertips pressing gently, enticing heat until it poured from her. She shook so violently, clinging to him, aching—

Over the rapid beating of her heart, she barely heard the tearing of her hose. His touch eased closer, deeper, and Sybil gave herself to the rhythm, parting her lips for his kiss, feeding upon the fire flaming between them. Heat pulsed from every taut nerve.

She cried out when his fingers entered her fully, an old terror pinning her heart. Then Duncan's scent, his heat, the sound of his breathing enfolded her safely. *Duncan... Duncan...Duncan....*

She could trust him, her body vibrating with the volcanic pulsing within her. She clung to him, flowed beneath the gentle directions of his hands and fought the building pressure rising within her.

His open mouth teased her skin; her throat; the rounded, aching tops of her breasts. Every molecule within Sybil waited to burst.... She couldn't...she couldn't— If he didn't—she didn't know what—but Duncan should. He should know what to do now when every nerve ached for—

"Oh, Duncan..."

"What? What do you want?"

"You know. Of course you know—" she managed breathlessly.

"Maybe. Say it. Tell me what you want."

His breath washed hot and moist across her skin, edging lower to the very peak of her breast.

Caught on the very tip of her passion, Duncan's hands moving on her, within her, Sybil believed she would explode at any minute. She shook, digging her fingers into the anchor that was Duncan as the waves washed hotter, beating upon her.

When his lips tugged at her nipple, Sybil fought the terrifying excitement, the throbbing within her pouring out in stars against a red haze. She wilted slowly, magnificently, certain that Duncan would catch her.

He swept her up into his arms and brushed a kiss across her lips.

Because she felt young and light and carefree, Sybil smiled against his damp throat. Then she began to giggle and couldn't stop. "Sorry. Nervous reaction."

"You weren't nervous a second ago and this isn't a laughing matter. Where can I put you down?" Duncan's expression was tender, yet bemused, sheepish but endearing.

She struggled to soothe him. "Sorry. Bad timing."

Duncan snorted, appearing very attractive in his rumpled, male look. Feeling very powerful and womanly for the first time in her life—other than their skirmish on his bed— Sybil cuddled close to him. "This isn't fair at all. Rather one-sided."

"Don't I know it," he returned grimly. "I'm going now."

Sybil studied him, this man who treated her gently.

He was the only man to touch her so incredibly intimately, to melt the cold. Duncan Tallchief was distinctly uncomfortable and wanting to soar back to his shadowy lair. Too bad. He'd chosen the wrong lady for sympathy. He'd started something between them, and she wanted more of him. She wanted to study every nook and cranny of his intriguing male brain…his psyche and his very fit body. There were parts of him that had seemed huge. An exploration when she was rested could satisfy her curiosity. She was very curious about anything concerning Duncan.

Carrying her easily, Duncan moved restlessly, and an idea struck her with the impact of a brick wall. "Duncan. This must be painful for you."

He flushed and began moving slowly toward the bedroom. He looked distinctly uncomfortable. "Not really. Not now. I...ah...well. It's not painful anymore."

She studied his grim, determined expression. "You... ah...didn't...ah..."

His dark, accusing look told her everything. The thought went soaring to her head, making her dizzy. Duncan was not immune to her lovemaking. He had exploded, too. She was sexy and all woman, able to affect a man who evidently had vastly more experience than she. She pushed his past experiences aside, because she wanted Duncan for herself. When he placed her on the bed, she held on to his shoulders. "Stay."

He kissed her and she caught his tongue, sucking it. She wanted to comfort him, to hold his head upon her breast and stroke him until the nervous energy within him eased. "Stay. Lie here beside me."

Duncan's expression was wary and uncertain. He closed his eyes and shook his head.

She'd actually told him to...to do several things. And he had, and now he wanted to carry all her wonderful moments out into the night. He wasn't going anywhere. Not if she could help it. Sybil locked her arms around his neck and tugged him over her. "There. Isn't that better?" she demanded as Duncan braced his arms tensely beside her head.

"For whom?" He shifted to one side and lay stiffly beside her.

Sybil yawned and laid her head on his shoulder. She nuzzled and pushed aside his shirt to find his skin, and pressed a kiss upon it. She burrowed her nose against the warm, smoothly covered muscle and decided to taste him. She licked him delicately. He tasted of soap and man with a bit of feverish salt tossed in. Quite delectable and her own homecoming present. "You taste good."

"Uh-huh."

Sybil skimmed out of her torn panty hose and cuddled

closer to Duncan, who was lying straight and rigid. She
pressed her breasts against his arm and looped her arms
and legs around him. He was hers. "Stay put," she managed between yawns.

"Yes, ma'am."

Duncan's deep, husky tone curled around her like a
warm, snugly blanket.

She dozed, and awoke with a silent scream on her lips.
Sybil lay very still, willing away the nightmare. She could
feel their rough hands on her...too many hands holding her
down, parting her legs....

The sheets were tangled around her legs and the nightmare began to shred as she clung to reality. A night bird
called and the summer wind brushed a limb against her
window. The shadows of her bedroom gave way to the
moonlight shafting into the room. There was the scent of
the mountains, clean air and pine trees.

The ragged, deep groan beside her caused her heartbeat
to kick up again. She turned to find Duncan sleeping beside
her.

Sybil forced herself not to move. He sprawled on her
cream-and-rosebud-spattered sheets, black hair gleaming on
her pillow. A ruffle lay against his jaw—delicate lace
against the hard line.

His thigh moved, hair coarse against her smooth skin.

Sybil eased the sheet up to her chin and pushed reality
into her senses. Here she was, lying beside Duncan Tallchief without the benefit of a nightgown. She edged her leg
away from his.

One glance downward proved that both of them were
naked. A quick flood of memories swooped upon her and
Sybil closed her eyes, shaking with the knowledge that
Duncan had touched her as no other man had. She had even
ordered him to...to taste her....

Duncan flung his forearm against his face. "Dad...Dad, I'm sorry...." The tortured cry had been wrenched from him; his tears shone in silvery trails down his cheek.

Comforting a grown man—a naked man—was far different from cuddling Emily.

His eyes flung open, staring sightlessly at her and filled with anguish. "Duncan?"

"Oh, God...I'm sorry...."

His tone was so shattered, so desperate, that Sybil reached to lay her hand on his cheek. He breathed quickly, still caught in his nightmare.

"Duncan?"

"I don't know if I can do it, Mom. But I'll try.... We'll stay together, the five of us. Mom?"

There were other frantic, jumbled sentences—a boy afraid of failing, fierce in his devotion to his family. She stroked his hair, hoping to relieve his nightmare. She saw then who Duncan was with his protection ripped away. He'd loved deeply, fought for those he loved.

"Duncan...come here...." Sybil eased his head to her breasts, rocking him, though his body almost covered hers. She welcomed the weight and kissed his forehead, holding him as gently as she would cradle Emily. "Duncan... shhh...."

Duncan sighed raggedly, tugging her close to him.

The next time Sybil surfaced from sleep, she heard the sound of her clothes dryer. She smelled brewing coffee and freshly showered male skin. She was being tucked in, kissed good-night.

Still more asleep than awake, Sybil reached for him.

Duncan's deep voice whispered in her ear, "More?"

"Mmm, please." She stretched luxuriously and gave herself to the rhythmic movements within her. Pleasure came softly, pulsing, tightening within her, until she melted gloriously. "Thank you." She was, after all, very polite.

Duncan's rough cheek moved along her throat, his smile slow against her skin. There was nothing soft about his body curving behind hers.

"I don't know if I'm going to live through this."

She flopped over, afraid that he'd escape, and clung to him even as she drifted back into sleep. She'd trap him in flowers and ruffles and keep him safe from the shadows.

Seven

$\mathbf{D}$uncan leaned against Sybil's kitchen counter, sipped his coffee and grimly tried to listen to Emily. The puppy chewed on his jeans; Duncan rolled him over gently, rubbing his sock-covered foot on the puppy's fat belly. Duncan would have rather been playing with a certain cuddly female.

Emily giggled and retrieved "Elvis." Duncan picked up bits about her calf, though his thoughts locked on the woman sleeping in a bed they had shared. Leaving Sybil just minutes earlier, removing himself from a luscious tangle of arms and legs, had been torture. His jeans were still damp from the dryer, and he wondered with humor if they steamed from the sensual heat gripping his entire body. Jerking on his socks, his shirt and a moderately welcoming expression for Emily hadn't been easy when every instinct and nerve he possessed told him to make love to Sybil.

In the morning light, Sybil's face had looked young and vulnerable, her lips slightly swollen. As she'd snuggled against him, her breasts had nudged his side, her soft leg sliding within his. She had very agile toes, walking them up and down his calf. She slept deeply, yet seemed in constant movement, arching and stretching luxuriously, which did little to calm Duncan's stretched nerves. But her cat-who-licked-the-cream smile and purrs did help.

Her delicate feminine petals had gently parted and moistly enfolded his touch. The need to sink deeply within her, to place himself within her tight, welcoming keeping, had risen too sharply. If he had moved with the heavy, primitive need surging through him, to thrust deep in her, spill himself into the tight pleasure, he might have hurt her, might have ruined what lay between them. He promised himself that the next time—

Emily spoke quietly while she sat on the floor, playing with her puppy and kitten. "Mom doesn't usually sleep this late. She must be really tired, because she works in the morning, when everything is quiet. I'm glad you came over this morning. You can see what she brought me. But I'm just glad she's home."

Calum, who had brought Emily over from Elspeth's, sprawled in a chair. He met Duncan's eyes; the understanding look held between the two brothers. "You know what you're doing, then," Calum said finally, and Duncan nodded.

A sleepy, deeply pleased feminine sigh slid from Sybil's bedroom into the morning. Calum's expression was humorous as he eyed Duncan and whispered, "The least you can do for the woman is button your shirt straight and put on your boots."

Emily, a younger version of Sybil, glanced at Duncan and studied his morning beard. She watched him slowly correct his buttons and holes and then looked at him. The girl was soft and sweet, yet the intuitive woman moved within her, shadowing her expression with understanding beyond her years. Duncan met her gaze with his steady one. There was nothing light in his feelings for her mother; his attraction was not a passing whim. The girl understood as she watched him and stroked her kitten. "I like to wear socks when I'm at home," she said finally in a quiet way he recognized.

Though Sybil might not want his presence this morning—or would she?—her daughter accepted and trusted him. Emily had picked her way through her reservations.

The bedroom door opened, and Sybil, her glasses askew and hair rippling wildly, stood in her new robe.

While Sybil stretched and yawned, Duncan shot a look at Calum. His brother was innocently studying the plaster design on the ceiling.

She blinked when she saw Duncan and jabbed her finger up to straighten her glasses, then she shook her head as if to clear it.

Duncan wasn't budging. If she wanted him to give her reassurance that last night hadn't happened, that she hadn't melted beneath his touch, hadn't pulled him into her bed, she was out of luck. And if she thought he'd run before dawn, she could think again.

Calum whistled a soft tune as Sybil tried to awake fully.

"Mom?" Emily jumped to her feet and ran to Sybil, enfolding her in hugs and kisses. Then Emily was bounding out the door to the car, anxious for her gift.

Sybil looked blankly at Duncan, then at Calum and back at Duncan. Her eyes widened and he watched a delicious shade of pink move up her throat. She scrunched the lapels of her robe over her breasts and swished the material to conceal her legs.

Duncan wondered if she regretted letting him touch her. If she regretted the closeness during the night. He inhaled and fought to remember what secret he had released, a memory that taunted him and danced beyond his recognition. He remembered his desperation, the pain, then the softness of Sybil holding him, whispering to him, easing him.

"I have to go—a trip to San Francisco. A hacker has infiltrated a security system and planted a worm—a computer bug—in it. It's eating its way through the company's memory banks. There's a hefty bonus tagged on to the offer, if I can nail the virus quickly." Calum rose, downed the last of his coffee and kissed Sybil on her forehead. Outside he spoke quietly to Emily.

Duncan handed Sybil a cup of coffee, then smoothed back a tousled length of warm, silky hair. She stepped back against the wall warily, looking up at him through glasses now steamed with coffee. He didn't trust what he saw in her eyes and placed a hand beside her head, blocking her slide away from him. "Good morning."

"Uh…good morning." She watched Emily and Calum through the window. "Ah…my, isn't it a pretty morning?" Sybil swallowed tightly and edged her coffee cup between them. Her fingers trembled on the cup.

"Sleep well?" Duncan wound a curl around his finger and tugged. He wanted her now, there on the sun-warmed tile of the kitchen floor. He allowed no room between them, taking her cup and placing it aside.

Her voice was very tight; the pulse in her throat pounded wildly against his fingertip. Her flush ran deeper.

"Quite well, thank you."

"You smile—a small, secretive and very-pleased-with-yourself smile—when you sleep. It's a sight a man appreciates and one to drive him mad. Those little purrs don't help, either."

"I must have been dreaming— You watched me?" Her bottom lip dropped open and she stared blankly up at him.

Duncan wasn't in the mood for giving her room to escape. He trailed his finger across her cheek and found the sharp row of her teeth. A tap on her chin and he followed the path of his finger down her throat, tracing the robe to the crevice between her breasts. "I watched you. Watched everything. I'm not likely to forget the heat inside you, not when I'm dying to have you. I want to bury myself so deep in you that we're one body and you're hot and tight around me. For a man, it's a beautiful thing to see a woman's body capture and hold tightly on to pleasure he's given her."

"I'm not certain that was gallant of you, Duncan. To watch me…you know."

Her unsteady, husky reply seemed so proper; a fragile, cool lily beside the raw tension humming within him. "Come to the house. I'd like you to see the cradle. I've cleaned away the old layers of varnish." Duncan could feel her sliding away from him, setting her barriers in place.

What had happened last night? What had slipped from his keeping into hers? Or had it?

"Old things, brought to life by those who care, are beautiful." Her whisper trembled on the cool, morning air. She lifted her finger to stroke his cheekbone, to feather across his lashes—

The screen door crashed open and Emily yelled, "Mom. Guess who's here? Gavin! Isn't that great?"

Duncan sheltered Sybil a moment, sensed her grasping at her proper moorings, and then he turned. The man dressed in an expensive suit and tie matched Duncan for height, but not for raw muscle. His stylish glasses glinted as he took in Duncan from head to toe—unshaven and standing in his socks near Sybil, who looked thoroughly mussed.

The man, younger than Duncan, bore just the cool class that would suit Sybil, while Duncan's raw edges could scrape her polish. He didn't like the man's quick frown, or the tensing of his body. Duncan recognized the protective stance in the man and the menace springing behind the mirror-like glasses. Duncan stood very still, keeping Sybil partly behind him.

Sybil's elbow nudged Duncan sharply as she stepped around him. He put out a hand and caught the sash at the back of her robe; he wasn't ready to share her yet. Especially with a man more suited to Sybil than himself.

The hair on Duncan's nape lifted as he recognized that this man fitted somehow into Sybil's life.

The man took a step forward, and Duncan tensed at his words.

"Sybil? Are you all right?"

He cared deeply; his fists closed at his thighs, his expression threatening Duncan. Duncan moved forward to the challenge, his chest meeting Sybil's back.

She shook free and stood very straight in front of him. He sensed that she was protecting the other man. Duncan rummaged through his battered emotions and found that he'd enjoy tearing the city from the man. He took a step forward and Sybil braced back against him, staying his movement.

"Gavin! How nice to see you."

"Sybil." Gavin's tight tone lacked warmth, his blue eyes locked with Duncan's. The city boy wasn't flabby. Nor was he backing up.

Sybil looked up at Duncan, then over to Gavin. "I, ah…"

Her hands pushed frantically at her mussed hair flying everywhere. Duncan blew a silky strand from his nose as she spoke.

"Ah…Gavin, this is Duncan Tallchief. You remember how I told you he had rescued Emily. He's…ah…just here to…"

She glanced down at Duncan's sock-covered feet, glued

to her kitchen tile, and she floundered, clearly ashamed of what had passed. "Umm. Duncan, this is Gavin James. He's…an old friend…we were once engaged. Would you mind pouring him coffee while I dress?"

Thorn pushed through the screen door, carrying his bowl. Duncan had forgotten the dog during the night and Thorn had apparently made the trip back to the ranch to retrieve his favorite food dish. He plopped it at Sybil's feet, looking up at her expectantly. His nose lifted at an unfamiliar human scent. Then, stiff-legged, his hackles raised, he bared his fangs at Gavin and growled.

Duncan saw Sybil's topaz eyes flash meaningfully up at him and then down at his dog. Beast and master had reacted instinctively to the new man in Sybil's house.

She scratched the animal's ears, then straightened. "Shame on you. This is Gavin. Duncan, has Thorn been outside all night? Ah…" Sybil placed a trembling hand over her mouth. She evaluated her escape routes—shielding Duncan's presence in her house—and came up with "Mmm. Duncan, would you please…?"

Duncan looked at her. On the morning after sharing Sybil's bed, he didn't feel like being civilized. He glanced at Thorn, who was still baring his teeth at Gavin. He knew exactly how his dog felt. Damned if he'd serve coffee and a smile to an ex-fiancé. Especially to a lover who probably had seen several delicious smiles. Who may have created them. Duncan fought the need to pit himself against something, and Gavin James was the closest— "No."

Then he scooped up his boots and walked out of her house.

"I have my vices," Elspeth admitted as the two women sat on the floor of her living room. "Saturday night. Old movies and a tub of buttered popcorn from the theater. How much better can it get?"

After two weeks of seeing Duncan at almost every turn, Sybil wasn't in a good mood. An encounter with the hard wall of his chest at the post office had almost caused her to latch both arms onto his neck and kiss that grim, accusing line of his mouth. He'd behaved as if she were having a convention of lovers in her kitchen. "You should have seen Duncan that morning. Gavin was no better. At any minute I thought my kitchen would be splattered in blood.... There was no reason for Duncan to act like a territorial male. None at all. Your brother is a rat. No offense, Elspeth."

"None taken. Duncan has been bristling nicely. You're doing a good job of payback. The women who have hunted him are rooting for you."

Sybil, comfortable in black shorts and matching T-shirt, studied Elspeth, who was also dressed in black. Both women had black streaks beneath their eyes—a camouflage trick, according to Elspeth. Sybil fingered her single, long braid, which matched Elspeth's. "Who would believe that you would lead me into crime?"

"Lori's ex-husband is being a rat. He's always been one and I didn't like him waving that...woman in front of his kids. Especially when they're on visitation with him and he's paying absolutely no attention to them. He's just hurting Lori for meanness, not because he wants the children. It seemed only fair to lure that skunk in his sports car, one Lori helped pay for." Elspeth swigged her bottle of flavored mineral water and burped delicately.

This facet of Elspeth—walking on the wild side—fascinated Sybil. "You are wicked. I can't believe I helped you. He'll find the popcorn trail to the car."

"No way. The skunk ate it." Elspeth shook loose her gleaming hair from the braid. It spilled down her back, catching the light in blue-black sparks. "You've got to do something about those two anonymous telephone calls.''

"I'll deal with them. They aren't very creative, a limited sexually explicit verbiage of what he'd do to me. I had the unpleasant experience before...years ago.'' *Just after the rape. The voices were muffled, threatening her....* She forced herself back to the present. "I can't believe I actually held that gunnysack while you looted Mr. Lockison's beautiful garden.''

Another delicate burp and a fond grin. "The things I learned from Fiona. Mr. Lockison pulled so many shady deals with his renters that they deserved a portion of his garden.''

"I can't believe we spied on John Wade. Last night, we actually took out our field glasses, lay in the grass and watched him—uh—sneak into Mrs. Snodgrass's house.''

In the light of the television screen, Elspeth's expression lacked pity. "He's there every Saturday night, just when he tells his wife he's out checking on his livestock. Mr. Snodgrass, as a deputy, is usually patrolling the other side of town at that time. Wade has blackmailed and harassed his last defenseless and down-on-her-luck woman. I'm merely documenting his visits around town. All it will take is a careful notation to each of his girlfriends and the cat is out of the bag. Oh, no names of course, except Wade's. That way poor, sweet Mrs. Wade just may be kept in the dark.''

Sybil lifted her bottle of mineral water in a toast. "A supreme plan. Congratulations.''

"Thank you. As I said, everything I know, I learned from my brothers and Fiona, who is marvelous on a caper. A real intuitive player. She'll be in Arizona for a bit longer, apparently locked on to the mother lode of causes.'' Elspeth tilted her head, listening. "That is Duncan's pickup. He must be just back from the cattlemen's meeting. He's taken a special interest in benefits for a disabled girl and her parents.''

''Forget I'm here, will you?'' Sybil hugged a sofa pillow to her and tried not to ache for the sight of Duncan Tall-chief.

His boots sounded on the back porch and Elspeth wel-comed him. In the next instant the lights clicked on in the living room and Duncan stood with his arms across his chest. ''Hello, Duncan,'' she managed. Just. How like him to leave his hat on, looking more like a desperado than when she'd met him.

A civilized man would have called her to discuss the scene in her kitchen. They could have had dinner and talked. Duncan preferred to glare at her as if she'd com-mitted a crime. After holding her, touching her so beauti-fully, he could have shown some sensitivity to her first-time awakening to him—and a houseful of people, including her daughter and an old friend. Sybil chose to ignore him now—a difficult task, considering how glad she'd been to see him that night. Just how many times did he think she had reacted to a man like that, opening herself to him? She shot a dark look at him and found him return-ing it. How could she ever expect him to act like a gentle-man?

''Fine. The two of you, dressed in burglar black and crowing over your capers with popcorn and old movies. Where's Emily?'' The edge in his tone wasn't exactly cud-dling.

''At a slumber party. Go away.'' She hugged the pillow tighter. She resented Duncan breaching the mother-daughter duet and playing the role of a father. Emily was her daughter alone and Duncan's tone implied he had rights. He didn't. With her or with Emily.

''I've come to let Elspeth cut my hair,'' he returned smugly, daring her to challenge his right to be there. He tipped back his hat and hooked his thumbs in his belt. "Unless you want to."

Sybil rose carefully to her feet and never looked away from him. There he stood, all six foot four of male arrogance, offering to let her cut his hair. To serve him. "I could do a very good job. Right down to your hard skin."

"Skin is good."

Duncan's reply was too slow and taunting, and every inch of her heated, as she remembered his hands running over her body.

"How's dear Gavin-boy?" he asked in a ruthless drawl.

He hadn't forgotten. With his glinting, narrowed eyes and widespread legs, locked at the knee, Duncan that morning would have put western gunfighters to shame. Now he was facing her in that same *High Noon* stance, waiting for her to make the first move. She threw up her hands. "If there is one man who can spoil a beautiful evening, it's you. I feel absolutely no reason to explain anything to you. You could have stayed and been nice."

"Nice." The word cut the air between them. "Yes. I could have stayed and shown off my manners. We could all have been very civil."

He smiled slowly, a wolfish, all-too-knowing smirk that brought the hair on the nape of her neck standing straight up. How like him to seek her out when she wasn't expecting him and when her defenses were down. Duncan jerked down the brim of his hat, shadows shielding his face.

One more second and she'd show him— Summoning every shred of the ladylike behavior she possessed, Sybil stood very straight. "Elspeth, thank you for the lovely evening. I'm going home."

He caught her arm as she swished by him. The pad of his thumb swooped and came away with the black beneath her eyes. His expression softened. "You look like Fiona, all filled with herself after a raid and ready to take down the first one who stands in her way. Who would believe that sweet Elspeth and her cool accomplice would make friends with skunks and raid gardens?''

"Next time you can help, Duncan. Now, come sit down and behave," Elspeth ordered, as if he were a little boy.

There was nothing innocent about the way Duncan's eyes raked Sybil's T-shirt. "Miss me?" he asked too softly, then scooped her against him and bent to take a swift, hungry kiss.

Sybil managed to walk home, her legs unsteady. Duncan's kiss had not been sweet or tender. It was a claiming and a challenge; she could either run or she could fight.

Marcella Portway's ancestry lacked any relationship to Spain. In the next week, Sybil had launched an all-out campaign to catch up on work and find the link to Marcella's desired royal ancestry. Indications so far were that Marcella would have to cancel plans to visit her homeland and castle.

Duncan's brooding cowboy image seemed pasted on Sybil's computer screen and the devastating kiss couldn't be unpeeled from her lips. Nor could his challenge.

After a blistering forty-five minutes, Sybil had been too curt with a well-known client. Pleased clients had led to better business; disgruntled ones could ruin her as easily. Marcella also tossed in the fact that there would be a handsome incentive if Sybil verified the link. She had added that Sybil's parents, in her elite social circle, would be also pleased. That sly reference to the strained relationship between Sybil and her family was little more than blackmail.

If Mr. Wade could be defeated, so could Marcella. "You'll have to find someone else, Mrs. Portway. I'll be happy to send you the files with my contacts so far. You might be interested to know that I did find an ancestor of yours who was a murderer. Then there's the French horse thief and rapist and the English one who was branded a coward. One of your grandmothers worked in a—she was a working woman who specialized in sailors.''

Marcella gasped, muttered a threat, and Sybil glanced outside. With Elspeth at a trade show, she was left with Elspeth's blackmailing project. Already dressed in black, she wove her hair into a single braid. With Emily spending another night at a slumber party, it would soon be her turn to host the giggling girls. It would be her first time as a hosting mother. "Good evening, Mrs. Portway. Better luck elsewhere.''

Forty-five minutes later, Sybil lay on the grass, her binoculars in place along with her notepad. Her mini-flashlight's beam caught Elspeth's neat handwriting: "For All Women Everywhere.'' Apparently defending the helpless ran in the Tallchiefs' gene pool. What else could be expected of the descendants of a noble chieftain and a wild-tempered Scotswoman?

She watched a familiar car circle the block and slide into the shadows to park discreetly. The lights in Mrs. Snodgrass's bedroom window blinked off; the stage was set. For a small town, Amen Flats was certainly busy.

The wind rustled the grass nearby as Sybil scanned the quiet town. Birk's pickup was parked at Maddy's and Lacey's motorcycle stood against the curb.

A firm nudge at her hips caused her to flip to her back. Duncan stood over her. "I might have known. Elspeth is out of town. Having fun?''

From her angle, lying flat on the ground, he looked a mile high, his hat shading his face. There was nothing easy in the wide stance of his long legs or his boots locked in the grass.

With the exception of her two escapades with Elspeth, Sybil had absolutely never done anything shady. "Ah…I was just…ah…'' She glanced around and found huge shapes looming in the moonlight. She hadn't known they were there, but since they were she might as well use them. "I was just studying the nocturnal habits of the buffalo. You know there are two kinds, the plains and the smaller black buffalo. Of course, the plains are larger, and—according to theory—then when the herd was almost extinct they cross-bred. Tracing the gene pools back to the original species is quite difficult—"

Duncan bent, latched a big fist to her black sweater and hefted her to her feet. He handled her weight easily, as though she were a child. No one had manhandled Sybil—with the exception of— She tried to dislodge his fist; it didn't move. Duncan did things on his terms and slowly released her. A woman who controlled her life and set her own terms, Sybil managed to hold her temper to a rumbling-volcano level. "I really don't like being manhandled, Duncan."

He grimly watched her dust herself free of leaves and grass. "Suit yourself. But one wrong move or a sound and that herd would make mincemeat out of you."

She wished she hadn't taken an instinctive step closer to him. "Uh...I thought Elspeth said they were more pets than wild."

Duncan picked a leaf from her breast and dropped it between them. "Right. Elspeth also knows a thing called keeping downwind and how to move and talk with them around. Is this where she said to be?"

"No...I could see better here...uh...Duncan?" Sybil peered around his shoulder to the huge shadow lumbering toward them.

His curse was short and disgusted. In the next minute, he'd scooped Sybil up in his arms and was running across the field. The heartbeat after he stopped, Duncan jerked her up against him and took her mouth.

Duncan threw his hat to a table and ripped off his gloves. Less than an hour ago, he'd manhandled Sybil. One look

at the buffalo bull catching her scent and seeing the rest of
the herd follow Old Apache toward her was enough to
freeze Duncan's blood. He'd acted instinctively and reaction to his fear—that she could have been harmed—had
caused the kiss.

So much for a man who knew how to cuddle frightened,
crying, lost children and make them feel safe.

Handling a woman like Sybil should be like touching
fragile silk. He looked down at his big, scarred, work-
roughened hands. "Way to go, Tallchief."

Every nurturing instinct he possessed told him that
within Sybil lurked a girl just budding into sexual awareness. She'd been scarred badly at a critical time and tossed
away by parents with hearts of ice. Elspeth and Fiona probably had better growing-up times, though they resented
their protective older brothers.

Just looking at Sybil caused Duncan to go hard.

He ran the back of his hand across his upper lip and
found sweat. A celibate man, he'd missed thousands of na-
tional averages in the sexual department and not another
woman had stirred him.

Duncan unbuttoned his shirt, dragged air into his lungs
and leaned against the wall. Until the old bull moved, Duncan had been admiring the neat curve of Sybil's backside.
He'd been remembering the few hours spent with her snuggling that bare softness against him.

Beside the fireplace, the old cradle gleamed softly in the
moonlight. *The woman who brings the cradle to a man of
Fearghus blood will fill it with his babies....*

Duncan snorted in disbelief, pushing himself away from
the wall. He moved to the fireplace and placed a boot on
the hearth. The old barn board with the Tallchief brand
stood on the mantel and Duncan traced the burned outline.
The stick man had lines radiating from the head, signifying

a full headdress. The brand lying beside the board was a remnant of cattle drives. There was a bit of red where Fiona had dipped the brand into paint and marked her calf. He gripped the hearth and remembered how he had planned to ask Sybil to go out with him. For her, he'd drag out his rusty manners and try his best at acting civilized.

He had no right to want Sybil.

They weren't a good match. He'd seen that clearly when Gavin James had arrived.

There was no way he could rein in his desire to possess and to protect her.

He had to protect her from himself, because around her his control slid to his boots.

Duncan ran his hand through his hair. She'd been handled roughly and was incredibly fragile, yet he was acting like the animals who had wounded her.

Her smile as she'd slept haunted him day and night. Duncan kicked the stone hearth lightly. A woman like Sybil had no idea of the raw passions stirring him.

Or that he felt like a half-grown boy, high on love, just looking at her.

A man used to western sounds and the silence of Tallchief Mountain, Duncan caught the sound of a motor revving in the distance. He turned to look out upon the fields below the house and saw headlights shooting into the night. Whoever had come to see him drove like a bat out of—

Duncan inhaled unsteadily. Sybil had picked a bad night to haul her classy but cute rear to his ranch. He watched, amused, as her car stopped, the headlights outlining cattle. They milled around the car as she honked, and Duncan shook his head. A city woman in the middle of the Tallchief spread was asking for trouble. In another minute the old longhorn bull would charge the noise—

Duncan almost started out the door to the pasture. His

horse would save time, if Sybil didn't start a stampede first. Duncan stopped, his hand locked to his hat. Her headlights still on, Sybil eased around the old longhorn bull and began walking toward the ranch house. One thrust of those long, sharply curved horns and Sybil— A huge, icy fist slammed into his gut.

Duncan moved quickly to his front porch and saw Sybil move safely away from the herd. He silenced his dog with a low whistle. Thorn, more wolf than dog, whined. His tail thumped the floor and his yellow eyes looked up to Duncan, waiting for the command *go*. "Lay off—she's not coming to pay a social call," Duncan ordered as Sybil marched up the road.

She searched him out in the shadows as though she knew where he'd be found. She scowled at him as she continued, hair floating from her face, framing the sweep of her cheekbones, the lift of her chin.

He knew he'd never see the sight again...a red-haired witch come calling on him, flouncing up his road wearing nothing but her temper and the Tallchief plaid. It ran across her breasts and over one very stiff, pale shoulder.

"Don't say one word. Not one." She didn't pause at his front steps, but continued walking past him. Was that steam coming from her body? Or a moonbeam waiting to slide down it? He envied the moonlight crossing into the room to touch her. He followed her into the living room, where she stood before the hearth in the Tallchief tartan plaid and western boots.

"That's quite a picture." Duncan breathed unsteadily and knew he'd remember the sight forever.

She threw up a hand, signaling him to stop talking. The other hand latched on to the old cradle.

He saw the other half of himself there, the woman fierce in her anger and tethered to the cradle. *The woman who*

*brings the cradle to a man of Fearghus blood will fill it
with his babies....* Duncan's heart lurched into rapid pace.

"You have no idea at all how to treat a lady."

"Have you come courting me, sweetheart?" he heard
himself drawl, though every nerve within his body stretched
painfully. "Because if not, you're in the wrong place at the
wrong time. Sweet Jesus. Aren't you wearing anything under that getup?" he demanded rawly.

"Not a stitch. I've come to meet your challenge, Mr.
Duncan Tallchief. So far, you've had things all your way.
Now I want equal terms." She pointed a finger at him.
"Your trouble is you have an empty nest syndrome.
You've raised your brood and now you're searching for
someone to tuck under your wing. I've been taking care of
myself for years. Count me out."

"The hell I will." He wanted to fill his bed with the
woman standing in front of him. Instinct told him that she
wasn't finished, and if ever he should rein himself in, it
had to be now. Sybil was calling him out.

He moved to the hearth to get a better view of anything
curved and feminine beneath the tartan. He caught a
rounded hip and a triangular shadow above one thigh—
Duncan locked his shaking hands to his belt. He was afraid
he'd say the wrong thing, touch her too hungrily....

"This could get rough. You had better tell Thorn to wait
outside. I don't want his feelings hurt. And don't count on
him for protection from me." Sybil stayed put until Duncan
had complied and returned to the fireplace.

She'd come for him. He balanced his hunger and his
fears and decided that he'd better clamp down any impulse
to touch her. He wanted her desperately enough to let her
make her choices. This time. For a man like Duncan, the
decision wasn't easy.

Sybil tossed her hair back. "I'm very angry with you,
Tallchief. You absolutely lack everything that is redeeming

in the other members of your family. Oh, I haven't met Fiona, of course, but I like the sound of her. Because your sisters won't allow you to bully them, don't think you can pick on me. If I want to lie on the grass at night, I will. I might just pet a buffalo.''

Two thousand pounds or more of buffalo and she wanted to pet one? He decided not to pose the challenge to her. In her present mood, she might walk her western boots and the Tallchief tartan right up to Old Apache. He tried a safer route. ''Your binoculars were glinting in the moonlight, sweetheart. I saw you from the road. If Wade had his mind with him, he could have seen you easily.''

''Details.''

Sybil began to pace in front of him and every molecule in Duncan's body told him to carry her to his bed. She continued stalking in front of him, allowing him a glance at a sleek thigh, quickly shielded.

''Emily is deeply attached to you. If you planned to use her to get to me…no, discount that. Your style is a direct hit. You swoop, Duncan Tallchief. SWOOP, in big capital letters. Oh, yes. Skip the wine and dine and dancing bit, the companionship, the relationship, and get straight to those devastating kisses.''

She stopped pacing and faced him. ''Oh, yes. As if you didn't know it. Your kisses aren't wet or sloppy. They're just there—swoop, bang, whop, mesmerizing. It's unfair. Okay…okay. The point is that you've been treating me like a minor partner. I'm not one of your siblings, one of your brood to care for, Duncan. I am a woman who has had to rely on herself. I've survived. Giving you a small portion of control over me isn't easy. Small? You want everything and it's too much without a balance in return. I refuse unequal terms in our relationship. Now, get this—''

Sybil slid the tartan from her body and folded it slowly while he watched, mouth drying and heart locked between beats. Delicately formed, Sybil's body curved perfectly, her breasts tilted to peaks in the moonlight, her waist small enough for his two hands. There was a rounded hip and a softly molded belly and then the dark mystery above her thighs. Enchanting him, she moved in a symphony of shyness, determination and defiance. The combination started his blood heating, pouring through him, and he wondered if his jeans could bear the strain.

At the last, she held the folded cloth against her, protectively, her breasts raised by the pressure.

Duncan knew a heavy pressure of his own as she sent him a curious look, her lashes fluttering down upon her hot cheeks. She'd taken her time and was tucking away the last of her doubts with the cloth. He owed her that—the gentle time of a woman—choosing her path. His own had been forged from the moment they'd met, when she'd come flying across Maddy's to claim him. Duncan held himself still, fighting his steely need for her.

He wondered whether his heart would leap into her keeping if she reached out a hand to him.

She smoothed the cloth into the cradle and stood slowly in front of him. She raised her chin, a fighter like him, setting her terms and fighting her fears. Duncan fought the need to hold her, to reassure her. But it was no easy matter for the both of them, and his hunting instincts told him to wait.

He traced the luminous pools of her eyes and found what he wanted: the steel to match his own. She held herself with pride, a woman who knew her mind.

Sybil's hair glowed around her, all silk and silver and scented waves spilling like a waterfall around her shoulders. "So here I am. I've determined that you may be the type of male who has to be dealt with on a base level, then work up from that. You've evidently inherited some of your grandfather's tendencies to pluck women up and run with them, discounting that the woman in question may have ideas of her own.... I've never done this before and it's crazy.'' She rubbed her forehead as if to clear it. ''I don't have the slightest idea how to proceed—''

He caught her to him, leaving her no room to fly. ''Is this what you want?''

''Desperately, Duncan.'' Then she began to grin. A giggle followed. ''You look so...desperate and dangerous. I...I'm nervous...I detest being tossed over your shoulder and I wish I could do the same right now and why don't you kiss me and why don't we...ah...well...I've decided to take the bull by the horns or...ah...uh...you know. I thought if making love is such a problem that we could get that out of the way first and work from there. I mean the other night, I...you...it wasn't fair. I have never come after a man in my life, never wanted one badly enough.''

''Let me get this straight. Are you offering yourself to me?'' He realized he sounded too rough, too demanding.

She smiled shyly, and the tight knot inside Duncan began unfurling. ''I'm nervous. I'm afraid I'll ruin this by being afraid.'' She looked away and he prayed she wasn't changing her mind. ''Gavin understood....''

''I'm not him. Lay it out.''

She ran her fingers through her wild hair, tears shimmering in her eyes before she dashed them away. He waited for her to run, waited for the pain—

Instead, Sybil stood on tiptoe to kiss him lightly.

''I won't hurt you,'' he heard himself whisper unsteadily, easing his arms around her so as not to frighten her.

''I know.... Oh, Duncan. You're shaking....''

Eight

Duncan promised himself he'd be very gentle, very slow with Sybil.

Then her hand floated downward, just skimming the hair veeing down his stomach. He sucked in his breath as her fingers toyed with his buckle. Both of Sybil's hands tried and failed to open his belt. Duncan groaned, unable to look away from her fingers fluttering upon him. He ripped open his belt buckle in one flip and met Sybil's nibbling kisses. They were sweet and cool and untutored and her fingers traced his jeans snap— Duncan tugged away the snap, leaving her to find his zipper.

She slowly slid the zipper downward....

"Leave the driving to me." Sybil's husky, uneven whisper almost caused Duncan to laugh. She kissed the curve of his lips and hesitantly touched the very tip of him.

He knew she needed to explore his body. She'd been forced, raped. Then from her actions, Duncan knew that her marriage had not been a tender one. On a sensual level, Sybil was young, and untried, and needed time to understand that his hunger, his body, was only that of a man who valued her. If she needed to explore him to satisfy her curiosity, and to reckon with her needs, he'd—

"Would you mind if we rested a bit?" he managed, just as she found the shape of him, pressing gently.

"Why?"

He sucked in more air and held his body taut. One more touch and— "I'm having a little difficulty with your project."

Her eyes raised to his, all innocence with her busy fingers purely sinful upon him. "Project?"

"You're getting to me, Sybil," he admitted grimly. He pulled back slightly, holding her away from him. In the moonlight, her breasts were tilted sweetly upward. He bent to gently nip and kiss each one. They were like shy, sweet doves, coming to shelter within the safety of his hands. "One more minute of those curious fingers and I can't promise anything."

Sybil trembled, her head back, her eyes almost closed. "Good."

He found his desire reflected in her expression, in the slow sweep of her tongue across her lips, moistening them. He ran his thumb across the taut bud of her breast, watched her inhale, then slowly, carefully, rolled her nipple between his finger and thumb. She shivered, her fingers digging into his upper arms. He breathed in her scent and admitted rawly, "I don't think I can make it to the bedroom."

"Good."

He counted her "goods," hoarded them. Still holding his gaze, Sybil began to ease to the floor and he followed her. He prayed his body wouldn't betray him, that he wouldn't—

He groaned as she parted her thighs, cradling him close

to her. Her heat fairly burned him, beckoning.... Duncan stroked her hair away from her face, letting her set the pace. Slowly....

Bracing his weight from her, just enough to let her breasts drag softly upon his chest, to nestle against him, he pressed his hips down gently. She'd been taken too roughly once and he wanted her to know that he wouldn't hurt her. Duncan framed her face with his hands. "We've got all the time you need, sweetheart. I'll be very careful with you. Tell me what you want and we can stop when you want. You're so small there, so tight."

Sybil found him and with one arch of her hips took him deeply within her. She cried out, and shocked, Duncan slid deeper until he thought he'd touch the very heart of her. "Are you hurt?"

Damn. He'd promised her. He was too rough with her.

Then he watched her smile slowly, her lashes sweeping along her flushed cheeks. Her hands caressed his taut back, his buttocks and down his thighs. Duncan had heard of women claiming men, and with her arms and legs binding him, her body tight and moist and hot around him, he knew that he'd been claimed to the hilt.

He watched her intently, her expressions reflected in her luminous eyes. He read tenderness and discovery, like a rosebud opening to a new day. He pushed back her hair, stroked her temples with his thumbs and kept her safe as she chose each heartbeat to stay with him. To let her know that he understood, that there was more than the meeting of their bodies, Duncan drifted kisses upon her lashes, her forehead, nose and cheek. "Stay with me," he whispered close to her ear, his heart fusing with the wild fluttering of hers. "You're so tight, so hot.... Let me in. I won't hurt you."

The smile playing around her lips told him her secret: that she had captured him and had her way. While her body eased to accept his, Sybil breathed deeply, her fingernails pressing into his shoulders. She flexed delicately, flowing beneath him, and Duncan knew he'd never made love like this, a tender game. She smoothed his taut shoulders as he tried to draw back and found himself taken too tightly to move. She seemed very pleased with herself, and if he wasn't mistaken—his world had just soared off into the moon—her feminine muscles were gently squeezing and releasing him. "You pounced."

"Yep. Swoop and took. You're not going anywhere." Though her tone said she was pleased with herself, Sybil frowned slightly.

He found himself grinning as she squirmed and adjusted to him; he treasured her determination. As the object of her concentration, he felt obliged to offer, "If you're uncomfortable, I can leave."

"I'm in control here, Tallchief. What's the process— Ohh...." Sybil arched her hips higher and cried out softly. She trembled, slowly lowering her body from his, only to rise sharply again. He treasured the tiny constrictions tugging at him and prayed his body would obey his will. Sybil's hands ran softly over him like the brush of rose petals. "I thought this would be horribly painful. It isn't. I...must have been thinking that it would be the same."

He mourned for the girl and cherished the woman. "You were ready for me. There's a difference. For my part, there is minor pain."

"Oh, Duncan! I didn't mean to hurt you...it just felt so right—so good." She raised her hips again and he groaned again. Pleasure had tossed her against him, her face taut with it. "Duncan? Duncan?"

He tried to wait, but the moist tightening within her set him off. He tried to tell her something, his words thundering—or was it his blood? This was Sybil—scents; feminine muscles; sweet, hungry kisses…this was his woman…a part of him as no other woman had been.…

The shadows were gone and he was warm.…

He found her breast, suckling, nipping, catching her bottom in his hands and lifting her, pouring into her. What he was, he wanted to be with her…to join with her. He fought his release and failed, heard Sybil cry out, her mouth against his throat. What was she saying? What was she saying?

She flung out her hand to grip the cradle, to tether them to it, and Duncan placed his hand over hers, a pledge to keep her safe.

The pounding of his blood echoed throughout the flashing colors of fire, higher.…

"I love you. Oh, Duncan…I love you so much.…"

Had her lips formed the words? Or did he want them so much he imagined them? Did her heart race to meet his?

After the pounding heat he held very still, listening, sensing, feeling as though he had completed a full circle. She was what had been missing in his heart, and she was his alone and he was hers. Sybil brushed back his hair from his forehead…

Warm. Sweet. Soft. Unwilling to release the missing part of himself, this tender captive, Duncan settled upon her, bracing his full weight from her. Their hands remained locked on the cradle; neither one had the strength to release it. With his thumb, he stroked the smooth skin on the back of her hand.

"You looked so fierce, so powerful," she whispered against his damp forehead.

"Was." He tried to breathe. He kissed her shoulder and smelled deeply of her fragrance.

"You're a pussycat, Mr. Tallchief."

"Thanks, I do my best. I've been saving up for this." If

he had had to move one toe, he couldn't have found the strength.

"It was right." She turned her hand to his, intertwining her fingers with his as he brought her hand to his lips and kissed the back.

He must have dozed, his head upon her breasts. Her heart slowed from its furious pace and he luxuriously stroked the curve of her hip. Half-asleep and very relaxed, Duncan decided there were advantages to letting a woman make up her mind. He weighed the pluses of being Sybil's captive, her raid successful. He was just summoning energy for a raid of his own, when she whispered against his ear, "You know, I could be highly fertile—"

Duncan's long lashes lifted instantly; they swept along her skin and tickled. His formerly hard body, draped so pleasantly over her, tensed. She could almost hear him thinking, damning himself for not using protection. But she didn't want him to say anything to ruin her moment. Their moment. When everything had healed within her.

Duncan moved suddenly, drawing her with him to stand. He lifted her into his arms and carried her up the stairway, taking them two at a time. In seconds, they were standing beneath the shower and he was soaping her very gently. His hand moved between her thighs. She should have been embarrassed; she wasn't. She felt lighthearted and young and thoroughly enjoyed Duncan's absolute mortification.

"I should know better," he said.

"I think it's my time to conceive." She slid the second volley of her idea to him on a platter of steam and spraying water. Gripping the cradle with his hand over hers while they had made love had caused brilliant images. Once she'd gotten past the shooting stars. Duncan, for all his raw edges, would be a perfect father.

Duncan closed his eyes, water glistening on his jutting

cheekbones and dripping from his forehead to his lashes. When he opened his lids, his expression was tender. ''I'm not certain, but you're teasing me, right? This is some odd humor from a redheaded witch who came strolling into my house to— Making a baby is a serious business, woman. If things are right between a man and a woman, and they want children, it's the most important thing a man can do in his lifetime.''

There it was, the warrior laying down the law, addressing her as ''woman.''

Sybil shrugged inwardly. She certainly felt like Duncan Tallchief's woman. Very well-loved and treasured.

''For a big man, you move quite quickly when frightened.'' She couldn't help laughing at his dazed expression. Unprotected sex shouldn't happen, but she was glad. In fact, she was flying. All the parts of her that hadn't made sense with Duncan leaped into a straight, logical line. She'd wanted him from the first moment she'd seen him brawling. He was hers to claim and she had. Faint heart did not apply to her actions tonight. ''The next time, I'll give notice before I pounce.''

''Do that.'' He continued to lave soap down her body, treating her breasts ever so gently. He kissed a red mark, his expression dark with regret. ''I promised I wouldn't hurt you.''

''You didn't.'' Sybil stood very still, entranced by this tall, tender man who had tended others before himself. She felt she was being worshipped, that he had placed aside everything but her. Beneath his care, she believed that only she was truly a unique woman to him. She pressed his hands against her breasts, kept them there and lifted her lips. Duncan's kiss exceeded her expectations, soft, seeking...

He hadn't given himself lightly, nor had she, and tonight would be the start of—

Sybil jerked back, looked at him and sputtered the word she had been forming— "An affair."

Her eyes widened. Other women had affairs; she didn't.

Duncan followed her out of the shower and into the bedroom, where she quickly found a discarded shirt and buttoned herself firmly into it. She'd never had an affair and Duncan was perfect affair material. "I think I'll see what's to eat," she said over her shoulder to the naked, glowering man standing in the center of the room.

"Now, get this straight...." He walked slowly toward her, all angles and smoothly moving muscles.

"Yesss?" She glanced meaningfully down his body and began to grin. He didn't bother to rephrase. He loomed over her, a tall, dangerous cowboy locked on to his prize. Then he bent, wrapped his arms around her and lifted her face to his lips. Her toes dangled above the floor. "Run that part about an affair by me again."

"You and me...and an affair. I've never had one in my entire lifetime."

"So what?" Duncan clearly lacked understanding. "Neither have I."

He'd shocked her. She'd been convinced by the way he'd kissed her, from the way he'd controlled his body, that he was very experienced. It was her turn to blink and reassemble.

Duncan leaned against the kitchen wall and watched Sybil. Dressed in his worn chambray shirt, she explored his shelves and refrigerator. The sight of her rounded, bare backside appeared each time she bent. At four o'clock in the morning, he would have preferred another enchanting session with a woman who had given every proof that she was committed to him.

"I love you.... Oh, Duncan, I love you so much...." The words were too clean, too new and fragile, riveting him.

He'd let her have her way, to his delight and fascination, and the payoff—her commitment—would be coming shortly.

She punched the buttons on his telephone. "I'd better check my messages."

As she listened, she turned away from him and her hand flattened against the wall. Her fingers trembled before she spread them on the wall and the set of her body tightened momentarily.

"Problems?" Duncan asked when she turned back, her expression taut.

She hurried to the stove and poured beaten eggs over sautéed green peppers, mushrooms and tomatoes. "Mrs. Portway. She's determined I know something about her Spanish ancestry."

He studied her as she passed, carrying omelets. Her grim expression didn't fit the easy way she could handle difficult clients. Something else bothered her. As a solitary man, Duncan recognized her privacy, and hoped that if she needed him, she would ask.

The portions on his plate wouldn't keep a bird alive, but he appreciated her efforts and the dessert that would follow.

The point was—he had her where he wanted her. With him. In his house and in his bed. He'd just let her keep pouncing and then he'd close the gate. It was just a matter of time before she said, "I do."

Marriage. The stark enormity of what he wanted with Sybil shocked him. He'd tried and failed once. They came from different worlds. Tallchiefs did not make easy relationships and were said to have backbones of steel. Sybil was too cool, too classy. Duncan settled back against the counter, tracking her movements. If she thought an affair would pacify what lay between them—

She whisked by again and he followed her over to the refrigerator and held the glasses while she poured orange juice. He was pushing the matter, but— "Earlier...when you vamped me the first time, what was that you said about fertility?"

She put the orange-juice carton back in the refrigerator and closed the door. She brushed by him and began buttering the toast, which had just popped up. She slathered on layers of butter. "Oh, you know. Emily was conceived my first time. And you...you were very with the project. Engrossed and looking like a fearless warrior. Shockingly so. You were very primitive...and sweet later. I watched you."

"I know." Duncan placed the glasses on the table and approached her. They had cried out together, their voices blending as their bodies had. He wondered if she knew how they had gripped the cradle together. That in the fiery storm of his passion, he'd heard *The woman who brings the cradle to a man of Fearghus blood will fill it with his babies....*" The idea that they could have created a life poured through him like sunlight.

He decided to be cautious about the matter. The decision was hers for now, yet he had to know. "Would it terrify you? To carry my child, I mean?"

"I was terrified once.... No, not now." She considered the idea, staring at the picture of the five Tallchiefs as children. They were black-haired demons, every one. Duncan had little doubt that his offspring would be civilized. He turned over the idea, warming to it.

He gathered his fear tight against him. Another woman had not wanted his "brats."

Sybil handed him a slice of toast and he bit into it firmly. She watched him chew and her eyes widened. She clutched the butter knife and pushed it through the butter and over to bump the plate of toast. It skidded across the counter; he caught it before it fell. "What's wrong?"

He was missing something. Sybil, tousled by passion, by

his lovemaking, was showing signs of retreating. "You're not wearing a shirt," she noted, looking down to his jeans.

"You're wearing it," he reminded her, and wondered where her mind was leaping to now. His was locked on the rumpled bed upstairs.

"This has all the markings of an affair, don't you think?" Her tone was a bit too cheerful. "I mean, here we are having a snack and I'm wearing your shirt and you're only wearing jeans and well…here we are, right in the middle of an affair."

While she might like the idea of an affair, it wasn't on his menu. "No. We're talking long-term plans here. People move in and out of affairs."

Her answer didn't please him. "I haven't. You haven't. Some of them last for years. We've generally been very careful—except with each other, this time. The question is, will a relationship work between us?"

Duncan knew he was skidding on new, unbroken and foreign territory of the female mind. He decided he'd better track her thoughts carefully. She took the remainder of his toast and scooped jam onto it. She studied the blackberry gob on her fingertip for longer than made him comfortable. Then she raised it to his mouth.

Duncan sucked the sweet blob from her finger; he sensed warily that he was performing exactly to her specifications. The hair on his nape stood up, as it did in dangerous situations.

"Mmm." Her tone considered something too abstract for him to center on.

Women were shifting elements he decided, not allowing her distance from him. He liked her on his lap while they ate. She seemed to enjoy feeding him.

On the other hand, he relished placing food in her mouth. When her lips closed around his finger and sucked, Duncan lifted her in his arms and ran up the stairs.

Before dawn, Duncan shattered twice more, only to be collected by the woman holding him. This time they had rolled to the floor in a tangle of blankets and passion. They snuggled together and the smirk on Sybil's face caused him to smile. "Amazing. Who would believe your resources ran to...? I believe I just raided your resources twice in short order."

Duncan found her breast and treasured the softness lazily. He ran his thumb across the tender tip and smiled when it hardened. "Counting coup. You've been listening to Elspeth's stories of our younger days."

"Aye. Let's rest and go for three."

Mist layered Tallchief Lake and spread upon the fields below Duncan's home. On the porch, Duncan stood behind Sybil, holding her in his arms. She wore nothing but the Tallchief plaid and a mysterious smile that pleased him. He nuzzled her hair, filling his senses with the scent of her, the feel of the woman who had completed him. With the dawn, their time had come to an end and peace lay between them.

"Duncan?" She turned to lift her face for his kiss and a drift of warm strands slid silkily across his chest.

"Mmm?" He could float into eternity, holding her quietly like this....

"You have to understand about Gavin. He's always protected me."

The man had come from Sybil's past and Duncan resented him. Gavin had the look of expensive breeding and manners, everything that a woman like Sybil should have. He could feel the past tugging at her, pulling her away from him, and he admitted his fear. "What is he to you? Now?"

She turned to hold him, snuggling beneath his chin. "He's my friend."

Duncan snorted, something he seemed to do more since Sybil had entered his life.

"Gavin has always felt guilty about me. His elder brother used him to lure me that night. He couldn't stop them and wanted to testify. His family wouldn't let him. When he could, he left them and has always helped me. Though relations between my family and me are strained, I care about them. Gavin votes my proxy at the family board meetings and lets me know the little things. How they look, if they talk about Emily at all—they don't.... So I guess—"

"You're friends," Duncan finished, and thanked the man who had sheltered Sybil. There, in the quiet morning with the mist enfolding them, Duncan asked again, "What promise to you haven't I kept?"

Sybil's fingers walked up his bare chest to his lips. "You said you'd dance with me. You haven't."

"I'm out of practice. I wanted to hold you in my arms—"

"You are now, aren't you? Holding me?"

He lifted her in his arms, filled with the beauty of the night past and the morning around them. She wrapped her arms around his neck, hands stroking his hair, as he began to waltz with her.

"Mmm. I knew you'd choose something old-fashioned and elegant," she murmured against his throat.

"Stay with me today." *Stay with me forever.*

"I can't. There's Emily."

Duncan hoarded other words to him as he waltzed, carrying her. *"Oh, Duncan, I love you so much."*

Nine

In the third week of August, Birk went to Arizona to post jail bond for Fiona. Then Calum and Duncan went to bail *two* Tallchiefs from the sheriff's keeping. During that visit, certain developers found that their underhanded crimes had "accidentally" surfaced.

Upon Birk's return to Amen Flats, Lacey promptly dumped a bucket of ice cubes over his head. Her work done in Arizona, Fiona headed for Montana on another environmental issue.

Wyonna grew stronger every day and had begun taking home education courses on the shelter's computer. She attended a seminar for women reshaping their lives and another one for administrating shelters. She changed her name, as though washing Jack away from her.

Duncan invited Emily and Sybil to his home for dinner and homemade ice cream. He surprised Sybil with a seafood pasta salad, served with sourdough rolls and fresh country butter. They watched the latest horror thriller, with Emily sprawled on the floor. Seated beside Sybil on the floor, Duncan ran his arm along her back. He tugged her back to rest against the couch, and other than playing with the tendrils at her nape and toying with her ear, he was very proper.

Lacey was right—Duncan's eyes were very expressive. In them, Sybil saw heat and storms and softer emotions that pulled at her heart. When his eyes drifted lazily down toward her breasts, she trembled.

Duncan took her hand just as the screen's vampire nipped a neck. He eased his fingers through hers, studying her pale, slender ones against his broader, tanned hands. Then slowly, so slowly, he raised her hand to his lips and kissed it.

Riveted to the television, Emily screamed, and Sybil's heart began beating again.

Duncan took them for walks on the mountain, pointing out a bear's cave, and deer in the meadows.

He was very courteous.

Too courteous. Sybil wanted to grab him and—

Just looking at him, especially his long, tanned body javelling into the lake, she wanted to taste what had begun. For the first time in her life, Sybil wondered if men could be flirts and teases. It was a new, disturbing thought that darkened when she was certain that Duncan was withholding himself from her.

She had gone to him that first time. But pride kept her from returning. Instead, she gave each kiss her best. She wanted him and he knew it.

Duncan Tallchief was the most contrary man she'd ever met.

The fourth week of August was the local fair and the first showing of Emily's pet calf. Emily, excited by her blue ribbon, was surrounded by leggy young westerners. Birk glanced in her direction and murmured one word: *"Boys."* Duncan's and Calum's heads went up, sighting the teenage boys surrounding Emily. In unison, the Tallchief brothers vaulted over a fence.

Duncan, Birk and Calum appeared menacing as they approached the teenage boys. All hard angles and brooding expressions, the Tallchiefs leaned against the corral. To protect Emily, they looked as though they could stand until the end of time. Elspeth shook her head. "You see what I mean? I don't know how Fiona and I managed. No wonder we were driven to... Well, I'd better not say. But the three of them weren't an easy match when holding our own."

The rodeo was Sybil's first; Duncan horrified her when he rode a bull named "Killer Deluxe." Dressed in a long-sleeved, cotton shirt, a western tooled belt, and jeans and boots, Duncan never looked more western male than when he strapped on flaring leather chaps and replaced his hat. With his leather-gloved hand wrapped in the bull rope and his other hand whipping the wind, Duncan rode the spinning, bucking monster from the open gate.

Sybil saw his essence then—grim, determined to win, all tough edges and whipcord power. The warrior within him terrified her.

She'd said she loved him. Unused to the emotion, she'd told him what lay within her heart. It had burst out of her, released by the beauty Duncan had created.

What did she know about love? What did she know about keeping it safe or nurturing it? Or blending lives?

Or taming a Tallchief?

The way Duncan rode his horse to where she sat in the grandstand, the way he crossed his arms over the saddle horn and just looked at her, sent chills up her spine. The crowd had quieted, watching her and Duncan, who showed no sign of moving. With the snow-capped mountains behind him, he appeared as enduring and hard as any western cowboy.

Next to Sybil, Elspeth sat very still, her proud profile revealing nothing. The soft curve of her lips told Sybil that Elspeth knew something no one else did, and it pleased her.

Elspeth seemed to have an unerring ability to tell just what her family would do in a certain circumstance.

Then, without warning, Duncan climbed out of his saddle, stepped across the grandstand fence and picked Sybil up in his arms. A man held his horse as Duncan settled her in his saddle and leaped up behind her. He rode around the area slowly, twice, and while she was fuming, he kissed her tenderly in front of the crowd. It was a light kiss, but a claiming one.

In the three weeks since Duncan had made love to her, Sybil could barely catch her breath. There were moments when just looking at him filled her with wonder—this strong man who could be so tender with Emily. He trembled when he kissed Sybil, devastating her and heating beneath her still-shy caresses. Yet he was too proper at times, and they hadn't made love again. Sybil ached in every fiber of her body for his lovemaking. His desperation had been her own.

To keep Emily from the traditional Tallchief thumb nicking and blood promise she wanted so badly, Duncan had pleaded for his abused thumb. Though Calum found an excuse, Birk had volunteered instantly. Elspeth had levied a threat against him, if he dared. It had to do with telling Lacey certain secrets. At the end of the passionate Tallchief argument, Emily agreed that she didn't need her thumb nicked. She decided to wait for a better time to argue her case.

Now, early September lit the mountains' aspens in flame colors. Mist clung in the meadows, and autumn's chill set-

tled in the mornings. Emily had begun her first experience
with public school, thrilled with wearing jeans and with
nature preparing for a hard winter.

Sybil traced her finger through a square of sunshine
crossing into her kitchen. She glanced at Elspeth, who was
visiting for afternoon tea. She looked nothing like the
woman who had shown Emily those riding tricks and
warned her not to try them.

Apparently all Tallchiefs had a wild streak, Sybil decided. "You should have seen Duncan last night. We'd just
gotten home from dinner and a movie and were just saying
good-night. I asked him in, but he's being very obstinate
about how things look. I am not the old-fashioned one
here."

She flashed an annoyed glance at Elspeth. "How things
look. That's a laugh. Do you know how embarrassed I was
when he just plucked me up and put me on his horse?"

"I seem to remember Mother complaining about the
same thing with Dad," Elspeth murmured with a light
smile.

"Well, anyway. Last night, there Duncan stood—wearing a scowl, with his hair all tousled, the way it is when
he's been running his fingers through it. It's getting long,
Elspeth. You should cut it."

"Me?" Elspeth's haughty tone said that she was no
longer responsible for Duncan's haircuts.

"You. The barber is afraid of Duncan and you know it.
I heard that once, he picked Joe up and hung him against
the wall. He seems to like picking people up—" Sybil
paused, thinking how magnificent Duncan looked with
longer hair. It gleamed with blue-black highlights and felt
so wonderfully crisp beneath her fingertips. Last night,
she'd tried desperately to sleep, recognizing that she needed
her rest for the morning's enormous new account. But
wanting Duncan in her bed had interfered.

Dreams of him standing tall and naked—except for a small loincloth—all tanned and gleaming and powerful...allowed for little sleep. Add to the backdrop of rugged mountains a huge tepee and an infant in the cradleboard he held, and the dreams would destroy any woman. Sometimes she saw a baby with straight, black hair sleeping in the Tallchief cradle—

Sometimes she dreamed of Duncan moving over her, his features taut and dark and desperate, his gray eyes tinted like shifting smoke in the night sky. He treated her so carefully, entering, filling her until he seemed to touch her heart.

Oh, Duncan...I love you so much....

Another telephone call had claimed the remainder of her peace. The man yelled obscenities at her when she blew a whistle into the phone.

The calls were sporadic and she suspected that Frank had a friend doing his dirty work. She believed he would tire of the game soon enough, and the calls seemed mild compared with those after her rape. There was an odd, ding-ding noise in the background and she'd kept tapes of the calls for legal use. Since she preferred her privacy, she'd decided against Amen Flats' law. They would just inform Duncan and she didn't want him concerned—a man who made up his own rules, he could be a disaster.

Sybil tore her flowery paper napkin in tiny shreds. Duncan was a difficult man. He could see how much she wanted him and his body gave evidence of his desire. Yet each time he set limits on his passion...on *her* passion. Sybil disliked his control, especially when she had locked herself to him last night. She looked at Elspeth. "You should have seen him last night. The word 'affair' came up and—"

"Don't tell me that you told Duncan that what you two

have is an affair?'' Elspeth lifted one black, fine eyebrow at Sybil.

''Well, I tried to. Actually, I asked when it was going to begin.... That I had made certain decisions and—'' She glanced at Elspeth. ''He seemed to grow three feet, looked horribly thunderous, his gray eyes flashing steel. I felt as if I'd stepped into the cave of some—''

''A Tallchief warrior, dear. By the way, it's true what he says about your eyes—they are the shade of topaz, and light like a tiger's when you're angry.''

''Yes, well. I've been a tad disturbed by him. He can be so— I'm not ready for what Duncan wants. Whatever that is. I've been under someone or another's rule most of my life. Duncan isn't an understanding person in matters like this, Elspeth. Since I've been on my own, I've always made my decisions alone.''

''Mmm.'' Elspeth's tone was noncommittal. She murmured, ''You're about to have a visitor.''

Duncan loomed outside the door, his horse tied to her picket fence.

Sybil glanced at Elspeth, who hadn't taken her eyes off her teacup. At times, Elspeth seemed to have the mystical powers of her shaman and seer ancestors. When Sybil opened the door, she tried a welcoming smile, which died. Looking all fierce and dressed in chaps, Duncan thrust a parcel into her hands, then bent to take her lips with a hard, hungry kiss. He lifted his head, pride flashing in his steel-gray eyes as he gazed down at her. Then, in the next instant, he was vaulting onto his saddle.

Sybil hugged the bulky parcel in one arm and covered her tender lips with her fingertips. Duncan shot one more hot look at her, then sat very straight, all broad shoulders and commanding man while his horse pranced toward Tallchief Mountain.

When Sybil finally turned, Elspeth was still sitting at her

kitchen table, looking amused. Sybil managed to recover. "Oh, that man. He just swoops and claims and then he's gone."

"He'll be back. What did he bring?"

Sybil tore the wrappings away, not folding them neatly as she usually did. When she was finished, the old cradleboard lay on the table, the pale, soft doeskin gleaming in the sunshine. The rich beadwork, blue and white and red, was intricate and perfect, portraying the symbols for chief, big mountain and woman. Good omen symbols shone in the rich, buttery texture. Fringes softened the oval-shaped cradleboard, which had been strapped to the mother's back. "It's beautiful."

Elspeth traced one of the fringes and smoothed the old beads. "It was Una's," she whispered. "Tallchief's markings are on the bent wood. See the mountain?"

Feeling dazed, Sybil poured herself into her chair. "What an odd thing to give me. I was certain we had an understanding that we wouldn't exchange gifts. I have never given him anything."

"I don't think Duncan has a gift exchange on his mind. But he does set rules that suit him." Elspeth's humor lit her eyes, crinkled in the corners.

"I can't accept something that is a family heirloom." Sybil adored the cradleboard, her fingers floating over the magnificent beaded handwork and soft doeskin.

Elspeth's humor became a soft smile. "My brother is making a statement, Sybil."

Sybil stared at the gift, her eyes rounding at Elspeth's implication. "No. He's desperate *not* to have children. I know because he…"

When she had mentioned her potential fertility, Duncan had rushed to cleanse her. She flushed under Elspeth's humored study. "Well, I just know."

"Perhaps he's thinking more of a lasting bond and the

cradleboard is symbolic of a union.'' Clearly Elspeth was amused at the whole incident. ''Symbolism is part of Duncan's heritage, you know. He listens to the sounds of the earth and to the animals. He's very respectful and observes some of the old ways.''

Sybil shook her head, disbelieving. ''I know that he meditates and that he collects relics of his heritage.''

Yet she'd seen Duncan carefully sidestep a plant or lift his head to watch a hawk soar.

Elspeth's hand covered Sybil's. ''We share a heritage, but Duncan more than the rest goes more inside himself. He's reverent of the earth and is very complex. We've all inherited certain insights, the ability to image people, and he sees a definite, interesting image where you're concerned. I believe you may have nicked his pride, dear. I really dislike informing you of this, but I fear you are in for a battle.''

''Whatever for?''

''You'll see. He's started to grow ferns. They are responding nicely.''

Sybil shook her head. ''Ferns are strange plants for Duncan to grow.''

''Yes. He usually collects herbs from the wild. This time, the image is different, I think. You're very exotic, especially when you're fighting with him. Your coloring changes into brilliant hues, too vibrant for a mountain cat, which blends with earth tones. At first, I thought a woman of fire. But you are too sleek and graceful.'' Elspeth sipped her tea and smoothed the doeskin. ''Mmm,'' she murmured again. ''So his time has come.''

The next evening, Duncan ripped his leather gloves away. The dying light caressed Amen Flats, the shadows of the mountain swallowing it. He needed to repair fences and store more hay in the barn before he thought about the woman who rode his thoughts. He patted his horse. This time he'd chosen a calico—or pinto—that had probably descended from his father's people. Tradition was as much a part of his life as the wind or Tallchief Mountain. Or the flame-haired woman tormenting him.

He plucked a delicately laced frond away from his fringed leather jacket. Ferns liked cool, shady places away from strong winds and heat. They had to be handled gently and responded to exact watering, a gentle misting.

She wanted games. An affair. A quick hunger of bodies that offered no commitment.

His pride nicked, he would leave no room for her to do other than to make a choice.

He'd chosen the way of tradition, bringing gifts to her in a time-honored way, riding a horse that was his alone. Duncan lifted his head to the evening, inhaling the town aromas of cooking evening meals. His truck would have been faster, but he'd wanted time to think, to listen to what was in his heart. He focused on Sybil's house; she was working at her computer, her office window framing her head and shoulders. Emily was probably watching television and trying to do her homework.

Sybil was a part of his mind and his body. He did not take that lightly, nor did he accept the fences she constantly erected between them. Cool, exactly placed fences that reminded him he had no claim on her.

But he did. When his heart beat for the sight of her, when a lift of her chin set his pulse pounding, when the sound of her voice soothed the restless pacing of the wolf within him, he knew she was his other half.

Whatever lay between Sybil and him, it had brought to life primitive instincts and passions he had not experienced.

The calico nickered as Duncan slid from the saddle. He'd expected the cradleboard to be returned. Perhaps it still would be when Sybil recognized his intentions. Maybe she hadn't had time to deal with it, her work taking priority over their relationship. He would expect that. She understood priorities necessary for survival the way few people did. He honored her thinking and counted each heartbeat that the cradleboard was not returned.

He longed for her. For the sound of her voice…the graceful movements of her hands like fluttering doves.

Duncan's tall body tensed. He'd fought the driving urge to have her. The entering of her body was symbolic, a treasuring of her as his heart. He would not cheapen either one of them.

She cared. But she fought what was within her, what the past had caused.

Or perhaps she wanted a man like Gavin James, one with city clothing and soft ways. One who knew the right things to say and when.

Duncan glanced at the tire swing he'd made for Emily. The girl had never had a simple swing hung on a tree and she'd cried. She'd never fished in a stream or been taught to treasure nature in the wild. At thirteen, she looked how Sybil must have looked, all coltish and promising. Emily possessed a sense of humor and Duncan mourned for Sybil, who would speak little of her life. He sensed it was too dark and cold for her to share.

This time when she came to the door he handed her the string of fat fish from Tallchief Lake. The light behind her lit the fire in her loosened hair and outlined her body within the long lounging gown.

Though stunned, she held the fish firmly—his gift to her—and stood on tiptoe to receive his kiss, and his heart leaped. The kiss was so soft, the brushing of his lips on hers, her scent enfolding him. The restlessness within him quieted, eased by this woman who was part of him and yet apart.

He heard the ring the second time and realized that Emily, engrossed in the lively, loud teen show, might not answer the telephone. Sybil, her eyes shaded with dark-gold tints, continued to look at him and reached for the wall phone next to her. As the caller, a woman with a sharp voice spoke, Sybil's eyes darkened.

Duncan watched her draw within herself, close the cool, tight fronds protectively around her. The woman's knifelike voice met Sybil's cool murmurs, as though she were waiting for a quick slash.

He took the fish from her and placed them in the sink. Sybil frowned at him, listening to the caller. He sensed that her mood had changed, that all the fences were in place. That she needed his protection. Yet the look she shot him was not welcoming, and he waited, understanding that this was a battle she needed to fight alone.

"No, I am not having a tawdry affair. I am not shaming the White name again. Duncan Tallchief is not to be investigated further. Yes, I did spend the night with him. I swear, Mother, if you interfere one more time with my life, I will make no promises about the shares that Grandmother left me. Furthermore, Mother…and Father—I hear you on the extension—I am not in your keeping any longer."

Her face flushed, she gripped the telephone with fingers that were white with tension.

Duncan watched her struggle, a tangled battle of frustration, love and anger. He waited until she'd hung up the phone, tears glittering on her lashes. She leaned heavily against the wall and closed her eyes.

He wanted to go to her, hold her, but saw that now she struggled with the past. A strong woman, Sybil preferred to fight alone. He hoped that one day she would lean against him. He made a movement to leave, and her topaz eyes, glittering with tears, opened. "My mother. She's worried that I've become involved. Not that she's ever cared."

He touched her cheek, rubbed away a tear with his thumb. "You love them."

It was enough that she placed her cheek against his palm, in his keeping. "The strange thing is, I believe they love me and simply have no idea how to show it. At first they were injured by the gossip—when Emily was born. Then the breach widened. They've never been demonstrative…but oh, Duncan. My mother sounds so old, so worried."

"Could it be that she knows? That now you are the strong one and she knows she has failed?"

Sybil shivered and stepped back, away from his keeping. "I don't know. Sometimes I see her or Father looking at Emily and—" She shook her head. "I don't know."

"She looks like you."

"Yes." Sybil's tender tone held pride.

In another minute, he would ask if she liked his gift, the cradleboard. He would ask her if she loved him….

A man of pride, Duncan moved away and into the evening shadows and the wind that told of winter's coming.

Two days later, Sybil smoothed the blue beaded mountain symbol on the doeskin moccasins. Another gift from Duncan, they had fitted perfectly, beautifully decorated in fringes and beads. When she tried them on with shaking hands, they clung to her ankles and calves.

His gifts were priceless heirlooms and she should return them. But they were a part of him and she found herself holding them close when she slept. She had to find something to give him in return…or force herself to return the gifts. She squared her shoulders and knew that Duncan would not be pleased. He was a man of pride…her pride was no small matter, pasting her together when her world had crumbled.

She leaned closer to the mirror, inspecting her eyes.

Dark-gold circles with a touch of flames stared back at her. "Topaz. Tiger eyes."

She felt like a tiger now, protecting her child and her home.

Dressed in a black business suit, with her hair neatly tamed, she turned to the mirror. While Duncan's gifts moved something deep and womanly within her, the obscene calls had to be stopped. Emily had almost answered the telephone last night. Sybil firmed her mouth and picked up the bag she had packed with copies of cassettes.

Fifteen minutes later, she parked her car near the filling station. She listened carefully as the cars ran over the rubber strip, signaling the attendant. Ding-ding. Ding-ding.

The sound was the same as the background noise in the tapes. She found Jack Smith immediately, hovering around the snack and drink machines with his buddies.

"Well, lookee who's here, boys." He leered at her. "Duncan Tallchief's little woman."

Sybil contained the fury within her and continued looking at him. He shifted restlessly, his leer dying. She was so glad that Wyonna had gone through with the divorce. Wyonna had not believed Jack's promises of reform. "Jack," Sybil said coolly, "I think you might be interested in these tapes. If you call my home one more time—or any of your friends do—or if you contact me in any way, I am turning the originals over to the police."

Jack's curse broiled the room. Sybil let him run out of breath, then she nodded and walked away.

She was just making tea, when Duncan entered her house. She knew that no amount of tea would calm the emotions he could fire within her. This time there was no polite rap on her door; sweeping into her home, dressed in chaps, he was like a full-blown mountain storm filled with lightning and thunder.

"You."

The flat, deep word was an accusation that raised the hair on her body. A gunfighter's expression would be more kindly. Elspeth had been right: Duncan was a warrior. But Sybil's control was running low. Facing Jack and his buddies had trimmed away a good measure. She needed every dram of control to deal with Duncan on any level.

She wrapped the teapot in a dish towel so the tea could steep, and lifted an eyebrow to him. "Yes?"

Then, because she wanted to waylay the war brewing between them, for whatever cause, she tossed him a diversion. "I hear you're growing ferns. That must be very relaxing. A tranquil—"

"You." Duncan's gloved hand shot out to clasp the back of her neck and draw her closer. His steely gaze cut at her, damning her. "With you around, I need all the tranquillity I can manage. What the hell do you mean by facing Jack Smith—and his so-called friends—alone?" he demanded in a too-soft voice.

"I prefer to deal with unpleasantries in my own way."

"Unpleasantries? They could have raped you right there."

She drew her head back from his gloved hand. "They wouldn't. Now, let me go."

He ripped off his glove and placed his fingers on her nape. His hands trembled as he caressed her and scowled at her. "Am I hurting you?"

"No. I just don't like being manhandled and you know it."

Duncan's eyes flickered and he slowly released her. "I know." He breathed deeply, the aroma of pine and leather enfolding her. "You make your choices about what affects your life. And how you will deal with them."

She found Duncan's dark, male scent and fought longing for him. "I had a problem. I took care of it in the quietest, most efficient way I know."

"Problem? So Jack has been making obscene calls to you for how long?"

"I've had them before and much worse." Her fingers shook as she unwrapped the teapot and poured the liquid into a fragile cup. With Duncan in a mood, she felt as delicate as the china.

On the other hand, who— "Just who do you think you are to talk to me like this?" she asked, her control slipping.

Pain ripped through his eyes, darkening them before he shielded his emotions. He spoke in a whisper.

"I'm someone you should have turned to."

She'd hurt him. Duncan the defender was used to taking people under his wing. She preferred to deal with the matter by herself. The Tallchiefs could be a high-tempered, avenging clan and she liked quiet and harmony. "Duncan...I...I am used to handling my situations by myself. This doesn't involve you."

He looked down at her, his eyes flashing steel. "Think again."

She tried to rally her thoughts, to reason with him. "Duncan, we each have pasts. You struggle with pain that you haven't told anyone about."

"Such as?" He was all hunter now, not allowing her any room. He folded his arms over his broad chest and stood, legs locked apart, watching her.

She caught the bruises on his knuckles, and touched them. The way he gazed down at her was as chilly as the bottom of Tallchief Lake. "Duncan. You didn't," she managed, studying him. "I don't want any brawls because of me. I detest fighting."

"It wasn't a fight, more like a lesson." His silence accused her. Then he said too carefully, "You told me you love me. Is it true?"

Facing Duncan Tallchief was far more difficult than facing Jack Smith. "You...I...we.... I believe we have a...a relationship of sorts. Neither one of us has seen anyone else—"

She found no comfort in his harsh expression. "I really should get your gifts and return them to you. They are much too priceless to give to—"

He snorted at that, looking all tall and western in his hat and boots.

The snort set her off. She saw his nostrils flare with it and his mouth tighten into a hard line. "*I* am trying here, Duncan."

"Cut my hair."

Like a flaming arrow, the order sliced into the space between them.

"What?"

"Elspeth won't do it anymore." The light caught Duncan's blue-black hair, touched his eyebrows and lashes and gleamed on his high cheekbones. Set in the shadows, his smoky gaze locked on to her.

Stunned, she took a step backward. Duncan remained as formidable as Tallchief Mountain. "I have no idea how to trim a man's hair. That isn't the topic here."

"I know. You're trying to remind me that I have no claim on you. You're trying to 'make nice,' and place everything in its righteous, cool corner. Sex, of course, is a different matter." The words cut at her.

He was too big and too dangerous to place in any corner, she thought instantly, desperately fighting to control her temper. "Duncan, I think we should both cool down—"

"Cool down? Just like that?" His mouth took hers, his arms wrapping her tightly against him. The heavy, rapid thudding of his heart hit her palm like a hammer. Her toes left the floor as his lips burned hers.

His need for her was too raw, his body thrusting against her.

But she wasn't afraid—this was Duncan…Duncan…the

word became a litany, raw with emotion and physical need to have him fill her, and only him. She buried her hands in his hair, his hat tumbling to the floor. Duncan eased her to the counter and moved between her legs.

His hand tugged at her jacket and found her breast, claiming it. His other hand found her bottom, opening to 'cup her tightly.

This was Duncan, elemental, passionate, meeting her desire and claiming her—

She cried out, needing him, her body weeping for his...her legs caught his hips, bringing him so close...so close and powerful.

Then he was shaking, burying his face in her shoulder and dragging in huge, unsteady breaths against her skin. He rocked her in his arms for one beat of her pulse. Then he moved abruptly away, as though tearing himself away from his very heart.

His thumb moved across her swollen, tender lips. The smoky tint of his eyes darkened; his expression slid to regret.

And then he was gone.

Ten

Duncan parked the rental car on the Whites' Seattle-mansion driveway. Rain slashed at the car, but the storm was no more elemental than what had driven him here—the need to see Sybil, to hold her. The lit entryway behind the pristine pillars was barely visible in the heavy downpour.

"Oh, Duncan...I love you so much...."

He gripped the steering wheel with his gloved hands. He was too used to his own rules. He should have called Sybil before he left to find the boy. The ten-year-old had become lost on a camping trip. He'd survived in a protected mountain cave until Duncan had found him. The boy was savvy once he'd discovered he was lost. His Boy Scout survival skills had kept him alive in severe weather.

While Duncan was in the area, he'd helped in a manhunt in the mountains. The killer was also skilled at survival and dangerous.

Duncan drew a steadying breath into his lungs. He hadn't slept in how long? Not on the flight from Denver. In the six days since he'd seen Sybil, Duncan realized that he'd had only minutes of sleep. Six long, hard days ago—that was the last time Duncan saw Sybil.

The Tallchiefs weren't an easy family to understand; their emotions ran deep. With the lack of sleep and his frustration, Duncan knew his usually calm nerves were stretched like bowstrings.

When Duncan thought of Sybil coolly entering Jack Smith's hangout, a place with a back room— He heard a crack and forced his fingers to release the steering wheel.

When he had called Elspeth earlier that evening, she'd told him that Sybil had left two days ago. Emily was attending school, staying with Elspeth.

He'd tried his message machine, praying that Sybil's voice would be on it, and it was. "Duncan, I'm leaving now. Don't try to contact me—" Static had blocked out her words and then, "I can't go on like this..." More static. "Our relationship has never been good—" Another message overlaid the rest.

She didn't want to see him again. A can't-be, you're-dumped message on a machine.

Duncan glanced at the streetlight, a dim glow in the sheets of rain. Sybil was probably making arrangements to return to the life she'd known.

He forced himself to breathe, and caught the scent of his last campfire. He glanced in the rearview mirror, and caught his savage scowl. He was too tired to be calm with her and shouldn't have come. He'd lost his temper and now Sybil was running from him. He couldn't leave it like that, couldn't write nice notes and leave telephone messages. He should have told her he loved her, should have said the words women needed to hear.

As Duncan walked past the butler, the man's expressionless eyes took in his battered western hat. Duncan hadn't shaven in days and his hair was past his collar. The butler's gaze slid to Duncan's flannel shirt, his worn and dirty jeans and scuffed western boots. "Sir? May I ask the nature of your visit?"

"To retrieve my wife. My name is Duncan Tallchief." Hell, he'd been retrieving everyone else— Duncan leveled a look at the butler, who backed up a step. Sybil was the other part of Duncan, and in his heart, he believed she was his wife. She should have waited. But since she hadn't, Duncan planned to—what? Capture her would be good, he decided darkly. He wasn't the kind to argue, but Sybil made him want to rant and yell.

The butler cleared his throat. "I see. And what, if I may ask, is her name?"

My heart. My own. My life. Duncan looked steadily at the man. "Sybil. I'm not in the mood for word games. Just get her."

"I see," the butler said crisply. "Very well. Wait here while I check with Mr. White—"

Duncan walked past the butler and into a well-lit, stylish room, a fire blazing in the fireplace. Dressed in slacks and a lounging jacket, a tall, gray-haired man stood slowly. A woman, an older version of Sybil, wearing an expensive sweater and slacks, came to the older man's side. "I'm calling the police."

"Do that." Duncan didn't bother to remove his hat. He watched the older couple take in his appearance—that of a dirty, tough cowboy. "But I'll have my say anyway. You're looking at your future son-in-law, and we're going to get a few things straight."

"Mr. Duncan Tallchief—" the butler started to say.

"Son-in-law?" both Whites asked incredulously, dismissing his name.

Duncan nodded. He peeled away his gloves and tucked

them into his leather belt. "I'll treat her well. You're welcome to visit us. You're welcome in our home. Until you hurt either Sybil or Emily. I've come to take her back with me."

"Now, listen here you—" Mr. White began.

"Dear…" Mrs. White's voice held a plea for patience. "Ah…sit down, won't you…ah…Mr…?"

"Tallchief. Duncan Tallchief. I'll make this short and sweet. I'm not in a good mood. I'm from Wyoming. I've just run six days without anything called sleep and have tracked a killer through a mountain range." When Mrs. White gasped, Duncan softened his image. "Don't worry. I'm not wearing my gun or knife. Just get Sybil for me, will you?"

He watched the Whites trace his features, picking out the darker skin tones of his Native American ancestor. Mrs. White sat abruptly; her hand went to her throat. Duncan was in no mood to be sympathetic. These people had wounded Sybil and left Emily unloved. "Are you going to get Sybil? Or do I do it myself?"

"So you're the one who has ruined her. I suppose Sybil should deal with the mess she has created this time." Mr. White waved the hovering butler to the task.

"Ruined her?" Duncan asked very carefully, as he sprawled in a chair. He draped one leg over the arm. If the inference was that Sybil was a loose woman— "It's been a long day. Why don't you explain that remark?"

"She's not herself. She's overly distraught and acting strange. Rather politely argumentative," Mrs. White explained anxiously. "We've been trying to reason with her. She could need medication and a long rest. She… mmm…has had other experiences and we've had to do the same. Though this time, she seems oddly determined in a cool manner. Do you, ah, know her background?"

"I do." Duncan caught Sybil's scent and slid his eyes

to see her leaning against the door frame. She was barefoot and her arms were crossed over her chest. He couldn't read her expression.

She'd expect him to act like a savage. He felt like one now. There wasn't an ounce of warmth in her parents. No wonder she preferred to keep her life streamlined and without the interference of emotional ties except for Emily.

She belonged in a mansion. Dressed in white, satin lounging pajamas, her flame-tinted hair tumbling around her shoulders, she caused his heart to stop. The ten feet between them was too far. Just seeing her settled the rage that had been burning in him. "Hello, Sybil."

"Hello, Duncan. Where are your chaps?" Her eyes drifted over him, her expression slightly amused. He hadn't bothered to do up the upper buttons of his shirt and her gaze brushed his chest, paused there, before traveling to his boots.

He wasn't amused. Every instinct told him to carry her away, back to Tallchief Mountain.

He caught the wiggling of her toes, and it reminded him of a mountain cat twitching its tail. She was enjoying his confrontation with her parents.

Mrs. White fluttered a handkerchief to her nose. "Dear. Sybil. Be reasonable. You can't possibly be…be enthused about this…this person."

"He has his moments. Now isn't one of them, apparently. He's got that brooding, dangerous hunter look on him, and I'll bet he's just gotten back from a manhunt. He's wonderful with Emily and beautiful in kilts. Wonderful legs."

"Goodness!"

Sybil lifted an eyebrow. "Didn't you get my message that I would be calling you soon?"

"The machine malfunctioned in the storm." Duncan forced himself to sit still. *"Our relationship has never been good.... He has his moments.... He's wonderful with Emily—''* Duncan clung to each word.

She might be enjoying tormenting him, but he wanted to hold her, to tell her that she was a part of him. He noted the lift of her chin and the sheltered anger of her eyes. Pride ran through her, just as it ran through him. "Did you miss me?" he asked bluntly.

"Mmm. Mildly. The last time we saw each other, you weren't exactly reasonable."

"Sybil." Duncan paused for breath, his control unsteady. "You know why, sweetheart."

"You came to defend me, didn't you? To tuck me under your wing, where nothing could hurt me."

"Is that so bad?" They were suddenly on elemental ground now, where it was too dangerous to move quickly.

"I came here to settle the past. You can't protect me from that. It happened. Our relationship—my parents and myself—has never been good."

Duncan inhaled sharply. The "relationship" she'd been talking about in her message was not with him but with her parents!

Sybil's deep-gold eyes locked with his. "Mother, Father, I want to introduce to you Duncan Tallchief. He's descended from a Scotswoman and the Sioux chieftain who captured her. Duncan has two sisters and two brothers, and each is very special. They're loyal and loving to one another. Duncan raises sheep and cattle on Tallchief Mountain. He is very good to Emily. His entire family has adopted her and she's determined to nick her thumb in a blood promise. Duncan and his brothers are her Black Knights and she is their princess."

Her expression darkened. "He wants me to cut his hair and wait on him. I've only just discovered why. He loves me. He cares so much, but he hasn't quite gotten the knack of telling me. I have high hopes for improvement. What is important for you to know is that he treasures those he loves. Treasures. He listens. He cares.''

Mrs. White gave every evidence of swooning as Sybil lifted her finger and curled it, signaling Duncan to come to her. ''But right now, Duncan is obviously tired and probably not sweet. Come to my room, Duncan. I'm afraid my parents can't handle any more Tallchief manners tonight.''

''Your room!'' Mr. White exploded. ''Not in my house. You are not taking this…this bounty hunter to your room.''

''We can go elsewhere.''

Sybil's challenge cost her; Duncan saw her warring with her love of her parents and her own course. Choices of the heart weren't easy. He prayed he was on her menu, and stood.

''I'd rather talk to you in private, away from here.''

''My terms, Duncan. I say here.''

He glared at her and found the tigress leaping from her eyes. He took a deep, steadying breath and knew that the gamble was too big. She wanted her way—this time. It was important in the battles with her parents. He nodded curtly.

''Goodness!'' Mrs. White exclaimed, taking in Duncan's height and size. ''You…you're so big. So…cowboy.''

Sybil's gaze ran coolly down him. She tapped her finger on her lips. ''Yes. Goodness, he is, isn't he? He's also not in a good mood, from the shade of his eyes and that black scowl. He's in his gunfighter-showdown mood and not exactly reasonable. The Tallchiefs are like that, but also caring, emotional and delicate. They have to be protected at times. So I'm taking him to my room. Good night, Father. Good night, Mother. We'll see you at breakfast. Come along, Duncan.''

''He's delicate?'' Mr. White's yell was pure outrage as Duncan followed Sybil up the winding, elegant stairway.

Duncan tensed at the shrill cry. It boasted of a bully's ownership.

On the other hand, he didn't like Sybil's "delicate" remark, either. Perhaps he had something in common with Mr. White.

"Sybil? Sybil, dear. You should put on your robe," Mrs. White called, following them.

Duncan noted the sincere concern in the woman's voice. Sybil turned to coolly look down at her mother.

Duncan's eyes were on a level with her breasts. She caught his hot look and flung it back at him, taking in his hat, opened shirt, dirty jeans and boots.

"Sybil, don't you dare take that man to your room. You always were a rebel and you've caused your own problems. How dare you bring your paramours here."

"If he leaves, I leave. And I won't be back. We'll talk all about this in the morning after everyone has had a good rest."

Her mother turned white. "You don't mean that. This…this cowboy is a bad influence. Just looking at the two of you, there on the stairway, your satin to his leather, anyone can see you're not a match. Dear, you have breeding and manners. He…he's a savage from Wyoming."

She seemed to wilt against the wall as Sybil just stared at her, then turned to continue up the magnificent stairway.

He forced his eyes away from Sybil's swaying backside, clad in satin. Unused to following orders, he wasn't happy that the woman he'd come to claim was issuing them.

She closed the door to the sumptuous bedroom and rounded on him, topaz eyes blazing. "Exactly what do you mean coming here? And telling Morris that I'm your wife?"

At a loss for words, frustrated and deeply tired, Duncan reacted immediately. He tugged her into his arms and found her mouth with his.

Sybil jerked her head back. "Oh, no. Not that darned Tallchief, mind-blasting kiss. I've been holding my own through the disasters of the past two days. You're not getting around this by kissing the daylights out of me."

"Fine. You can kiss them out of me." Duncan leaned down slowly to brush a kiss on one corner of her lips, then the other. "You taste like honey."

Sybil closed her eyes, leaned slightly toward him for an instant and then firmly pushed her hands flat against his chest. "Duncan, you look like living death, and if I let you run over me now, I know I'll regret it. You've got your defender look written all over you and I won't have it. Not now."

Beneath the satin her hip was curved, full, all woman. He squeezed slightly and brushed another kiss against her cheek. Her breath caught and her hand lifted to smooth his stubble-rough cheek. There was tenderness beneath her touch and Duncan almost sighed as she stroked him and asked, "Why are you growing ferns?"

He caught her bottom lip with his teeth. She tasted like cinnamon and silk. "They remind me of you. I've been studying them. Cool. Private."

She laughed shakily. "I was cool and private. Before you."

When her fingers began unbuttoning his shirt, Duncan captured them and lifted them to his lips. "I'm dirty."

"You're always very careful to be gentle with me, aren't you? To touch me with reverence."

He rubbed his nose against hers. "Your parents are probably aghast."

She grinned at his use of the proper word and continued unbuttoning his shirt. "Yes, probably. We've been battling for two days now. They're not at all happy with me."

She pushed him toward the bathroom and, when his back was turned, patted his bottom. "Now, off you go. We'll talk later."

For a moment, Duncan stood absolutely still, his body

taut. He devoured the thought that she had patted him affectionately. The way a man might pat a woman. The light gesture from her, his first, stunned him. It was no light thing when a woman like Sybil demonstrated affection. Obviously Sybil felt she had that right.

Obviously he liked it. It was an encouraging little demonstration that perhaps she wasn't tossing him out of her life.

Duncan felt the tension ease from his tense shoulders. He could deal with Sybil's feminine hand on his backside. "Do that again."

This time her touch was a caress, accompanied with a light kiss on his shoulder. "That's nice," he said, meaning it.

"Go."

Duncan bathed, then shaved with her razor. Her scents clung to the bath. Pretty, expensive Parisian oils and salts lined the luxurious tub and ferns of every kind stood beneath the huge, etched windows. He hurried and prayed that Sybil was in a gentle mood. He didn't trust the banked fire beneath her lashes. He swung open the bathroom door and stepped into the room, a towel around his hips.

Mrs. White was standing by Sybil, and her eyes widened. She glanced nervously at her daughter. "Is he safe?"

Sybil smiled, her eyes slanting with humor. "I hope not. Out, Mother. I'm going to marry this man as soon as possible. We'll talk over breakfast."

Mrs. White's diamond-studded hand gripped the door frame as Sybil began to close the door. "Dear. Dear, you know the guest room can be ready in minutes. Ah... wouldn't that be more comfortable?"

"No. He's tired and he needs me. He's come all this way for me. Shoo, Mother."

"Well, I...dear, will you be all right? We could have him forcibly ejected."

Sybil laughed outright. "I doubt it."

"But you know, dear, a wedding takes months of planning. There's the guest list—" Mrs. White's eyes grew large, as though she'd just realized there might be more Tallchiefs attending the event.

Sybil placed an arm around her mother and bent to kiss her forehead. "Don't worry, Mother. The rest of them are quite tame."

Duncan noted that Sybil was trying to comfort her mother. When hugged, the older woman had tensed, but then had settled against her daughter. Perhaps she knew it was time to change, to let the past go and adapt to the future.

When the door closed, Duncan forced himself to prowl around Sybil's room, studying it. All whites and pinks and ruffles, with a huge, canopied bed filled with more ruffles. Dolls peered from a packing box. "I want Emily to have them. My parents want them to remain in the White keeping," Sybil murmured. "It's a minor tug-of-war, but an important step forward. They've agreed that my daughter should have them."

He saw the pain moving through her before she turned to him. "You're here to carry me off, aren't you, Duncan Tallchief? You actually think that you can just—well, you can't. Not this time. You've complicated a few things, but nothing I can't deal with. You've just escalated what must be done, the meeting of terms. I love my parents, and deep down, I believe they love me. So I had planned a nice, quiet balancing of our relationship. A gentle nudge in the right direction. Then here you are, the perfect picture of a western bounty hunter."

"Are you going to marry me?" His voice sounded coarse, unsteady, raw with the emotions lashing him.

She avoided the answer he wanted to hear. "You could have waited to be invited, you know. But, then, you missed me, didn't you?'' She slid his words back to him on a platter.

''Yes. Are you leaving Amen Flats?'' He would move to be near her. A modern relationship tuned to air flights and schedules wouldn't do. He needed her too much.

She walked slowly, gracefully, to him and tugged the knot of the towel away. ''Come to bed, Duncan. Rest. You look so tired. We'll talk in the morning.''

Unused to having his schedule set for him, Duncan stood very still. ''You've planned a lot of morning talk, sweetheart.''

''Yes, but not now. Come here.'' She eased onto the cream-tinted satin sheets and waited. She crooked her finger again and blew him a kiss. ''Come here, big man. I won't hurt you. Don't look like you're expecting a tiger to pounce.''

''I could use that guest room. Or a motel.''

''I know, you're old-fashioned. You can't go anywhere because Morris is washing your clothes. Nothing else will fit you. I just want to hold you. You look so worn. Come to me, Duncan Tallchief. I'll keep you safe.''

Duncan climbed into the bed carefully. It creaked with his weight, and in the shadows he found Sybil watching him. He lay very still, his nerves raw with wanting her. To hold her, to make love to her, to show her with his body how much he loved and cherished her. Fear that he might hurt her, that his passions ran too deep for his control, stayed him.

In the shadows, a quick movement of lace and ruffles brought Sybil's satin-covered body over him.

''You are mine, Duncan Tallchief. Mine. Got it?''

He tenderly placed his hands on her waist and she smiled, bending to kiss him lightly. Her hand smoothed the hair on his chest. ''So proper. Not comfortable with lying beneath my parents' roof?''

Her fingertip toyed with his nipple. "It's my house, really. Upon the event that I marry. I've been defending you for two days, Duncan, and doing a neat job of it, too. I never really cared to battle my parents over anything, anyone...except Emily. Then you show up, looking like a gunslinger out for trouble, and tomorrow I'll have to soothe them all over again. Getting my parents used to the idea that I'll be living in Wyoming and married to a Tallchief is something I had hoped to do gently. The dolls were just a minor ploy in my plans."

His throat dried instantly and his fingers tightened on her waist. His heart raced painfully.

Sybil squirmed closer. "I bought a haircutting set. I've been taking lessons."

He decided that he'd better remain quiet and let her take the lead. "You have?"

She played with his hair, trailed it over a lacy ruffle and studied the contrast. "Your heart is beating like a tom-tom. Try to relax."

"I could do that a lot easier if you'd run the marriage thing by me again," he returned unsteadily.

She laid another raven strand against the cream-and-pink lace. "Layering, I think. I hope you'll be patient my first few times...of course, I could try with someone else. Calum or Birk. Elspeth has such lovely long hair that I wouldn't dare."

"What's hair got to do with anything?" he demanded.

Sybil bent to kiss him and snuggled close, her arms around his neck as they shared the pillow. "It was important to you that I cut your hair. At first I thought it was ugh-me-male whimsy. Then I remembered how you looked when my hands touched you—that stark, waiting desperation. You like my hands on you. I believe that to you it was symbolic of a commitment from me. That I would care for you. I think, by the way, that you'll be very easy to tame," she added clinically, then bit his earlobe.

"You do, huh?" Duncan tried to think as she moved his hand to cover her breast.

"Thinking near you isn't possible. I needed distance to place everything in line. You told me with the cradleboard and with the other gifts, didn't you?"

He treasured her softness wound tight around him, the lovely curve of her breast that she had given to his care. "Yes. I found words would not come."

Her hands smoothed his cheeks, tracing a series of small cuts. He'd been too anxious to come to her. Her eyes were gentle upon him. "You've kept your fears locked to yourself for so many years that you don't know how to tell me...it's all right, Duncan. I know how hard it was for you and that emotions move deeply within you which I can't understand. But I know that you love me, just as I know that one day the words will come easier."

She bent to kiss him. "Last night, I dreamed I told you that, and you picked me up and ran to your tepee. There you did wonderful things with me. I was wearing a wedding band—so were you." Her lips brushed his throat.

Duncan rolled, easing her beneath him. For a moment they stared at each other in the shadows, then Duncan tugged at her elastic waistband, a gentle suggestion. "Did you like that dream?" he asked very carefully.

"Yes," she whispered, her fingers dragging through his hair and caressing his taut shoulders. "Yes."

Together they removed her clothes and Duncan settled easily upon her, viewing the picture she made. With her hair tumbling over the pale lace, her body flowing, warming to his. His eyes ran down the length of their tangled limbs, the melding of her breasts with his tanned chest. In the shadows, the tiger-woman flickered, challenging him, loving him.

He slowly bent to take her breast, to suckle her tenderly, this woman he loved. She tasted of honey and promised the future. He nipped her gently, caught the heat moving through her, the dampness of her body preparing for his.

Cautiously Duncan rested against her, fearing that he would rush, when he wanted his body to tell of his love. She bit her lip and lay beneath him like warm silk, opening, inviting him to her care. She trembled now, her hands fluttering lightly across his shoulders.

Duncan pressed his parted lips to the smooth flesh of her other breast, and found the tight bud waiting for him. She touched him, soothing his length, coaxing him within her moist folds. When he eased deeper, she closed her eyes, taking her pleasure within her. She trembled and softened and flowed beneath him, around him, yet Duncan treasured the flush riding her face, the pulse pounding in her throat. There would be other times, when he would want her quickly, fiercely. But now they were sealing the marriage that would come and he wanted to take each moment into his heart.

In the night, her eyes were tender upon him. "You fill me so completely. More than this, my gentle lover, you fill my heart."

He raised her left hand to his lips, kissing the finger that would wear his ring. "In my heart, we were married that first time."

"Yes. I think I knew it when our hands locked on the cradle."

Duncan closed his eyes, not daring to hope that she would want his child.

"I expect to make the legend come true and fill that cradle with your babies, Duncan."

Her words brought emotions so primitive they ripped through him and he could not contain them. Duncan groaned, straining to withhold his driving need to release himself within her. She gripped his arms and raised her hips, receiving him deeply. He tried to be gentle, caressing her breast, taking it to suckle deeply. All woman and power, she rippled beneath him, capturing him in a tangle of arms and legs and moist power. He was hers and she was his, and they were of one soul, one body, one heart. When she tightened her caress, straining, meeting his kiss desperately, crying out his name, Duncan felt himself tumbling, spilling, giving himself to her. He shattered on the pinnacle of their storm, heard himself crying out to her that he would love her until the stars were no more.

Gently, so gently as an autumn leaf settles to the ground, he settled upon her. Sybil claimed him gently, easing his head to rest upon her breasts. "You say such lovely things, Duncan Tallchief," she whispered shakily against his ear, her hands stroking his back.

He had heard himself telling her things that lay within his heart, images of her as his wife, his love. That she filled his heart the way the sun fills the sky. That she was his dove, his other half, his heart. That she had made his soul take flight, and when he saw her his heart fluttered like the heart of a small rabbit sheltering in the bush. That his life lay within her hands; that dawn was no more beautiful than her.

Duncan kissed the flushed side of her throat. "They're true...." Within the warmth of her body, tangled in her care, sleep dragged him away from what he wanted to say.

During the night, she came softly to him, enfolding him. Then before dawn he awoke, fearing a dream. Sybil lay cradled beside him, fragile and pale, her hair tumbled around them. He bent over her, anxious to see if he'd hurt her in his passion, filled with the wonder of her loving him. Her lips curved slowly as he touched them, his hardened body brushing her soft hip.

When he bent to kiss her breasts, Sybil's hands and body caressed him. "Again?"

"Yes," he whispered against her soft stomach.

"Yes," she returned, receiving him like silk meant for his touch.

Epilogue

Almost one year later, Duncan lay in the tepee he had built near the lake. The early-August night was cool, animals moving in the meadows, the owls hooting. In the center of the tepee was a small fire, which lit his wife and the baby nursing at her breast.

The firelight caught the tangle of her hair, loose around her bare shoulders. His daughter's blue-black shock of hair contrasted with Sybil's glowing, ivory skin. The baby's blanket was spread across her lap—a soft Tallchief tartan woven by Elspeth. Sybil's wedding ring glowed on her finger; he wore the matching one.

This was their retreat, usually shared by Emily, who was now attending a weavers' fair with Elspeth. Sybil's daughter thrived in her new life, just as her mother did.

Sybil discovered a beautiful Tallchief tradition, that of the Bridal Tepee. Though made of modern canvas, the tepee signified that a Tallchief had claimed a true love. When

Tallchief realized how deeply he loved Una, his captive bride, he had constructed a beautiful new tepee for his love. Down through the Tallchief generations, the Bridal Tepee was a statement of commitment and bonds of the heart, a home to nourish that love and shelter the family that would come.

Sybil wanted her new husband alone; he had been very, very good throughout the formal wedding that had pacified her parents. In fact, he had wooed them into a begrudging respect for the man who loved their daughter. Duncan and Sybil spoke their vows again in the tepee, and Sybil had worn the beaded doeskin shift, a Tallchief legacy for brides. She'd come to him, humbling him with promises that she would keep for a lifetime. He'd given his heart to her and his pledge, taking her gently, reverently, as though together they would put away the past. For the rest of his life, Duncan would see his bride lift away the soft shift and come to him. To their new life.

At first the Whites were stunned with the small considerations he gave them—pictures of Sybil with Emily. Pictures of Emily grinning, her hand upon the new life nestling in Sybil's body. Though their relationship was tenuous, the Whites did accept Emily, and Sybil lost her tenseness around them. In a stiff, formal way they were trying to relate.

"I love you, Mrs. Tallchief," Duncan whispered. At times he could not believe their happiness, or that their child, Megan, suckled at her breast.

"I know, and I love you," Sybil replied, the dark gold of her eyes catching the firelight.

In the flickering light, the old cradle seemed to glow, waiting for the baby—

The woman who brings the cradle to a man of Fearghus blood will fill it with his babies....

Duncan met his wife's mysterious, sultry look. When the

baby lay safely in the cradle, she would come to him. Then he added his thoughts to the legend—*and she would capture his heart.*

*   *   *   *   *

TALLCHIEF'S BRIDE

To Kerry and her Ava Gardner traits.

When a man of Fearghus blood
places the ring
upon the right woman's finger,
he'll capture
his true love forever.

Prologue

————

Wyoming October winds whipped Tallchief Mountain; fear chilled seventeen-year-old Calum Tallchief. Duncan, his older brother by a year, and Fiona, his ten-year-old sister, were missing. With the experience of a mountain tracker, Calum listened to the night and pushed through the lashing pine boughs. The night clouds swept aside briefly, allowing him a glance at the white crests of the waves on Tallchief Lake. In a small, quiet meadow, high on the mountain, leaves tumbled across his parents' new graves.

The five Tallchiefs had just been orphaned. Matthew and Pauline Tallchief had stopped at a convenience store to buy a pizza for their children; they had interrupted a robbery in progress and been killed instantly.

Afterward, Calum had buried himself in his dad's small, tidy office, trying to make sense of the family's home and Tallchief Cattle Ranch accounts. Wrapped in grief, he had forgotten Fiona's desperate fear that her brothers and sister would be torn apart. As the youngest, she needed reassurance constantly.

Calum stopped, glanced at a herd of deer passing to a lower meadow, and heard Duncan's low, quiet voice, carried on the cold, unrelenting wind, and followed the sound. A branch cracked in the bush behind him, and Birk, Calum's younger brother by a year, spoke to Elspeth, just fourteen. She answered in the quiet, soothing tone that reminded Calum of his mother. He fought the tears burning his eyes and dashed them angrily away.

He had preferred the logic of numbers to a grieving ten-year-old sister, and had barricaded himself behind the safety of accounts. There was no logic in the murder of their parents. The circle was not complete. The unfinished cycle, that of his parents growing old and holding the grandchildren they wanted—

The wind passed through the trees on the mountain, and Calum remembered his father's gray eyes lighting with love as he looked at his wife. Matthew Tallchief's voice had come from his heart, the quiet, deep sound of a man's certainty. "Wait for the right woman, son. There's more than the body's fire between a man and a woman. And when the right woman comes along, she'll lead you on a merry chase, you with your numbers and plans and logic. You can't arrange love, son. It comes waltzing into your life when you least expect it. Turns things upside down, and things happen fast after that. Can't say it's all logic and roses. But it's worth every minute."

His parents had had more than enough love to keep their family warm and to give to others when it was needed. Then, with two shots, they had been ripped away.

Was he frightened for himself? Maybe. Was he frightened for the others? Yes.

"Calum, listen to your heart," his mother had said. How could he listen, when it was filled with grief and fear?

He moved into a small clearing near the lake to find Duncan holding Fiona up against him. Her pale legs dangled down his longer ones. She had been carefully wrapped against the cold in a thick quilt made by their mother. The wind whipped against them both, sending their black hair flying in the moonlight. When Duncan turned slowly to look at him, Calum saw the startling reflection of his raw anguish and fear in his brother's expression.

Calum moved close, blocking the wind and meeting Duncan's eyes, silver in the moonlight, over Fiona's head. They were men now; they had lost a portion of their boyhood when they tracked their parents' murderer. Calum remembered how, riding on horseback, the Tallchief brothers had tracked the murderer into the mountains. Only the Tallchiefs possessed the skill to track at night, and the sheriff had known it. Matthew Tallchief had taught his sons well, and at dawn they'd ridden back to Amen Flats. Bruised and shaking with fear, the murderer had cowered and walked behind their horses. He'd been glad to see the sheriff, running to his protection.

The three sons of Matthew and Pauline had nodded grimly to the sheriff and ridden away as men. They'd returned to the ranch, where Elspeth had been keeping Fiona safe.

Calum's heart tore as he read Duncan's fear and knew it for his own. It would be no easy feat to keep them all together and the mountain for their own.

Could they keep together?

Could they keep Tallchief Mountain and the ranch?

As the oldest, Duncan would try to do both. The mountain was their inheritance, the same as their gray eyes, given to them by Una Fearghus, a Scots bondwoman captured by Tallchief, a Sioux chieftain. In the end, she'd tamed him, and they'd settled upon the mountain; the rocky cliffs and lush meadows had reminded her of Scotland.

Calum blinked away his tears as he met Duncan's anguished stare. Calum swallowed and, to hide his fear and grief, muttered tightly, "So you've got her. You should have left a note."

Birk and Elspeth arrived, the wind slashing at their coalblack hair, an inheritance from their Sioux great-greatgrandfather, Tallchief.

Then Duncan reached into the pitch-black night, lifted his hand into the cold wind and united them.

Later, Calum would think of that night as magic, when somehow Duncan managed to snag upon an idea. He added glue to the need to survive as a family, to keep their inheritance. "Aye!" they had shouted, raising their thumbs to the whirling tempest in the night sky. "Aye!"

Though it was no game to survive, alone and too young, the five hurled forth their childhood names upon the cold wind—Duncan the defender, Calum the cool, Birk the rogue, Elspeth the elegant and Fiona the fiery.

They had a job to do—good grades, no trouble, each working to keep Tallchief Ranch.

The five Tallchiefs also pledged to return Una's lost dowry—sold to keep Tallchief Mountain—to the family.

They would each seek and find one item of the dowry. A ring with three garnets held in a Celtic design fell to Calum.

He promised the others and himself that he would find it. Because the seasons had to have meaning, and the circles had to be completed.

One

"You'd like me to find whoever is sabotaging Unique. Is that correct?'' Calum Tallchief interrupted the frustrating man. Seated in front of Unique Import-Export's chairman of the board, Calum preferred to slice through chitchat; he wanted to finish this assignment quickly, all the ends neatly tied. Then he wanted to find a family heirloom that had been included in his great-great-grandmother's dowry. Calum wanted the Tallchief heirloom returned to his family.

Calum Tallchief was very good at tying loose ends. He kept his life neatly packaged, and soon he would have the ring. It had been traced to Denver, which stretched out and glistened in the morning sun beyond the executive office.

The son of a mountain tracker and the descendant of a Sioux chieftain, Calum did not trust the uneasiness that ran up the back of his neck. Maybe it was because all Tallchiefs got restless in October, the month when their parents had been killed and when their stormy emotions rode near the surface.

Emotions? Calum kept his tightly wrapped, except when in the midst of his family. The ring had not been important in his life, though he had given his pledge long ago, when the five Tallchiefs, newly orphaned, had raised their hands to the night sky and shouted, "Aye!"

He'd been too busy surviving to claim the ring. Calum inhaled slightly. Just like his marriage, the ring represented unfinished business.

Roger Olson, chairman of Unique's board, lightly touched his hair and his bald spots. The early-October sunshine drenching Denver's streets skimmed through the office window to gleam on his head and on the hand mirror he'd been using. "Before someone put hair remover in my styling gel, I had a head of hair, too. Even my private washroom isn't safe. It's a case of business *and* personal sabotage, Tallchief. That's why I hired you to find whoever is doing this and protect me."

Calum glanced at the washroom door. Anyone could have picked the lock. Fiona, his youngest sister, could do it behind her back in one second flat.

He rolled his shoulder within his gray suit jacket. His six-foot-four-inch body resented the long drive to Denver from his home in Amen Flats, Wyoming.

The stone that had been Tallchief's nestled warmly against Calum's chest. Worn smooth with age and bound by a leather thong, the stone had been given to Calum by his father. Matthew Tallchief had known when he met his life's mate, Calum's mother; he had given her the stone, an obsidian, in a tradition that had begun with the first Tallchief and was now passed on to Calum. For a time, Calum had set aside the stone as he built his career. October and the search for the ring seemed good reasons to wear Tallchief's mark. Roger Olson continued to drone, and Calum shifted restlessly. "If someone is sabotaging Unique, Inc., there will be a trail. I'll find it," Calum stated.

"You're the best corporate hit man in the area—" Olson began, then noted Calum's quiet, cool look. "Okay, okay, you're supposed to be a top-notch corporate investigator. I just want this mess cleaned up and fast."

Olson glanced at Calum's glasses, then down the length of his expensive tie and across his broad shoulders, clad in the light gray suit jacket. His envious gaze rose to Calum's neatly clipped straight black hair, another inheritance from his great-great-grandfather, Tallchief.

Olson preened in the mirror, a fiftyish man trying to look thirty. "I'm a researcher, too, a pretty good one. I checked you out."

"Did you?" Calum asked slowly.

Olson didn't recognize the cool invitation of a professional, used to getting information and giving none. "You're a cool one, Tallchief. You're thirty-six and widowed. You've got an older brother, Duncan, who's got a ranch on Tallchief Mountain—he's done some work finding kidnapped children—and you have a younger brother and two sisters. You live in Amen Flats, Wyoming, a wide spot in the road. You're part Scots—guess that's where you get those cold gray eyes from—and part Sioux…guess that's where you get that black hair and your dark coloring. You come highly recommended by the firms you listed in your résumé."

Again he glanced down Calum's tall, lean body, then sucked in his belly. He eased his suit jacket over his stomach. "You don't talk much, but I'm pretty good at selecting people."

Calum nodded and noticed Olson's eyes cutting to his secretary, who had quietly entered the office. The woman, dressed in a navy blue suit with a long skirt and practical pumps, passed through the room to place a stack of papers on the desk. A pencil was thrust through the dowdy, tidy knot of hair on top of her head, and she wore no makeup behind large glasses. Her cheekbones were high, probably a Slavic inheritance, and matched the angle of her mouth, set in a firm jaw. A streak of gray ran from her temple into the severe knot. Olson's expression dripped with lust, his stare locked on her prim, buttoned-to-the-throat white blouse. He showed his teeth in a leer before the woman nodded and turned to leave.

Calum noted her ears, and the tiny holes of missing earrings. Her glasses were probably purchased from a discount rack, and the lenses struck him as nonprescription glass. Her suit was modest and inexpensive.

Olson's gaze dropped to the woman's ample backside, lost within the folds of her loose jacket, and skimmed down her legs.

Calum noted that her legs were shapely, and too thin in proportion to her hips. The woman exited the room without a sound, the door closing behind her and leaving a delicate scent of jasmine.

Olson released the air he had been holding, since he'd sucked in his stomach. He glanced at Calum and leaned forward on his desk. "My secretary. Excellent work. Quiet, efficient. Knows how to keep her mouth shut... Two to one she's a virgin. Takes a bit to get them to come around, if you know what I mean. I'm in the mood for a virgin, and I've been checking her over. I'll bet she's real hot. The quiet ones always are. I like a woman with big hips."

When Calum continued to look at him, Olson flinched. "Now get this, Tallchief. A man has a right to...you know what I mean, play a bit on the side. This sabotage business is overlapping into my private life. I don't want my wife to know. It could be real messy if she or her old man found out I was getting a little excitement once in a while." Olson jabbed a finger at the portrait of the man behind his desk.

"I've been keeping this mess secret. That old man would kick me out in a minute if he knew I couldn't handle this. So it's just best if my wife or the old man doesn't know about your function here."

Calum listened to the slight rustling of paper coming from the intercom. He reached over to click it off, unnoticed by Olson. The man was sloppy about business and his relationships.

The older man smoothed the missing patches of his hair. "Play ball with me on this, Tallchief, and I'll see that you get all the business you can handle."

Calum inhaled slowly. He had more than enough work. He'd picked this offer from a stack of others because he wanted to look for the legendary Tallchief ring, which his sister Elspeth had traced to Denver.

His great-great-grandmother Una's dowry had been sold to keep Tallchief land. Calum's older brother, Duncan, had recently placed a Tallchief baby in the cradle he'd vowed to reclaim.

Was it October or four-month-old Megan that had started the restlessness within Calum? Or was it the challenge of his older brother's keeping his part of the promise to reclaim Una's dowry? Whatever the reason, Calum's tracker's instincts told him it was time to find the ring.

While Olson droned on, Calum automatically noted incidents he wanted to check out, yet his mind was on the ring. He supposed he had inherited the tendencies of all Tallchief males to keep what they considered theirs. He wondered whimsically whether he should have found the ring a long time ago to place on his wife's finger, then pushed the thought away. He preferred clean logic to the clutter of legends and whimsy. Sherry had died in a car accident five years ago; he'd never know whether the ring could have made their marriage strong.

While Olson continued to drone on, Calum listened on

a professional level. On another level, he considered the success of his quest for the ring and his family. Elspeth, as keeper of Una's journals, and Sybil, Duncan's wife, were a good team. Sybil's occupation was recovering antiques and working in genealogy. She had helped Elspeth track the ring. Both women were graceful, cool, and powerful when set upon their course.

Sybil's purpose seemed at times to be focused on distracting Duncan and tormenting him into a smile, which she could do easily. Duncan, Sybil and Sybil's daughter, Emily, had bonded for life, and Megan had only added more joy.

Megan. Calum loved to hold and cuddle her. He tensed and shifted restlessly. It was true—October unleashed the Tallchiefs' emotions.

Olson's voice cut into Calum's thoughts. "I pride myself on picking the right man. Under that classy look, you've got an Indian look, Tallchief. A tough, cold look that would go a long way if you caught someone in a dark alley. Or draw good-looking women—" His eyes brightened, and he asked hopefully, "Say, how about if you and I go to a night spot tonight and relax a bit? I know you don't have a wife to account to."

"I have plans. Some other time?" Calum didn't like anyone rummaging through his private life, and he didn't want to socialize with Olson. He wanted to prowl through Unique's vacated offices after business hours.

The secretary entered the room again, moving just as quietly as before. Calum noted the slight slope of her shoulders, sometimes typical of office workers. He stood slowly, as Tallchief men were taught to do when a woman entered the room. Olson, taking the hint, leaped to his feet. He placed his hand with familiarity on the secretary's shoulder, clearly oblivious of her body's distinct recoil. "This is my secretary, Talia Smith. Talia, this is Calum Tallchief. Mr.

Tallchief is serving as an advisor on one of my pilot projects. You'll probably see him poking into things. Help him if there is anything he needs."

"It's nice to meet you, Mr. Tallchief," the woman said very properly, in a low, well-modulated voice that bore a slight Texas twang.

Talia pasted a tight, pleasant smile on her face. Calum Tallchief had trouble written all over him. From what she had heard before the intercom was switched off, Olson had hired an expensive bird dog to check out the problems at Unique. Unlike Olson, Tallchief spoke little, asking precise questions in an even-toned voice.

He probably never shouted. Talia, who had grown up in a passionate, demonstrative and loving home, did not trust quiet men.

Calum had uncoiled himself from the chair with the grace of an athlete. The sunlight coming from the large windows glinted off his stylish glasses. The light slid in a blue sheen across his black hair and shone on his high cheekbones and hollowed, lean cheeks. Dressed in an expensive suit, Calum Tallchief reminded her of a steel stiletto, lean and deadly.

She chanced a brief, pointed look behind his glasses and found narrowed smoke-colored eyes framed by jet-black lashes. There was nothing comforting in the hard set of his jaw, or in the line of his mouth.

Beneath the suit jacket, he wore a pocket protector, just like every other corporate nerd she'd known. Nerds could be dangerous. Corporate nerds had brains that clicked like calculator buttons. This one looked as if he hadn't seen fun since time began.

Calum Tallchief towered over her five-foot-eight-inch—with heels—height. Her eyes were level with his expansive, Armani-clad chest. The gray-and-blue-striped tie was too perfect. Beneath Olson's overpowering cologne, Calum's scents of soap and a lime-scented after-shave were masculine and to the point.

To the point, Talia repeated mentally. This man did everything methodically and for a reason. Calum inclined his head and extended his hand to her for a handshake. "Ms. Smith."

His voice was deep and cool, making her think of danger just beneath the surface. He reminded her of a deep, quiet pool that she'd dived into from a rocky Acapulco cliff. The currents running beneath the gentle waves had almost drowned her. Talia stared at that large, tanned hand, with its neatly clipped nails. Hair slightly flecked the back. The hair at her nape lifted slightly as she slowly took his hand.

His fingers enfolded hers in a firm handshake that was soon gone. A layer of calluses lay in his broad palm. His eyes lingered, studying her closely. His gaze took in her glasses, purchased to disguise her long lashes and eyes, then slid from her left eye to her right one, their blue color concealed by tinted brown contact lenses.

Great. All she needed was a supersharp iceman, a corporate hit man, from the sound of it before the intercom clicked off. She'd listened to Olson's every conversation, and he'd never noticed, until today. Very likely it was Calum Tallchief who had noticed, not Olson.

Mentally she spit out a word in Swahili which translated as *elephant dung*.

Talia nodded, forcing her expression to be bland. "Do you need anything from me, Mr. Olson?"

"Not now, honey. Maybe later," he added with a meaningful leer that she let slide off her. She'd put up with his leers for months while she quietly destroyed him. Then she remembered that she was shy, dowdy Talia Smith and feigned a quiver, looking down at the floor. In the four months she had been working for Olson, it had taken every ounce of her willpower not to attack him. He'd go down in a soft flow of blubber, probably a whiner....

Talia felt Calum's stare on her back as she left the room in her practiced sloped-shoulder walk. Once in the outer area, her cubicle, Talia allowed her aching shoulders to straighten. She briefly rubbed the binding across her full breasts, relieving the uncomfortable pressure. She glanced in the mirror and checked the color on her hair. None of her naturally pale blond roots were showing. She'd achieved the dowdy brown color perfectly. She touched the gray hair extension she had added at her temple; it held firm.

She blinked her eyes—she was getting used to the tinted contact lenses. The fake, slightly hairy mole remained firmly pasted to her throat.

Talia stalked to a file drawer and jerked it open. Just great. Things had been perking along just fine until Olson finally showed a single dram of intelligence and hired an investigator. Talia muttered the Swahili word for elephant dung again. She flipped through the report she'd done on Calum Tallchief for Olson. Tallchief was a numbers genius, a widower, good references, resided in Amen Flats, Wyoming...brothers, sisters... Worked his way through college while helping raise his younger brother, Birk, and the two sisters, Elspeth and Fiona. Part owner of Tallchief Cattle Ranch, managed by brother Duncan. Respected family. An office in his home in Amen Flats, managed family investments. No record of— Talia snapped the file shut. In her two-week stint as a detective's assistant, she'd discovered how to identify a doctored background check. Calum Tallchief had supplied little but a list of references that Olson had apparently checked out.

Talia tapped the file with her short, neat nails. She glanced at them, a part of her disguise. She couldn't wait for revenge and for long, red-hot nails. Until then, she wanted to prove that Olson would pant after a woman who didn't wear short skirts or figure-revealing clothing. She would give him no cause to think she was available.

For four long months, she had been slaving for Olson, carefully plotting how to destroy him.

Seven months ago, Olson had sexually harassed Talia's sister. Jan, a sweet young housewife who badly needed a job, hadn't known how to handle Olson's unwanted attention. Within three months from when he hired Jan as his executive secretary, Olson had destroyed her life. Jan had been afraid to tell her husband about Olson's blatant pursuit. Eventually, Jan's husband had come to believe she'd taken a lover; Roy had walked out. Jan had been shattered and had returned to the Petrovna family home in Texas. Roy remained inconsolable in Denver.

Talia's father, Michael Petrovna, part Russian and part Apache, wanted to kill him, or at the least tie him down on an anthill and pour honey over his "overactive parts." Her brother, Alek, a tough newspaper correspondent, wanted to slaughter Olson, first in the news and then in an isolated alley. Anton, another brother and a business genius, wanted to bankrupt Olson. Talia, just in from surfing in Hawaii, had barely managed to convince the three Petrovna males to let her do the job. She believed a slow disintegration from the inside of Olson's business was the best revenge. She wanted to drive him so low that he would contact Roy, admitting his deeds. Talia was experienced in creating chaos. It was her unique talent.

Talia placed a glass against the door and listened to Olson drone and to Calum's quiet, short questions. She didn't trust a man who spoke little and looked too much. Calum Tallchief had noted her missing earrings.

She would wear tiny pearl studs the next day, a neat recovery. Olson would probably take that as a come-on, and that was unfortunate. She wanted him to come all the way, to box himself in so perfectly that there could be no mistake about who was chasing whom. Talia shook her head and moved away from the door, just as Calum Tallchief opened it.

His cool glance slid to her, then to the glass on her desk. Great. This guy might put two and two together, something Olson was incapable of—even after she'd she planted a computer virus in his accounts-tracking system.

Talia hunched her shoulders and slid into her desk chair. She placed the earphones on her head and began transcribing another boring, overworded threatening letter from Olson to a client. Then she caught Calum's fresh-soap-and-male scent and inhaled. Just what she needed, a professional, oversize, cool corporate bird dog nerd. There probably wasn't a thing running around in his brain but numbers.

Olson came into her cubicle, and she decided to let the giant magnet in her purse stay there. Drifting it over the computer tapes that held the company's entire resources of customers would have to wait for another time. The magnet would wipe out the tapes, and restoring the information base would take months of costly marketing time.

Olson's meaty hand weighted her shoulder. He bent close to her ear to whisper, "Be nice to the guy, honey. Take him around, show him what he wants."

"Yes, sir," she returned, neatly stacking her work and rising to her feet. Her artificially padded hips bumped the desk. Talia readjusted them with a rubbing motion of her hand.

Calum Tallchief opened the office door for her. He continued to open doors for her. He must have learned that in Nerd Basics. She introduced him to the heads of the departments, waited while they briefed him on schedules and procedures, and then took him to the next department. The man she was baby-sitting drew women's eyes like magnets.

By the end of the day, Talia had decided that Calum had the mental tenacity of a bulldog. If she avoided a question, he managed to circle back to it. A regular listmaker, with all the checks in place. At quitting time he'd had the building's plans spread on the conference table. He'd looked just as immaculate as when the day began, as though he had been dipped in cool plastic. She'd watched him methodically track air vents and heating systems. Darn. Just when she had figured out how to eject a stink bomb every time Olson flushed his private toilet.

Then there was that nasty business of demanding that Sleazeball toss away all of the toiletries in his private washroom. Her neat dusting of itch powder on the toilet paper roll had been foiled when Calum requested a new one.

Anyone who had a high-security lock for the washroom within one hour couldn't be trusted to think normally. Any nerd with calluses on his palm was not normal.

Calum Tallchief wasn't ruining her plans for Mr. Sleazeball. Too bad that all that gorgeous, neatly clipped jet-black hair might start falling out the next time he combed his hair. At just the right, critical moment, she'd manage to drop in a tidbit about an article she'd read: It was true that in certain stress environments, baldness was catching. He needed to go elsewhere, because she intended to create a stress-mountain.

Talia smiled tightly. She'd never destroyed a nerd before, but if she had to disassemble Calum Tallchief to get to Olson, she would. In her experience, nerds went haywire when something unexplainable got tossed into their path. She'd just have to find that certain something.

From the conference room, Calum watched Talia and the other employees get onto the city bus. He glanced quickly at her personnel file and found it too clean. Then he moved quickly into her cubicle and sat at her desk. A secretary usually knew more than anyone, and she had access to Olson's washroom. It was a start. A quick search revealed nothing, except that the desk was too neat.

Too neat worried him. He stashed away that fact and turned on her computer. It was linked in the system, as was everyone else's. He inserted a disk that would automatically try a series of access codes that she might use. *Jerk* popped up right after *Jane*. Calum pushed everything else from his mind and dusted her computer for fingerprints. He lifted a good set, made a few calls to technicians who would work off-hours. He flipped through her personnel file, noted that she was approaching forty, had never been married and had recently moved from Baltimore; Maryland was supposedly her native state. Calum tapped the form just once; Miss Smith was definitely a Texan. Then he began prowling through her computer.

In the morning, Calum opened the door for Talia as she entered. Today she was wearing tiny pearl studs and a shapeless dark dress with a tiny rosebud print. "Good morning, Mr. Tallchief," she said pleasantly as she slid her large, unfashionable purse into a drawer. Calum wondered just what was in that bag. Talia Smith played an exciting game, though she did not look it. A new employee, she had quickly learned how to infiltrate the computer system. One huge list of clients had been tampered with, the addresses all the same—"Blue Moon Road."

She opened her desk drawer and searched the contents, and her expression chilled momentarily. Then she smiled at him, her eyes skipping down his taupe suit. "You're here early."

He sat on the chair opposite her and noted the grim line of her untinted lips. Calum tossed her something to chew on. "I slept here."

The tiniest bit of anger flashed in her obviously tinted

contact lenses. "Really? Couldn't you find accommodations? I'll be happy to find you a room, if you wish."

"Thank you, but I'm comfortable here."

"I see," Talia said, her voice clipped. She began briskly organizing her desk for the day. In a few moments, she noticed that he hadn't moved. She peered over the top of her glasses. "May I help you find anything, Mr. Tallchief?"

The polite nudge to get him out of her way didn't work. Calum traced the small, firm line appearing between her dark brows. He hoped he was interrupting her schedule for sabotage. He also noted that the tracker within him was stirring. "I'm waiting for Olson."

"He should be here at any moment. I have to make coffee in his office. He likes it to be ready when he arrives. Would you like a cup?"

"Yes. Thank you." He rose to follow her into Olson's office. "Do you always make coffee for him in the morning?"

"Yes. Always. He likes his desk tidied and the blinds opened and a sweet roll waiting for him. Excuse me." She left to return with a large, nutty sweet roll and placed it on the expansive desk. "I'm sorry. I only bought one. Would you like something?"

"No, thank you." He'd noted the sweet roll she had hidden beneath a napkin. The scent of coffee wafted through the room, and he longed for the fresh, clean mountain air of Amen Flats. Calum thought of Elspeth's freshly baked bread and berry jam. A sweet ache shot through him. The Tallchiefs were a close family, bonded by love and hard times.

Duncan had been the first of the Tallchiefs to prove the truth of a Tallchief legend—*When a woman brings the cradle to a man of Fearghus blood, she will fill it with his babies.* To their marriage, Sybil had brought Emily, a teenage daughter the Tallchief family adored. Then gray-eyed, black-haired Megan, with her baby scents—

He wondered briefly what mischief his brother Birk and Lacey MacCandliss were up to, battling away at each other. The Tallchiefs had unofficially adopted Lacey. Her childhood had been abusive, and though the rest of the Tallchiefs adored Lacey, she'd never ceased to be the thorn in Birk's life-style.

Duncan would be wallowing in the love he had waited for, had deserved for years. Sybil would be putting Megan, their baby, down to nap. She would start her work then, hunting for family history or maybe a lost antique. Sybil's nemesis, Marcella Portway, wanted Sybil to find a royal Spanish gene in her family tree, and she refused to be dislodged from Sybil's clientele.

Elspeth would be at her loom—one that Tallchief had made for Una—her home serene and filled with the scent of herbs and freshly baked bread. Calum frowned. Elspeth worried him. As a girl, she and her mother had worked on Una's journals, and now Elspeth spoke little of her quest— the paisley shawl. Once she'd been excited about the Tallchiefs' legends and suddenly, after a visit to Scotland, Elspeth did not speak of the shawl.

Then there was Fiona, the youngest Tallchief and a rebel down to her bones. Perhaps that was because as a teenager she had had to strain to be very good in the older Tallchiefs' keeping. One wrong move, and the authorities would have been ready to claim her. Fiona had found ways to take out her moods on the family, if not the world. Now that she was grown, if there was a cause—human or animal rights, pollution or government injustice—Fiona would be in the midst of it. Calum hadn't received a notice to bail her out of jail lately, but he expected her call at any time. Things were too quiet in Montana, the location of Fiona's present project.

Then Calum turned his mind to the job he had taken and watched Talia Smith prepare the office for Olson.

Olson steamed into the room minutes later, curses heating the air around him. He slammed an invoice on the desk with one hand and a bouquet of flowers with the other. "I'll find who's responsible for this, and when I do— Some jerk has doubled our order for frozen Swedish herrings and had them shipped to a holding warehouse in Africa. That was no typing error. We're just building that market, and they'll have to be gone before their shelf life runs out. We'll have to sell cut-rate. *If* they are still frozen."

He plopped into his chair, took a big bite of sweet roll, munched on it and thrust the bouquet at Talia. "Here, honey. There's a present on your desk," he muttered, glaring at Calum. "What have you found?"

Then Olson scowled at Talia as she was leaving. "I tried to call you last night. I thought we might do some work at your place—or the corporate apartment. Where were you?"

Clearly dismayed, Talia's hand rose to her cheek as she turned to him. "Oh, dear. I'm so sorry. I must have fallen asleep early."

Olson scowled at her briefly. "Yeah, well…okay. But if you want to go up in Unique, you've got to play ball, got it?"

She nodded demurely. "Yes, sir. I understand that it is sometimes necessary to work at odd hours."

"Now you've got it, honey. Why don't you run along and open your present?"

When Olson demanded results, Calum reported finding the "Blue Moon Road" addresses and that he had restored the proper ones. The older man patted the too-curly wig he had adopted and looked nervous when it slipped. He punched the intercom, and Talia responded in a professional tone. Olson muttered, "Anything Tallchief wants, you do. Okay? Did you like the present?"

There was a pause, and then Talia said very quietly, "Thank you for the Hot Nights and Passion perfume. But I couldn't possibly accept such a gift. A bottle this size is terribly expensive, isn't it?"

"Baby, you're worth it." Olson leered and preened at the same time. He picked up his hand mirror, lifted the toupee, glanced at his missing hair and scowled. Without clicking off the intercom, he glanced at Calum. "Just a matter of time, Tallchief, and I'll nail her."

Calum turned off the intercom. He decided not to mention the potential of a sexual harassment suit. No one had brought charges against Olson, though office gossip had insinuated that he had been very busy. A scan through the personnel files showed a high percentage of women who had entered and then left the company. Motives for revenge against Olson wouldn't be hard to find.

"I don't think this will take long," Calum murmured. Meanwhile, he decided to keep Talia's mind and fingers busy.

Calum walked into Talia's cubicle to find her stuffing an opulent perfume bottle into a drawer. "Mr. Olson is always so generous," she murmured.

"How do you feel about that?" Calum asked, noting an assortment of other gifts in the drawer.

"I wouldn't want to hurt his feelings by refusing him. I need this job," she said softly. She sniffed, and he noted the teardrop hovering on her lashes.

He was a sucker for tears and sniffs, though the world didn't know it. It was in his Tallchief genes, and his sisters knew it well. From the look of her, Talia Smith was probably sheltered and couldn't picture being roughly used on Olson's desk. "Would you mind calling this list of pawnshop and antique shops and asking about a garnet ring? Here's a drawing to help you describe it," he said, placing Elspeth's drawing on the desk.

Her lashes fluttered, and she looked down, the perfect picture of a victim. Her shoulders slumped, and she sniffed once more. Calum fought to keep his protective tendencies under control. He decided grimly that Olson wasn't going to destroy another innocent woman, not even one who was disrupting the company. Then Talia murmured, "It looks beautiful. I'll try very hard to find it. Mr. Olson said to accommodate you."

Calum inhaled sharply. He disliked Olson's sexual harassment of his female employees. Her tone implied that Olson wanted her to share sexual favors with Calum. Though it had been some time since his wife had died in the accident, Tallchiefs weren't sexual butterflies. Talia made him feel like a heel for associating with Olson.

He found himself reasoning that perhaps she had had a valid reason for having Olson sign a document changing the company's health policy. Female employees were now allowed to stay home with sick infants. Calum doubted that Olson had known what he was signing, or that the policy had taken effect. His signature was also on a huge order for unmarketable artwork. While bits of trails led to Talia's desk, she didn't deserve being cornered by Olson. "It's a family ring," he explained too sharply. "I would appreciate your efforts, but only if you have time and it doesn't interfere with your professional standards."

Calum left her office with a feeling that he was going to pay dearly for not turning Talia Smith over to Olson. He'd protected his sisters all his life, and he suspected that Talia was benefiting from the Tallchief traditional respect of women.

Over the next three days, Calum noted and was disgusted by Olson's obvious pursuit of the unattainable Talia. Her boss never missed a chance to stroke her arm, and his gaze on her ample hips dripped with lust. The day he followed her into the copier room, Calum was on the point of entering to protect her. Within minutes, Talia exited the room, an untidy stack of papers in her hand, her face flushed and her blouse loosened. She glared at Calum and puffed by him, her wide hips swinging. Olson opened the door, drew his jacket over the huge inkstain on his belly and smiled curtly. "Just a little accident. Come into my office. I've got problems."

Calum followed, remembering Talia's furious expression. He didn't blame her for cooling down her boss.

Olson shut his office door. "You're good, Tallchief. But I have to tell you that someone knows where the company apartment is, and they are playing with me. Last night I was there…uh, you know…entertaining on company business…when the fax rang. Now, here I am, getting mellow with a red-hot— Uh…I was working hard. Here comes this fax that says, *Bozo, hanky-panky isn't company business. What would Daddy think?* That's all I need, someone turning me in to my father-in-law. I want this jerk out of my life. Do something!"

Calum studied the fax. The words had been clipped out and pasted on, and the message sent from a commercial service. The clue wasn't worth tracing; the sender had probably used an alias and a disguise. He almost admired the sender. Almost.

Two

That night, Calum leaned back into the shadows of the alley. Seventeen stories up, Olson was scheduled for an after-hours massage in Unique's corporate apartment. The exclusive penthouse could only be accessed by a security key. Olson had the only key to the new lock, suggested by Calum.

Calum caught the scent of the trees planted in the concrete sidewalks and a drift of cold, crisp night air. Above the street lamps, the stars twinkled just as they would over Tallchief Mountain.

Calum traced a woman walking briskly down the street. She reminded him of his wife—tall, black hair and white skin, efficient, business written all over her, carrying a briefcase. As a sensuous woman, Sherry had liked men to admire her, in business and in private. For a time, the marriage had purred along smoothly, carefully planned by both of them. Yet just months after their marriage, small arguments, distasteful to them both, had arisen like a bed of nettles. A beautiful woman, Sherry had viewed marriage as a shield from which to test her flirtations. Though Calum missed the long, hot nights in her arms, he didn't miss the jealousy that she could easily ignite. He wondered briefly whether he shouldn't have looked away when Sherry played her femme fatale role, enticing men to her like bees to honey.

They'd never been friends; lust hadn't allowed the time. Sherry had been his first strong attraction; they'd wanted each other immediately. They'd both been up-and-coming executives. Marriage had seemed logical to them both, and the heat had continued for several months into their marriage.

When his jealousy first began, Calum hadn't liked the dark side of himself.

Sherry had wanted an upscale corporate life. She had come into his life a sexually experienced woman, and he'd found himself looking at her old lovers when they socialized. Maybe he should have been more— Sherry's car had slammed into a truck just after a flaming argument. Calum would carry that guilt with him for an eternity.

He'd run that argument through his mind a thousand times. Sherry had wanted to "cultivate" a potential investor at a private dinner with him. When Calum ordered her to stay home, she'd tossed at him everything she hated about their lives—and no, she wouldn't live in Amen Flats...ever....

She never had.

Perhaps his expectations had been too high. Calum had expected his parents' deep love to develop in his own marriage. Matthew and Pauline's marriage had been ideal, their lives bonded by love, children and the land. Duncan had found that love with Sybil.

Visits to Duncan's warm, busy home emphasized the

stark emptiness of Calum's life. Perhaps that was why at times he preferred to stay away from Amen Flats or to lurk in his sterile modern home.

He adjusted his collar against the cold night air. At thirty-six, he was likely experiencing a nesting urge, a biological need to produce another Tallchief baby. Calum exhaled sharply. He'd wrapped himself in computers and his profession, a neatly crafted, logically safe lair in which to brood alone. Lately he had been feeling the loneliness of his life. And his bed, to be honest. His body was protesting abstinence, and his life seemed uninteresting.

He liked routine, neatness and logic. There was no reason Talia Smith's little tricks should excite him even slightly. Yet he had enjoyed strolling through her computer gambits and unraveling them.

Calum's eyes narrowed against the glare of streetlights as he traced a figure moving swiftly toward the building. His mind lingered a moment on the past, the warmth of a woman moving in his arms, under him. The scent of love-making— Maybe he'd wanted too much from Sherry, a beautiful woman who loved the admiration of all men. Maybe he was still half in love with her. Because the memory of their lovemaking haunted him. That was why he preferred sleeping on Unique's boardroom couch, rather than in an empty bed—when he could sleep at all.

After his computer screen was turned off and the business deals completed, reality painted his life in cold, empty colors. Though he loved his family, there was a big, illogical hole inside him. Only investigating financial packages or firms, or tracking down a corporate mischiefmaker like Olson's, eased whatever drove him.

Guilt? If their marriage had lasted longer than those few months, would it have survived? Maybe he wasn't cut out for the warmth of a relationship, though he had tried.

He shifted restlessly, pushing his hands into the pockets

of his black leather jacket. Nights of sleeping in Unique's conference room had aggravated an old rodeo injury, a rib long healed. Back then, the Tallchiefs had badly needed the money to survive as a family.

A slender boy dressed in the apartment building's valet uniform entered the well-lit foyer. He nodded to the watchman, showed his identity badge. Calum leaned against the brick wall and noted the lights dimming in Unique's suite. He went back to waiting with the patience that had earned him a reputation. Suddenly, a motion above him caught his eye.

A window opened; a black boot, followed by slender legs and a body stepped out onto a narrow ledge that ran beneath the penthouse. Calum moved quickly, taking the elevator to the fifteenth floor and quietly entering the hallway. It was two more floors up to Olson's penthouse. Calum listened at a suspect apartment door for a moment, then deftly picked the lock and entered.

The valet jacket was tossed over a chair. From the open window, Calum saw the intruder angle around a corner and begin edging upward. He threw a grappling hook and began to climb.

Calum stepped out onto the narrow ledge. Whoever was scaling the building knew what he was doing. Using a rope and scaling hooks, the slender man was dressed in black and wore a black cap. He wore a mountain climber's safety belt, which was attached to the rope. He swung out from the building, expertly bounced his feet against it and swung around the corner. Calum inched his way to a safety ladder and then to the dangling rope.

The intruder was now on the ledge near the penthouse and extracting something from the bag at his waist. Calum took a deep breath, tested the rope and pushed away from the building. He swung around the corner, landed neatly on

another narrow ledge and looked into the blackened face
of a startled boy.

The boy muttered something that sounded like an African curse with a Texas twang.

Calum noted the black glove gripping the windowsill;
the boy's other hand held a camera rigged for night shots.
"Hello. Having fun?" Calum asked pleasantly.

The boy jammed the camera into a bag at his waist and
began inching backward on the narrow ledge.

"Let's make this easy," Calum began, dismissing a
woman's high giggle within the apartment. "You come
down with me and I'll see that the charges are less than
what they should be."

He didn't like the curt tone of the intruder's curse. "Be
reasonable. You could get killed. Blackmail isn't worth it,"
he said slowly, fighting his rising temper.

The youth was agile, leaping to another ledge and flattening himself against the wall. Calum glanced downward,
took another breath and followed. He never lost his temper,
but working with Olson hadn't helped his mood.

Calum sucked in his breath as the youth missed a step,
angled for a foothold and began searching for an escape.
Calum didn't want to panic the boy; it could be fatal. When
he was young, Calum had had a few antics of his own, and
his good luck had held. The boy's luck might not. Calum
talked quietly. "There isn't any way out. I've got you. Take
it easy and you'll be safe."

The youth reached upward to grasp a window ledge, and
Calum noted the high line of a woman's bosom and the
neat curve of a firm bottom, running into long legs that
ended in black boots. Her cap slipped off, tumbling down
into the night's abyss. A long, smooth swath of hair un-
furled and ran down her back.

She glared at him, her eyes glittering within the black
face paint. "Would you mind getting off my ledge? In case

you haven't noticed, it's occupied." Her tone was proper and indignant.

His hand shot out to grip her wrist. She released her grip on the ledge, and they overbalanced. Calum grabbed the ledge and drew her closer at the same time, steadying them. He looked down into Talia's furious expression.

Despite a precarious position seventeen stories above the street, Calum found the situation amusing. He glanced down her trim, athletic body and fought the immediate jerk of his awakening body. "Did you forget your hips, Miss Smith?"

"Stop leering. You look like Olson," she snapped, trying to pull her wrist away. Her skin was warm and supple, smooth and soft, beneath his fingers.

"I'm not exactly happy," he muttered. Seventeen stories above the ground, a mayhem-causing female smelling of jasmine had just alerted his deprived sexual needs.

Olson's voice sounded inside the penthouse. "Come to Daddy, Little Red Riding Hood." Calum glanced into the window and saw Olson's bare backside running into another room. He was following a blonde dressed in a red bonnet and scanty lace briefs.

Talia watched the blonde's flight. "She could use a workout program and less heavy sauces in her diet."

Calum sought and found a latch. He picked the latch and opened the window. "You seem experienced. Maybe I should let you do this. Get in."

Her eyes widened briefly and narrowed. "Look, guy. You can't just pick me up on a ledge and then start telling me what—"

He pushed her into the room.

"I've got plans for the evening, big boy. Sorry," she said lightly, and turned. "Some other time."

Calum caught the back of her climbing belt before she took the first step away from him. Olson's giggle sounded, closer now, and Calum jerked open a closet door and pushed his captive into it.

"Just what do you think you're doing—?" she began before he placed his hand over her mouth.

While he was checking out the dark linen closet, she bit him, hard. Calum tensed, pushed his face down to hers, and between his teeth, said very softly and distinctly, "Shut up. Or I'll open this door and explain your little plan to destroy Olson."

"Nerd," she muttered after a full second of debate passed through her narrowed eyes. "Stop crowding me, you jerk. You're taking up all the space and all the air. You know that sleazeball deserves a good dose of blackmail."

"Lady, you need to be taught some manners, and there is a stiff penalty for blackmail." Calum rubbed his injured hand and tried not to think about the soft flow of her body bumping against his. When she squirmed, he locked his hand on her climbing belt and jerked slightly. "You're not going anywhere."

She straightened, and the top of her head butted his chin. The movement knocked his head against a shelf and caused his glasses to bump painfully against his nose. Her slight satisfied smile told him that Talia Smith deliberately created accidents to suit her.

Olson's call entered the dark closet. "Come to Wolfie, my little feastable."

"Ohh, my big strong daddy…" the blonde cooed.

Talia's boot heel stood on Calum's toe, and he wrapped both arms around her from the back and lifted her off the floor. "You put me down, you big bozo!"

"Bozo," he repeated. "I bet you had a hard time finding that word to cut out for your fax pasting job."

The feminine bottom squirming agilely against his lower belly caused Calum to go very still. His body reacted irrationally to Talia's. This was the wrong woman, and the wrong time to be distracted. In a hushed whisper, he spoke into her ear. "You've got two choices. Hold still and I'll give you a chance to explain, or it's out the door, and probably into Olson's bed. He'll blackmail you in a minute."

"He's got nothing on me, and he deserves everything he gets," she snapped back.

He reluctantly admired her style. She wasn't giving up easy. In a way, she reminded him of Fiona, his youngest sister, whom he'd pulled out of more scrapes than he could remember.

"But I do have something on you, Talia, a lot of somethings," he said quietly, logically, then left her to chew on that bone.

She opened her mouth, closing it as the sounds in the other room increased. After a time, Talia muttered, "That is disgusting."

Calum blew a strand of silky jasmine-scented hair away from his lips. Talia was in constant, if small, movement, her body brushing his with every turn. His lower body was heavy with need, much to his disgust. "Hold still," he ordered.

"Make me," she shot back.

Calum felt a small muscle contract in his cheek. "Fine," he said coolly before he lifted her jacket collar to a hook and hung her on the wall. He jerked a pillowcase from the shelf and tied her wrists; another pillowcase tied her ankles.

"Cute," she muttered darkly after a long moment.

"From your expression, I doubt that anyone has ever tried to make you do anything," he whispered over the faked sounds of the blonde's ecstasy. He rubbed his injured nose. Talia was a disaster, worse than a hurricane.

"You have no idea what I can do," she told him threateningly.

"That?" Calum asked, nodding toward the sounds.

His question was effective; her mouth clamped shut and she glared at him.

Calum leaned back against the wall. Temporarily safe from her kicks and elbows, he shot a quick inventory down his taut body and found it still aroused. The scent of jasmine enfolding him didn't help. He closed his eyes and wished for a nice, safe, logical problem. "I have no idea why I'm in this mess," he muttered to himself.

"There's no explaining nerd types," she answered in a logical tone, and then was quiet.

After a few more moments in which Calum tried to dismiss the amorous noises coming from the other room, he asked the question that had been grating on him. "Nerd?"

"Pocket protector. Glasses. Briefcase. Mind like a calculator. No fun at all. The good part is, you don't wear your belt up under your chest and your boring ties match."

"Thanks for that much." Calum closed his eyes. The air was filled with her womanly scent. He knew his nostrils were flaring, trying to catch every whiff. He hoped Olson would leave soon.

"Why are you so quiet?" she asked, long after the sounds of the room had stopped. "Can we leave?"

Calum wished he hadn't just remembered that the last time he was with a woman had been during his marriage. He'd grown used to accepting his quiet, well-ordered life—pre-Talia. "I want to get out of here just as bad as you do."

"Ah! That's because *now you're my accomplice.*"

He glared at her. She was smirking. "Untie me, big boy. We're now birds of a feather that stick together."

"Hang there awhile and cool off. I think they're about to leave."

She blinked, clearly surprised. "That was quick. No after-sex cigarette in bed? They just get up and go? That isn't how it happens in the movies," she stated firmly, then flushed. "Well, that's not how *I* like it."

Calum stared at her for a second, then eased the door open, saw that the apartment was vacated and lifted Talia from her hook. Outside the closet, she waited patiently while he untied her. Then she leaped to the couch and placed her hands in a karate-style position. "Okay, let's have this out right now. You've messed up my caper. I'm not backing away from Olson until I have his big hairy nose quivering with fear. And I'm not letting you get away with hanging *me* on a hook, buddy."

Calum placed his hands on his hips and studied the woman bouncing as she waited for him to make his move. He shook his head and wished he hadn't been distracted by the soft flow of breasts beneath her black sweater. He studied her billowing mouse-colored hair and felt the muscle contract in his jaw. "I have to get away from you, or I will throttle you," he said as pleasantly as he could.

"Okay. Go. By the way, your hair is standing out in peaks and your glasses are crooked." She peered at him. "Hey, I think your jaw is swelling...maybe it's bruised. You should take better care of yourself. Maybe you're accident-prone. I'll see you in the morning and we can talk over old times, pal."

Calum ran his hands through his hair and straightened his glasses. "I should have—"

She shook her head. "It's my charm. Irresistible even to a nerd." Then she walked to the window, jammed it open and began to step out.

Calum grabbed the back of her jacket, and she turned on him. "I'm not going anywhere without my ropes and hooks."

He grabbed a fistful of the front of her jacket and pushed her back, controlling his strength because she was a woman. When he was on the ledge, he shook his head.

Here he was, retrieving a blackmailer's scaling gear; he should have been dragging her to a police holding cell. Maybe he would, and then clean up the mess at Unique and—

Talia closed and locked the window, leaving him on the ledge. With a flourish, she jammed a small bit of plastic into the latch and wrapped the drapery cord around the lock handles so that they couldn't be picked. She drew out her camera, focused it on him and took his picture. She blew him a kiss and strolled out the door, her hair swaying down her back.

"This is my caper, and I'm not leaving because of a little push and shove from Iceman. Okay, okay…he was definitely heated last night, and definitely all man," Talia muttered to herself on her way to work the next morning, dressed in her usual disguise. She prepared the office and went to look for Calum Tallchief. Talia wanted to propose an offer that he couldn't resist—the problem was finding the right nerve. She doubted that Calum had soft spots— he *had* tied her up and hung her on a hook—but she pushed that thought aside, as well as the thought nudging her all night, that he wasn't aroused by her body.

She thought about disappearing—she could be very good at that. But she wanted Olson pinned to the wall.

When she didn't spot Calum, she swiftly left her office, carrying her big purse. The computer banks were on hold, humming nicely and waiting for work. Talia glanced out into the hallway and eased her purse open, her fingers finding the huge heavy-duty magnet.

Calum loomed beside her, looking just as cool as the day he had arrived. She noted a distinct glint behind his glasses, a rather smoldering, smoky look in his gray eyes. Talia's fingers released the magnet back into her purse. Calum plucked her purse from her, peered inside and shook his head. "Figures."

Then he walked off, placing the strap over his shoulder as if it were his bag.

Talia muttered her elephant-dung curse several times in his direction. She tried not to notice his long-legged stroll and his broad shoulders that narrowed down to lean hips. He reminded her of a mountain puma—big, graceful, solitary and powerful. And his male arrogance reminded her of the overprotective men in her family, the ones she had escaped at the first chance.

Talia deeply resented Calum's easy overpowering of her, and the way he had confined her. The closet episode had brought back her dislike of staying in one place for long and the boredom of tedious romantic commitments. At eighteen, she'd been a wide-eyed bride deserted at the altar; she'd been running ever since.

By 11:00 a.m., Olson had already stroked her arm and offered the first two sexual innuendos of the day. Alone at her desk, Talia traced the drawing of the ring Calum had given her. It was a lovely old thing, a Celtic design enclosing three large garnets. She checked off the name of her last query. If she could find that ring before he turned her in, she would have something he wanted. They could trade. He would go away, and she could continue—

Calum strolled into her cubicle, carrying a file folder and her purse. He tossed the purse, lightened by the removal of her best magnet, onto the desk and slapped the file down on it. "Read it and weep. You can buy me lunch, away from here. Set it up, or Olson will hear some interesting information about his secretary."

"You're enjoying this, aren't you, big boy?" She didn't trust his too-pleasant smile or his glinting eyes. She flipped open the file and ran her finger down the list of her misdemeanors, slight infractions that even Papa Petrovna didn't know about. Talia narrowed her eyes and growled quietly. If her own papa, the chief of police, didn't know she'd tampered with that politician's big television moment and rigged his slacks zipper to stay open, how could Calum?

Her family name, fingerprints, correct age—thirty-three—and life history spread before her. Her ship was sinking.

Darn. On top of that, Calum Tallchief had definitely sent sensual tingles up her spine. A closet spine-tingler. Trust a nerd to pull that one off.

Up close and disheveled, Calum had caused some unpredictable warmth and weakness in her legs. The sight of his gray eyes darkening as they locked on her bouncing breasts had stopped her.

She prayed for a bird of paradise to fly over and bomb Calum's black, arrogant head, then began furiously dialing pawnshops and antique shops. She got Nose—the street name of a man who was a human bloodhound—on the trail. At eleven-thirty, with no results, she closed her eyes and resigned herself to her fate. She made a luncheon reservation for Calum Tallchief and herself.

She chose a busy, jam-packed deli, and two sauce-dripping meatball sandwiches packed with onions. Dressed in an immaculate light blue suit, Calum looked perfectly at ease as he sat back, studying her. She noted with malice that he had managed his sandwich perfectly, while hers dripped steadily. She shifted uneasily within her hip padding and removed her knee from the intrusion of his hard one.

He tapped his fingers, and she jumped. "Is that a nerd method of Chinese water torture? *What?*"

"What." The word didn't have a question in it. It was flat and demanding.

"You know, Tallchief, I've always thought that nerds

were flat-sided, one-dimensional. You turn them sideways and you've got nothing. No heart, no fun, nothing. What now?'' she added tightly.

"Tell me why Talia Petrovna from Texas and other places has her mind on destroying Olson."

"The guy is a dog."

"True, but not good enough reason for your little disasters. Try again. You're just one step away from jail, Petrovna." His eyes skimmed past her fake mole, down to the rapid beat of her pulse. He reached out to strip off the mole, then dropped it to the floor. His expensive Italian loafer covered it.

She rubbed the slight burn on her neck; she didn't trust him. A guy who could spot fake moles wasn't normal. He moved too fast, and she didn't like his use of "little disasters." She had worked hard to bring down Olson; she had created beautiful, enormous disasters. "What's your motive? Do you think I'd tell you and give you the stuff to turn me in? No way."

"That's what I thought. That's exactly why you're taking a necessary leave of absence to visit your sick mother. Starting today. You're coming with me."

"Where?"

She didn't like his steely look, or any man giving her orders as if he had that right. "Look, guy. You may be enjoying this, but I'm not trading one slimeball for another. There's no way you can blackmail me into sex. Jeez, I'm unqualified for nerd sex. I think I feel faint—"

Calum slowly eased back the edge of his jacket. The pocket protector and pens were missing. A small trickle of fear ran up Talia's nape as he smiled blandly. He reminded her again of a mountain cat—twitching its tail while waiting for her next move. She sensed that he was enjoying their encounter. Talia managed a threat. "You don't have a chance with me, Tallchief. Remember—you were the one locked out on the ledge last night. Not me.''

She allowed herself a smirk. ''I've got your picture, Mr. Tallchief. Such a fierce, dark scowl. My, my…''

''Times change,'' he returned easily.

She deliberately peered at him. ''Do you know that you've got the strangest movement in your jaw? The swollen side. Is that a muscle contracting? A facial tic? Well, buddy, if you think I won't make your life miserable, think again. Once I finish Olson, I'm on to ruin your—''

''You're not making my day now,'' he interrupted her in a low tone that caused her fingers to tremble on the pickle she had stuck in her mouth. ''Are you going to eat that pickle or—?'' He inhaled sharply. ''You're paying. Don't forget to leave a tip.''

On the busy street, Talia dug her heels into the concrete. Calum had a grip on her arm that didn't hurt, yet he managed to drag her along in his wake. Talia preferred to choose her own path. ''I want my hooks and my ropes back. I paid a fortune for them. Okay, I'll have to pay a fortune for them, if I don't get them back to— Well, never mind. Someone who is in the business. Rental fees are high on that stuff. I'm not going anywhere with you.''

She cursed in corrupted Russian as he walked off and she was forced to run to keep up with him. He looked down at her coolly before she could open her mouth. His glasses glinted like round mirrors, and the sun caught blue sparks in his neatly clipped hair as he said, very evenly, ''You're coming, you irritating little fireball, and one more curse from you, in whatever language, and I'll—''

Talia almost missed a step when his arm swung out and his hand rested lightly, possessively, on her waist. He easily drew her to his side. She had the miserable feeling that Calum would not give up easily, and that he'd chip away at her until he found her motive.

She emphasized the natural sway of her hips to test him. His reaction was immediate; his hand tightened on her padding, and his glance down at her was pure annoyance. She liked annoyance, but not the swift darkening of his eyes. Calum Tallchief, nerd, had definite warrior tendencies.

The sick-mother ploy worked easily. Especially when Talia's substitute from the secretarial pool appeared—tall, stacked and blond. The woman oozed a sexy welcome when she saw Calum Tallchief. "Disgusting," Talia muttered.

At nine o'clock that night, Calum looked in the rearview mirror at the car towed behind him. "Saboteurs shouldn't drive red convertible sports cars. Bad for a low profile."

Talia tugged at the handcuffs linking her to the four-wheeler. "So now you tell me. I never go anywhere without my car. I really didn't appreciate you plucking its poor little distributor cap off. I'm really good at that trick myself, so I knew where to look. Oh, and darlin', where did you put that, by the way?" she asked lightly. "In the back, with my things from the apartment? I've never had anyone move me before. So nice of you to save me the effort, and to be waiting for me to get off work. Now, about that distributor cap. If I were you, I really wouldn't mess with me on things like that. I don't like ramrods, or men who think they know what's best for me. I have a brain—I think."

In response he glanced at her disguise-dress and shook his head.

In the light of the dashboard, she noted that stubble darkened his jaw, giving him a dangerous look. The rolled-back sleeves exposed strong, hair-flecked forearms. A dark whorl of hair nestled in his opened shirt collar. The large hand easily moving the steering wheel looked as if it never released anything it wished to hold. She definitely sensed that she was being carried off to the dark, secret lair of a warrior. He seemed rather lonely at the office, prowling around like a Doberman, sniffing out her best-laid efforts. Her mother would probably want to bake him pies and fatten him. Jan would probably like him, and Alek and Anton would immediately take him into their hallowed male club, and Papa, too. When disturbed, Calum had...a dangerous edge, she decided. There was something magnificently male about him. *And she didn't like being controlled by overbearing males.*

She shivered and stared out into the night. She'd already had a sample of his strength and agility. Calum Tallchief moved fast, he was too smart, and he wasn't to be trusted. "You come close to me, Tallchief, and I'll break anything within reach."

He snorted; it was a disbelieving masculine sound.

"You know, a girl can't trust a guy who doesn't talk much. Communication can make friends." Talia leaned her head against the seat. She felt too drained to fight much tonight. Despite her dislike of Calum, there was a safety to him. He could easily have turned her in after the penthouse caper. Maybe she could work on some hidden gallantry, prey upon his sympathy, she thought sleepily. "I'd really like to know where we're going. A forwarding address for good old Mom, so she won't worry?"

"Go to sleep, Petrovna, and try not to curse me in whatever languages you've collected in your busy little life. After you tell me what I want to know, I'll know what to do next with you."

"Nice guy, Tallchief. Watch your toilet paper." Dozing, Talia thought she saw his mouth curve and smile lines crinkle beside his eyes.

Calum stretched in his cot, inhaling the fresh, cold morning air. He dozed, listening to the stream running not far from the cabin. October splashed the color of sunshine upon the Rockies' aspens and covered the tops of the mountains with snow. The deer were moving to lower meadows, and the warrior within him stirring.

This was his inheritance, his special place on Tallchief Mountain. In the shadowy single room, he opened his eyes to see Talia glaring at him. She looked nothing like the sleeping woman he had carried inside the cabin. She had curled into him as he lifted her from the seat and snuggled her face against his throat. The delicious purring noises she made had reached inside him, tormenting him.

He turned on his side and opened one eye to watch her tug on the handcuff attached to her cot's post. A variety of clothing littered the floor, evidence that she had had difficulty in finding the right escape outfit. Somehow she had managed to shed the baggy dress and tug on very tight jeans that showed every curve of her hips and long legs. She wore expensive running shoes, ready to leave immediately.

She moved, bending over, and Calum swallowed, his body jerking to full alert.

Talia wore a bright blue top. The elastic strip across her breasts revealed that she was not wearing a bra and that every curve was all woman. Calum swallowed again. Above the elastic, her breasts flowed with each tug. Calum's body responded almost painfully. He closed his eyes; she was a disaster.

He groaned mentally and tried not to notice the delicate jasmine scent that had filled his cabin during the night. The subtle scent had aroused him, wafting gently through the smells of wood smoke.

She glanced his way and continued to drag the cot stealthily after her, making her way toward his slacks, slung over a wooden chair. "Going somewhere?" Calum asked lightly.

She straightened immediately, her eyes rounded innocently. Her handcuffed hand clutched the cot's post. "Who, me?"

Dressed in jeans and nothing else, he stood up quickly, stretched and put on his glasses. The careless stretch and yawn had taken great effort; his body ached, rigid in every muscle, with sexual need. He didn't appreciate his body's awakening to Talia's.

Talia stared at him. She looked down his body, then up again. "Nerds don't wear jeans," she said, as if stating a well-known fact. "Not worn ones with light spots in appropriate male areas. Or ones that hang low with the front snap open. My auntie Em, Calum! You're tan all over, and you've got...*muscles!*"

She took a deep breath as he moved to uncuff her and to easily shove the cot back against the wall. "You're not fitting the perfect nerd picture, Tallchief."

He tried to ignore her dipping elastic top and the crevice of her breasts. Her rounded eyes on his body had every nerve dancing on sensual alert. Then, shaking his head, he reached to quickly tug up her top. The brush of her silky breast remained on his fingers after they slid away. He shook his head again as Talia backed up against the wooden door, her hands behind her. She smiled sweetly at him and batted her lashes. "No phone, darlin'. How do I dial room service?"

Calum knew he'd feel better after coffee, and he began to quickly stoke the old stove. "The door has a hidden lock, Talia. Save your energy. And...put...on...a shirt." He tossed one of his to her.

The next instant, Calum ran his hands over his face. The image of Talia in his shirt wasn't helping his temporarily unstable need to fit her body against his. He glanced at the smooth sway of her hips and knew she walked like no other woman he'd known. She had a walk that would easily draw men's eyes, and Calum didn't intend to be one of her conquests. Talia's sexuality was like her perfume—invasive, feminine and unwanted. He concentrated on preparing their meal. He didn't intend to come close to that illogical, sexual flash point with a volatile woman like Talia. Ever.

Calum frowned. He would choose his encounters logically, and Talia wasn't on that schedule.

Talia wandered around the cabin, peering out the windows, while he prepared biscuits, eggs and bacon. She ate ravenously, and daintily reached to take his last strip of bacon. She munched on it and eyed him with speculation. "Okay. I'm ready to confess. The way I figure it, you'll be considered as my accomplice now. How did you explain your absence from the job?"

"Logically. I needed a few days to research leads." Calum noted the cream and sugar she poured into her coffee. "Are you going to drink that or play with it?"

"I like sweet things, Tallchief. And nice guys. Listen, I might as well tell you up front, don't torture me. I've never thought I'd be good at that. If you've brought me here, to God knows where, to let the chipmunks listen to my screams, I'd rather not frighten the wildlife. If you don't mind."

Calum crushed the paper napkin in his hand. He'd brought her here to protect her from herself. Now the idea seemed insane. "Petrovna, the thought appeals."

Talia leaned forward, and Calum tried to force his eyes away from the deep crevice between her breasts. She seemed unaware of how she could stir male needs. Calum decided that was a practiced skill, just as Sherry's had been. No woman would be that unaware of how badly a man could want her, how the small cabin intensified needs—

Talia looked at him intently. "You're up the creek, Tallchief. You've done the deed. We're in cahoots now." Then she spoke slowly, distinctly, as if explaining to a child. "You're in this with me. Together we could really do a number on old Sleazeball. We could avenge every woman he's taken advantage of.''

Calum couldn't remember when any woman had distracted him the way Talia did. The thought was disconcerting. The rumpled bed behind her set him on edge. He could easily see tossing her upon it.

Calum scowled at her graceful fingers. He realized how his great-great-grandfather Tallchief must have felt when he tried to toss Una onto the tepee pelts. Calum had never tossed a woman beneath him, nor would he. He pushed the illogical thought aside and met Talia's narrowed eyes.

''Why did you bring me here, Tallchief?'' she asked warily.

''You might not believe this, but you remind me of my sister.'' She had reminded him of Fiona, when he first discovered what she was trying to do. But in the same cabin with her, and after a discussion with her brother, Alek Petrovna, that motive shredded to bits. ''Fiona is always trying to protect someone, something. But you were in a position to get hurt badly, or prosecuted. I wanted to give you a chance.''

''Oh, right. Uh-huh. Sure. Mr. Galahad to the rescue. I don't trust you. You're on Olson's payroll.''

''So are you.'' Calum found his fingers locked around Talia's wrist. The woman raised his hackles, and he resented it. ''Now you. You've gone to a tremendous amount of work. Why?''

She tried to tug her hand away. ''Oh, nothing to do. Bored, I guess.''

He released her wrist slowly. ''Olson has really stepped on your bad side, hasn't he? Did you know one of the women?''

She sat back and crossed her arms over her chest. ''You can't make me talk. *Unless* you agree that you're with me.

That you'll either help me, or ignore what you find. I've got people to protect in this caper.''

Her expression softened as she ran her finger around the rim of her coffee mug. Calum realized that whoever had her thoughts at that moment also had a portion of her heart. The tiny well of jealousy springing up in him shocked him. He hadn't found a lover in his background check on Talia Petrovna, though he'd learned that men drooled after her. It didn't help his nerves to know that he was one of those men. ''I'll do my job, and you, Miss Talia Petrovna, will eventually tell me what I want to know. By the way, did you return those hooks and ropes to Vinnie the human fly?''

She smiled coolly and met his eyes. ''Fingerprints again, I suppose. You rat, you found Vinnie by lifting his prints. Now that is low-down and devious.''

''You'll do the dishes if you want any more food, Petrovna.'' Much as he resented that his protective instincts seemed locked on this woman and that she little appreciated what it could cost him, Calum found a primitive excitement racing through him that he didn't trust. He realized that at some level, Talia affected his warrior instincts; his logic told him that the whole matter was nonsense.

His body told him differently.

She leveled a meaningful stare at him. ''If you know what's good for you, you'll give me my distributor cap and send me on my way. If you don't let me go, you have absolutely no idea what I am capable of.''

Calum studied her set face. He knew what she would do once he released her. He wasn't ready to let her go. Something deep inside him wanted to prolong his Talia Petrovna misery. ''You'll go straight back to mayhem, sabotage and Olson.''

''You've got it, Sherlock.'' She lifted an eyebrow. ''There's no way you could have gotten that information

on me unless you contacted someone I know very well.
Say a family member. Someone I grew up with.''

He sipped his coffee and waited. Without the tinted con-
tact lenses, Talia's blue eyes darkened as she glared at him.
He watched with interest, as she seemed to be building up
to explode, which she did. She threw a cup against the wall.
It rattled across the floor as she glared at Calum. ''Alek
Petrovna is a rat! Don't believe anything my brother says!
How much did he tell you?'' she asked warily.

''What was in the file, and he asked me to keep you safe.
He said you'd tell me the rest. I'm waiting.'' Alek hadn't
asked, he had yelled and demanded that his little sister be
in one happy piece the next time he saw her. He expected
regular reports, and he had put Calum through an investigation that was tight and thorough, with double checks.
Alek was extremely protective of Talia, and he'd promised
torture if anything happened to his little sister.

The passion coloring Talia's cheeks and lighting her eyes
fascinated Calum. She was a symphony of color and movement.

Talia shook her head and closed her eyes. ''Okay. I'll
take care of Alek, right after I take care of you, right after
I take care of Olson.''

''That's a long list.''

''I'm up to it.''

Three

Calum tried to keep his attention on his computer screen. He systematically ran through Tallchief investments and tried to keep his mind off the pacing, furious woman sharing his cabin. With difficulty, he forced his eyes from the elegant sway of Talia's hips to thoughts of her sister, Jan— January Petrovna. Alek had not offered information about his youngest sister; Calum was certain that Talia's revenge had something to do with Jan, who he'd discovered had worked for Olson.

At odds with her striking looks, Talia's financial savvy fascinated Calum. Her wise investments provided her with an uncommon income and allowed her the freedom of mobility—to step into trouble at will. Talia invested cautiously and took risks. Her game style was unique and profitable; she wasn't the simple headstrong go-for-it woman as she appeared.

Alek Petrovna had not been difficult to locate. A call to

his wire service about his busy sister, and Alek had called immediately from a war-torn country. Concerned about his sister, the tough journalist had yelled over a bombardment of shells. He'd checked out Calum's credentials within minutes and wired the information needed about Talia. He'd promised to check up on his little sister and roared with laughter when Calum described her antics.

Yet Alek had not revealed Talia's motives, and he hadn't said much about Jan.

The fire crackled in the stove, warding off the cold weather. By midafternoon, Talia had stopped threatening Calum, though he had begun to appreciate her creativity. She was too quiet, sitting on her cot and watching the afternoon mixture of rain and early snow trickle down the window. From the shadows, she'd been studying him closely, seeking out his weak points. Now she was somewhere else, and the expression on her face was soft, with a whimsical curve to her lips. Her slender, pale fingers traced the rain trails slowly; she was the image of a vanquished challenger. He wondered what her next move would be.

Her last one had been to hurl another cup at him. He'd caught it and smiled tightly. "Thanks. I was just getting ready for some more."

He clicked off the computer and stared at her.

After a moment, she stared back, her expression hardening. The light touched the angles of her face, softening her fierce expression.

"Okay. You want to do this the hard way, Petrovna?" Calum began. "We'll do it the hard way." He began to mentally arrange his questions about her motives.

Ignoring him, she stood up, jerked off his shirt and began to stretch. She parted her legs and eased her body to one side, touching the toes of one foot, then the other. The warm-up exercises caused Calum to inhale, every molecule in his body locked on the flow and rhythm of Talia's. So much for his plans. He wanted her; his body was taut. "I'm going outside."

She continued to ignore him, and Calum stepped outside. He realized that he had slammed the door; he realized that he was standing in the freezing rain, shivering, when the cabin belonged to him. He stepped back inside to find Talia rummaging through his traveling bag. He leaned against the door and folded his arms over his chest. At least the movement kept his hands from reaching for her delectable neck. "The distributor cap isn't there."

"Cut the chitchat, Tallchief. I'm not in the mood." She began to run in place.

Calum forced his gaze to remain above her shoulders, on the irritating angle of her stubborn chin. "You're a spoiled little witch who has run amok your entire life. You've got your father and brothers and every other male you've come in contact with under your thumb." He paused for effect. "But you are not going back to destroy yourself."

"Alek will pay," she returned grimly. "It must have been easy to connect him with me, given a name like Petrovna."

Then Talia paused, looked at Calum thoughtfully and grabbed a towel, blotting it across her forehead.

Calum watched her glide toward him, taking away his breath. Talia placed one hand on the door, beside his head, and smoothed his hair with the tip of her finger.

Calum found himself holding his breath and relishing her next move. The woman intrigued and fascinated him, despite his aversion to problem people. Talia had Problem pasted all over her. He fought falling into the warm scents of jasmine and overheated woman enticing him.

She studied his face and ran the tip of her finger over his ear. She touched his bottom lip and trailed her finger down his chin. "You know, this could be fun. Together, we could level Olson."

"Fun?" Though Calum kept his expression steady, every nerve in him wanted to paste Talia's body against his. He wanted to feed upon that generous soft mouth—

"Mmm... Think about it." Then she turned slowly and walked away from him, the sway of her long, straight hair almost brushing her hips.

Calum closed his eyes, shook his head and forced himself to concentrate on how he was getting out of this mess. He'd always been in charge of his life, but for one dizzying moment, he'd felt like a butterfly on the tip of a pin, or a moth drawn toward a light.

Calum shook his head. At two hundred pounds and more, he was no butterfly-moth. And there was no reason he was here with this maddening woman. He hadn't thought out a plan; he'd simply captured her and whisked her to safety. Olson wasn't getting her.

He grimly decided to blame his actions on the Tallchief males' protective genes.

"There are big wild animals out there," Talia stated slowly, watching the night through the window. "What are they?"

"Take your pick...moose and bear. A hungry wolf or two." Calum resented how Talia looked now, her face pale, her eyes shadowed and rounded. She seemed deceptively fragile. Her slight torment should have pleased him; it didn't. With her hair in a ponytail and dressed in his shirt and her jeans, she looked like a young girl. He could deal with the girl image and keep Talia on a level with Fiona.

Like hell.

Talia had skin like silk, she walked like no other woman, and every molecule of him heated just from looking at her.

She moved closer to him. "I want to go home, Tallchief."

Calum turned off his computer and looked at her steadily. "We can go anytime you tell me what I want to know. And when I have your word that you will leave Olson alone."

She glared back. "You'll pay," she said finally. "Petrovna's Law. I am very good at what I do."

He lifted an eyebrow. "You think it's pleasant being in your vicinity? Tell me what I want to know and we'll work from there."

A coyote howled and, with a fearful gasp, Talia hurled herself against him. She wrapped her arms around him and shivered, just once. Calum found his arms locking around her, resisting slightly as she stepped back. She stared at him. "Sorry. I forgot you're the enemy."

Calum dealt with the immediate need to lay her down and love her. She glanced at him resentfully. "Okay, okay. Stop glaring at me. You're big and hard and strong, and I got scared for just a second. It won't happen again. Just how long do you plan to keep me here? You should know that nothing is going to keep me from ruining Olson. Nothing."

"I am," Calum stated quietly. He forced himself not to look at the slope of her breast where her shirt had come unbuttoned.

"Darlin', the day some paid-for hit man stops me, that's the day I'll turn it in for an apron and a houseful of kiddies."

"Don't press your luck." Calum almost smiled at the image. *Exotic* described Talia, like a colorful butterfly. He couldn't see her in the role of a housewife.

When Calum stepped outside for firewood, he returned to the door to find it wouldn't budge. He pushed his shoulder against the wood and pushed slowly, forcing it open.

Behind it, objects crashed, furniture slid and Talia cursed. Within minutes, Talia had stacked the contents of the cabin against the door. He stepped over a chair, then over a cot mattress, and neatly placed the firewood in the box. In a blur of motion, Talia raced by him, out into the freezing rain.

Her athletic stride took her quickly down the rough road.

Calum was faster, and when he reached her, they went down into the mud and the snow. A thrill like none he'd ever known before shot through him; he'd captured a woman he wanted very much. He stopped breathing, focused on her and exhaled sharply. He shook his head to clear it; he preferred a sensible life—without Talia.

"Get off me, you big lug," she stated between heaving breaths that dragged her breasts up to his chest. She squirmed beneath him. Calum discovered he'd firmly inserted his leg between hers. The movement startled him; it was primitive and possessive. His body flexed in reaction, his thigh pressing higher as she glared at him. "Now you've gotten me dirty."

"I ought to—" Beneath the layers of sweatshirts and the heavy coat, he felt her body against his. A tropical heat surged through Calum, stunning him.

Calum held very still, too aware that his thumbs were stroking the fine inner skin of her wrists. He realized that he was lying between her legs and that her thighs were quivering along his.

In the next second, he was on his feet, his chest heaving as he tried to calm the need to crush her mouth beneath his. He locked his knees to stop the shaking of his body, wrapped his fist in the jacket she had taken and pulled her slowly to her feet. He lowered his face to hers and spoke very softly. "Get back to the house."

Talia stared at him for a moment. She fluttered her

lashes, taunting him. "But, master, I'm dirty, and there's no bathroom there."

"We'll manage," he returned tightly before giving her a light shove toward the cabin.

While Talia was bathing in a tub of heated water behind a wall of blankets, Calum shook his head. He found himself close to muttering, something he'd never done before meeting Talia. The cabin was warm, steaming, and scented of female flesh. Calum ran his hands over his face and grimaced when he felt the bruise she had left on him from the window incident.

When she placed her bare feet on the floor, Calum found his gaze locked on her ankles, revealed by the blanket. His hands could wrap around them easily. She was humming, and the blanket moved as she bumped it. Talia emerged, dressed in hot-pink pants and a tight long-sleeved pink sweater. Calum's mouth went dry at the sight of her nipples, thrusting at the knit fabric. A sensual punch landed in his midsection and slid lower, lodging heavily and uncomfortably in an area he considered very private. She closed her eyes, giving herself to the erotic motion of drying her hair with a towel. "Oh, this is good. The first time I get into a real bathroom, I'm having a soak that will last two days."

The purring, sensuous noises she made as she dried her hair weren't helping the rising desire within him.

He wondered whether she purred when she made love, and his body lurched into desire.

She was very quiet as he handcuffed her to the cot. He didn't trust her innocent, friendly smile, and he took his bath quickly, sliding into clean jeans and drawing on a thermal shirt. He shot her a warning glance as he turned off the light.

After a night of his body hardening each time her cot creaked, Calum finally fell into a fitful sleep. When he awoke, the room was freezing. A bottle, nudged by the wind, rolled across the table and hit the floor. Talia's cot was empty, and the window was not tightly closed.

He found her expertly hot-wiring his four-wheeler.

The next evening, Talia sat on her side of his vehicle. Calum Tallchief was interesting, once she'd peeled back his sleek edges. She noted that occasionally now he muttered a bit. In her experience with Petrovna males, muttering was good—a sign that she was getting to them, wearing down their overbearing, controlling behavior.

This guy was big and bleak and tasty. Not that she'd ever really tasted a man, except for a few really indulgent and unsatisfying kisses. Deep within Talia Petrovna lurked an old-fashioned girl, raised with traditional family rules. Only her family knew that despite her travels and antics, she was basically old-fashioned. An outdated good girl. Alek and Anton loved to point that out to her. They tactfully avoided references to her one try at a wedding—the one at which she'd been jilted at the altar.

But Calum raised a certain challenge, and she never passed up a really good one. What woman could ignore Calum's towering wall of dark, tangy secrets? She was certain that pain lurked in his past, and— Darn, that brought out the need to comfort him again.... As if human Dobermans could be cuddled. Still, when first seen in the mornings, with his hair rumpled, his body aroused against his tight jeans, and his magnificent chest... If she wasn't anxious to destroy Olson, she might—

Talia glanced at Calum's profile. Right now, he was singed around the edges—a minor mishap during her first experience with a wood stove. The pink sunset traced his angular, hard face as he turned to lift one black-singed eyebrow at her. She smiled tentatively. "Now tell me your master scheme again, darlin'."

were already moving into an argument about the car and how fast it could race. He noted their motorcycles parked in front of the tavern. He wasn't the only one; Talia's stare had locked on to the fast, elegant beasts. "Don't even think about it. I know you placed first in the High Mud Bike Ride."

She smiled innocently at him and fluttered her lashes. "I have other skills. You'll be sorry if you provoke me into using them."

He reeked of the smoke that Talia's diversion had caused in the cabin. Before the stove had burst into a small flame. A particle of soot fluttered from his head to his nose, and Calum blew it away. Another night with Talia and he'd be— Calum rubbed his hand over his unshaven jaw. His hand came away coated with soot.

His home, a sleek, modern wooden affair with a rambling yard, settled into the evening shadows of Amen Flats. It didn't surprise him that the lights were on in the house and Elspeth was waiting for him at the gate. She carried a woven lunch basket. Elspeth always sensed his homecomings; he could almost taste fresh bread and a tasty casserole. He shot a glance at Talia, who was studying Elspeth. "She's my sister. Be nice," he ordered curtly as he stopped the vehicle.

"Aren't I always?" Talia asked sweetly before opening her door and sliding out. She moved toward Elspeth gracefully, purposefully, and the hair on Calum's nape lifted. He hurried to her side. "Elspeth, this is Talia Petrovna. She's going to keep house for me. For a time."

Talia smiled warmly, and Calum blinked. Her smile could have charmed Duncan's mean longhorn bull into acting like a frisky calf. "I'm so pleased to meet you, Elspeth."

She looked away from Elspeth's quiet stare, which moved slowly to Calum, then back to Talia. "Aye." Elspeth's voice was as soft as her gaze upon her brother, who shifted restlessly. "Aye," she said again, in a tone of approval.

"Nay," Calum shot back darkly. "Not in a trillion years."

"Petrovna, did you say?" Elspeth frowned slightly, as though tracking the name through her memory.

"Yes. My brother is Alek Petrovna, a journalist. You may have heard of him."

Elspeth hesitated, then answered lightly, "Perhaps." Elspeth looked as though she knew something that Calum or Talia did not. "I'm pleased that you've come here," Elspeth said quietly.

"For a time," Talia stated.

"A short time," Calum added firmly.

Talia's smile was angelic. She flicked a particle of soot from his ear and reached up to pat his head. "Calum is helping me between jobs."

"Mmm... I see," Elspeth murmured, rising on tiptoe to hug and kiss her brother. She stood back, smothering a grin. "Calum, you smell like smoke, but your singed look is becoming. I don't believe I've ever seen you so... distracted." She studied him. "Strange."

"Calum got all bothered when I turned the damper on the stove. There was a bit of smoke, and a teeny fire. He has a murderous temper, you know. I couldn't help it that his clothes got a little scorched. He shouldn't have tried to put out the fire by himself," Talia informed her, and smiled sweetly at Calum. "He mutters, you know. Who would have thought it?"

"I do *not* mutter." The fire had been her last ploy at the cabin, the turning point at which he decided that he couldn't stand another night with her tossing in her cot.

Or watching the very feminine sway of her hips. Now

that they'd moved to his house, he hoped she would do her mind-stopping exercises in the privacy of her room.

While the small holes of his clothes were still smoldering, Calum had almost picked her up and—for just that instant, he almost tossed her on the cot.... Talia had glared at him, curiously unaware of the sensual danger he presented. Curiously. Almost naive about his painful need of her, especially when her hand had brushed his thigh and pressed against him as she squirmed.

That hand had stopped him. On the cusp of pressing it firmly against his body, Calum had managed to push her away.

"Strange," Elspeth murmured with an impish smile. "We call him Calum the cool."

Talia laughed outright. "Calum the cool. I'll remember that. By the way, tell me about Duncan."

"Duncan the defender." Elspeth's tone was affectionate. "He's our older brother, and until now I thought *he* was the dark, moody one."

"Calum is just having a bad hair day. Tell me more about your family, Elspeth."

"No." Calum released the breath he had been holding and pushed his hand through his singed hair. "Not tonight."

Talia fluttered her lashes. "Petrovna's Law includes tit for tat. Elspeth, what is this about a family ring? I'm helping Calum find it. I understand you traced it to Denver."

Calum stared at the mountains and rocked on his heels. Somewhere there was a world without Talia, a quiet, steady, predictable world.

"Our great-great-grandmother had to sell her dowry to keep Tallchief Mountain. We've each pledged to bring back one item. Calum's search is for the ring." Elspeth smiled at Calum meaningfully. "The Tallchief dowry has legends."

When a man of Fearghus blood places the ring upon the right woman's finger, he'll capture his true love forever.

Elspeth didn't have to voice the legend; it hovered in the crisp October air between them. Calum didn't like the amused light in her eyes as she turned to Talia. "You must be tired. There's supper waiting in the warming oven, and I hope you like your room. I put some bath salts near the tub and laid out fresh towels. I need to get back to my weaving now. I have a new order of shawls waiting to be filled. I'll check to see if you need anything tomorrow. Good night, Talia. Calum." Then she moved gracefully into the shadows.

"She's beautiful," Talia murmured. "There's something very different about her…soothing. I like her. How did you manage to call her and tell her I'd be coming?" She eyed him darkly. "Don't tell me you had this whole thing planned."

"I didn't call her. Elspeth just knows." He didn't like explaining his family to Talia.

"Really? She's a psychic? What do you know about that! And in such a tiny town, too. What do people do here for excitement?"

Calum watched as Talia studied the rugged, snowcapped mountains in the distance, turning as she looked out over Amen Flats. Then she turned to his house, studying the angular contemporary shape, his own design. "Where's the big, tough black yard dog? A perfect pet for you."

"I don't have pets."

"Mmm… Women?"

"Stop pushing." She nettled him. He could have any number of pets if he wanted them. Female clutter didn't fit his life-style. Calum followed her up the walkway with a sinking feeling. He tried not to notice the distinctive feminine sway of her hips. In a half hour, everyone in Amen Flats would know that he had brought a woman home.

Even now, the telephone lines were probably hot with the news.

For now, he had Talia on a tether. And he had no idea why he had placed his professional reputation in danger. He found himself staring at Talia's hips as she ascended the stairs, heading straight for the bathroom. He closed his eyes and shook his head. He needed sleep; his nerves were drawn too tight. The sooner he was rid of Talia Petrovna, the sooner he could get his life back on track. He waited until he heard the bathwater running, and then he began to make calls.

Talia emerged from the bath; she now felt up to battling Calum. "You've got quite the little security system here. Not that I tried the windows or anything… It's a wonder what a bath can do for a girl—"

Calum, freshly showered, stood waiting for her at the bottom of the steps. He took her breath away. Water gleamed on his coal-black hair—a drop caught on his bare chest—and the smooth black stone gleamed on the leather thong. There was a primitive edge to Calum Tallchief, one she wanted to explore. In jeans, with his shirt opened, Calum was all sexy male.

Until she looked at his scowl, his black eyebrows jammed together and the muscle contracting in his jaw. His eyes dropped to midway on her chest, and he shook his head. She glanced down at the nightshirt she loved; it was worn thin and revealed her breasts. She instantly crossed her arms. She'd never been shy about skimpy clothing, but then, she'd never met a man like Calum. He caused her to feel very feminine and aware of how much she'd like his mouth on hers. She remembered his weight between her legs as they lay in the mud and the snow. The movement of his thigh nudging her intimately was firm and knowledgeable. She'd danced away from men who pursued her too closely; Calum had the look of a hunter, of a man not easily put off.

Talia inhaled sharply. She didn't like being pushed and locked into corners. Out of his business suit and clearly at home, Calum wore his warrior arrogance like a big danger flag.

"Here. Put this on. You look cold." He took off his shirt and tossed it to her. He watched grimly as she put it on. "Button it."

He lifted a pale strand of her hair, studying it in the firelight. She sensed that he could easily wrap his hand in it and tug her to him. Talia eased back slightly as he studied the various light shades. "A blonde. I should have known you'd dyed your hair."

"I've always liked basic brown. Goes with everything. But it was time for a change." Talia inhaled the scents of soap and freshly showered male. The cloth was still warm from his body. When she made no move to button it, but met his gaze, Calum moved closer and began to button the shirt. She studied his big hands, moving slowly, efficiently down the cloth, and wanted his touch upon her. She moved closer, watching him now as his knuckles brushed her softness. She reacted instantly, her nipples peaking, shocking her. When his eyes darkened to the shade of night smoke and flickered down to her breasts, her heart stilled.

Talia found her hand opened on his chest, her fingers pale against the black hair and darkly tanned skin. Beneath her palm, Calum's heart pounded in a fascinating rhythm, drawing her to him. Talia moved instinctively, as she always did. She caught the black stone around his neck in her fist, pressed her body against his and rested her head upon his chest. He felt good—warm, steady, comfortable. She nuzzled the hard padding of his chest and inhaled more of his delicious scents.

A telephone rang somewhere, and Talia was left standing

and swaying without Calum's support. She frowned at him as he answered the telephone. No man had ever moved away from her. *That's my role,* she decided, slightly outraged. Of course, she'd never reacted to a man as she had to Calum. She glared at him. He didn't know anything about her rules, but he would learn.

Calum scowled back at her from the kitchen, looking dark and dangerous as he pressed the receiver to his ear. "Fiona, why are you calling?" His eyes flickered to Talia as she moved closer and waited, hoping to hear more. He turned away, presenting her with an expanse of broad back that fascinated her. She reached out a finger to stroke a muscle running across his shoulder blade, and he looked down at her over his shoulder. "Yes, I brought a woman home. We're here together. She's going to keep house for me. No, I didn't find the ring yet, but I will. Yes. I just told you that I brought her home. Hell, no, I'm not like Duncan carrying off the woman I want—" He glanced impatiently at Talia, who was standing very close. "Would you mind?"

"No," she returned innocently, and eased closer. "Just how many women have you carried off to your cave?" The jolt of jealousy surprised her. She dismissed it as anger at the man temporarily foiling her plans.

Calum inhaled and spoke into the telephone, "Fiona, we'll talk later, okay? And stay out of trouble. Montana is a big state. Find a cause to keep you busy. Call me when it's bail-bond time."

Talia watched, fascinated, as Calum's expression softened. "I worry about you, too. Don't forget to call when you need me."

"Girlfriend?" Talia asked as she followed him into the kitchen.

"Sister." Calum began cutting warm bread, and Talia couldn't wait to butter it.

"Is this real homemade butter?" she asked, munching away while Calum placed a hot casserole on the table.

"You could help."

"Help what?" she asked between delicious bites of buttery warm bread.

"Set the table. You're supposed to be my housekeeper."

Calum stared at her mouth, and Talia found her heartbeat kicking up to warp speed. "So you said. I think it's sweet how you thought of my reputation. How many women have you had here?" she heard herself ask. If other women had seen Calum's dark smoky look in this same house...if he had buttoned them into his shirt...such a sweet, protective gesture...she'd— His gaze had fallen to her mouth and lingered, warming it. She licked a crumb from her bottom lip as he traced the movement.

Unprotected from the sudden lurch of her heart, Talia glanced at the assortment of small potted plants on the cabinet. Munching on her bread and butter, she moved toward them and away from Calum. The tiny, fragrant leaves bobbed beneath her light touch.

"Herb starts from Elspeth. She likes to give things she likes—" Calum glanced out into the night, and then at Talia, as if wondering where he could stash her. When a light knock at the door sounded, his deep voice was almost a snarl, and he moved in front of Talia, almost protectively, backing her into a corner of the cabinet. She hopped up and sat on the counter, one hand on his tense shoulder and the other holding her buttered bread. She liked touching him.

A man as tall as Calum, but more heavily built, entered the kitchen. He wore his grim look like a cloak, though his eyes—the shade of Calum's—lit with amusement.

"Hi. I'm Talia. Mmm... Interesting," she managed around a mouthful of delicious bread. "He looks just like you, Calum. Same steel-colored eyes, same dark skin and black hair, same— I like the cowboy getup. Boots, hat, gloves... Mmm... Is that apple pie?"

"Fresh from the oven. My wife, Sybil, sent it for you. She'll be over in the morning with Megan, our daughter. Emily, our other daughter, will stop by on her way from school, if that's okay."

"I'd love to meet everyone. Calum has told me so much about the Tallchief family," she lied.

"So you've finally caught one, Calum. Elspeth said it would be soon." The other man's voice held amusement. He removed his hat in a lovely cowboy gesture and nodded to Talia. "Ma'am, I apologize for my little brother. He's not usually so poor-mannered. I'm his big brother, Duncan."

Talia leaned to whisper in Calum's ear. "I like him. He's sweet."

Calum moved back slightly, and his large hands found her knees, resting beside his hips. She concentrated on the erotic circles his thumbs were drawing on the inside of her knees.

Talia reached across Calum's shoulder, extending her hand for Duncan's handshake. "Calum has had a bad day. He's tired," she explained sweetly, and noted that Calum had tensed immediately.

Duncan chuckled. "Elspeth said he was slightly singed when you arrived. He had soot in his hair."

Talia noted the muscle leaping in Calum's jaw as he said, "Put the pie on the table. Thank Sybil for me, and—"

Calum stood very still as Talia draped her arms around his shoulders. "I'm his very own live-in housekeeper," she said teasingly, while blowing in his ear.

Duncan burst out in guffaws. Calum's skin heated beneath her touch in a slight but noticeable blush. "I want pie," Talia stated over the wild thumping of her heart. But with Calum's muscled back nestled against her, she wondered whether she didn't want another dessert—one with a protective, rather sweet attitude.

Four

When the sun rose the next morning, Talia began shoving away the furniture she had placed against her bedroom door. She accidentally dropped a chair and bit her lip, pressing her ear to the door. With luck, Calum would be sleeping, or engrossed in his computer, and she could make it to his vehicle—

"Can I help?" The masculine drawl stopped Talia. She sat heavily upon the old chest and shook her head. The door opened; she gripped the chest as it began to slide across the floor, carrying her. She hopped off as Calum leaned against the door and nudged her carryall bag aside with her toe. His eyes ran down her black sweater and leggings. She'd added the Hessian boots as a touch of her passionate and daring Russian inheritance. Calum wasn't the only one with dynamic ancestors. She always felt up to any caper dressed in black and with her hair neatly tucked in a single waist-length braid.

"Oh! Hello. Just a little furniture arranging. I hope you don't mind. I put rugs beneath the legs so as not to scar the beautiful wood flooring." She eyed Calum's bare chest and the corded arms crossed upon it. The black obsidian, secured by the leather thong, nestled on gleaming coarse hair. Her fingertips tingled with the need to grab that stone and tug his mouth to hers.

On the other hand, Calum wasn't that easy to move, or to dismiss. She might not be able to walk away unaffected from his kiss. She definitely didn't want Calum's kiss.

"Afraid that I might enter your boudoir during the night, Petrovna?" The sensuous masculine challenge wrapped around her. The warm color of night smoke, his eyes traced her body. He smiled lightly at her tall, polished boots.

She braced her legs apart and placed her hands on her hips. Her boots matched anything perfectly, from tight leather miniskirts to long, dynamic dresses. And in a pinch, they were great in mountain snow.

"The day I'm afraid of you, I'll give away my bangle bracelets." He smelled great. That dark, dangerous, mysterious scent, layered with a brisk after-shave. She could easily get used to the sight of him wearing jeans and smelling great. But she could see that he wasn't buying anything. She was losing her touch. She decided to treat him lightly…if she could. Her chin went up a notch. "Are the breakfast croissants ready?"

Calum stared down at her. "Petrovna, give up. Promise me you'll leave Olson alone and we'll call it quits. I'll clean up your trail, and we can both go our own ways."

"How you sweet-talk me, Tallchief. Dream on, big boy. I'll call it quits when I have Olson begging for mercy. I want him to face every life he's ruined." Talia waltzed past him and took the stairs to the kitchen two at a time. Calum was too alert this morning, focused on her. She preferred not to play the mouse to his cat. "Nice house, by the way.

Love the light wood contemporary furniture against the dark paneling. Perfect for plants and lots of stuff.''

Within the hour, Calum was holding his dozing baby niece close to him and cooing at her. In the midst of a sterile kitchen packed with gadgets, the timeless scene of man and baby caused Talia's heart to do flip-flops. Obviously taken by his niece, Calum leaned against the counter while Sybil, Elspeth and Talia sat at the huge table. The only softening colors in the spacious kitchen were those of the small potted herbs on the window and Elspeth's woven place mats.

The image of a Western cowboy, dressed in worn flannel shirt, shearling vest, jeans and boots, Calum could have posed for a calendar. His four-month-old niece cuddled against him. Megan stirred in his arms, her gray eyes, so like Calum's, finding Talia. Talia barely breathed, aching to hold the baby, yet startled by how much she ached for a child of her own.

Calum's darkened gray gaze met hers, and for a moment Talia's heart stopped. Something caught like gold dust on the sunlight between them. Then she swallowed and wondered if she wasn't catching a flu, and was momentarily weak with it, rather than with the image of a cowboy holding a baby. Calum eased Megan into Sybil's arms and leaned back against the counter, sipping his coffee and studying Talia. She forced her stare away from him; Calum had dangerous edges, and she had just touched one of them.

''It's all in Una's journals.'' Sybil rocked Megan, who was sleeping on her lap. ''She came to this country, an indentured servant, and was captured by Tallchief, a Sioux chieftain. She tamed him, and together they built a life on Tallchief Mountain.'' She kissed Megan's jet-black hair. ''Duncan and his brothers share certain instincts inherited from their great-great-grandfather.''

''This plaid is beautiful.'' Talia, still reeling from the

effect Calum had upon her, traced the place mats Elspeth had woven. "This shade of green is marvelous."

"It's the Fearghus plaid, with adjustments. Dragon green for the fierce chieftains of the Sioux and the Fearghuses. I believe my brothers have that same proud fierceness when tested. The vermilion red is to recognize Tallchief. He must have paid dearly to marry a woman not of his blood. He gave up everything for her, and loved her deeply...after she tamed him."

"Tell me more about your family." Talia glanced at Calum, who shot Sybil and Elspeth a dark warning look. "Why don't you run along, darlin'?" she asked him, and wondered whether she could tame him. Did she want to?

Did she want to become involved with Calum? She considered the notion, She'd avoided romantic entanglements her entire lifetime. She'd avoided men like Calum, quiet, unpredictable men with shadows and edges. They couldn't be trusted; she'd found that out the day she was to have been married. And after living with the dynamic, emotional Petrovna males, she preferred men who were easily managed and who let her waltz away easily.

He reached for his Western hat and took a deep breath that lifted the hard planes of his chest. "I'll be back for lunch," he stated meaningfully, and shot a dark look at Talia.

She returned it with a kiss tossed into the fragrant air. The muscles in Calum's jaw tensed instantly. Then he nodded to the women sitting at his kitchen table. Talia studied his taut backside and rigid shoulders as he walked out to a pasture where an Arabian stallion gleamed in the morning sun. With the stark Rocky Mountains, tipped in snow, as a backdrop, Calum presented a delicious picture of the cowboy. The black beast whinnied and reared, his front hooves pawing in the air. Then he raced away into the pasture, tail high and flying. In a moment, he raced back to the gate to stand meekly as Calum saddled him.

Calum's efficient movements came from experience. He had lost his city look; he was all rugged Westerner.

Talia hadn't realized she was staring, fascinated by Calum's Western image. His hands soothed the horse, and Talia shivered. When he held Megan, Talia's resolve to lead an independent life had turned to warm butter. The appealing picture of the two Tallchiefs, uncle and baby niece, could make a woman wish for—

Duncan rode up to him on a more heavily built horse, and another, younger version of the Tallchief brothers appeared at Calum's side. They rode toward the huge jutting mountain known as Tallchief.

"Calum and Duncan are so much alike. Yet so different." Elspeth sipped her tea and studied her brothers, sitting tall in the saddle. "Birk is like them, too, despite his lighter side. My three older brothers bore the burden of growing up too soon. They rode off like that when our parents were murdered. The three of them were the only men capable of tracking in the mountains at night. I stayed behind to care for Fiona. I knew they would catch him. My father had taught them well. He'd been taught by his father, and so forth, back to Tallchief. I wanted to go desperately. I did resent not being able to go with them, but they don't know it. In a pinch, I can track as well as they."

Talia touched the small scar on Elspeth's thumb. "That looks like Calum's."

"Aye." Elspeth's tone was gentle, loving, and her eyes were warm. Talia sensed that the Tallchiefs' "Aye" meant that their emotions ran deep. Elspeth continued, tracing the plaid. "There was a night on our mountain, with the fierce October wind howling and Tallchief Lake lashed with white waves. Our parents were lying beneath the cold ground, and we were all afraid. It was Duncan who reached

into the night to pluck an idea, a way for us to survive as
a family, to keep our heritage.''

Elspeth paused, caught by the past, then continued,
''When we were very young, the five of us had cut our
thumbs and mixed our blood...to our mother's horror. She
was a passionate woman, in the few times she was angered.
I remember her calling out Dad and leveling him for encouraging us. Suddenly he became very romantic. We
played with swords and we shouted 'Aye!' as Una's chieftain ancestors had. The Tallchiefs were also quite good at
spears and bows and arrows.''

Talia ached for the five orphans facing the world, none
of them certain about the future. She had been tucked in
the safety of the Petrovnas until she managed to escape.
Except for visits, she preferred not to stay too long. They
were in a family ruled by traditions, and they wanted her
safely married, inevitably presenting an array of overbearing potential husbands. She preferred a life without the con-
finements of marriage.

Elspeth's expression softened. ''We each had special
names, and we still do—Duncan the defender, Calum the
cool, Birk the rogue, Elspeth the elegant and Fiona the
fiery. And that night, Duncan called us out to do our best.
We raised our scarred thumbs to the sky and pledged that
we would survive. That night, we wrapped our heritage
around us to keep us safe.''

Sybil reached out to touch Elspeth's shoulder. ''You
used the legends?''

''The legends. Aye...'' Soft memories lay in Elspeth's
tone. ''The legends served to calm our shaking hearts. We
were so frightened, and we needed more to survive than
our wills. So we clung to what we knew and cherished. The
stories written by Una and held dear by our family since.
The legends pasted the safety of the past around us. We
literally wrapped ourselves in that security.''

Elspeth touched Megan's soft black hair, then straightened. Her expression indicated she was looking back into the past. "Una described her dowry, sold to protect Tallchief Mountain. Each item of the Fearghus bridal dowry carried a legend, and we pledged to find an item and return it to our family. We spent our family time discussing it, to lighten the load we all carried. Duncan was to find the cradle, and Sybil brought it to him. The legend came true— *The woman who brings the cradle to a man of Fearghus blood will fill it with his babies.* Calum has pledged to find—"

"The ring," Talia said thoughtfully, interrupting her. "And what was its legend?"

Sybil smiled at Elspeth, who was smoothing a table mat of the Tallchief plaid. "Calum will tell you the legend soon enough. He had paid dearly to keep us together, scraping pennies and paying bills and keeping us afloat. It wasn't easy keeping a growing family in clothes and food. Fiona was just ten when it happened. I was fourteen. My brothers were deathly afraid a well-meaning matron would snatch us from them. It almost killed Fiona to mind her manners, but she did."

"Elspeth, you helped, too. Keeping the house going and your brothers in hand couldn't have been easy." Sybil soothed Megan, who stirred, awakening. The baby opened her gray eyes to stare at Talia.

Talia's heart lurched instantly. She yearned to hold the baby, to cuddle her. She shivered, unused to her maternal instincts surfacing. She wrapped her arms around herself protectively. She didn't want the warmth of this family, or the enchantment of this small town, with its freshly baked pies and laughing children.

She wanted nothing of Calum's to enfold her, to fascinate her.

She wanted freedom, and mornings without great-looking, great-smelling, sultry, gray-eyed cowboys. "Tell me about Tallchief's stone, the one Calum wears."

"That was the first stone Una threw at Tallchief. It wasn't her last. She was just as proud as he was. In the end, they loved each other. Would you like to hold Megan?" Elspeth asked softly. Then Sybil was placing the warm child within Talia's arms. A tiny hand gripped Talia's pinkie while Megan watched her steadily.

Talia swallowed and moved her little finger, enchanted with Megan. She looked up to see Sybil and Elspeth smiling softly. "Aye," Elspeth said.

"Aye," Sybil returned.

"My brother has already taken you to his cabin, hasn't he?" Elspeth asked.

"Yes. We, ah...needed a break in the drive," Talia answered, distracted by Megan's cooing. She found herself cooing back, something she had never done.

Megan clasped Talia's single braid and took her heart.

Later, when Sybil and Elspeth were gone, Talia called her mother, assuring her that she was safe. Her mother promised to send her clothing and, with a smile in her voice, told Talia to stay out of trouble. Then Talia called Marco the Fence and asked him to contact Vinnie and Nose for a lead on the ring. Marco the Fence promised to get back to her.

After a quick search of the kitchen, Talia found the grocery's telephone number. The clerk seemed stunned when she placed a delivery order. "A woman in Calum Tallchief's house? You bet. We'll have this delivery over there in no time. Oh, sure. We have watercress.... Er...uh...we'll send someone down to the creek for fresh-grown. I can't believe it. Calum brought home a woman. Hey, lady, are you the one with the red sports car hooked to the back of his rig?"

"I am. I'm his new housekeeper. My car seems to be missing its distributor cap. I'd love to locate a new one before winter settles in. I hope you have a wonderful fish market here—" Talia frowned as the clerk's snickers became roaring laughter, apparently shared by the other customers.

The groceries arrived within half an hour, and the deliveryman never stopped grinning. "Hot dog. Calum brought home a woman," he exclaimed as she signed the bill.

"Is that a novelty?"

"Huh? Oh, no, ma'am. Brings 'em home all the time. Herds of them. Tall...short...all kinds. Lots of women," the clerk answered, and chuckled as he closed the door behind him. He motioned to a passing truck and ran out onto the road. Several pickup trucks stopped, with the drivers looking and pointing and grinning at Calum's house. Then the sheriff's patrol car passed by with the emotionally charged music of an Italian opera, and the small convention dispersed instantly.

Talia packed away the groceries, then explored Calum's home. Of wood and stone, the house was sleek and functional, revealing little about the man. Elspeth's weaving perfectly tempered the sterile browns and creams. Upstairs, Calum's closets and dresser were neat; in a framed picture, a younger, happier Calum held a beautiful woman dressed in a wedding gown against him. A small pain shot through Talia's heart; Calum had loved deeply. She ached for all the bright expectations of the groom, and for the hardened man Calum was now. There was no denying the blatant sexuality of the blue-eyed, black-haired woman. She had a haunting face and a lush body that curved intimately against Calum's. The faces in the photograph smiled at Talia, making her uneasy. The woman and Calum had already been lovers, and judging by the way the woman's

hand rested possessively on Calum's flat stomach, she'd
wanted him then.

Talia's fingers shook as she replaced the photograph. She
didn't want to know Calum's secrets or sense the heat running between the people in the photograph. She closed her
eyes and placed her hands over her stomach. Calum still
loved the woman, keeping the photograph when nothing
else feminine remained in the house. His private bathroom
bore his scent, his shaving gear neatly arranged. She leaned
against the wall, stunned by her sudden need to see him.
Unused to needing anyone, to a sense of homecoming,
Talia shook her head. She wouldn't have Calum affecting
her, deterring her from her revenge. Nor did she want to
realize the torrid sexuality of his past.

She bit her lip. She'd never been jealous, but now there
was no denying the hot crush of it. Just that much more
reason to run like the very devil from him...

She picked the lock of another room and entered the
shadows of a different century. A bow and a beaded,
fringed quiver of arrows hung on the wall with a brilliantly
colored war shield. A large wooden bowl was filled with
balls of homespun yarn. Carved wooden spoons and trench-
ers lay beside it. A length of Tallchief plaid lay tossed
aside, and Talia held it high. The kilt would look gorgeous
with the man's ruffled shirt hanging on the wall.

Elspeth's weaving was beautiful. Talia studied the plaid
and then laid it aside. She lifted the cuff of the shirt to her
nose. Calum's scent swirled around her, a mixture of soap
and male.

She moved through the shadows, touching what was evidently very dear to Calum Tallchief. A huge old knife
gleamed, stuck deep in a weathered board bearing the Tallchief brand, a stick man and a mountain.

A blanket of Native American design covered an old,
comfortable couch, out of place in Calum's modern home.

Another wooden bowl, full of amulets and beads, gleamed in the dim light. Drawn to it, Talia lifted a delicately crafted necklace of blue and red beads.

A folded pale doeskin vest, exquisite with beaded flowers and fringes, lay soft beneath her fingers. Talia touched old ledgers, the books worn, yet obviously treasured. She lifted a framed photograph of the Tallchief family. The adult Tallchiefs looked at each other with love, their happy brood cuddled against them. Talia's fingertip traced Calum, already wearing glasses. He'd been a bright-looking, angular boy, his happy expression bearing no resemblance to the man he was now. Talia mourned the shadows of his life.

The door opened slowly, and Calum filled it, a broad-shouldered Western male with his legs spread in a show-down stance. Talia swallowed, and a little warning trickle of fear shot up her spine. "Can I help you find anything?" he asked, too softly, as he removed his glasses.

His face was shadowed, yet there was no mistaking the set of his shoulders as he walked toward her. She realized instantly that she had found his deepest center, his heart's lair, where he was vulnerable and yet protective of what was his. The lifting of the hair on her nape told her that Calum considered everything in this room his, including her. There was no mistaking the purpose of the graceful male moving toward her. She would pay for entering his privacy. Talia backed against the wall and tried to paste a fearless expression on her face. "Home so soon, darlin'? Gee, that's a great kilt. I bet you'd look marvy—"

One of Calum's big hands flattened on the wall beside her, and the other wrapped gently around the nape of her neck. His thumb began to move slowly, caressing her skin. His voice was too soft. "Your heart is beating like a frightened rabbit's. Are you afraid of me, of being caught here?"

"Get…back…" Talia flattened against the wall. Close to her, Calum was too big, too powerful, and too dangerous.

She'd always loved a good challenge, and that was what all six feet four inches of Calum Tallchief offered. She could meet him any day, on any plane. "Move, Tallchief."

"When I'm ready."

She wasn't waiting. She pushed hard against his stomach and found it unrelenting. Calum's hand slid from her neck to her back, and flattened her against him, in a movement so quick she couldn't protest. "Lady, you are nothing but trouble."

She'd never been possessed, held so tightly that her heart beat against a man's. Instantly her body dismissed the clothing between them, her hunger and fascination startling her. Something dark, fierce and primitive stilled and heated the air between them. Then Calum moved, and Talia found herself tumbling onto the spacious woven couch.

In the shadows, he lay over her, his weight confining but not hurting. Fascinated by the shadows of his face, by the heat burning between them, Talia managed to breathe as his gaze swept her mouth and lingered on her throat.

A taker, she thought distantly. A man who would not be denied. Nor would she.

He had not hurt her; he waited for her to answer the sensations running hotly, tautly between them. Calum was controlled now, waiting for her permission. He would leave her—if she wanted. He'd given her a choice.

Softness shifted within her, answering, soothing, wanting. She fought the need of her hips to lift to him, and feared the demand of his body against hers. Talia lowered her lashes to shield her emotions. The position was too intimate, too demanding, and Calum suited too well the role of the dominant male possessing a woman he wanted.

Her heart lurched wildly. She'd lived her life with excitement and sometimes danger, but Calum represented a feast of both. She would take this moment. She placed her hands on his shoulders and gripped him.

His eyes held hers as his hand moved slowly to cover her breast, to enclose the unbound softness, gently, firmly. He sucked in his breath, and she trembled. Or was it him?

His hand rested upon her possessively, not moving, not hurting. "You're frightened, aren't you?"

"I'm not afraid of anything, Tallchief," she managed, in a voice that was too soft and husky to be threatening. Her fingers pressed into his shoulders, yet did not force him away. She caught her breath as his hand opened, his fingertips smoothing her skin.

Slowly his eyes lowered upon her body.

Unable to deny herself, Talia looked to where her black sweater had come free from its buttons. To where his hand covered her bare breast.

There in the shadows, she watched his thumb move slowly across her nipple, peaking it.

Unable to look away, Talia met the glitter of his gray eyes. "You're heavy, you know."

"Am I? Are you uncomfortable? Why are you shaking?" Though his tone seemed almost clinical, hot steel flashed in his eyes.

"That's you, Tallchief."

He shifted between her legs, only layers of denim separating his desire from her. "Petrovna, you're burning like a furnace. If I put my mouth on that fine white skin, you'll ignite."

Her breath caught. She fought the need to grasp his arrogant black head and bring it to her breast. Her fingers fluttered upon his taut shoulders.

"Your eyes are huge. What do you want me to do?" His voice was deep, mysterious, fascinating. "This?"

He slowly eased aside her sweater to caress her other breast. She cried out, arching to his touch and thoroughly shocking herself. Then, with a moan, she locked her arms around his neck and tugged at him.

Calum didn't budge. "You're used to having things your way, Petrovna. Not this time. After what I've been through with you, I like having you under me and obedient."

"*Obedient?* Don't you dare think for one minute that you can use sex—"

Calum slowly lowered his head and took her mouth. He tasted of everything she wanted—passion, mystery, heat, storms…. She allowed his tongue to enter her lips, taking up the fascinating rhythm with her own. Then he began to nibble on her bottom lip, tugging on it. He bit gently on her earlobe, his breath swirling warmly, roughly, upon her skin.

His kiss tormented, possessed, teased, lingered and took. She was vaguely aware of the purring deep in her throat. Her legs moved along his, allowing him deeper into the cradle of her body. She thought she heard him murmur, "Jasmine and silk," and then she gasped as his hot face fitted against her throat, his kisses over her skin leaving heat as they passed.

His open lips found her aching breast, tugged at it, and she cried out softly again, sensitive to the erotic suckling. Calum's hand moved down her body, cupping her hips, lifting her to him. There was a movement at her waist, and she gasped as his warm hand flattened possessively on her bare stomach. "Calum…"

She bit his throat—a slight, instinctive nibble—because he tasted so good.

The sound running through his throat pleased her, a rough, deep yearning.

She almost cried out as his fingers found her, stroked her, warmed her into flowing, melting honey. She held him tightly and gave, moving her hips higher, undulating and lifting herself to his touch. Calum's breath caught, and his hand gently eased away. "What are you doing?" she managed when he lifted his head, looking down at her with an amused tenderness.

"You're very tight, Petrovna. Chances are you're a damned hot, wet, eager, jasmine-scented virgin. I might have known you couldn't be trusted to play fair." Yet Calum's voice was soft, his lips moving across the tears on her cheeks.

"I might not be," she threw back at him in her defense. "But thanks for the anatomy lesson, anyway." She wished she wasn't shaking violently and that he wasn't wearing a beguiling, pleased masculine smile. Trust a man like this one, a methodical, low-down, no-good expert kisser to discover she hadn't been—

"So, despite all your accomplishments, you haven't been touched. And you ignite when my mouth is on you."

"I do not. I was faking. You are terribly out-of-date. Everyone knows that men like that sort of thing. At least in my experience, they do." She ached horribly from the need to have him touch her. Tears burned her eyes. She realized with horror that she was shaking fiercely. "Don't you kiss me, Tallchief. I despise you. I'd rather kiss Godzilla with two heads."

"You like kissing me, Petrovna. Admit it." He chuckled; it was a disarming sound. Then he shifted, drawing her to his side, and placed her head upon his chest. Talia wished that she hadn't cuddled instinctively closer to his hard body, that her leg hadn't ensnared his and that her arm hadn't wrapped around his waist. He wasn't going anywhere just yet. She wasn't ready to release him. Beneath her cheek, she could hear Calum's heart racing.

He stroked her temple, and rocked her against him. She felt a little as Megan must have, warm and safe and cherished. "Better?" he asked in a tender tone that disarmed her.

She wouldn't admit her needs, not if he poured honey

on her and placed her on an anthill. But she wouldn't let him go, either. She flattened her hand on his chest and traced the breadth slowly. She traced Tallchief's stone, a part of Calum's inheritance. Beneath the worn flannel shirt, his nipples peaked against her palm. She slowly moved her palm again, fascinated by the hard nubs. Calum sucked in his breath as she moved her hand downward.

She wanted to touch him. To enfold his strength in her hand and explore— He caught her wrist and drew her hand to his lips. "Don't."

Talia stared at him. She scrambled over Calum, pausing as a big hand smoothed her bottom in a caress. Then she made the mistake of looking back at him.

He sprawled there in the shadows, all delicious male, a grin on his face. She blinked at the tenderness and the soft invitation in his voice. "Come here, Petrovna. You're shaking in your boots."

The hair on the nape of her neck lifted. She glanced down his hard body to find his jeans very tight across his hips. His blatant sexuality frightened her. Or was it herself and her need to feast upon him? She'd never let a man come so close to her, touch her, place his mouth upon her and tear the very hunger from her femininity. Talia blinked. Calum was very pleased with himself, this arrogant, sexy, all-dynamite male that she couldn't possibly have let— She backed up and gripped a ball of yarn. For once she didn't trust herself. She pelted him with yarn balls as he slowly rose, his shirt opened by her fingers, and walked to her.

Talia, who never blushed, found that her face was hot. She eased back into the shadows, hoping he wouldn't notice. Calum very gently buttoned her sweater, and the sweetness of the gesture almost caused her tears to return. "What's for lunch?" he asked gently.

She sniffed, uncertain and wary and not pleased about the blush running hotly down her body. Calum wasn't playing by her rules. She'd have to find that darn ring and free herself. Olson needed— "Lunch?"

He smoothed a strand of hair across his hand and wrapped it around his finger, studying the shades. "You're the housekeeper, remember? You're supposed to cook for me."

"Listen, you jerk. I have never liked the idea of me Tarzan, you Jane—"

He ran his thumb over her thick braid and drew it to her breast. His fingertips grazed her flushed cheek. "Wear a bra from now on, Petrovna. My brothers will be here shortly. Birk is unmarried and looking."

She lifted her chin. She didn't want to be enchanted by Calum's hot sultry look. No man had a right to be that enticing. "You just can't trust nerds to be what they're supposed to be anymore," she stated haughtily, before walking out of the room on unsteady legs.

Behind her, Calum stated softly, "Petrovna, you've got a bad habit of wanting the last word. I find that a challenge."

She sensed then, with a trickle of fear, that Duncan Tallchief wasn't the only Tallchief male with possessive carry-woman-home tendencies.

Calum placed a boot on his fireplace and surveyed his ruined kingdom. He glanced at his previously uncluttered living room, where boxes of Talia's clothing had been opened and scattered everywhere. Emily, Duncan's stepdaughter, had arrived with her kittens, now playing amid a stack of frothy lace lingerie. A red lace teddy had been tossed on one of his lamps, and a huge chest of costume jewelry, all of which made noise, was open. Talia had screamed with delight when her things arrived, and, fascinated, Calum had stood back to watch her rip open the boxes and tear out the colorful clothing.

She enchanted him, a woman who seemed worldly-wise but who'd blushed furiously, her eyes huge, when he approached her upstairs. He'd found her in the midst of everything that was dear to him, and his instincts had told him that she belonged to him, that she was his and where she should be. His first impulse had been to lay her down and make love to her amid the treasures of his family, his life.

He wanted to be in her, to be captured by her warmth, held close and—

Calum's entire body ached to claim Talia's and to cherish her. The knowledge rocked everything that was safe within him, the barriers that he had placed around his heart.

He was still shaken by her virginity. She'd ignited under him, and the feel of her skin beneath his mouth would torture him for hours. The movement of her hips arching up to his touch could drive a man insane— Her blush had sent him walking on air.

Later, at his kitchen table, Duncan and Birk were eyeing tiny watercress-and-cucumber sandwiches. Emily had run all the way from school, stopping only to pick up her kittens, to meet Calum's guest. She'd arrived breathless, with a carload of boys following her. Duncan, Birk and Calum had immediately gone to the porch and glared at the boys, to Emily's horror.

Talia carefully ladled asparagus soup into bowls; it was uncommon fare in beef-and-potatoes Amen Flats. Dressed in a hot-pink top tied in a knot beneath her breasts and a long sarong-style skirt over skintight pants, Talia added basil sprigs to the platter of tiny sandwiches. Her artistic flourishes caused her bangle bracelets to jingle. The crystal drops flowing from her ears caught the sun and lit her skin. Calum scowled at the length of straight blond hair swaying down to her waist as she moved. He found himself staring at the undulating sway of her hips. No woman should move with that sensuality.

Talia caught his glare and tossed him a challenging smile. She patted him on the top of the head as she passed to sit by Birk.

Emily grinned up at Duncan as he frowned at the soup. The teenager touched the rhinestone beauty-queen tiara on her head, evidence of Talia's jaunt in the glamorous world of the pageant runway. "Eat up, Dad. It's just good old everyday asparagus soup."

Fresh in from taking cattle to a lower pasture on Tallchief Mountain, Duncan and Birk eyed the tiny sandwiches suspiciously. "Grass," Duncan stated finally, after probing the watercress.

"She's a gourmet cook. Took classes in France. Burned up a top chef's kitchen. He went into a sanitorium to recuperate." Calum's body vibrated with the need to take Talia. Every time she came close, he caught the scent of jasmine that arose from her skin. He wanted to order everyone out and kiss Talia until she melted.

He wanted those soft lips on his. She'd just thrown him a curve, and he was still reeling from his emotions. He began to feel the weight of Alek's and Papa Petrovna's concern. Despite Talia's sexy look and adventures, she had no idea what an aroused male could do.

Calum frowned at the tiny watercress sandwich. He resented her threat to his life and his control and his reputation. He understood the chef's lawsuit against the cooking school for letting Talia into his class.

Talia shrugged, and her bangles tinkled. "André wanted more flames in my cherries jubilee. I gave them to him. I couldn't help it if the curtains ignited. You know, I'd love to do a really good bouillabaisse with French bread. Is there a good fish market here?"

"Ma'am, I'd be happy to take you fishing. Tallchief Lake offers some of the best there is." Birk's grin widened, and for the first time, the keen edge of jealousy pricked Calum.

"*I'll* take her." Calum eased the delicious asparagus soup into his mouth and tried not to look at the woman who had folded gracefully to the floor to cuddle a kitten. Calum had compromised his reputation, linked up with a woman who acted like a temptress but whose body had never been touched, and had just agreed to spend his afternoon fishing, when he should have been tearing out her secrets. Talia nuzzled the kitten, and Calum felt himself go weak. Alek Petrovna would skin him alive if anything happened to her. Talia was set on ruining Olson, who was probably very experienced at forcing and blackmailing women.

Calum's house was infested with Tallchief men, an array of sexy and colorful clothing, a woman who wanted to cook bouillabaisse in beef-eating rural Wyoming…and a younger brother who was leering at Talia— Calum wanted to pick her up and run to his favorite spot on Tallchief Mountain. He scowled at Elspeth's woven place mat. An action like that—carrying off Talia—would prove she had gotten to him. He was a controlled man, a logical man. He did not allow his emotions to rule him.

Calum looked up to see Duncan grinning broadly at him. "Find that ring yet?" Duncan asked.

"I will," Talia said confidently as she stroked the kitten on her lap. "I'd love to hear the legend attached to it."

"He didn't tell you? Mmm… That's why we call him Calum the cool. Has to do with—" Birk began, then closed his lips when Duncan lifted a warning eyebrow.

Calum stared at her and noted the slightly swollen curve of her lips caused by his kisses. *When a man of Fearghus blood places the ring upon the right woman's finger, he'll capture his true love forever.*

Without thinking about the consequences of his next move, Calum stood. He placed his hat on his head, then grabbed a warm jacket and stuffed Talia into it. He stooped to pluck her up and place her across his shoulder. He walked out the door, carrying a startled, indignant woman. Duncan's and Birk's laughter followed him. They stood at the door, grinning, as he placed her on his Arabian stallion and swung up in front of her. Birk came at a run, bearing Calum's extra jeans, a bag of collapsible fishing poles and a tackle box. He tossed the jeans to Talia and swung the bag over the saddle horn. ''You might need this, brother.''

''He's going to need more than that. You can't just sling me over your shoulder like that. I am not a sack of potatoes,'' Talia stated warningly.

''I'll say,'' Birk returned appreciatively with a grin.

''Dibs.'' Calum heard himself mutter the Tallchiefs' boyhood term for possession. He disliked the unstable emotions coursing through him and the knowledge that Duncan had claimed Sybil, using the same word. The woman seated behind him wearing a filmy skirt, body-molding pants and tall black leather boots would make any man act irrationally. Calum realized that he had just placed his hand, gloved in rough work leather, possessively upon her knee. Talia had very nice knees.

''Hey, Birk!'' Duncan called from the steps. He wrapped his arm around Emily, at his side. ''Lacey just called. She wants you to know that she's bought all the roofing nails in Amen Flats. She hopes you won't be late on that roofing contract.''

Birk's grin died. He scowled and stalked toward his horse.

''What's that about?'' Talia asked, holding her breath as Birk raced his horse for a fence and cleared it beautifully.

"Don't ask. Lacey MacCandliss and Birk have been warring for years. She's a builder, and his competition." Calum stopped talking.

Talia smiled behind his back. "Gotcha. You almost told me something I wanted to know. You could make this all easier if you'd tell me everything I want to know and if you'd let me find that ring and if you'd trade me Olson for it. As my accomplice, I'd think you'd want to make things easy for me."

Calum turned slightly, looking over his shoulder, down at her. His expression told her that nothing would be easy with Calum Tallchief. She'd have to fight him every step of the way. He lifted one thick black brow, then turned around, leaving her with his broad back.

Talia smiled and wrapped her arms around him. She leaned her cheek against his back and cuddled close to his warmth. There was just something old-fashioned and sweet about the way he'd plucked her from the midst of his family. This man had touched her intimately—because she'd let him—and she wallowed in the thought that she had shocked him. "Did you love her?" she asked, her heart stopping as she waited for his answer.

His answer took a long time. She sensed him considering the past when he returned, "She's never been in my house. She hated the country." Calum's answer snapped back to her on the chilling wind.

She slid her hand inside his jacket and found the stone. He allowed the trespass, and she snuggled closer, surprised that she wanted to soothe him and wrap him safely in her arms. "Then…you never took her to your cabin, either, right?"

She edged higher, and watched, fascinated, as Calum's cheek flushed. "Shut up, Petrovna," he murmured easily, and pressed her hand to the stone.

Her heart did a happy little flip-flop. "You know, Tall-chief? I'm getting to you. I'll have you right in the palm of my hand before you know it."

Five

"Calum yells? I thought Birk was the only Tallchief male who did that." Lacey MacCandliss grinned over the mug of "brewski" with which she had just toasted Talia. It was Tuesday, ladies' night at Maddy's Hot Spot. Sybil, Elspeth, Lacey and Talia were sharing a table, upon which Maddy had placed a vase of battered silk roses. The forgotten price tag on one dusty rose trembled when Lacey removed her battered work boots from the table and her chair hit the floor.

Talia continued her story. "All I was doing was standing on a log and rolling it on the water to angle for a better place to fish. I just happened to be holding the stringer of fish we'd caught, and when he yelled, it slipped from my hand. I'm an expert logroller…learned how in Canada…the lumberjacks were only too happy to teach me. Calum didn't have to dive into the lake and push me to safety. He could have unbalanced me, and that water is so cold. When I was ready, I could have simply walked the log back to shore. When we rode back to the house, I couldn't tell if his teeth were gritting or chattering. I hope he doesn't catch cold. He is in a foul and evil mood, for some reason.''

Talia smiled to herself. Though she had been terrified when Calum dived into the water, he had responded magnificently to her administrations when they arrived home. For a moment, she'd thought that he might tug her into his hot, steaming shower. The thought had appealed; Calum, she had learned, was a very sensual man, and one who touched carefully, gently. She would have trusted him to take her into his keeping; she'd wanted him desperately, wanted to hold him and soothe the pain that she sensed lurking near his leashed emotions. Then he'd muttered something to himself and firmly closed the door. He had glared at her and muttered again when she made him lunch—this time with a dark, menacing tone—but had drunk every drop of her chicken soup. She was getting to him. No doubt about it.

Talia grinned at Lacey, who had come soaring up to Calum's house on her big black motorcycle. With a getaway driver at hand and a chance to nettle Calum, Talia had hitched up her tiny black skirt and hopped on the back. Ladies' night at Maddy's was just what she needed. Maddy, the beefy bartender-owner, served lemonade, nonalcoholic beer, and drinks for those who wanted them. A former pro football player, he had covered the pictures of naked ladies with sheets and had saturated the tavern with flowery air freshener in honor of the female customers. He wore a black T-shirt without holes, and a bow tie. A lemon sucker replaced his usual cigar. Patty Jo Black, a sizable farm wife with a steamy voice dipped in rhythm and blues, played rock and roll on the piano.

A big banner, painted by a ranch wife with five children, was spread across the mirror Maddy protected in every

fight. The banner read No garden planting, childbirth, or
Intelligent and Beautiful Children stories allowed. The
ladies of Amen Flats relaxed, teased each other about the
latest hunk's taut backside, discussed soap operas and relaxed around the tavern. Sybil, dressed in a classic gray
cardigan set and slacks, smiled at Talia. "Duncan yells
sometimes—I just thought I'd share that. It's really quite
lovely when he does. I find a good out-and-out battle in-
vigorating at times—he's usually so controlled."

Elspeth shook her head. "My brothers never yelled while
we were fighting to stay together. Those times were grim,
with the child authorities wanting to take away everyone
but Duncan. He was just eighteen, and took legal responsibility for all of us. We had family friends, but we were
so frightened back then. I remember Calum working all
night at accounts—juggling them—until a couple hours before the school bus arrived and then going to school. Even
in our darkest times, they quietly shielded us, and they
never raised their voices."

Sybil's sleek, knotted hair gleamed like rich copper as
she leaned closer; a faint sprinkle of freckles dusted her
nose. Sybil had had her own dark times. She understood
fear, and to lighten the moment she shared a secret about
Duncan. "The thing that Duncan does even better than the
Tallchief kiss is roar magnificently. He looks so horrified
when he's discovered he's yelled. Poor baby. Since Emily
has turned fifteen and is wanting to date, he's really been
distracted. His brothers have joined him in protecting her
against marauding teenage boys."

"The Tallchief kiss?" Talia remembered Calum's mouth
tormenting, teasing hers, fascinating her into a dark, stormy
world heated by the pulse of her own heartbeat.

"They should bottle it." Sybil grinned. "The first time
Duncan kissed me, I—" She flushed elegantly. "Actually,
he's quite...passionate." Her blush deepened.

Elspeth snorted delicately. "Surviving as a teenage girl who wanted to date wasn't easy in our family. My brothers frightened every male in the territory. The three of them would just stand there, thumbs hooked in their belts, legs spread like gunfighters, and stare. That's all it took. A simple Tallchief staredown, and the boys ran for safety. Fiona and I were outraged."

Sybil grinned. "That's exactly what they do. Look deadly, when they're really just big pushover pussycats. They're perfect with Emily, except when it comes to her growing up and dating. She loves them, but is planning revenge with a party at our house. Duncan is chaperoning. Birk is to assist. I believe Calum's last crime was plucking a prime candidate right from her pucker. She thinks Talia is a great payback."

"*Moi?*" Talia lifted her eyebrows innocently. She liked these women and their warmth. Lacey was a recognized member of the family. With short black curly hair and a height well under the Tallchiefs', Lacey was quick to grin, yet elements of sadness lay beneath her surface.

Lacey glanced outside Maddy's tavern to the well-lit street. "Calum's four-wheeler is out there. I see three heads, probably Duncan and Birk with him. Emily is staying overnight at a friend's, but Duncan probably has Megan with him—they're starting the car, probably to warm it up. Ladies' night at Maddy's has always driven Birk nuts. He can't stand the thought of women being holed up without him. He is so disgusting around women, such a flirt. But Calum surprises me. I never heard of an employer keeping such close tabs on his housekeeper."

Elspeth shook her head. "I was hoping no one would notice them. Megan is having a wonderful time out there with the three of them doting on her. They're probably doing some bop-shoo-wop song for her right now. No doubt my brothers are overheated while Megan is perfectly

comfortable. They're probably discussing how silly it is to
have a baby out on an October night.''

Talia glanced at her. ''You seem to have a sixth sense
regarding your family.''

''It's a shaman thing, and maybe a bit from Una Fearghus's Celtic ancestors,'' Lacey offered. ''Elspeth feels it
sometimes about me.'' She met Elspeth's quiet gaze. ''Like
the time Elspeth knew my mother— Well, my mother
wasn't a happy woman, and she took it out on me. Elspeth
told her mother. I never saw Pauline Tallchief in a high
temper but once, and that was when she called my mother
out. That was what she did—called her out and promised
her, not threatened her, but promised my mother what she
would do to her if anything happened to me. I never saw
my mother so scared as when she saw Pauline Tallchief.''

Lacey traced the top of her beer mug thoughtfully. ''I
grew up eating more at the Tallchief table and being protected by them than in my own home. Pauline rocked me
on her lap as though I was one of her own, and took care
of me when I was sick, too. They all did. At school, the
Tallchiefs were right there when things got bad for me.''

Elspeth's hand rested on Lacey's. ''We've always loved
you.''

Talia caught the tears shimmering in Lacey's eyes before
she turned away. Lacey shielded her pain well. She glanced
at Talia. ''Elspeth made me a kilt, just like the rest of her
family. You should see the three Tallchief brothers dressed
up in kilts and ruffled shirts…all dark and dangerous and
snarling at the world because of it. But they do it because
it means so much to Elspeth. Darn near takes my breath
away. Put Elspeth into the picture and it's worth a tear. So
tell me, Talia, how did you meet Calum?''

Talia flicked a silk rose petal. She wasn't looking forward to another night in Calum's house. After Calum's
devastating warm, slow kisses, and his gentle hands trea-

suring her, heating her body, she'd remained one big blush. She didn't like him knowing that she wasn't all that worldly. She glanced at the women, saw their strength and decided that they would understand. She told them the truth about Olson's sexual harassment of January, and how he had destroyed her happiness, and other women's as well. How Calum had prowled through her crimes and wanted her to ignore her revenge.

"Men," Sybil muttered darkly.

"They don't understand," Elspeth stated gently, but her gray eyes had a steely glint that reminded Talia of Calum's concealed temper. "He shouldn't have interfered. You were doing a marvelous job."

"I agree with you, Talia. You were taking the only course to really teach Olson a lesson and protect other women from the same fate. Olson's downfall definitely needs a feminine touch." Sybil glanced toward the street. "Sometimes Tallchief men are so protective of us that they forget we have needs of our own—a sisterhood thing. I thought Duncan would explode when he discovered that Elspeth and I were...well, keeping tabs on our own sleaze-ball here in Amen Flats. It was nothing more than a few documented accounts of Sleazy's visits, with some excellent night photography involved."

"Duncan was worried when you went on a stakeout in that field with the buffalo. But it is important to help another woman on a level that does her the most good," Elspeth added.

"I'm for it. As a kid, I went through things with sleazes like Olson—men my mother brought home. Sometimes they need more than a legal slap or a thinning of their pocketbooks. They need something potent enough to shake their slimy guts and put fear in them. Any way I can help?"

Talia sat very straight and smiled primly. "Actually, there is." She flicked a mischievous glance at Elspeth. "I really wouldn't want to cause the Tallchief family problems, but I do have a debt of honor to complete my mission.''

Elspeth glanced toward the men sitting outside in the vehicle. She tilted her head slightly and studied the roses. ''Good. Birk and Duncan are leaving. Duncan is afraid that Calum's sneezing will make Megan catch cold.... You're going after Una's ring, and you want to trade it for a release from Calum. You want to finish the job you started, with no interference from him.'' Elspeth lifted one sleek, questioning eyebrow at Talia.

''You guessed it. Petrovna's Law. We always finish what we start.''

For an instant, Elspeth's fine black brows drew together, her gray eyes darkened as though remembering something unpleasant. ''Does you brother, Alek, always finish what he starts?''

''Petrovna's Law,'' Talia stated firmly with a nod.

''Has anyone ever finished anything for him?'' The steely edge in Elspeth's soft voice startled the other women.

Lacey recovered with a quick grin, nodding toward a well-built male at a nearby table. ''I'd like to finish plenty with him. Nice buns.''

Sybil, Elspeth and Lacey looked at each other. They began to grin. ''Shall we tell her the legend of the ring?'' Sybil asked.

''Not just yet. I really think that is Calum's place,'' Elspeth murmured, her eyes lighting.

''Yeah. Let her find out on her own,'' Lacey said with a cheeky grin. She dangled the key to an aged commuter plane. ''Will this help? If you can manage a takeoff from a paved country road. I borrowed it from a client to scoop all the roofing nails from the nearest towns. Then I called Birk's logical shipping supplier and anonymously questioned his credit. Birk wasn't happy.''

* * *

Five days later, Calum lowered a small, sleek jet into
position. He placed the landing pattern between the two
rows of torches on the desert. Prince Kadar Abd al Jabbar's
men stood beside the fine blooded Arabian horses, calming
them as the plane dipped neatly through the night onto the
runway. As Calum taxied to a stop, the desert night spread
out upon the endless sands of the small, primitive country,
far from civilization.

Calum resented his anger, a gift from Talia. When he
first discovered Talia had come here, terror had gripped
him. Anything could happen to her. Gradually he'd worked
his way through fear to anger. He preferred anger when
dealing with Talia; it was safer. He was letting his emotions
show. Talia's latest escapade was too dangerous, far more
so than Olson's blackmail. He hadn't discovered her getaway until Wednesday night. He'd forgotten how effective
Elspeth could be as an accomplice when she set her mind
to it. Disguised as Talia, Elspeth had walked to his home
while Talia borrowed Lacey's motorcycle and commuter
plane.

Calum hadn't had an old-fashioned cold since childhood,
but he had one now, thanks to Talia's logrolling incident.
When Calum's bad mood and temperature rose, Elspeth had
felt obliged to explain that Talia had gone after the ring.
Four days of headaches, fever and sneezing had primed
Calum for his personal revenge on Talia Petrovna.

Calum regretted the language he'd used on Marco, Nose
and Vinnie as he tracked Talia by telephone and sipped his
hot lemonade remedy. Alek Petrovna's yelling hadn't
helped Calum's headache or anger. The Petrovnas were
emotional people, and multilingual. Calum didn't want to
know how the Russian threats translated, he just wanted to
get his hands on Talia. She had entered a world where

women were still considered chattel, despite Kadar's firm
hand in changing his small country.

From a bed laden with tissues and aspirin, Calum had
managed to pacify Olson and track Talia. She'd made contact with Marco, Vinnie and Nose. Vinnie had sold a ring
answering the description of Una's to a sheikh at the Denver airport. The sheikh had been en route to Cairo, then to
his small, primitive kingdom nearby. Talia had imperson-
ated a stewardess, traveled to Cairo and jumped the next
camel train to follow the suspect sheikh. After Calum's call,
Kadar had simply located her and purchased her.

Kadar welcomed Calum as he stepped from the plane.
"My friend! So you have come to claim your butterfly,
no?" He hugged Calum warmly, then motioned to his man,
who slid a billowing cloak around Calum's shoulders and
adjusted a flowing headdress around his head.

The sand, blown by the fierce wind, stung his face, and
Calum expertly tucked a portion of the headdress across his
face. "Kadar, I thank you."

Kadar chuckled and nodded graciously, in the custom of
his country. "Your tone is that of the frustrated hunter.
True, the woman is maddening and skilled in almost anything, especially disguises. After so many women hunting
you, it pleases me that you have met your match. I have
followed your instructions. She is being prepared now by
the women of my tribe. They only consented to leave their
luxuries and homes to play the nomads of their ancestry
because I told them of your love for the woman and how
she flees you. In the name of romance, they help you, but
also mourn that it is not one of them you wish as a bride.
Or a love slave. So this one you want enough to come after
her, to keep her safe, no? This is the first woman that I can
remember who causes the fire to come to your eyes. Maybe
to your heart, eh, old friend?"

In his native robes and poised in the desert night, Kadar

looked like a sheikh of his ancestry. Actually, he was a modern man, infuriated by the age-old status of women in his country. As a ruler and politician, he battled to protect his country and to bring it into the contemporary world. Together Kadar and Calum had fought terrorists and slave traders, and Kadar's thumb bore the Tallchief scar. Calum grinned. "Fiona is fine."

While skiing in a Swiss resort, Calum had saved Kadar's sister from an avalanche. Kadar had instantly invited Calum and Fiona—both were on vacation—to visit his palace, and Fiona had caused trouble from the first moment.

Kadar snorted. "That one in there with the evil temper. She almost caused a revolt when you brought her to my palace. Nor is this woman gentle. My bodyguard is sulking back at the palace. She has bested him in wrestling. Is that Russian she curses in so fluently?"

"Among other things. She likes to revert to Apache threats of ants and honey."

Kadar frowned thoughtfully at Calum as they walked to their horses. "If you call for help, we shall both be embarrassed. You know, my friend, I have never seen you so emotional. Do not snort so, you will frighten the horses. I think you are like the stallion catching the scent of the mare, no?"

Talia tugged the tiny beaded bodice downward. The red silk garment was tight, and cut very low to emphasize her breasts. She jingled when she moved, because of the bells on the filmy gold-and-red harem pants. The distance between the bodice and the off-the-hip harem pants showed a smooth expanse of her waist. The golden rings on her toes glistened in the light of the lamps scattered around the elaborate tent. She shook her head, and the string of pearls across her forehead quivered. The tribe was quiet now, and she was left with two hulking bodyguards who watched her closely. An elaborate feast had been prepared by the women flowing through the massive tent. Above their veils, their sloe eyes watched her curiously. Behind a film of curtains was an immense low pallet, scattered with tasseled pillows.

Talia shuddered and wrapped her arms around herself. Her body had been bathed, pampered, scented and oiled for the sheikh who was expected to arrive later. Arabic was one language she hadn't studied, but there was no denying she was in a fix. She felt like the primed and stuffed Thanksgiving turkey, properly buttered, ready for the man who was to arrive. She was certain it wasn't Kadar. He didn't act interested in her at all.

She swallowed the fear that had been nagging her since the sheikh, her previous owner, discovered her trading rock-and-roll tapes to one of his wives for the ring. The sheikh was fat, and greedy for her. He'd reluctantly sold her to a rank-pulling prince, who had arrived in full native garb, with a scimitar at his side.

In the midst of bartering, the sheikh had forgotten about the ring. Talia hadn't. She looked down, checking the ring securely tucked in the perfumed crevice of her breasts. All she had to do was steal a camel, make it across a freezing desert and slip back into her cozy stewardess outfit.

A dark-eyed woman moved swiftly toward Talia, clucking softly, comfortingly. She dabbed a silk cloth at Talia's eyes, which were lined with kohl. ''Women should stick together,'' Talia informed her, and tried not to sniff. ''I really could use good old nerdy Calum and his protective Tallchief genes now, you know.''

The woman nodded as though she understood and sympathized. Talia sniffed again. ''Petrovnas don't give up. Calum is the sort of sweet guy who leads a nice life in a small town—and I did like his family. Little Megan is a beautiful baby, with the Tallchiefs' gray eyes and black lashes.'' She shook her head at the woman, who was looking up at her sympathetically. ''But, gee whiz, my auntie Em. Calum is a great kisser, but he doesn't understand Petrovna rules. He's overly protective, and exactly what I do not want after Alek, Anton and Papa. Calum can be very sexy, though. The first time he—well, you can't understand anything, so I can speak freely—I felt like I'd been claimed when he...''

She tried not to flush and shook her head. Calum's large hands had moved over her sweetly, possessively. His coaxing lips on her breast had drawn a taut, heated, trembling response from feminine areas she hadn't known were that sensitive. She almost wished he was here to share the sumptuous bedding with her. She'd saved herself because she valued her first experience with a man. The way Calum had looked down at her tenderly, she had known he would treasure her. She closed her eyes, hoarding the moment. Calum had fitted against her perfectly, and she had felt so safe. She could use a dose of his safety now. ''It's just that I really don't want to be claimed, you know. I've been under the Petrovna males' protective thumb, and I like my life now. Lots of action and travel. Then he had to hold this baby, see? I never knew I had nerves so deep in my body, like I wanted—okay, like I wanted to have a baby...his gray-eyed, black-haired baby. Now that was frightening. I can't imagine living in one place or settling down. The whole thing is scary.''

The woman smoothed Talia's long hair and murmured sympathetically as Talia continued listing her woes. ''I just hope the prince didn't buy me too cheaply. That wouldn't be good for my ego.'' She studied the gold slave bracelet on her wrist and one on her ankle, and the tiny bells attached to them jingled merrily. ''I do like the shade of red you used on my nails and toenails. Too bad you don't understand what I'm saying.''

"My dear, you should be honored that the Desert Hawk, blood brother of Prince Kadar, has chosen you to warm his bed," the woman murmured as she moved gracefully away from Talia. While Talia dealt with the woman's perfect English, she paused before opening the tent's flap. "Many women have wanted him, yet he comes a long way to see his gift from Kadar."

"Wait! You *can* speak English!" Talia ran after the woman, stopped by the two burly guards at the tent's opening. She listened intently to the clamor outside the tent, shouts rising above high shrills and— Talia backed away as the guards parted and two big men stepped into the shadowy tent. She recognized Kadar instantly, but the other man stood in the shadows, his face shielded by his headgear. He motioned to Talia to come closer, and she shook her head. One of the guards gripped her arm and brought her into the light.

Kadar moved to a tray filled with liquors. He poured two small glasses and handed one to the other man in the shadows. "My brother, Hawk of the Desert, this is the woman I wish to give you. Turn around, woman, so that my brother may see you."

Talia resisted the guard's easy turning of her body. She looked at Kadar over her shoulder, her hair whipping around her body. "Now look here—you have no right to buy and sell women."

The Hawk loomed over Talia, his cloaked shoulders and headdress flowing around him, blocking out everything else in the tent. His black eyes glittered, coursing slowly down her body, then back to her face. Cloth concealed his jaw, and the scent of horses and leather and man wafted around her.

She took a step back and bumped into the bodyguard. He grunted painfully and removed his foot from under hers.

"Quiet, woman. She is scrawny, Kadar. Not at all enticing," the man's deep voice stated arrogantly. He came closer, only his dark eyes showing between the layers of his headdress and cloak. His finger lifted and slowly traced her breasts above the ornate low bodice. He lightly prodded the soft flesh above the bodice. He peered down at her scowl as the guard held both of her upper arms. "She is scrawny, Kadar."

The man's big hand opened and slid slowly down Talia's side, fitting in the indentation of her waist and resting on her hip. When she eased aside, his fingers were firm. He studied her navel and the soft swell of her stomach, then possessively placed his hand over her stomach. Talia sucked in her breath, because the man's eyes were burning into her. "Look," she began breathlessly as his hand circled to her back, flattened and tugged her against his unrelenting body. "Oh—"

"My dove, why do you tremble?" he whispered in a husky, deep voice. Then he bent to whisper in her ear, "You want me, yes? You want to twine those long legs around me and let me drink of the wine of your body, nourish me from the strawberries upon your pale breasts and warm me with your silken hair, do you not?"

"No!" Talia trembled at the image of the Hawk's dark body spread upon her own. She longed for good old safe Calum. She arched back, her hands outflung. "I can pay you back. I'll go into hock. I'll borrow—"

In the shadows, Kadar laughed softly, and the Hawk's dark eyes glinted with humor. "The woman could not entice a hermit. She has nothing seductive about her. Making love with her would be like caressing a board. I find my body runs cold at the thought."

"Well. That's okay with me. Let me go." Talia watched the Hawk sweep through the tent to sprawl in the shadows beside Kadar. The two men watched her intently as musicians began to pluck small stringed instruments in a seductive beat. The wind fluttered the tent walls with a rhythm that matched the fear within Talia.

"Do not talk. Dance. Try to interest me with your scrawny body," the Hawk ordered, sipping his liquor. A woman entered with a plate of hot, spicy food and watched the Hawk with hungry eyes as she served the two lords.

Talia stood very still and tapped her toe. When the bells jingled, she stopped.

Kadar leaned toward the Hawk and grinned. "She refuses. Shall I turn her over to my men now? Or just stake her in the burning sun?"

"Perhaps she is shy. Perhaps she does not know how to please a man, or to dance as a woman."

"No and yes. I've had dance lessons." Talia inhaled, then exhaled quickly. "Look, Kadar…Hawk. If I dance for you, is that a fair trade? I mean, will you let me go?"

"Begin." The Hawk sprawled in the shadows, his dark shirt and trousers flowing along the tasseled pillows. Kadar rose in a swirl of robes as he nodded and left the tent, indicating that the musicians, the guards and the woman should follow. Outside, the musicians began again, their beat seductive.

Talia slowly moved one shoulder, a concession to the dance Hawk wanted. She tapped her toe once.

"Or we can go to bed," the Hawk murmured, a motion of his hand indicating the sprawling, pillow-laden pallet behind the silken curtains.

Talia rotated her other shoulder, a bit more quickly. She bit her lip. She swallowed and began to sway with the music, intending to dance as long as the Hawk stayed awake. Then she'd borrow that huge-looking dagger he'd placed on his discarded cloak, slit a hole in the tent and escape. She moved toward him in the lamplight and refilled his glass to the brim. "You must be very thirsty after a hard day at riding the desert."

"I prefer your body without clothing." The Hawk's hand flicked open one tiny pearl button on her bodice. Then he reached for the glass and drained it slowly, while keeping her startled stare locked with his. "What is this?" The tip of his little finger caught in Una's ring and tugged.

"That is the reason I came here. I need the ring to—"

She didn't trust the way his expression immediately tensed, the way his eyes pinned hers. Talia leaped to her feet, clutching the tiny bodice to her. This man frightened her.

She saw none of Calum's tenderness in the hot-eyed Hawk. She held her bodice and poured another glass of potent liquor for him. With any luck, he'd pass out and she could make her escape. All she had to do was dance and keep his glass filled, and then she'd make her way back to Calum. She wanted him to hold her and comfort her. She would take his ring back to him and finish off Olson and find a way to make Calum her first lover. She'd soothe the shadows within him. He could do with a little chaos in his life. And a little tenderness. She would find her way back to him, grab the Tallchief stone and seize Calum Tallchief.

"Drink up. I feel like dancing."

Six

When at last Talia slept on the carpet, Calum lifted her in his arms and carried her to his bed. She hadn't noticed that his glass had been regularly emptied into a vase. Her sensuous dance, a subtle mixture of eye-popping quivers, had strained his body until he wondered if he'd recover. Her dance had been a war of wills, and for once Calum couldn't rely on his control. Finally, clearly exhausted, she had danced slower and slower until she had wilted magnificently upon the lush, huge flowers of the carpet. Una's garnet ring gleamed bloodred on Talia's finger, and Calum raised it to his lips. He had placed the ring upon her finger, and he would keep her safe.

Talia purred softly in her sleep and pressed against him as he wrapped them together in the thick silken quilt. Calum eased the string of pearls away from her forehead and gathered her closer. Talia, in a seductive mode, was a sight Calum didn't want another man to experience.

He slid the tinted black lenses from his eyes and placed them in a container. Black eyes went well with the deeper tan he had acquired under Fiona's old sunlamp.

"Mmm…Calum…" she murmured drowsily against his throat, and eased a long leg over his, her arms encircling his neck.

He held very still, his body aroused against her softness. He realized suddenly and to his horror that droplets of sweat had appeared on his forehead. Even sleeping, the woman was a disaster, a willful, thankless—

She moved over him, her hips undulating slightly against him as she whispered drowsily, "Darn. I ache all over. I know you're just a dream, but I'd really like to—"

Calum nuzzled her ear. The concession reached inside him; he realized how tenderly he felt toward her. She'd come home to rest, like a tired kitten, and he wanted to cuddle her.

"Calum, do you suppose you could…" He thought she was sleeping, but then she moved restlessly, placing his hand upon her breast. "Mmm… Like that." Then she slid off into sleep, leaving him cupping her breast and his body aching.

Talia hugged the silken quilt up to her chin. This was her second night in the tent, and desert nights were cold. Though he was gone, Hawk's presence filled their bed. He'd been off doing desert things during the day, and the entire tent had been stripped of anything she could use for clothing to escape. Again, she had been bathed, kneaded, buttered in scents and oils and left to await Hawk's arrival. Because she was aching from hours of dancing for Hawk, Talia had asked for several baths and massages during the day. It had become clear after her first tentative tries for clothing that the entire encampment was loyal to Prince Kadar's blood brother, the Desert Hawk.

Talia held up Una's ring, the three bloodred garnets set in a golden Celtic design. At least she had the Tallchief ring. The gold slave bracelets, with their bells, jingled on her wrist and on her ankle. She sniffed and dabbed the quilt to her eyes, drying them as the wind billowed inside the tent. Wind billowing in the tent was the signal that someone had arrived; it was more effective than a doorbell.

She heard Hawk speak quietly to the serving girl who had brought him dinner.

The tent quieted, and the lamps were extinguished. Talia's heart raced until the Desert Hawk swept into her veiled bedroom. He wore his robes. "So my bride anxiously awaits me," he murmured in a deep, satisfied drawl.

"Bride?" Talia went very still and blinked. "I missed that part."

He lifted a brow, his eyes black and smoldering in the dim light as they swept slowly, possessively, over her. Talia pulled the quilt up to her shoulders, only to have it slowly pulled downward by a stronger hand. He stared at her body, which instantly flushed. "So shy? I thought we dispensed with that last night."

Talia pressed her thighs together and ran a thorough quick inventory of her intimate parts as Hawk knelt down on the bed.

"Run that bride part by me again?" she asked, edging away from him.

"Surely, after last night, you have no doubts as to my claim. How you danced with ecstasy for me. Come here, my desert lily, let us begin...."

Hawk eased beneath the quilt, and Talia scooted to the other side of the bed. Talia stared at him. "Now, just a minute—"

Talia shivered, then flushed. She was finding it hard to breathe, and she stood, holding a fringed pillow to her as a shield. "Don't you have a camel to wash?"

The Hawk's dark eyes glinted in the shadows as he studied her. "Come…no need to be shy, after last night. You want me. Say it. Say it, or I will make you say it."

For the first time in her life, Talia Petrovna was scared. "Uh…I…I can't. I've got this sweet guy at home. Calum Tallchief. He's rather sweet—"

"You have no other man but me," the Hawk stated, in a low, primitive tone resembling a panther's growl. "But you amuse me. Tell me about this man."

"He loves computers. I think he's buried himself in them because he's mourning his wife. She was killed in an accident just months after they married," she managed.

He frowned thoughtfully. "Surely he would not like computers more than a woman as fiery as you. Tell me more."

"He likes order, which drives me nuts. His clothes are all organized in his closet…dull gray suits—" She sucked in her breath as Hawk rose from the bed and stood staring at her.

"You are shy. Yet you want me."

"I want only one man." Her voice surprised her; it was strong and firm.

His black eyes probed hers. "You love this Calum?"

"He's sweet. Safe and controlling. He reminds me of my brothers and my father. Very old-fashioned."

Talia cried out as Hawk slowly walked to her, lifted her and carried her to the bed.

He tossed her upon the pillows, and when she began to scramble away, he caught her ankle and gently dragged her back, following her down into the sumptuous bedding. He caught both her flying wrists in one hand, held them above her head. "My dove, you will tell me of this Calum. Now."

She wiggled beneath him, then as his gaze shot down her pale body, she stilled. "I told you. Calum is sweet and old-fashioned."

"Sweet?" Hawk bent to taste her inner wrist, lightly running his tongue across it. His big hand eased down to possessively claim her hips and raise her to him. "Like this?"

"He's more…mental. He's very controlled. He wears a pocket protector."

"Ah, I see. A boring nerd. Yet you cry out beneath him? You want the heat of his body in you, filling you to the hilt, taking you to ecstacy—"

She looked away and flushed as he stared down at her body, pale against his, his eyes glittering beneath his lashes. "We're very…very hot for each other," she managed valiantly, and tossed back a phrase as eloquent as his. "My skin tingles with each touch. His eyes are the color of the mountain storms, or as clear and hard as steel. He's delicious, like a nice, tasty…pomegranate or a cherry sundae with whipped cream."

She changed the fruit-and-ice-cream image to one more masculine. "Like a big black stallion. With stormy eyes. Mmm…hot. That is how I feel with him. All that, and he manages to be rather…innocent and sweet, too."

Hawk lifted a black eyebrow. "Hot? You want him? Even though I want you? Even though the bud of your desire awaits my touch? Even though the promise of your body comes from the perfume of your skin, the honeyed liquid of—"

"That is very descriptive language," Talia managed shakily.

"My hot-blooded temptress, I fear I am too tired to amuse you. Perhaps tomorrow night," he murmured after a yawn. Then he eased away and turned his back to her.

Trembling, Talia stared at him. *Who was he to be scheduling lovemaking she didn't want?*

"Come." Hawk reached behind him to draw her arm around him. He sighed and nestled his hard-muscled back against the pillows. "We sleep. Perhaps, if you are good, I will take you in the night— Ouch!" He rubbed the hair on his chest that had just been pulled, and then he chuckled, flattening her hand on his muscled stomach. "Oh, no, my pigeon. Your impatience for me must wait."

"We can't sleep all night like this," she began, and found that he held her gently when she tried to move away.

"Mmm, *chérie*. Can we not?" Hawk snuggled deeper in her clasp and breathed deeply.

Talia decided not to test her good luck. When Hawk slept deeply, she'd grab the nearest camel and—Talia yawned and closed her eyes; she'd rest until then.

In the night, she dreamed Calum was kissing her thoroughly, and she reveled in the slow, dreamy sensuality of being well loved from head to toe. Of being touched intimately, and rising to the delicious torment of his hands and mouth, to the loving that took her higher until she burst. Then the gentle whispers of Hawk awoke her—

The Desert Hawk! Her eyes popped open to full morning, and she lay very still, running through an inventory of her body. She knew instinctively that he hadn't touched her. Talia was waiting for him when he entered the veiled bedroom. He didn't stand a chance. "Real clothes would be nice. Just any old thing you could spare." She shivered and drew the quilt higher. "You've got to let me go."

His arrogance flicked at her. "I cannot. You are mine. You wear my ring."

"It's my ring. I traded it for Huey Lewis tapes. I'm going to trade it to Calum for—"

"Admit you do not care for this Calum."

"He's a great guy. I may even love him. I may want to bear his child. The Tallchiefs have beautiful gray-eyed children—" Talia's defiance was rewarded by Hawk flipping her onto her back.

He lay over her, arrogant, strong, and easily stilling her. "You *may* love him?"

"I have a…certain tenderness for him. I've been saving myself for a sweet guy like him."

He bent to nuzzle her throat. "Have you?"

Hawk began to grin, and then to chuckle. He reached to light the lamp.

Slowly Hawk removed his robes and tinted lenses, and Talia found herself staring up into the hard, determined face and gray eyes of Calum Tallchief.

"You!" Talia yelled indignantly, and flung herself at him.

An hour later, Calum sat behind Talia on his horse. Wrapped in his cloak against the chill, she sat very straight, with a heavy guilt around her. She hadn't spoken to him since that first "You!" She refused to be logical, to discuss the lesson he hoped he had taught her.

Calum began to feel very uneasy; the ramrod set of her shoulders was not forgiving. Talia was an emotional woman; perhaps he had gone too far. "It was for your own good, Talia. To teach you a lesson. One wrong move and you'll stay here with Kadar until I deal with Olson."

Unused to dealing with a woman he wanted desperately, Calum resented his lack of past experience.

Talia eyed him over her shoulder, then turned away, her shoulders rigid. Calum inhaled grimly, guiding the horse easily toward the waiting airplane. He glanced at the ring on Talia's finger, the bloodred garnets catching the morning sun, and wondered why this one woman could drive him to distraction. He preferred her temper and Petrovna curses to her silence.

That night at Calum's house, Talia noisily barricaded her room while Calum called Alek. Her brother roared with laughter. When Calum carefully added they had shared a bed, Alek swore passionately and demanded to know Calum's intentions. "Keep her," Calum responded, listening to more furniture thumping against the walls. "We're not to the logical discussion point yet."

"Logic?" Alek began to laugh again. "Whose? Yours or hers?"

Talia burst into Calum's office, her hands on her hips, her legs wide in their knee-high black-heeled boots. Her breasts shimmered palely above the black leather bustier. "Did we or did we not have sex?" she demanded.

"*Sex?*" There was a brief pause on Alek's end of the telephone line before he started yelling in an outraged tone. He muttered something between curses, and another dark, menacing male voice began yelling. A woman began wailing about her sweet little girl without a white wedding dress. She used the word *beast,* frequently, and Calum realized that he was probably the beast in question.

"Talia is all right, and in mint condition," Calum managed steadily before hanging up the phone. He caught the statue Talia had just flung at him.

"You mean—? You mean to tell me that I wasn't seductive enough—? That you really weren't interested—? What am I, boring? How dare you!" she stated indignantly as the phone began ringing. She jerked it from its cradle and snapped, "Alek. Papa. This one is mine." Then she slapped the receiver into the cradle. "You low-down—"

He tried logic. "Talia. When I make love to a woman, she knows it."

She tilted her head, her eyes darkening dangerously. Her voice had a deadly, controlled purr. She was wearing black, her black boots braced wide apart, her hands on her hips. She looked glorious, powerful...enchanting. Talia whipped back a gleaming pale strand of hair. "You mean that, as a man, you pick the time and the place?"

"Rules, Talia. Men usually—" Calum ran his hand through his hair. It had been a long, hard, silent day, and Calum ached to have a calm discussion with her, to reason with her about the danger in which she had placed herself and to explain that someone had to take care of her. He would wait until Talia's mood burned itself out, and then they'd have a nice calm discussion—

"Whose rules?" she demanded, grabbing a fistful of his shirt. He winced as she pulled the hair on his chest with it. He hated wincing, Calum decided darkly. Only Talia could extract that expression from him.

"My rules." Then he reached for her, tugged her into his arms and kissed her hungrily.

What began as frustration became a softness flowing between them. Talia's lips lifted for his, shifting, brushing, heating.... Calum held very still as she eased closer to him. He didn't trust her, not a bit— He carefully placed his hands on her waist, because they badly wanted to wander to softer places.

To his surprise, she melted against him and snuggled her face into his throat. "Calum, why did you come after me?"

He lowered his lashes to study her. There he was, all ready to be logical and explain the danger.... But the vulnerable tremble in her voice could be faked.... She could be gathering ammunition to— Calum flung all caution to the winds, and realized to his horror that he was absolutely involved with the life and adventures of Talia Petrovna. He nuzzled her cheek, and sensed a homecoming when she held very still. He cautiously pressed closer and sensed a warmth that he had missed his entire adult life. He kissed her temple, then her cheek, then eased her head upon his shoulder. She was his to take care of, his life's mate. He rubbed the back of her head, experimenting with the places that might soothe her. She began to purr softly, the response encouraging him.

Talia looked up at him, and he smiled tenderly at her. He went light-headed with relief.

That was what he wanted with Talia. A life of holding her, of children— He wanted to claim her, to make her his, to care for her, to protect her and hold her in his arms. He found her pouting lower lip and bit it gently. Talia sighed and placed her hands on his cheeks. "Tell me, Calum. Tell me why you brought me here. Why you came after me, and why you brought me back here. Tell me."

She held very still as he kissed her cheeks, her lashes, her nose, and brushed her chin. "Calum. Words. Say them. I need to know."

Calum wrapped her in his arms and stood very still. He'd never shared his heart with anyone, and he wasn't certain he could. Talia nestled closer and sighed. "This is good. But, Calum, you know I can't let you get away with this. Not without a good reason."

The question slid across his lips, a raw invitation that he knew she'd refuse. "Will you stay here with me?"

"Calum, you must have loved her so much." The illogical sequence of her statement caught him broadside. Leave it to Talia to shift from the required yes or no. Their conversation was on a different plane now, a very iffy plane, and a wrong answer could send her running.

Calum realized that he had to express himself to her, a difficult task for a man who shared nothing of himself. He realized with a sinking feeling that Talia was giving him the opportunity to tell her how he felt. A cold fist slammed into his stomach as he realized that he might fail this important test. He'd always found his privacy safer, but now he risked losing Talia— He moved away from her, and ran his hands through his hair. He stood to look out at the mountains, his hands tucked into his back pockets. "Sherry demanded, and got, male attention. She was beautiful and we—were passionately involved. We were either fighting or loving. I wanted more. Logically, we had to have some middle ground for the marriage to survive. Some common interests—''

Talia moved against his back, taking his hands from his pockets and wrapping her hands around his waist. She leaned against him, nuzzling his back. ''I was jealous,'' Calum continued, lacing his fingers with hers. ''She liked that…called it 'our common interest.' I thought I could handle the situation, turn it into what my parents had, something solid. We were on our way up, young, hungry, savvy executives. Our marriage should have worked. But our fights got more intense, and after one, Sherry got into her car and ran into a truck.''

Talia rocked him gently and kissed the back of his neck. ''You can't control love, Calum. Or people.''

''Love? We had nothing like that. It ended that night. Maybe I could have stopped her, I don't know. I'll never know if we could have strengthened our marriage and made it last.''

''You were shattered. You think it was your fault.''

He hated admitting his vulnerability. ''Maybe. I just know it ended wrong.''

''It wasn't a clean wrap, with all the ends neatly tucked in place.'' Talia moved around to slide into his arms. She looked up at him, smoothing his cheeks. Calum gave himself over to her fingertips, letting them soothe the slicing pain within him.

''Calum, I'll stay here, and you go out into the world and do your warrior deeds. Joust with Olson. I suspect that you're just like all the Tallchief males, despite your modern-man exterior. But I'm not going to make it easy for you. I've never done this before, and I'm definitely not going to release you until I've had my full revenge. My brothers and Papa won't be happy with you if I stay. You can certainly count on them arriving in full temper, demanding that you marry me.''

Her gaze slid away from his. ''I... You have no idea how embarrassing they can be. Please don't take their threats seriously. I have no intention of getting married. I get this terrible choked feeling just thinking about it.''

''Will you stay?'' Calum fought the fear within him. He didn't want to lose her, and it wasn't like Talia to concede easily. He could be making a mistake by leaving her—

''Yes. You can trust me to stay. But I don't promise to make it easy on you, you rat. I can't deal with secrets, and you're loaded with them. I suspect you inherited your stoic silence from your great-great-grandfather. I'm not the settling-down kind, and I'm still very miffed at your interference in my capers. That Desert Hawk escapade still deserves payback. I count on you for logic. You scare me, Calum. You're a man who wants everything, and—'' she frowned up at him ''—I'm not certain I can fit into your life, even for a short time. Any man who would make a woman wonder if she hadn't just dreamed they'd... they'd made love...''

Calum lifted a mocking eyebrow. ''How do you know we haven't?''

She didn't trust his teasing expression. ''I think I would remember. From now on, don't play games. You're too effective when you do, and I don't trust you.''

''Rules? From Talia Petrovna?''

''I'm making new ones for you.'' She frowned up at him. ''Oh, Calum, I'm so scared. This isn't what I want. *You* aren't what I want. I've never wanted an affair with a man like you...possessive, dominating, macho, scheming, devious—''

''Affair?'' The word slammed into Calum, but he decided not to confront Talia until he had considered his options. An affair with her wasn't the long-term commitment he wanted. "After you're safe from Olson's reach, we'll discuss everything logically. Together." He understood. She wasn't used to letting anyone share her life. Neither was he.

She shook her head, and a sleek swath of hair swirled around his wrist, soothing him. "Logically? Calum, you never change."

"I will try. Just don't leave me." Very gently, Calum enfolded her in his arms. She held him fiercely, and for now, it was enough.

After he kissed her at her bedroom door, Calum stopped in the hallway and looked back at her. He didn't trust her expression. Talia had plans, and leaving her now could mean disaster. Taking her with him would definitely be a disaster and put her in danger. He found himself anticipating what her next move would be, and he walked back to her. He removed the stone from his neck. "Will you wear this?"

She accepted his placing of the stone upon her, a ceremony that he discovered was very important to him. She accepted his light kiss and moved slowly backward into her room, closing the door firmly against him.

Calum stared at the door. Talia definitely had plans of her own, and they included a measure of revenge against him. Calum found himself smiling.

In the morning, Talia walked Calum to his car. She'd decided to teach Calum a lesson—to take revenge upon him for his interruption of her capers and for using logic when he should have used romance. Talia allowed herself a small smile. Her disguise this morning was the first of many. Calum would learn not to interfere with her life. He would soon learn that living with her was not an easy road.

Because Calum was a delicate man, Talia realized that his male ego demanded that he take care of the Olson situation. She also realized from life with her family that the male ego was a fragile flower and honor had to be served.

His arm had been around her, his hand resting on her hip. He hadn't said anything about her hair up in curlers, her cutoff sweatpants and T-shirt or his old flannel bathrobe. He didn't seem to notice her mud mask, though she didn't trust the humorous glint in his sea-gray eyes. She'd promised to stay, but she hadn't promised to make it easy for him. She wanted to let him know that she wasn't always glamorous or sweet. But she also wanted him to know that she wasn't a wilting Nellie when times got tough.

She handed him his briefcase and sighed. "You'd better do a good job on Olson. Are you certain that you don't need me? I mean, I can be ready in no time. I'll go like this— I can change in the car."

"That's an interesting offer. But I want you safely away from Olson. From the messages on my recorder, he's out for blood. But no more than Alek or your father. After all, what's one more enraged male? No, you stay here, out of temptation's path. You were right about them asking my intentions. Your father demanded that you have extra locks on your door, with one key—yours."

She looked away as he paused, studying her intently. She would have to lay down the rules for her family, to protect Calum. She wouldn't have him forced into marriage, or into a commitment to her.

She eyed the man she'd once thought of as a nerd. All the danger of the Hawk was there, just below the surface. She smoothed his suit-clad shoulder and straightened his lapel. Calum's eyes flickered with suspicion; his large hand locked firmly on her hip. "What are you up to, Talia?"

"Me?" She fluttered her lashes. Calum smelled delicious, all freshly showered and shaved. She touched his gleaming black lashes. Not every cowboy could play a sheikh like Calum. "Trusting someone else to pull a caper isn't that easy,'' she admitted reluctantly. "You don't know what you're asking of me. I'm not a damsel in distress. I can take care of myself. I'm a hands-on person.''

"You stay out of trouble.'' He kissed her nose, his hand caressing her waist. "I'll take care of the hands-on.''

His sensual challenge made her catch her breath. She studied his expressions. It was all there, the tender desire, the need, the danger, and the shadows of his past.... She ached for Calum's dark side, the pain kept tightly inside him. And the loneliness that he had not shared with anyone. "I'm not promising anything, and I want to know every detail. Calum, it is important that you do not use physical violence on Olson. I detest violence. I don't expect you to lower yourself to physical vengeance—it's so crude. That is exactly the reason I did not want Alek, Anton or Papa involved. I have confidence in your logic, without brute force.''

"So you trust me?'' The question was laden with meanings she didn't want to consider.

"I have a certain faith that when you promise to do a job, you do your best,'' she returned. He chuckled, and she loved the deep, rich sound. She, Talia Petrovna, was now playing the waiting housekeeper, while her knight leaped into his black four-wheeler and rushed off to save the kingdom.

She *did* trust him. Good old logical Calum. She lifted aside his suit jacket to find his pocket protector, neatly lined with pens. The sight was reassuring. Talia realized that she wanted him wearing his official gear when he was within reach of other women.

She realized with horror that she was slightly jealous and very possessive.

Calum was going to where women would find him enchanting and probably try to— "Wear your pocket protector.... Uh...protection for your shirts.''

He frowned curiously, and she wondered about protection. Specifically about Calum and protection and herself.

About gray-eyed Tallchief babies and Calum.

About sharing his life. About giving and taking and sharing. She realized there was one area in which she would not share Calum Tallchief—that was with another woman. He looked too luscious to release into the wild, too tempting to expose to other women. She blinked. Except for his darkened gray eyes upon her and his alert expression, he was the same old Calum, corporate troubleshooter.

Talia inhaled the fresh, crisp late-October air and went dizzy. She, Talia Petrovna, who had always waltzed away from deepening relationships, wanted to cuddle Calum. Not every cowboy would appreciate a goodbye kiss from a woman with a mud mask on her face and curlers in her hair. It had taken her an eternity and ten empty frozen orange juice containers to create the proper curler look.

She wondered if Calum knew she had crept into his bed last night and cuddled up to his broad, warm, safe back. She grinned up at him as he studied her curlers as though he were placing her in a picture frame. His intent stare caused her to be nervous. "Like it? The little-housekeeper outfit?"

"I get the idea that you're out for revenge, and this outfit is just the start. By the way, your distributor cap is back on."

Talia grinned. "My, my… Do *you* trust *me?*"

"In some things, yes." Calum moved to shield her from curious eyes. He ran his fingertip slowly down her throat to her breasts and then across them. His hand flattened gently, finding the stone beneath her clothing. "You're up to something, and I've got the feeling that I'm going to pay for collecting you. Whatever you decide to do about me, just stay here. I want you safe. My family will take care of you," he whispered slowly, meaningfully.

She realized that now he was vulnerable, asking instead of ordering her.

She frowned slightly, feeling childish at being bothered by his admission of desire for his wife. Talia was inexperienced, and— He moved her hips against his taut body. "You do that to me, Petrovna. Every time I look at you. Last night, very little kept me from coming to you. I'm glad you came to me."

She flushed, uncertain of her need of him. "You should have told me you were awake. I couldn't sleep and needed something to cuddle. You're warm and hairy, like my favorite old teddy bear."

He laughed outright and drew her hand lower to cover him. "And not exactly soft." He placed her hands upon his cheeks, turning them to kiss her palms, one by one. Over their joined hands, his eyes were dark and making promises that frightened and excited her.

Calum's warm gaze slid from her to over her head. His smile died as he watched Birk approach them on his motorcycle. Talia watched, fascinated, as Calum's features hardened and his arm reached out to draw her close in a possessive gesture. She thought the gesture was sweet. His kiss wasn't. It left her dizzy and hungry. Then he nodded curtly and slid into his vehicle and drove off.

"Wait!" Talia motioned to Birk, then hopped on the back of his motorcycle, and they sped off after Calum. He pulled over to the side of the road with a wary, resigned expression on his face. "What is the Tallchief legend that goes with the ring, Calum?"

Birk turned his back, clearly giving them privacy. Calum stared at the road, at Birk, then lashed a glance at her. He distinctly looked cornered, as though he were looking for an escape. "I suppose you'll threaten me with dire consequences if I don't tell you." His sigh was heavy with resignation. "Come here."

GET 2

HOW TO GET YOUR
2 FREE BOOKS AND FREE GIFT!

1. Peel off the MIRA sticker on the front cover. Place it in the space provided at right. This automatically entitles you to receive two free books and an exciting mystery gift.

2. Send back this card and you'll get 2 "The Best of the Best™" novels. These books have a combined cover price of $11.00 or more in the U.S. and $13.00 or more in Canada, but they are yours to keep absolutely FREE!

3. There's <u>no</u> catch. You're under <u>no</u> obligation to buy anything. We charge nothing – ZERO – for your first shipment. And you don't have to make any minimum number of purchases – not even one!

4. We call this line "The Best of the Best" because each month you'll receive the best books by some of today's hottest authors. These authors show up time and time again on all the major bestseller lists and their books sell out as soon as they hit the stores. You'll like the convenience of getting them delivered to your home at our special discount prices . . . and you'll love your *Heart to Heart* subscriber newsletter featuring author news, horoscopes, recipes, book reviews and much more!

5. We hope that after receiving your free books you'll want to remain a subscriber. But the choice is yours – to continue or cancel, anytime at all! So why not take us up on our invitation, with no risk of any kind. You'll be glad you did!

6. And remember...we'll send you a mystery gift ABSOLUTELY FREE just for giving "The Best of the Best" a try.

SPECIAL FREE GIFT!

We'll send you a fabulous surprise gift, absolutely FREE, simply for accepting our no-risk offer!

Visit us online at
www.mirabooks.com

BOOKS FREE!

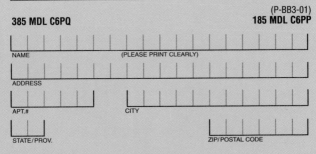

Hurry!

Return this card promptly to GET 2 FREE BOOKS & A FREE GIFT!

The Best of the Best ™

▶ DETACH AND MAIL CARD TODAY! ▶

Affix
peel-off
MIRA
sticker here

YES! Please send me the 2 FREE "The Best of the Best" novels and FREE gift for which I qualify. I understand that I am under no obligation to purchase anything further, as explained on the opposite page.

(P-BB3-01)

385 MDL C6PQ   **185 MDL C6PP**

| | | | | | | | | | | | | | | | | | | | |
NAME   (PLEASE PRINT CLEARLY)

ADDRESS

APT.#   CITY

STATE/PROV.   ZIP/POSTAL CODE

Offer limited to one per household and not valid to current subscribers of "The Best of the Best." All orders subject to approval. Books received may vary.

©1995 MIRA BOOKS

The Best of the Best™ — Here's How it Works:

Accepting your 2 free books and gift places you under no obligation to buy anything. You may keep the books and gift and return the shipping statement marked "cancel." If you do not cancel, about a month later we will send you 4 additional novels and bill you just $4.24 each in the U.S., or $4.74 each in Canada, plus 25¢ shipping & handling per book and applicable taxes if any.* That's the complete price and — compared to cover prices of $5.50 or more each in the U.S. and $6.50 or more each in Canada — it's quite a bargain! You may cancel at any time, but if you choose to continue, every month we'll send you 4 more books, which you may either purchase at the discount price or return to us and cancel your subscription.

*Terms and prices subject to change without notice. Sales tax applicable in N.Y. Canadian residents will be charged applicable provincial taxes and GST.

...k began chuckling, and Calum scowled at him. He ...ed at her, his expression that of a brooding, resentful ...ale. "Now isn't the time, Talia."

"Now, Tallchief." She wasn't budging an inch.

His scowl deepened, and his tone was neither sweet nor romantic as he explained the legend. "When a man of Fearghus blood places the ring upon the right woman's finger, he'll capture his true love forever. There, that's it. Are you satisfied?"

Stunned by the romantic legend, Talia looked down at the ring on her finger and then at Calum. "It's just a legend. Don't get terrified," he muttered darkly. "Be here when I get back."

"Oh, fine. The ring is supposed to be special, and you've wasted it on me." Tears burned Talia's lids. Here was a perfectly wonderful romantic legend, and Calum had no idea of the value— Calum closed his eyes and shook his head. She'd wait for him—something she'd done for no one else. She'd be trustworthy—and perhaps even prepare him for the woman who *should* wear the ring.

Meanwhile, it fitted her perfectly and looked wonderful against her skin. Just as Calum did. He was actually a nice big snuggly teddy bear, of a species temporarily endangered by Alek, Anton and Papa Petrovna. She'd have to keep him safe for his "true love." "Goodbye, Calum, darlin'," she whispered meekly.

He scowled, clearly not trusting her tone. His expression ran through a series of dissecting, curious and suspicious looks that Talia returned with a blithe smile. "Go on, now. Shoo. Ride off and fight the world. Joust. Throw spears. Call if you need backup...."

She watched his vehicle drive away, aware of his uncertain study in the rearview mirror. She waved happily to him. "Poor Calum. He really needs me, Birk. Doesn't he? As a housekeeper," she added cautiously.

"Ah, yes. I purely believe he does. His life has been too easy up until he met you." Then Birk began grinning "You intend to teach him a lesson, don't you?"

She grinned back. "Come back to the house for breakfast. I've got lots of orange juice. I'll tell you about Calum when he was the Desert Hawk. I knew all along who he was and that he was out to give me some sort of obscure lesson. He's such a romantic."

Talia ignored Birk's disbelieving snort to glance down at the gleaming garnets. She liked wearing Calum's ring to remind her of him. She tightened her hand into a fist, keeping his ring safe.

Seven

That afternoon, Lacey's parachute drifted closer to Talia's. "What do you mean, it's nice for a time? The Tallchiefs aren't the kind of people who drift in and out of lives, Talia. They've been taking care of me since I can remember. Calum isn't the kind of man to take a relationship lightly. He took his wife's death very badly. He was totally dedicated to preserving their relationship, and she put him through hell."

Talia concentrated on the cow field below them, their target landing site. "He's delicate in some ways. I'm afraid I'll hurt him. He's got this thing about ends being tied up neatly. I don't know that my life is neat, or that I can change. I've always detested order and systems, and Calum wants everything. I'm just not a built-to-stay person, Lacey."

Talia glanced down at Duncan and Birk, on the ground, their hands on their hips as they looked up. "Look down there. Look at those frowns. Calum is just like them, afraid for me. I've lived a life of doing as I please. I'm past the idealistic stage of my girlhood. At my age, a good percentage of women have been married and divorced and are struggling to survive.''

''You're afraid.'' Lacey's blue eyes were serious, framed by her helmet and her windswept mop of black curls.

''Basically. And I resent promising Calum that I would stay here. He's like that, expecting things from me.''

''What do you expect from him?''

''I'd like him to be happy. That's why I agreed to stay, because it seemed to comfort him. And to teach him a lesson for his own good.''

Lacey laughed out loud. ''Yeah. Right. No selfish reasons tucked in there at all, right?''

They sailed on the wind, lowering slowly into the pasture. ''I do not like domineering men. My family is filled with them. Calum shows the same tendencies. Eventually—'' As they expertly landed in the field, Talia looked at Duncan and Birk. They stood, long-legged Westerners framed by a backdrop of snowcapped mountains. The grim set of their jaws, and their arms, folded disapprovingly over their chests, reminded her of Calum.

A long-term relationship with Calum wouldn't be good for either one of them. Rules weren't for her—except Petrovna's Law.

She touched the Tallchief stone beneath her scarlet jumpsuit; the garnets on her finger caught the brilliant afternoon sunlight. She wore the mark of his possession, light tethers to a relationship she hadn't wanted.

Calum didn't need more pain; he'd had enough. So had she.

Talia inhaled with resignation. ''My family won't understand if I stay. They'll consider it my first commitment. You don't know them. I've been running from that long white dress for years. I don't want Calum forced into anything illogical."

Lacey laughed again; it was a musical sound. "Duncan didn't want an affair with Sybil. I doubt that Calum would stand for anything less than a wedding ring."

"He can be just awful. Arrogant and rude. He gets this warrior attitude about me, and I rise to the bait every time. He's old-fashioned and outdated and it sets me off. I'm still furious with him over that Desert Hawk incident. I lost a measure of confidence on that caper. I'm usually quite successful. He was totally arrogant, and payback is definitely needed."

"You're afraid, and none of what you're saying really is enough reason to walk away from something good."

Talia closed her eyes and let the old pain swirl around her. "I can't go through it again. I almost got married once, and he walked at the last minute." The memory slammed deep within Talia, who realized her pride had not yet been salved. She vividly remembered the people sitting in the church, saw their sympathetic expressions as she escaped her shame, dressed in her wedding dress. Talia hated the tears that began flowing easily, chilling her cheeks.

Lacey gave Talia a quick hug. "Calum keeps his promises. The Tallchiefs always do." Lacey spoke quietly and from years of experience. She bent to scoop up her parachute from the ground. "Take a note. The Tallchiefs are bred to hold what is theirs. Calum has never looked at a woman like he looks at you."

"The whole thing is scary."

"Think of it as jumping out of a plane. Or surfing the best wave yet. Or climbing a mountain. Maybe a relationship is something you have to work at. Like an acquired skill."

Talia scooped up her parachute. Calum was years ahead of her in certain skills, like lovemaking. She intended to catch up and make it an equal game; she was a woman of action, and not one to wait. She studied the sheer wall of rock on Tallchief Mountain and knew it was a challenge she had to take. "I'm dying to scale that— So what about Birk and your relationship? It's definitely not a smooth one."

Lacey looked at her with surprise. "You're kidding. The only relationship Birk and I have is the Tallchief family. I'm almost one of them, and that's why I have the right to bring his arrogant nose down a notch. And I wouldn't try scaling that rock wall without help."

The two weeks away from Talia were the longest of Calum's life. In the second week of November, he drove urgently toward Amen Flats, aware, to his distaste, that he was breaking the speed laws—something he had never done. He didn't trust Talia to be where he had last put her. His four-wheeler soared through the moonlight as Calum grimly concentrated on the very neat wrap-up job he'd done, extracting Talia and the Petrovnas from suspicion.

Volatile in-laws-to-be like the Petrovnas had to be protected.

Calum gripped the steering wheel tightly and swerved around a lonely curve, the tires squalling and spraying fallen leaves.

In one week and one month, she'd turned the order in his life upside down. He had tossed away caution and decided to marry Talia Petrovna. That would eliminate interference from the protective Petrovna males. Marriage would keep her near, touchable, and under control. All he had to do now was make himself appealing as a life mate to Talia. He would approach her with logic...once he found her.

She was frightened of the commitment he badly wanted.

Calum cursed the man who had deserted an eighteen-year-old girl at the altar.

Alek hadn't meant to let that tidbit slip, but to Calum, Talia's past experience explained everything logically.

Calum pushed away his fears that he might not appeal to Talia. He did not want to be compared to her passionate, yelling, protective male family members. He wanted her to see him as...valuable. A commodity she wanted very much.

Not that he could trust Talia. The morning he left, she'd tucked him in his car too easily. He'd had two long, tense weeks of waiting for her to pounce on Olson. After the first week of nightly telephone calls to her, Calum's body had ached. He did not doubt that Talia had deliberately underlined her husky, unspoken invitation to him on the telephone. He glanced at the reflective eyes of deer at the side of the road, and barely missed a skunk. He braked carefully, so as not to alarm the animal. His hands, encased in black leather gloves, ached from gripping the steering wheel, from the tense fear consuming him.

Cleaning up after Talia had required a second week—Talia's ingenious sabotage of Unique's systems had taken time to unravel. Calum allowed himself a tight, proud smile. He impatiently loosened his designer tie. Talia showed an aptitude for computers, and was capable of wrecking any system.

Including his personal safety-protection system. Sherry had been very capable. Calum scowled at the silvery disk in the sky and knew that only one woman could make him howl at the moon. Talia had been very effective. He wanted her on another level than sex—though at the moment, a good dose of it would have calmed the tension humming through him. Visions of her shimmering in red and gold and dancing for him in the desert haunted him.

Calum grimly forced away that body-jolting image and

concentrated on driving. She hadn't answered his calls the second week, and Olson had felt the brunt of Calum's taut nerves. He almost regretted rapping Olson's knuckles with a file dedicated to sexual harassment statements from former employees. Jan and Roy's marriage was one among many that had suffered. Added to Olson's blatant misuse of company resources, Calum had plenty of ammunition to force the sleazeball into a tight corner. Olson had gladly set up a trust to anonymously pay cash to those he had injured. Then he'd made the mistake of pushing Calum, who dissected his past errors with the neat, effective skill of a surgeon.

At the time, Calum had controlled his need to brawl, to vent his frustration about Talia. In the end, Olson had whimpered for his job, which disgusted Calum. He really needed just one shot at Olson, a physical one, but the man's cowering had stopped him. That end would have to remain untied. He'd countered with an anonymous file, sent to Olson's wife. As a woman scorned, she would know how to use the information effectively.

Calum turned his mind to Talia. If she knew how badly he wanted her, how he lay awake wanting her in his arms, she'd be frightened. Hell, he frightened himself. Lovemaking with Talia approached an obsession that he wouldn't let out of control. She deserved tenderness, and the knowledge that he was committed.

Okay. He was committed to getting Talia into bed. But he wanted their relationship to have everything she deserved. He wanted a strong foundation. He would learn how to relate his emotions.

All right, so he didn't know if he could give her everything she needed. He didn't know about loving a woman the way Talia deserved, a sweet, old-fashioned love like his parents'. After Sherry, he doubted that he was capable. But he'd give Talia everything he could, starting with marriage. Was it enough?

Calum reluctantly admitted he hadn't given everything to his wife. He'd had sex with her, nothing more.

With Talia, his emotions caught him, tossed him in a jasmine-scented wind with passion and with tenderness. She excited the primitive hunter in him, stirred the lover who touched her with trembling hands, as if opening a delicate flower especially made for him.

He had to give her time to adjust, yet his instincts told him to claim her.

The tires squalled as he rounded a corner. Calum realized that he had never really tried to seduce or invite a woman into his firmly closed inner sanctum. There was no reason to expect Talia to act like other women—she'd just stepped into his life.

A cold mountain mist enveloped him. *Was she gone?* Her frumpy-little-housewife disguise zipped through his mind again. He studied the car ahead of him, and the woman snuggled close to the driver. That was what Calum wanted, Talia snuggled close to him.

His lower body coiled into a hot, heavy knot as he remembered her beneath his touch…the soft, fragrant petals of her body—

Calum gripped the steering wheel with aching hands and shifted restlessly in his seat. Hell. He wasn't a kid anymore. He knew all the dirty facts of life, and he hated loose ends. He'd kept his life neat. Then Talia had bewitched him. Moved right into the aching abyss he called his heart and started dreams of home and babies and warm, cuddly nights when they were ninety. He couldn't remember excitement before Talia. Calum pushed down on the accelerator, passing the lovers' car.

He was an idiot to think that her role as his housekeeper was believable. He felt like a sitting duck, waiting for disaster, which would arrive at Talia's choosing. One of his rules had always been self-protection, never leaving himself open to disaster. With Talia, he had little choice.

He sped toward an empty house. He couldn't remember ever wanting to return home so desperately as he did now. And Talia was gone. No doubt he'd catch her scent, and that would have to be enough. He'd rest for the night, lick his lonely wounds and then track her. Wearily Calum stopped the car and studied the darkened house. He'd find her, and hold a very tight rein on the passion that engulfed him every time he looked at her. His need for her went much deeper than lovemaking, he admitted tiredly, extracting himself from his rig. The angles of his contemporary home loomed cold and sterile in the moonlight, like his life without Talia.

She was gone. He was certain of it. The fire and gold she'd brought into his life was gone. The thought lodged in Calum's mind like a cold, hard brick. He felt drained and old.

For once he dismissed his laptop computer, leaving it in the car. He braced himself against the house and began to walk up the walkway to his porch.

A low, feral growl stopped him. An experienced hunter, Calum realized that the dog was big and mean and ready to protect his territory. "Easy, boy."

The massive dog moved slowly, his growl deep and menacing. He planted his four paws firmly apart, ready to defend his home. The huge hot-pink bow artfully tied around his neck was at odds with his bared fangs. Calum braced himself against the beast's assault and moved slowly toward the house. He was tired, lacking sleep, and not in the mood to wrestle with the fanged monster. The beast prepared to spring, and Calum leaped to a nearby tree. After shaking the monster's fangs loose from his slacks, Calum swung neatly upward and onto the roof of his house. He eased his way into a window that he had purposely not rigged for alarm, opened it and dropped to the floor. He padded along the shadows of the upstairs hallway. Tomorrow he would deal with the dog, which continued to bark threateningly outside.

Calum caught the scent of jasmine and decided against checking Talia's room. He couldn't bear empty closets, a neat, barren room. A kitten meowed timidly from the shadows of his bedroom. Emily had no doubt forgotten one of her kittens. Calum picked up the kitten and tucked it against his body. He stroked the tiny, warm, snuggly form, and it curled into him. He would have preferred Talia doing the same, he decided whimsically. He placed it on the bed, a small comfort in the cold emptiness that enveloped him. He undressed wearily, methodically putting away his clothing. Calum glanced at his empty bed; there was no reason to fling away his clothing and hurry.

Calum slid into bed—a cold, lonely bed, except for the kitten that came snuggling close, purring. Loneliness engulfed and chilled him. He rubbed the kitten's stomach, too drained to do more than absently notice the one-o'clock cuckoo sounding from downstairs. Remnants of Talia's time at his house would surely haunt him. Just as her voice on the telephone, husky, sexy, inviting, had set him off. He'd found himself picturing what she was wearing—and dreaming of taking it off.

Calum sighed slowly and listened to the silence of his home. A silence he had preferred, pre-Talia.

A board creaked, and Talia strode into his darkened bedroom. She lowered the hair blower, raised as a weapon in her hand. "Exactly what have you done to upset my dog, Calum? Now you just go outside and make friends with poor Olaf this minute. He's insecure enough, after his previous owner's shabby treatment. By the way, you are not one of Santa's reindeer. Please don't tromp across the roof, frightening me."

Calum flipped back the blanket, then tugged it away from the hissing kitten, who had been buried. He was on his feet in one movement and striding toward her. Talia stood her ground as he slowly noted that she was wearing his chambray shirt, and that her long legs were outlined by moonlight. He noted the deep crevice in the unbuttoned front, and the pert lift of her breasts against the cloth. He wanted to toss her on his bed and ask questions later. Instead, he took the hair blower from her hand and placed it on a table.

He faced the woman who had consumed his waking and sleeping hours. In the moonlight, Talia's hair spread across her shoulders, gleaming like a silver mantle against his shirt. Her eyes were huge and dark in the shadows, and her lips— She was right where she was supposed to be, where he had left her. A pink, fluffy rush of exhilaration swept through him. She had waited for him…there were no unresolved loose ends. His plans to keep her remained intact.

Calum reached for her and pulled her tightly against him. He realized he was shaking. He tucked Talia's head under his chin and, elated, smiled into her hair. She hadn't left. He tried to push away the fear that still held him. He asked her carefully, so as not to frighten her, "Where have you been? Why didn't you answer my messages?"

She snuggled close to him and kissed his chest. "I've been right here, playing the busy little housekeeper. And I've been starting a community theater, a tremendous amount of rewarding work—mostly during the evenings, when the actors come in from ranching. I think I've finally found my calling. The grand opening is set for December. Elspeth has promised that the Tallchiefs, dressed in full traditional garb, will be at the reception. I can't wait to see you in a kilt."

For the moment, Calum bypassed the threat of wearing

Elspeth's kilt in Wyoming's notorious cold winds. He stroked Talia's silky hair, smoothing it down her body. "You're better than a kitten," he mused happily, and found himself grinning.

He placed his thumb beneath her chin and lifted her mouth for a long, hard, satisfying kiss. Things weren't so bad after all. He wallowed in a joyous jasmine-pink cloud.

"The dog... His name is Olaf...." Talia reached up to place her arms around Calum's neck and nuzzle her face into the curve of his throat and shoulder. "He won't stop barking until he knows I'm safe and that everything in the house is peachy. If he wakes up the puppy, we'll spend all night trying to get him back to sleep. The sheriff stops by and shines his spotlight when he hears Olaf. The sheriff loves opera, and Olaf howls when he hears a soprano."

"Can't have that," Calum agreed rawly as Talia nibbled his throat. He didn't care how the monster had come to claim his home. The dog wanted to protect Talia, just as fiercely as her brothers and father did. As Calum did. Now he understood the dog's threatening stance perfectly.

Calum frowned as the dog's excited barking continued. If Calum could just get Talia settled in his bed, everything would be fine. He wanted no spotlights, no barking dogs, no whining puppies. He didn't care how they had all come to claim his home, he just wanted to hold her close.

"Come back to bed when you've finished making friends with Olaf, darlin'."

Calum held very still, letting her invitation soak in, testing it, as Talia moved away from him. Standing by the bed, she slowly unbuttoned his shirt, dropped it to the floor and eased into the spot he had just vacated. He watched, fascinated, as she snuggled down in his bed. His heart rate wasn't the only thing to kick up. He caught a glint of gold in the moonlight. "You're wearing the ring."

She frowned at him, and stroked her finger. "I like it. I

just don't like how you placed it on my finger. There I was, exhausted from belly dancing for you, fast asleep, and you slipped it on my finger. The next time you decide to do something that romantic, I want to see you coming. The Tallchief stone was a nice save.''

She wore his ring. She'd waited for him. Unused to free-wheeling emotions, Calum reeled at the knowledge. He knew now why people sang from rooftops. Why Duncan hurried home to Sybil every chance he had. Why flowers bloomed and birds sang.

Calum hurried through the dark house to quiet the barking dog. Olaf planted his huge paws firmly on the porch and bared his teeth, growling dangerously. Calum spoke quietly—there was the puppy and the kitten to consider. Calum didn't want Talia to be distracted tonight. ''Now listen up, you black monster. This is my territory, and my woman waiting for me. Shut up and you'll get a nice juicy steak in the morning.''

The dog's massive head tipped to one side and then the other, his expression one of curiosity. Calum held out his hand and let the animal sniff it cautiously. ''Okay. Give me tonight, and it's everything you want tomorrow. An insulated doghouse. The shoe of your chewing choice. A lady friend. Just don't bark. Deal?''

Olaf tried one halfhearted snarl, then plopped down on the porch, his head on his legs. Then he rolled over, belly up; it was a clear invitation. Calum crouched to rub his belly. ''That's better—''

Olaf flipped to his feet and began snarling as a patrol car slid to a stop in front of Calum's house. The sheriff's spotlight pinned him. A loudspeaker broadcast an order: ''Freeze. Just raise your hands and stand up.''

Olaf began barking fiercely, standing with four legs locked in front of Calum's crouched nude body.

''Okay, Sheriff. You've got me.'' Calum slipped the

huge hot-pink bow from Olaf's neck. He impatiently looped it over his aching hardness, raised his hands and stood. The sheriff's guffaws sounded immediately. Lights appeared in the house down the road as the sheriff's laughter crackled across the loudspeaker. "Naked as a jaybird, huh?"

Calum scowled at the sheriff, who slowly drove away to the radio's emotional violin music. As usual, the sheriff had forgotten to release the broadcast button on the loudspeaker. Olaf howled. A warning shot, then two, sounded from neighbors wanting sleep. A small herd of deer grazing near Calum's house took off in the moonlight. Calum held very still. *He did not want the puppy awake.* Olaf shook his massive head, ears flying, and plopped down on the porch. He whined, wanting his bribes now. Like Olaf, Calum had an immediate need, a painful one for the woman upstairs in his bed. He kept the pink bow firmly lodged low on his body and eased back into the shadows of the porch. "I know how you feel."

When Calum stepped into the room, Talia drew the quilt up to her chin. She wasn't exactly certain she was doing this right—but Calum had looked so lonely, so needing. After two long weeks away from him, she needed to hold him tight and know that he was safe. Her revenge could come later. The kitten was safely asleep on her bed, while Talia didn't feel safe at all in Calum's bed.

To claim a Tallchief could be a dangerous game. She realized the full impact of staying in his bed, waiting for him to settle the house. She realized her fear, the physical pain that would occur as she shared her body with him. Talia trembled; she wanted to claim him in a primitive way, to make him her captive, her lover. The antique ring gleamed richly in the moonlight, her bond to Calum.

Talia shivered; she wasn't certain she wanted bonds

other than the psychic claiming she sought tonight. A conventional man, Calum was certain to rebel—

No doubt he wasn't happy about being caught naked on his front porch. Outlined in the faint light coming from the hallway, his body was streamlined with powerful long legs and broad shoulders that she craved to smooth. His stance, legs apart, body tense, reminded her of a warrior just back from battle and ready to be comforted by his woman. A primitive surge of pride engulfed her. She pressed her hand against the Tallchief stone. "I feel a bit like Una."

He shook his head. "What?"

Talia realized she was trembling. Calum was edgy, a violence shimmering beneath the surface. She wanted to hold him and soothe him. "You've got that warrior look, Calum Tallchief. You've been out defending the tepee, and now you're back and looking—"

"Hungry?" he asked, too softly. "You could say that." Then he turned and eased the bedroom door closed, locking it. "Let's define the ground rules right now. Why are you in my bed?"

She temporarily tossed away a lifetime of running from dominating, protective males and let the quilt slip off one shoulder. Calum responded very satisfactorily. "Talia, I want a logical explanation. If this is some kind of revenge, it's a dangerous game to play." His voice was raw and dark with hunger.

"Get into bed, Tallchief. I want to hold you, and you can tell me about Olson." She patted the empty space beside her. He looked so weary, shadows under his eyes, lines on his forehead and beside his mouth. "Oh, Calum…"

"I want to settle this. If I get into that bed—I can't promise—"

"To be logical? Come here. You can't settle everything to your satisfaction, at least not tonight. I have major plans." Talia ached to hold him, to soothe the tension humming through him. She looked at him sharply. "Calum, you didn't hurt Olson, did you?"

He moved through the moonlight, a tall man bound by his pride. "I don't suppose we could save the details for the morning, could we?" Then he eased over her, the quilt between them. He impatiently dismissed a froth of ruffles by her head. His hands trembled on her cheeks, and she turned to kiss them. "Why are you here, Talia, in my bed?"

Calum needed details. To forage them out and lay them neatly in a row. He needed her reassurance that everything was proceeding according to plan. Talia locked her arms around his shoulders and settled comfortably beneath him. She stroked the taut muscles rippling across his back. "Tell me how you feel, Calum. How you feel about me. I have to know."

"You want it all, don't you?"

"You could have had Kadar send me home. You didn't need to come after me."

"Oh, yes, I did," he stated firmly, his hand gently easing the quilt down until he was looking at her breasts in the moonlight. The black stone slid into the palm of his hand, just as Talia wanted to. Calum slowly covered her pale breasts with his hands and bent to kiss her. The kiss was gentle and seeking, with leashed hunger. Talia arched up to him.

Calum drew away the barrier separating them and slowly resettled between her legs. He stroked the length of her body slowly, smoothly, his hands caressing and warm down to her knees, her ankles. He kissed her shoulder, placing his hard face against her throat. Talia closed her eyes and shivered. "Calum, this is not a time for control and logic."

He chuckled against her skin. The curve of his mouth changed to a kiss, and then another. "Petrovna's rules? It's been a while. I'm trying to get the logical sequence straight. Tell me what you want.''

''You.''

Calum eased slowly to her side, so that they lay facing each other, their legs intertwined. His callused hand lightly skimmed her body, flowing over her rib cage to her waist and then to her hip. His fingers pressed into her softness, in a possessive gesture. The slight tremble in his hand told her how much he wanted her. She loved the heavy, rough weight of his thighs, the heated, smooth length nesting comfortably against her lower stomach. Calum drew her knee higher, smoothing her thigh and then her bottom, cupping her and rocking her gently against him. She locked her leg around his and pressed her nails slightly into his shoulder. He wasn't leaving her.

''We'll stop when you want.'' The dark, raw hunger in his tone reached inside her lower body and heated her.

Talia closed her eyes and bit his chin, licking its rough texture. ''Good old Calum. I know I can trust you.''

''Can you?'' The taut male challenge caused her to open her eyes.

''Calum?'' The heat in his body reached out to hers, softening it. She wanted him fiercely, wanted to ease him, to love him, to make him hers.

Calum parted her legs, gently tormented her softness, and she cried out in her desperation. ''Take me, Talia. Place me where you want me,'' he ordered rawly, softly, tenderly, against her hot cheek.

He shivered when she first touched him, and her hand moved away from the silky sheath of heated male. She touched him again, this time firmly, caressing, marveling at his strength. Calum kissed her cheek, her eyelashes, her nose, and then sank hungrily upon her mouth. ''Open for me, honey....''

She cried out, took a deep breath and placed Calum

gently at the petals of her aching, tight sheath. He held very still as she squirmed beneath him, uncomfortable with the blunt, heated pressure pressing intimately against her. "This won't work."

"Okay."

"What?"

"If you say it won't work, it won't work." His heart was beating heavily against her breasts. His eyes narrowed, the moonlight drawing shadows from his lashes. Then he grinned, a careless, boyish grin that shot right into her heart.

"I worked very hard to escape a houseful of dominating, protective males, Calum Tallchief. I'm used to every possible male trick to challenge me. You're not getting away with this easy-okay business. Not now. You're years ahead of me in lovemaking, and I am determined to catch up."

Calum wrapped a strand of hair around his hand and drew her down for his kiss. "You're very hot and very tight. I don't want to hurt you. I'm not exactly in control tonight, thanks to two weeks of untangling the very neat job you did on Olson."

"Why, thank you, darlin'." Though Calum appreciated her good work, he wasn't imposing logic and schedules on her lovemaking. "I thought you said we'd stop when *I* wanted." She studied him, the seductive curve of his lower lip, the rumpled male within her web. The first lover she had ever wanted.

Lover. A jolt of heat shot through her, her lower body melting against his. "Help me."

Calum reached into the bedside stand and opened a small packet, preparing for her. Then he held her, soothed her with more kisses, until he thought he would— Calum leashed his primitive need until Talia lay warm and pliant in his arms, arching against him.

He looked at her for a very long time; she nodded, realizing that Calum was asking her permission and that she trusted him. Calum found the entrance he sought, opening her gently with his caressing fingertips, and very gently pushed deeper against the tight barrier. "Tell me to stop now, Talia."

"No. I won't." Her nails bit into his shoulder, and Talia frowned, slowly forcing them from him. "Oh. Sorry—"

Talia's flustered, hot, desperate look caused Calum to go light-headed, in contrast to the heavy desire smashing through his taut body. He smoothed a strand of hair away from her damp cheek. A sense of tender pride swept through him. "If tonight goes as I want, I expect a few small woundings. You might even decide to nibble a bit on me."

"I'll try to keep everything under control. But don't you dare stop now. It's time you knew that I'm not exactly the submissive— I'm very good at holding my own— Oh!" Her fingers pressed into his shoulders, and Una's ring gleamed in the moonlight.

Calum took her soft gasp into his mouth as he eased deeper, slowly filling her, pausing to allow her to adjust, stretching her. He lay still, his body very tense, his expression a mixture of hunger and concern and tenderness. Talia dug her nails into his shoulder. "Don't move. I hadn't expected— Oh! Oh! Calum, you can move now." Calum eased deeper, and Talia held her breath, lying very still against him.

She closed her eyes, itemized their joining and what it meant to her. She'd already known when she made her decision to make love with Calum Tallchief. She was a traditional woman in many respects, and she knew that he was the man she wanted. The man she had waited for. Calum wanted her and cared for her.

This was her decision. She could do this.

He was hers, and she cared for him. This was a commitment that was not light, because Calum was not a man

to let his body rule him— She lifted her lashes to study
Calum. She smoothed the taut shiver running down the
length of his arm. She kissed the rigid, damp line of his
jaw and knew what the effort of letting her explore her
thoughts at a sensual moment had cost him. "Yes," she
murmured against his mouth. "Yes."

Calum groaned shakily. "Do not move."

Good old Calum. He knew just when to toss out those
challenges. Talia wrapped herself around him and rolled
onto her back, drawing him over her. She nipped his shoulder, and Calum's body surged instantly, lodging fully, to
the hilt. She wiggled her hips and grinned at his shocked,
fierce expression. "Gotcha."

This was her fierce lover, the man she had waited for,
the man who was now within her power. A gentle man, a
good man, one who weighed his decisions—and he had
decided on her. Her desert sheikh, her sweet little Hawk.
She promised herself distantly that when she got better at
this particular event and at handling Calum, she'd repay
him for the Hawk's tantalizing, sensual role. Despite the
uncomfortable stretching of her body, she loved his weight
on her. A flowing warmth curled through her, and the tight
sensation eased. She fluttered her lashes against his cheek,
thanking him for his gallantry. When control was needed,
she could always trust Calum. She wiggled, adjusting to
the hair providing an erotic nest for her breasts. She moved
her softness against him experimentally, and Calum shot a
fierce, hot glance down to their bodies. Talia inhaled and
chanced a curious glance downward, following his gaze.
Dark and light, hard and soft, woman and man. While he
studied her with a dark, intense look, she gently tightened
around him.

Calum braced himself with his hands and glared down
at her. "Petrovna—"

She raised her hips again and caught him. He was hers.

Their kiss ignited, hot, stormy, hungry. She held him tightly, felt him deep within her, aching when he withdrew, following him, keeping him close. Calum's kiss sought hers, his heart racing against hers. Talia felt the cords in her body draw tight, keeping him, pressing him close. The rhythm of storms drew her higher, tossing her into the red-and-gold mist, and then there was only Calum...Calum...

In the flames, she turned to see their hands joined. Her pale, slender fingers, twined with his darker, larger ones. The old ring gleamed richly on her finger. *When a man of Fearghus blood places the ring upon the right woman's finger, he'll capture his true love forever....* The stones were the color of blood, the pulse beating within her, the heavy, full throbbing of Calum's body locked within hers. Bloodred—the blood that came from tearing away from one life and entering another...her body torn apart and then completed... Red—the color of life, of babies fresh from their mother's nest. The Celtic design swirled like fire, flowing from the ring into Talia's body, running through her veins, heated by each brush of Calum's lips upon her parted ones. By his breath flowing upon her skin, his body withdrawing, then flowing deeply, strongly, into her raised, undulating one.

Red and gold.

Fire and heat.

Waves of fire, of exquisite pleasure...

The height of their passion startled her. Caught her on the edge of fire and heaven and burned, exploding within her.

Calum... She heard his muffled shout, her victory, her lover striding through the storms with her. Then the incredible heat, the throbbing deep within her, gently eased, and she began to drift wonderfully, warmly, down to snuggle in Calum's arms. Talia kissed his chest and clung to him, unwilling to let him move away, frightened by her emotions.

She'd always dismissed romantic entanglements. She'd just given her heart to a complex man, one who could hurt her badly. He wouldn't. She'd hold him and warm him and love him.

She hated tears. They crept from her lids to his chest, and she clung tighter. Calum had kept her safe. His heart was slowing now, his hands stroking her gently. He kissed her forehead and rocked her against him. Good old safe Calum. Her warrior. Her lover.

He tipped up her chin to lick a tear away. "I'm sorry."

She lightly tugged a whorl of hair on his chest. Here she was, Talia Petrovna, woman of the world, feeling very shy and delicate. Calum had taken very good care of her, though it had cost him, the strain showing on his intense expression. "You'd better not be sorry. You're my first lover, and I thought I did a reasonable job."

"Very reasonable," he returned, in a tone wrapped in humor and tenderness.

She dived into the tenderness, wallowed in it, as he rose to pad to the bathroom. For a musing moment, she admired his strength when hers had fled. He returned with a basin and warm water, placing it carefully beside the bed.

She sensed that what he was about to do, the cleansing of a woman newly taken by a warrior, was an unspoken, unwritten tradition of the Tallchiefs, and perhaps the Fearghus chieftains. Shy of him, Talia tried to take the damp cloth, her thighs trembling as he urged them apart with large, gentle hands. Calum eased her hands aside, indicating with the silent gesture that he had taken responsibility for their passion. That he would tend his commitments to her. She trembled while he administered the age-old lover's ceremony, the tender cleansing, the intimate opening of her body with his fingertips, an unhurried endearment.

Tears continued to flow from her lids, dripping to dampen the pillow. Calum's tenderness, the male ceremony in which he cared for her body, had shattered her resistance. When he was finished, he placed his open hand on her stomach, smoothing it. "This was your first time."

The words were husky, running deep through his emotions. Calum's expression softened. He brought her hand to his mouth and kissed Una's ring. "Thank you, Talia... honey."

She bit her lip, almost crying out at the beauty of what had passed and at Calum's tenderness to her now. He studied her, smoothing her hair out upon the pillow they had shared...touching her lips, her throat, and skimming his open hand down her body, all the way to her toes. He caressed her arches and lightly shackled her ankles, then skimmed his hand back up to her throat. Slowly, as though he were absorbing her body into his memory by touching her, he followed her arms, tracing the feminine muscles down to her wrists. Slowly, methodically, he laced his fingers with hers, bringing their palms together. He found Una's ring and drew her hand to his lips, cherishing it with an intricate, tantalizing, erotic design of kisses. Then he turned her palm to his mouth, treating it just as carefully, just as intimately.

"Thank you," he whispered again, and this time the moonlight ran silvery and damp across his lashes.

She touched his cheek. "I missed you, Calum."

"I missed you, too, honey." Calum eased slowly down beside her, pulling up the quilt to cover them.

When she lay against him, he held her close. "It won't hurt that way again. We'll wait, and you can choose the next—"

Her finger, resting upon his lips, stilled the rest of his sentence. She gathered him close and safe and Talia sighed against his chest. She'd waited two long weeks to have him in her clutches; the sound of his deep voice on the telephone the first week had been too much. She draped a leg over him and snuggled closer. The dark, stormy edges of Calum Tallchief had gently settled, for a time. She knew then why Tallchief Lake reminded her of Calum—the smooth calm covering deep currents that, when lashed by the elements, could rise into a torrent of white, fearsome waves.

Perhaps Una had sensed that about the Sioux chieftain who had captured her. That beneath the warrior's stoic arrogance, emotions ran deep and true, emotions that a woman could cling to. Talia sensed that she knew Una very well, that when the warrior calmed, he needed care and tenderness, and that his allegiance ran deep. Perhaps Tallchief had tended Una, just as Calum had cared for Talia's newly opened body.

She inhaled unsteadily, fiercely joyful that she had kept herself for this moment, when intimacy was treasured by a man she adored.

He'd just called her *honey,* an endearment. Calum wasn't the sort of man to issue endearments on a regular basis to every woman. She hugged that comfort deep in her heart.

She lifted slightly to find her captive sleeping deeply. A masculine contrast sprawled across the ruffled pillow shams and flowery printed sheets, Calum looked carefree and vulnerable. Talia inhaled deeply, wallowing in her victory. She ran her foot slowly down her captive's hair-roughened shin, fondly patted his firm rear, and settled down to sleep in his arms.

Eight

Before dawn, Talia crouched in the kitchen with the kitten and the puppy. They required regular small feedings, and had just been fed and were settling down to sleep. The regular sound of Olaf's claws on the front porch had continued all through the feeding, the dog patrolling his territory until the house settled. Olaf had acted slightly jealous of the puppy and the kitten, though he seemed pleased when they frolicked over him and between his paws. He didn't grumble when they tugged on his ears, just lifted his jowls in a doggy grin.

Because Olaf needed to know that he hadn't been displaced, Talia took special care to open the door and speak quietly to him. She absently noted his pink bow, looped over the doorknob. She tossed him a doggy biscuit and padded back through the living room.

She glimpsed a movement in the dark kitchen, then Calum moved through the shadows and scooped her up in his arms. Talia cuddled against him, instantly alerted to his aroused body beneath her hips. He held her tightly against him, his expression fierce and stark. His heart pounded heavily against her breast, as though he had just run a gauntlet of torture.

Talia had no doubt that Tallchief had looked just as fierce when he claimed Una. She knew how Una must have felt, the feminine tenderness of a woman welcoming the man she had chosen. A woman's choice, that of balancing her mind and her body. To select her lover was the ultimate choice. She smoothed the hard planes of his chest and placed her palm over his racing heart. For all his calm and steel, Calum had been frightened when he awoke and found her gone. He'd reacted instinctively, seeking her out and holding her.

Talia placed her arms around his shoulders and stroked the taut muscles of his neck. She saw then the pain that Calum covered so well; it hummed through him like a vibrating wire. Pain brought by the sudden loss of his parents and by his wife's death. "I'm not going anywhere, Calum. Except back to bed."

"Mine." The statement was flat, arrogant, possessive, and yet a vulnerable uncertainty lurked beneath it. A man who liked things completed, he would want her by his side in the morning. And that was exactly where she wanted to awake, taking equal responsibility for her actions. However, the warrior technique would not suffice in daylight. She'd allow him the night.

She placed her hand on his jaw, caressing him softly. His head went up a notch, an arrogant warrior tilt to it. Calum and Olaf were more alike than she had first thought. Both lonely, battle-scarred warriors, wary of a tender hand.

Talia held Calum closer. He needed her. Talia kissed the damp side of his throat and cuddled closer. She gently bit his shoulder, then licked the small wound, and Calum relaxed slightly. For a time, Calum was her very own.

He carried her up the stairs and placed her carefully upon his bed. She smoothed the flowery sheets, this nest she had prepared for them. When she opened her arms to him, Calum gently eased down upon her. Talia ached for him; she intimately adjusted her body beneath his and took him gently, slowly, inside her. Calum trembled, then went very still. The tension humming through him frightened her...yet she clung to him, soothed him, spattering tiny kisses on his hard forehead, his glossy straight lashes and jutting cheekbones.

Calum gave himself up to her hard, fast kiss, moving instinctively deeper within her, burying himself possessively.

He withdrew slightly and Talia looked at him.

"Tonight changes everything, honey. I'm upping the ante." The arrogance returned, mixed with tenderness, as Calum lowered himself again, resting very deep within the throbbing warmth of her. He kissed her hungrily, scooping her hips in his palms and lifting her high as he moved, very slow, very controlled, against her. She didn't have time to think about what had changed or what ante had been raised as Calum gathered her closer, making her a part of him.

Then Calum bent his mouth to her ear, kissed it and began to tell her how he felt, close and tight within her. Talia's blush deepened, her body straining against his hard one, as she found the rhythm of the dark, powerful storms, the urgency of Calum's raw, deep tone taking her higher. He was her warrior, her lover, taking, giving, tantalizing. She held him tight and flung herself into his keeping.

Later, when they had burst together and drifted slowly back to reality, Calum carried her into the shower and treated her just as gently as the first time. She was too tired to do anything but move into the shelter of his arms.

The morning sun crossing into the room awakened her. Talia hugged the night to her; here in this flowery garden was the male she had captured and brought to her lair. An admirable trophy, one she had waited for on a primitive level. Instincts, thought Talia. Marvelous, good, old-fashioned instincts. He looked delectable against the mauve flowery print sheets and the ruffled pillow shams she had added to his bed. Since she had been sleeping in it, she'd wanted to feel comfortable, and she'd never liked Calum's sterile white sheets. He lay sprawled on his side, his arm and a heavy thigh crossing hers possessively, his morning beard darkening his strong jaw. His usually neatly clipped hair had grown shaggy, gleaming blue-black against his dark skin. A dark mat of hair covering his chest veed downward, and Talia inhaled as Calum's body began to change.

His drowsy gray eyes opened slowly, and a sensual curve replaced his usually grim mouth. "What you see is what you get," he drawled huskily.

Startled, Talia jerked up the sheet, tugged it away and wrapped her body in it. She walked shakily to the bathroom. She wasn't quite ready to deal with Calum in a playful mood just yet.

He'd changed the rules, she decided as she showered, needing privacy.

Calum Tallchief had changed the rules and the schedule. She would have to watch him very carefully. She knew full well how Petrovna males dominated and protected their women, and she wouldn't let Calum take her freedom.

She reached for a towel and caught the glitter of Una's garnets—*When a man of Fearghus blood places the ring upon the right woman's finger, he'll capture his true love forever.*

Talia carefully removed the ring. She knew herself too well. She resented day-to-day living, the kind needed to forge a strong relationship. She resented domineering and

traditional men who occasionally acted like warriors, claiming their rights.

Tonight changes everything.... I'm upping the ante....

"I am not acting miffed, Elspeth." Calum tracked Talia
with his frown. She moved easily among his entire family,
serving them breakfast with ease. Calum tried not to notice
her graceful saunter, the sway of her hips that was like no
other woman's. "Just because a whole horde of Tallchiefs
land on my doorstep my first morning home, *why should I
be miffed?*"

She flushed as she glanced at him and looked away suddenly. Calum cursed silently. Talia needed his reassurance
that he hadn't taken her lightly; she needed to be cuddled
and cherished.

Calum the cool—his nickname taunted him.

He glared at the family he loved; an infestation of Tallchief males and accompanying females, along with Olaf,
an unnamed puppy and kitten and Duncan's huge wolf dog,
Thorn, prevented him approaching Talia on a romantic
level.

He had awakened amid flowery sheets and ruffles and
had stepped into a shower scented of Talia, allowing him
to prolong the new softness in his life a bit longer. The
feminine clutter across his bathroom counter had fascinated
him. He'd picked up a lacy bra drying on the towel rack
and run his fingers over it, dreaming of softer fare.

Why had she taken off Una's ring?

The ring had gleamed when they first made love, as
though loving made the colors richer, forging them in red
and gold. Calum's body hardened painfully as he remembered Talia's uneven, soft cries, the delicate pulsing of her
body tight around him, flowing beneath him.

He cursed silently. He was a traditional man after all,
slightly proud that his woman had held her body for him,

that he had taken her— Calum realized that his thoughts were not politically correct; nor were they those of a contemporary male. When terms like *maiden-shield* dropped into a man's mind, he definitely needed to update himself.

Talia placed a glass filled with *biscotti* on the table. Her breast touched the nape of Calum's neck, and his lower body lurched with a painful reminder of how he had hoped to spend the morning. In bed with Talia, sorting out the logical flow of their relationship.

They'd known each other one month.

He still didn't trust her to drop her revenge on Olson so easily.

Talia probably had an alternate plan in effect right now. He was off balance, sensuously hungry, and uncertain. Calum detested the combination of emotions disrupting his life. He simply wanted Talia back in his arms, back in his bed and committed to him.

He realized with slight distaste that greed had just stepped into his life.

Calum scowled at the kitten nestled against Talia's body. He knew instinctively that when plans went into motion before they were fully developed, anything could go awry.

Logically, he should have been the one to initiate their lovemaking last night. He followed Talia's path to pick up the whining puppy, tracing the sway of her hips; he resented this knowledge that the moment of seduction, and therefore the commitment he wanted to get from Talia, had been taken away from him.

Talia had claimed him before the ground-level foundation of commitments and promises had been properly laid.

Laid. The word dropped like a stone upon him. He had been laid, well and good. Drawn into a flowery bed of ruffles and jasmine and— He realized he was scowling. Talia just…counted coup, Calum decided darkly in terms of his Sioux chieftain grandfather.

A modern woman, she had taken the initiative in their lovemaking. While he appreciated her need of him, Calum realized darkly that he was old-fashioned and needed the courting stage.

Roles. Male-female. Ceremony. He wanted ceremony and courtship and a long-term relationship with Talia. She could easily bolt when faced with restrictions of a conventional relationship.

Olaf padded after Talia, eager for a petting, reminding Calum of himself. The comparison grated at him.

He rummaged back through time, to his needs in his marriage. They had been starkly devoid of the tenderness he felt for Talia.

From the drift of the conversation when he arrived downstairs, Talia had invited his family for breakfast. An impromptu affair to which Sybil brought an apple pie and Elspeth brought freshly baked bread. Duncan had placed a gallon jar of creamy cow's milk on the counter.

Talia periodically unscrewed the container, dipped her finger into the cream and sucked it. Calum inhaled sharply, suddenly aware of how much he wanted her. He jerked out his only defense. "I do not like flowery sheets or ruffles."

The Tallchiefs' black heads jerked in his direction. Calum glared at Talia, who lifted her eyebrows.

Duncan looked amused, Sybil hid a grin, and Elspeth's lips curved softly. Birk cheerfully slid into the too-quiet void. "I've been here every morning. Had to. You should appreciate the new greenhouse I built onto your house. Talia says fresh herbs are the best and you require the very best." Birk bit into a chocolate *biscotto* and washed it down with vanilla-flavored coffee. He grinned blithely at Calum, who scowled back. "Every good housekeeper needs an indoor herb garden. She's ready to start making flavored vinegars—says there's a real lack of them in Amen Flats."

Calum almost winced at the "housekeeper" remark. His

family had accepted Talia. But she had placed Una's ring aside.

In the cheery buttercup-yellow kitchen softened by woven cotton rugs, Talia settled like a butterfly against the counter. She contemplated Calum over the puppy, who was licking at her chin. With a braid of garlic and chili peppers on the wall next to her, Talia looked very Slavic and very cool.

She had given herself to him. The thought stunned him. Uneasily, he studied her expression. It was the look of a satisfied, victorious cat who had just caught the mouse she wanted. Calum's trickle of uneasiness rose up the nape of his neck.

As the flow of the Tallchiefs continued around him, Calum began to hate cute, cuddly, lovable puppies and kittens. He didn't remove his gaze from Talia. She was too quiet.

She wore a single braid and her knee-high boots, and she was dressed in black. The typical ready-for-action Talia costume. Olaf grinned up at her. The phone had rung multiple times this morning. While Duncan discussed the family's cattle business with The Tallchiefs, Calum had noted darkly that most of Talia's calls were from single males. From her comments, Calum also noted that Talia's play, *Nachos and Nanette,* needed work before presentation. His experience as a substitute reviewer told him that, even in rural Amen Flats, she'd be cut to ribbons. To protect Talia, he decided to watch rehearsals and offer his help. He wanted to be a supportive mate.

He wouldn't have anyone booing his bride.

"By the way, Calum the cool…" Elspeth said softly, firmly. He stopped his report on family investments to listen to Talia speaking on the phone. Elspeth continued, amused by her brother's distraction. "I'm not clipping your hair again."

Duncan and Sybil shared a tender look. Though Elspeth cared carefully for her brothers, she renounced care of them when she believed the right woman was at hand. Sybil leaned to kiss Duncan, Megan sleeping safely in his arms.

Then Duncan's sea-gray gaze slowly turned to Calum. "Have you picked out a spot on the mountain, Calum?"

Calum hesitated, fearing that Talia might feel too constricted by the knowledge that his family expected him to claim her. According to her file, Talia had no problems leaving a situation that did not suit her. He needed time to make himself enticing. A month was not time enough for her to know his best selling points or for him to offer marriage in a romantic way—where *he* had the advantage of choosing the moment of seduction. He tried a diversion. "How is the women's center going, Sybil? I know Lacey and you have been helping."

"What spot on Tallchief Mountain?" Talia's question plopped out into the brightly furnished kitchen.

"I'll explain later." Calum realized with horror that he had just flushed. As boys, the Tallchiefs had planned to set up their family tepees on the mountain. Duncan had snatched the past and tossed it at Calum with a grin. Calum trembled a bit when Talia dipped into the cream again and sucked her finger. "I thought you might want to ride with me this morning."

"Uh…" Talia went very still. Her blush was a contrast to her wide-eyed innocent look. "Actually, I'm a little stiff this morning—from my new yoga exercises. I've got the housekeeping to do, and the play in the afternoon. I'll have to hurry—"

Calum got very slowly to his feet. He'd hurt her last night, and now the barricades were going up. Any minute, she'd be packing. He rubbed the back of his taut neck and glared at her. The cuckoo he hadn't seen yet sounded ten times. It set off the sound alarms he had automatically turned on when he came downstairs.

While his family burst out laughing, Calum walked stiffly to the alarm box and punched in the disconnect code. He caught a scent of jasmine, remembered the fragrances and feminine clutter in his bathroom and knew that he wanted anything Talia wanted. "Fine."

Then he walked to her, drew her into the scented sanctuary of herbs and kissed her. Talia wilted afterward, cuddling comfortably against him. His fears ebbed and eased. She was where she was supposed to be. She ran her fingers through his hair, and he fell into the soft blue depths of her eyes. "Everything will be just fine, Calum. I know you need reassurance. I'm sorry I'm not experienced at morning-afters. You won't have to worry about that again."

Making sense of Talia's statement cost him the better part of the day. He'd repeated Talia's "won't have to worry about that again" statement out loud to find the baseline in it. Did that mean she wasn't going to bed with him again?

From his experience, it was best to move swiftly, effectively, upon differing bargaining points. For that reason, he had spent the morning and early afternoon clearing his work calendar and referring clients to another corporate bird dog. He checked the budget for the women's shelter and the Tallchief family accounts for which he was responsible. He wanted everything running smoothly, so that he'd have the entire winter to hook Talia, to lay aside her fears that he was a boring nerd and that a marriage with him was reasonable and not overly structured or confining.

In the socks Talia had sloshed with bleach, he padded out to examine his formerly sterile and quiet home. Talia had left his streamlined office alone, but the rest of the house blended herbs and Native American rugs and throws, and she had carefully arranged the memories of his past throughout the house. There were newly framed pictures of Duncan's family, as well as an antique copper water heater filled with a huge bouquet of eucalyptus and dried wild-flowers. Antique jars caught the day's light in tints of blue and purple. Candles of every scent, shape and color lurked in unpredictable places. A Cheshire cat pillow sat on his modern staircase, grinning at him.

His former starkly modern home had a pleasantly clut-tered look, a warm look that said *home*.

Olaf had seemed abandoned when Talia left for her busy day, so Calum had let him into the house. The big dog padded at his side, a friend in a newly cluttered world. He howled as the cuckoo leaped out of its walnut house and baited him repeatedly. Because the kitten and the puppy were crying, Calum picked one up in each hand and tucked them close to his body. They quieted after a few sniffs at his scorched shirt, and together they all set off to discover Talia's creation.

For a moment, Calum had stood riveted in his living room, bound by a creative festival of colors and nostalgia. The Tallchief branded board hung above the mantel, the leather-sheathed hunting knife hanging from it by leather thongs. Comfortable pillows spattered the couch and ranged onto the floor. He approached his rearranged bookshelves carefully. Talia's how-to books and cookbooks spread across an entire shelf.

Laundry spilled from the utility room into the hallway. Calum's shirts hung from a rack, a mass of scorched wrin-kles. He touched the scorched imprint of an iron lightly. The mark, shared by the one on his collar, was endearing.

Calum had taken an assortment of telephone messages for Talia, fed Olaf, the puppy and the kitten and quickly made a pasta salad for Talia's lunch. He also wanted to be prepared in case he could manage to get her upstairs or downstairs or in the kitchen. He was just fantasizing about the kitchen table when Talia breezed in, laden with groceries.

For all his plans for step-by-step action, Calum grabbed her, lifted her to the countertop and placed his hands flat on the counter by her hips. "What do you mean, I won't have to worry about *that* again?" he demanded.

Talia smoothed the ironed wrinkles covering his chest. "Your glasses are tipped and steamed, and you're upset. Goodness, darlin', you can look so fierce."

"*Upset* is an understatement. What did you mean, Talia?" Calum placed his glasses aside.

He closed his eyes while Talia gently soothed the bridge of his nose, where the glasses had left marks. "Calum, you really are a fragile person. You're off balance because I...well, I had you last night."

Her assessment was accurate and nettled him. He caught her left hand and brought it to his mouth. "That's debatable. Why aren't you wearing my ring?"

"Because..." Talia took a deep breath and set her chin. "It's not logical. The ring is meant for a true love, Calum. Not for the object of a man who has just discovered that his life is missing—" she flushed before going on "—certain creature comforts."

Calum narrowed his eyes. "Translation—you mean a nerd who has just discovered sex."

"You're terribly old-fashioned, Calum." She held up a finger to stop his next argument. "You will not offer to pay me for housekeeping. We're on a fine line here, and if my family found out you were paying me *and* sleeping with me, they would be offended. *I* would be offended. It isn't wise, in the employer-employee sense of the word. The Petrovnas would have to have revenge. I couldn't protect you."

She paused and smoothed his taut jaw. "By the way, thank you for reuniting Roy and Jan. My sister called me.

That was a neat piece of cupid craftsmanship…sending romantic notes to Jan and to Roy and gradually explaining Olson's part. How did you know that Roy wouldn't confront Olson?''

Calum had approached Roy cautiously, and together they had decided that Olson's scorned wife could better exact justice. Calum dismissed everyone else but Talia. He tilted his head, his mind reeling from Talia's verbal curveball. ''Let me get this straight. *You* are using logic?''

''Basically. Just general deduction stuff. Sorry about the plumbing in the downstairs bathroom. They're not making pipes and wrenches like they used to.'' Talia hopped off the counter. She flicked a glance down at his jeans. ''Calum, you should wear your jeans longer. Above-the-ankle length doesn't do anything for you.''

Calum ran his hands through his hair, hesitated with growing fear, and followed her look. His jeans, dotted by white bleached spots, were at high-nerd level.

Talia patted Olaf and gave him a treat. ''He reminds me of you, Calum.''

Calum studied the big, scarred dog briefly. ''I don't know why.'' Then he moved toward Talia, and so did Olaf.

Talia turned to him slowly. ''Calum, I'm moving to Lacey's house—''

''*What?*'' He stared at her, ready to pluck her up and run with her. This was the day after the night she'd given herself to him— Calum reeled at the dark anger enfolding him.

She began quickly unpacking the groceries. ''She's remodeling that old bordello and has lots of room. She needs me.''

Calum stood very still. His world was crumbling, and he couldn't find the right words to stop Talia from leaving him. He really wanted the tender option of gentle persuasion. ''*She* needs you?''

Talia's hands shook as she avoided facing him. Calum took small comfort in the fact that she wasn't as cool as she seemed. His heart was racing as though he were fighting for his life. Maybe he was. "Stand and fight, Talia. You're up to it," he said, very quietly.

She turned to face him, her expression serious. "This isn't a showdown, Calum. We both could lose."

Calum took her face in his hands and lifted it to his. "Take a chance, honey. Take it with me."

A tear dropped onto his thumb as Talia closed her lashes. "Calum, we're so opposite. I'm an extreme person. You like to think things through. Or sometimes you do. You are very methodical, Calum Tallchief. It's frightening."

"You're afraid of me, is that it?"

Her eyes opened. "Absolutely not. There are times, though, that I'd like to demolish you."

"So stay and do it."

"That sounds suspiciously like a challenge, Calum. You like neat packages, and I don't. I could demolish you easily."

"Just try it." Then he placed his lips on hers and folded her body against his. Calum tucked his chin over the top of her head and stroked her tense body. He noted that Talia did not relax easily against him, but held herself slightly apart.

Nine

Talia gripped the rock face with her gloved fingertips, pitting her strength against Tallchief Mountain. She needed the challenge to exorcise the tension humming through her, tension caused by one Calum Tallchief. She tested her safety rope, attached to nails hammered into the red rock surface of the cliff. The wind howled around the iced rock, buffeting her. "Stand and fight," she muttered as a pebble bounced downward, forcing her to huddle against the rock face. "Is this the OK Corral or what?"

She pounded a stake into the rock and attached her safety line to it. Calum wasn't easy game. So what? She'd always liked challenges. So why had she been crying? Talia swallowed the tight emotion in her throat. She'd actually fallen asleep in a tiny cave, exhausted from the emotions that Calum managed to drag out of her.

She eased her climbing boot slowly to one side, found a secure ledge and placed her weight on it. A snowflake slid down her cheek, and another landed on her nose. She inhaled the freezing air, savoring it, and inched higher on the rock face. Her up-to-date gear and clothing kept the cold at bay.

Extreme exercise had always helped her think better. Yesterday, Calum had cost her three male actors just by sitting in the theater during practice and glowering at them. *Nachos and Nanette* was her first play; he shouldn't have propped his boots on the chair in front of him, crossed his arms over his chest and snorted at every beautifully sculpted punch line.

She'd decided not to embarrass him in front of his friends, saving her thoughts for later. Calum had stuffed her into her coat and walked her home. His hand on the back of her waist, guiding her across the street, and the way he shielded the cutting mid-November wind from her, had made it clear that she was his woman. She resolved that, as a contemporary woman, she shouldn't have been so grateful for his tall body blocking the wind. But then, she had always suffered from periodic bouts of self-preservation.

When he'd opened the door, delicious food scents ensnared her. One look at the candles, the flowers, the lit fireplace and the expensive wine and she had backed against the wall. The beautifully wrapped gift by the flowers had looked ominous and threatening to her freedom. She had caught Calum's dark, determined and wary look and run for her room and locked the door.

Talia breathed deeply, aware that sunshine no longer warmed the unrelenting rock. An expert climber, she jerked down her knit mask and readjusted her goggles. "Stand and fight. Is that a thing to say to a lady?"

She muttered the African elephant-dung curse. Of course Calum would know how to challenge her; she hadn't found how to challenge him.

Rocks dislodged under one foot and bounced down the cliff. Talia eased higher, then pounded another nail into the flat red rock surface. She tested it, and when it held, she began to inch upward.

Just one sultry look from his smoke-gray eyes and she began to melt. Thoughts of him had probably caused her slide down thirty feet of sheer rock earlier, her safety line and a friendly root saving her.

She wasn't meant for small towns and family men who held gray-eyed, black-haired Tallchief babies. Beautiful antique rings with legends of lovers weren't her style; she wore dynamic modern jewelry. She panicked when she thought of committing to Calum Tallchief.

This morning, Calum Tallchief had worn the stone around his throat, nettling Talia. When she arrived in the kitchen, he had been flipping pancakes expertly, dressed in worn jeans and nothing else. Every instinct Talia possessed had told her to go to him and lay him upon the kitchen table, to feast upon him.

She sniffed the cold air, scented with Tallchief Mountain pines and fresh earth. She'd never stayed in one place too long, and the longer she stayed in the Tallchief home nest, the more difficult it would be to leave.

A rock came loose in her hand and skittered down the face of the cliff. Talia's elephant-dung curse hit the icy wind. She couldn't trust Calum. He hadn't said anything when she infiltrated his computer system. He didn't seem to mind the feminine clutter in his bathroom; she'd been certain that would unnerve him. "There is no explaining him sometimes. Unorganizing his closet was a piece of art," she stated breathlessly.

A blast of winter wind hit her, flattening her against the cold surface. Talia glanced at the clouds that were bringing darkness sooner than she had planned. Her boot found a rock; it dislodged when she placed her weight upon it. Sleet began pelting her, and Talia realized that she had to reach the top of the cliff quickly. Apparently the weather on Tallchief Mountain was just as volatile as one Calum Tallchief.

Her fingers slipped, numbed by the sudden cold temperatures. She realized that she'd been running on anger and on nerves caused by Calum.

He had "possessive, traditional male" written all over him, and that was a commodity she'd avoided for a lifetime.

A fresh blast of sleet iced on the rock, and her glove slipped away. Talia realized with horror that she had thoughtlessly placed herself in danger. The cold penetrated layers of clothing and silk underwear now, and her fingers were too numb to grip properly. The safety line had iced, and a mixture of sleet and snow pounded her. Her sleepless night and her exhaustion had taken the last of her resources. Her nap had consumed precious time. She flattened against the iced wall and began searching for shelter, a small niche like the one she had napped in.

If she couldn't find shelter in which to rest, she would continue scaling the cliff. Survival training would serve her once she was in the pines, and then she would make her way down easily after the sun warmed the rock. She glanced at the forbidding late-afternoon sky and knew that Tallchief Mountain could be enclosed in a winter storm for days.

Someone would miss her; a big SOS or a bonfire would draw attention to her....

A pebble dislodged from above her, and above the howling wind, she heard Calum yell, "Petrovna, I'm getting tired of waiting for you!"

Talia gripped the rock face tightly; her heart raced. She leaned back carefully to look upward. "Calum?"

Against the cloudy sky, he loomed over the top of the cliff, his legs braced wide and his hands resting on his hips.

Hail pounded his worn Western hat and bounced off his shoulders, which were covered by a warm shearling jacket. He began swirling a lariat against the gray, stormy sky. "Come on, Petrovna. Don't be difficult. Just take the rope and make it easy for the both of us."

"This is my gig, Tallchief. Who invited you?"

"You did, precious." His tone was too confident. She decided not to ask the when and how of her invitation to him.

From her precarious position, she tossed him a reminder that she wasn't precious or sweet. "So how do you like your closet, Tallchief?"

"It's a real piece of art, Petrovna. I like ties wrapped around my mismatched sock-balls. Now take the damn rope and haul it up here fast." The rope dropped neatly by her side, his order impatient.

Talia closed her eyes; coated in ice and clinging by her fingertips from a sheer cliff, she had no option but to accept his command. To salve her pride, she tossed out her best comeback. "I resent your tone, Tallchief. You cost me three of my best actors. It's not that easy to find men who will cooperate and wear tights in this town, you know. And I did *not* write a boring play. *Nachos and Nanette* is a highly sophisticated comedy with a deep, heart-wrenching message. Just how did you get up here?"

"I took the horse trail, city girl."

"Of course, a horse trail. I knew that." Reluctantly Talia agreed that she hadn't been wise to approach the cliff on Tallchief Mountain in the face of a winter storm. She resented being the object of Calum's rescue and that she had no choice but to take the rope, inserting her foot into the loop he had prepared. She grabbed the rope to wrap it around her waist and tugged the line twice; the rope drew her slowly, carefully, up the side of the cliff. Talia used her chilled hands and feet to grasp rocks and roots; she eased onto the top ledge and grasped...Calum's worn Western boot. She stared up at him as his hands went under her arms; he lifted her easily to safety and tugged off her iced goggles.

She'd forgotten his strength; when they made love, he'd been so gentle— He stood back, his collar turned up against the wind, his hands on his hips, his legs braced apart. He looked as much a part of Tallchief Mountain as the rocks and the pines and the snowcapped mountains beyond.

She stared at the rain freezing to his black beard; the clean-cut Calum she knew shaved twice daily. Slowly she met the cold, steely glint of his eyes, shadowed by his hat. A trickle of fear slid up her spine. This was the real Calum Tallchief—dark, stormy, dangerous. This would be the side of him that his parents' murderer had seen that night, civilization stripped away. Calum looked like an old-West gunfighter, a well-worn revolver strapped to his jeaned thigh. His eyes cut coldly down her black-clad body. "You looked like a damn ninja crawling up the face of that cliff. Are you all right?"

"I'm just fine." She was lying; her muscles ached, her body was frozen and trembling from fear and exhaustion. Now she faced a towering, angry cowboy who looked about as warm as the cold rock face of the cliff. A short distance away, his horse stood with the rope attached to its saddle horn. She noted that the horse was not the elegant Arabian, which was probably related to Kadar's, but rather a seasoned cow horse used in a rodeo.

"Gee, that felt great. It's a great day for—" she managed lightly before he scooped her up in his arms and loped through the hail to a tepee settled in the pines. His strength startled her again; she remembered the Desert Hawk's easy control of her.

Calum deposited her none too gently upon a thick bedding of sleeping bags, furs and blankets. "Okay, city girl.

You've had your fun. Now get your clothes off and get into that bed. You'd better be in it when I get back.''

Talia studied the interior of the tepee. ''At least you haven't murdered any animals to make this. Imagine, insulating canvas with— She took one look at his grim, dangerous expression and decided that getting into bed was just what she wanted to do. She sat up and began to strip away her gloves. Her numbed fingers caused her to be clumsy, and Calum cursed darkly. He ripped away his leather gloves, crouched in front of her and began unlacing her climbing boots. He grimly stripped away her clothing, extracted warm rocks from the sleeping bag and stuffed her into it. She decided now was not the time for chitchat, and attempted a friendly smile.

Calum scowled back at her, tugged his hat lower and jerked on his gloves before leaving.

Talia examined the tepee, which was protected by boughs layered around it. Smoke rose in the center of the tepee, drifting around the blackened pot over the fire, and an ancient coffeepot sat on a flattened rock; the flowers were frostbitten and wilted, and the elegantly wrapped package of last night was battered slightly. An unopened bottle of wine sat near scented candles.

Calum entered in a gust of sleet and snow. He tossed the saddle and tack into a corner, ripped off his hat and expertly sailed it to rest on the saddle horn. The gloves followed, and then his coat. He secured the tent flap, crouched by the fire and warmed his hands near it. He continued to ignore Talia while he ladled soup into a bowl and poured coffee into a steel cup. Talia studied the tense muscle contracting in his jaw and decided to let him open the conversation. She tugged the sleeping bag up to her chin.

But, since waiting ran against her nature, she decided to open with a tentative, prim, safe ''Thank you, Calum.''

He snorted, looked at her and shook his head. He handed

the soup to her, a thick, delicious clam chowder, and the mug of coffee. Then he sat, stripped off his revolver, wrapping it expertly in the gun belt, and placed it aside. He began eating his meal, ignoring her.

She decided to open with a compliment, a silence-softener. "The chowder was absolutely delicious. Thank you, Calum."

"Leftovers." His single word reminded her of the beautiful meal he had prepared the previous night.

"Leftovers are always good."

He grunted. She decided she was making progress. There was the possibility she could pacify his unjustified bristling. "Is the horse cozy?"

He stared at her as if she'd asked how the tropical storm was doing outside. "Just peachy."

Talia hitched up the cloth that had slipped from her bare shoulder. She tucked it under her chin and began undoing her damp single braid, spreading her hair around her shoulders to dry.

"Petrovna…" Calum's tone held amusement. "We're lovers, remember?"

"I wouldn't exactly say we're lovers, darlin'," she managed to drawl carelessly as Calum began to draw off his boots. She watched, fascinated, as he cleared away dinner and arranged her clothing to dry.

Towering over her, his rugged face and beard lit by the fire, Calum looked down at her. "Feel like talking? What made you decide to try to climb Tallchief Mountain with a storm brewing?"

"You upset me." To her mortification, she began to cry.

"*I* upset *you*," Calum muttered darkly.

Talia dashed away the tears dripping from her cheeks. "Thank you, Calum Tallchief. I haven't cried since I was eighteen, and see what you've done." She flung out a hand helplessly. "Get into that bed, you said—just like you had the right to say it in that way. You don't."

Calum's hands stopped unbuttoning his wool shirt. He glowered down at her. "The hell I don't. You're my woman, Talia. The only one to make me mad enough to... Okay, so I'm not into spanking, but watching you slide down an ice wall for a good thirty or forty feet before you snagged that root and your safety line caught you? About then, I wanted to put that cute fanny over my knee and paddle you like Fiona needed as a child."

"I would not like that, Calum Middle-Name Tallchief."

"Like?" The word was fired back at her, as though shot from a six-gun. "Now get this, Petrovna. When a man sees the woman he *loves* acting like an idiot on a dangerous, icy cliff, he starts thinking all sorts of things. For one—he'd like to have a life with her...a safe one, maybe with kids. He'd like to see her grow old and—" Calum ran his fingers through his hair, then he began undressing grimly. "We'll talk about this when we both settle down."

Love? Talia sniffed and dried her tears. She'd taken him so deeply into her body, until she felt she'd burst with the fullness of him—*and she didn't even know if he had a middle name.* Lit by the firelight, Calum's face was weary and hard, lines deep across his forehead. "I don't know that I'm up to that love part," she stated carefully. "Even if I were, you shouldn't have flung it at me like an old shoe."

"Move over." Calum, stripped down to his boxer shorts, slid into the sleeping bag with her. She eased to the limits of the bag, away from him. He folded his arms behind his head and stared at the smoke drifting through the top of the tepee. "Go to sleep."

"Calum, you're acting overly emotional."

He snorted and continued to stare at the smoke. "A

climber died four years ago in weather situations just like this. He came down like a rag doll."

"You were afraid for me." Talia placed her hand on his chest, surprised that his heart raced beneath her palm. "You're still afraid."

"I've been afraid before. Go to sleep." He glanced impatiently at her and wiped away a tear from her cheek. "You look like hell, Petrovna, all big-eyed, and your hair—" He gently lifted a strand away from her cheek and placed his hand on her head, rubbing her scalp with his fingertips.

Talia turned her head to look at him. "Why do you do that?"

Calum's rugged yet whimsical expression fascinated Talia. "You're touchable, Petrovna. You respond instantly. You actually purr."

"That's ridiculous. You make me sound like a cat—"

"Kitten. A soft, cuddly kitten. One that I want to hold very much." The tenderness in Calum's expression ensnared her.

"Are you asking?" she asked when she could manage a breathless whisper. She really hoped he was asking.

"Come here, honey. Let me hold you." Calum's expression was wary and vulnerable, yet he made no more moves to take her into his arms. He was leaving that choice to her.

Talia needed his arms around her. She pushed aside her fears of being hurt and slid into his arms. He eased aside her hair, and Talia carefully placed her head upon his shoulder. Calum tucked the sleeping bag up tight to her chin and rocked her gently. He exhaled slowly, and she realized that he had been waiting for her to choose him, holding his breath out of fear that she wouldn't. Talia stroked the hair on his chest and settled more heavily against his solid body.

She looked at the flames, gave herself to his warmth and safety and began to relax.

The wind howled outside, and Calum stroked her hair, nuzzling her forehead periodically with tiny, comforting kisses. "Better?"

She nodded slowly and closed her eyes, the fight for her survival ebbing away from her tense muscles. In the next instant, Calum sat up, ripped away the sleeping bag and studied her body. Flattened on the bedding, with her hands covering her breasts and lower, Talia glared up at him. "Don't you dare."

Calum's broad shoulders rippled in the firelight as his hands moved slowly, expertly, over her body. "Now is no time to play doctor," she muttered when he studied her from head to toe, found the slight scrapes on her knees and spread antiseptic on them. She noted the quick, efficient way he applied adhesive bandages and an automatic healing kiss. "You've done this before."

He covered her with the sleeping bag, then tossed wood on the fire. "Fiona's knees and elbows, on a regular basis," he explained curtly. "I knew you wouldn't let me look until you were relaxed and not on the defensive. You are a very defensive lady, Talia. You let me come only so close, and then the doors swing shut. It's a matter of trust, and you don't trust me."

She'd hurt him. She sat up beside him, drawing his discarded shirt up to her chin. "Calum, we've known each other just over a month—and you were gone for two weeks of it."

He stared at her over his shoulder. "And you wanted me when I got back. A woman doesn't give herself that way unless she cares, honey." Calum reached to take her hand and bring it to his lips. "I told you once that you'd see me coming the next time. Here."

"Calum…" She flushed, aware of how shy she was with

him. Images of their loving danced in the firelight, along with images of his tenderness to her later. He'd just told her, in anger, that he loved her....

He placed the wrapped package in her lap, watching her. "I wanted to give this to you last night. Open it."

Talia's hands shook as she unwrapped the package. Nestled in tissue was a beautiful Native American bag. Smooth, flat designs alternated with beads. Carefully folded beneath it was a beaded doeskin shift.

"The bag is decorated with porcupine quills and is called a parfleche bag. I want you to have it. It was Una's, a gift from her husband." Calum traced the beaded cerulean flowers. "This was Una's bridal dress. Sybil wore it, and I've asked for it until the next bride of the Tallchiefs accepts marriage."

"Oh, Calum, I couldn't possibly accept these...." Talia dashed away the tears burning at her lids. "I've never cried so much since—"

Calum eased her into his lap and wrapped a blanket around her. She listened to the wind passing through the pines and to the beating of his heart. She felt so safe; she wouldn't have moved if she had the energy. "You are a persistent man, Calum Tallchief. I sense that you operate by wearing people down, or boxing them into situations. I do not like boxes, though I am presently worn down. You have no idea what a life with me could be like. You don't know what you're asking of me. I'm a contemporary woman, a free spirit. I could never accept your basic warrior act and a structured lifestyle."

"I'm asking you to trust me, honey."

She ran her finger down his bearded cheek. Calum kissed her fingertip, his eyes dark and serious as they met hers. She lifted her lips slightly to his and brushed a kiss across them. "There are ways that I absolutely trust you."

She kissed the corner of his mouth, then the other. She

eased her fingers into the warm, sleek texture of his hair,
tilted her head slightly and fitted her mouth upon his.
Calum tensed, but held very still beneath her light kisses.

She allowed the blanket to fall aside and locked her arms
around his neck, pressing her body into his. She eased him
backward, aware suddenly of how easily a big man could
be moved when he wanted to be. Calum drew the sleeping
bag up to cover her back as she settled upon him. In his
arms, she felt warm and safe, and she knew that sleep had
begun to enfold her. "I'd like you to make love with
me...." she heard herself whisper.

She heard his wistful groan before she drifted into sleep.

Talia awoke slowly, just as she was moving over Calum.
His hands were locked righteously on her waist. His lashes
gleamed in the firelight, shadowing his eyes. She touched
his cheeks, smoothed the dark beard and ran her fingertip
across his brows. His hair ran sleek and cool through her
fingers as she settled upon him, taking him within her
slowly, as naturally as she breathed his scent.

Calum held very still, his body taut, as his hands caressed
her hips, claiming them with splayed fingers. Then he
moved swiftly, easing her beneath him, filling her in one
thrust. Talia lifted her body to him, and then he was where
she wanted him—

His mouth took hers in the hungry way she wanted, and
she gave herself to the fire igniting between them.

She awoke the second time to find Calum fully dressed,
braced against the saddle, his legs stretched out to the fire.
Daylight had penetrated the top of the tepee, and the fire
was dying between them. She met his dark gaze, felt the
tug of desire, and something gentler, more frightening,
stirred within her. A tiny spray of sparks shot between
them, and she realized that tears were slowly falling from
her cheeks. "What do you want from me, Calum?"

"Only what you want to give."

"The legend—the ring is meant for your true love, Calum. I can't wear it."

"Afraid? I didn't think you would be afraid of me, Petrovna. Or my love." His challenge curled, too softly, around her.

"You know very well that we are a bad mix. A combustible one."

"*Combustion.* That's a very apt word. So the way you see our relationship is that when you're ready to move on, that's it? You just take me when you want me? You set the terms?" He threw his coffee into the fire, creating a dying, hissing sound that matched the feeling in her heart.

Until she remembered that she had taken Calum too quickly, that his body had flowed deeply into hers, so perfectly that— Talia leaped to her feet, her head hit the tepee's canvas. She began hurriedly dressing, while Calum watched grimly. "Now what?"

"Oh, nothing," she returned airily, plopping down to lace up her boots. She glanced at him as he began to fold the bedding. She wanted to get away from him, to think; thinking near Calum seemed impossible, especially with the scents of their lovemaking enfolding her. His body smelled wonderful— Talia cleared her throat. "I think I'll just be going now. Thanks for everything."

His hand caught the back of her collar. "This is no have-me-and-leave-me hotel, honey. You are going back with me, Petrovna, sweetheart. The safe way."

"I sense that in some way I have upset your sensibilities, Mr. Tallchief."

"Always the last word, Petrovna?"

She opened her lips, but decided from the way Calum was looking down at her that perhaps, for this time alone, he could have the last word.

The next morning, Elspeth replaced the telephone in its cradle. Her classic black sweater displayed her willowy body, which flowed into a long wool skirt of the Tallchief plaid. "That was Sybil on the phone. She thinks that Calum was being high-handed in not letting us help take care of you last night. My brother probably hovered over your bed all night, just watching you breathe. To catch a cold with a Tallchief male around is no simple matter. Though I really wish you would have been here when Calum was so ill after the logrolling incident. Sybil is also very frustrated with Marcella Portway's missing royal Spanish gene. Marcella is determined that she has royal blood and a family castle somewhere in Spain. She doesn't want to believe that her ancestors were of the ordinary mix."

Talia pushed Marcella's desired genealogy away and cut to news of Calum. "Calum was ill?"

"He caught cold, and could have developed complications. When they're ill, all Tallchief males are horribly evil-tempered."

"I feel so guilty. He didn't tell me."

"He'll tell you what suits him."

Talia dealt with this news; she had caused Calum actual harm, and yet he had come after her, playing the Desert Hawk. Elspeth studied Talia beneath her lashes and traced the tiny rosebuds on her china cup. "So Calum took you to our parents' graves?" Elspeth asked quietly.

"Yes, this morning. It's so beautiful there in the meadow with the tall pines around, almost like a chapel. I felt as though Calum was sharing something precious with me. Oh, Elspeth, he was hurting so…all of you must have been devastated…Calum looked almost…like a little lost boy there in the snow by your parents' graves. I ached for him. All of you must have loved your parents deeply and still miss them." Calum's expression of deep grief had touched Talia, and she had moved close to him. His arm had come around her in a natural gesture, drawing her nearer.

The hours in Elspeth's home soothed Talia, who couldn't deal with Calum's cool, polite manners since he'd brought her back to his house. He'd gone off to chop firewood with his brothers. In his dark, ominous mood, she had no doubt that he was throwing tomahawks and running down game in his moccasins.

Talia inhaled the scent of herbal tea. "I'm very uncertain about this entire project. Calum is not an easy man to understand. For instance, how could he stop his entire career and decide to spend the winter at home?"

"Have you asked him?" Elspeth's black hair gleamed in the brilliant morning light. Her gray eyes were much softer than Calum's steel-shaded ones, yet Talia sensed that when Elspeth was tested, her Tallchief inheritance would hold like honed steel. Behind her stood Una's huge loom; on the floor sat a huge basket filled with yarns matching the Tallchief plaid. Lengths of dyed wool from the Tallchief Ranch's Scottish sheep hung from the wall in rich array.

The scent of herbs and baking bread blended with the harmony in Elspeth's quiet home. She had been studying Una's journals; they lay open on the table, along with Elspeth's notes.

Talia traced Una's script with her fingertip. She deeply loved the man who had captured her and whom she had tamed. "It is not easy to communicate with Calum. We've known each other only a short time."

"Una's legends were true enough with Duncan and Sybil. Once Sybil brought the Tallchief cradle to him, Megan's birth was certain. My stern, grim brother was destined for a household of women. He's their great big spoiled pet, and proud of them." Elspeth placed Talia's hands apart. She looped dark green yarn around them and began winding it into a ball as they talked.

"Which piece of Una's dowry have you claimed to return to the Tallchiefs?"

"A paisley shawl of fine merino wool, dark red, like coals lit by fiery tints of yellow and orange. Una describes its pattern and texture beautifully."

"And the legend?"

Elspeth flushed slightly and looked away. "There is something about the lady huntress taming a scarred warrior, and ice and fire. I haven't been able to read that part clearly yet, because of damage to the old pages. I'm not certain I want to. It definitely is more complex than the other legends. Una has blended it with a legend from our Sioux heritage."

She smiled quietly at Talia. "I've just started a new Tallchief pattern and need more yarn. Calum works regularly from his home. He helps regularly with the Tallchief Cattle Ranch and sheep shearing, and with wood gathering and with family events. For instance, before Megan was born, Calum cancelled everything and made her wear a beeper. Not only did Duncan carry one, but so did Calum and Birk. Poor Sybil was weighted down with every emergency contact device possible, including a flare signal. When she was allowed to drive by herself, my three brothers ran an ongoing spy mission, networking with the entire town and neighbors."

"I think you're being evasive about your legend and I think Calum can be very...centered."

"You mean when he wants something, he's very dedicated to obtaining it? Like a hunter." Elspeth avoided the return to her legend.

"Yes." Talia frowned at the rhythmic motion of Elspeth's hands. She fought the slow anger riding her; Calum would know about birth control, an important matter to be discussed by both participants. "He has old-fashioned ideas."

"My brothers are like that, especially when they care. They can be overpowering, just like our great-great-grandfather was with Una. They can be...devious."

"Devious. Like Calum's Desert Hawk. He still hasn't paid fully for that." Talia scowled at the journals.

"They are challenging." Elspeth finished the ball of yarn and studied Talia. "You realize that you're just exactly what Calum needed. He needed a good challenge, and the gossip in Amen Flats is that you are his fast game."

Elspeth smiled. "That was quite the sight—to see you riding on the back of Calum's horse, wrapped in a blanket against the cold and huddled to his back. The travois—the tent poles dragging behind the horse—carried the tepee and camping gear. The image dates back to Una and Tallchief's time, when he first captured her."

"Captured? You think Calum has captured a bride?"

"Umm...it was only an image, probably a false one." Elspeth's tone was noncommittal.

Talia remembered Calum's body lodged deeply within hers, the fire rising between them, the beating of their hearts— "You realize that he told me to stand and fight, don't you? What kind of a man would say that to a lady? To me, a Petrovna?"

With her hands free, she leaped to her feet and began to pace. Locked in her thoughts of Calum, Talia touched the huge old spinning wheel near a window cluttered with bundles of lavender and sage. "Now Calum has me sounding like Papa," she muttered.

Elspeth seemed lost in thought for a moment, then carefully placed the ball of yarn in the huge wooden bowl near the loom. "By the way, did you know that Calum is an expert climber? He was the only one qualified for the rescue operation."

"I wanted to think. He makes that difficult—" Talia

rounded on Elspeth as the other woman elegantly poured tea. *"He climbs mountains? Rescue operation?"*

Elspeth's gray eyes met Talia's. "The climber who died had panicked. He was told to wait for Calum. He didn't. He fell to his death, right past Calum."

"You mean, he was fully qualified for rescue and he let me struggle up to grab his boot? He let me freeze on that sheer rock and didn't help?"

Elspeth's cool, amused look took in Talia's taut body, her flushed face and her furious expression. She stood up to take Talia's hands in her own. "Would you have wanted him to interfere? In some ways, you and he are alike...you like to do things your own way. Calum has traveled all over the world. He rescued Kadar's sister from an avalanche, and he's a champion skier. He also reviews Broadway plays for critics who can't. He's been searching for the best challenge yet. If I'm not mistaken, he's found what he wants. What do you think?"

"Calum reviews plays?" Talia ran through Calum's comments and weighed them. They were professional.

"Mmm... He's led an interesting life." Elspeth smoothed her sleek black chignon with an elegant hand. Then she smiled warmly. "Interesting tidbits about my brother, eh?"

"I'd like to take his thick neck between my hands and—" Talia stopped pacing back and forth in the serene kitchen. She stared at Elspeth, who was standing hands on hips, legs spread. Talia looked closely at Elspeth's grin. "You're enjoying this. You're deliberately feeding me tidbits about Calum."

"Aye, captive bride of the Tallchief. That I am. I've had my fill of Calum Tallchief, and it's time for another woman to share that burden. He's told you he loves you, and you're on the run. Get him to wear the Tallchief kilt. I'm counting on your help, and don't listen to his moans about the cold wind sweeping up his backside.''

Elspeth smoothed her fingertip over the Tallchief plaid neatly folded on her worktable. From beneath her glossy raven lashes, she studied Talia's expression, and then Elspeth smiled slightly. "The bridal tepee is a lovely Tallchief tradition, but I really didn't know if Calum would—"

Talia rounded on her. *"Bridal tepee?"*

Ten

Freshly showered, Calum rinsed his old-fashioned straight razor in the bathroom sink. Electric razors served a purpose, but not for the heavy beard he had acquired in the past two days. Talia's climbing escapade, and the woodcutting and hauling, had prevented his usual ritual. He'd needed the physical exercise of chopping wood and hauling it to his home; he'd needed to think. In his home, Talia's jasmine scent prevented that. Now, with a better grip on his emotions, he'd planned a logical meeting of the minds with Talia, and, hopefully, a meeting of their bodies to confirm her agreement with him.

He met his reflection in the mirror and shook his head. A man couldn't haul his bridal tepee around forever, waiting for his chosen bride to decide to come to him. But that was exactly what he did, unfolding and establishing the whole process yet another time, deep in the woods of Tall-chief Mountain. Life with Talia could exhaust a man in multiple ways. A woman of action needed adjustments in the courting game; for her, he was willing to skip certain pleasures, like conventional dating, for the present.

Calum ignored the small dollop of shaving cream that dropped onto his chest. A regular shaving time would be impossible with Talia nearby; he could cope with that easily, but not with the abrasions his beard left on her skin. He wiped the razor blade on the towel draped around his neck. He'd been a little evil-tempered with Talia. It wasn't every day that a meticulous man realized he was so stoned with love and passion that he'd forgotten to use protection. He'd fallen into Talia's tender hands like a ripe fruit, dismissing his plans to tell her about his feelings. The word *laid* taunted him.

He clung to the moment when she'd given herself to him, wrapped himself in that small security.

The squall of Talia's red sports car coming to a stop outside his home caused Calum to pause. Olaf, who had been curiously studying Calum's shaving techniques, bounded past him, followed by Ivana and Igor. Amid the hectic, happy barking of the puppy, who had begun imitating Olaf, the front door slammed. The sound of Talia's boots marched through the house. She paused in the kitchen. He frowned at his image in the mirror and began a slow, studious swipe up from his jaw, drawing away the white foam on his cheek. He smiled grimly, realizing how much he liked Talia hunting him, coming for him. This time he was ready.

Talia flung open the bathroom door, stepping into the room immediately. "Here you are! I read your comments, Mr. Professional Reviewer, Top Mountain Climber, Champion Skier, and I—"

She blinked; her gaze jerked down his body. "Calum. You are shaving in the nude."

"True," he returned pleasantly, and continued shaving.

Determined to shoot at him whatever was nettling her, Talia continued, "I've just come from Elspeth, and—"

"And?" Calum patted away the remaining foam and turned to her. After a lifetime of Elspeth's delicate manipulation, Calum had known she would intervene in his romance of Talia. He'd known it from Elspeth's first approving "Aye!" He braced himself....

Her eyes skipped down to his arousal and widened. "Uh...I'll talk with you later."

Calum threw the towel around his neck to the floor in one swift, impatient movement. "I've got plans for later. You're on my schedule *now,* dear heart."

"You brought a bridal tepee up to the mountain. Everyone saw us come down." She backed up as he advanced a step. "What plans?"

Calum took another step. "It's called tradition, sweetheart. Much to my amazement, I've found that I'm a traditional man where you're concerned. You're the only woman who has mattered to me enough to admit that I am not a contemporary man. I had planned a romantic evening the night before, which frightened you. It seemed a shame to waste a pot of good clam chowder, so I decided you might want something hot at the end of your, what?—caper?—in freezing weather?"

"You did all that work for clam chowder?" She backed up against the wall. "Just what are your plans for later?"

Calum leaned down to place his cheek along hers. His body hummed with the need to hold her, yet he feared frightening her. He was afraid enough for both of them. He nuzzled, then gently bit her ear. "Romancing my bride in my own time. Without her skipping from A to Z and seducing me before I'm ready. You move too fast, Petrovna. I fell into your hands like a ripe fruit up on the mountain. Do you know how I feel about that? I'll tell you."

Talia trembled. She shook her head. "I'm not really a

very good housekeeper, you know. I just stayed to irritate you, and— Oh, by the way, I found the envelope of your suggestions on the kitchen table. Thank you for the wonderful helpful hints on *Nachos and Nanette....*''

Her breath caught as the tip of his tongue toyed with her ear. ''Petrovna, shut up. I had major plans for the use of the bridal tepee, which you squashed. You frightened me badly by climbing up that cliff. Then you had me. I was shocked and not in a pleasant mood when I realized you'd struck again. Counted coup and had me, laid me out and took me, before I could explain exactly how I feel. A bridal tepee is not the place for anger, which you had aroused in me. That is why I didn't pursue my plans for the tepee further. Take a note, Petrovna. Not only did I forget protection—something I've never done before—there's tradition. Courtship. Rules and terms. A woman like you could emasculate an unsuspecting man.''

''Not you,'' she breathed unevenly after a quick glance downward. Calum allowed his masculinity to lurch heavily against her stomach, which she sucked in instantly. ''You're tender and considerate and... You forgot protection? I mean, a methodical man like you—that discovery alone must have been shattering. An untied end, so to speak. Do you love me?'' she asked hurriedly.

''Enough to try again, which any man with good sense wouldn't do. Let me phrase this very carefully, Petrovna. You could be carrying my baby. How do you feel about that?''

When her shock turned to surprised wonder, he pounced. ''You're a quick mover. It would be just like you to take what I've given no other woman and create a child before our relationship is thoroughly resolved. I can deal with that complication. In fact, I welcome the possibility. If you do.''

He proceeded quickly, before his dreams could consume him. Before he could pick her up, close to his heart, and race up the stairs with her. "You move fast, and I'm trying to catch you on the run. I want you to know that the lack of prevention *wasn't* on purpose. That I am not trying an old trick that my great-great-grandfather probably used to keep Una."

Her hand went up to his cheek. Her eyes were gentle upon him. "Why, Calum. You've shocked yourself. You're in a stew as to how to handle me and the situation."

"I have a backup plan, Petrovna. Logic always prevails. I want you to know that from now on, I will always be very careful with you in every way."

Talia eased slightly away from him and out into the hall-way. "Calum, you could, ah…catch cold. Exactly what are your plans for tonight?"

"I would like, with your cooperation, to begin the basis of a long-term relationship. I want to romance my bride and tell her what is in my heart. Like the first step in ne-gotiating a lasting proposition." He let her feed on that as she took one step backward and hit the stairway. "Keep in mind, Petrovna, that you are a fast-moving woman. I am just doing my best to cope."

She took a step up, her eyes on a level with his. "I sense that you are very fragile right now."

He snorted in disbelief, and she took another step. His eyes jerked to her breasts, rising and falling within the tight black sweater. He could almost taste the delicate nubs, the softness cupped by his hand. "I feel as hard as iron," he stated with confidence. He asked again the question she had not answered. "How would you feel if you found you were carrying my child?"

"Tallchief, I took you because I wanted you. Is this an even-Steven sort of gig? Where, ah…you would like to repay certain, ah…scores?"

"I am not going to throw my love at you like an old shoe, if that's what you mean." A trickle of anger ran through Calum as he recalled what she had said. "You were right. I should have picked a better way of telling you. It's not a phrase I've used often."

She continued to back up the stairs as Calum advanced upward. "Okay—here's how I felt. I felt you…pulsing in me, so deep that I didn't know where I stopped and you began. You completed me and I completed you. We were one. I thought then, 'How marvelous…how wonderful… You are mine, Calum Tallchief. This is beautiful.' And then I realized I was crying with the beauty of it, a timeless essence of how life goes on…of what you gave to me, and how I wanted to protect and nourish your gift."

Her softly spoken words stunned him in midstep, wrapped around his heart and hugged him. He forced away his light-headed joy and proceeded. "Will you be my bride tonight? Will you let me tell you the things that are in my heart?"

In the shadows, she met his eyes. "I am so afraid, Calum. I thought I could handle my emotions. Where you're concerned, I can't."

"Share them with me." Upstairs now, Calum cradled her cheeks in his hands. "Make me a part of you tonight, Talia."

She closed her eyes, tears spiking her lashes. "It is important to you that…we use the tepee?"

He would not lie to her, as badly as he wanted the night to tell her of his heart. "It is important. But we can stay here. Or I will leave you alone. You decide."

Her lips trembled, and still she did not meet his eyes. "You are so…traditional."

"It is my wedding night. One like I haven't had before. Nor will I again. Come with me."

"Yes," she whispered unevenly, so quietly he had to lean close to hear. "Yes, I'll come with you."

* * *

"Love is a circle," Calum whispered unevenly when she stood in the tepee's firelight, clad in the doeskin shift.

He tossed away the warm sweat suit and maxicoat that she had worn riding on the horse behind him. Calum quickly stripped away his own clothing; the stone lay warm upon his chest. He stood very straight, letting her see his obvious need of her. The ceremony was age-old, that of a man and woman coming together, knowing that their lives would forever be intertwined, as their bodies soon would be.

With her hair undone and loose around the shift, Talia allowed Calum to replace the garnet ring to her finger. The tent billowed with the night wind that sighed in the pine boughs overhead. "Why do you want me?" she asked quietly, as Calum brought their joined hands to his lips.

"You make my heart glad. You fill me with wonder and joy."

"You haven't asked me to say I love you."

"That has to come from your heart. What you give me now is enough."

The doeskin fringes fell away from her arms as Calum lifted one; he brushed a kiss on the inside of her elbow. In this moment, Talia's eyes softened upon him, stroking his face with a tenderness he hoped to nurture. "Come to me," he whispered as her trembling fingertips brushed his lips.

He lightly kissed her forehead, her eyebrows, her lashes, and straightened, easing away from her. Talia's eyes shimmered in the firelight. "You make me feel like I'm shining, Calum."

He feared she would change her mind, but then she lifted the shift slowly and discarded it. Talia's long, pale limbs gleamed in the firelight as she slowly lowered herself onto the bed he had prepared of soft old quilts, sewn by his mother and grandmothers. Talia's movements stirred the scents of sweet grass he had placed beneath the pallet; he caught her jasmine fragrance and her exotic, intimate womanly scent.

Calum stood still, absorbing the picture of her hair, flowing over the pillows and the warm soft quilts, over her shoulders. He prayed there would be other times, but this one would be locked in his heart with their first loving.

"Come to me, Calum," she whispered above the sound of the fire and the drumming of his heart.

He came with purpose and touched her reverently, lightly. First her face, brushing her lips with kisses, then her throat. She trembled as he touched her breasts, his rugged face warm and strong against her throat, his kisses heating her skin. She waited, breathing unevenly, washed by emotions of joy and of fear. She curbed her need to take him quickly as Calum eased her fully into his arms, a gentle abrasion of rough skin against her own. Of his heat and his length stroking her thigh.

Beneath her palms, Calum's back rippled as he moved over her very carefully, fitting his length to her.

She respected his need for tradition, for this moment, letting him lead her.

Calum rested above her, his eyes light within his tanned, rugged face and the scented shadows. Braced on his forearms, he smoothed a strand of hair from her cheek. His expression was tender, yet fiercely proud, his fingers trembling as they stroked her cheek.

Talia dived into the sensations he arose within her, the tenderness she felt for him now. The joy for what would come. She eased her thighs apart, admitting him to the cradle of her body. He waited, his heart pounding against hers, his body taut. Their eyes locked as she moved her hips, lifted to receive him, and he slid home, deep within her.

For long heartbeats, he lay very still, stretching her to

the limits, easing deeper. He filled her with himself and with the wonder of the marriage ritual.

The elemental ceremony caused her to cry out, a tear sliding from her cheek. He kissed away the dampness and laid his head down beside hers. "Listen to our hearts," he whispered against her hot skin. "We are one."

He moved slowly, thoroughly, within her, and the storm crashed within them, flinging them into the heat and the thunder. When she burst, she held to Calum, gradually floating back to the safety of the soft old quilts scented of sweet grass. She dozed and awoke to his cleansing, his tenderness.

His radiant grin took her heart and stunned her for a heartbeat. She grinned back. "Taking a captive groom isn't that hard."

"Isn't it? Now that sounds like a challenge, honey." Then he bent to kiss her in a shocking place. While she dealt with that tender assault, he licked her navel, then found her breasts. Calum took one into his mouth, suckling deeply, alternating with gentle bites. .

While the first joining had been dreamlike and beautiful, Talia sensed that he no longer needed to observe tradition. She held his head to her, heard his hungry sounds of pleasure. The delicate pressure caught fire, cords heating throughout her body, lodging deep within a place Calum had just filled. Her body tightened desperately, and she knew that this was the mating of bodies, as well as hearts and souls.

Calum trimmed the shocking, primitive needs enticing her body. He kissed her hungrily, his tongue finding hers, drawing it into his lips to suckle. She tasted him, locked her hands to his strong shoulders and allowed herself to fly. His body flowed against hers, tormenting, heating, retreating.

She pushed against him, locked her arms around his neck

and bit him. "You're not going anywhere, Calum Tallchief. Not now."

He laughed aloud, startling her. The deep rumbling sound vibrated against her breasts, sensitized by his tender treatment. Talia bent to find his nipples, suckling the flat, hard nubs. She grinned against his chest as Calum groaned hungrily, his tall, strong body hers to tempt and to heat. She licked his navel and Calum's big hands locked to her head, drawing her upward for his openmouthed kiss. "Take it easy, Petrovna."

Raw emotion coursed through his deep, uneven tone. She had him now; he was her game, her captive. She moved her leg over him experimentally, allowing her heat to warm his hard thigh. Calum's hand found her then, his palm caressing her in gentle circles. She flowed against him and nipped his nipple again. His ragged groan was a sharp protest, his body taut against hers.

Calum's fingers slid to caress her. He touched her and she bloomed, heated and moist, at his stroke. He nourished a tender bit within her, slowly, delicately, and Talia began to vibrate, her blood pounding. "Calum?"

"You are so hot, vibrating with heat—" When she would have taken him, Calum resisted, smoothing her body with big, strong hands. He took her hips within his hands, cradled her against him and rocked gently, undulating against her.

The tiny contractions caught Talia unaware, lifting her higher, and she gripped his shoulders tightly as her body was riveted on a peak she didn't understand. When she could breathe again, she met Calum's teasing kisses and opened her eyes to see his tender smile. "You think this is funny, Tallchief?"

"Beautiful. I think you are beautiful." His fingers stroked her again, and a tiny convulsion of pleasure raced through her, causing her to gasp.

Calum raised her fingers to suckle them, his gaze locked with hers. Talia reached lower to touch him, and Calum held very still as she fitted her hand around him. "Don't," he ordered rawly as she began to experiment. "Just don't."

He fused his mouth to hers, and she took. She lost a sense of tomorrow or yesterday and found only pleasure in looking at him. "Tell me what you like."

"I love you, Petrovna. All of you. You fascinate me. Each moment with you is exciting. But if you mean in relation to this—" His hands swept meaningfully over her body, drawing her close to him. "Your breasts. They fascinate me."

He turned her over to study them. Then bent to kiss the tip of each one. "They're pink and soft and tasty."

Riveted by his expression, Talia forgot her shyness. He caressed her aching breasts equally and placed his splayed fingers over her soft stomach. "I like this. It's gurgly and warm and—"

His hand slid lower, curving over her. His expression was changing intensely. "You're fragrant here, honey. Like a flower."

"That's how I feel when you touch me…like a flower opening, becoming beautiful," she admitted shyly.

"Petal by petal…" Calum stroked her lightly, and she bloomed beneath his touch.

He trembled, desire sharpening his features, his hair disheveled by her fingers. He eased over her, drawing her knees high to kiss the tender insides.

He slid to fill her, and she cried out, locking him to her. He pushed deeper, his breath warm against her cheek, her throat. She turned to meet his hungry kiss, and the words flowed from her lips to his. "Calum. Calum. Calum. I love you."

The fierce pounding of their hearts rose and heated and thundered through their pleasure. Calum bound her to him with strong arms, and she captured him with her limbs and her mouth fused to his. They moved higher in the incredible pleasure, found each other and cried out. Her shattering was followed by his, and she heard his muffled shout. Talia smiled against Calum's shoulder as his body pulsed deeply within her. She'd taken him, and with an age-old wisdom, Talia realized that they had bonded, mated, in a way she would never forget.

"Stop smirking, honey," Calum muttered drowsily against her throat.

She stroked his tall body, relaxed now upon her. He was vulnerable now, hers to protect. "Shh… Go to sleep."

Calum eased slightly aside, but stayed locked within her. During the night, he stirred, filling her once more, and Talia rose to meet him. "I love you," she cried out, taking him fiercely.

Calum listened to the silence of his house. They had returned home midmorning on the second day. After their hurried shower—Calum really enjoyed that shower, with the water sluicing between them as they made love—Talia had kissed him, dressed and soared out of the driveway in her red car. She'd been humming, ready to capture the world and to redo her play. Calum had unpacked, started lunch and laundry, then settled down to catch up on his messages and accounts.

Olson's redemption was progressing according to plan. His wife had tied him to the rack, and he was definitely paying. Calum smiled at Olson's dropping bank account balance. Calum had gotten the bank's permission to "audit anytime" when he worked for them. He tapped out a computer note to Olson's private machine—"I'm watching."

He found another message waiting for Olson and scanned it. "You jerk. Keep your hands in your own pockets, lover boy. Big Sister is watching." Calum grimly erased Talia's message; Olson just might match his ex-secretary to Calum's new bride. The tenderness in their bridal tent, and Talia's crying out her love for him, were not going to be disturbed. Calum wanted everything running smoothly.

As smoothly as possible, with a volatile, unpredictable woman like Talia.

Calum checked on Sybil's progress in locating another Tallchief cradle; the Sioux warrior had built and sold others to support his growing family. She muttered about Marcella Portway's missing Spanish royal gene and said she'd locate a cradle soon, running through old auction summaries and antique stores' inventories.

Freed from Ivana and Igor, who were curled together, sleeping, Olaf placed his head on Calum's knee. He whined softly and Calum rubbed his ears. "I miss her, too. It's a one-step-at-a-time proposition with Petrovna, soon to be Tallchief. I intend to romance her out of those Hessian boots and add a wedding ring to Una's Celtic band. We've got all winter."

"I love you...." Talia had cried out, her body throbbing against his.

Calum inhaled, realizing that his loins were indeed old-fashioned and lust-prone when he thought of Talia—the woman he considered his wife. There was more, of course, an emotion that ran on a level that bonded heart and soul when the heat had passed.

Calum realized that he was slightly and old-fashionedly shocked by Talia's volcanic response to him. He hadn't known how much had been missing from his marriage. The completion was there, the feeling that the circle was completed when he lay in her arms. When they talked softly, or played.

He realized he was grinning like a boy. Talia caused him to feel that way—light, young, carefree. He'd told her about the Tallchiefs' struggle to keep together as orphans. She'd understood and told him about her "long white dress phobia."

They were communicating, and everything was proceeding along nicely.

Talia stepped into his office and found him sitting at his computer. Their eyes locked; she walked toward him in the long-legged, hip-swaying slow walk that dried his throat. Her short skirt flared as she eased her leg over to straddle him in the chair. "Hello, darlin'. Doing your methodical investment thing?"

"I checked on your freewheeling investments. You're an intuitive player, and a good one." Calum found her moist and hot to his touch. "You do everything well."

"Why, thank you, darlin'. It's nice to know I'm appreciated." Her tights tore in his hand as Talia ran her hands over his cheeks. "I miss the beard," she whispered huskily. Then she bent to nibble on his jaw, his throat, and took away his breath when she suckled him.

With a new confidence, she found his confined desire, stroked him lightly and tugged open his zipper.

When Calum could speak again, his heart pounding like a running stag, and Talia had wilted warmly upon him, he muttered.

She forced her head up to kiss his jaw. "Mmm?"

"Ambushed again." He lowered her to the floor and began slowly unbuttoning her sweater. "Let's take it slower this time."

"You'll have to keep up. I am a woman of action—" She inhaled as he began to kiss her throat and breasts. Her fingertips dug into his shoulders and she bit his neck gently as he proceeded to pleasure her. "Oh, my…Calum, you are a thorough man."

"Mmm… I manage to get there, honey."

She fluttered her lashes against his throat. "I've got news for you, darlin'. Calum the cool has got to go. The name no longer applies."

Eleven

The first week of December, the curtain came down on the last act of *Nachos and Nanette*'s first night. Talia held her breath; the audience rose to its feet, clapping and whistling. She beamed, elated—her first play was a success, thanks to Calum's well-placed criticism. She'd touched the hearts of cowboys and ranchers and farm wives and merchants. The local undertaker wore a grin. A section of stern-faced Native Americans had nodded their approval.

Life in a small town wasn't that bad.

Waking up in Calum's arms was fantastic.

Lounging in his shirt and socks and arguing over who read the comics first was quite pleasant.

She hadn't thought that a traditional man would play house-husband while she worked to perfect the play. Calum practically dressed her in the morning and tucked her into bed at night. He listened and encouraged and saw that she ate regular meals; he'd handled her business investments that needed immediate attention. He'd pacified her family, promising to bring her home soon. His foot massages were wonderful. Tonight he understood her fear of failure, her need to wear her battle gear, the black sweater and tight pants and Hessian boots. He'd even polished them for her, along with his Western boots; Megan had helped by drooling upon the leather.

When Talia was discouraged about the play, he'd known just how to challenge her. When the applause began, he had vanished from his seat. Everything was perfect—she wanted to share her victory with Calum Tallchief.

She'd find him, drag him into a locked closet and toss up his kilt. Talia hurried down the hallway to the reception room and flung open the door.

The Tallchief clan stood together, dressed in white ruffled shirts, kilts and the Fearghus-Tallchief plaid draped from shoulder to hip. Elspeth, looking very feminine, stood in front of her tall, grim brothers. Sybil held Duncan's hand, a smile touching her lips, her eyes warm upon him. In Birk's arms, Megan was a miniature replica of the Tallchiefs, with her gray eyes and glossy black hair. Birk didn't mind the wet spot on his shoulder from Megan's nibbles, a child teething on loved ones. Lacey, looking like a Scots elf amid the towering Tallchiefs, grinned up at the males' glowering expressions.

Calum walked slowly toward Talia, a tall, dark man with fierce, stormy gray eyes.

The pure white of his shirt contrasted with his dark skin, the ruffles a contrast against his rugged face, the dragon green and Tallchief vermilion catching the overhead light. His jet-black hair gleamed; her fingers recognized the crisp texture, the way it curved on his nape. His shoulders, broad beneath the layers of shirt and plaid, blocked out the soft, knowing smiles of the other Tallchiefs. The kilt moved around his long legs, sheathed in plaid stockings.

"Aye!" the Tallchiefs shouted cheerily behind him. "Aye!"

His hand stretched out to her, large and callused. Strong enough to keep her. Gentle enough to exquisitely pleasure her.

His steady smoke-gray eyes held hers. He came to claim her as his bride, with a binding legality this time. To change the present, to take her to the future. To place a gold band beside the garnets she wore, to make her his... To make her a part of him and the Tallchiefs. To transport her into age-old traditions, into a love that frightened her to her very core.

Battered by her old fears, her uncertainties and her new love, Talia reacted instinctively to protect herself. She fled down the hallway and hurled herself up the stairs to the rooftop.

The cold December wind hit her, taking away her breath. She leaped to another building, keeping to the shadows of a chimney. Then she hurried across the night shadows to a flat building, dropped to the fire escape and ran down it. Ten feet from the street, she held the bars and dropped gracefully to the ground.

A horse moved from the night shadows into the light of a street lamp. Calum sat in the saddle, still dressed in his ruffled shirt, plaid and kilt. "Having a nice time?" he asked in too soft a voice.

"Oh, hello, Calum." She began walking hurriedly on the sidewalk, the hoofbeats sounding behind her.

"Talia." Her name echoed like a shot in a showdown.

She pivoted on him, tears streaming down her face, emotions ripping through her. Against the night sky, he looked as huge as some dark knight coming to claim her. Talia dashed away her tears and backed away from his approaching horse. "I'm scared," she admitted, shaking violently.

"No one said this would be easy."

She tried to find comfort in his tone, and couldn't; it lay hard as steel between them. She could accept him, love him, trust him…or she could walk away. Calum Tallchief tossed the challenge at her without giving an inch. He sat in the saddle, the winter wind rippling his shirt and plaid and kilt.

She wore his family ring; it gleamed in the night as she held up her hand protectively. Calum wanted to place another band on her finger; he wanted more….

"I love you, Calum Tallchief." She dashed away the tears freezing to her cheeks. She wanted him to scoop her up, warm her and tell her that he loved her in that sweet, dark, hungry way of his.

"Oh, Calum. I do love you," she whispered to the freezing night wind, and realized that she was crying, her fist pressed to her lips, her body trembling.

He'd left the choice to her….

The second week of December, Calum walked through Denver's elegant downtown section. Past the buildings and the streetlights overhead, the stars twinkled on the velvet night. A week without Talia grated on his sleepless nights.

He'd placed his love at her feet. He'd taken a chance that she loved him enough to step over the bridges that separated them; he'd meet her more than halfway.

Calum tugged up his black leather jacket collar against the biting wind. He dreaded Christmas more than ever, an outcast from the dreams he savored of Talia snug in his arms, laughing up at him, the future spreading before them.

"Aye!" The Tallchief cry echoed in the deserted streets, the cheery Christmas decorations mocking him from shop windows. He'd wanted to woo her in his arms, to gently ease her into the idea that he wanted the years with her.

Calum glared at the elves in a window, working to wrap presents for under the Christmas tree. In his heart, he was a married man, yet she'd nicked his pride. Her dismissal of commitment, of designing a future together, had wounded him.

"Aye!" His family had flopped out his intentions too quickly and frightened Talia. He'd read the fear widening her eyes, causing her face to pale.

His heart had shattered, tumbling down his damned kilt to his feet, when he saw Talia run from him. He'd give her only so much time, and then—

Calum noted a shadow sliding alongside his, a slender, agile shadow, and his hopes leaped by twenty stories.

He strolled into a darkened alley, and the shadow followed. A hard object pushed against his back. "Put your hands against that wall and spread 'em."

Calum obeyed, his palms flat on the building's bricks, and waited as the scent of jasmine curled around him. A soft hand brushed the nape of his neck; bangle bracelets chimed by his ear. "Don't get any ideas about turning around. Hold still while I frisk you."

"I might not have what you want." Calum tensed as two hands cupped his buttocks and squeezed gently.

"Oh, you do. An ample amount." A slender, pale hand slid to his chest, three garnets set in a Celtic design gleaming in the dim light. They disappeared beneath his sweater and grasped the polished stone around his throat. When her fingers released the stone, they slid in a caress across his chest and slowly down to his stomach.

Calum's heart kicked into double time when Talia's softness gently nudged his back and slid upward until her lips bit his ear. "Hold very still. Don't get any ideas that you can get away from me now."

He braced himself against a trail of kisses down his throat, and the feminine hands splayed possessively over his flat stomach. They slid lower, circled his waist and slid up inside his jacket to caress his taut back. She eased against his body, and nudged him with her hips. "Don't you dare move, Calum Tallchief. I've got you now. You are mine, darlin'."

She hugged him fiercely, and when Calum started to move, she tucked a small box into the front of his belt. He slowly took his shaking hands from the brick wall and opened the velvet box. A man's broad wedding band gleamed on the red cloth. "I love you, Calum Tallchief. You're just old-fashioned enough to consider this a dowry. Petrovna's Law. Equal terms. Are you going to stand and fight, or—"

Calum pivoted, clasped her in his arms and lifted her until her toes dangled inches above the street. Talia hurled her arms around his neck, her legs around his hips, and kissed him breathless. She leaned back momentarily to remove his steamed glasses and tuck them in his pocket.

"I've been taking lambada lessons," Calum said between hungry, teasing kisses. He'd noted Talia practicing as she cooked. The notion of dancing the sexy Latin-American steps with her pleased him, as she did. He gently squeezed her soft hips in his palms. She was wearing her black outfit, her Hessian boots locked firmly around his hips. That was good. When this lady came calling in Hessian boots, she meant business.

"I know. I've been tracking you. You need lots of practice. You need a dance partner who will keep you on your toes and not mind your nasty temper. One who will stand and fight you when you get overbearing and too traditional."

"Mmm... Private lessons?"

"Very private. Tell me why you want me?" Talia's husky question revealed her vulnerability to the commitment she had made to him tonight.

He kissed the sensitive corners of her mouth. "Because of your passion. Because of how you make me feel. Because of how my heart lifts just looking at you, you irritating little witch. You make me happy.''

For a moment, she just stared at him. ''It's a circle, isn't it, Calum. You complete me, love.'' Talia ran her fingertips across his lips, her eyes glowing up at him. ''It all happened so fast... I should have trusted you.... I realized later how much I hurt you when I ran—''

''Shh... You're here now. I love you, Talia.'' He kissed the tip of her nose, the damp spikes of her lashes.

Talia cradled his face in her hands, her thumbs brushing his lips. She looked at him with soft, glowing love. ''You're my great adventure, my exciting challenge for the rest of our lives. You're my nerd, my Desert Hawk, my cowboy, my warrior, my friend...and, best of all, my love. Will you wear my ring? Will you marry me, Calum Tallchief?''

He fused his mouth to hers and held her close to his racing heart. ''Figure it out.''

Breathless and soft against him, Talia smoothed his cheek. ''There you go...challenging me. Take me somewhere where I can help you make up your mind. I want the whole works, the bridal gown and the hungry groom. I want my bridal tent after a wedding in which Petrovna and Tallchief men will probably shock the guests. I want to see my mother's face when she cries, and I want to cry at our children's weddings. I want to see my father slightly tipsy and boasting what a fine catch his little girl brought home. Alek and Anton will be grim at first, and no doubt run you through some ceremonial male gauntlet—''

Talia lifted her face to Calum's lips. He kissed away her tears, her friend, her lover. She kissed his lashes and found them damp, this gentle, emotional, traditional man whom she loved. ''Tell me the legend again....''

Calum held her closer, this woman he loved and who loved him in return. Against her lips, he whispered tenderly, "When a man of Fearghus blood places the ring upon the right woman's finger, he'll capture his true love forever."

"It's true. Forever, my love." Their eyes met and promised.

The bloodred stones on the golden ring gleamed on Talia's finger as she stroked Calum's tanned cheek. "So, my loving, traditional husband-to-be, what do you know about seeds?"

He blinked, refocused and shook his head. "Seeds?"

Elspeth ran her fingertip across a pine bough laden with snow. She gathered the Tallchief plaid shawl around her against the winter night. Tallchief Mountain loomed above the moon-trail on the lake. Circles were age-old, binding the past and the future. Calum's circle was complete; his heart had claimed another who loved him just as much. Elspeth inhaled the scent of smoke and pine; the wind fluttered the tendrils around her face, they clung to her skin. Duncan and Calum had found their heart mates, their souls wedded for eternity. Calum had another Tallchief cradle hidden away for the time when it was needed. He would cry unashamedly then, a warrior humbled by his blood's continuing, by the woman who loved him and who gave his child life.

From the mist upon the cattails and reeds swirled a warmer wind; it circled Elspeth, toyed with the glossy black ends of her twin braids and caressed her cheek. She nuzzled the Tallchief plaid, her lips curving. Another love would be coming soon. Which Tallchief would it seek?

"Aye," she whispered softly to the shadows. "Aye."

*   *   *   *   *

TALLCHIEF FOR KEEPS

To my Valentines at Silhouette—
Melissa Senate, Isabel, Lucia and Tara

You're wonderful!

Legend of Una's Paisley Shawl

When the Marrying Moon is high,
a scarred warrior will rise from the mists
to claim his lady huntress.
He will wrap her in the shawl and carry her
to the Bridal Tepee and his heart. Their song
will last longer than the stars.

Prologue

In the kitchen's early-morning shadows, fourteen-year-old Elspeth Tallchief wrapped her mother's hand-stitched quilt around her. Pieces of the five Tallchief children's lives colored the quilt: outgrown clothing neatly arranged, each telling a vivid story. There was a square of her mother's apron and her father's lucky red shirt, woven by her mother and torn by a ram at shearing time.

Elspeth gripped her mother's favorite cookbook tightly against her. In the large, airy room beyond the kitchen, her mother's giant loom stood waiting for her shuttle. Her quilt rack hung close to the ceiling, ready to be lowered. But Pauline Tallchief would be not weaving or stitching quilts again.

Tears burned Elspeth's lids and she fought the tightness in her chest, dabbing at the tears with the quilt of memories.

Four days ago, the aroma of her mother's famed apple pie had filled the farm kitchen; her jars of fruit and jam lined the pantry. In the silence of the house, Elspeth could almost hear the echo of her mother's gentle laughter.

Elspeth recognized the wild rage running through her, the high fury that was said to have come down from her great-great-grandmother, Una. Elspeth noted distantly that she'd never been so angry, so torn by emotions, not even when tormented by her brothers. Perhaps it was the pride of her Sioux great-great-grandfather that prevented her from throwing dishes or raging at her parents' death.

The old quilt and her mother's cookbook were Elspeth's armor, because her brothers and sister were depending on her. She glanced at the old loom, supposedly her great-great-grandmother's. It would comfort her in the dark and frightening hours, because she was just as strong as her brothers and they were already preparing for the hardships ahead.

Outside, the cold October winds stalked Tallchief Mountain, rustling the dried aspen leaves over two new graves in the family cemetery. In the fields sloping up the mountainside, Tallchief cattle and sheep huddled together against the wind.

Down in the valley, the small town of Amen Flats, Wyoming, lay sleeping. All was the same and yet different, because in Amen Flats's jail was a—*life-taker*. Elspeth supplied the bitter tag for a man who had changed the Tallchiefs' lives.

Elspeth turned to the sound of stocking feet padding across the old house's floorboards. Her three brothers loomed in the shadows.

Only hours before, the five orphaned Tallchiefs had gathered at Tallchief Lake. Amid the winds and under a round, silvery moon, Duncan—the eldest at eighteen—had vowed to keep them safe and together. They had all pledged to find their heritage, their great-great-grandmother's lost dowry that was steeped in legends.

Elspeth clasped the old cookbook closer, the one with

her mother's beautiful handwriting and favorite recipes of each Tallchief child.

Her brothers moved closer to her, their gray eyes as light and fierce as Una Fearghus's, their Scottish great-great-grandmother. Jutting cheekbones, slashing brows and gleaming black hair were gifts from Tallchief, their Sioux great-great-grandfather. Long-legged Westerners, they knew how to deal with cattle and killers, but a woman's tears of mourning would send them fleeing for safety.

"Fiona is sleeping upstairs with her cat." Duncan's soft voice curled around Elspeth.

"Ten years old or not, she'll have to be up in the morning and on the school bus." At seventeen, Calum had always been practical, but now his voice had a new note of steel.

"It's three o'clock in the morning, but we'll all go to school tomorrow." Birk touched Elspeth's hair to comfort her, but she shook him off.

Wrapped in the old quilt, Elspeth stood in the center of the kitchen and faced them, her head high, her own gray eyes flashing like steel. Her strength was forged from the same fierce blood and pride. "I don't know why that man had to kill Mom and Dad when they stopped for pizza at the convenience store. I don't know why *only* my brothers had to be the ones to track their killer down...why all of you thought you were the only ones Dad taught how to track by moonlight. The sheriff knew you were the best trackers, let you go after him, and you brought him back—walking behind your horses and only a bit bruised after what he'd done. I should have been there. I should have gone. I can ride just as well as any of you...better."

"You had a job to do—"

She dismissed Calum's practical statement, noted Duncan's helpless expression and glanced at Birk. His boyish grin was gone, his jaw set and grim—the picture of a boy who had become a man overnight. Her temper rose, consuming her fury and the helplessness at their parents' murder days before. Her control shattered, cracked like ice. She shivered, shook free of what they knew her to be and stepped into the fire of her rage. "So you took off, hunting the killer. Elspeth the elegant was ordered to tend Fiona the fiery. She needed me, and so I did, though I wanted to throw a knife right through that murderer's black heart—I can, you know—I can throw a knife or shoot a bow or a gun as well as any of you. It's just that I prefer...never mind what I prefer."

She preferred her mother, alive and well, and dancing in her father's arms, kissing him. Elspeth dashed a tear from the old cookbook, clutching it tighter. It was hers now, just as her brothers and Fiona were. She'd tend her family, but right now she would have her say.

With the flat of her hand, she pushed the broad chest of each of her brothers, one by one, and stepped back to face them, her long nightgown swirling at her ankles. "Poor, dainty Elspeth. Elspeth the elegant...isn't that what I'm called?" she asked, referring to names they called each other in play. "Isn't that true, Duncan the defender... Calum the cool...and Birk the rogue?"

"Aye." The word rumbled slowly from her brothers' throats, and Elspeth lifted her head, determined to hold on to her pride.

She lifted the tiny scar on her thumb before their noses. "Aren't I one of you, a nick in my thumb to prove it? Didn't I raise my thumb to the storm just two hours ago and pledge with you to do my part?"

"Aye!"

Elspeth shed the quilt. She wouldn't let her brothers see her weak. "You'll pick up your shorts and socks, and I'll set a schedule. Mother would have no one visiting a dirty house, and neither will I."

"Aye." The rumbling male voices came stronger, more fierce. It was said that Tallchiefs had backbones of steel, and now they would be tested, each ready to do his or her part. There would be no Tallchief Ranch on the county auction block or brothers and sisters torn apart. At eighteen, Duncan would try for legal guardianship, and Calum's methodical business brain would plow away at the family and ranch accounts. With his brothers, Birk would take his new share of hard ranch work. Fiona also would try something new—minding her p's and q's at school, taming her wild side until she got home.

Elspeth recalled the plan that Duncan had plucked from the fierce night wind and clouds; she held it before her brothers like a sword raised in a challenge. She paced before them, faced them like a general facing his troops. "Tonight, beside the lake, Duncan held Fiona close, promised to keep her safe and all of us together. As he says, we're wrapping our heritage around us to keep us safe and together. I will continue as Mother and me were doing, reading Una's journals. We'll each search out and bring back to the Tallchiefs some beloved piece of her dowry that was sold to keep Tallchief Mountain."

She ran a fingertip over a place mat her mother had woven, and an icy sword cut through her. She'd learned to weave on her mother's lap.... Elspeth's bottom lip trembled before she firmed it and faced her brothers, hovering uncertainly around her, wanting to protect her. She wouldn't let them. She wouldn't crumble and show her fear because she had no less pride than they did.

She gripped the place mat, crushing it to her with the cookbook. "Stand and fight, Tallchiefs. Isn't that what we've always said in hard times? Tonight we tossed an 'Aye' into the storm to guarantee our safety. Duncan says we should have family meetings and report on progress of finding Una's dowry. Each piece has a legend, though Mom and I couldn't translate the shawl's. I'll find Una's shawl, the one she brought from Scotland, and I pledge to bring it back to the Tallchiefs.''

She searched her brothers' taut faces, mourned for their boyhood that had been murdered days ago and flung herself into their arms.

"Stand and fight...." She allowed the tears to flow, dampening the shoulders of her brothers, wrapping them in her arms and keeping their strength around her. "We'll be safe. I promise you. I'll keep us safe and so will you. There will be no one finding fault with how we're dressed or what we eat or if we do our homework. We're staying together.''

"Aye!" The four Tallchiefs pledged at once, and for a moment, Elspeth thought she felt the caress of her mother's hand upon her cheek.

"Aye," she whispered to her mother's kitchen. "We'll be safe. Sleep well."

One

The month of March came to taunt Elspeth with a birthday that never came and yet would never go away. Elspeth came to Tallchief Mountain to mourn the loss of a baby that had never been born.

Bound by blood and love, the Tallchiefs had left her alone on their mountain to face her demons—when winter protested its death and the scent of spring lurked nearby. As she listened to the wind outside the tepee her brothers had fashioned for her, Elspeth sat upon her pallet and loosened her single braid. She'd combed her sleek black hair around the beaded shift that once was her English great-grandmother's and Elspeth touched the elegant beadwork, its points forming the Tallchief Mountain symbol.

Every year at this time, she came to Tallchief Mountain to mourn, and her brothers had wanted to ensure her safety during her retreat. When she arrived today, she'd found the tepee ready for her, fresh wood cut and stacked nearby. Fish waited in the lake's weir for her dinner. Inside the tepee she'd found a bag of Tallchief wool to hand card, the routine and rhythm giving her peace at the evening fire. There were bundles of her favorite herbs neatly hung from a cross pole, a blackened teakettle, a china pot with a matching cup and saucer—all the necessities Elspeth would need. Another cross pole held the branch waiting for her free-style weaving. She had in mind a wall hanging, the first of an exclusive contract with a Denver art dealer. She'd needed only a backpack filled with her clothing, her Navajo spindle and her Tallchief tartan shawl.

She gathered the soft length of green-and-blue wool to her, holding it tightly. Elspeth closed her eyes; she needed this respite from her family, though she loved them more than herself.

Duncan's second marriage brought him joy, and Calum's new wife would have his baby. Engaged twice before, Birk was circling Chelsey Lang, a gentle heart and a good friend. Always a rebel, Elspeth's sister, Fiona, fought her current war against "predators of the environment" in Wisconsin.

Una's journals spoke of the loss of her dowry, sold to protect Tallchief Mountain. To each item was attached a legend, and two of the legends in Una's dowry had come true—Duncan and Calum had claimed their true loves.

As a girl, Elspeth had dreamed of Una's paisley shawl and the legend attached to it. She'd pledged to find the shawl and bring it safely to the Tallchiefs, but the relevant journal entry had been smeared, perhaps by tears, and the legend had escaped Elspeth.

As a woman, one night in Scotland had her wanting to forget the legend entirely.

When she had returned home from Scotland, she'd ripped the page from Una's journal and torn it in pieces. Regretting that her temper had ruled her and that she'd destroyed part of her inheritance, Elspeth had then placed the pieces in an envelope for safekeeping. There would be no true love legend for Elspeth now; she no longer believed in a love for herself. She wanted the paisley shawl now for the beauty of the merino wool, the fiery golds and reds blending in a paisley design. More, the shawl was hers by right of an inheritance, and she wanted it wrapped around her like her family.

Elspeth traced the bold vermilion streak she had added to the Fearghus tartan on her lap. The red stood for the Native American Tallchief blood, and its addition to the tartan indicated that the two fierce clans had been woven together. She was restless; perhaps it was the seer blood passed down to her through her Scottish great-great-grandmother, added to the shaman inheritance from Tallchief. A woman bred from warrior chieftains would be restless on a day like this, when the wind tossed the black waves of Tallchief Lake and the mountain jutted into the mist. The untamed tempest and the isolation of this special place quieted the stormy darkness within her.

Una, a bondwoman captured by an arrogant Sioux chieftain, had reveled in the tempest. But Elspeth wanted no more storms in her life; she'd had enough pain to last her two lifetimes. She wanted the rest of her life to be as smooth as the doeskin shift she wore, or the silk thermal sweater and pants beneath it. She'd put order into her life, wrapped the safety around her like the blue-and-green tartan, and so it would stay.

In the center of her tepee, smoke curled upward, soon caught by the fierce wind.

Alek Petrovna had been her fierce wind, taking her innocence upon an ancient Scottish stone and giving her a child. Elspeth the elegant was taken by a laughing gypsy of a man after a few traditional dances around the bonfire.

"As good as I've had," he'd said as though comparing dinner fare, rather than making love. "Is this enough money?"

Bit by bit, she'd pasted herself together, warmed herself with the joys of her family, and now, at thirty-three, she'd finally found a measure of peace. She wanted quiet now, and Calum's marriage to Talia Petrovna, Alek's sister, could destroy that.

Elspeth held very still, drawing the sounds into her—winter wind whipping the snow-laden trees, branches snapping beneath the weight. Mist shrouded the mountain, and somehow that comforted her, a reminder of the fierce elements that had always been there since the beginning of time.

She studied the tepee slowly, considering the neat contents and the branch-rack waiting for her new wall hanging. Her unique designs had drawn attention at the last weaver's fair, and with pride Elspeth had signed a generous contract for her work. She had constructed her life as tightly as her weaving, carefully planning the threads of it. Only in March did the fabric of her life weaken, and she came to Tallchief Mountain to strengthen herself in an age-old tradition.

Talia Petrovna's marriage to Calum would draw Alek to the Tallchiefs. Elspeth wanted to be strong when next they met—and she knew that day would be soon.

Alek Petrovna cursed as he ducked a pine branch laden with snow and ice, only to have another hit his scarred cheek.

Alek impatiently snapped the branch and tossed it aside. He had scars earned from years of reporting on wars. Not one of them compared to the pain caused by the black-haired witch he sought, Elspeth Tallchief.

As a journalist specializing in war zones, he'd seen too many orphaned children. He'd ached for years for a child of his own, only to discover that Elspeth Tallchief had hidden his...what? A boy...a girl?

Alek's research had been thorough. Not even her family

knew of his child...and Elspeth's. She'd hidden his child away so neatly that not even the Tallchiefs knew her secret. He'd get it out of her. One way or another, he would make Elspeth dance to his tune.

So she would camp on a mountaintop by herself, would she, when March caught the Rocky Mountains in a wintry shroud? "Damn fool idea, setting up a tepee in zero-degree weather. Her brothers shouldn't have—''

Years of covering stories in frozen war zones had prepared him for the elusive, dangerous trail that wound upward to Tallchief Lake. The mountain soared, bleak and ominous, against the gray sky. Mist layered the top, obscuring it and a fierce wind threw the pine branches at Alek, like blows to a warrior running a gauntlet.

Elspeth traced her bloodline to Sioux, but Alek's tracking ability had come from his Apache ancestor...as perhaps had his need for revenge.

He thrust aside another punishing branch. He'd find Elspeth Tallchief, dig her out of her safe hole and make her pay for what he'd missed, that precious time a father spends with his child.

Alek fought the tight pain in his chest, the cold that invaded his flesh, though he was dressed in layers of clothing and a heavy Arctic parka. His Russian blood reveled in the freezing temperature, heated by the passion of anger that had churned within him for months.

He leapt over a broken limb, his boots sinking into a mound of snow. He'd only just discovered Elspeth's little secret when he'd had to go on assignment. He'd made a promise to a dying friend that he would complete the project. Now Alek had missed an additional four months of his child's life by covering a senseless war and trying to stay alive through it.

Talia's wedding photos had arrived last December in the middle of a storm, the sound of thunder matching the battery of gunfire and the rockets. Tucked neatly into his sister's wedding party was, unmistakably, one Elspeth Fearghus. *Tallchief,* he corrected bitterly.

He wiped away the snow that clung to his beard, tossed it away just like Elspeth had done his child. He'd set his traps for her, one by one, and she'd have a fine time escaping him.

Alek stepped into a clearing, searching the shadows enfolding the lake. Outlined against the fierce, wind-tossed lake was Elspeth.

Her long black hair flew up and away in the wind. In the dying light, her face was blurred, a pale oval turned to the mist high on the mountain. She leaned into the wind as though it were her lover, as though something wild and fierce within her matched the icy blast. Her fringed leather shift offered little protection against the cold. Her legs were encased in leather with thongs laced around them to keep them tight.

She walked slowly by the black fury of the lake, blending with the elements rather than fighting them. The wind bowed and battered the cattail reeds bordering the lake; it pasted the shawl and her shift against her, the dim light revealing the trim, lithe outline of her body.

Alek controlled his need to rage at her; control ran contrary to his impulsive, passionate Petrovna blood. So she thought she was safe here, did she, a lady strolling through a winter storm? A private retreat away from her brothers and family where nothing could harm her?

Family wouldn't keep her safe against him, not this time. Alek stripped away his gloves and fished for a small box from a safely buttoned inner pocket designed to hold camera film. The earring, a fragile affair of dangling beads that ended in a silver feather, seemed to leap into his hand and nestled there, taunting him—as it had hundreds of times before—with the memory of that night.

He smoothed his thumb over the earring. He'd come through hell to face this woman and to claim his child.

"Alek." The name cut through the emotion that tightened her throat.

He stood in the shadows of the pines bordering her clearing. There was no mistaking the set of his shoulders beneath the battered parka or the arrogant stance of his long legs clad in camouflage print.

He shoved back his parka hood, and that same black stare locked on her, this time without the laughter. His hair curled wildly, tossed by the wind, and there was nothing gentle in his set jaw darkened by stubble.

One look at Alek Petrovna, and Elspeth fought a wild rage she hadn't known since her parents' death.

One look at Alek Petrovna, and she knew he'd come for her, like a black wolf facing his prey.

The first time she'd seen him, almost five years ago, she knew that fire stirred between them—like flint striking sparks on flint. They'd come together, full circle, and with the look in his eye and the emotions unravelling her, they would surely lift swords—

Elspeth inhaled and held her breath, steadying her impulse to run from him. Alek wouldn't raise her emotions, not this time. She'd worked through her pain, and now it was ashes.

Elspeth straightened and watched him walk to her, that swaggering, loose walk of an athletic big man, focused and sure of his purpose.

Alek didn't stand near her; he loomed over her, his black eyes locking with hers. "Say something."

Just like that. A demand drawled in the deep tones of a Texan, skipping the pleasantries. He was nothing like his fair-skinned, light-hearted sister Talia.

"Hello, Alek."

She noted the scarring on his left cheek and throat; she remembered as though it were yesterday, instead of almost five years ago, the burned-smooth texture beneath her fingertips when they made love. A new scar ripped through a black eyebrow, and another ran from his bottom lip into his chin.

"Hello, fair Elspeth. Or should I say sister-in-law? We're related, aren't we?" He pushed the fact at her like a spear. "Too bad I missed the wedding. I was trapped by the siege for two weeks." He caught the wild spray of her hair in one big hand, taming it. "But I'm here now."

In the next heartbeat, Alek lightly jerked her head back, lifting it for his inspection. "Older," he murmured, not sparing her in his appraisal.

"Wiser." She eased her hair away from his grasp, and wondered if anyone escaped Alek Petrovna unless he granted permission. But she would, because she'd already paid the price.

"Where's my child?"

His question slammed into her, shattering the layers of protection she'd pasted around her. There was no way he could know—Elspeth fought for the smooth level of her tone. "Please explain."

The line between his brows deepened. He spaced the words precisely, a predator more than a journalist marshaling facts. "Our child. I know the how of it. Where is it? *What* is it, a boy or a girl? And again, *where is our child?*"

She refused to let him tear open her private wound. She wouldn't let him push her back into her pain. Elspeth straightened her shoulders, meeting his searing stare with her calm one. "I've just put tea on to steep. If left too long—"

"Dismissing me? Just tell me what I want to know, and then I'll leave. I want to see my child."

She would not allow him to pounce in and out of her

life so easily. "But you'll come back because you're angry. More than angry. You want to hurt me."

"Damn right I do. And I will," he shot at her in a low, passionate voice. His lips tightened. "You should have told me. I'm easy enough to find."

Elspeth glanced at Alek's powerful six feet four-inch body, then lifted her chin. She had given him more than what was safe, and now she owed him nothing.

"I know your strength, fair Elspeth, and your passion. You can clasp a man dry...wring a child from him, then— Is the child mine or—?"

She gripped the Tallchief tartan shawl to keep her hand from flying at his face. She refused to enter a verbal duel with Alek, now or ever again.

The doctor had thought her baby had been a boy....

She lifted her face to the wind, letting its bite cool her heating temper. "You'd better leave. More snow is coming." Then she turned and walked toward her tepee.

No sooner was the tepee flap closed behind her than Alek ripped it open and stepped inside in a blast of wind and snow. She let him loom, his head angled from the slanting, insulated canvas of the tepee. Elspeth ignored him; she knelt to toss wood on the fire. She watched the flames lick and grow, and then settled to pour tea into a china cup. She folded the tartan and glanced up, only to find him glowering down at her. His anger vibrated in the small space.

She resented his harsh presence in the soothing tepee, draped with bundles of herbs. The disquieting scent of an enraged man swirled through the small space.

He opened his fist, broad palm up. Her mother's silver-feather-and-obsidian-bead earring gleamed against his dark skin. Elspeth's grandmother had given it to Pauline Tall-chief as an engagement gift. The earring looked fragile in Alek's scarred palm. "You lost this that night. A village woman, a midwife, gave it to me last fall. She said that by the look of you, you were 'breeding' when you left Seonag two weeks after we met at the festival.''

Elspeth sat upon her pallet and clasped her arms around her bent legs, resting her chin on her knees. She studied the fire and wished Alek Petrovna back into the past.

He threw his gloves down and ripped open his insulated jacket. ''Well? Where is my child? How old is it—he…she—now, four?''

Elspeth slowly lifted her head to face him. She wouldn't give in to the temper that flickered at his taunts. She'd dealt with a houseful of wild Tallchiefs, every one of them difficult and arrogant, and nothing could be gained by facing Alek on this primitive plane.

For a moment he held her eyes, then ripped off his coat and tossed it into a corner. While Elspeth forgot to breathe calmly, he ripped the dangling beads and silver feather from the stud and slowly pushed it through his right earlobe. Blood ran freely from the wound, dripping onto his thick sweater.

''Alek!'' She leapt to her feet, grabbed a towel and lifted it—

His fingers circled her wrist, staying her. ''I'll wear your mark, you bloodless witch, until I'm damn well ready to remove it.''

He took the towel and sent her sprawling upon the neat pallet. As he placed the cloth to his wound, his black eyes slowly, insolently studied her body.

She knew he was taunting her, driving her to the edge, making her remember that night with the huge silver moon when he'd spread her beneath him, anxious for her first taste of this laughing, passionate lover. ''Alek…there is no child!''

Heartbeats later, as he stared coldly at her, her words

echoed in the tepee. She'd never spoken the secret buried in her heart, and now it tore her apart once more.

Alek slowly removed the towel, ignoring the steady flow of blood. "No? Another lie, like the name you used when we met? Fearghus. Yes, that was it...Fearghus, not Tallchief."

She hated giving him anything. "Fearghus was my great-great-grandmother's name. I used it to make connections, to make my studies easier—"

"Ah, yes. The American weaver woman, they said, come to Scotland to study the Paisley shawl at its Scottish roots and to dig out some legend about the one you inherited. Now tell me about my child."

"Alek..." Elspeth swallowed the pain that had never dimmed. From his sister Talia, Elspeth knew how deeply the Petrovnas cherished their children. Perhaps he needed peace just as she did, and then he would leave. "There was a baby. I miscarried—"

In that instant, Alek paled, his eyes closing as the knuckles on his fists turned white. A vein pulsed in his muscled throat, standing out in relief, and his nostrils flared, dragging air deep in his lungs. Then the next heartbeat, he crouched before her, his brilliant eyes damp and cutting at her from beneath fierce brows.

"Damn you! If it's true, not another lie, you must have taken something...did something. You discarded my baby like dirty laundry without the slightest care about...the father. Then you ran back here where you'd be safe, tucked away in this nest of Tallchiefs. Oh, yes, I've researched the entire family and I'm good at what I do. They won't be able to help you.... Well, nothing can protect you now, Elspeth. Not from me. You've given me no choice—"

Elspeth leapt to her feet; she couldn't—wouldn't—stop the anger welling up and bursting from her. Alek had stepped into her life, wrenched her pain from the past and spread it before her. If he believed she had deliberately lost their baby... She hit his chest with the palms of her hands with enough strength to send him sprawling backward.

Elspeth slashed a dark look at him as she stalked back and forth over the small area near the fire. She stooped to toss the bloody towel into the fire, wishing Alek were as easy to remove from her life. The towel ignited, and so did her temper. "Your baby. Your choice... Pushing earrings through your ear—"

"Earring. One ear. Singular."

"Oh, yes. You're a journalist, aren't you? Five years ago, you were off for a little romantic holiday before you returned to the wars. What was that you said when you were done and ready to be on your way—'As good as I've had. Thanks for the good time'? I burned that wad of money you tossed at me, Alek. Thanks, but no thanks."

Because he looked so shocked, she saw no reason to spare him. She doubted that anyone had cut Alek down to size, but he'd forced her into a corner. "I've never told anyone, Alek. You want the clinical details? Fine. I'll send you the doctor's name and the hospital in London. I was studying with a talented weaver, a distant relative, when—"

She dashed away the tears flowing down her cheeks and folded her arms protectively across her body. "Damn you, Alek."

She closed her eyes, waves of pain crashing over her again. Elspeth felt herself sink to her knees, heard her trembling whisper above the cold mountain wind. "He was only three months into term, Alek. According to the doctor, it was for the best.... For the best..." she said, repeating the phrase that had echoed through her heart for years.

She hated the sobs tearing out of her, and pressed the tartan to her face to muffle them. She was naked now, stripped of control by Alek Petrovna, and she hated him for that.

Two

Elspeth's cries tore into Alek; he hadn't prepared for this...*twist,* he decided was the right word. A story twist that didn't make sense for him. He'd planned a methodical revenge, not the softening within him.

Well, hell, Alek thought, suddenly drained of all his revenge, his motivation for bringing Elspeth to her knees. He'd planned his revenge, devising a plot that would tether Elspeth to him. He'd intended to take his revenge methodically, slowly. He'd hated her for hiding his child, for leaving him with an ache too deep to bear.

There was no child to hold in his arms....

The ache grew within him, even as his hatred for Elspeth eased. The miscarriage had torn her apart, her sobs proof of her mourning. Elspeth had wanted that child as desperately as he—Alek read that knowledge in the aching curl of Elspeth's body, her fingers gripping her tartan length. She'd always mourn the baby—

Alek carefully placed the china cup upon its saucer when he wanted to smash it. He rose slowly, a healed broken bone or two aching now. He stood very still, his fists clenched at his sides, bracing himself against losing a child he'd never known.

Elspeth lay curled upon the woven blankets. The sobs came raw, straight from her soul.

He swallowed, moistening a throat clogged with emotion.

Alek closed his eyes, listened to the wind howl beyond the canvas and saw Elspeth as she was back then—dancing passionately around the Scottish bonfire. He saw her lie upon the ancient rock, her face flushed with desire, her lips swollen from his kisses. Half-drunk on native brew and whiskey, he'd thought of her as a moonlit goddess with slender curves and dark, mysterious places. He'd teased her, enchanted with the chase…loved her—took her virgin body for his own. She'd tasted of life, a drink he'd needed to remember his attachment to the human race.

He'd wanted that child desperately, because he wanted his life to go on, a damn Petrovna trait. Then, too, the selfish gene within him needed more, a healing only the gift of a child could offer.

"Elspeth…" He crouched by her side and placed his hand on that sleek hair, lightly, tentatively, afraid that she would push him away. "Elspeth, don't cry."

She dashed his hand away.

He hated the sound of crying. He'd heard enough for a lifetime. He wiped his hand across his face, steadying his shifting emotions. Alek gently placed his hand on her head again. When she did not push him away, he stroked her hair lightly down to her shoulder.

The silent sobs racking her body shot up his arm, straight to his heart.

There was nothing he could do but lie beside her.

Alek held very still, allowing his tears to flow down his cheeks. When she didn't draw away, Alek stroked her hair, drew the tartan plaid around her and whispered her name. He laid his arm gently across her back, so as not to frighten her. He wanted her close to comfort her, and yet for his own need, as well. They'd created a baby between them, and he wanted to linger in the thought before burying it. "Elspeth...shh."

She turned her face to him, a blur of black eyebrows and lashes and shimmering eyes. "You're crying."

The tip of her nose almost touched his. Her breath swept across his lips. "You'd better go. The snow has begun."

He fell into gray eyes shimmering with tears and cursed himself as he whispered, "How do you know?"

"Listen to the wind...." she whispered unevenly, and instead he heard his heart beating slowly, cautiously.

"I'm not going anywhere." Alek's lips touched hers once, lightly. "I'm sorry for that night." Was he? That night had given him hope that the world was still pure.

Tears shimmered in her eyes, and her look was disbelieving. He kissed her again to soften the past, a kiss much like those he gave his sisters when they ran to him with scraped knees. Then Alek forgot everything but the taste of Elspeth's lips. He licked a tear from them and she stiffened, drawing away.

"How dare you!"

Alek traced the black hair crossing her damp cheek with his fingertip.

He watched a single swallow move down her elegant throat. He kissed her again, softly. "The child would have been my first."

Her lids closed, but he wouldn't allow the dismissal. He slowly brushed his lips across hers, finding one corner of her mouth and then passing to the other. He remembered the clean smell of her, the scent of wind brushing through the heather and then, when she lay trembling and warm, the intimate scent of a lover. He remembered how sweetly she had given herself to him, as though she would not touch another lover in her lifetime.

Alek damned his tears and the emotion welling up in

him. Without a care for his plans to make Elspeth pay, Alek buried his face in her throat and clung to her.

Elspeth held very still in his arms and then, with a sob, she wrapped her arms around him, holding tightly. She began crying again, and this time he rocked her against him. She cried until exhaustion allowed no more and the fire burned low. Alek tucked his chin over her head and drew the shawl over her carefully. Tonight they mourned a child.

Alek watched Elspeth sleep, drained by her emotions. While the firelight flickered on her too pale face and gleamed upon her black hair, Alek's mind moved through his discovery that there was no child.

For months, he'd built his life around a plan for revenge, to hurt Elspeth and to claim his child.

He could not claim the child, but he wasn't ready to leave Elspeth alone—not just yet. Not until he'd untangled the twists and examined them, and sorted through his emotions, laying them to rest. He knew he would not rest until his feelings were resolved, like digging out ends and pieces and shaping them into a composite story…making sense of the whole and how he felt.

He wondered if he could ever rest…Elspeth had tormented him since that night in Scotland.

The stick he'd been holding snapped in his fist. Unsettled after his wife's death, he'd taken Elspeth's virginity and placed his child within her womb.

He'd hurt her that night, walking away from her. But he wanted no more emotions then, to haunt his mind, his heart.

Elspeth had faced pregnancy alone—she should have found him…it wasn't his fault that he didn't know.

Still, he wasn't without sympathy for her—for any woman stranded by a man who gave her a child and walked away. Young and alone, Elspeth had suffered the brutal loss alone. Alek fought the guilt riding him. He'd never thought of himself as one of those irresponsible men, denying their actions.

Elspeth sighed and shifted restlessly on her pallet and

Alek held his breath, waiting for her to settle. Then his mind began to move into the puzzle, trying to stabilize the whys and the hows and make sense of them to his satisfaction. He needed a measure of peace and Elspeth's torment had left him none.

He'd changed her life. According to the townspeople and to Talia, Elspeth had changed dramatically after her visit to Scotland.

After her loss of a child....

After her loss of innocence....

Alek shifted restlessly, uneasy with his thoughts. He'd run on the steam of revenge for weeks, months, and now he felt empty and guilty and aching.

His story with Elspeth was unfinished and he wanted it resolved, needing the last line and the last period in place. This time he couldn't walk away too soon.

Alek remembered Elspeth that night, all fire and excitement and glowing with happiness.

He saw the woman upon the pallet, sleeping, drained by tears, a shadow of Elspeth-the-girl. She intrigued him still; he knew and disliked the thought. There was fire in her, temper and rage, all locked inside her until he'd arrived. Alek doubted that few people had seen what he'd just experienced, those locked thoughts of Elspeth, now freed. He wondered what else lurked beneath her cool surface.

For the moment, he had her and he'd keep her close until he unraveled whatever ran between them...until he solved the mystery of whatever nagged his heart and mind about Elspeth Tallchief. She wouldn't dislodge him easily—not until he was ready....

What was that she'd said that night? The Marrying Moon? What did it mean to her?

After one last glance at Elspeth, Alek settled down to sleep and prayed that he didn't dream.

Elspeth awoke when Alek moved to toss wood into the fire. He crouched by the flames, looking like a Gypsy with

his wild black ringlets and the earring pushed into his earlobe catching the light. The barbaric act surprised Elspeth
again, at odds with the expert way he poured tea from her
china pot into a cup. He refilled her teakettle and placed
its handle on the iron bar over the fire. Taking care, his
hands too large for the task, Alek placed the china cup and
saucer nearby, and the scent of mint tea swirled up to her.
"Drink your tea."

She sat up quickly and wrapped the tartan around her.
She ached, drained by crying, and wondered if she had aged
a hundred years. She stared unseeing at the fire, pitch shooting sparks, and resented Alek, a marauding invader in her
quiet sanctuary.

The line of his jaw was unforgiving, and his eyes shadowed as he studied her. "What's to eat?"

The intimate tone of his voice shocked her. Elspeth
scrambled to her feet and found that he'd removed her moccasins. She sat quickly and jerked them on, binding the
leggings with leather thongs to her knees. When she pushed
back her long hair, Alek looked amused.

"It isn't as if it was the first time I removed your clothing."

She fought a sharp retort and smoothed her shift. She
realized that Alek's scent clung to her, just as it had that
night.

The sounds beyond the tepee told her that it would be
foolish for Alek to leave. He knew it, too. "I'm staying the
night, and we've got to eat. You can either tell me what
you have in your pantry, or I'll dig it out," he murmured,
watching her as she wrapped her tartan around her and
prepared to leave. Alek's hand caught her wrist. "Where
are you going?"

Away from him…to the silence she needed to restore her
balance. He'd seen into the wounded heart of her; she'd
give him no more. "There are fish in the weir. The baked
potatoes under the coals should be done now. There's butter
in a tin near my loom."

"Good." He grinned, that charming, careless, boyish grin that had won her heart. She steeled herself against a man who could cry for a lost child and who could sweep away a girl's heart with eyes that promised laughter.

Elspeth stepped away from him and into the welcome bite of the freezing night air. She took her time retrieving two trout from the weir, listening to the coyotes and the night, to the sounds of branches snapping under the weight of snow...to the sound of her heart. She'd known for months that her life would change; the restlessness within her would not deny it. She'd known that Alek would come to see his sister, Talia, newly married to Elspeth's brother.

Beyond a smooth, moonlit span of snow, Alek loomed in the trees, a huge bear of a man, watching her as though he thought she would escape him. Elspeth refused to give him any pleasure and ignored him as she returned to the tepee—until he stepped into her path. "What was that you said, about the Marrying Moon on that night?"

"I can't remember, Alek. Please step aside."

How could she forget? When she was growing up, she'd plucked the legend's words from various references in Una's journals. Before Scotland, Elspeth had believed and clung to their hope, dreamed about them, certain that the shawl and the legend would bring her true love. Though she didn't know the entire legend, those words had brought her peace in hard times.

"Uh-huh. Sure, you can't remember." He took the fish from her, hefted them appreciatively, then looked down at her. "I'll find out. Facts, Elspeth. I'm good at digging them out."

She let that challenge pass and entered the tepee. Alek stepped inside moments later with the cleaned fish, invading her privacy and taking far too much room. Accustomed to fending with soldiers in the wild, he took the sticks by the fire, skewered the fish and propped the ends of the sticks against the cooking rocks. "Handy, aren't I?" he asked as the fish began to sizzle and cook, fat dripping into the fire.

Elspeth decided to ignore whatever Alek threw at her. She folded her tartan neatly, arranged the pallet and tried to dismiss the alien scent of a man amid her familiar ones. A contrast of vivid passions, Alek was an uncertain commodity, one she couldn't afford in her neatly structured life.

"Everything neat and in its place, right? Elspeth the elegant, isn't that what they call you? There's Duncan the defender, Calum the cool—although my sister seems to have him heating nicely—Birk the rogue and Fiona the fiery. Then there's Elspeth the elegant, the secret keeper." Alek reached across a mound of her clothing and the bag of uncarded wool. He picked up Una's wool cards and rubbed them together, testing them and Elspeth. "Tallchief Cattle is managed by Duncan, who holds most of the shares, and the land is in all your names. Calum manages family investments."

She braided her hair into two sections, tying off the ends with leather thongs, aware that Alek watched her. She wouldn't give him a drop of insight into her. Elspeth resented his digging at her life—and his touch upon her possessions, upon her. No doubt he'd interrogated Talia quite thoroughly. Elspeth ignored Alek's probes, scraped aside the coals, found the baked potatoes and placed them on a cooking stone to keep warm.

Alek pushed on, nudging the silence Elspeth had drawn around her. "Talia told me about a Tallchief custom, that of the Bridal Tepee...where newly marrieds share their first days." He studied her tepee and settled upon the empty branch waiting for her work. "Mmm. Let's see. You've never been married, or at least none of the Tallchiefs know of it, and you don't date. You go to weavers' fairs, take custom orders at a good price and, so far as I can tell, your role now is that of a maiden aunt, a mentor for the family— but then, you can't be a maiden, can you? You've raised them and now you're happy living on the fringes of their lives—rather like an old maid...the friendly aunt...your niece Megan's baby-sitter and the reliable mentor for a new Tallchief bride. Talia speaks highly of you.''

She resented the dark flash of temper he drew from her, slashing like a sword across the fire at him. Alek's eyes narrowed, meeting her challenge. ''The Marrying Moon, Elspeth. What is it?''

She ignored him and lifted the teakettle aside; Alek's hand shot out to cover hers. She fought to remain impassive; his fingers were dark and long and blunt and covered with scars. The scars had been fresh when he'd first touched her.

He leaned close to her, and there was nothing gentle in his expression. ''I'll find out. Your great-great-grandmother Una Fearghus was quite the historian. Talia thinks reclaiming the dowry is romantic. I know of Duncan's and Calum's legends, but not yours...could it have to do with a Marrying Moon, whatever that is?''

Elspeth inhaled slowly. Alek's keen mind could forage for details somewhere else. ''Let go.''

''When I'm damn ready.'' Alek released her hand and sat back.

They ate quietly, tension humming between them. At last he lay back with the ease of a man used to discomfort in wars, drew his coat around him and slept deeply.

Her earring caught the firelight and gleamed in his ear, taunting her. The earring had been her mother's, the mate to it safely tucked away. How dare Alek Petrovna intrude into her life again?

Elspeth shivered slightly. She'd known from the first moment she saw him laughing at her in Scotland, catching her in his arms to dance around the bonfire and dropping a teasing kiss upon her lips, that Alek Petrovna would change her life. She'd known when he first touched her that he would become a part of her life. Back then she'd believed Una's journals, that there was a Marrying Moon, that hearts bonded magically and forever beneath it.

She'd never been touched or kissed in the way that Alek had that night on that ancient Scottish stone. She'd known forever that she couldn't, wouldn't, be touched lightly and that, in her lifetime, only one man would hold her heart.

Alek didn't qualify. Not a man who used Elspeth as comfort for his dead wife, a woman he'd loved.

For years later, she was disgusted by what she'd done, making love with a married man. Months ago Talia had dropped the tidbit that Alek had been mourning his late wife on his visit to Scotland.

The past lay cold and hard behind her. Elspeth cleaned away the meal and sat to do her evening carding. Pushing the cards against each other and taking the neat roll of wool away gentled the stirred emotions in her. She'd never forgotten or forgiven him. The legend's words taunted her…*Marrying Moon, scarred warrior, shawl, mists*…she tossed a soft roll of wool from her cards into the smoldering fire, wishing she could rid her mind of those haunting words as easily.

Suddenly Alek propped himself on his elbow and stared across the fire at her. "I'm not done with you, Elspeth, not by a long shot. I had a right to know about my baby and I was easy enough to contact." He gave her a hard, promising look, then lay down again.

She managed to doze, only to be awakened by Alek's cry. "These kids need food, shelter, medical attention! He'll lose that leg…. Oh, God, look at the little girl…come here, baby…. Oh, no…she's dead…. Honey…do you know where you live? Her parents were killed—"

Elspeth ached for what he'd seen, for the children. She wrapped the tartan closely around her and steeled herself against Alek's tossing and muttering. His life was no part of hers, and she would be glad when he was on his way….

"Alek Petrovna…" Elspeth muttered as she passed the shuttle through the taut wool on Una's loom. She banged the beater down, pressing the sage green into the pattern. His name grated in the large, sunlit room, filled with a weaver's clutter—a basket of shuttles and foot-long spindles filled with wool from Tallchief sheep, dried bundles of flowers, leaves and stalks hanging from the wall and a shelf lined with jars filled with berries for color. Skeins of every color hung across one long wall, filling it from top to bottom. Her collection of Navajo drop spindles—notched at the top, with a disk near the bottom of the shank—hung on a peg.

Neatly folded throws rested in a stack, ready for shipping. Each was of natural color and had taken a solid week to lay on the warp and to weave. Clearing her work calendar to allow time for the new Denver gallery contract hadn't been easy. Perhaps that was why she'd needed her retreat more this year. Or was it because the seer and the shaman blood in her sensed that Alek would be rising out of her past?

Elspeth regretted that moment when she'd broken for the first time in her life. The one person she did not want to see her wounds was Alek Petrovna.

She gathered her dark red shawl around her, the natural color from her favorite ewe at the ranch. She stared at the sett on a smaller loom—the repeated pattern of mauve-and-cream lines passing regularly through the dark brown background. The shawl was a gift for Talia, and its gentler colors would suit her fair coloring.

Alek's statement, rich with pride and arrogance, seemed to echo in the quiet, airy room—*You can't stay up here by yourself. It's too dangerous. You're coming back with me.*

Elspeth inhaled and straightened as she remembered him challenging her. *Of course* we *can stay up here. If you won't let me stay in your tepee, I've built shelters before. We can be neighbors.*

In the end, Elspeth had been forced to trek back down to Amen Flats with Alek. Her home offered protection from him that the wilderness could not provide. She resented the way he looked at her, as though contemplating how she would have looked carrying his child. He wouldn't get to her, not this time. The tiny, quiet town of Amen Flats would soon bore Alek; he'd go on his way and—

Elspeth glanced out her window, past her herb garden, to see Talia, striding toward her house, black Hessian boots gleaming. Olaf, a huge black dog of mixed breed, bounded at her side like a puppy.

Alek, as dark as Talia was fair, wore his parka over a navy turtleneck sweater and canvas trousers layered with pockets and tucked inside his laced hiking boots. With their arms around each other, Alek and Talia were clearly happy. Alek had shaved, and his grin flashed at Talia, and then darkened and died as he met Elspeth's gaze through the glass.

A warning prickled, then skittered up her nape and beneath her skin; with trembling fingers, she smoothed her single braid and gathered the dark red shawl closer. She didn't doubt that Alek had contrived Talia's visit this morning. *I'm not done with you, fair Elspeth....*

Talia entered Elspeth's kitchen, her arm tucked into Alek's, and swooped to kiss Elspeth's cheek. Talia was four months into her pregnancy, and her unpredictable emotions were definitely on the happy side today. She beamed at Elspeth through happy tears and hugged her. With Alek in tow on one side and Elspeth on the other, Talia looked like a child at Christmastime, blinking through her tears.

"I'm so happy. Now everything is perfect. Calum and Alek talked about everything last night—that's why Calum didn't come, since he's catching up on some work. Alek cooked a marvelous dinner last night—oh, Elspeth, he's finally settling down. We won't have to worry about him in those awful wars anymore. Mom cried when he told her he was planning to settle in Amen Flats."

Alek met Elspeth's startled look and arched his scarred brow. Elspeth forced her hand to steady as she poured herbal tea into the china cups and saucers. "How nice. I was just ready for tea. Join me?"

"Love to." Alek's Texas drawl raised the hair on the nape of Elspeth's neck. He swept away Talia's woolen wrap and tossed it to a chair. Elspeth didn't like the way he arranged his parka across the back of her kitchen chair, as if he intended to stay.

She sliced the freshly baked loaf of whole-grain bread—she'd fairly attacked the rising dough, a substitute for bashing Alek and rendering him out of her life.

"Sleep well, fair Elspeth?" he asked too softly and too innocently.

"I always sleep well." She lied. She'd had dreams of Alek as he was that night in Scotland. A huge, laughing man whose lips had lightly touched hers and with enough magic to take her soul. The curve of his mouth had enticed her, mobile and generous and so soft she could fall into him with the brush of a feather. His chest had gleamed in the firelight, his heartbeat heavy with passion. Her stomach contracted almost painfully as a memory slid by—the moment he'd given himself completely to her...

"There's Calum. I knew he couldn't stand to be away from all the fun!" Talia dashed out of the kitchen.

Through the kitchen window, Elspeth watched Talia run toward Calum, who was scowling and clearly admonishing her about the dangers of pregnant women running. She leapt upon him, and he staggered back under the onslaught of her momentum and her flurry of tiny kisses.

"The Tallchiefs are fertile...Duncan's Meggie was born before they'd been married a year, and Talia was likely pregnant when she married Calum. They're very happy...a good match," Alek murmured softly at Elspeth's side.

"Yes. She's been wonderful for Calum." While she loved her sister-in-law, Alek was another matter. He stood too close, his heat invading her clothing.

Alek trailed a dried stalk of lavender down her cheek and close to her ear as he whispered, "'When a man of

Fearghus blood places the ring upon the right woman's finger, he'll capture his true love forever.'''

Elspeth pivoted instantly, only to be pushed back against the counter by the closeness of Alek's body. His hands locked to the counter at her hips as he studied her. His thumbs brushed her hips, jolting her. No one touched her casually, much less caressed her with familiarity. She sent him a look that would send another man running, but Alek leaned closer.

"Calum placed Una's garnet ring on Talia's finger, and the legend came true. What was Duncan's legend? The one about the Tallchief cradle? Ah, yes... 'The woman who brings the cradle to a man of Fearghus blood will fill it with his babies.' Sybil and Duncan had Megan, a little sister for Emily, Sybil's daughter, didn't they?"

He'd been prying at her life again, firing her resentment of him. When Elspeth frowned at him, Alek leaned closer. "I'll find out, fair lady Elspeth. I'll find out about the Marrying Moon and the legend you guard in that cold heart—"

Elspeth lifted her chin and met his black, raking stare. "I think you should make this easy for all of us and leave."

He chuckled at that. "Tell me about last night. Did you dream of me?"

"You overbearing, conceited and stone-headed oaf." Elspeth knew in that moment why Una had once dumped cold porridge over Tallchief's head. Why LaBelle, her grandmother, had tied Elspeth's grandfather Jake to a chair.

"True," Alek returned undaunted. "But from the way you kiss, I doubt you've been practicing since that night. Almost five years have passed—rather, four years and nine months—and I would have thought—"

Alek flicked a glance at the window, to Calum and Talia, wrapped in each other's arms. "Did you really expect life to turn out beautifully after that moment on the rock? Did you really think that one night—a brief sexual episode— would bind us happily ever after?"

"You...back off!" Elspeth despised her low, threatening

tone, yet she hated Alek's taunts more. He'd come too close, cutting her nearly to the bone. Five years ago she'd thought just that—that she had met her mate, that they had bonded. But Alek had ruined that fairy tale by calling out his wife's name and devastating Elspeth before he went on his way.

Now he pushed on. "I've had months to forage in your life, putting the pieces together, Elspeth. A Bridal Tepee— a Tallchief tradition—the Sioux equivalent of a honeymoon palace. Hmm…and you have one alone…. Tsk-tsk, what am I to think? That you've been pining for me, your lost lover?"

Alek leaned over her, but she refused to move back. "Is that temper darkening those gray eyes? Or is it passion, fair Elspeth? I think you still want me." Then he stepped away, leaving Elspeth clasping the counter for support.

Calum walked into Elspeth's kitchen carrying Talia. "She shouldn't be running," he stated with a proud grin as he lowered his wife to her feet. She stood on tiptoe to kiss him, and Calum beamed down at her.

"Sit," Talia ordered after taking Calum's denim coat away. Calum towered over his fair wife, grinning sheepishly while she smoothed his black hair and straightened his collar. Quiet, methodical and a professional investigator for companies with problems, Calum had captured Talia, claiming her for his own, almost instantly. Talia hadn't made the chase easy, and still didn't, keeping Calum on his toes.

When he sat, Talia plopped happily into his lap and snuggled against him. "This is nice. I'm so glad Alek is moving here. Though that was no reason to stick that earring in his ear—a commemorative moment, he said. I cleaned his ear last night, and then he rammed the earring back in again. He said it was a keepsake and won't give details."

"It was a very private moment." Alek met Elspeth's searing glance.

"I hope it was properly sterilized." Elspeth smiled lightly and showed her teeth.

"Thank you, Elspeth," Alek returned too easily.

This town isn't big enough for the two of us, and I am not the one who will leave. Elspeth ran the shocking thought by and decided that if she wanted to, if Alek pushed her far enough, she would extend her own brand of welcome.

Calum frowned and glanced from Alek to Elspeth and back again. Her brother knew her too well, despite the protective cloak she'd drawn around her.

"Elspeth, come sit."

Alek was there, pulling away her chair and waiting for her to slide into it. She refused to look at him. He slid into a chair next to her, and she edged her thigh away from the intrusion of his. Alek pushed his thigh firmly against hers and continued, "This Marrying Moon thing really interests me. That's what you went to Scotland to find out about, wasn't it? Talia said that you couldn't read the entire passage in Una's journal and wanted to find the original legend. Maybe I could help. I'm good at translating rotten handwriting and bits of phrasing—like putting together a puzzle. I'd like to read Una's journals if I may."

"No." Elspeth didn't spare him pleasantries, and for a moment, Talia's eyes widened. Calum glanced sharply from Alek to Elspeth and cuddled Talia closer.

Talia stepped into the silence. "Alek, Elspeth has just signed a marvelous contract with a Denver art gallery. It's an exclusive contract…much more money than the custom work she's been doing for her clients. Oh, she's marvelous, taking bits of people's lives and blending them with wool and textures and colors. The gallery wants her to specialize in Native American designs, and if she wants, she can blend artifacts into the hanging. She did a sky, mountain, lake and meadow hanging for Calum and me, and it was gorgeous…a living harmony of blues and browns, something quiet and forever, you know. The wool was from Tallchief sheep, and she'd gathered the natural dyes from the Tallchief mountain.''

Alek reached to rub Elspeth's dark red shawl between his finger and thumb. ''She does beautiful work. I've seen the Tallchief tartan and kilts. She must be a very patient woman.''

Elspeth fought the simmering temper threatening her; she didn't care for him discussing her as if she weren't there.

''She learned from her mother. She designed the Tallchief plaid from Una's journals.'' Like a child, bursting with excitement one minute and then sleepy the next, Talia settled closer to Calum. She took his hand and placed it over their baby. Una's garnet ring gleamed bloodred as Talia caressed his hand. ''Everything is going to be just great. Alek is shopping for a car—one he can restore. I hope it's got a comfortable back seat. He was known for his necking and hot lips while in high school, almost more than his awards in writing.''

''I agree. We're going to be just one big, happy family. You know, I've missed necking in back seats.'' Alek looked at Elspeth and showed his teeth in a bland smile.

Talia snorted delicately. ''You and Anton—Anton's our other brother, Elspeth—steamed up a few windows in your time.''

Alek flashed her a grin. ''The steam was to keep my nosy sister from seeing how bored I was.''

''Amen Flats is a typical small town. There's not much excitement here.'' Elspeth traced the woven place mat with her fingertip. She didn't want to think about Alek Petrovna's hot lips or his necking tournaments in back seats.

''I'm staying.'' Alek's statement came back like a shot. Her fingers trembled, and her cup clattered against its saucer.

Ah! Alek thought, Elspeth doesn't like to be pushed or teased. She prefers the comfort of her shadows. Yet what he wanted, to find the heart of the woman, to understand his fascination with her—in the turn of her lips, the fire in her smoky gray eyes—would require a bit of prodding and testing.

Alek inhaled abruptly. The need to hold Elspeth close and soothe her, comfort her, ran through him like a freight train, winding him.

He wondered if she ever laughed—she had before their night in Scotland. He wanted to see that smiling curve of her lips, the happiness in her eyes.

Alek let his lashes drift down to shield his eyes—sometimes Petrovna eyes gave too much away.

With Elspeth, he had an uneasy suspicion that he would always want more.

Three

"Duncan...Calum...Birk...I will not have you interfering with my life." Elspeth snatched the loaf of freshly baked bread away from Duncan's reach. She swooped to pluck the plate of farm butter from Birk's poised knife. She placed the cutting board with the bread and the butter on the counter, then seized a buttered slice just before it entered Calum's open mouth. "I am not a young girl needing my three big brothers running interference for me. It wasn't wanted when we were younger, and it definitely isn't now. All of you stop."

"Eating?" Calum looked meaningfully at his empty hand and then lifted an eyebrow at her.

"You know very well what I mean. Stop sniffing at the trail of something you think is disturbing me. With April coming this week, I'd think you'd have fields to plow and seed to sow." Elspeth resented the sharpness to her tone; her brothers meant well and loved her.

Birk and Duncan leaned back in her kitchen chairs with almost the same expression—like wolves protecting the pack's only pup. Her three brothers crossed their arms over their chests and studied her.

Duncan was the first to speak. "One week ago you came back from the mountain together. You were wearing a big Keep Back sign. Alek is wearing your earring in his ear—I'd recognize LaBelle's gift to Mother anywhere—and you're—"

"Frothing," Birk supplied. "She's beating her loom to death at warp speed—no pun intended." Birk, younger but no less protective than his brothers, watched her with shadowed gray eyes. She recognized the determined set of his jaw and the narrowing of his eyes, a reflection of a stubborn gene shared by all the Tallchiefs.

"Birk, you are almost engaged to Chelsey Lang. Why don't you pay attention to her instead of me?" she asked too quietly.

"I pay plenty of attention to Chelsey. I just may marry her, but that doesn't enter this discussion."

"Chelsey is far too sweet and too sensible to marry you." Elspeth had fought their protective instincts all her life, matching wits to keep them from suffocating her. She sipped her raspberry-leaf tea. "Let's have this out here and now. You three have been hovering around me since the day Alek arrived."

"How did Alek get the earring, Elspeth? The last I remember, you were wearing it when you took off for Scotland." A methodical thinker and well paid for it, Calum began laying out the facts.

"You're not yourself. I don't like it." Duncan's statement was blunt, demanding an answer.

Birk glanced at her studio. "You're weaving night and day, Elspeth. You've got circles under your eyes. You always weave when you're upset. You almost killed that bread dough. What's wrong?"

"I think I'll have a little talk with Alek." Duncan glanced meaningfully at his two brothers.

"I am weaving more than usual because I want to complete my orders before I start with the gallery. Duncan the defender...you will not," Elspeth tossed at him.

"Aye, I will," he returned doggedly. When a Tallchief used the word *aye,* it was a pledge.

Calum dropped a tidbit that didn't ease her stormy mood. "Alek bought the old newspaper office. He's planning to put the *Sentinel* back in business."

Birk stepped into the battle. "I'm lending him some power tools. He's just bought the old Potts place—"

"He didn't!" Elspeth held her breath. "The Potts place? Next door?"

A contractor by trade, Birk nodded. "It needs work from foundation to roof. Alek said he's got nothing but time. Says after all he's seen torn apart, he wants to rebuild something."

"He's a busy little boy, isn't he? He'll have to pick somewhere else." Elspeth regretted the bite to her tone. She glanced out the window to the old house, overgrown with trees and shrubs. She quickly poured a bracing cup of tea to settle her nerves. At the moment, she felt as if she could weave a road straight up to Tallchief summit and back down again. She took a sip, disliking the unsteady emotions caused by the mere mention of Alek Petrovna.

"You'll be neighbors," Duncan stated as though willing to set up a fortress to keep Elspeth safe.

"I'll talk to him." Calum, married to Alek's sister, was primed to investigate whatever storms Alek had created for Elspeth.

Elspeth discarded the safety of silence; her panic stayed. "Calum, spend anything from my accounts to buy him out."

"It's not worth what he paid for it, Elspeth," Calum reasoned after a glance at his brothers. "And he'll want to make a profit."

"What is it with you and Alek?" Birk studied his sister.

"I will not have that man living on my doorstep."

Duncan pulled on his leather gloves. "You're right, Birk.

She's too sensitive about Alek. We'll have to find out why. If she won't tell us, he will.''

Elspeth's brothers stood up, flinty eyed and powerfully built westerners ready to protect what they held dear.

Elspeth rounded on them, her hands on her waist. "Back off.''

"This isn't like you, Elspeth," Calum reasoned. The three of them, all inches taller than her five foot nine inches, looked at her steadily. "Alek isn't the kind to play games, Elspeth.''

"He wants you." Duncan tossed away Sybil's hours of tutoring his curt manners.

"It's more than that," Calum added. "There's something there, running between them. Talia doesn't know anything other than that Alek has been interested in Elspeth's life. My wife is hoping for a little thing between you called romance.''

"Romance? With Alek?" Elspeth's fingers wanted to grab a shuttle and let it fly through the weave, easing her emotions. Instead, she grasped at the hope Alek would disappear. "He'll get tired of Amen Flats. In a way, he's like Fiona, always searching for something, as though a piece of them was missing and needing an anchor to make them whole. There's not enough excitement here to keep him interested.''

Women. Alek Petrovna needed action and a variety of women. She chewed on the thought. Alek wouldn't be satisfied until he'd pitted himself against the hardest assignment or a woman who fascinated him.

"Maybe he's found what excites him more than anything else…it can move that way between a man and a woman sometimes. In the past week, I've seen how Alek watches you—when the family is together. Sybil and Emily agree." Duncan now drew in the support of his wife and his fifteen-year-old stepdaughter.

"The earring, Elspeth. Why is Alek wearing it?" Calum prodded.

For once, Birk was too quiet, then he stated slowly, "Elspeth hasn't been the same since her studies in Scotland five years ago. She's more cautious and she's built walls, not letting anyone come too close. Lacey, who practically lived with us after Mother faced down Mrs. MacCandliss about her treatment, or lack of care of Lacey, said the same. Now that I think back, Elspeth was as much of a fighter as Mother—once her dander was up. Not as wild as Fiona, but subtle and effective. I haven't seen that since she returned from Scotland. Except for her midnight forays to Tallchief Mountain."

"Aye," Duncan and Calum stated together. The word sounded like the growl of wolves who had sniffed the danger near their pack.

"Haven't you three got something to do?" Elspeth asked more sweetly than she felt, and reached for Duncan's ear. One tug widened his eyes. One by one, she pushed them out her door.

The old Potts place sat in full view of her studio, and Elspeth gripped a shuttle tightly as she stood before the large windows lining the room. She looked past the large rack of beams that served as her wool-dying shed, her gaze skimming her dead herb garden and resting on the house next door.

Alek was there, piling old boards, limbs and weeds into a huge pile. Dressed in his laced boots and worn camouflage clothing, he moved easily, powerfully, leaping over a branch before hauling it to the pile. He tossed the For Sale sign on top with the air of a man who was sinking in his roots to stay. A tall, powerful man, Alek braced a boot on a stump and surveyed the house. With his back to her, Alek was all long legs and wide shoulders.

No man should have that much black, curling hair, nor look as if he hacked at it with a knife when it got in his way. It glistened in the sun, touching his shoulders and mocking her. Her fingers itched to trim it, to cut it as she did Birk's—but with her hands near Alek's hair, she didn't trust herself not to pull hard.

Elspeth wished Alek and her brothers into another country.

She studied her new work, which was just beginning to take shape. The design waited for her, springing not from her usual paper layouts, but from something simmering inside her. Elspeth sat at the rack that had been used by her mother and grandmothers before her and chose a tan wool. Whatever beckoned to her from inside the design had waited and now wanted life—it simmered and heated beneath her fingers.

Alek hadn't expected his smoky-eyed neighbor to welcome him with a tuna casserole, freshly baked bread and a smile. And she hadn't.

In his new house, Lacey MacCandliss, a petite, curly-headed elf and adopted member of the Tallchief family, raged at Birk, who yelled back. The two contractors had taken time away from competing long enough to help Alek with the basic necessities of safe electricity and major plumbing.

He'd expected Elspeth's offer to buy and Calum's methodical dissection of why he might want to consider another home. Calum was already questioning Alek's motives and Elspeth's reaction to him.

A tall, cool blonde with cornflower blue eyes had stopped to introduce herself. She had been distracted by Birk's yell at Lacey and had listened intently to them. "I'm Chelsey Lang. Birk and I are going together. He's busy now or I'd talk with him. Tell him I came by, okay?"

Alek nudged a loosened foundation stone back into place with his boot. He'd planted himself near Elspeth's castle, near enough to spot her looking at him through the huge windows of her studio.

Alek blew her a kiss.

She reached to the side, and shades slashed down between them.

Little kept Alek from leaping over the picket fence that separated them. On a second thought, he began working the rotted old fence free from the ground and dragged it into the pile to be hauled away. He wanted no fences between Elspeth and himself, on any level. Thorns from the old rosebushes raked across his hands and arms, and when Alek could no longer avoid it, he looked at his scarred hands.

His palms were soft, and he wanted calluses from working outside in the fresh air. He wanted roots and growing plants and babies.

He wanted a woman to hold in his arms at night, to hug in the morning—Alek fought the churning, cold pit inside him. He didn't know if he could put down roots, but hell, he would try.

When Elspeth had entered his life, he'd been a desperate man, one wanting to survive. Now he wanted more than to survive. He wanted a life here in Amen Flats. He took the leather gloves from his back pocket, an inheritance from Mr. Potts, who could no longer do yard work. Alek intended to get his calluses and along the way, he'd get Elspeth's secrets.

At forty, he should have been immune to teenage sexual hormones raging in his body. But one look at Elspeth, and he wanted to examine firsthand just how long she could remain untouched.

He worked furiously, needing the late-March wind cooling him and the labor to dull the fine edge riding him. That damn soft promise of a mouth had haunted him for a week, no less enchanting than the first time he'd kissed her. She had tasted as sweet as the Scottish heather smelled in the night air; the taste of her haunted him. He swiped the sweat from his cheek and whipped a handkerchief from his pocket, tying it around his forehead. He pitted himself against the disaster of the yard with an intensity that eased his need to pull Elspeth against him and kiss her until she melted.

His conscience didn't help, especially when the townspeople chatted with him about his neighbor. Full of life and as fierce as any of the Tallchiefs, she'd laughed and gone off to Scotland. Una's shawl had come from the Paisley town mills in Scotland, where Elspeth had journeyed to seek her heritage.

According to Mr. Potts, the whole town had seen her off, and then Duncan and his brothers had brawled with any takers. The townsfolk cherished friendly brawls—a tradition in Amen Flats. Fiona and Lacey had jumped into the fray, banging heads and riding shoulders. At some point, Birk had tossed Lacey over his shoulder and carried her out into the street, instructing her to stay put and safe. She was on him instantly, landing a punch in his stomach and crawling up a ladder that wouldn't support him. Birk had yelled threats to her, watching her cross the rooftops to Maddy's Hot Spot Tavern. Then he'd stopped to accept a kiss on his cheek from an elderly woman who had changed his diapers. He helped her carry her groceries from the store into her car and accepted another kiss before he stalked back toward Maddy's.

The sheriff had ignored the brawl at Maddy's request. The lawman had turned up his radio, an Italian tenor shrieking loud enough to set off the town's dogs.

Stories about the Tallchiefs saturated Amen Flats, and sorting them out, Alek found that Elspeth's adventures had stopped after visiting Scotland. *He'd changed her life, shredded it with one night.*

Alek jerked a rotten post from the ground, tossing it onto the pile. He was responsible for the Elspeth who had returned to Amen Flats: she'd built a home for herself, was too cautious about relationships and had settled into her safe castle, weaving into the night.

Alek's shirt tore and he ripped it away, just as he wanted to rip away the past and his guilt. Yet she should have told him— He switched on the tape player, turning up the passionate Russian folk music that stirred his blood.

"Alek." Elspeth's call stopped Alek as he braced his bare shoulder against a loosened post supporting the back porch.

Dressed in a loose cream blouse over a long chambray skirt and moccasins, Elspeth picked her way over the rubble. The ends of her dark red shawl, wrapped tightly around her against the biting wind, reminded him of the flying banner of a lady going off to war. From the yard, she looked up at him on the porch. Alek leaped to the ground and strolled to her; he wanted to see every expression on her face and know when he had fired her passions enough to ignite.

Alek studied her braids, wound like a coronet on top of her head. Oh, yes, he wanted to see her ignite. To lose that fine hold on her emotions. He'd seen her heart break, and to soothe his guilt, he needed the heat of her temper.

She backed up a step, pleasing him. Like it or not, Elspeth Tallchief had been affected by him. He admired the way she lifted her head; she wasn't a woman to give herself easily and yet, she had five years ago. Why?

"You can't do this, Alek. You cannot move in next door to me."

He laughed at that. He'd always gone where he wanted, and this would be his first home. "Says who?"

He enjoyed the way she struggled for control, the flash of smoke in her eyes and the flush spreading slowly up her cheeks. The reluctant skip of her gaze down his sweaty chest and then the control that took it upward to meet his eyes caused his senses to leap. Without effort, Elspeth possessed more sensuality than any woman he'd ever known, and he resented the lurch of his body. Alek studied the quickening pulse along her throat and found himself lost in the clean smell of her—the scent of wildflowers and herbs, and Alek breathed very slowly, inhaling a light, exotic scent. *Elspeth.*

Her sea-gray eyes darkened, stormed and locked to his. The pulse in her throat pounded heavily, and Alek wondered what she'd do if he placed his lips upon it. She inhaled and he found himself wondering if she wore lace or plain white lingerie.

Elspeth's breath came out in a hiss. "It won't work—you living next door to me."

"I'll live where I want. You lit a flame or two before you left for Scotland, and the locals say that Tallchiefs have a backbone of steel. You've changed, Elspeth."

"I've changed for the better. If it comes to rooting you out, I will."

He stroked a gleaming strand of hair away from her cheek, tucking it back into the black braid flowing down her breast. Unable to stop, Alek allowed his fingertip to slowly move downward. Elspeth stepped back instantly, her eyes flashing with anger.

"Why don't you make it easy on yourself and tell me about the legend? Your edges are showing, fair Elspeth." Edges, he thought, nice little edges to explore, to fit together until the puzzle was complete.

"I wonder why." The whip in her voice took him by surprise. She leapt to the porch and switched off his tape player. Without thinking about the why of it, Alek leapt up to the porch and bent to brush his lips across hers.

She jerked back, flattening against the old boards, her eyes widening with surprise and then narrowing as her temper flared. He reveled in the blaze of emotions, trolling a fingertip down her flushed cheek.

Then Birk yelled at Lacey, doors slammed and Elspeth frowned up at Alek. She spoke in a controlled tone, the effort clearly costing her. "Amen Flats is a small, boring town. Other than for Talia—and she shares my beliefs about overly protective brothers—there is absolutely no reason for you to be here, Alek. Especially living next to me. I don't like noise while I'm working, or half-naked men parading in front of my studio window."

"So you've noticed me." He leered at her, pricking at her edges. What right did she have to keep all that heat bottled inside her, when the scent of her caused him to steam? "It's beautiful you know, when you weave. Your arms and hands are flowing, artistic, and there's a time-lessness about your movements. But I wondered what you thought about when you wove and now I know. You ogle men from the corner of your eyes, Elspeth-mine. It's nice to know you admire me, that I am the object of your lust." Alek delivered the taunt and watched her struggle for con-trol. For effect, he reached out a sweaty arm and flexed his muscle. He was showing off like a teenager, trying to get a girl to notice him. Alek tossed the mocking thought aside, and gave himself to studying Elspeth.

Her gaze slowly skipped to his arm; she wasn't as im-mune as she pretended to be. When her eyes locked to his, they were steel gray, shooting sparks at him. "Lust doesn't come into it. What do you think you're doing, Alek?" she asked too carefully, her face very pale.

"Settling down, fair Elspeth. Making my nest. Issuing a town paper in two weeks. The middle of April is a won-derful time for a first issue. I'm shopping for a work truck and a Chevy classic in that order. Take care of business, that's Petrovna's law—finishing what I start. What do you think I'm doing?"

"I think that you are being stone headed and totally ob-noxious. You thought you had a score to settle, but there is no score now. And there is no Petrovna law in Amen Flats. Leave me alone."

Alek took a step closer. "We're not done, Elspeth. Not by a long shot."

"Back off."

"Stand and fight. Isn't that what the Tallchiefs say?" Alek caught her scent, clean and yet exotic, and realized that his body was taut, remembering that night.

"There will be no fight, Alek."

"No? Because *you* say so?" He knew the air had shifted

between them, warmed by the past and enticed by the future. He leaned closer. "You think you can cut me out of your life? Forget that I would have been the father of our child? I can still see you, smell you, after all these years. What was that about the Marrying Moon, Elspeth? What did you mean that night?"

She gasped slightly and moved back. Alek took her wrist. Her pulse fluttered and raced beneath his fingertips as he brought her wrist to his lips. "You knew what you were doing, Elspeth. It was there in your eyes, heat and smoke burning me."

"I knew what I was doing, but not that you needed a substitute for your wife. I didn't know you were grieving for your wife until Talia told me last October, when Calum brought her here." The words were hushed and rapid, held too long and now rushing out. "Do you know how I felt after and for years later, thinking I had given myself to a married man?"

Pain and guilt over hurting Elspeth tore at him; instincts told Alek to protect himself against her barb. "I didn't know you were a virgin until it was too late. You were twenty-eight, and ready."

"And you took."

Alek's head went back. The truth hit him like a fist. "And we made a child. I want another."

He hadn't meant to state the thought, the need to be a father, but once the words caught the wind, he knew he meant them. He saw into Elspeth Tallchief, the strength in the silence, the fire rising out of the smoke. Then the fine control leashing her emotions. He'd wanted children, ached for them, dreamed of holding them in his arms. If Elspeth would have come to him, perhaps he could have—

Yet that high pride of hers—and his own actions—kept her from notifying him.

If he'd never known about the child, perhaps the ache would have been less...but now he'd had a taste of the dream, and so the loss had deepened.

And with it came a new kind of bitterness.

They both owed each other a dream, Alek raged silently. They owed each other a child.

"This won't work, Alek. You'll get tired of whatever game you're playing and move on."

"Sometimes you have to dig beneath the surface…make things happen." He lifted an eyebrow to spear at her with his gaze. "I always finish my stories and tie up loose ends. I happen to like puzzles, Elspeth. Get used to it."

Sunlight skimmed along her lashes as she glanced beyond him. Anger flashed, steely, hard and bright before she looked up at him. "You have a visitor, Alek."

Alek stepped back and glanced at a young woman with too-tight jeans. He recognized the hungry smile; the casserole dish she carried caused more excitement than her look.

To set Elspeth simmering, he turned to greet the curvaceous blonde bearing his food.

Laden with scents of mountain pine and newly tilled gardens, April 1 usually entered Elspeth's open windows as she wove. The sound of Alek's power saw ripping through lumber grated; the sound of his hammer caused her headache. His dented pickup needed a muffler badly, and when he wasn't working on the house, Alek tinkered with the truck. This drew the Tallchief brothers and a host of teenage boys, complete with the teenage girls tagging after them—to say nothing of the boys on bikes. The rubble stacked in his backyard grew daily, and big new windows now faced her house.

A meandering line of daffodils divided their properties, punctuated by the old rosebushes, which Alek had trimmed. At least she'd have the roses this summer, some small token after he'd invaded the quiet street.

Elspeth longed for the old Kostya place, which bordered Duncan's ranch, but it wasn't for sale. There she could have her privacy with no irritating, half-naked, muscle-flexing, arrogant, grinning Alek Petrovna.

Elspeth kept to herself, finishing Talia's present and the order of woolen throws. She sketched her new wall hangings for the exclusive contract. The dealer already had several of them, and when they were first shown, the price would be outrageous.

Outrageous.

We made a child. I want another.

She wanted to free herself of Alek's statement, to stop it from tearing into her thoughts. Yet that *I want another* remained, despite her will, nagging at her. It seemed just as permanent and irritating as the man himself.

To free herself from her new neighbor, Elspeth pitted herself against the heavy loom until her body ached. Alek had women running after him, eager for a taste of the worldly bachelor who was settling down in Amen Flats.

Elspeth firmed her back. Alek could flirt with an army of women bearing casseroles, and she wouldn't notice. He could flex his muscles and—Elspeth inhaled sharply. Alek's muscles had been the object of her wandering eyes, and she regretted that. She jerked down the beater and regretted that, too, because she'd made the weave too tight.

Then she glanced out the window. Alek stood on a ladder, hammering away at the rain gutter, his body taut. The sun glistened on his muscles, which were pulsing with each blow. Elspeth found she was holding her breath and let it out in a rush. Alek did not affect her, not in the least.

Just then, Alek wiped the sweat from his forehead with one hand and caught her gaze. He blew her a kiss.

Hours later, Elspeth smiled at Sybil, Duncan's wife, and kissed her niece, Megan. "How is Marcella Port-way?"

Sybil groaned dramatically at the mention of her client. "That woman will drive me to fake her ancestry. I've never done that, but the thought appeals—just to get rid of her." A genealogy expert, Sybil had been hired to track Mar-

cella's family gene pool to a Spanish nobility that didn't
exist. "By the way, Duncan has been worrying about you."

"Are you scouting?" Elspeth watched Megan toddle to
her mother. At ten months, Megan was already a handful,
ready to explore.

Sybil laughed and kissed Megan's black hair. "Something like that. Come on, Elspeth, don't tell me that Alek
isn't appealing. He's got all those rough edges that women
love to smooth out. Add all that charm and the dark, Gypsy
look, and any woman would be happy to have him interested. He's very romantic and absolutely enthralled with
Talia's pregnancy. Now she has four men clucking over
her."

Elspeth helped Megan crawl up onto her lap and handed
her a tea cookie. "I'm certain some women would find him
fascinating."

Sybil laughed outright and grabbed Megan's fingers before she could snatch Elspeth's notebook. "Elspeth Tallchief, you know very well that Alek is interested in you.
He's flirting outrageously with you. Sharlene Davis almost
fainted when he pushed your shopping cart at the grocery
store and you walked off and left him. You've avoided him
when possible, and he's not giving up."

Sybil kissed Megan's soft cheek. "Didn't Una call it the
awakening? That's what it felt like when Duncan came calling. It was as if I'd been waiting for him all my life, maddening creature that he is."

"Una said the awakening is when a man comes calling
softly, when he places himself in a woman's care, needing
the softness within her. Then she awakes, cherishing the
gentleness he's shown only to her, wanting to heal his scars
with her touch. If I have shadows under my eyes, it's because of hammers and saws. Alek is too—"

"Passionate, Elspeth—passionate, emotional, fierce and
proud. He likes to laugh and play and flirt. He's everything
Talia is and more—heavier, deeper, as though he's been
tempered by life's hardships. I'm a survivor and I've rec-

ognized that something horrible prowls through Alek in his dark moments. From what I know of him, his wife died tragically. His scars are from trying to save her. They'd been in love since they were teenagers, and he had to give permission to unhook the life-support equipment that kept her alive.''

Elspeth's fingers trembled slightly, and she held Megan tighter. She refused to think about the texture of Alek's face that night, how he had taken her exploring fingertips and kissed them.

The brisk knock on her kitchen door startled Elspeth, and she rose, holding Megan on her hip, to open it. Alek, a carpenter's pencil tucked above his ear and dressed in his usual tattered olive drab T-shirt and worn jeans, looked at her through the screen door. Megan, spoiled by the Tallchief males, squealed and leapt at him as Elspeth opened the door.

Alek reached for the toddler, cuddled her and grinned. ''Now, this is a girl who knows how to greet a man. She's got good taste, too...blackberry jam. Want to share, kitten?''

Megan laughed and held up her fingers to Alek's mouth, and he sucked them noisily, making approving noises of how she tasted.

Elspeth moved back slightly, overpowered by the way Alek stormed into her quiet home. ''Come in, Alek.''

He tugged her braid as he passed, reached for the platter of freshly baked cookies and handed Megan one. She giggled and offered it to him. Around the granola cookie, Alek said, ''Thanks. The smell of these things has tormented me for hours.... Sybil, how's the article on genealogy coming? I need that for the first edition.''

''I'm just polishing it. Emily is thrilled about the paper and the column you've opened for budding writers. Mrs. Freeman has the older circle working full-time on stories about pioneers. I understand you're just getting the newspaper in running order and then you'll step back.''

"I'm working with Brad Klein. He wants to stay in the area and use his journalism degree. If things work out, he'll take over pretty quickly. It's a shame that all the equipment hasn't been in continuous use. It's like a woman left to waste when she should be loved." Then he turned slowly to Elspeth. "Hello."

She stiffened; his Texas drawl was back, intimate and sexy and curling around her. There was no mistaking the message in his eyes as they lowered to her lips. Elspeth hated the heat moving up her cheeks and the quick amusement in Alek's expression. He swept a finger down her cheek and tapped her beneath her chin, startling her with his play.

"She's shy." Alek grinned at Elspeth.

Sybil laughed. "Elspeth doesn't know how to take you. I think Megan and I need to be going along."

Megan pursed her lips at Alek, and laughing, he bent to give her a kiss. A bit of Megan's blackberry-jam feast transferred itself to Alek's cheek and stayed there.

Minutes later, with Megan and Sybil gone, Elspeth faced Alek, who leaned against her counter, long legs crossed at his ankles. She tried to keep from looking at the juicy glob of jam stuck to his unshaven cheek. "Shouldn't you be leaving?"

"Nope. I've got business here. I'd like to do a story on Una's journals. Or would you consider doing a story on weaving?" He munched on another cookie.

"My family inheritance is private, and there are other weavers. My mother taught them, the same as she taught me." Elspeth snatched the remainder of the cookie from his fingers and tossed it away. She grabbed Megan's washcloth and swiped at his cheek. "I should think you would have enough food in your house. Every woman in Amen Flats has brought you a casserole. You could have opened a restaurant."

"Every woman but Elspeth Tallchief. Bothering you, is it?" Alek's expression darkened. "If you don't know how to take me, then I'll have to make certain you figure it out, won't I?''

Elspeth refused to answer to his bait and began to move past him to the safety of her workroom. ''You may leave. I have work to do.''

Alek caught her wrist, smoothing the fine skin as he studied her hands, more slender and lighter in his. Then he took them and placed them on his cheeks, her left palm against his scars. Alek closed his eyes, and when they opened, Elspeth stepped back, frightened. There was too much heat in him, skimming over her, needing something she did not want to give. Alek would have to fight his private wars by himself.

''Please leave.''

''Do you know how much I needed you close to me that night? How much I've thought about you—?'' His voice was uneven, raw with emotion that startled Elspeth.

''Alek—'' Her thumb brushed the scar on his lip, and Alek pressed it there. Unable to move, to look away, Elspeth met his black eyes. She saw his pain again, the shadows enclosing him.

Only minutes ago he had laughed at Megan; now he was serious, lines deepening in his forehead. ''I am sorry, Elspeth. I should have handled the matter better.''

''The *matter*? As in you should have worn a brown suit in lieu of a blue one?'' She fought to draw her hand away, fought to keep her fingers from stroking his lined brow.

''I made love with you, Elspeth. There's a difference.''

''And you would know, wouldn't you?'' she demanded bitterly.

Alek took her hand against her will and lifted it to his mouth, pressing his lips to the center. Over their hands, he looked at her. ''It took some time before I sorted out what had happened. I was riding an emotional maelstrom that night, and making love to you confused the issue. I moved through the next weeks like a sleepwalker—lucky to keep my life, in some cases. But I knew that whatever happened that night went deep with us. You were twenty-eight, Elspeth. Most women have experience by then...you didn't. Why hasn't there been someone to care for you?''

She trembled and fought the panic rising in her. Alek was prowling too close. "Alek, this has gone far enough."

Alek took her hands and placed them over his heart. The steady, heavy beat pushed at her palms, and Elspeth looked away, aware that her senses were racing, that after all the years, she was affected by Alek. The knowledge still startled her.

"I need answers, Elspeth. You are going to give them to me, like it or not." He bent to brush his lips across hers. The second time, he leaned closer, and Elspeth held her breath as his lips lingered over hers, brushing, warming. He was asking now, needing—

Alek inhaled quickly and straightened away from her. "That's how it is, Elspeth-mine," he murmured, and was gone.

Elspeth flattened back against the wall for support and found herself shaking.

Whatever had passed, the bond that she knew they'd forged that night remained. It shimmered and tangled between them, twisted and heated and forged like an ancient Celtic design. She'd known from the moment he'd come to her side, his eyes hot and laughing, and his hand taking hers...

Elspeth placed her shaking hands over her face and tried to control her emotions as she had since that night.

Yet her instincts told her that it was the same as when she'd first met Alek, the heat and the need to claim him for her own...to bond with him...to meet him on a plane where they both demanded and both gave— Was it true? Did she bond with Alek so deeply that even with their past, he could still affect her on a level that she did not want to revisit?

"No." Elspeth firmly reined her impulse to seek out Una's legend of the shawl, to place the pieces together and try to unravel the words. The words came to haunt her—*scarred warrior...placing the shawl...the Marrying Moon...tepee....*

Before her encounter with Alek in Scotland, she'd believed the words would unravel into a romantic truth just for her. Now she had no illusions.

"No. I will not let him interfere with my life," she promised, and forced herself to walk to her loom.

Four

"Alek Petrovna, Jr., don't ignore me." Talia, dressed in overalls and a sweater, picked her way across the rubble of Alek's new office. She tottered on an uneven board, and instantly Alek and Calum swooped upon her. Two big hands gripped each side of her overalls at the waist and lifted her over the board. She glared up at them, both with a big hand on her shoulder to steady her.

"Wouldn't want the baby to get hurt." Alek rubbed Talia's gently rounded tummy.

"The percentages say that we'll have a girl," Calum stated, and bent to kiss his wife. He caught the back of her overalls in his hand, tethering her and drawing her back to him. "You've been up all night practicing. Tell him."

She stared at her husband and stated indignantly, "I was merely baking baklava. You didn't have to sit in the kitchen and placate me with nods and hmms."

"Sweetheart, it's darn hard to sleep with you marching in your Hessian boots and muttering in corrupted Swahili. The Russian folk music didn't help, either." Calum kissed her nose. "You were stewing, precious. I'll leave and let Junior take his medicine. Make certain you're home in time to take your nap, or I'll be hunting you."

Talia snuggled against him, contented and loved. "Well...okay. Just because I know you'll send out Duncan and Birk and probably Alek, too. But I want a kiss first."

After Calum had left, Alek noted, "That was some kiss. He'll be steaming all afternoon."

Talia grinned. "Calum is in that 'gee can I...is this good for the baby?' stage and too ready to protect me. He needs reassurance and pampering."

"I'm glad you're together." Alek glanced at Elspeth's house and tasted her mouth again. He inhaled and stuck his hands in the back pockets of his jeans.

"You're mooning over her, Junior. I never thought I'd see the day when hard-to-catch Alek had it bad." Talia slid her arm around him to soften her tease. She leaned her head on his shoulder. "You just don't know how to handle yourself around her. Elspeth can't be pushed, and you are...you've got that 'ugh, me man' look around her, just like you want to toss her over your shoulder and run off with her."

Alek snorted. The raw hunger prowling his body wasn't easily denied. The sound should have deterred Talia, but she plunged on. "I've got experience with that look. Sybil agrees. Both Duncan and Calum had quite recognizable 'ugh, me man' looks and flames in their eyes when they decided they wanted us. Both of them just swooped, and you've got that same look. Take my advice, Alek...Elspeth isn't the kind of woman who appreciates a swooper-taker."

Talia rounded on Alek, her long, straight blond hair flaring out to catch the sunlight. "Junior, you're tired and you need someone to share your life and diversify your focus. You keep pouncing on Elspeth, trying to corner her at every family gathering, and she'll take you down."

"Stop calling me Junior— Will she?" The prospect fascinated Alek; he wanted Elspeth out of her shadows. If he was right, the contract in Denver would make a distinct change in their relationship.

"She's just as tough as her brothers. They had to be, carrying more than teenagers should to survive. Pride and steel has been bred into them for generations."

Talia placed her hand on his shoulder, her blue eyes concerned. "Alek, I won't have you toying with Elspeth. She's too rare and she's been wounded, though we don't know from what. Sybil agrees. We haven't told her brothers. They're old-fashioned about a woman's honor and very protective of family. Emily at fifteen is having an awful time with the Tallchief males, but no more than Fiona and Elspeth had as girls."

Talia touched his scarred cheek, her blue eyes soft upon him. "Move carefully, Alek. Elspeth's isn't the only wounded heart around. You've been needing an anchor for years. Just to look at you makes my heart ache. Until you look at Elspeth, and then I think...I think there just might be hope, because if there's anything you like, it's a challenge. The Tallchiefs aren't an easy game, but worth every minute of it."

"Elspeth is too quiet." He'd done that to Elspeth, put the walls up.

"She's very controlled, like Calum in a way. He doesn't share himself easily, even now with me. We're working on that. Elspeth doesn't share with anyone, not the things that are deep in her heart. I've often wondered what would happen if Elspeth decided she wanted to claim a man as her brothers have claimed loves. She just could be explosive, Alek."

"Am I supposed to be scared?" Alek had a quick flash of Elspeth, aroused and ready to fight him. He liked the image, savored it.

"A normal man would be. Petrovna males sometimes lack...shall we say delicacy and fear of an enraged woman?"

* * *

That night, Alek stepped back from the flames soaring against the night sky. Despite his hours gearing up at the newspaper, teaching and writing articles, Alek was restless, his emotions taut. The discarded boards and rubble ignited, matching the primitive need that had grown within Alek throughout the day. The flames reminded him of his wife crying out for help, her clothes burning—that was a distant nightmare.

The firelight illuminated a tall, strong pine tree, the top swaying in the night wind. His night with Elspeth vibrated through him, the heat of their bodies, the pagan way he had claimed her, the pounding of hearts and of bodies flying through passion.

Alek inhaled sharply and rubbed Elspeth's earring. Primitive…pagan…alive…happy—that was how he'd felt that night. As though nothing could keep him from…from having his woman.

He tossed a board on the flames and scowled as it ignited.

Two hours later, the fire had burned itself down to coals. Familiar now with Elspeth's daily schedule, Alek glanced at her home. A slender, curved body passed into the night, heading toward the fields. "Well, well. Things are looking up, Elspeth-mine," Alek murmured. Edges, he thought, all those nice little interesting edges to keep things from getting boring.

On a Saturday night, Amen Flats's single street was busy. Birk's motorcycle and Lacey's truck were parked at Maddy's Hot Spot. Carefully choosing her site on the field overlooking Amen Flats, Elspeth kneeled to unroll the blanket she'd draped across her shoulder. The occupants of the grass field—a buffalo herd—grazed peacefully a safe distance away. She took out her binoculars and notebook, braced the thermos of hot jasmine tea against a fallen limb and lay, stomach down, upon the blanket. She needed to escape the sight of Alek fighting his demons, his fists bunched, his body taut as he stared at the dying fire.

Elspeth knew he thought of wars and the fire and his wife. She shook her head, tossing the past away into the fragrant April night. Elspeth applied herself to the task she enjoyed, that of protecting Amen Flats in a subtle but effective way. Angela Tremany had been stalking Alek for two weeks. But Angela was also pressuring a younger man with a wife and newborn son. Angela's past record said she could be successful, the hunt more satisfying than keeping what she had caught. Alek could take care of himself, but young Stephen needed protection. And Angela did not want to lose her wealthy older husband.

Angela's silver sports car cruised down Amen Flats's main street, then parked in the lot behind Stephen's office. Elspeth jotted the time in her notebook and picked up her binoculars. Dressed in a bustier, a thigh-revealing skirt and huge sunglasses, Angela slid into the office door.

A branch broke near her, and before Elspeth could jump to her feet, a big hand flattened on her back, staying her.

"My, my. Look what we have here," Alek drawled as he crouched beside her. Dressed in a black shirt and black jeans, Alek looked as if he could face any street gang. His shoulder-length hair curled damply to his shoulders; the moonlight caught on his scarred lip and skimmed across his broad shoulders. He'd showered, the soap scent clinging to him, blending with the fresh spring-earth fragrances.

Elspeth allowed him to turn her; she didn't protest as he eased her knitted cap from her hair and smoothed her single braid to her chest. She wouldn't fight him on any level, and soon he'd get bored. "I thought you were roasting marshmallows."

"This is more fun. What are you doing?"

Elspeth glared up at him. "Let me up."

"Sorry. Can't. You look too good that way." His amusement threatened her control, and his hand, though firm, gently held her wrist.

"I don't want to hurt you, Alek."

"Try, why don't you...." He issued the invitation in a slow Texas drawl and blew a kiss at her.

She moved quickly, but Alek's large hand splayed between her breasts, pushing her back. She lay quietly, barely breathing as he looked slowly down to his hand on her black sweater. He frowned, smoothing the softness gently, his fingertips trembling. His tone was deep and raw and achingly uneven. "Elspeth—"

Elspeth shifted restlessly. She wanted to clasp Alek's hand against her, to take his mouth. But kissing Alek meant she'd be opening herself. "I don't want to go over this again."

"No? Your heart is racing beneath my hand." His thumb moved, sweeping across the hardened tip of her breast. She gasped, trying to shield her emotions and failing.

Alek leaned closer, his black eyes gleaming in the night. "I'll have what I want from you, Elspeth—Petrovna's law. We finish what we begin." Then he bent to pull her against him.

For a heartbeat, she let down her guard, feeling very feminine, delicate and soft—then the hair lifted on the nape of her neck. This was Alek, a man bent on revenge.

His lips moved against her ear, sending tingles down her body. "So this is what you do before you go to the theater on Saturday nights and collect your free tub of popcorn. This is why Duncan and Calum don't want their wives with you on a Saturday night—you're a troublemaker, Elspeth." He nipped her ear. "What's next? The old movies you rent at the video store? Well...sweetheart, I like old movies," he said, imitating Humphrey Bogart.

The second stroke of his thumb set her temper simmering. His grin caught the moonlight, igniting her, and Elspeth reacted instantly. She grabbed his shirt and pushed hard, intending to leap free. A lifetime of pushy brothers had taught her a thing or two.

Alek grunted, fell back and swooped out an arm to catch her, jerking her lightly toward him.

Instinctively Elspeth straddled him and pinned his wrists beside his head. His body lurched just once upward against her, and he shuddered before lying beneath her. "Elspeth, I do believe that you are not always shy."

Elspeth realized to her horror that Alek was aroused.

"Now, this is more like it," he drawled in a deeply pleased tone. His wicked expression challenged her. "Ah-ha! The dominant position. I like games, especially ones with you. So you've tossed me on my back and straddled me. I'm your prisoner, Elspeth. I yield. Now what are you going to do with me?"

They both knew that he could easily overpower her, and Alek grinned up at her. He lifted his hips playfully and bounced her upon him; the movement forced her—an experienced horsewoman—to clamp her thighs tighter against his hips.

In her lifetime, no one played with her, treated her lightly. "This is no game, and we're not teenagers. I am going to get up, and you are going to let me." She braced her hands on his chest, aware that Alek's body thrust at her through the layers of their jeans.

"I feel like a boy around you...." The admission was dark, begrudging, and the look in Alek's expression denied her freedom. Beneath her, Alek was big and solid, his heart pounding against her braced hands. "How long do you think you can run from me? From what happened?" he asked softly, easing her hand to his mouth and brushing his lips across the palm.

She braced herself awkwardly above him, her breasts too close to his face as Alek slowly looked downward.

When his teeth nipped her fingertip, she refused to be intimidated. "I am not running from you, Alek."

"No? Then let's talk about it." He sucked her finger and sent her a look that said he wanted to taste her from toes to forehead and back down the other side. A bolt of heat

shot to her lower stomach, startling her. Alek watched her
as he slowly licked and sucked another finger.

"Alek..." She could almost taste his mouth on hers—
fierce, hungry, delighted, tormenting—but fought the softening heat of her body and tried to breathe quietly.

"I knew we were making a baby that night, your heart
pounding like a wild bird against me. Why didn't you stop
me?"

Elspeth closed her eyes against Alek and the memory of
that night, of Alek poised to enter her fully, shocked by her
body's resistance.

Alek caressed her back, kneaded muscles taut and aching
from hours at the loom. He went right for the tight knots,
working them. Elspeth fought to hold her body still when
it wanted to arch against him.

"Do you know what it does to a man to know he's been
the first and probably the last man to love a woman?"
Alek's voice was husky, deep, sweeping through her.

"Let me go, Alek. You've had your fun." In another
minute, she'd be arching to the motion of his hand.

"Not yet, Elspeth. Not until you stand and fight and we
settle what is between us. Not until you tell me what Una's
journals say about the shawl's legend."

There was no softness in him as he rose to stand over
her. He pulled her to her feet, and Elspeth stared at him,
her mouth open. Alek Petrovna dared to treat her as if she
were a child.

*He wanted to treat her like a lover, the evidence bulging
against the confinement of his jeans.*

"What are you going to do with that?" he asked in that
slow Texas drawl, and looked down at her fist. "Go ahead.
Take your best shot."

She knew where to punch to knock the air from his in-
flated ego...but she wouldn't. Moonlight glinted off the
edges of his teeth as he grinned, daring her. She wouldn't—

Then she did, and heard the satisfying grunt and the whoosh of air.

Elspeth tried to walk away slowly, then she began to run.

In her house, she ripped away her sweater and jeans and slid into a cool, old-fashioned gown, racing for her loom. She didn't want to know what was inside her, why she ached to have Alek hold her close and safe. On another level, her body recognized her first lover and ached with stark, primitive needs she didn't want to acknowledge.

She slid through the familiar, comforting shadows of her home, passing Una's journals on the living-room floor. Next to them was a huge wooden bread bowl, filled with arrowheads she used in her wall hangings. Elspeth probed the buckskin scraps, stick men painted on them, and found the envelope containing the pieces of the shawl's legend. She closed her eyes, willing herself back to safety. Suddenly she needed to know about the legend of Una's shawl. Her hands trembled as she shook the pieces from the envelope, and they tumbled into a square of moonlight on her woven rug.

Her fingers trembled as she eased the pieces into a page. The ink had been blurred by moisture, and the lines wavered, emotions sweeping from Una to the paper. *The Marrying Moon.* The moon had been a huge disk that night, lighting Alek's fierce expression and bathing their naked bodies in silver.

Melissa! Alek's cry had echoed through the night, spearing into her, killing her dreams.

Elspeth turned on the lamp, holding the pieces of paper up to it. Her instinct told her that Una's legend and Alek seemed entwined from that night.... Both were too close and too dangerous.

"A scarred warrior"—the piece fluttered from Elspeth's fingers, and she replaced it, running her finger across the other words: "mist," "mountain," "wind." References to a shawl punctuated Una's journals, but the entire legend was only on this page. It amused Una that Tallchief found the shawl so lovely, and she had blended a legend from his ancestry with hers. On another page Una had written,

Heat lives in the shawl. When a warrior wraps his lady love in it and the Marrying Moon is right, they will know the flames. I think my coppery-skinned husband blushes when I tell him this and he remembers that night beneath the Marrying Moon. He won't say the words, but he knows that something passed between us that night that would unite our souls forever.

Elspeth squeezed her lids closed. She'd believed so deeply from reading Una's journals that if she could just find the shawl, romance would come to her.

Romance was a foolish, girlish dream waylaid by the necessities of survival and coming upon her later than most.

Elspeth rummaged through a file she had created years ago while trying to find the shawl. The shawl had been sold with the rest of Una's dowry to protect Tallchief land, and passed through several hands and then out of the country. Elspeth wanted that shawl desperately now; it was hers, and with it in her keeping she would be safe.... She wanted all the bits of the Tallchiefs' lives tucked safely within their keeping. They'd learned early to depend only on themselves in dangerous times, and she clung to that knowledge now.

She sensed the room's shadows shifting, and Alek tossed her gear onto the sofa. "You forgot this when you ran away. You've got quite a punch for someone who is supposed to be elegant and coolheaded."

She wanted to take *cool*, wrap it around his neck and squeeze tightly. "Get out."

He glanced at the journal and the torn pieces of the page. "That tells about the shawl, doesn't it? You've pledged to return it to the family. It bothers you that you've dropped your quest."

Alek braced his western boot on the low rock hearth beside her. He leaned closer to her. "Let me tell you something about quests, Elspeth. Either seek them out with everything you've got, run them down and claim them...or forget them. But I don't think you can forget the shawl. Would you like help?"

Elspeth came smoothly to her feet, thankful for the long cotton gown, high at the neck and sweeping her toes. "Leave, Alek."

His gaze swept down her loosened hair, to her breasts, taut against the well-washed cotton. He closed his eyes, and a muscle tightened in his jaw, a vein throbbing heavily in his throat. Then his eyes cut to hers. "If you would have told me about the baby, I would have married you...taken care of you. We could have made it work."

Her body jerked in response to the passion in his expression. "Stay away from me, Alek."

"Not likely." The bitter lines around his mouth deepened, and then he was gone.

An amateur playwright, Talia Petrovna demanded a party at Maddy's Hot Spot after the success of her Saturday-night play, *Beer and Boomerangs*. With the *Sentinel* ready to hatch, Alek should have been working with Brad.

The newspaper was what he wanted, to start that beautiful old equipment running, to write about small-town USA, Amen Flats, about new babies and tomatoes the size of basketballs. But words didn't hold him now; images of Elspeth distracted him too often to hold the thread of the story.

Full circle, Alek thought. He wanted to come full circle with Elspeth and this time to play for keeps.

He almost regretted Elspeth's contract with the Denver gallery. Almost. He'd set out to force her into interacting with him, and the contract would do that. Now he wanted time alone with her, without brothers to rescue her and without convenient separate living arrangements. The gallery would provide an ideal environment to manage the elusive Elspeth.

Manipulative? Yes. Hungry for her? Yes and yes. Used to being alone, without tethers, Alek turned the idea.

He'd left it to her to tell her brothers about their past, and she hadn't yet. All hell would break loose the moment they knew.

Alek lifted a beer, blew the foam off it and nodded to Maddy for another. The beefy bartender chewed on an unlighted, worn cigar and waved to the sheriff's patrol car on the street. Maddy plopped a pitcher of beer on the table and groaned. "The sheriff has all the dogs stirred up. He's left his mike button on again. It's bad enough the sopranos are in heat, but does he have to try to sing with them? Jeez, he sounds like nails on a blackboard—throw in a bull moose in mating season."

Birk Tallchief—without Chelsey in tow—lifted the edge of a sheet draped over a painting of a nude woman. He peered under it. "I like that tall, fully stacked look. I don't know why you're desecrating good art."

Alek's gaze slid to Elspeth at another table. The long, lean look appealed to him.

Maddy's thick neck shortened as his jowls sank into his battered black T-shirt. "Women. They're delicate. Don't want any of them offended. Did you ever watch any of those temperance movies? The women stormed bars, took hatchets and smashed them to smithereens. Scared the hell out of me."

Alek watched the lines of dancing couples. "Line dancing. Whatever happened to men holding women against them, you know the old thigh-nudging thing and dips? The way a girl snuggled to a guy and he had both hands free to roam? The old blowing-into-her-ear thing? Slow dancing had its moments."

Talia laughed and cuddled against Calum. "I think someone is in a romantic mood...you're outdated, Alek."

"Is that so?" He surveyed the room, his gaze focusing

on the woman he sought. Seated at a table with Sybil, Elspeth was deep in an intense conversation. Dressed in a black turtleneck sweater, loose slacks and a shawl, Elspeth had been snatched from her house by Talia. Elspeth's black hair was twisted in a fat, gleaming knot that caused Alek to want to loosen it, to feel it sift through his fingers. Small silver disks resembling moons dangled from her ears. *The Marrying Moon*...

Alek's fingers went to his earring, a new habit he'd recognized when thinking of Elspeth. The sight of her standing in that old-fashioned gown had had him wanting to pick her up and cradle her, soothing the past and giving her new memories.

Duncan and Calum and Birk shared an expression. Birk clapped a hand on Alek's shoulder. His wry tone was understanding. "Son, you're horny."

"Could be. The urge comes upon me infrequently, but I'd say I was ripe now." Alek looked straight at Duncan, who had already tensed.

"Pick someone else." Duncan's tone was low, primitive, a man protecting his loved one.

Calum studied Alek. "It's more than that. There's something running between them. He's set Elspeth on edge."

Edges. Alek should have been satisfied that the Tallchiefs recognized the cracks showing in Elspeth's life. He wasn't. He wanted to smooth those lovely, secretive edges. The Tallchiefs knew something brewed between the eldest Tallchief sister and himself, and Alek had no doubt that he'd be called out if they knew it was a baby. From what he'd heard of Fiona, the sister causing trouble in Wisconsin, she'd raise hell if she knew.

Tonight his thoughts were drawn to necking in a back seat and the taste of hunger on Elspeth's lips....

Talia stood instantly, clearly prepared to smooth any tense moments between the Tallchiefs and her brother. "Come on. I've been waiting for this." She tossed a tape at Maddy. "Play that, will you?"

"Like I have a choice," Maddy grumbled, and padded off to the tape player. "Probably some stuff with fiddles that think they're violins."

The high-voltage sounds of a Russian folk song filled the room, surprising the country-music dancers. Maddy went down behind the bar, protecting himself from the barrage of plastic roses used as table decorations that came flying at him. Talia moved into the open space, placed her Hessian boots in position and lifted her arms. "Alek?"

He groaned and rose slowly to his feet. He glanced at Calum. "You should be doing this. Anton and I will give you Talia's Petrovna dances. She has no idea if they are authentic, but it was either that or eat her meals of an indefinable origin."

"Alek!" Waiting for him, Talia clapped dramatically and stamped her boots.

"Do something, Alek. My wife is pregnant. See that she doesn't hurt herself," Calum ordered in the tone of a western gunslinger.

"You'll have to learn this, Calum. No more of that Latin smooth stuff if you want to keep up with the Petrovnas." Alek glanced at Elspeth and knew he would dance for her.

Talia began dancing, moving her boots to an intricate step and weaving to the music as it grew faster. Alek picked her up and held her as he lifted his free arm, going around and around. Talia laughed, and together they began an intricate, fast-paced dance, boots stomping. They shouted and swirled around the room with Talia laughing up at Alek. When the music was almost finished, Alek lifted her and gently twirled her into Calum's waiting arms.

Another fiery folk tune caused the western crowd to groan. Alek's heart pounded with his exertion, and with another passion. He knew what he wanted. He walked across the room to stand by Elspeth. The room quieted suddenly, and he sensed that everyone was watching; he didn't care who knew that he was coming for her. Elspeth glanced at him and flushed. Before she looked away, Alek caught the smoky anger in her eyes.

Smoke and steel, he thought. Heat. Passion. Soft mouth and gentle heart.

In the next instant, Alek caught Elspeth's hand, drawing her to her feet. He lifted her high, treasured her slender body in his hands and slowly lowered her against him. She'd been smiling as Talia and he danced, and the curve of her mouth remained, enchanting Alek. He caressed her lower lip with his thumb, brushing the soft indentations at the corners.

The magic was still there, coursing dark through her gray eyes. Was it the passionate music still playing in his mind, his body? He tossed that thought away; Elspeth had made his body pound, his heart need. Alek ran his finger beneath her chin and lifted it. Slowly, taking his time, he placed his lips on hers and waited. After a long heartbeat, her mouth lifted to his, pushing slightly, returning the brief kiss.

Alek caressed her waist, lost in the feel of her softness vibrating beneath his hands.... She began to respond slowly, magnificently.

There, Alek mused. There was the edge, the silvery gleam of passion streaking in her smoky eyes.

The hoots and wolf whistles started, then stopped when Elspeth drew herself up and stared at the crowd, which quieted immediately.

Alek stepped back and nodded. He'd thrown down another challenge, and Elspeth's cool veneer had begun to melt. He chose to leave her, let her simmer for the moment. Because if her protective walls began to crumble now, Alek didn't trust himself. He turned his back and walked away, and in every step sensed her uncertainty. He'd touched her, reached for her bruised heart, and gotten inside for a moment. However Elspeth liked to hide in her quiet shadows, in her loose clothing, she wasn't immune to him. Nor could he walk away from her unaffected; he'd wanted to carry her out into the moonlight and— His hand shook as he raised his mug to drain it. He didn't want to feel tenderness for Elspeth. Nor the need to lock himself close to her, thrust into that lean body of hers and let her satisfy his hunger.

Alek shifted restlessly. A forty-year-old man who had seen everything and done most of it shouldn't be desperate for a taste of a woman who didn't want him.

The three Tallchief brothers got slowly to their feet, and three forbidding frowns pinned him. Instantly Sybil, Lacey and Talia swooped and drew the brothers into a western two-step dance.

Alek propped his boots on an empty chair and met Elspeth's dark stare. He watched as she slowly rose and gathered her shawl about her.

Alek caught her at the door, his hand shooting past her head to open it. Elspeth did not look at him, but swept out into the night. Elegant, he thought, pure elegance of a lady who is just about to lose her temper.

Alek caught her within ten steps, walking along with her. She slanted him a cool look. "I prefer to walk alone."

He looked at the round moon and inhaled her fragrance and kept walking beside her. "It could be dangerous."

Still keeping his gaze, she snapped her fingers and instantly, Olaf and Thorn appeared from the shadows. Talia and Duncan's huge dogs were gentle with children and dangerously protective of the Tallchiefs. The sheriff, playing a Caruso tape loudly, paused on his drive through town. Both dogs howled, lifting their heads to the moon. The sheriff turned the music down, and the dogs quieted. His spotlight hit them.

"I can tell when those dogs are around that the Tallchiefs are together. Who's that with you, Elspeth?"

"Talia's brother, Alek."

"Alek Petrovna? The guy on television? Heard he's putting out the old newspaper in another week. See if you can get his autograph, okay?" The sheriff's patrol car glided down the street to Caruso's vibrating tenor.

With his finger, Alek scribbled "Petrovna" on her back.

She jumped, glaring at him. "How dare you! Don't think you can pick me up and kiss me like that, Alek. It looked like…like a claiming…as though you were making certain that everyone knew that you wanted me…as though you were pasting a big She's Mine sign on me. Everyone saw— and then you had the nerve to—''

"Hey, the sheriff asked for my autograph, okay?" He bent nearer, enjoying her heated expression.

"Oh!" Elspeth turned and walked a few steps with him at her side. She rounded on him again. "Never—repeat, never—write 'Petrovna' on me, and while I'm at this, don't ever kiss me again, Alek."

"I like kissing you, Elspeth-mine. I'd like to catch up on that necking, too." To reinforce his statement and to ease his need, Alek bent to brush his lips across hers. "Ah, you're a fierce woman, Elspeth. When you come calling for me, I might be half-afraid to step into all that passion. You'll have to hold my hand and woo me."

"If I came calling for you, Alek, it would be to end this."

"End it, but first you'll have to stand and fight me. You'll have to clear out what's between us," he challenged, then bent to kiss her ear and blow into it. "You're hot for me, Elspeth…sweet on me. Admit it."

Her head went back, but before she could slash at him, Alek jerked her into his arms and placed the tip of his tongue exactly in the part of her mouth. He kissed her thoroughly, fitting the slender, taut shape of her body to him, absorbing her into his loneliness, feeding upon the warmth stirring within her. Then Elspeth's lips moved to his, and her head slanted and rested upon his shoulder, cupped by his palm. Something savage, haunting and painful settled within Alek as he held her. He wrapped his arms around her waist and lifted her against him until her eyes were at a level with his.

"I like touching you and kissing you, Elspeth."

When he placed his face in the curve of her throat and

shoulder, her fingers hovered, then stroked his cheek. Her heart raced against his skin. She tensed, her voice a whisper. "Do you?"

"It's not necking, but it's a promising start," he admitted.

"I've never necked."

"Then you're behind, too. Care to catch up? My pickup has new upholstery."

"That rattletrap. Whatever you paid for it, it was too much."

"I've never had a chance as an adult to putter and repair, to make things right. I like it."

Her fingers splayed through his hair, played with the curls and touched the earring. "Petrovna, we both know that you can't stand here all night, holding me like this. You'll get tired eventually."

Then Elspeth bent her head and nipped his lip. She said quietly, "Thorn...Olaf...come," and the two huge dogs leapt, bracing their paws on Alek's back, waiting for Elspeth's next command. "You'd better put me down," she said quietly. "They might think you're detaining me."

She was wrong. He could hold her all night. "I'd like to. Or you could detain me, like you did that night you played detective."

"There are people who need protecting. You don't."

She'd needed protection from him that long-ago night, and he'd been too wrapped in his grief and passion to recognize it. "Who held you when you cried, Elspeth?" he asked quietly, lowering her to her feet.

The flash of emotion in her expression told him more than he wanted to know; Elspeth had never allowed anyone to comfort her since the death of her parents. She'd always been so strong for the rest of the Tallchiefs. Yet he'd held her that night in the tepee and knew how terribly fragile she was.

This time, Alek didn't try to hold her when she moved

away. He shoved his hands into his back pockets to keep from reaching for her as she walked away.

The taste of Elspeth lasted long into the night. To keep his sanity, Alek began writing queries for the shawl. Clive Hardeness in London was friendly with a group of specialized antique collectors, and he would be a good place to start. Alek rubbed his earring and looked at the midnight light in Elspeth's studio. He would have what Elspeth sought and he would know why she had whispered, "The Marrying Moon."

Five

"Elspeth!" Mark Redman hurried across the gallery's office to greet her. Outside the gallery, May sunshine spread like warm butter over Denver's streets.

In Amen Flats, the *Sentinel* had become a three-week success story. Alek had worked night and day, giving her some reprieve from the noise next door to her. There was no reprieve from the jump in her heart, the tightness of her throat each time Alek looked at her. Focused, she corrected. Alek had focused upon her and was testing her, playing games that didn't interest her.

She told herself that again...that Alek's games didn't appeal. He was out to prove something, and she wouldn't have any of it. She could hold her distance, she told herself, and he'd get bored. While she was away from Amen Flats, she'd forget his taunting kisses and the way her blood heated at his torments. She'd return to Amen Flats, restored and without thoughts of Alek.

A pleasant businessman in his thirties, Mark wore a loose

silk shirt and slacks, and his long hair was in a ponytail. He took in her leather vest, chambray blouse and woven belt, long skirt, soft moccasins. He grinned as his practiced fingers traveled over her woven bag. "Perfect. Just the artsy look that sells. Keep the braids, will you? Sometimes we get an artist who looks just fine, and then the night of the opening, they go off and change it."

Mark touched her vest's leather fringes, decorated with beads. She didn't mind his examination of her woven belt, the intricate, ancient designs. "Perfect. You look great in the Tallchief plaid, too. We've sent out invitations to our clients, and they'll love to meet you. You saw the brochure we did on you? I want you to be comfortable about how you're managed."

"The brochure was wonderful, and the braids are here to stay." Elspeth allowed Mark to hold her hand. She liked him, this easygoing man who had stopped by her booth one day and asked about her work. An expert on wools and textures, Mark had presented a comfortable advance on the contract to deal with his gallery exclusively for two years. She saw no problem when he'd asked her to promote her work by making appearances.

Mark studied her face. "You're tired. Probably scared about the showing and working too hard. Take the day to rest, will you? We've got to wow them tomorrow night."

"I'll be fine, Mark...if your assistants don't think my driftwood for free-form wall hangings are firewood. They're from Tallchief Lake."

"We'll take care of them. You're comfortable with the showing schedule we worked out? You're okay to travel with the exhibits after the showing? Having the artist there to explain technique will add up to sales. Did you bring me anything new?" Mark rubbed his hands together; he sounded like a child at Christmas.

She liked the friendly way he draped his arm across her

shoulder. Then she moved away, unused to comfortable men. "I have new pieces. They're out in my van."

Mark pushed the intercom buzzer. "Make certain Ms. Tallchief's things are taken to the apartment, will you? Bring her work to me." He winked at Elspeth. "I can't wait. My partner says you're certain to set record sales and your price will go up. He'll be at the opening tomorrow night. He's the one who really liked your work in the first place. He's already bought several pieces."

"Really? That just shows he has good taste. I look forward to meeting him. Who is he?"

Mark chuckled. "He's the silent end of the deal. He bought in as a silent partner in December. Prefers to handle his own introductions. The guy has a big past—has traveled everywhere and has made a bundle in investments. He's a celebrity wanting to remain anonymous, and I respect his wishes. I like him, and he's been good for building a new clientele. It's kind of cute to see a big tough guy go all woozy over your work. He touches it as if he revered every thread. Once he pointed your work out to me, I recognized your talent right away."

After two and a half months of Alek invading her life, Elspeth looked forward to Mark's offer of the gallery's apartment, to traveling with the exhibit for the next two weeks...and escaping Alek Petrovna.

Mark showed her around the gallery, explaining to her about the natural light bringing out the colors of her work. Mark latched on to her weaving like a mother hen picking over her chicks.

"What's this? Not your usual," he said as an assistant brought in one of her new works.

The hanging was slender, lacking the Native American elements of her other work. The tightly woven, hand-spun wool had leaped into her fingers, pale stripes of mauve and tan. In places, she'd used a fork as a beater, keeping the weave tight and heavy. In others, the weave was looser, freer. The weft, running horizontally, was tighter in places, giving a curve that flowed throughout the piece. She'd kept the frame simple to highlight her weaving. The colors heated to gold and dark red, circling a pale cream center with one burst of brilliant vermilion, then eased to deep waves of mauve and tan.

Mark skimmed his hand down the uneven, nubby texture. "Emotion vibrates in this. The colors shouldn't work, not in that design...but they do. It's almost alive beneath my touch. What's the theme? Life? No, nothing so broad. Its message is infinite, too deep to explain—the heat and feeling in it just fly out. Is it titled? We'll have to put something really pricey and obscure sounding on it."

"I haven't decided." The colors had come to her at sunset, the dying light glistening in the wool, the texture—now smooth, now rough—presented shadows upon its surface. Elspeth didn't want to think about what she had created, or why it was different from the rest. The design and texture had sprung from her heart, unfettered by her plans and sketches.

The making of this work had cost her, wrung something from her that both hurt and gave joy. The elements in her other work sprang from her heritage, but this was new, coming from her alone.

Mark jotted a note. "Names...titles, hike up the price. Make a list. We'll pencil it in later. By the way, my partner has ordered some dresses for you...for the promotion events. They're pricey, but just the thing to present you this first time."

"Mix...mingle...talk wool. Make sales." Mark glanced down at Elspeth's cerulean blue silk gown, which was supported by two tiny straps. A shimmering fringe ran across the bodice, then the gown clung, defining her slender body

until it flared from her calves to her feet. Mark eyed her
hair, pulled straight back into an elegantly twined chignon.
"Wow! What a babe!"

Elspeth shot him a frown. Her stomach ached, and she
rubbed her palms together. "Don't grin. You know I'm
nervous. You have no idea how I dislike this...packaging.
The clothes in the apartment are too many, too expensive
and...exotic. I feel naked enough with my work on display." She resisted telling him about the mountain of seductive lingerie, scraps of lace and satin she'd found among
the clothes.

"Just part of the game...don't want a little-villager image who sells cheap." Mark flipped the blue topaz beads
at her ear. He touched her bare upper arm. "You've got
muscles, kid. It's exciting to know that a strong woman
created your work. Just a selling point my partner thinks
will work as we package you for the public."

"I'm not the exhibit. My work..." Elspeth began. Her
head throbbed, and in another minute she would return to
her room. The gallery was packed, brightly lighted and everything she wanted to avoid.

The guests wanted too much, picking at the pieces of her
life. One woman wanted to know if Elspeth had children,
and how nice it was to pass a feminine tradition down to
children.

Elspeth ignored the familiar pain and answered that her
works were her children.

"I must have that," a woman told her husband, pointing
to the untitled hanging. "I'm not much on that Native
American–theme stuff and plastic arrowheads, but this
would be great in our bedroom—it's so sensuous, so
erotic."

"Plastic arrowheads," Elspeth muttered to Mark.

"Shh."

Mark leaned closer to Elspeth. "Do more like that...the erotic stuff. We'll pick up another clientele—"

"Not a chance—"

Mark turned, his expression lighting as he shook hands with Alek Petrovna. "Hey, guy. We've been waiting for you. This is Elspeth Tallchief, one talented weaver woman."

Alek, dressed in a collarless black silk shirt under an expensive suit jacket and loose slacks, loomed at her side. His brows and lashes gleamed in the bold light, his cheekbones cut at angles across his face and there was nothing soft about his mouth and jaw. His scars and shoulder-length, unruly hair only added to his dangerous look, drawing women's eyes. Alek did not look away from Elspeth. One eyebrow lifted, mocking her. He took Elspeth's hand and raised it to his lips. He did not let it go at her first tug.

The shawl draped around his shoulders was fringed and elegant, fluttering as he moved. Elspeth noted the merino wool and the fiery gold-and-red design made in Paisley, Scotland.

Una's shawl.

She almost ripped it from him, but didn't only because she treasured the fine work and her heritage. The man was another matter. Alek had found a new way to enter her life. The shawl was his declaration. Aware that the crowd was focused on Alek, a tall, striking man dressed in a suit and a fiery feminine shawl, she rounded on Mark. She sheathed her fury in a whisper. "Is this your partner? Is this the man that I'm supposed to travel with, to the exhibits?"

She could feel the snarl of anger curling in her. Alek should have looked silly in the shawl; he didn't. The soft, fiery texture only enhanced his dark skin and black, amused eyes, and she hated him more for that.

Surprised by her hushed fury, Mark was alarmed. "Well, yes. Alek is my partner. He pointed me to your work. I'm glad he did. The first pieces we sold brought a hefty price, but with this showing that will go up. Elspeth, this is Alek—''

She rubbed her temples, her headache pounding. ''I know who he is. Mark, you should have told me—''

''I'm her admirer. Let's not belabor details, Elspeth. Mark, don't sell that piece. It's her best work, and let's show it off.'' Alek reached out the flat of his hand to caress the hanging in a blatantly sexual manner that took her breath away. Then he wrapped his arm around her waist and eased her through the crowd, despite her resistance. ''I knew blue would look good on you.''

They were on the patio and alone. Elspeth jerked free and gripped the wooden railing. In another minute, she'd— ''What do you think you're doing?''

Her earring gleamed in his ear, challenging her.

Clearly bothered by Alek's commandeering and Elspeth's unexpected temper, Mark strolled into their battlefield. He looked worriedly from Elspeth to Alek. ''Is everything okay?''

''Go away, Mark,'' Alek murmured. ''She's just a bit nervous.''

''Yes, please, Mark. Go away. I'll be fine.'' Elspeth wanted Alek to herself. She wanted to strangle him. He'd invaded her life and now her heritage. When they were alone, she said, ''I want that shawl. How much?''

''You'll have to fight me for it, love. Or you could tell me about the Marrying Moon.''

Every nerve in Elspeth's body stretched taut. No one had ever dared to toy with her, to push her as Alek had done. She wasn't certain how she might react, but with Alek the prospect excited her more than weaving. ''You deliberately packaged yourself in something that is mine. This could be war.''

"Mmm. I'm not going anywhere. Do your damnedest."
He leaned to brush a kiss on her nose, playing with her.

"You'd better take care of it. You chose this—" her
hand swept down her gown "—and those bits of lace called
lingerie. Alek Petrovna, you are a jerk.... Where did you
get that shawl?"

"As a matter of fact, Talia picked the lingerie. I told her
I wanted to give a woman friend something nice. Since I've
been out of the lingerie game for a while and you were the
wearee, my taste ran to bare flesh and nothing else. She
has matching styles that she wears for Calum alone. The
shawl is from a Paisley shawl collector. Sybil described it
to me perfectly. It needs a broach, don't you think?" Alek's
hand caressed the shawl.

She couldn't let him get away with that. Elspeth caught
his curls in her fist and drew his face down to her level.
He didn't deserve kindness. He'd invaded her privacy; she
didn't intend him to leave unmarked. Alek's kisses had
been hot and hungry, leaving her without a complete
thought. She intended to do the same to him and maybe
more. Elspeth tossed away the red flag of caution tugging
at her; Alek needed a lesson, and she intended to give it to
him.

"Here's a challenge for you, Mr. Petrovna."

She intended the kiss to be sensual, but she hadn't prepared for the instant tenderness he returned, the gentle
tempo of his lips brushing hers lightly and hers following
his. He tasted of everything she'd missed and everything
she wanted to grasp selfishly for herself. Unaccustomed to
greed, Elspeth reeled in the need to vanquish Alek, to pit
herself against him. She moved closer, allowed her body to
lightly touch his. Alek tensed, the movement satisfying her.

No, it didn't. Nothing could satisfy her but bringing him
to his knees.

A siren wailed in the street below as Elspeth trailed a

fingertip down his cheek and watched his expression harden. Because she knew she must, Elspeth stood on tiptoe and lightly kissed the scar on Alek's lip.

He jerked her to him, wrapped his arms around her waist and hauled her into the shadows of the potted bushes. Elspeth gripped the shawl with both fists. "Alek, you're over your head."

"Am I? You'll have to show me, won't you?" Alek's hands went beneath the soft shawl. He touched her breasts lightly, tracing the shape of them. Elspeth breathed quietly, uncertain now. His prowling fingertip slipped beneath the bodice and stroked her softness. She wanted to be immune to his touch, to walk away unaffected. Alek leaned close to her, placed his scarred cheek against her smooth one and stood very still, allowing her the freedom to walk away. He wasn't holding her; he breathed heavily, his fingertips smoothing her breasts, following the shape of her slowly. Then his hands cupped her breasts firmly, possessively. He bent slowly to place his face in the curve of her throat and shoulder. Her heart pounded heavily, racing.... The woman in her stirred, softened and wanted....

Elspeth closed her eyes. Alek wasn't taking; he was giving himself to her care. Nothing could have been more effective.

His lips moved, kissing her throat, and she feared to breathe, her fingers fluttering against the soft wool around his shoulders.

She wanted him against her, deep inside where heat forged them as one—where the pounding of their blood couldn't be defined as his or hers.

She'd have him frothing and then she'd walk away, leaving him to simmer in what he had started. There would be no Petrovna's law where she was concerned; Alek had tossed her a challenge she couldn't resist.

Elspeth slid her hands under his suit, caressed his chest

and placed one palm over his heavily beating heart. Alek tensed, then ripped away the shawl and his jacket and caught Elspeth close again. "Touch me. Make me feel, Elspeth."

He pulled the pins from her hair, releasing it and burying his face in it. Elspeth fought the emotions rising in her; she was too susceptible to Alek's tender touch.

Alek bent and lifted her in his arms. He raised her to kiss her throat. Elspeth dug her fingers into his shoulders, shaking, fighting. She hesitated, poised at the edge of a dangerous abyss, hovering between staying in the shadows and taking what she desired.

Desire. Heat. Hunger.

Alek's heated face pressed against her throat, and he dragged aside one strap of her dress with his teeth, instantly claiming her breast with his lips. Shocked by the intimate heat, the laving of his tongue, Elspeth tensed, caught on the edge of surprise and delight. Another flick of his tongue, the edge of his teeth, and she fought the fire rising in her, stepped into heated space and gave herself to the gentle suckling until she was shaking. She pressed his head against her, running her fingers through the black curls and gave herself to the heat of his mouth, the sensations coursing through her, the need to be alive, to take, to give. When Alek lowered her, she raised her arms to capture him and gave him her mouth.

He was gentle, tempting her tongue with his.

She was on fire, wanting him closer.

This was Alek, her Alek, her lover and— He groaned unevenly, shaking in her arms, exciting her. His hands trembled when he touched her lightly, and it wasn't enough. Elspeth nipped at his throat, and Alek shuddered; his hands smoothed her hips, then locked to her and pushed her against his steely need. His palms ran down her thighs, trembling, easing the gown higher until he touched her soft,

quivering thighs. His fingers explored the lacy elastic of
her stockings and then found the satin lace covering her
femininity.

She moved slightly, and his fingers caressed the damp
satin, sliding inside to the heat— "Alek!"

His body supported her as the pounding, the intimate
clenching, began, riveting her until she climbed the peak
and then gently, slowly melted against him.

Alek shook, taut with need as he kissed her and soothed
the tremors running through her. "Elspeth," he whispered
hoarsely against her loosened hair.

His tone sent her tumbling into another time, when another woman's name crossed his lips.

Reality and shame came creeping softly to her. She
wanted to walk away and couldn't, her legs still trembling.
Alek had taken her beyond what she wanted, to prove she
could take him down—

He smoothed her hair, drawing her head to rest on his
chest. "Let me hold you."

Alek rocked her gently, and Elspeth gave herself to a
safety she hadn't known since her parents died. She should
have moved away; she couldn't. She closed her eyes and
knew that she didn't want to think, to fight him...not now.

"You are not a nice man. I think I'm going to kill you,"
she said finally, faced with the reality of a gallery filled
with clients already curious about her. She had to get away;
she'd exposed her needs. She trembled and waited for Alek
to speak. In another minute, she'd shatter....

He brought her hair to his lips, his eyes burning as he
looked down at her. "Blush is definitely your color."

Alek turned her and began combing her hair. She shivered, emotions streaking through her; she'd just threatened
to kill him—not seriously—but she intended to nick him
in a few places where it would count.

The novelty of being tended startled Elspeth; usually she was the caregiver. "You've done this before."

Of course he had; Alek Petrovna had devoured experienced women. "I had baby sisters. Anton couldn't be trusted not to tie their hair in knots."

She didn't believe him, not for a moment. Alek had touched her with experience.

Mark suddenly appeared in the lighted doorway. "Come on, Elspeth. They want to meet you. She's been nervous all day, Alek."

"She's relaxed a bit." Alek's Texas drawl was back and filled with amusement. He stared down at her, the angles of his face rigid and reflecting his desire for her. She'd done that much at least—raised his desire. A quick learner, she could have him panting and giving her the shawl....

He jerked her hair lightly, forcing her to look at him over her shoulder. "You'll have to work a bit harder to get that shawl, my fair Elspeth," he whispered huskily.

"You think I...?" She began to wonder if her hands would fit around Alek's thick neck.

Mark came closer, clearly curious about Alek combing Elspeth's hair. Alek made one long braid, then reached to neatly tear away a fringe from her bodice, which he used to tie off the braid.

Mark moved to Elspeth's back. "Good job. Gave her a neck massage, did you? Good for tense muscles. I should have thought of that—the Native American look mixed with a contemporary businesswoman. You missed a strand, Alek. Do it again."

"Do you want to?" Alek was not amused.

"Heck, no. You won't catch me braiding a girl's hair. Your hands are shaking. Alek, you look like you want to strangle someone. Be cool, guy. She'll be okay—"

"I think tomorrow I'll strangle you slowly," Alek muttered darkly.

"Will the two of you stop?" Elspeth wanted to escape Alek's touch and her shattered emotions and the people waiting for her.

Somehow she managed the evening, taunted by Alek wearing Una's bright shawl around his broad shoulders. Folded triangularly, the fiery red-and-gold point shot off one shoulder, the fringes dancing as he moved. He wasn't prettily handsome, his features too rugged. The scars on his cheek and lip enhanced his masculinity, and the soaring scar in his eyebrow needed a woman's touch to smooth it.

Looking like a dangerous pirate, he caught the attention of a lush brunette, who snagged his arm. He smiled down at her, and the woman issued an open invitation by leaning closer and licking her glossy lips. A blonde slid her hand through his other arm, and Alek laughed outright at something she said.

The blonde pushed her breasts against him and spoke intently. Alek leaned down to listen, the woman's red lips almost touching the earring—LaBelle's earring—and Elspeth found her hand curled into a fist. His hand rested on the woman's waist—

Elspeth lifted her head. He had held her only minutes ago, his tall body rigid and trembling against hers. Now he had another body against him and another one just as willing. Alek's charm flashed across the room to Elspeth, and she tossed it back with a light "no, thank you" smile.

He said something to the women and moved purposefully through the gallery crowd toward Elspeth. She wouldn't move away from his advance; she wouldn't give him the satisfaction. When he came to her side, she leveled a cold look at him. A swaggering, arrogant, hot-for-sex pirate was exactly what she did not want in the arena of her life.

Alek placed his hand on her waist and walked her across the gallery. As they stood in front of "Untitled," his hand dropped an inch lower to rest on her hip, fingers splayed possessively. Pushing, she thought. Always pushing.

"'Untitled' is very erotic. What about titling it 'The Second Encounter'?" Alek had loosened the top buttons at his throat. Elspeth recognized the mark on his skin; caught in her startling passion, she had nipped at him.

Alek rubbed his temple, fighting a headache. He was tired and drained, fighting years of sleeplessness and the constant need of Elspeth. The steady sensual humming in his body wasn't helping his concentration. He clicked off his computer laptop and stood, stretching cramped muscles. Dressed only in his shorts, he padded to the bed in the gallery's lower apartments and lifted the shawl against him. He had pushed Elspeth too hard, and tonight the walls had gone down. Whatever Elspeth felt about him, there was no mistaking her passion or her need to take him down. It had frightened and angered her, raising the color in her cheeks and deepening her smoky gray eyes.

He loved her.

He'd begun to hunt her with rage and then a clinical, cutting revenge, tethering her with the contract. Along the way, he'd fallen in love with her. Maybe he'd always been in love with her since that haunting night in Scotland.

A noise drew him to the empty, darkened gallery. Elspeth, wrapped in an old flannel robe, stood before "Untitled," studying her work. Wool drifted from her hand, as though "Untitled" had drawn her from her weaving.

Alek closed the door, allowing her privacy. He drew the shawl across his cheek, pressing it against his face. The merino wool was soft and light with a life of its own…he wanted Elspeth to want him as much as she wanted the shawl. If he came to Elspeth now, he'd want to make love with her, and though tonight had shown him a flash of her

passion, he wanted more than a quickening from Elspeth.
He wanted her awakening.

"All right, Alek. You've had your fun. I'll buy Una's
shawl. How much?" Elspeth leaned back against the van's
passenger seat and faced the passing scenery. After a week
of press interviews and parties, they were on their way to
the first exhibit in another gallery.

She could have walked out, dismissing the contract. But
she was a Tallchief, bred to honor commitments. Until her
obligations were met, Alek had her within reach. He'd
waited, and now they were alone. Alek rubbed LaBelle's
earring. "The shawl is not for sale."

When she turned to him, her sunglasses like mirrors,
Alek placed a dried apricot against her lips. Elspeth had
her vices, he'd discovered, and dried apricots were definitely a priority. Hand-feeding Elspeth was an experience
he savored. Or was it torture to watch her lips curve around
the morsel, her teeth bite into it? She'd actually taken what
he had offered. He rubbed her lip with his thumb and
sucked an orange tidbit into his mouth. "The shawl re-
quires the legend."

"It's my heritage," Elspeth muttered around the apricot.

"So's the legend. They're a package deal. You give me
one, and I give you the other."

"The Paisley mills in Scotland produced excellent work
from the early 1700s on. The shawls are pure art. Only
a—"

"I admire art," he stated, comfortable with whatever
names she would call him.

She stared at him, one sleek black brow lifted in disbelief. "You blockhead."

"Sweetheart. Baby-doll." Alek grinned when Elspeth's
mouth curved slightly.

"I'm not a baby-doll. You've got the wrong woman,
Alek."

"Have I?" Alek tugged her sunglasses away; he wanted to see her eyes, watch the color change shades with her emotions. When he told her what lay between them, he wanted to see her eyes. "I haven't been with another woman since that night, Elspeth."

Again Elspeth lifted a disbelieving, sleek eyebrow in his direction.

That grated. "You're not making this easy, Elspeth. I'm sharing a bit of Petrovna insight here. My sex life is a private matter."

"Oh, I'm sure," she murmured too easily.

Alek passed a truck and, after checking his rearview mirror, swerved back into the lane. He glanced at her rigid expression, the set of her jaw. Elspeth had plenty to chew on; she might as well hear more. There was nothing like baring his soul to a woman who would walk away from him the moment she could. Okay, he was a sucker for pain, Alek thought as he plunged on. "I loved Melissa. I told her not to come to me, not to enter the war zone, but it was our anniversary and she wanted...us to be together."

Alek tightened his fingers on the steering wheel, his knuckles white with tension. He swerved to avoid a squirrel and dropped back into the terror years ago. "The rocket was a direct hit in the tiny room. It exploded instantly, and Melissa screamed. I'll never forget the sound of—shrieks, blind, terrified, shrieks of pain—"

"Alek..." Elspeth touched his hand; he locked her fingers with his, bringing their clasped hands to his thigh.

He took her hand and brought her fingertips to his mouth. "I'd seen everything by then—hungry orphans, starving elderly, mass graves in war-torn countries. Melissa's dying was—"

"Alek, those things are in the past." Elspeth's voice ran on a thin, trembling thread, snaring him with her emotions.

He kissed her palm, studied her slender, capable fingers.

"The past is with us, just like my scars, and I want you to understand. After...I knew what I had to do, to hurt you...to make the break clean. You had your whole life ahead of you, and I had nothing. Maybe I got scared, so I said what I had to and left you."

Her wary expression hurt him more than he'd expected. He pulled a small, worn envelope from his pocket and handed it to her.

She carefully opened and eased a tattered woven swatch from the envelope. Her fingers trembled, running over the wool. "It's mine. I was studying mordants to set the color and used copperas on this. The dye is a heather olive."

"I found heather sprigs and the swatch stuck to my clothing. The heather crumbled right away." He'd crushed it, diving under twisted barbed wire. The swatch was all he'd had left of Elspeth, a silly little bit of cloth that had reminded him of life and tenderness and hope.

She looked down, then away into the mountains, the sunlight skimming her high cheekbones and sweeping down her bare throat. There beneath her lightly tanned skin, a vein pulsed heavily, and Alek prayed it was because she thought of him.

Six

"Alek, this isn't working. You're intruding into my life. *I do not like you acting as though I am your possession.*" The storm outside equaled Elspeth's raw emotions. A week and a half of Alek invading her life, snaring her into sleepless nights, was taking a toll on her nerves. She opened the apartment door to Mark, who had returned to the gallery's apartment with cartons of Chinese food. She helped him place them on the coffee table, then sat on the couch and began filling their plates.

She'd missed the closeness of a family, eating together and sharing small talk over the table.

Alek glanced up from his laptop computer, a pencil shoved over his ear. In a startling change from whatever interested him to complete absorption with her, he spoke quietly. "I have to get this story done. Why don't you tell me what's bothering you? Don't spare my feelings."

"I *was* telling you, Alek." Thunder crashed as he watched her with interest. "You're steaming, Elspeth. Come on, let it all out."

"Will you two kiss and make up?" Mark complained.
"It's safer out there in the lightning storm than in here with
you. You've been like this since you got back from that
last trip. Neither one of you look like you've had a minute's
sleep."

Elspeth placed the points of her chopsticks on his chest.
"You mutter when you're distracted, Mark. Alek hovers.
You both are—"

She inhaled a quieting breath and began again. "I am
not used to being pampered...to being tucked in at night.
He physically dragged me away from my work and plopped
me in bed, Mark. He brings me a breakfast tray in the
morning. Alek actually told a very nice man that he didn't
deserve one of my hangings."

She ached from the long day, traveling to the showing
with Alek, and she...she didn't want to share herself with
Alek, who watched her carefully from what she ate to...
Elspeth had just noted that his hair needed trimming and
he'd lost weight. Alek Petrovna was not a man to care for
himself, his needs untended. Her gaze skimmed him, from
dress shirt to worn jeans and socks. He needed a shave and
someone to care for him. She glanced at his rumpled shirt,
opened at the collar and revealing a soft curl of black hair.
She didn't want to care—

"That *nice* man was trying to pick her up. He stroked
the painting, put his hands on it while he was looking right
down her dress. We're going back to Amen Flats." Alek
glanced down Elspeth's loose pink sweater, her black
slacks and her bare feet. Elspeth curled her toes, aware that
Alek's close inspection raised her senses to a danger level.
With him, she felt feminine and cherished; she didn't like
the feeling, nor the sense that Alek wanted to make up for
not being close when she needed him. Elspeth realized suddenly how empty her life had been since that night.

Thunder rattled the windows, storm clouds rolling across

the sky outside, and she felt as fragile as the bouquet of roses Alek had ordered for the apartment. He'd also ordered the potted herbs running along the window, their scents giving her peace in an emotional war zone that was Alek. Restless now near him, she rose to cut chives, wash and chop them over their food.

Mark looked at her, then leveled a stare at Alek. "Elspeth, any time this jerk makes moves you don't like and you want me to do something, I will. I'm pretty good in a gym."

She had been afraid of this. Alek could shred Mark and walk away untouched. "I shouldn't have said anything. I have brothers, remember? Alek is just going through a phase, and I can handle him."

"A phase…and I am not your brother, sweetheart. We're going home," he repeated softly, watching her.

Mark's expression said that he had an investment to protect, if not Elspeth. "Going home? She's got two more showings in as many days."

"Alek, I am honoring my agreement."

"But you'd rather be home and you know it." Alek eyed her, a muscle contracting along his jaw. "You were playing with something you have no idea how to control."

She lifted an eyebrow. Who was he to tell her what she wanted and if she was flirting? "Don't I?"

She'd scored a hit; Alek scowled at her. "We're going home. Elspeth needs her family, and they need her. She likes to bake." Alek frowned and continued typing.

Elspeth stared at him. There was no limit to his arrogance. How could he possibly know what she needed?

"That's me, just the little homebody. I *love* to putter. Take me out of Amen Flats and I'm just lost without my puttering." Again Elspeth enjoyed the quick flash of anger in Alek's expression.

He reached for his cup of cold coffee, downed it and

turned back to his computer. He'd ignore everything when engrossed with an article, and when he was hungry, he ate whatever popped into his hand from cold food to candy bars.

Elspeth finished her meal. Alek continued punching keys and ignoring the food that Mark was devouring. Alek fascinated her, from his high-hell moods to his tenderness with children and the elderly. Elspeth found herself picking up a sliced carrot with her chopsticks; she lifted the morsel to his mouth.

Alek stopped typing, clicked off the machine and slowly turned to her. His lips opened, and Elspeth placed the sliced carrot within his mouth. He chewed and swallowed, and Elspeth slowly placed a chicken morsel to his lips. He fascinated her, restless and concentrating on his writing one moment and then easily managed by the offer of a food tidbit.

Big, tough, impatient Alek Petrovna sat quietly while she fed him, his eyes gleaming beneath heavy sets of curled lashes. "I could get used to this," he murmured unevenly.

"Don't. It's either see that you eat vegetables or deal with Talia."

"Okay. I'll get you off the hook." In a move that she had seen her brothers employ, he stretched his arms up and then laid one across the back of the couch. His hand settled on her shoulder; Alek's thumb lazily caressed her throat. Though she knew his intent, she tried to ignore the immediate response in her.

Finished with his food, Mark cleared away his dishes. "Just take good care of her, Alek. She doesn't look any better than you do. The next time you decide to stake out a woman, count me out. I'm glad you got this one here, though. She's fabulous. Elspeth? Call me if you need me— for anything. You've got my beeper number." After a level, ominous look at Alek, Mark exited the apartment in a crash of thunder.

Alek leaned back against the couch, his gaze locked with Elspeth's as she fed him another morsel. His fingers caressed her thigh, then slid to draw her legs over his thighs. His wary expression reminded her that he'd seen everything, had no delusions about mankind and yet wanted to believe in fairy tales.

"What are you doing?" he asked huskily when she placed the plate aside.

"In the time we've spent together, I haven't seen you eat an entire meal. You eat on the run, Alek, anything and everything, hot...cold, and too much coffee. By the time you get to them, your sandwiches are dried."

He nodded slowly. "Okay. If it's important to you, I'll work on regular, balanced, sit-down meals. What else?"

"I doubt you have any idea of what a balanced meal is." Elspeth carefully picked through her thoughts about Alek. First of all, Alek could take whatever she handed him; she doubted she could make a dent in his ego. "You wear socks with holes. You're messy. You shout. You're volatile, Alek. Emotionally expressive. You snarl and threaten and intimidate." Then she flung the worst of the lot at him. "And...you gesture too much. You're much too...dramatic one minute and laughing the next. To top it off, you've been too darn easy lately."

"Gee, I guess it's my Petrovna blood," Alek returned, unbothered. "You can shout back. You can handle it. You can even laugh if you want." Alek tapped her nose with his fingertip, then lifted her to his lap.

"Idiot." She braced herself away from him. He handled her as though he had the right to touch her. "Alek, I am not Talia to tease, or little Megan to be cuddled."

"Shut up, Elspeth-mine. I like cuddling you. You could

cuddle me. We could grin together,'' he teased with eyebrows lifting suggestively.

She looked down at Alek, studied the harsh jutting cheekbones and deep-set, almost slumberous eyes beneath curling lashes that no man had a right to own. Rain patterns on the window shadowed his face, and she knew there was nothing sleepy or laughing about Alek Petrovna. Against her, his body was hot and tense, humming with needs she didn't understand but wanted to match. The storm outside suited her emotions; she wanted to rip away Alek's clothes and—

Elspeth wearily closed her eyes. Alek had moved into her life and turned it thoroughly upside down.

''Don't think about it, love. Just rest.'' Alek tugged her head down to his shoulder and stroked her hair. She could have, should have, moved away, but instead settled her cheek onto the novel cushioning of warm muscles and the slow, safe beat of his heart. Elspeth rested there lightly, curved to Alek. Years ago, she'd been held like this, cuddled to her father…she couldn't remember being so safe.…

Elspeth awoke to Alek's scent clinging to the pillow beneath her cheek. Her clothes twisted around her. She'd slept heavily.

In a heartbeat, Elspeth leapt to her feet and stalked toward the sound of water running in her bathroom.

She ripped open the bathroom door; the sight of Alek shaving in the nude stopped her. The profile of his body was beautiful, rippling cords and hollowed at his haunches, his legs spread, feet bare upon the tile. She avoided a full frontal view and skipped to his legs, bulky at the thigh— the scars angry.

Alek turned to her and lifted his scarred eyebrow.

She advanced, careless that he towered over her, dressed in nothing but the white foam on his jaw. She wanted to drag him back to bed...or just have him where he stood. "Just what do you think you're doing?" she asked rawly. She realized that she had thrown up her hands and forced them down, making fists at her thighs.

Her eyes flicked to the foam clinging to the hair on his chest...then jerked to Alek's flat nipple. She forced herself not to trace the line of hair going downward—she grabbed a towel and held it up to him. Alek lifted that eyebrow again, then slowly looked down to the intimate bulge in the hanging material.

The atmosphere in the small room shifted and stood still. In the mirror, Alek watched her, his face expressionless. "You slept with me. All night." She didn't believe it was true, not yet.

"Uh-huh. That I did." Alek rinsed his razor and continued shaving as though they spent every night together. Because he had moved, she was forced to shift the towel.

She stiffened at the sight of the delicate pink razor in his hand and took it away from him.

Alek patted his face dry, slashed away the towel and turned to her, hands on hips. There he stood, towering over her, hair damp and spiraling from his shower. Droplets of water shimmered on the hair on his chest and on his shoulders—a deep jagged scar running across his left one. She wanted to place her lips on it and— Elspeth refused to allow the hunger in her; she refused to look down.

"You're not a comfortable woman to sleep with, but I needed to hold you. A simple, old-fashioned, basic need of a man who needs to sleep one entire night with one special woman. I should have spent that night with you, Elspeth. I should have held you close to me and tucked your fanny neatly against a part of me that is in a constant and hard state, thank you very much."

"You could take care of that...need easily enough. You've had enough offers since I've known you." Elspeth straightened, horrified that she had sounded like a jealous lover. She threw out her hand. "You could have slept all night with—"

"You're gesturing wildly, Elspeth. My, my. So I'm not the only one." He took one step toward her, then another, and slammed the door shut behind her, backing her up against it. Alek glowered down at her. "Yes, damn it. I could have had women. But I slept with you. I wallowed in the event. Hell, I probably glowed. I dived into your scents, the texture of your hair, like a love-starved teenage boy, too hot and too hard. You sprawl, Elspeth-mine. You sprawled, took up the bed and nearly made me embarrass myself. You are a restless sleeper, and your hands are very busy. I am not wool to be woven or to be plucked or caressed."

His body heat burned her, ensnared her. "I'm not discussing my sleep habits—"

"Oh, you're not?" he repeated too softly. His face lowered to hers, his eyes savage and blazing. "Get out."

His hardened body lurched intimately against her, and Elspeth flattened to the door, fighting her need to touch him, to soothe...or just pit herself against him and show him that he couldn't walk into her life and shatter it.

"Yes, you little disaster. I'd like to carry you back to bed and keep you there until we've erased that first time. Until you're sweaty and limp and cuddly. Oh, yes, Elspeth-mine. Don't look so shocked. I'd like to lick the sweat from your breasts, watch it gleam on them and pearl on your body. I'd like to slide against you, frontal, side and backside. I'd like to suck and bite and kiss you until you—"

He hesitated, studied her, only to begin again. "Good. You're shocked. I need to be locked to you, in you. With you, Elspeth, until barriers of flesh burn away," he repeated. "But you're going to have to make your own decision. You're going to actually have to take the first step because, if I did…if I did…"

Alek closed his eyes and groaned; he pivoted away from her to latch both big hands on the countertop. The counter cracked, and he cursed. "Out."

Alek realized he'd been staring at the computer monitor while his mind drifted to his neighbor. Elspeth had closed herself away from him and moved through the next showings with cool detachment. His brand-new "necking" car stood in his driveway, unused. A ladybug crawled across the window screen and he followed its progress until his rosebud came into focus. The bud was nothing to compare to the fiesta of color next door, or scented geraniums brushed by the June wind, but it was respectable and it matched his Chevy, waxed and chrome shining in his driveway.

A man had to have more to caress than the big steering wheel of a car he'd always wanted, Alek decided with a sigh.

The *Sentinel* of Amen Flats required little tending, taking shape in Brad Klein's hands. Alek leaned back in his chair. The article could wait. The newspaper boys were hitting their marks without destroying more than three windows and a newly potted vase. Alek's gaze drifted back to the rosebud.

The bud was madder red, the fiery shade that reminded him of Elspeth. Heat lay in Elspeth's work; he'd seen it in "Untitled." He saw it in the new work she'd begun. The vibrant colors softened, swirled, enclosed and burst, her style changing.

School had ended in the last week of May. Amen Flats settled into its Saturday-afternoon routine of lawn mowers buzzing, children yelling and riding bikes and people visiting on sidewalks. Riders hitched their horses to anything that didn't move, and the scent of home cooking lay on the town like perfume. The aroma of baking didn't come from Elspeth's kitchen; she was weaving as if it could carry her away from Alek.

"Too bad, kid. Like it or not, I'm here to stay." Alek traced the Rocky Mountains, rugged peaks attacking the sky. He sucked in the fresh, pine-scented air and the fragrance of herbs growing in Elspeth's garden.

He'd take what he could get from her.

His mind wasn't on the cat-chasing-dog news in Amen Flats, but Elspeth. He rubbed his temples, fighting a headache. She was probably creating one of those sensual masterpieces that dried his mouth just looking at them. He'd played a stupid game with the contract. Now he knew that he'd sink to any depth to be with her, and the thought nicked his pride. Mark's raging sit-down discussion about how to treat women didn't help.

Elspeth's van whizzed into her driveway; a second later, her back door slammed.

Duncan's pickup skidded into Alek's driveway. Duncan pushed out of the cab like a bull out of a rodeo stall. Alek could use a good brawl, and the dark expression on Duncan's face said he'd like to oblige.

"Well. My, my. Things are looking up." Alek moved through the storage crates in his living room, the remodeling of his kitchen, and opened the old back door with enough force to tear one hinge away, then stepped into his back yard. Duncan was big enough and hard enough to take Alek's frustration. Mark had offered to bash Alek for trapping Elspeth in the contract. Mark with his fancy silver shorts and boxing gloves wasn't Duncan, used to good old-fashioned tavern brawls.

Alek eyed Birk, who had just pulled his pickup to a stop on the street. Two of the Tallchiefs had come to visit; all he needed was a third brother.

When Duncan found Alek, he ripped away his leather gloves. Something that looked suspiciously like dried oatmeal clotted on Duncan's black hair. There wasn't an ounce of fat on the rancher, Alek noted with satisfaction. He'd hate to take advantage of an out-of-shape, outraged brother. Alek also noted that Duncan's mood didn't leave much room for gentleness, and he appreciated that, too.

"This won't take long," Duncan stated. "I don't like you shoving Elspeth into corners. Something is wrong, Petrovna, and it started when you came to Amen Flats."

Alek leaned against the small shed. Things were looking up. He glanced at Calum, who had just strolled into the backyard. He nodded at his brother-in-law and met a scowl. Alek was up for taking all three brothers at once. "Elspeth wouldn't tell you, would she?"

Duncan glared at him. "You're not sleeping with her."

"I'm not?" Alek drawled the insinuation. *One damn night. I should have been holding her in my arms every night for years and doing more than sleeping…with maybe a sleepy child or two between us at times.*

Now wasn't the time to think of children with Elspeth; he went woozy and mellow and disgusted with himself. When Alek bared his teeth in a leer, Duncan's fist shot out, clipping Alek's jaw. He rubbed it. "That was a good one, Duncan. Don't count on a second."

Things had been too sweet, too boring, Alek decided instantly and grinned. Amen Flats wasn't boring at all, not with the Tallchiefs on the prowl.

"She's special. You'll get more if you don't leave her alone."

"She *is* special and she can make her own choices." His punch connected solidly with Duncan's jaw. Alek rubbed his fist as Duncan staggered back a few steps. "Don't just stand there, Birk and Calum. Do your damnedest," he invited, and licked the blood from his lip.

Calum leaned back against a wall and crossed his arms over his chest. "I've got a vested interest in seeing that neither one of you get hurt too badly. You might know, Alek, that this is all about Elspeth dumping Megan's oatmeal over Duncan's head. He wanted to know your intentions."

Birk swept out a gracious hand. "Eldest first, Duncan the defender. Save some for me."

Duncan glared at Birk. "I changed Elspeth's diapers more than you. And by the way, if you don't start making moves soon, you'll be too old to make a cousin for Megan."

"Worry about yourself, old man. I'm working on it."

Duncan rubbed his jaw. "That was a good one, Petrovna. You're solid, but let's see just how tough you are—" Then Duncan's weight sent Alek to the ground, and matched for size, the two men rolled, battering away at each other.

Ah, the glory of it, Alek thought, a friendly romp in the sun—just the thing to ease his taut nerves. Duncan's fist slammed into his side and knocked the wind from him. Alek paid him back, and the two rolled across the newly plowed patch of earth where he'd planned his garden. Amid the grunts and the savage sounds of bone meeting flesh, Alek gasped under a wall of icy water.

Duncan grunted and flopped to one side, and the two big men lay there, side by side in a cold pool of muddy water. Birk and Calum roared with laughter, and Elspeth walked with dignity to the water faucet and turned off the hose. Alek enjoyed a good view of her swaying hips before Duncan hauled him to his feet. She walked back to Duncan and Alek, who had looped their arms around each other companionably and awaited their comeuppance. They looked at each other and tried friendly, innocent grins. Things were definitely looking up, Alek decided.

"She's mad," Duncan noted as the flat of Elspeth's hand hit him in the chest and sent him a step backward.

"Brawling." Elspeth's single condemning word lashed out at them. She'd convicted and sentenced the offending males.

"Just letting off a bit of steam, Elspeth-mine. I'm glad you came. Why don't you just go inside my house and make some brownies or something, will you?" Alek watched, fascinated at the lift of her chin, the blaze of her eyes burning him. She moved suddenly, her sleek hair fanning out, gleaming blue black in the sunlight, and his heart flip-flopped. He took in her taut breasts beneath the clinging red sweater with long sleeves and the new jeans that clung to curves he wanted to caress. Neatly packaged, Elspeth's supple muscles attracted him more than would a lusher combination. Everything about Elspeth was feminine, soft and yet tempered with strength that said she would hold what she wanted.

Yep. That's my woman, all right, Alek purred mentally. He just hoped she wanted him.

Her eyes narrowed. "I'm done with patching bloodied lips and swollen eyes, Alek Petrovna. I've lived with these three, watched their stupid caveman games. You're not adding to the trouble."

Alek was floating, high on the sight of Elspeth aroused to a fine, dangerous temper. He stroked a sleek strand back from her hot cheek, and her head went back. She flashed him a look that shot straight into his gut, twisted it and sank lower to heat and harden and ache. Alek tucked that look to his heart; she was glorious, a proud, hot woman that he wanted to toss over his shoulder and run—Alek glanced at the scowling Tallchief males and decided to wait.

The three brothers looked sheepish beneath her quick, raking stare. Clearly Elspeth could pull rank and intimidate with the best. This was the real Elspeth, Alek mused, elegant even as the shutters went up and darkened steel gray eyes changed to fire.

"Be gentle, Elspeth-mine. I've got a few bruises already. Will you kiss them and make them better?"

Air hissed between Elspeth's teeth, the tone a warning.

Good. This was what he wanted, honesty between them. She was mad and letting it show; in another minute, she'd broil him. Intoxicated with the heat rising in Elspeth, he'd take a few more bruises from her and be glad of it. Alek grinned and tugged her hair, wrapping a strand around his fingers to enjoy and to torment her. With her, he felt like a teenage boy showing off.

She studied him from muddy hair to muddy boots and back up again as if deciding which piece of him she'd like to sample first.

He hoped it was his lips and pursed them appropriately for her kissing.

Her eyes went black, boiling with temper.

Calum straightened and stopped grinning. "Take it easy on him, will you, Elspeth? He'll be an uncle to my baby."

Without looking at her brothers, Elspeth tossed over her shoulder, "He asked for this. Go bother someone else."

Duncan shifted restlessly, a muddied, rough cowboy towering over her, with a guilty little-boy expression.

"What a woman. Right now, I'd say she could take all four of us and leave us in the mud," Alek drawled, his breath catching as her eyes flashed at him. He winked at Duncan with the eye that was not swelling. "She loves me."

Elspeth muttered darkly to herself, a delight to Alek.

"Uh-uh. If she did, she'd take you down herself. You'd be wearing kilts—like the rest of us with a cold wind blowing up your backside." Duncan grinned at his sister, who had slashed a look at him steely enough to freeze spring. He stepped away from Alek. "Ah…you're on your own, Alek."

"Juveniles," she muttered quite clearly.

"Just boys having a good time. You'd better start sewing." Alek grinned and slowly placed the muddy tip of his finger just on the end of her nose. He almost laughed as she went cross-eyed and quickly recovered, glaring at him.

The sheriff's patrol car pulled up, complete with his latest opera and dogs howling. His bullhorn rattled the windows of every house on the block. "I thought you Tallchief boys gave up brawling since two of you got married. Now, Birk I'd expect it from, especially since Lacey— Never mind."

"They've been missing it, and I'm innocent," Birk called back to him. He waved to the line of trucks stopped on the street. In town for Saturday shopping, people enjoyed a show from the Tallchiefs. Birk watched Sissy Mayors strolling by in her short shorts, and tossed a tidbit to the sheriff. "Petrovna has a thing for Elspeth. What did Lacey do?"

He glanced at his brothers. "I do not trust that little witch past anything. Since she bought that old bordello, she's been twice as bad."

Elspeth groaned, closed her eyes and shook her head. Her cheeks flushed slowly, and she turned a glare on Birk that widened his eyes. "Chelsey is too sweet for you, Birk the rogue. You'd mow her down too easily. Now take Lacey—"

"The hell I will. Elspeth, you try to match me with Lacey, and I'll—"

The sheriff's loudspeaker blared, inciting a new round of howls from dogs. "Oh, hell, Birk. Everybody in town knows that Petrovna is sweet on Elspeth. He's passed up some choice offerings, all heated up and engines running. How's Petrovna doing? Don't hurt him too bad. He's doing a real nice article on western law and Caruso for the paper. He just interviewed me.''

''He can hold his own,'' Calum yelled. ''It's good to know the uncle of my baby isn't a pansy.''

''Not a one of you will ever taste, smell or come close to another loaf of my bread,'' Elspeth stated too quietly.

She took one step toward Alek. There wasn't anything sweet or soft about her, but enough passion to ignite them both. She took another step and struggled for control; the shutters began to come down as she pressed her lips together. He couldn't allow her to retreat. He dipped his head to kiss her and found what he wanted, the heat simmering inside and waiting for him. Unable to stop himself, Alek wrapped his arms around her, lifted her against him and gave himself to her care.

He placed his hopes and dreams on his lips, asking her to taste them. He promised her his heart and asked for hers. He sank into the taste of what she had held apart, of the precious core of her—to the softness and the heat.

Elspeth's arms went around his neck, and she took. She tasted like wine and hunger and temptation all in one. There in the spring sunshine, she kissed him until he forgot the limits, the sweetness he wanted to show her, and sank into the heat of what she offered. When the kiss was done, Elspeth looked down at him, her hair spilling around their faces. The world spun and tilted and stopped in a halo of glittering sunshine as her thumbs caressed the corners of his lips, her eyes dark and mysterious. She was all woman, and his heart, the other part of him—

She'd been like this that night in Scotland, and he prayed there would be more times when she'd look at him as if nothing else mattered.

After a time, Duncan cleared his throat. ''Aye,'' he murmured. ''That's what I thought. But I wanted to make certain.''

Elspeth pulled her gaze away from Alek's and turned to Duncan, her face still flushed and her lips swollen. The drowsy look in her eyes did not match the taut press of her body within Alek's arms. Her arms, locked around his neck, loosened; her fingers trembled as she placed them lightly on his shoulder. He held her there, her feet off the ground, and admired her dazed expression, as though she didn't know what had snared her but had enjoyed the taste. He intended to give her more than a taste.

"Aye," Birk and Calum agreed, borrowing the term from their great-great-grandmother.

Duncan reached out a friendly fist to punch Alek's shoulder. "Come out and help us lay fence. We're needing an extra hand. There's a beer in it for you, and Birk has a sweat lodge near the creek. After a nice icy swim in the lake, Sybil won't know—" Duncan glanced down at his muddy, torn clothing and muttered a curse.

Elspeth had shocked herself; the proof crawled up her throat in a beautiful pink, coloring her cheeks. Entranced by the wordless movement of her mouth as she looked at the crowd that had gathered on the street, Alek grinned. "Shocking, Elspeth. Just shocking. Here you are making out with me in broad daylight."

Mrs. Schmidt, who had been Elspeth's first-grade teacher, called, "Elspeth Tallchief, are you all right?"

Elspeth's lips moved wordlessly, and her hands flopped helplessly on his shoulder. Because he was in a generous mood and floating on Elspeth's kisses, Alek called, "She's just fine, Mrs. Schmidt."

"You be nice to her, Mr. Petrovna. She's always been a nice girl."

"Let...me...down." Elspeth braced herself and pushed away from him.

Alek lowered Elspeth to her feet. He'd prefer taking her into his bed.... The struggle for composure cost her; Elspeth straightened her sweater, smoothed her hair and attempted a cool, detached smile. She failed when she glanced down at her sweater to find two muddy patches where her breasts had pressed to Alek's. He admired the sight, peaks pressing against the material and then the wild flush sweeping up her checks.

He didn't reach out a hand when she sagged, but let her straighten by her own will. She'd have pushed him back in the mud and then he'd have to wrestle her down into it for a kiss. "Aye," he said, borrowing from the Tallchiefs. "You'll do."

Sun glinted off her lashes as they narrowed, and Elspeth turned to elegantly pick her way across the muddy garden back to her house.

Alek folded his empty arms, ached for her, and tilted his head to admire the fine sway of her hips.

Birk hooted. "Petrovna is in love."

"Petrovnas can be a fast game," stated Calum from experience. "Elspeth is picky."

Duncan looped an arm around both brothers. "She can handle it."

Calum elbowed him. "You'll be sleeping on the couch tonight, older brother."

Duncan winked at him. "Making up is the best part. It's worth a night on the couch."

"She hasn't decided she wants me yet." Alek spoke to himself. He stroked his muddy beard. "I'll have to make myself even more enticing. It doesn't usually take this long to have them swooning over me. Five seconds, tops."

Birk guffawed at that, and Calum grinned.

"I'd say she's thinking about having your scalp right now. You could work some of that off by helping us with the fence." Duncan placed his western hat on his head and braced his legs apart, grinning at Alek.

Alek suspected Duncan worried about Elspeth...that

Alek would cross those few yards to her home. "Tucking me under your wing, Duncan the defender?"

"You could call it that. A few years ago, you wouldn't be standing on two feet now. She can rip the earth right out from under you before you know it. I've got firsthand experience, and I'm wearing Megan's oatmeal. From the look of Elspeth, one wrong step and you could be wearing some bruises."

"It would be worth it."

"I know the feeling," Duncan returned with a grin that brought a quick, pained frown and a finger to his swollen lip. "At least we know you can handle yourself. Come on, girls, let's fix that fence."

Seven

Elspeth shook. She managed to walk to her kitchen table, poured the alfalfa-mint tea she'd just brewed into a cup. She stared at leafy bits at the bottom of the china and spread her trembling hands flat on the table.

She'd taken one look at Duncan and at Alek; a lifetime of experience with bristling males had told her they wouldn't be civilized. She'd swept out of her home, leaped across a bed of sweetwood herb and had feared that she wouldn't reach them in time.

Alek had stood there with one eye swelling and had blown her a kiss. "Swaggering, arrogant..."

Her home seemed to quiver around her. Thyme and sage, bundled and hanging by her kitchen window, seemed to twirl in her flooding emotions.

Her studio was the same; her loom caught the sunlight from the windows. Skeins of dyed wool hung from pegs and the spinning wheel. Everything was in its place, and yet her life had changed.

She had cared what happened to Alek.

Her kitchen was neat as usual. Her new weaving projects consumed her, as though she were pitting what snarled and heated and brewed inside her against the wool. She reached for a skein colored with madder root—a fiery red—and gripped it in her fist.

Violent. That's how she felt about Alek.

Elspeth sifted through her emotions concerning Alek. No. Violence wasn't enough. Primitive suited her emotions better.

A reluctant glance out the window caused her to shake her head. Alek stood beneath the hose, his ruined shirt hanging on a branch. He stretched his arms high over his head, and Elspeth's mouth went dry, her body instantly quickening.

She wanted to feed upon him. To take and to give, to bear him to the mud and—

She touched her swollen lips, still hungry for the taste of his promise, his dreams...if only he hadn't offered her his dreams....

''Aaagh!'' Elspeth lifted her teacup and forced herself to sip slowly. She knew men were boys, and boys liked boasting and brawling. She shouldn't have jumped to defend Alek against Duncan, who used to fight to ease his demons before marrying Sybil. But the sight of Duncan moving purposefully toward Alek sent her flying to rescue Alek.

She ran a fingertip across the rose design of her teacup; Alek made her feel like a rose—delicate, soft, beautiful. She glanced at the shadowed mirror and found her flushed face in it, her lips swollen and ripe.

She inhaled the scents of her herbs to calm her nerves and found Alek's, lingering on her skin. ''Beast. Arrogant—''

Beast. The word echoed in her mind, reminding her of Una's description of Tallchief:

A swaggering, arrogant warrior of a man, accustomed
to women doing his bidding and fetching for him. The
worst of it was he knew how gloriously beautiful he
was, even with his battle scars. I'll bring the beastly,
mule-headed giant of a man to his knees...I swear it.
He mocks my size and feminine weakness, but there
are other ways, softer ways. I have nothing so fine to
capture this Tallchief man-beast but the shawl.

The shawl. Suddenly she had to know the legend. Elspeth
shook the pieces of paper detailing the legend to the table
and began to arrange them. Under a magnifying glass,
Una's handwriting defied reading. After a few frustrating
moments, Elspeth called Sybil and asked her advice about
duplicating the page. Minutes later, Elspeth hurried down
the street to the printers and asked them to enlarge and
darken the pieces.

When she arrived home, Sybil was sitting on her doorstep with her camera and magnifying lens. "We can shoot
the pieces outside in a few minutes with natural light and
have pictures in a snap. Meanwhile, I am *not* a happily
married woman," she stated. "Your brother is a huge,
brawling, full-of-himself boy. He walked right into the
house, kissed me with his swollen lip—right while my client Marcella Portway was on the phone, pestering me about
her blasted royal Spanish gene. He actually eased me down
to the floor and held me there, all muddy and bloody
and...Mrs. Portway raged on about her royal blood while
he kissed me silly."

Sybil blushed. "There Duncan was, huge, ragged and
bloodied and grinning like a baboon. 'Don't blame me. I
did it for Elspeth,' he said. The strange thing of it is that
he seems to like Alek.

"I could use a good cup of tea. I left them all with
Megan, who is teething and not happy about anything. That

should keep them from fighting. Duncan is cooking tonight, planning to wine and dine and candlelight me out of sleeping on the couch…and just maybe he will.''

Elspeth and Sybil went inside and Elspeth prepared and served tea. ''I remember when you entered a brawl at Maddy's to defend Duncan.''

Sybil sniffed elegantly. ''I had to. There he was having a fine time when I needed him to rescue Emily. He was the only one who could track her kidnapper and find her.''

''You'd do it again.''

''Of course. Alek shouldn't pick on Duncan just when he's properly tamed. Now show me what you have. I wondered when you'd get around to this.''

Elspeth pivoted to Sybil with a thought that plagued her. ''Do you think a man can be celibate for more than five years?''

''I do. But he'd be a hungry one—'' Sybil's eyes widened. ''Five years. That's about when you went to Scotland, isn't it? Before you changed? Don't tell me that Alek has wanted you for five years— Don't tell me that you knew him in Scotland and you and he and— So that's what's been going on between you. Something happened before…. Oh, yes! Tell me.''

''No. Duncan will get it out of you…there'll be more stupid, overgrown boys' brawls, and then Talia…I do not want to think about what she would do. She shouldn't be upset now.'' Elspeth decided not to ask Sybil more questions; she was too sharp, her mind trained to connect hidden implications.

''Mmm. I see what you mean. But Duncan can't get *everything* out of me.''

Elspeth shot her a disbelieving look. ''He's getting good.''

''I can still hold my own. By the way, I know all about Alek's little contract. You know it equated to the Tall-

chiefs' capturing their brides, don't you? That old macho
thing about beating their chests and dragging off their
women.''

"He's apologized for the contract. He was rather sweet
about it. Alek had his reasons.'' Alek wanted to make her
pay, to run her down, push her around and swagger off
after his revenge. He ached for a child, a need coursing
heavily through him to produce an offspring, to have his
line continue in the world after he was gone.

Elspeth swallowed. It must have cost Alek to back up,
to apologize, but he had. She shook her head, clearing it.
She had to find a way to exorcise him from her life, to peel
him away from her heart.

Sybil sighed with dreamy longing. "I get all fuzzy when
Duncan apologizes. I don't know whether to take a broom
after him for his crime...or to kiss him senseless. The light
should be fine now. Let's go take those pictures. From
there, we'll use computer tracing. The pictures are just double insurance.''

Alek sat on his porch and drew the shawl across his bare
chest. He tipped the chair back against the new siding and
settled into his thoughts. A brawl, bruises and hard physical
labor couldn't tear away his need to see Elspeth. Neither
the sweat-lodge steam nor the freezing dip in Tallchief
Lake could cool what she had ignited with one sultry look.
He knew better than to push Elspeth now. He'd done
enough with that damn, stupid contract.

He'd had his reasons, Alek argued against himself.

At ten o'clock, Amen Flats was settling in, lovers getting
steamy and older folks holding hands.

The old tomcat who had claimed Alek yawned and
curled into a corner. Sporting a chewed ear-and-a-half, the
gray-striped tom yawned and yellow eyes looked at Alek
as if to say, *Well, this is what to expect, chum...one ear*

chewed to hell and lonesome on a Saturday night. You get used to it.

"Speak for yourself." The shawl, light and soft, whispered across his skin, the fringes tangling in the hair on his chest. He rubbed them against him and wished for Elspeth's hair. Alek propped his western boots on the railing, settling in for a long, lonely night. An owl soared across the sky, and Elspeth's front door creaked. She was probably coddling the hungry strays at her back door. Alek grimaced…maybe he was a stray needing a home and he certainly was hungry. He tried to ignore the lurch of his heart and damned his weakness for her.

Marcy Longfeather cruised by in her convertible and blew him a kiss. Gossip said that Marcy could age a man in hours. "Call me anytime. I'm in the book," she called to him.

Marcy held as much appeal to him as cold oatmeal. He'd never liked a woman who slid her hand into his back pocket when he wasn't prepared. A hefty supply of multicolored, super-duper condoms, waved beneath his nose at the local coffee shop, brought out her cold-oatmeal appeal. He preferred— He preferred Elspeth.

Alek glanced at Elspeth's darkened studio. She was probably weaving those mind-blowing hangings by candlelight, the graceful movements of her arms telling a story that would ignite any red-blooded male. Alek groaned because now he knew that Elspeth sometimes wore only a T-shirt to weave. Visions of the taut peaks of her breasts, the gentle, soft weight swaying to her movements, had haunted his sleepless nights.

He inhaled the cool night air and watched newly hatched moths cluster around a street lamp. Caruso's music drifted from a distance away, and dogs howled. Alek smoothed the shawl across his chest. It was going to be a long night.

The tom sniffed the air; he leapt to his feet like a young

cat, arched and stretched. With his tail high, he pranced lightly down the steps, headed for Elspeth's house and welcoming female company.

"Deserter." Alek reached for a can of beer and stroked the shawl. His fingers curled to the can, then released it as Elspeth moved quietly up his porch. The single black braid swung down her neat white blouse and dangled at her waist. He admired the loose fit of her gray slacks and wanted to strip her then, taking her on the front porch.

"Here." He tossed the shawl at her. "It's yours. Forget about the contract. You're free."

"You don't like my work?"

Alek spread his scarred fingers and studied them. He didn't want to hurt her on any level. "You're talented. There's not another artist like you. But you're not under any obligation to produce for the gallery. I'll see to it. It was a stupid move on my part."

"How kind of you. And you're right. It was stupid. Mark agrees."

Was that a smile lurking in her tone? Because he felt too exposed, too raw and aching, and wanted his pride, Alek plopped the chair to its feet and stood. He pushed his hands in his back pockets to keep from grabbing her. "Well?"

Elspeth's slender fingers flowed over the shawl, and his body jerked into a tight knot. She touched it reverently. "It's beautiful. No wonder Una loved it so."

"It's yours. You should have it."

"Thank you."

She placed it around her, and Alek went weak. He brushed the tangled, fiery fringes with his fingertips and found them shaking. The shawl flowed, clinging to her slender body, fringes catching the soft night breeze. She looked exotic and yet untouched. But Alek had touched her, had taken away something that she would never get back. "You look good in it."

Unused to compliments, Elspeth bowed her head. When her head came up, her expression sent him reeling. She frightened him, and Alek took a step backward. "I don't want you to feel...obligated on any level."

Her lips curved, enchanting him, and she slanted him an amused look. "For a shawl? Come on, Alek. I could have taken it any time I wanted."

"From me? I doubt it."

"You know, there's just something about taking you down that appeals." She took another step toward him, and the look in her eyes caused him to blink. He hadn't expected the sultry look, as if she had chosen to feast upon him and was considering where to start.

He took a step back and found his hips against the railing.

She came close to him, placed her hands on his shoulders and watched him. She was taking him apart, examining him with those smoky gray eyes and trying to see beyond bones and scarred skin. He wasn't a mystery, yet Elspeth kept hunting what ran beneath the surface. The shawl's fringes caught on his skin, lifting with his sudden breath.

"What are you doing, Elspeth?" he asked unevenly, uncertain of himself and of her. In another minute, he'd be lifting her in his arms and devouring her. He had to get her out of here, to a place where she'd be safe.... He sucked in his breath as she leaned closer.

"I'm waiting for you to kiss me, Alek. To see if you're all show for my brothers and the town, or if you really mean it." Her fingers touched his face, smoothing the stubble there.

She touched the earring, and Alek's knees began to weaken. "Games, Elspeth?"

Her mouth curved again, secret and feminine. "Are you going to show me your house? You've been in mine often enough. You've been hammering and sawing until all hours of the night. Something must have changed." Elspeth moved to the door and waited, the slender line of her nape as vulnerable as Alek felt. He opened the door, and she moved inside to the darkness.

Inside his house, Alek's fingers found the shawl, gripped it and tugged her back against him. His arms instantly encircled her, his face pressed close to hers, caught by the fresh and exotic scent of her skin and hair. "You like playing with fire, do you?"

Against his cheek, her smooth one moved in a smile. "Maybe you're the one in danger."

She eased away, and Alek let her go. He pushed his hands in his back pockets to keep from grabbing her.

The shawl whispered secrets as Elspeth studied the house, and Alek sensed that another woman had worn it and had called up a man, beckoning to him. In the dim light, the soft material gleamed and dipped into her waist, traced the slender curve of her hip. Alek washed a fast, hard hand over his unshaved, taut jaw; in another minute, he'd be drooling.

"You've opened up the rooms…there's more space. I'm glad you didn't use contemporary furniture." Her fingers smoothed an old piano, battered from years of use at Maddy's Hot Spot. Alek had liked the thought of happy people, clustered around the old piano and singing to the music. She glanced at the mantel, filled with framed pictures, and picked her way around unpacked cartons. Her fingers trailed over the shells he'd collected and set to catch the dawn's light. She wandered into his office, touched the paper clutter and his computer. She studied his desk—two file cabinets set a distance apart and topped by an old door. "This is the heart of you, isn't it?"

The heart of him thudded heavily, needing her warm and soft against him. Because he was afraid he'd frighten her if he pushed too hard, he asked, "What about going down to Maddy's?"

Elspeth lifted an elegant eyebrow. "And face what you did to me earlier today?"

"No, I suppose not."

"Thank you for that much." She picked up a rock painted with a child's hand, then moved to the swatch she'd woven in Scotland. She turned and studied the room, littered with bits of his traveling years, bits of people he wanted to remember. When she touched a framed picture of a little Eurasian boy and girl, Alek said, "Marta and Ben. I help them by one of those foster-adoption plans."

"And these?" Elspeth touched other pictures of children and Alek nodded.

There was a picture of an Asian girl, blushing as a bride with her husband standing proudly near her. "Those two were young teenagers, living in cardboard boxes. They entered a medical training program and now they're married."

"With your help?"

When he nodded, she lifted a picture of Doug Morrow, an arm draped around Alek. "The frames are new."

"This is the first time I've stayed in one place long enough for frames. The pictures were getting battered. That's Doug Morrow, a friend. When I was in Scotland this last time—I had some notion of finding a woman I'd met years ago."

Alek shook his head. "It seems so long ago, and it was just months. I thought I'd go there and...find you...see if you were happy. It didn't turn out that way. I was on my way here when Doug got sick, calling me to complete his assignment. I said I would. The assignment delayed my trip here."

She glanced at her work, a blend of earth and sky and mountains wrapped in mist and sharpened by a spear thrust diagonally through it. Elspeth roamed to the pictures of his immigrant great-great-grandparents. "All immigrants of that time have a look, don't they? Dressed in black, half afraid and half joyous that a new life was theirs for the taking. I can picture Una lugging her precious dowry, some of it in the shawl on her back."

"Mine came from Russia. They were probably thinking about how soon they could get to Texas heat."

Heat. Despite the cool night, Alek's palms were damp, and his hands shook. If he touched her— He jammed them deeper in his pocket.

Alek followed her to the kitchen, remodeled and gleaming, too clean and uncluttered. Her fingertip traced an open manual to the pasta machine. "Very nice…a new bread machine and a pasta machine and an electric wok."

He didn't want her to know that he ached for her fresh bread and that he'd tried to make his own, that he didn't know how to make a home. "I'm not exactly a homemaker, but I'll learn."

If she found that old stew pot under the cabinet, she'd really think him off center. He loved the idea of that old pot bubbling with enough food to feed an army of kids.

She glanced down at the assortment of kitchen gadgets on the counter. "You're certainly prepared. No more dishes from gorgeous blondes?"

"I'm waiting for a herd of them to turn up now."

She opened the cupboards to see the old dishes he'd bought at an auction. Talia had teased him ruthlessly; she had relented when she saw how he treasured them despite the chips. "These are lovely. They're from the Winscotts, one of the first pioneers in the valley. They had eleven children and loved each other deeply. The table was theirs, too. Mr. Winscott had to make more leaves and supports as their family grew. He wanted the entire family to sit down at once, every meal, and so they did."

Alek had felt that, the love in the chipped dishes and the handcrafted table, scarred by years of use. He sensed the children eating greedily and then bouncing up from the table, filled and ready to play. It pleased him to eat from the same dishes, to imagine that his children would be settling on his knee to be rocked and cuddled and burped. Lost in that dream, he could forget that the meals he ate were prepackaged and frozen.

"The rocking chair in your living room is the Mulveneys'. Mrs. Mulveney was six feet five inches and of ample proportions. She loved rocking children, sometimes three at a time. All of their children were rocked there, and most of the Tallchief clan, too," Elspeth added, jarring him. He sensed that she had dipped into his thoughts.

The seed packets on the table embarrassed him. He wanted to grow herbs, to wallow in the scent of them in his house as he had in hers. Comfortable in the shadows, Elspeth touched and smoothed and explored—he wanted her touching him in the same way. Elspeth probed into the desperate, lonely heart of him and exposed his raw edges. "Why are you here?"

She touched his cheek, then stood on tiptoe to nibble on his lip. "Questions. Ever the journalist, aren't you? You've been over here, hoarding a collection of things that no one wants anymore. Why?"

"My lifestyle hasn't exactly allowed me to have a houseful of furniture or dishes." That was true enough, but he wanted bits of happiness of other homes. Because he wanted a family and a home and was too proud to admit his need.

Alek gripped her upper arms, then her wrists as her arms slid up to his neck, around it, drawing him close to her curved body. Elspeth, on the prowl, could frighten any man who thought he could control what lay within him. "We'd better go somewhere else."

He'd hurt her now if they made love. He wanted to make this time tender and last until the dawn came and then start all over again. Elspeth moved against him, and Alek hardened instantly. The sound of his voice came raw and uneven as the shawl whispered between them. "Elspeth..."

For an answer, she held him tighter. Alek eased aside the folds of the shawl to lock his hands on her waist. "Elspeth!"

She held him tightly, refusing to be eased away. Her thumb ran along the scar on his shoulder. Then she looked up at him and grinned for the first time. "I've shocked you, Petrovna. Admit it."

He blinked, uncertain if Elspeth had really sent him an impish, five-thousand-watt grin that sent him reeling. Tonight he wasn't certain of anything. The shawl's fringes clung to his fingers as he forced her away gently. "You're inexperienced, Elspeth-mine. You have no idea of what you're doing."

"Not up to it?" Her tease was followed by a quick smile that enchanted him. Her hand lay flat on his chest, toyed with the hair there and slowly, slowly moved downward.

"You wouldn't—" When her fingers skimmed down his stomach, he jerked back against the counter and gripped it with both hands. "Elspeth!"

"Yes, Elspeth. Remember my name, Alek. It's Elspeth." Elspeth slowly unbraided her hair, combing it around her. The shawl slid from her shoulders to rest over the back of a chair.

Alek latched his fist in the soft material, warm from her body, and found that he couldn't think as Elspeth began to undress. She unbuttoned her blouse and tossed it to a chair. Alek's mouth went dry when she reached behind her to unfasten her bra.

She tossed the white cotton scrap at him, and he crushed it in his fist. She kicked aside her flats and, veiled by the heavy swath of hair, she stripped away her slacks. Her practical white panties slid down her slender thighs, revealing the dark triangle between her thighs. Alek shuddered, every muscle in his body tightening into a knot.

The moonlight coming through the window slid to caress her body, to outline it in silver as she took the shawl from him. Then she draped it around her and began slowly ascending the stairs. Alek, taut and shaking, traced the flowing movements of her body beneath the shawl, the fringes swaying along the slender, strong backs of her thighs, the cloth caressing the sway of her bottom.

Alek realized that he was alternately cold with fear that he would hurt her and hot with need that rose with stubborn pain within his body.

Then Elspeth paused, looked down at him over her shoulder and lifted an elegant, expressive eyebrow.

Elspeth listened to the movements downstairs as Alek locked the doors. The cats howled near her house, the sound grating on her nerves…not exactly romantic music for her adventure into tasting Alek.

''Untitled'' hung on Alek's wall, mocking her. It was very sexual, a woman's translation of intimacy, colors locking together, exploding— Elspeth groaned silently. She should have known he'd buy the wall hanging, outlined in the moonlight, a monument to what she was about to do.

It was no casual thing coming to Alek, following the needs of her heart and body. She studied the room, bits of other people's lives mingling with Alek's family, his friends. The braided rag rug on the floor, well washed and familiar, probably had once belonged to Mrs. Potts, who was fond of cutting off buttons from ruined shirts and braiding them into rugs. The buttons were likely in the antique blue glass jar. The lovely old quilts neatly folded on a chair ached for a proper bed.

She'd passed a small room, cluttered with tools and lumber and a crib folded against a wall. There was a tiny rocking horse.

Alek wanted a family. While he could afford better, Alek preferred to retrieve old pieces, to lug bits of lives back to his house.

Elspeth pressed the heels of her hands to her eyes. He wanted a home, deserved one.

He'd gone to hell and back when he'd discovered there was no child. He knew more than her family knew about her—

Oh, fine. She'd gotten herself worked up, raging and pacing in her house and mourning her lost powers given to her by her seer and shaman ancestors. She'd meant to set Alek on his ear, to define the rules of his life interrupting hers, and then she'd seen into the very heart of his need to have a home and family.

Oh, fine. She should have walked away. She should have placed their night in Scotland into a drawer—wove it into her wool or buried it. Some secret part of her, uncontrolled by her will, wanted to tuck that night close to her— Elspeth forced down the panic streaking through her.

Alek had been pushing her and she didn't like it. While her mind didn't quite trust his motives, on another level she needed Alek to prove that she had emotions, that she was a woman and not a shadow. Alek definitely made her feel feminine, exciting.

Was she using him? Definitely. She needed him to complete a restlessness within her. To be cherished and held and yes, loved.

Was she wary of him? Yes. Alek wanted her to have the shawl, giving the prize to her too easily.

Elspeth had never liked easy, or trusted it. She preferred to claim the shawl herself, as a matter of pride. Was he yielding the field to her? Not likely. Alek Petrovna had definite fighting tendencies that excited her own.

Why was she here, in Alek's bed, waiting for him? The answer came back, true and strong. Locked deeply inside her was the need to hold Alek close…to have him so close that nothing could separate them…not the past, or the future he kept pushing at her…. She wanted…no, she needed to be complete once more, as a woman felt with a special man. And for whatever happened in the future, tonight Alek was very special.

She wouldn't be pushed; she would make up her own mind about Alek and what he was to her.

He'd wooed her with his love of family treasures, the simple things harvested into his home. He'd touched her with his children, obviously cherished.

Deep inside Elspeth lurked the fear of Alek leaving her again…devastating her with words. She acknowledged that fear and tended it, even as she knew that Alek moved gently through her heart. She would keep that part of her locked safely away.

Yet here she was, waiting—naked—in his tiny cot for him. Elspeth drew the shawl against her as she thought back to Una's legend, which she had reconstructed with the aid of Sybil's photography trick.

When the Marrying Moon is high, a scarred warrior will rise from the mists to claim his lady huntress. He will wrap her in the shawl and carry her to the Bridal Tepee and his heart. Their song will last longer than the stars….

Tallchief had wanted Una to add the Bridal Tepee to the legend so that the legend became a blend of their bloods. Sybil had cried and held Elspeth's hand as the legend was revealed before their eyes. Una had cried as she wrote, the

teardrops blurring the ink. A hand stronger than hers and
untutored with a pen had drawn Tallchief Mountain and a
man and a woman by the tepee.

In the end, Una had captured her captor, and the shawl
had been her weapon.

A tiny shiver skimmed along Elspeth's bare skin. The
legend didn't—couldn't—apply to Alek Petrovna and herself.

Elspeth surveyed the spartan room, littered with Alek's
battered suitcases and clothing. She recognized the huge
bureau of the Samuelsons and framed pictures of Alek and
Talia with their family. Propped against a picture of Talia
and her sister was a picture of the Tallchiefs at the wedding.
A circle had been drawn around Elspeth's face, the enlarge-
ment resting next to it.

He'd come through years and crossed continents to find
her.

Elspeth lifted her head as his footsteps rose surely to the
door of the room. He paused, then moved into the bathroom, and the shower ran. The water stopped, then silence.

Alek loomed in the doorway, framed by moonlight skimming his shoulders and down his spread legs. He hadn't
given her the concession of a towel around his hips.

She wasn't making concessions, either. "You will not
come to this bed with thoughts of your wife, Alek Petrovna.
Not with my weaving on your wall."

"I wouldn't think of it." His tone bore arrogance and a
taunt and just enough uncertainty to curl around her heart.

He moved to her, filling the room. He'd hurried, droplets
gleaming on his shoulders. A deep scar crossed his ribs,
another rode his hip and the moonlight caught the smooth
expanse of healed burns. Alek appeared battered and tough-
ened by years, his cheekbones rugged and darkened by
stubble, his jaw tense. The dim light angled off his broken

nose, LaBelle's earring gleamed in his ear and Elspeth ached to feel the soft flow of his curls against her breasts.

She gripped the shawl tightly and forced herself to continue, "That is my price, Alek Petrovna. I will not have you take me with a sense of guilt. I'll know it if you do and I will not forgive you. Pretty apologies won't work."

"Pretty...?" He tensed, the moonlight shafting over angles and taut muscles and cords that ran down his arms to his fists. His feet locked to the pool of moonlight on the old braided rug. The heavy muscles of his legs stood out in relief; his desire jutted into the silvery light, startling Elspeth. Or did her body startle her, desire streaking through her, cords igniting, clenching, heating?

A shudder ran down Alek's body. "I can promise not to hurt you...but I can't promise to forget that night completely." His voice was ragged, rimmed with naked, deep emotion.

"You won't hurt me. I ask that you try to forget."

He took a step. "They say you inherited both seer and shaman powers. What do your senses tell you about me, Elspeth?"

She already knew. "That whatever happens, you will try to please me."

"I will be careful." His promise came firm and raw.

"Do and I'll kill you."

Alek's grin was slow in coming. "Now, that's my girl."

For a moment, Elspeth was startled. She'd never been anyone's girlfriend; she hadn't allowed the possessive tone from anyone, not even her brothers. She found herself blushing as Alek came to the cot and stretched out slowly beside her, his hands behind his head. She lay there, the shawl drawn to her chin, and wondered what to do; her confidence of moments ago had vanished.

"We can lie here and admire your weaving technique, or you can simply take me...I'm yours," Alek murmured,

his body heating her side like a furnace. He lifted a challenging eyebrow at her. "Lost the mood? Have a headache?"

"You're taking up all the space." She couldn't breathe.
Alek smelled like soap and man, his heat warming the
shawl. Her breast brushed his arm, and he tensed. Alek
tugged her over him and wrapped his arms around her.
Beneath her, he was all hard power and vibrating male, hot
and rigid against her stomach. One hand stroked her bottom
leisurely while his other hand prowled dangerously close
to her breast.

He tugged at the shawl. "You wouldn't want it damaged,
would you?"

She drew the shawl from between them and let him take
it. His eyes flicked down her body; his features hardened,
a flush rising up his cheeks. There was nothing sweet about
Alek, nor in the desperate way he wanted her.

"What now?" he asked with interest after tossing the
shawl to a folding chair. "Ready to make your move?"

Elspeth settled closer, placing her flushed face in the
shelter of his throat. Alek's hand smoothed her side, lingered along her ribs, then rose to cup her breast. "You're
trembling."

He kissed her forehead, her lids. He tasted her gently,
brushing his lips across hers, tempting her. She could have
killed him for being so tender...for taking time to place
protection between them. For trembling so badly that he
ruined his first effort, cursed and had to try again.

Elspeth smoothed the taut cords of his neck, his shoulders and the hair covering his chest. As her fingertips
brushed his nipple, Alek went taut, shivering. His look at
her was fire and desperation, his body burning hers.

She lay quietly as he moved over her. "Open for me,
Elspeth," he murmured when her thighs trembled, then

closed against his intrusion. "It's all right, love. We'll do what you want, when you want."

Braced away from her, Alek ran his hand down her side, pressing his fingers into her softness, lingering on the curve of her thigh. The night breeze coursed through the window's curtains, bearing the scent of the mountains, an elemental blend of time and passion, and Elspeth gave herself to it, allowing Alek's touch to open her legs.

He held very still, then bent to place his lips upon her throat. "Your heart is leaping out of you. You can touch me."

She placed her hand on his chest, and beside her throat, Alek's mouth curved into a smile. He nipped the side of her jaw. "That wasn't exactly what I meant."

He cupped her breasts, cherishing them, lifting them to torment with gentle bites and then catching the peaks deeper, suckling her until she cried out, holding him to her.

He tensed as she moved, his body intimate against hers. She accepted the tip of him, holding her breath, and fought the slight pain of his intrusion. "Am I hurting you?" he asked.

There was pain, but she wouldn't let him leave her, not now. Elspeth pressed her legs against his hips, her face hot against his throat. "Don't leave me."

Alek groaned and, when she raised her hips slowly, taking him fully, he cried out, trembling. This was what she wanted, Alek close to her, a part of her, despite the slight pain.

His body began to move, hips thrusting down on hers, filling her. She held her breath, aware of the mechanics of sex and yet startled that he desired her.

"Elspeth!" Alek's hushed shout tore from him, his hands clamping on her thighs.

Elspeth smoothed the heavy muscles of his shoulders, rested her palm over his racing heart.

"Elspeth-mine..." Alek struggled for breath, and Elspeth shivered as her body heated, moistened and tempted.
Her nails dug slightly into his flesh as she bent to kiss the
scar running across his shoulder and the one slicing his
eyebrow. Her breasts dragged slowly, softly against his
chest, the hair sensitizing her nipples, hardening them. The
new sensation caught her, and she moved beneath him.

"Elspeth," Alek began, and stopped when she kissed the
scar on his bottom lip. He groaned and held very still. "Do
not move. Just don't move."

He trembled, cords standing out in his arms, his throat,
his body barely joined to hers. Alek's fist wrapped in her
hair, turning her face to him. He took her lips deeply, answering the savage need. He shook violently, trying to lie
still, his hands braced at her head. "Don't you dare move,
Elspeth."

His desperation was a challenge that she took, lifting her
hips to capture him.

She'd forgotten, the weight and heat of him stretching
her, and fought the cry tumbling from her lips.

Alek muttered a frustrated curse, then he found her
breasts, kissing and suckling them quickly now, his body
urgent; the sound of her hunger came, shocking her. This
was Alek, Alek soothing her, caressing her, telling her—
telling her what? She'd captured him, run him down
through the years and tethered him. Elspeth rose to find his
face, the pounding within her too loud to hear his words.
She stroked the scar on his eyebrow with her thumb and
slid her fingers through his hair, locking his to hers. She
lifted again, her body taut and pounding, but she had to see
him, to watch him move through his passion. Alek was
beautiful above her, his face all rugged angles and tense
cords. His eyes were brilliant, black and hot as he lifted his
hips slightly. He stretched her gently, filling her until she
cried out again.

His body plunged into hers, and she tossed him back. Again. Then the frantic, desperate rhythm began, Alek breathing as if his heart had run the fastest race, as if he ran to the edge, waited for her and then shot off into the heat. His cry came from the depths of his soul, as if he'd shattered there, lodged in her.

Just beyond her reach, whatever she sought taunted her. Alek drew her shaking body to him, his heart pounding beneath her cheek. He ran his hand down her back, caressing her and then covered her with a quilt that had warmed other lovers.

Elspeth snuggled close to him, mourned the moment of separation and sighed as Alek kissed her. She gathered him to her; for the moment, he was hers and the shadows were gone.

Una's shawl moved in the night, the moonlight playing over the shimmering colors, the fringes swaying gently in the breeze.

When the Marrying Moon is high, a scarred warrior will rise from the mists to claim his lady huntress. He will wrap her in the shawl and carry her to the Bridal Tepee and his heart. Their song will last longer than the stars....

For a moment, Elspeth fought tears and wished the shawl's legend was true.

Eight

Alek allowed Elspeth to slip from the cot. He fought the urge to drag her back to him—as if he had the strength to do anything but drag air into his lungs and regain his sight.

Elspeth had taken him and left the shawl as if it meant nothing to her. As if making love with him meant nothing.

He lay in the shadows, his arms behind his head, winded, filling his senses with their past lovemaking. Beyond his window, Elspeth's screen door creaked, and the night settled around him.

Alek rose to study Elspeth's dark house; there was no light. She liked moving through shadows, becoming one of them. He reached for a bottle kept on his dresser and poured a quick neat whiskey. He hadn't had a drink since December—when he'd first seen Elspeth in Talia's wedding picture—and he badly needed one now. The glass was halfway to his lips when Alek realized that Elspeth had not climaxed in his arms.

Nor had she on that night in Scotland.

She'd accepted his passion, soothed him later, but she had not fully entered the fire....

Alek sat abruptly, locked his fist to the sheets bearing Elspeth's scent and shook his head to clear it.

He began tracing their passion. He'd been intent on her pleasure that first time, then had lost himself and gone over the edge. He plopped the whiskey glass down on a stack of magazines and licked a drop from his wrist.

Alek forced himself to breathe. Melissa had been more like his sister than his wife. Their lovemaking had been tender and sweet, and Melissa had been shy their entire marriage. They'd been cautious, wanting children, but when wasn't he blazing a career in foreign wars? He'd known the moment he'd poured himself into Elspeth that he'd given her the deepest part of his being....

Elspeth wasn't sweet; lava ran beneath the surface. Yet she had waltzed through their lovemaking twice, never experiencing the full measure. Her heat ran just below the surface untested, and his body knew it.

Alek lay back carefully on the cot, bracing the glass on his naked stomach.

Elspeth had had him and left him. She'd gone back to her safe shadows and left him with the shawl, a reminder that she kept her secrets, and the Tallchief legend, to herself.

Preoccupied with the wrongs done to him and feeling fragile, Alek almost admired the curses boiling out of him. He threw the glass against the wall, glared at the shards mocking him in the moonlight and lurched to his feet.

He jerked on shorts and stepped out of his window and onto the huge oak-tree limb. Two more limbs, and he was within jumping distance of Elspeth's roof.

He stepped into her bedroom window and listened to the sound of her shower. Alek waited, prowling in the room scented of her and the lily of the valley blossoms in the old vase. Moonlight filtered through the window, running across the bed's old, hand-stitched quilt. He scooped her blouse and slacks from the bed, caught the scent of their lovemaking and crushed the material in his fists, flinging it to a chair. Because their precious daughter was about to be exposed—her cool veneer ripped away—Alek draped a lacy handkerchief over the framed portrait of the Tallchiefs.

Elspeth entered the room in a scent of soap and lavender. The sight of her naked body—breasts tilted high, the dip of her stomach, the curve of her hips—caused him to suck in his breath. Alek's hand latched to her wrist. "I don't like being used."

She turned on him, damp hair flying around her bare shoulders. "What?"

Alek stood back and kicked the door shut with his heel; he crossed his arms, fearing that he'd shake her. There was no kindness roaming in him now for Elspeth Tallchief. "What just happened in my bed?"

"I don't know what you mean."

"Anytime you want to play games, honey, just let me know the rules first, okay? You wanted to exorcise that night. Get rid of me, then come home, tidy up and forget the whole thing happened, right? Well, it did. It happened with me."

She frowned and backed up a step when he advanced. "Of course it did."

Alek picked her up and tossed her to the bed, following her down. He held her damp hair in one fist and braced above her. "It goes like this, Elspeth. When you come calling for me, plan to share breakfast with me."

She moved beneath him, the scent of her soap sending him precariously near taking her right then. He studied her. She wasn't afraid; rather, a keen anger had begun to brew. Good. He could deal with her anger, not her fear of him.

She shivered, control skimming along her voice. "Alek, I didn't know there were rules to this."

"You thought you'd just wander over, have a bit of sex with old hungry Alek, lay there, let him take—" Alek bit off a curse, then continued. "You come home, take a nice shower and drop off to sleep, right? Or was it more like, 'I think I'll give Alek whatever he wants and then he'll go away.' I've never been a nice guy when I want something, Elspeth darling. Don't count on my sympathy."

He was just getting wound up. He wanted Elspeth to understand everything boiling out of him. "You play hardball, Elspeth-mine, and I don't like it."

He'd never talked to a woman like this, pushed her, held her forcibly still beneath him. Of course he loved Elspeth Tallchief—that was a given—but a man had his pride. He'd just realized that he'd never given Melissa the deepest part of him, poured into her everything that he was, that he would be.

A fresh tide of anger and frustration ripped through him. Elspeth's face registered shock. He bent nearer to hear her whisper. For the first time, Alek began to realize that Elspeth had no idea of true fulfillment.

"It wasn't like that at all." Her lips quivered in the moonlight, and Alek bent to taste them. "I thought—"

"You thought you'd complete the circle and this time *you'd* walk away, correct?" he shot at her, his heart raw and exposed.

Alek found himself hard, wanting her. Elspeth eyes widened as his desire lay upon her stomach. "Oh, yes. I want you again, Elspeth-mine. I ache with it, hard. Not a little 'Oh, I think I'll get this off my calendar,' but damn hard, right down to my toes and back up to the pounding in my brain, not to mention other parts of me. Baby, this time, you can come along for the journey, too." Alek smoothed his hand down her leg, enjoyed the rippling of her muscles

as she tensed and followed them back up to the soft, fragrant center of her.

"Alek!" Her soft cry of panic stopped him; it skittered
through her eyes.

He hadn't meant to frighten her. He cursed himself rapidly, silently in whatever languages he could manage. His
hands shook as he caught her close, drew her up to him to
scan the terror in her light gray eyes.

"You don't know what this is all about, do you?" he
asked, studying her shocked, flushed face.

Her flush ran all the way down her slender curves; he
could feel it warm against his skin. "Sex. I suppose you
want sex. I know the mechanics. I've lived on a farm. Alek,
it's late and we've just— I thought you were finished."

*Finished with me...the same as before...when you
pushed away and left me on that stone, alone and torn—*
Alek went cold, just sensing the words Elspeth could be
thinking. Then he'd ripped her apart with words to protect
her, to protect himself.

There were times for words and there were times for
loving. For touches and tenderness that Elspeth deserved.
Alek found himself smiling down at her; maybe they were
both new at the loving game. "This time, I'll do the thinking, okay? Not that your little foray left me much for
brains."

Alek carefully placed his lips on hers, fused the shape
of his mouth to hers, hoping to stamp the memory of this
loving over the others. He kissed her until she softened,
hungry little sounds coming deep in her throat. Gently,
Alek reminded himself, gently. He cupped her breasts,
cherished them, then the softness of her stomach and the
mound below.

The hard thud of his blood, pounding at his temples,
stopped him; he shoved back the desire to have her too

quickly, reminding himself that this was the woman he loved, a treasure opening to him, damply, softly....

Hunger flowed in Elspeth now, arching her body to the sweep of his hand, her arms locked around his neck, her mouth fused to his hungrily.

She made love silently, Alek thought in the last remaining reasonable cell of his brain. He treasured her sounds, wrapped them against him and waited for her to say his name.

Elspeth tensed as he traced her soft opening, spreading the folds delicately with his fingertips to find the moist, taut bud; Elspeth bolted at first, then writhed beneath him, making outraged, frustrated noises. She flung back her head, her hair flowing around her, and raked him with her eyes. The moonlight caught the edge of her teeth, biting into her lip. "Alek!"

There was nothing cool about her now, the heat shimmering in her eyes, her heart hammering against his, lips trembling. Her fingers dug into his shoulders, anchoring him. "What do you want?"

"I want to spend the night with you. Naked. Here in this bed or in mine. I want to wake up to you, to hold you. It's a simple matter." Alek kissed her with the stark hunger raging inside him. He trembled when her lips slowly parted for his tongue, when her arms came out to lock around his neck and her body undulated in a quick, satisfactory movement beneath his.

"Don't push me, Alek," she warned, even as her lips bit his shoulder and her nails lightly raked his back. Her breath swept unevenly, rapidly across his skin.

"Wouldn't think of it," he murmured as he moved away from her, drawing away the old quilt. Elspeth's fingers dug into his arm, and he tensed, bracing himself against the fresh wave of desire. This time, she would know how he felt, shattered upon her just a short time ago.

Alek rested his head upon her breasts, nuzzling them and giving her time to adjust to him again. His hands stroked her breasts, her ribs and locked to the restless, quivering movement of her hips. Or was it he who needed to slow down and gather control? When Elspeth shivered, he opened his mouth on her breast and let her know how much he needed her. She jolted up, her hands ready to push away and then cradle his head against her.

Alek smoothed her restless, heated body from shoulder to ankle. "I want everything this time, Elspeth."

She murmured a protest as his hand smoothed her inner thigh, moving to cup the fragrant nest of curls. "No, Alek, don't."

"Don't what? Do you want me?" If she didn't— Sheer terror swept through Alek, freezing him.

"Yes. Yes, I want you. But like before—"

"Oh, no, sweet Elspeth. I'm not letting you set the rules this time. This time you won't lie quietly and let me have you. This time you'll have to step into the fire with me."

She breathed heavily, her body trembling beneath his. "No. I won't—"

Yet her body—soft and moist and welcoming—parted for his fingers. Elspeth's thighs pressed together, her hands shaking on his shoulders as he began to kiss his way downward. His tongue in her navel brought a shudder and an unwilling groan. A thumb sweeping across her hipbone brought her arching upward. She moved with his hand now, flowing restlessly, her fingers anchored in his hair.

He held her still as the first small quivers tightened around his fingers and Elspeth's nails bit into his shoulders. "Alek, no. I can't take—"

"Yes, you can. But I'll stop if you want. Do you?" Alek gritted his teeth, waiting for her answer. For her and for the future he wanted with her, he would force himself to do anything.

Her fingers dug into his shoulders, and a ripple shot through her body, pleasing him. "Don't stop," she whispered unsteadily.

He smiled at that, rising to sink into the delicious heat of her mouth, drinking in her unsteady breath. She gave and gave, demanding more, slanting her lips against his, and then Alek began his thorough passage down her body.

When his mouth touched her, Elspeth's hushed cry trembled on the night air. She squirmed beneath his touch, and Alek locked her to him until she trembled and went still. Her body arched to his touch as his lips took her breast, suckling, gently biting it and laving it with his tongue, and then he found her, lifting her to him. Elspeth's body jolted into a taut line, the delicate contractions within her began, giving him pleasure. He held her there, poised on the tip of her desire until the tightening slowed and Elspeth went limp, her hands locked to his damp shoulders.

She barely moved when Alek slid into her, rested over her, kissing her gently. "I didn't know," she whispered against his lips.

He moved his hips, filling her, and a second set of contractions began. This time Alek flung himself over the edge, his body thrusting into hers.

She cried out, fighting him and her, her body flowing beneath him, heating, shifting, tightening. Alek gave himself to the storm, reveled in it until it burst, raging through him. This time, she had taken and given, her heart pounding against his.

Alek cradled her against him, rocking her as the last shudders vanished. He tipped her face up to his and found what he wanted in her expression, a woman who'd been thoroughly loved and had loved back, a drowsy and sated look that filled him with pleasure. He ran his thumb across her soft, swollen lips, treasuring her. "And that is how it's going to be, Elspeth love. No self-sacrifice, no guilt…just the loving.''

Still wrapped in her passion, shaken by it, Elspeth smoothed his cheek with her fingers. The touch was light, exploring him as if she'd just discovered him. She skimmed his throat, his shoulders, all the time looking at him with soft, drowsy eyes, her body tangled with his. ''Stay.''

As if he could stand. As if he was anything but one boneless, fuzzy grin wrapped in rose blossoms. He almost laughed at the thought, but the effort was too much. Instead he smoothed his chin over her hair, letting it tangle, web across his skin. Alek had poured himself too deeply within her to be free, had given her a part of him that he hadn't shared with another woman. Elspeth nestled against Alek, her legs tangled with his, her heart slowing as she slid into sleep.

Elspeth awoke to birds cheeping, the pink light of dawn entering her bedroom window and Alek's mouth upon her breasts. His hands caressed her stomach, her legs. ''This isn't fair,'' she protested even as her body opened to receive his hard one and her lips opened to his.

Alek's hands ran beneath her hips, lifting her, his mouth feeding upon hers. He locked her to him until they moved as one, sharing body and skin and hunger.

She locked her hands to his hair and held him still for her kiss, and then the contractions started. Pleasure rolled through her, taking her. She held on to him, refusing to release him, his body thrusting into hers just as she wanted.

She wanted the primitive heat, the hardness of his thighs, his hands shaking yet gentle upon her heated skin. ''You smell delicious,'' Alek murmured, running his hands down to her ankles and locking her legs around his hips.

Elspeth gasped and braced her hands on his chest. ''Alek, I can't—I can't take any more.''

"Dare you." His wicked grin set her off, caused her to fling herself into the fire. His fingers reached between them, and Elspeth splintered into fiery shards. Minutes later, she managed to flop her hands from his sweat-damp shoulders. Alek showed no signs of moving, a single lid opening slowly. "Now, that is how it's done, Elspeth-mine. At least between you and me."

She grabbed his head and kissed him with the last of her strength. Alek settled down upon her breasts, and with a feeling of coming home, of safety, Elspeth stroked his hair and slept.

She dozed and awoke again to Alek's hand shackling her wrist and terror in his voice. "Come on, kid. You're okay. I'll get you out of here."

His legs threshed the sheets, his body taut and sweating. He pushed her away, fists gripping the sheets, feet moving. "I can't take it anymore...what happened to loving kids and keeping them safe?.... Yes, damn it, I'll finish your assignment, Doug. Just don't die...."

Elspeth placed her hand on his arm to wake him from his nightmare, but he flung it away. Tears gleamed on his lashes, trailing down his face. "Damn it," he cursed as if that labeled his pain. Then a brisk burst of a harsh language and a shift to a Latin-based one, probably French.

"Alek." Elspeth smoothed his hair and his cheeks as he tossed beside her. "Alek, you're here now. With me. Alek."

"Damn it," he said finally as if mourning the world while he moved from nightmares to reality. Alek's hand swept out to grasp her hair to tug her close to him.

She saw his nightmares lingering in his eyes. "I'm here, Alek."

"Did I hurt you?" he demanded hoarsely as if he'd die if he had.

She touched his damp lashes and remembered how he

had cried with her about the baby. "No. You didn't hurt me."

He sat upright, turning his back to her. He washed his hands over his face hard, fighting the nightmare. "I could have. Damn. I could have."

"But you didn't, Alek." She ached for Alek, needing to comfort him. Elspeth sat up behind him, stroking the taut muscles of his back, his neck. She rose to her knees and folded her arms around him, rocking him gently. He allowed her petting, and she placed her face against his throat and rocked him. "I could get used to that."

"You're here now. Safe with me, Alek. Don't think about tomorrow." The words surprised her, she who had always thought of consequences and of tomorrow and of safety. First for her family, then for herself and now for Alek. Elspeth leaned her head against his shoulder and enclosed him with her arms until his shudders stopped completely.

He turned to her, tracing her face as if locking himself to a dream he wanted very much and shoving away the past. "I hate being weak like this. Sometimes I wake up— Elspeth, I could have hurt you. I wish…I wish we'd met before…when I hadn't seen too much."

"Wishes are for the taking," Elspeth whispered, and kissed him. She wished that he'd never awaken to his terrors again. "Here and now."

"Are they?" Alek cupped the back of her head and pressed her lips to his.

She floated beneath the tender assault, wrapping her arms and legs around him to moor him in the present, safe from the past.

"Sweet Elspeth-mine," Alek murmured, and the kisses changed, heated and they began again.

Alek reached for Elspeth and drew her against him, spooning her body against his beneath the quilt. His hand ran down her curves to the heat he sought. He lost himself in the fragrance of her hair swirling around him. Birds chirped outside her window, and children yelled in the street. This was how he wanted to wake up every morning. He nuzzled her throat, found the awakening pulse with his lips, ignored her sleepy protest and began to kiss her. Her bottom shifted on his lap as she snuggled back to him, sighing.

Alek closed his eyes and let his hands roam over his captive. With luck, he could keep her here all day—he smiled and wallowed in cuddling her against him.

"Well, well," Birk noted with an edge in his tone, and Elspeth tensed, her fingers digging into Alek's wrist.

"I suppose this means a wedding, Elspeth." Duncan's tone suggested tar and feathers for the man who had dishonored his sister.

"What if they're married already?" asked Sybil in a dry tone.

"Not a chance," stated Calum.

"Stop it, all of you," Sybil ordered, balancing Megan on her hip. In a tactic to deter Duncan, who was already moving toward the bed, Sybil plopped Megan in his arms. "There. You will not interfere with Elspeth's life."

"She's our sister," Birk stated in an outraged tone.

Talia laughed outright. "I think they look cute together. I've never seen Alek look so outraged. Isn't Elspeth gorgeous? And sweet. I think she looks sweet. At least neither one of them look like the living dead now."

"I'm going to beat the living crap out of him," Calum stated too coolly. "That contract was bad enough."

"What contract?" Talia asked, pivoting to her husband, the sunlight showing off the tiny mound of their baby.

"Duncan Tallchief, you told," Sybil stated, outraged. She plucked Megan from him and placed her on the bed.

The toddler scrambled toward Alek and, with a squeal, launched herself upon him. Sybil stopped Duncan from retrieving his daughter. He glared at Alek as if he'd stolen another female away from his nest.

"I demand to know what Alek has done, Calum. You would keep this from me, a Petrovna?" Talia's tone caused Alek to feel sorry for Calum.

"Tallchief," Calum corrected in a flash.

"Duncan Tallchief." Sybil's tone said she had plans to teach her husband a lesson. Duncan had the good sense to look sheepish, all six foot four inches, two hundred thirty pounds of him.

Alek sat up, propped a pillow behind him and said, "I'll get you off the hook, Duncan. I arranged for a two-year exclusive contract in Denver. She's too good, and I wanted to see her work hanging where people could enjoy it. I also wanted her away from the pack of you, so that I could persuade her that she likes me."

"You weren't on assignment?" Talia asked.

"My assignment days are over, kid. It was a plain case of wanting to get Elspeth alone, and all of you, standing here right now, are proof of that need."

"Why, Alek. You're a romantic," Sybil murmured. "And you knew Elspeth before, didn't you?"

Elspeth let out a loud, protesting groan and closed her eyes. He took her hand, but she shook him off.

"We met five years ago when she was studying in Scotland. When Talia's wedding pictures arrived in December, there was Elspeth. I wanted her then and I want her now. It's as simple as that."

He waited for that one to sink into the Tallchief brothers. Click. Click. Click. All three brothers' scowls locked in place. Alek frowned back.

"Nothing is ever that simple," Calum stated, already digging at facts, placing them in a neat row.

Elspeth groaned and flipped to her stomach, jamming the pillow over her head; Alek placed his hand over the curve of her bottom. He answered Megan's kiss and admired the satin ribbon she pointed to on top of her head. "Pretty, Meggie…Elspeth apparently is not taking appointments today."

He placed Megan over Elspeth's bottom and let her bounce as though riding her rocking horse. Elspeth groaned aloud as Megan gurgled, delighted.

"She's never been afraid to face us," Duncan stated, outraged. "You, Petrovna. Outside."

Elspeth groaned again and wiggled up to sit beside Alek. She placed a pillow between them. Megan launched herself at her aunt, and Elspeth cuddled the baby against her. "Go away, all of you."

Just looking at her with Megan started him thinking about— He sat back to admire the picture Elspeth made, rosy and warm from a night with him, a blanket tugged up to cover her breasts. He found a long strand of her hair and brought it to his lips. "She isn't an easy woman, but faced with a shotgun wedding, I'd sacrifice."

"Shotgun wedding. Try another century." Elspeth's snarl caused him to grin. Alek soaked in the sight of her, hair wildly flowing around her, cheeks flushed with outrage and eyes leveling hot, steely threats at all the males in the room. "Petrovna, shut up."

"Yes, ma'am."

After a warning look at Alek, Elspeth turned on her brothers. "Have I ever, ever butted into your love lives? I had plenty of opportunities between the three of you. When you were teenagers, it's a wonder your zippers held the strain."

Alek wanted to lick the gleam on her shoulders, but instead tugged on her hair. "She's feeling a bit testy and worried about my reputation."

"I thought I told you to—"

Birk glowered at Alek. "Huh. What did she do, drag you here? You outweigh her by a good eighty-five pounds."

"My, the testosterone in this room is fairly bubbling," Talia noted with delight, inching away from Calum's restraining hand. "This could be the makings of a new play."

Alek ran his finger along Elspeth's hot cheek and jerked it away before she bit him. "She came after me. This wasn't my plan at all. I'm a regular old-fashioned guy. I'd prefer necking and dating and picnics and the regular route to…ah…a relationship. But there she was, determined to have me, and what could I do?"

Too incensed to speak, Elspeth looked at him as though she'd like to tear him to bits. He jerked when her fingers pinched his thigh. After a quick search and another pinch, he captured her hand and brought it up on the blankets to hold it.

Elspeth's muttering was the frosting on Alek's well-devoured and sated cake. He knew he was glowing and grinning. "At least she's not indifferent to me."

"Idiot."

Duncan snorted, drawing on his leather gloves. "I've got a field to plow." He glared at Alek and then at Sybil, who was smothering a grin. "I've got work to do. Any time, Alek. Name it."

"They don't call him Duncan the defender for nothing." Sybil gave way to her grin.

Talia straightened the curtains at the windows. She glanced at the tree limbs connecting Alek's open window to Elspeth's. An experienced troublemaker, Talia knew exactly how Alek had traveled to Elspeth's bedroom. "So, Elspeth. Are you keeping that dinner date with Jeremy Cabot? Or does this change things?"

Elspeth tried to reclaim her hand from Alek and couldn't.

"Alek and I are not going steady or engaged. Of course I'm keeping my date with Jeremy."

That stopped Alek, who was foraging for his shorts with his toe.

Sybil cradled her cup of coffee and sat on the end of the bed. "Don't glower, Alek. Mmm. Tell me what you know about Una's shawl, the one she seduced Tallchief with?"

"I did not seduce Alek," Elspeth stated firmly, edging away from Alek.

"I found the shawl. Used it as bait." He jerked her back, glowering at her after a full minute of trying to identify one Jeremy Cabot, a man soon to die. "Is that the idiot that runs the office at the feed-and-grain store? The piece of blubber who tries to fit himself into that tiny red sports car?"

She sat very straight and smoothed her hair. "He's always liked me. It's been only lately, since his divorce, that I've thought he might have possibilities."

Talia leaned against Calum, whose expression said he was putting lots of twos together. "You know, this reminds me of home, Alek. Remember when all of us piled into Mom and Dad's bedroom and Dad kept trying to shoo us away?"

"Una's shawl?" Duncan repeated too slowly in a tone resembling a growl.

"Get lost, and take your posse with you. Now." Alek didn't want to deal with the Tallchief brothers right now; they could take him apart later. He took Elspeth's wrist; Cabot wasn't getting her. Elspeth glared at him and tried to reclaim it. She picked up the pillow.

"You hit me," he stated a heartbeat later, and blew a feather from his lips. He slashed a hand down his face and glowered at her, the woman who had swung the pillow with enough force to tear it. He blew away another feather, tumbling down his forehead. Outraged that she would attack him after a night of lovemaking, Alek stared at her. When she didn't act as though she'd apologize, Alek wrapped the quilt around his waist and stood.

He looked out into the morning sunshine. The sheriff was parked on the street, binoculars focused on Elspeth's bedroom window. Beside him stood Elspeth's first-grade teacher, Mrs. Schmidt, shaking her head. A squad of little boys on souped-up dirt bikes stared with blatant interest and open mouths. Alek cursed; the boys would learn soon enough how a woman could make a man act like an idiot.

"That's mine," Birk stated as Alek reached back to grab a kilt that had been flung over a chair. A spool of thread attached to the hem rolled to the floor.

"I'm sure you won't mind me borrowing your skirt, under the circumstances," Alek returned. He stepped into the kilt, ignored the sewing pins jabbing him and crossed the limbs amid hoots and whistles from the Tallchiefs. Once in his bedroom, Alek slammed down his window. The phone ran a second later, while he was debating about which wall to take down. "Yes?"

He knew it was Elspeth by the soft breathing at the other end. She probably wanted the kilt back, but he served her a warning instead. "You date that jerk, and I won't be held accountable."

String circled Alek's ankles, and he traced it from the kilt's hem back to Elspeth's window. Duncan appeared, grim faced, and jerked something between his leather-gloved hands. The thread at Alek's kilt went limp.

Elspeth strained for control. "Alek Petrovna, don't you dare hurt Jeremy. He's been my friend for ages."

Alek crushed the shawl. He intended to disassemble Cabot. "Will all that lard fit into a bucket?" he asked in a too-pleasant tone.

Then he looked at the kilt he wore and smiled grimly. For the moment, he was wearing it just the same as the rest of the Tallchiefs. He began to wind the thread around his fingers. He was keeping as much of Elspeth as he could.

"What's that noise?" Elspeth asked as Sybil and Talia began laughing. Megan squealed in delight.

Alek finished his thread recovery and glanced out his window. "Why, Elspeth-love, I believe that's your brothers' chain saws."

"*What?*"

"It looks like they're cutting off my access route to your boudoir."

Her outraged gasp did wonders for his bruised ego. Alek slowly replaced the phone on its cradle. Beneath his window, Elspeth, dressed in a faded flannel robe that exposed her legs magnificently swooped upon her brothers. The revving chain saws died as they backed away from her accusing finger and found themselves against her house.

Though Alek couldn't hear the words, from her expression, they weren't pleasant ones. The brothers' expressions changed from outrage to frustration. Duncan began arguing with her, Birk threw down his western hat and Calum shook his head. Talia and Sybil stood on the porch and laughed. Elspeth threw up her hands. She pointed to the new flower bed the brothers had tromped.

"Huh. Look at that," Alek mused as Elspeth stalked to the water faucet and turned the hose on her three brothers. After they were dripping and Sybil and Talia doubled over with laughter, Elspeth began pacing in front of them, her flannel robe flying around her legs. Duncan, Calum and Birk stood rigidly against the wall, until she pointed at them and scolded. One by one, they spit a distance. Elspeth shook her magnificent mane, threw up her hands and stalked into her house. "I love it when that woman gestures. She's showing a real flair for it," Alek murmured.

The three brothers tromped and huffed and cursed and in the end packed up their chain saws.

Suddenly Alek felt much better and took the stairs two at a time on his way down to make breakfast.

He whistled while he fixed his cereal. After plucking away several pertinent pins from the back of the kilt, Alek sat down and propped his feet on another chair. He listened to the birds chirp, the revved-up teenagers' trucks prowling on the street and settled into a happy cloud of morning-after—

His back door opened and slammed. "Alek! Where are you?" Elspeth's tone was not sweet.

"In here, my love. Would you like breakfast? Have you come to court me or to drag me off to that shotgun wedding?" He was groggy on dreams, daft on making love with Elspeth and mellow with contentment. There was just something about seeing his lady love protect him. "You know Amen Flats isn't really that boring—"

When cold milk and soggy cereal ran down his head and onto his shoulders, Alek shivered. Then he grinned and licked a flake from his cheek. He leered at the gaping flannel robe and the curve of her breast. "Things are certainly looking up, Elspeth-mine."

"Jerk." She ripped his shorts from her pocket and dropped them on his head.

"I'll treasure that endearment forever." Alek sat very still as Elspeth lifted the carton of milk and slowly poured it over his cereal and his shorts. He tilted his head to better appreciate the slope of her breast. "Are you going to make me spit, too?"

He got a delicious view of a taut, dark nipple when Elspeth threw up her hands. "I used to make them settle their differences that way—spitting contests to see who could spit the farthest."

"I love a passionate, dominating woman," Alek murmured, and leered up at her. "Let's try whipped cream next time."

* * *

"Whipped cream…" Elspeth's hand reached for the bed sheets, hovered and then she decided to leave them. She dusted the feathers from it and remembered how outraged he'd been, feathers drifting around his black, shaggy head and shoulders.

She picked up the abused pillow, and Alek's scent clung to it.

A wave of stark longing washed over her, startling her. She couldn't want him again. Not after last night, her body still aching from his. Yet images of Alek flashed through her mind, forcing Elspeth to brace herself against her emotions as she always did. She quickly made the bed and took a long, thorough shower, and the images returned. Alek, dressed in Birk's kilt, created a memorable picture. Complete with breakfast cereal and extra milk, he looked delicious. He had sat very still while she poured, then smiled hopefully up at her with milk dripping off his nose.

His little-boy expression had changed too rapidly back to a dark, passionate one. He'd wiped his face with one big hand and leveled a glare at her. "You date Cabot and—"

Elspeth had reacted instantly, hooking one foot beneath the legs of his chair and pulling, sending him sprawling down in a mass of muscled, hairy legs and tangled kilt. She'd placed her bare foot on his cereal-spattered chest. "Hmm. Threats. Take a note, Alek. Don't ever threaten me…I have lived with arrogant, threatening males all my life. I have experience in dealing with them."

Then, disgusted that Alek had provoked her and lay grinning as if he'd single-handedly won a football game, she had tried for an even tone. "I think I need to get out more," she had stated elegantly before returning to her home.

She'd broken every rule that she'd ever made—losing her temper with Alek Petrovna. There was no reason she shouldn't date Jeremy and add to a growing list.

Elspeth rummaged through the lacy lingerie she'd stuffed

into a pretty flowery box and selected a white lace bra-and-panty set. Her body told her that she'd strained every muscle while making love to Alek, and a few she hadn't known existed. "And that is how it's going to be," he'd said after their lovemaking.

There was nothing sweet about Alek's lovemaking, not at the center of it, while he held her on high on that fiery, throbbing pinnacle and still demanded more— Who was he to make rules about their lovemaking? To say what and how and when?

She couldn't forgive him for unleashing her emotions, for exposing her need of him.

"Shotgun wedding," she said, repeating Alek's light concession. She had no intentions of getting involved with Alek.

She was involved. For starters, she never wanted Alek waking to his nightmares alone. He should be held and tended and loved.

Elspeth groaned. She knew herself, the old-fashioned steel built into her. She ran her hand across her mother's quilt, the one she'd been holding that terrible night long ago in the kitchen.

Alek Petrovna had come from another time, from another world in which she'd given herself.

She'd changed. Or had she?

She'd changed, the proof lodged in her body.

Elspeth placed her hand over her eyes and sat upright. *Elspeth...* She recalled his murmur, close and hot against her. She didn't trust Alek Petrovna; he was far too experienced at games and always pushing her, prodding her about what she'd locked inside. The shawl's legend was none of his business. She'd tossed it and her romantic dreams away after returning from Scotland.

Elspeth shivered and reached for her jeans, drawing them on and zipping them. She sucked in her breath and glanced at the light scrape marks on her stomach caused by Alek's morning stubble. The rough denim material rubbed against the sensitized flesh of her thighs, and Elspeth groaned.

This morning, Alek's back had shocked her, pink lines showing where her nails had scraped him. A rush of heat shot through her, and Elspeth groaned again. She quickly drew on an old blouse she hadn't worn for years. Alek had demanded everything, kissing her intimately, touching her. He'd handled her gently, firmly, committed to extracting the ultimate from her.

Elspeth let out an unfamiliar, long, frustrated groan.

She shook her head. Sex with Alek shouldn't have gone so far, nor taken her so high, nor should gentler emotions tug at her now.

Elspeth threw up her hands. What did she know about sex? She'd been unprepared for the shattering, and no amount of preparing could have shored up her walls, her protection.

It was eight o'clock. Elspeth shivered and swept the lacy handkerchief from her family portrait. At least Alek had that much decency before he planned his raid.

Downstairs, for the first time in her life, her loom held little interest. She was too restless. Elspeth forced herself to sip her morning herbal tea and then work her hair into one long braid. The sounds coming from next door said that Alek had set out to remove another wall—or tear his house apart. She listened intently and decided she liked Alek Petrovna worked up and frustrated.

Elliot Pinkman, an older man needing to supplement his retirement income, came to till her garden and haul away brush. "Mornin', Elspeth. You're looking in the pink. Flushed, sort of. You been baking?" Elliot sniffed the June air. "Nope, can't smell that good bread of yours. You sure look worked up. Alive. Full of it. Haven't looked that way in a few years."

"I've...I've been moving my loom, Elliot. You know how big it is. I've got to get back to it." Elspeth quickly made her retreat and glanced at the mirror. She placed her hands on her hot cheeks and released the taut, frustrated "Aargh!" to the shadows of her home.

Elliot knocked at her door. "I could help you move that loom, Elspeth."

"Thank you for asking, but it's all right now," she lied. Nothing would ever be the same again, not with Alek dipping in her life.

Jeremy called, clearly aware of the morning's events. He wanted to confirm their dinner date. Jeremy hesitated slightly before asking her if she had a "thing" for Alek Petrovna. Her "We're neighbors and Talia is his sister," pacified Jeremy, who had been hovering around her for years, even during his marriage.

This morning, Elspeth decided to ignore her garden, ignore her waiting loom and Mark's messages on her answering machine. She slapped sandwiches into a backpack and drove to Tallchief Cattle Ranch.

The time had come to visit her parents, resting high on Tallchief Mountain. When she'd returned five years ago, she couldn't bear taking her shame to them—that she had loved a married man and had taken his child.

Her mother had always told her that a special love waited and Una's journals had supported that belief. Elspeth had returned with crushed dreams and chose to mourn her baby alone. Though she thought of them often, her parents' love had been so perfect that it seemed they should rest, undisturbed by Elspeth's dark storms.

She'd missed the visits with her mother, as daughters do, and now it was time to share her life with them.

Like a violent summer storm on the mountains, Alek had changed her life yet again. Her parents needed to know about him.

Alek. She refused to surrender to him easily. Years ago, she'd tasted heaven in his arms, certain that life would grow richer and love would come to call. Those dreams were dashed too soon and that trust was hard to regain.

Did she trust Alek? Not quite. He pushed too much, moved too quickly and wanted too much. She wasn't ready to give her deepest heart, the privacy she kept as her fortress. She doubted that now she could give that part to anyone...

A man who could and had changed her life, Alek wanted everything. Elspeth clung to her safety, weaving it around her like a shield. As a girl, she'd lost her parents, and then Alek.... She feared another loss would take her deeper into the shadows....

She needed this visit to quiet the sadness within her. Her parents had missed so much of their children's lives and now it was time....

When she arrived at Tallchief Cattle, Duncan had saddled Delight, a sturdy brown-and-white mare. He'd always known when she needed to ride up the mountain; they shared the Tallchief intuitions.

As he watched her strap on her chaps, Duncan's expressive eyes told her he worried but that he understood. He nodded to her and held out the reins. Elspeth placed her western hat on her head, nodded to her brother before placing her foot in the stirrup and rising to the saddle. Duncan didn't say anything, nor did she; the Tallchiefs understood that dark moments roamed within them and needed privacy. She took the trail to Tallchief Mountain, passing through the shadows of the pines up a rocky stretch and over meadows filled with grazing Tallchief sheep.

It was the first time she'd taken the trail to her parents' graves in those five years.

Nine

Chipmunks ran up the red bark of the pines, and rabbits crossed Delight's path as she carried Elspeth upward. In an aspen clearing, Elizabeth Montclair, Elspeth's great-grandmother, had met the son of Una and Tallchief. Liam Tallchief, a half blood, had fought his captors who wanted him to dishonor Elizabeth. To save her sister, Elizabeth had agreed to shed her pride, marry the savage in his customs and take him into her body. Then Liam had followed her to England to revenge his pride, his seed taken from him unwillingly by the English heiress. She'd given up everything to be with him, to return to Tallchief land.

The mountain sun burned through the trees, and a lizard baked on a lichen-covered rock. Scarlet Indian paintbrush blooms quivered in the wake of scurrying ground squirrels.

Elspeth lifted her head and sighted a cliff where LaBelle Dupree, her grandmother and a reformed international jewel thief, had hidden her treasures. LaBelle had been a bit of a tomboy, something like Fiona, always into trouble, and she'd loved intrigue. Nothing satisfied her like plucking fortunes from the wealthy. Until Jake Tallchief had turned up at her fancy soiree and blackmailed her into marriage. Jake had only wanted to capture her, to prevent her from hanging or worse, and tuck her under his wing. LaBelle, once faced with a man she couldn't push to do her bidding, had fallen deeply in love with him.

Now LaBelle's earring was Alek's.

Elspeth slid the reins through her fingers and glanced up at the clear blue June sky. Her ancestors had loved deeply, and she would settle for nothing less.

Alek had carried the woven swatch with him for years.

Elspeth ran her hand across her damp lashes, not wanting to believe the tenderness in Alek's arms, the gentle, reverent way he touched her.

A doe bounded across the path, startling Delight. Elspeth calmed her in a soft, gentling tone. The sound reminded her of Alek, whispering wild, exotic things to her, treasuring her with his body....

A hawk swooped down in a grassy meadow, reminding Elspeth of Alek. In a cave beyond that meadow, Pauline Dante, the first woman judge of Amen Flats, had been held hostage. Matthew Tallchief, her childhood nemesis, and a sheriff's deputy assigned to protect her from threats, had tracked the kidnappers and rescued her. There in the meadow, he'd won her heart by reciting Greek mythology.

Elspeth stood in the saddle, absorbing the mountain's familiar sounds and scents. Her eyes swept the valley below, a blend of rich fields, winding roads and the small town of Amen Flats. She stretched, her muscles aching from Alek's lovemaking and from riding. Elspeth inhaled the pine scents and knew that she'd never pitted herself against anyone, any challenge, like Alek.

She'd never felt more alive.

She believed in her senses, in what they told her before

the happening; they'd told her that Alek would be coming and that he would change her life.

Lovers' whispers swept through the pine branches, and Elspeth shivered because they sounded familiar, the tone the same as Alek's and hers.

Delight grazed in the meadow while Elspeth settled near her parents' graves. She folded her arms over her knees and let the tears roll down her cheeks.

She'd created a safe nest, and now he'd come to tear her loose.

The wind whispered along her body. It caressed the tendrils of hair near her face, and she remembered her mother's words, *Love isn't calm, Elspeth. It's fierce joy, rising out of your very soul. Love can shatter and hurt and, if it's real, it will take the wear and become stronger. There are no guarantees, nothing but the tenderness in a man's eyes that's just for you. When your time comes, honey, take a chance.*

Elspeth crushed a bluebell stalk. Alek's black eyes had been very tender. He'd placed his face into the hollow of her shoulder, a gentle, sweet gesture from a hard man.

Elspeth held the wildflower bouquet and thought of the heather that Alek had given her that night. She'd taken one chance with Alek Petrovna. Could she withstand another?

You sense things, probably because of your seer and shaman blood. Duncan has a bit of the gift, but not as much as yours. You'll know, Elspeth, when the man is right. You'll feel like you're walking on air when he looks at you. There's a fever in your blood that is only for him.

Elspeth had been too full of thoughts about Alek; he'd washed away the premonitions she'd come to expect. Even now, she saw flashes of him wherever she looked, big arrogant and bold, pushing...pushing....

Elspeth placed her forehead on her arms, braced over her knees. Alek moved too quickly; he was too passionate, too ready to laugh or to rage…or to kiss her as if all his dreams were wrapped up in her.

Your heart will know, even if you deny him, dear. The Tallchiefs are a complex brood, and I've always known that love wouldn't come easy to you.

At five o'clock in the afternoon, Amen Flats's Main Street began settling in for the weekend. The scent of apple pie and backyard barbecues hung in the June air. High-school boys in their spotlessly waxed trucks and cars cruised up and down. The butcher hauled an extra order of hamburger into the local drive-in. Trucks and cars were already parking near Maddy's Hot Spot, and the sheriff had slept in that morning to prepare for Friday night and payday on the ranches.

At eight o'clock, the ballfield lights would flick on for the start of the first softball game. Families would sit on blankets lining the field, and babies would sleep through it all.

A hay baler prowled down Main Street, on its way for repair at Powell's Machinery. Forced to move aside, a tractor ran up on the sidewalk, the driver cursing and slapping his battered Stetson. Dirty from working in the fields and building fence, a truckload of college boys home for the summer whistled at Sexy Sue, who wore a gold chain around her waist and had just gotten a brand-new rose tattoo on her ankle. According to gossip, Sexy Sue had pierced more than her ears, and the boys were drooling to know just what.

With Megan strapped to his back, Alek sorted through his thoughts. He'd grown up in a town just like this, his teenage hormones lusting after another version of Sexy Sue before Melissa.

When it came to Elspeth, maybe his hunger hadn't changed. Alek stared at Jeremy Cabot leaving the feed mill in his red sports car. Jeremy did not return Alek's unwavering stare. Alek managed not to flinch when Megan's wet fingers investigated his ear and a certain warm dampness spread down his T-shirt. When Cabot's sports car shot out of sight, Alek cursed the intricacies of diapers with sticky tabs; his engineering attempt had been admirable, if lopsided.

Outside the newspaper office, Alek crouched in the midst of the dirt-bike squad. Bundled to his back while Sybil shopped, Megan alternately cooed and giggled and jabbered at the boys surrounding her.

Alek liked the feeling of the toddler on his back almost as much as he liked her in his arms.

"They're girls. I can shoot off a ramp, fly up ten feet, spit another ten feet and still come down on both tires." Jimmy Lattigo, the biggest of the ten- to twelve-year-olds, wanted a steeper ramp to jump his bicycle.

"Who says we're girls?" Ace Wheeler demanded. "You're lucky you don't drown when all that spit flies back in your face."

"Jimmy is a show-off. Watch this." Mad Matt, his baseball cap on backward, glared at Jimmy and spit a perfect arc into the street.

"Nice shot, Matt. I always thought the best riders were the most careful. They finished, while the ones showing off laid on the pavement, bleeding their guts out." Alek tightened the sagging bicycle chain for Killer McGee. The raging discussion was a mix of air gauges, wheelies, tire treads and Annie Jones, who wanted to kiss the entire gang.

Alek had been amid other children, hungry, damaged ones. The grins on these faces said that no one was hungry and the biggest problem was soap and fleeing Annie Jones's mushy kisses. It eased Alek to know that in Amen Flats, most parents took care of their children and that they could sleep at night without fearing for their lives. There were images of children he would never forget.

"He's been in wars. He knows everything." Shark Malone's freckles caught the afternoon sun. Shark didn't know that Alek had failed the diapering rodeo twice before succeeding—somewhat.

Alek reached to ruffle a boy's unruly hair, and another small boy—Tyree—timidly placed his hand in Alek's. His mother had made Jimmy take Tyree, and Jimmy wasn't happy about a kid brother in tow. Alek knew the feeling; as a boy, he'd been mortified when stuck with Anton and his sisters.

A horseback rider came down the center of the street, and people came from their offices and stores to watch.

Alek stood slowly, keeping Tyree's hand in his. Maybe he needed the boy's support; maybe he needed to take a breath before he passed out. Electricity played along his skin, and his pulse rate zapped into overdrive.

Megan squealed with delight and bounced on Alek's back as she recognized her aunt.

Elspeth sat straight, shoulders back, the wind tugging at her dirty and torn blouse. Each movement of the horse caused a soft movement of her breasts. Her hair, loose around her shoulders, rippled and gleamed, black as a crow's wing. The chaps covering her jeans were as worn as her western boots. Her gloved hand rested on her thigh, and the other skillfully managed the reins.

Beneath the straight brim of her black western hat, Elspeth's eyes were steady heat, searing Alek's. She stopped the horse directly in front of him. There wasn't a shadow touching her; she was all steel, all woman and knew what she wanted.

Alek sucked in his breath and knew that what Elspeth wanted, she would take. Maybe it was Una's shawl…maybe, just maybe it might be him. His brain swarmed with dreams and hopes, while a solid ache lodged low in his body, turning his thighs into stone.

Elspeth's mare held still as the squad hopped on their bikes and circled Elspeth on Main Street.

Birk's pickup, laden with a portable concrete mixer, slowed to a stop. Calum, laden with grocery sacks of Talia's latest craving, placed the sacks on Birk's hood. The brothers stood side by side, legs spread, arms across their chests, their faces impassive.

"She always was the best horsewoman around," someone murmured behind Alek. "Her mother rode like that. Straight back, eyes that could see into a man's soul and find the dirt in it. She was a judge right here in Amen Flats. I saw her mother wound up, one day, and Elspeth right behind her. The two of them came after Lacey MacCandliss's mother. You could feel the spit and fire coming off them when they rode into town that day. Everyone knew that when Pauline Tallchief rode like that on horseback and came into town by herself, someone had stepped over the line. Though only a bit of a girl, Elspeth was right at her side, riding straight backed and looking like steel. Never knew what they said to Ms. MacCandliss, but she didn't treat her little girl as bad after that."

Lee Braker picked up the Tallchief story. "The Tallchiefs all pulled their weight when they lost their folks. Sometimes they're plenty hard to understand because of those times. Every one of them has that Tallchief steel, clear through. Elspeth took on her mother's chores right then and never complained. She was a champion trick rider when she was fourteen and making a nice penny at it, too. Or else she was at her loom, earning another penny, or in the kitchen trying to keep her family fed."

As Elspeth sat straight, watching Alek, he knew he'd pay hard for loving her. Deep down, there was the steel that had kept the Tallchiefs together, and they'd fight when

pushed. But from the look of Elspeth now, the fights would
be out in the open, not in the shadows of the past. It was
worth the battle. She didn't give an inch, her expression
unreadable, and Alek wanted it that way; she had a right
to her privacy.

Tyree's eyes were enormous as Alek walked with him
to Elspeth. The four-year-old boy clung to Alek's leg, peering up at her. "He's afraid of the horse," Elspeth noted
curtly.

Alek slowly took in her hat, the faded pink blouse, jeans
and boots. "Did you get it settled?" he asked, even as he
knew the shadows had shifted in Elspeth.

She'd gone to the mountain, searching for answers and
a measure of peace. He ached for her, because she'd torn
herself apart along the way. Alek wanted to reach for her,
to wrap her safely in his arms, but knew she'd have none
of that tenderness between them now. Sunlight slanted
down the set of her jaw. Sometime during the day, she'd
cried, a tear streak dragging across her cheek.

Elspeth ignored Alek's question; she'd answer him when
she was ready and not before. She tipped her hat western-
style, and went dizzy with the sight of Alek. On the afternoon after their loving and subsequent cereal dumping, he
was dressed in low-riding jeans, a faded T-shirt and a teething infant's drool on his shoulder. He stood there, combat
boots locked to the pavement the color of sundown, his jaw
set, a tense muscle working beneath his dark skin. Slashing
cheekbones, soaring black eyebrows and beautiful, curling
lashes ran into a nose that had been broken and then to a
tight, scarred, unforgiving mouth. She preferred that mouth
in its natural sensual curve or widened in a grin that softened his face. When he fused his mouth to hers, assaulted
her senses—

She gripped her thigh with her glove and remembered
Alek's big hands soothing her. Raw-boned, big and tough,

there wasn't anything sweet about him—until he tasted her, because that's surely what he did, tasted. There in the dying light, shadowed by the mountains she loved, Alek stood amid the children he deserved. The infant strapped to his back could have been his own. Alek wanted a family and he wanted her. Fear shot through Elspeth, and she gripped the reins tighter, startling Delight.

She wouldn't know how to keep him when the excitement outside Amen Flats beckoned to him. She couldn't bear loving him one day and then finding him gone the next.

She didn't know how to trust her emotions; she'd kept them locked and safe too long.

"We're planning a Fourth of July soap-box derby," Alek said, and she knew that he wanted something from her that she wasn't ready to give. The currents were there, running through Elspeth's eyes, though her face remained impassive.

"I've never ridden on a horse like that. Can I ride on your horse?" Tyree asked shyly, and Elspeth shivered in the late heat of the day.

Alek realized suddenly that Elspeth kept her distance from children this age. She looked strong enough to take anything now, and he decided to push her a bit more; Alek wanted her eyes to flash and smoke at him. He bent to lift Tyree to his hip. "She's got a hot date tonight. She might not want to right now."

Elspeth shot him a look that would have made her brothers take two steps back. Instead, Alek took one toward her and pushed again. "I bought the Kostya place."

The moment he'd seen the old ranch, he knew it suited Elspeth; laden with flowers and vegetable gardens, the yard spread into fields and the fields spread into mountain meadows. He could see Elspeth rocking a baby on their front porch, running after a toddler and swinging a child.

He could see her in the old house, busy at her loom or walking and spinning on the huge old wheel on the front porch.

Alek's heart skipped a beat as he saw her in the old bedroom, dressed in yards of old-fashioned nightgown and waiting for him.

The mare pranced backward; Elspeth's soft mouth firmed, sunlight catching on the edge of her jaw, spilling down to her breasts, flowing with the horse's restless, side-stepping prance. "The Kostyas haven't wanted to sell their ranch."

Smolder. Steam. Heat. Alek pushed her again. The lady had a chip on her shoulder, and he liked prodding it into a precarious tilt. "I'm from Russian stock, and they knew a Petrovna once. They like the idea of ties to their homeland continuing their ranch and want to retire into town. I traded them this house and any modifications they want. They're in their new motor home, headed to a South Dakota reunion of their native village."

Elspeth narrowed her eyes. "What are you going to do with their ranch?"

"Grow things." *Hold you. Kiss you. Love you. Marry you. Make children with you. Adopt children and give them homes. Keep them safe and then love you more.*

"You're not a rancher, Alek. It isn't easy."

"I'll learn what I have to. I'll make mistakes, but I'll learn." *I've made mistakes with you—I'll learn what makes you happy.*

Delight pranced beneath Elspeth, and she ran a gloved hand down the mane's neck, soothing her.

Alek stood and waited for her to make her call; he realized that he hadn't known the meaning of fear until now. Living in war zones, lit by rockets and bullets, hadn't prepared him for the freezing terror that she might not want him on a permanent basis.

If she didn't, he'd get drunk first and fall apart later and pick himself up to try again. She'd have a hard time getting rid of him. He locked his boots to the pavement and waited.

Elspeth's brothers walked to Alek. Birk lifted Megan from Alek's back and cuddled her on his hip. "Say 'Birk,' Meggie. Birk is your favorite uncle. You're wet, kid. Uncle Alek needs diapering lessons, doesn't he?"

Calum snorted and placed his hand on Alek's shoulder as they watched Elspeth manage the mare easily. "Women," he said, as if the word explained the intricacies of the universe. "Elspeth the elegant can take the heart out of you when she rides. She hasn't in years."

She's got my heart now. Alek crossed his arms over his chest. Because if he didn't, in another minute he'd be up on that horse, taking her out of town.

Elspeth smiled at Tyree, a strand of hair whipping along her cheek and flowing into the wind. "Her name is Delight, and she's the gentlest horse on the Tallchief spread. Her grandmother was my first horse, and they both loved little boys the best. Do you really want to ride with me?"

"I...I guess so." Tyree was too scared to know that Elspeth rarely came close to children this age; Alek ached for her.

Tyree's thumb was almost in his mouth when his big brother pushed it down firmly. "If you wet your pants, you're in double-dutch trouble, shrimp."

Tyree turned slowly to his brother and from his look, his brother would pay for that one day.

"I've never ridden in a soap box. Do you think I could ride in yours?" Elspeth asked Tyree, distracting him from the wet-pants shame.

Tyree's eyes went wide. "You never? You can sure ride in mine."

Alek lifted Tyree in front of Elspeth and envied the little boy. She placed her hat on his head and wrapped one arm around him. With the other, she guided the mare through her paces, circling the street slowly, then trotting, then stopping, shifting directions and repeating the fancy steps.

Alek went lightheaded just looking at her. The dying sunlight caught on Elspeth, her hair swirling around her, and his heart stopped. Somewhere violins played—he was certain of it—and rose blossoms fell like rain. Maybe it was rain, sparkling in sunlight. Maybe it was moonlight and angels singing. He tossed in butterflies and magic fairy dust and listened to the uneven flip-flop of his heart. He dragged in a necessary breath of air and hoped no one heard it come out as a lovesick sigh. He locked his knees, because they were getting weak at the sight of Elspeth's taut body, moving as one with the mare, controlling her.

"Welcome to the pack, Petrovna. You're in love," Calum remarked dryly. "You're also drooling. The thing about all this is that from now on, you won't have an idea what hit you. By the way, did you know Megan wet your back?"

"Babies, laundry and a spare tire around his belly. Having to explain a beer at Maddy's and why the dishes weren't done. It's all downhill from now on," Birk added, and returned Megan's wet kiss.

"Getting up at midnight and waking up the grocer when she wants pistachio ice cream with kraut." Calum rummaged through the grocery sacks. "Good. I didn't forget the pickled artichoke hearts."

"Gag," Mad Matt commented, his finger in his mouth.

"I think I'm going to swoon," Alek stated, meaning it. The Tallchief brothers' eyes widened, and then they began to laugh, rolling laughter that turned the townspeople's attention to them.

Mrs. Schmidt began to weep, and Maddy wiped a tear from his eye with a bar towel. He gave the towel to Mrs. Schmidt, who blew her nose on it.

An old cowboy, bent by years of ranch work, drew out his harmonica and began to play "The Yellow Rose of Texas."

Alek leaned back into the shadows and knew that if Jeremy Cabot put one finger on Elspeth, he was—

Jimmy peered up at Alek and asked, "Who's dead meat?"

Elspeth struggled out of Jeremy's arms for the twentieth time that night. The effort cost her; she ached from head to toe and back again. She'd discovered that a man's hands could be sweaty and soft. Then the tiny muscles within her body reminded her of her night with Alek. There was nothing soft about Alek, all hard angles and strong, rippling muscles...he'd demanded and took, and she'd given and demanded more, hungry for him.

Jeremy's flabby body pressed against hers again; it seemed as if she were fighting a living, sweaty swamp. She'd regretted her impulsive date with him from the moment he placed his hand on her knee—which was an immediate event, once they were in his car. Jeremy's sneaky looks at her thighs beyond her new short skirt disgusted Elspeth, almost as much as his eating habits.

Sideburns did nothing for his chubby face and fat lips. His shirt barely closed over his round belly, a middle button severely strained. She'd liked him while they were in school, but Jeremy had truly gone to pot and to pork. Somewhere between shy Jeremy with glasses and this Jeremy with busy hands, he'd lost that sweetness that she remembered.

"Let's not say good-night just yet," Jeremy crooned, sneaking another appreciative look at her thighs. "You are a strong woman, Elspeth. Uh...I don't suppose you'd ask me in for a drink?"

"No, I don't suppose I would." If Jeremy tried one more

move, he'd find out just how strong she was. He was her first experience with a man who— She realized suddenly that Alek hadn't forced his hands on her. When Alek leered, something rose out of her that wasn't disgust, rather the need to pit herself against him. In one day, her male menu was certainly varied—from Alek to Jeremy.

She eased up and out of Jeremy's tiny sports car, her horse-riding muscles protesting every move. "Good night, Jeremy. It's been an experience."

"But honey—" Jeremy glanced at Alek's porch light, which had just flicked on. Alek came onto the porch and stretched, then folded his arms across his chest. "Uh…I'll call," Jeremy muttered, and sped away.

Alek stared at Elspeth through the night and a bird swooped between them. She stared back, and a ripple of excitement shot through her. She decided against talking to him, rehashing her miserable first date with Jeremy, and walked slowly to her door, aware that Alek's gaze followed her, daring her to start something with him.

"Have fun?" he drawled in a Texas tone that sparked her temper.

"Of course." She wouldn't let him know that the evening rated a total zilch.

"Lady, you've got an attitude. Next time, let me know when you want to go out."

"What makes you think you'd get top billing?"

This time, Alek's voice was menacing like an approaching thunderstorm, with all the lightning bolts ready to zap. "Like I said. You've got a real attitude."

"Suits me," she returned airily when every muscle in her body reminded her that Alek had made thorough love to her the previous night. Elspeth decided she would pick when and where, and Alek could look all he wanted. There was just something about Alek that created in her the need to walk in a leisurely manner, letting her short skirt work slowly up her thighs. Mail-order catalogs definitely had advantages in tiny Amen Flats; once she'd started ordering an updated wardrobe, Elspeth had had to force herself to stop. She really enjoyed short skirts against her thighs.

She shot Alek a look over her shoulder and watched him sizzle, his brows jamming together fiercely, his body taut. Elspeth stopped outside her door and blew him a kiss, just as he had done to her.

If he would have just come to her, she could have— But he didn't, and that nettled Elspeth.

Whatever Alek Petrovna was, he wasn't flabby or unexciting. Just looking at him gave Elspeth pleasure. Pleasure was one thing, excitement another, and desperation to have Alek kiss her yet another.

Once inside her house, Elspeth passed by her loom and realized suddenly that today was the first time she had not spent hours weaving or spinning or carding.

She groaned, her muscles aching as she made her way up the darkened stairway. Once in her chamomile-scented bath, scrubbed free of Jeremy's busy hands, Elspeth leaned her head back against the wall and closed her eyes.

At nine o'clock in the evening—after one hard, long day and the night preceding it—she should have been exhausted. She wasn't. Usually in this mood, she would be at her loom...but it didn't soothe her tonight.

Alek had stood in the midst of the boys with Megan strapped on his back as if he'd last forever. As if he'd come to her to stay. As if nothing could keep him from her. His wide grin had caused her heart to flip-flop, and the answering twinges in her thighs as she rode told Elspeth that she wasn't finished with Alek, not just yet.

He'd bought the Kostya place, a beautiful homestead with natural meadows and fields plowed by mules. It bordered the Tallchief land, and Duncan had been trying to buy it for years. The Kostyas were a beautiful elderly cou-

ple, steeped in their Russian background and mourning
their son, killed in a minor revolution. Alek would appeal
to them, a man needing a home, scarred by life and pain,
ready to laugh, ready to love—

Elspeth groaned and shook her head. She was high on
fresh air, playing with her lambs and freedom. She'd
needed the day on the mountain, the visit to her parents'
graves and the reminder that their love had touched her life.
She soaped her leg, lifting it to survey the strong yet slender
line. Alek had possibilities, if properly trained.

Distance, she decided. She needed proper distance from
Alek to balance what she needed. A friendly relationship
wasn't possible, not now. He was pushing her too much,
offering to sacrifice himself to a shotgun wedding, a willing
victim of the Tallchiefs.

Alek Petrovna would have to learn how to behave.

She ached in every muscle possible, and yet she
wanted—

Elspeth rose, dried slowly and lay upon her bed. Alek's
scent caressed her, and she pressed her face to the pillow
they'd shared. Elspeth flopped to her back and watched the
moonlit ceiling of her room and groaned. However she'd
strained her body today and made a fool out of herself by
showing off in front of Alek, she had to face him again.
Today she'd reclaimed a part of her life and she wanted to
tie up one last loose end. Alek had no right to give her
Una's shawl, to make it so easy for her. She had left the
shawl because the *giving* bothered her. *What was hers, she
would take.*

Tonight, Elspeth was up to reclaiming the shawl and
whatever else was hers. If Alek interfered…she smiled into
the night and hoped he wouldn't make it easy. She wasn't
an easy woman and she did so enjoy challenges, the hunter
in her lifting to the scent even now…

Alek could be ruthless, withholding what she needed;

another man would have come to her tonight and tried an apology. But not Alek—he only offered to be her victim in a shotgun wedding.

She could have strangled him for that.

Elspeth dressed slowly in black shorts and a black T-shirt. At eleven o'clock in the evening, Alek's lights were off. Elspeth watched as a sleek black convertible pulled up in front of his house and Alaina Michaels, complete with bottle in hand, waltzed up to Alek's porch.

He rose out of the shadows on the porch; Alaina's hips swayed beneath her short dress as she moved toward him.

Elspeth suddenly decided she needed to top off her day with a glass of wine.

She went outside, lit her candles, sat on her front porch and plopped her moccasin-covered feet up on the railing. She rocked back in the chair, tilting it against the wall and decided Alek could be replaced anytime, anywhere.

She sipped her wine, trying to ignore the tussle on her neighbor's porch. She tried to convince herself she'd find another Alek Petrovna tomorrow; she'd just go out and pluck one just as sizable, just as exciting, off the shelf. He was a common-variety stud, confident of himself—damn, she hated his confidence. No, she hated his teasing more.

All in all, little kept her from bounding those few feet to Alek's porch and ripping Alaina's willing body from his.

Elspeth inhaled. Alek's body was hers. She'd claimed him five years ago. "Dibs," Elspeth muttered, and poured her fourth glass of wine. She kept trying to ignore Alaina's whimpering sounds and Alek's sexy rumbling.

She closed her eyes and melted at the image of Alek, naked and aroused.

Alaina's convertible squealed off into the night, and the sheriff's car cruised by, sopranos nicely muffled. He trained his spotlight at Elspeth. "Everything okay, Elspeth?"

She lifted her glass to him. "Just peachy."

"You okay?" he persisted, clearly worried that Elspeth Tallchief was having a glass of wine.

"My neighborhood livens up this time of night. Sometimes the cats squall and it's hard to sleep," she returned as the sheriff's spotlight hit Alek, also sitting on his front porch.

"Petrovna, how's my feature article coming—you know, the one about me?"

"It's done. Who won the game?"

There was only going to be one winner in the Alek-Elspeth match and that was her.

"Had to leave it early," the sheriff called. "Some teenage boys with too much beer in them decided to face down Apache, that old buffalo. They made it up a tree, where he's got them pinned. I'm going back there to check that no one gets hurt. If I have my way, they're staying in that tree until their parents collect them in the morning. I'll have someone call you on Monday. My boy is a top player in the town league, you know. We won big time. They need a shortstop. Maybe you could try out."

"Maybe I could. I'll be waiting for a report on the game."

"Maybe you could help me out next time I need a deputy quick. The Tallchiefs usually help out. Duncan's got a real name for it. I hear your dad is a sheriff."

"He's retired and growing orchids. I'll be there if you need me."

The spotlight swung back to Elspeth. "Caught Calum naked out on his porch again. He was picking a bouquet. Looked guilty as hell when I spotlighted him. Had to pull Lacey off Birk. Seems he didn't like what she said to Chelsey Lang, and now the almost-engagement looks shaky. Guess I'll be going then. Uh…Elspeth, it's a couples team. What do you say about trying out, too? You're in shape…I saw that today. Nobody could ever ride like you, except your mother. Something to see, all right.''

"I'll think about it," Elspeth lied, then she took her glass into the house to answer the telephone.

Fiona went right to the reason for her call. "What happened today? I called Calum. Uh…I'm in a bit of trouble here in Wisconsin and needed some…uh…advice. He's helping me."

"What kind of trouble?" Elspeth smiled; Calum had left a message on her machine. Fiona had pushed an attorney's nerd-boy son into newly poured concrete and sat on him— with only his head above the surface—until it hardened. Nerd-boy didn't like the handcuffs he'd been tricked into wearing, or the concrete overcoat. At twenty-nine, Fiona was moving more quickly now, and Elspeth sensed that her sister had almost finished her wandering.

Fiona explained curtly, then switched to Elspeth's life. "This guy Petrovna, Talia's brother. He's tough, Elspeth. I met a journalist friend of his, who told me a lot about him. He's been there, done that. I really wouldn't…mess with him if I were you, Elspeth. He's not your type. I hear he has Una's shawl. If I were there, I'd get it back for you. Calum thinks that earring Alek is sporting is Mom's from LaBelle. I don't care what Duncan says, I think I should come home and rescue you. You're too sweet, Elspeth. Too elegant to deal with a guy like that. He's nothing like Talia at all. There's absolutely no reason for him to be in Amen Flats, and I don't believe that newspaper malarkey for a minute. There's our family honor at stake, you know."

Because Elspeth had had enough of other people in her life for one day, she cut Fiona's advice short. "Yes, why don't you come home? Joel Johnson asked about you the other day. He misses you. Says Amen Flats is dull without you. Micah, Steele and Taggart said they hoped you'd never come home—but they were very nice about it."

"Those nerds. You know how I—"

Elspeth smiled and lifted her glass in a toast to herself. "Don't worry about me, Fiona. Or Una's shawl and Mom's earring. Just come home when you can. Megan is growing fast, and Birk is teaching her to say he's her favorite uncle. Duncan is happy. Talia is blooming and driving Calum nuts."

"I like that. Calum never lets anything get to him. It's fun to see Talia broadside him. They were so beautiful when they got married in December." The silence at the other end of the line said that Fiona did miss Amen Flats despite all her declarations of never coming back to wither away in a boring dirt town.

"I went to see the folks today." Elspeth ignored the stab of pain.

"I hope you took a bouquet of bluebells. They were Mom's favorite."

"I did. I love you, Fiona."

"I love you, Elspeth."

"Aye," they said together, and hung up slowly, without saying goodbye.

Birk's pickup skidded to a stop outside, and she watched him stalk up the walkway. She met him on the porch. He wasn't mulling over Chelsey in Elspeth's house or spending the night on her couch. She wasn't baking his favorite bread in the morning to soothe him. Tonight she had another agenda and a date she was determined to keep.

Birk nodded to Alek, who nodded back and said, "Nice night."

"Depends." Birk plopped down on Elspeth's front steps and slammed his Stetson against his hand. "Man. For two cents, I'd take Lacey over my knee and paddle her."

"The last time you tried that, you lost. You're a lot slower than she is. She went right over the top of you."

Birk glared at her. "She knew that branch wouldn't hold

me. You know what she told Chel? Never mind. You'd just laugh. I'm not in the mood for advice tonight.'' He frowned at her. ''Hey. Do I smell Chablis or a wine cooler? You?'' he asked, frowning at her.

''Me. I'm not giving away advice tonight or making you a snack after my kitchen is all clean, and I'm not cutting your hair. I think Chelsey has good sense. I like Lacey. Go away.''

''Uh-huh.'' His response said he knew more than she did. ''I'm headed home for a brew and a bath. Take it easy, Elspeth the elegant.''

She loved her family, but tonight she wanted them off her front porch and off her telephone. Birk's pickup sailed out into the night, and Elspeth glanced at Alek. He hadn't moved, his bare feet still braced up on his porch.

''Nice night,'' he said again, and stood.

His stretch caused Elspeth's mouth to dry. The porch light caught the powerful sweep of his shoulders, glanced off the ridges of his stomach and highlighted his thighs. She realized she was straightening to see more of him and closed her mouth abruptly. After Alek entered his house, the porch light clicked off, leaving her alone with her thoughts.

Elspeth watched moths circle the streetlight. First of all, Alek had a shawl she wanted and an earring that was also her inheritance. She shook her head because it was getting a bit light and concentrated on Una's legend.

When the Marrying Moon is high, a scarred warrior will rise from the mists to claim his lady huntress. He will wrap her in the shawl and carry her to the Bridal Tepee and his heart. Their song will last longer than the stars....

* * *

Alek glanced at the clock in his living room. At two o'clock in the morning, he sat in Mrs. Mulveney's old rocking chair, his jeans unsnapped at the waistband, and waited. From the look in Elspeth Tallchief's steely eyes as she'd ridden into town, she'd decided to reclaim what was hers.

He tried to give her the shawl, and now she'd have to take it...and him, if his luck held.

Jeremy was lucky Elspeth had left his sports car when she did. Jeremy wasn't the real problem, and Alek curled that comfort around him. Jeremy had simply intruded on a very private battle, one that Alek intended to win.

Elspeth's endless legs in a short, hot, red number had lodged an uncomfortable hardness low in Alek's body. If making love to Elspeth happened a second night, he didn't intend to wake up to the entire Tallchief clan and end up in kilts and feathers.

Like the summer thunderstorm brewing on the mountains, Alek sensed that Elspeth would make her move tonight—if Alaina's visit hadn't put her off. Somehow he doubted that anything could put Elspeth off from what she wanted. Alek hoped she wanted him.

Outside, the wind whipped at the rosebushes he had planted in the front, and upstairs he heard the first creak. Alek smiled; he hadn't expected Elspeth to use the tree route. He rubbed his earring, listened to her progress across his new roof, and then a board in his bedroom creaked.

Alek bent to pick up the blanket roll and the picnic basket he'd prepared. Then he slipped out of his house into the night.

Ten

Elspeth pulled her van into what used to be the Kostyas'
driveway; she parked next to Alek's pickup. She placed her
hand on his hood, which was still warm.

Moonlight filtered through the old oaks sheltering the
house. Out on the mountain hillside, sheep seemed to float
over a hill. Cattle grazed in the fields, and Yakov and Yuri,
the Kostya mules, looked at her from the corral. A white-
eyed sheepdog ran from the sheep to her. "Hello, Fadey."

Fadey panted, accepted her ruffling of his black-and-
white pelt, then bounded back to his sheep. Protective of
the Kostyas, Fadey wasn't a dog to give his affections
lightly or to trust trespassers on his property. The dog knew
Alek well to have let him pass. So Alek had been coming
here, making friends with the Kostyas, had he?

Elspeth crushed Alek's note in her hand. She'd found it
beneath a rose, lying upon his cot. "The shawl isn't here,"
he'd written in that bold script that few could read. Nothing
could keep her from Una's shawl tonight, nor from Alek.

After a stop at the newspaper office, a call to Talia and Duncan, another sip or two of wine, Elspeth knew that Alek Petrovna had barricaded himself in the Kostya farm place.

Only Alek would know that she wanted this homestead desperately and he'd plucked it from her. Though she loved her house, she'd dreamed of having this farm, of tending the sheep and milking her cows. She'd dreamed of placing her mother's things amid new ones. She'd thought to make the Kostyas an offer, but she'd been…tied up with life. She phrased the thought carefully. She hadn't taken the time, and now Alek had scooped a dream away from her.

She bent to pet Sophy, the barn cat winding around her feet, and studied the darkened two-story house with the opened front door. The Kostyas didn't trust electricity, and a lamp glowed within the old house, spreading a square of gold upon the front porch.

Elspeth ripped off the note pinned to the front door: "Make sure you shut the front door and blow out the lamp. Sorry I missed you."

"Aye. You'll be sorry, Petrovna." Elspeth went back to her van, retrieved a flashlight and her tartan plaid—if he played games in the mountains, she'd need the warmth. She quickly braided her hair into a single rope, then began looking for signs of Alek's passing. His boot prints were too big to miss, tromping through a newly plowed field, headed straight to a glade near a stream.

The man couldn't grow anything but roses. How did he expect to take care of a farm? As her father had taught her, Elspeth turned off the flashlight and let the moon guide her, noting a bent stalk, a freshly broken twig on the path to where her mother and she had often gathered sumac berries, goldenrod, wild rose hips and blue lupine flowers for dye.

She hadn't tracked in years, since before— Elspeth pushed that time away, on her way to run down Alek.

Elspeth entered the shadows of the pines, slipping

through them to watch the bubbling stream. She reached up to pull a black, curling hair drifting from a pine cone; she lifted it to the moonlight. ''You need a haircut, Petrovna.''

Higher on the mountain, an owl shot high into the sky. Elspeth bent to trace a boot track and another, then stood and straightened, drawing the tartan around her. Alek was headed to the meadow that she'd just passed the day before. From the distance of his footprints and the depth, he was loping up a mountain.

''You'll have to run faster than that to keep ahead of me, Petrovna,'' she muttered, inhaling the clean mountain air. Nothing could keep her from running Alek into the ground.

Alek wasn't an easy man, but he didn't have to make the catching so hard, Elspeth thought, pressing her hand to her side and panting. Every muscle ached, including some she didn't know she had, until Alek pushed her over the edge. He liked edges, did he? She intended to give him plenty of them.

She moved quickly over rocks and fallen logs, tracing his path. Every muscle ached, her head throbbed and Alek had Una's shawl. She stepped into the meadow, panting, sweaty and dragging herself every step. *She'd caught him!* Elspeth paused at the edge of the meadow, the light of predawn shimmering in the dewy flower field between them.

He'd been waiting, praying she'd be safe.

His heart lurched just looking at her cross the mountain daisies almost reaching her bare thighs. Did she come for the shawl, neatly folded and tucked in the basket? Panic skidded up his back and coiled low in his gut. He wanted her to want him more than anything she'd ever desired in her lifetime.

Elspeth took her time in coming to him, and with each step Alek forced himself to breathe. Almost black, her eyes locked with his, the dim light catching her high cheek-bones, glistening in the length of her blue-black hair. He saw her take in his bare chest, the scars on it, the hair arrowing low to his jeans. Alek placed his hands in his back pockets, afraid that he would touch too soon when he wanted her to come to him. To love him. To hold him and let him love her. He'd settle for half a love—his for her—and yet knew that Elspeth would have nothing so easy.

On her way to him, through that sea of daisies, Elspeth was proud and ready to fight. He'd linger on the sight all the days of his life. The tops of her bare thighs glistened with dew; Alek sucked in air and remembered the strong feel of them beneath his touch, wrapped around him. He waited for her to speak, to make the first move.

She slanted a glance up at him, not making it easy. "You have the shawl."

"It's yours. Take it." Would he ever forget the look of her, a huntress on the prowl, ready to take him down? He clung to the hope that maybe, just maybe, she wanted him more than the legendary shawl.

She circled him slowly, dragging her fingertip around his waistband until she stood in front of him. Her fingertip reached to touch his scarred lip lightly. "Where did you get this?"

He caught the scent of her, one he'd remember until eternity. "Minding an orphan, stuck in the middle of no-man's-land and scared as hell. I was running, carrying Danny, and went down in shrapnel. Danny made it out without a scratch. I had a stitch or two."

In another minute, he'd be dragging her to him. He glanced at her breasts and wished he hadn't; her shirt was damp, clinging to her and showing every curve. Her nipples peaked against the light cloth, and Alek's mouth dried. He strained to keep his mind on her questions, but his body was strained, as well.

"Did you adopt him?"

Whatever roamed in Elspeth's sea-gray eyes told him that she would choose what happened between them. He kissed her roaming fingertip. "He's enjoying a family here in the States, adopted and safe."

"How did you break this?" She touched his nose.

"Back in Texas and again in Germany."

Elspeth touched the scars on his neck and cheek. Alek shuddered just once; it wasn't easy feeling like a Christmas package about to be opened and inspected. "Do my scars bother you?" he asked hoarsely, surprising himself.

"I like texture," she murmured, tracing the smooth old scars along his cheek and throat.

He snorted at that. "Texture. Now, that's a name for it."

"Interesting texture," she corrected, and his heart went still, waiting.

Her fingertips drifted over his bare chest lightly, circling each nipple. Her feather-light touch roamed to his shoulder, skimmed his back and trailed down his spine as she moved around him, giving him nothing but her heat and the maddening scent of her body. Her finger trailed over his wrists, touched his palms, locked to his pockets. He shuddered as her lips touched his back, soothing an old scar caused by shimmying under a wire barricade.

"You made me come looking for you, Alek. I know the look of a planted trail, and that's exactly what you did, breaking branches as you went, swaggering heavy enough to plant a good print. You should know, the bear and cougar on Tallchief Mountain aren't exactly friendly."

"I passed some of the wildlife on my way up here. They seemed friendly enough." He'd worried, guilt biting him until minutes seemed like hours. He'd timed the moment her van arrived at the Kostyas' former farm and the time it took her to cross the meadow. He'd traced her progress with his binoculars. She was good, stopping to mark his passing, trained by her father. The Tallchiefs should have let her go with them, tracking on the mountain that night her parents were killed. Elspeth had been put in her place, and Alek wanted to give some of that back. He knew how he'd feel if he were left behind. She'd not been allowed to go with them that night, but tonight she'd prove to herself that she could. Yet if anything had happened to her, he'd—

He arched against the stroke of her lips on his back. He needed to breathe—he'd stopped when she began touching him. He sucked in air, filled with her scent.

She stood on tiptoe, leaning against him, her lips against the corner of his mouth. Her hands smoothed up to his neck and locked around him, fingers playing in his hair.

He wouldn't grab her, drag her closer yet to him. Then he did, hands splayed across her long back. "Come here, sweetheart," he whispered against her lips, and caught the taste of wine and woman and desire.

"I'm here." Elspeth bit his lip, kissed a path to his earlobe, and her tongue toyed with his earring. "You couldn't make this easy, could you?"

"And have that family of yours arriving on our doorsteps?" he scoffed. He breathed deeply, savoring the twin press of her breasts against him. "I've got plans that don't include them."

She smiled against the curve of his throat, her fingers digging slightly into his shoulder. "Tell me."

First I'll tell you I love you and watch that sink in. Then, because you'll look so flustered, I'll damn myself and go all the way, telling you all my dreams. Instead, Alek bent to scoop her bottom in his hands, dragging her body upward. She locked her legs around his hips, her arms looped around his shoulders as he hoped she would.

"If we go down, you land first," she whispered. "I didn't come all this way to be crushed."

"I'm hoping you came for just that reason." Alek tossed away his smile. "Trust me, Elspeth." *Trust me with your love, trust me to love you.*

He kissed her in the faint light, told her he loved her with his lips. She gave him back heat, hunger and what he needed. Alek slanted a look down at her wicked smile. She filled him—quite simply filled him with pleasure just looking at her. He felt tipsy on pride, daft on dreams and full of himself. "So you tracked me, did you?"

"Did you doubt that I could?"

Pride was there in her voice, and despite the fears shrouding him, Alek grinned.

"Arrogant, intellectual gypsy meathead." But she locked her hands to his cheeks and fused her lips to his. It was a rough taking, hunger dancing on her tongue and sucking, tempting his desire until he trembled and went weak kneed. He felt like a chocolate to be savored before the having.

The having. "I love it when you talk dirty, Elspeth-mine. You keep doing that, and we'll go down. Did you come for the shawl?" he asked roughly when he could drag his lips from hers.

Would her pride let her say the words that he needed? Would she admit she needed his body, if not his love? He saved her pride by taking another kiss and lowering her to the blanket he'd prepared.

He spread her hair upon the old quilt, one stitched by loving hands and one in which children had slept, lovers had talked intimately. The shadows had them now, dawn rising on the rugged crest of the mountains.

Then Elspeth lifted against him, her hands gripped his hair, her mouth hot on his. Her hips moved restlessly against his sweeping hand. "Hurry, Alek. I can't wait."

"Not this time, love," he managed to say, and wondered where he got the strength. His pride barely in control, Alek needed some sign she cared, that there might be a chance she'd take him to her heart. He smiled grimly, quickly, mocking his uncertainty. He needed a measure more to salve his pride. He smoothed the soft line of her stomach and lower, the excitement racing in him, battling with the punishing stab of desire.

"I came for you," she whispered against his mouth, setting flame to the tinder burning in him.

"Did you?" he had time to whisper before dragging her to him.

Her hands flew between them, touching him, igniting him. She gasped as she pushed away from him and quickly shed her clothing. Alek groaned, shucking his jeans and cursing when they lodged at his ankles, halted by his boots. Her hands flew to touch him, to cradle the softness gently and stroke him until he groaned outright. They stared at each other, panting, dragging air into their lungs, then Alek managed to drag off his boots and kick away his jeans. He bent to take her breasts, to cherish them.

"Alek," she cried out wildly, locking his head to her.

He touched her intimately, felt her pouring into his hand, waiting for him, gasping. Alek jolted when she touched him again, this time with possession, dragging him back to her, over her.

He'd go blind, locked in the pulse of her, lodged deeply as they rolled from one edge of the blanket to the other. Elspeth cried out, her hips lifting quickly to him, her arms and legs gripping him to her.

Alek lost himself in the scent of her hair, in her body taking his, the drag of her breasts against his chest, nipples taut. He suckled hard, surging deeper into her, so deep he lost himself and gave himself to her. Poised in the heat, skins aflame, bodies locked, Elspeth pried his head from her breasts and forced him to look down at her face.

Elspeth was flushed, hot, ripe, succulent...sweet, tender...necessary Elspeth.

"Say my name, Alek Petrovna. Say it," she demanded unevenly, her body rippling beneath his, quivering with the effort of holding the heated flight away, until she got her due.

He tried to focus, his arms trembling with the effort of giving her what she wanted…what did she want? If she wanted the world, he'd give it to her. "Elspeth. Elspeth. Elspeth. Love…my love."

She clenched him with her legs, claiming him, her hands wrapped in his hair, her breasts shining damp and peaked in the sunrise. Alek allowed himself a quick look downward, to her stomach quivering against him, to the pulse of her straining against him. Then there was no time for thinking, for taking images into his mind, for dissecting the whys and the whats. Passion came curling out of him, squeezing him, and still he kept hold of Elspeth, caught the dimming of her eyes as she loosed her desire, caught it, held him, their bodies, heartbeats raging, rushing as one.

Alek cried out her name, pledged himself to her and poured himself into her.

The rippling constrictions had already begun deep within her, and they went flying into the dawn, pitting their strength into the ultimate release. He quite simply shattered, giving her everything. He watched, fascinated, as she took pleasure into herself, her eyes bright with it, riveting him, until his eyes closed in his own pleasure.

When Alek could force his eyes to focus, to see Elspeth drift lightly back to him, to go wonderfully, beautifully limp and damp against him. She managed a weak kiss when he offered it, allowed herself to be caught close and fast. Alek listened to the beating of their hearts slow. "Elspeth," he whispered against her damp brow, and smoothed the curve of her hip, keeping her near, their bodies joined.

"You watched." Her voice dragged like velvet on him, warm and rich with lovemaking.

"You were beautiful." Again, another treasure to tuck in his memories when they were old and rocking their great-great-grandchildren on the front porch.

"You didn't swoon," she stated slowly in a tone that made him grin. Elspeth Tallchief was a very satisfied woman. "My brothers bet each other that you wouldn't swoon with my kiss. I wanted a really good swoon."

"I'll try when I can see again," Alek promised with a kiss. "Talia told me about the famed, mind-blowing Tallchief kiss. I'd say you've got it."

She grinned up at him. "Just the kiss?"

His hand skimmed appreciatively down her hip, squeezed her softness. He wouldn't give her what she wanted; she'd have to take it from him. "You're a fast learner. What if I were delicate or sensitive and you came at me like that? Why, I'd be shocked."

The lift of her eyebrow mocked him. Her hand flopped from his shoulder and slowly, slowly slid to his ear. "You're wearing my mark, Petrovna. Remember that. You said Elspeth."

"Elspeth-mine." There were rules to this game; he was no easy lover, nor one to walk away. "I'm sorry about the first time."

She traced the earring thoughtfully. "I understand now what happened to you. You're a passionate man, Alek. Not one to give himself lightly. When we met, you were hovering between two worlds."

"Something like that. They got tangled at the wrong time, and I hurt you."

"Now that we've got that straight…" She smiled and skimmed her hand downward until he sucked in air. She touched him just at the spot of their joining, and Alek surged, desire renewed. Elspeth lifted, braced her elbow across his chest and touched him again, smiling enchantingly down at him.

He toyed with her hair, fragrant upon him. "Be careful, little girl."

She laughed at that, startling him. She bent to flick her tongue over his nipple, and Alek caught her chin, brought her curved lips to his and whispered, "Elspeth. Elspeth. Elspeth. Have I told you that I love you?"

She tensed against him, and he held her tight, lodged deep in her body, their passion humming gently, ready to ignite or to die. Her eyes flickered, wary, her fingers digging in his shoulder. "You don't have to say that, Alek. It isn't necessary."

He took her mouth, dragging her against him, fighting for his dreams. "But it is. I'll probably pay dearly for saying it, for loving you, because when it comes right down to it, Elspeth Tallchief, you are a greedy, greedy, savage woman. I didn't stand a chance."

He let her chew on that tidbit and held himself still when he wanted to make love with her.

She toyed with his earring and shot him a challenging look. "You're saying that I enticed you. That I gave you little choice but to make love with me. Here. Now."

He nodded. "Little choice. You've run me down. There was little I could do but let you have me after all your effort."

"Petrovna, you're half the size of a house. Don't tell me I've winded you." She grinned, teasing him. The sight dazzled him; he fell into it, wallowed in his sheer joy.

"Not quite," he said, satisfied that she wasn't denying him. Or that something more than desire could be moving through them. Then, just to keep the balance right and in his favor, he began loving her all over again.

In the midst of the daisies, Alek stood, sunlight flowing over his bare shoulders and making Elspeth catch her breath as it spread across his chest. She'd awakened without him, groggy from lack of sleep and high on the lovemaking that had crept into her very bones. She awoke craving Alek, moving her hand upon the empty, wrinkled blanket, awoke to Una's shawl covering her.

She'd panicked, icy with fear. Could she trust herself? While Alek seemed to know exactly what he wanted and was ready to declare his love, she moved at a slower pace, needing to sift through her emotions.

If she gave herself too freely and gave too much because Alek pushed her, would she ever be certain that the choice was really hers? There was the heaven of the past hours— lying with Alek, challenging him, meeting his passion and her own—and then there was fear that her hurried decision could harm them both. At dawn, she'd trusted what moved between them. But would it last when put to the test? He'd walked away before—

In a frenzy, Elspeth tossed away the shawl. She'd dressed hurriedly, ready to run Alek into the ground if needed, and then to give him the lesson of his life. She surged out of their bed, ready to hunt, and then she saw him picking flowers, and her knees went weak.

Of course, he'd had her twice the night before she tracked him to the mountain and twice more as dawn became morning. No wonder her thighs quivered and her knees almost buckled. No wonder her heart raced at the sight of him. *I love you....*

Love had happened to her brothers and would come to Fiona when the time was right. The Tallchiefs were bred for loving families. But she'd never imagined Alek loving her. Elspeth fought for the visions that would come to comfort her, and all she could see was Alek standing in the morning sun, holding a bouquet of wildflowers out to her. She blinked, waiting for an image to tell her what to do. She felt the thumping of her heart, racing against her breast, the softness of her body where Alek had been and a light, flowery, lacy sense that she was a woman, all woman, and desired.

Alek looked as if he'd been rumpled, steamed, and had during the night. The look suited him, she decided.

As if to test her mood, Alek held out the bouquet of wildflowers shimmering with morning dew. "Good morning, Elspeth-love. You're thinking hard enough to scare me."

"You could use a good dose of scare." What was he doing? *Trust me...I love you.*

Then Alek smiled, a whimsical little smile as if he were wishing something from her, and her fears went tumbling into the wildflowers. There he was, everything she wanted. Cocky, irrational at times, grumbling, laughing, passionate—a huge, tender, delectable morsel. Her heart sailed out of her, desire slamming into her, tightening her throat, dancing along her skin. Elspeth began to run toward him. Her T-shirt landed in a patch of bluebells. She hopped on one foot, tugging off one moccasin, ran two steps and tugged off the other.

"You're on my land, Petrovna."

Who did he think he was to leave her alone in their bed, the scents of loving snaring her before she woke fully? Oh, he'd have to pay for that one, she decided. She unzipped her shorts on the run and shimmied out of them.

The sunlight glinted off his teeth, this huge bear of a man she'd come to claim.

"Pay for being on your land, am I?" He stood there holding his bouquet and grinning like a boy who'd just won the prize.

She flew across the meadow. She wanted to plunder and take; it was her right, she'd run him down.

"You know you are. You know exactly where you are and what happened here. You've researched the Tallchief family. You knew everything." Elspeth leapt upon him, and Alek grunted with the impact and caught her close as he reeled backward. They went down in the field of flowers.

She pinned him beneath her. She straddled him as she had before and knew that he'd let her take him down. She sat on him, her palms on his chest, and studied him, this new Alek that she'd captured.

"You're full of yourself, Tallchief. What are the rules on this one?" Alek asked as he tucked a bluebell into her bra.

"You'll have to pay the price for being on my land and for stealing the Kostya place from under me." She tugged a whorl of hair on his chest. "And that awful contract."

He brushed the hair from her cheek, his expression tender. "I want a long-term contract with you. One that says you'll be waking up beside me every morning." *Elspeth...I love you.*

Unable to dance along that dangerous dream, Elspeth slid back into reality. "You really shouldn't have bought the Kostya place, Alek. I wanted it."

She was glad he let her change direction.

"It looked like home to me. You can bring me a blueberry pie or come milk the cows—" He sucked in his breath as her fingers went to his jeans snap. The angle of his jaw hardened. "Watch that."

Too bad. She had her own agenda. He'd stepped over the enticing line and looked as necessary as the wildflowers strewed across his chest.

Elspeth ripped away her lacy bra; she arched and stretched and looked down to see what she wanted—the heavy hunger shadowing Alek's face, the taut, carved edge of his cheekbone and firm dip of his mouth as he fought for control.

She skimmed the flat of her hand down his chest, following the V of hair lower, until Alek's hand gripped her wrist, staying her. "Take it easy, Elspeth-mine. I'm feeling sensitive this morning."

She fell upon him, fused her mouth to his and gasped as his arms came around her, hard—just the way she wanted. She wanted Alek to hold her as if he'd never let her go.

He rolled her over, unzipped his jeans and sprawled heavily upon her.

She was waiting, eager, locking her fingers to his hair as she dived into the kiss, the hunger of his mouth, feeding upon it, nipping his lip.

Alek groaned unevenly, tore away the scrap of lace separating them—she didn't give him a chance to pause to reconsider. Elspeth reached to glove him, to bring him to her.

Later, when her bones had melted from their passion, Alek smoothed her body, gentling the aftershocks of their lovemaking. "Elspeth-mine, you're seriously denting my ego. I've just made love for the first time with my boots on and my jeans around my ankles. To pay for that infraction, you'll have to go out with me in my Chevy. We can neck—"

She tensed, rummaged for enough strength to lift herself. "You mean a date, Petrovna?"

"With my best girl. I'll pick you up. We'll cruise Main Street, stop at the drive-in for burgers and shakes, cruise some more and then neck ourselves blind."

They were lying in the meadow, the morning sun bright overhead, and at any minute all of her brothers could appear on horseback.

"Just neck?" She grinned before his hand cupped her breast and his tongue laved the hardened tip. She skimmed down to taste his nipple.

After a quick lurch of his body and a groan, Alek reached to bring her lips to his. "You're getting really good at this, Elspeth."

Eleven

"My Russian is definitely shaky, but Alek studied it and he's always correcting me. Alek never speaks Russian to you?" Talia asked, her tone incredulous. Seated at the same table, Lacey and Sybil looked at Elspeth, waiting for her answer.

"Not to any of us," Sybil offered. "He's a complex man."

"Hmm. No more than the Tallchiefs." Talia tapped her fingers on the table. "Let me think about this."

At Maddy's Hot Spot piano, Patty Jo Black sang a husky, sensual rhythm-and-blues number after a day of canning green beans. A sign hung over the door on Tuesday night—No Husbands Allowed Or Males Of Any Kind. No Boring Smart-Children Stories Allowed. Maddy's luscious-nude paintings had been properly covered by sheets. Maddy had placed paper doilies beneath the tables' bottles of plastic roses, some with price tags dangling in the breeze from the air-conditioning.

Maddy buzzed by with a tray of iced-lemonade glasses. He sidestepped Miss Loretta Mulveney of the pioneer Mulveneys and owner of Amen Flats's only bookstore. Miss Loretta had wanted Maddy for years, since his first wife left him, but he was wary of aggressive women. He jumped; lemonade glasses clinked as Miss Loretta sneaked him an appreciative pinch on his backside. She batted her lashes at him and he flushed. A beefy ex-football player, Maddy pirouetted away from Loretta on one toe like a ballet dancer. To his credit, he never lost one glass on his tray. He plowed righteously forward to the protection of his bar. Miss Loretta picked up her lemonade and sashayed to him, decked out in a gauzy new number that looked like a drifting tropical bouquet.

At seven months into her pregnancy, Talia smoothed the small ball of her stomach in the short flirty skirt. She plopped her practical flats—Calum had studied the construction of shoes and wooed her into wearing them—on another chair and rummaged through her thoughts. "I love my Hessian boots. Love tromping in them. Calum said if I'd wear these double uglies now, he'd wear skintight leather pants after the baby came—just while I was teaching him Petrovna family dances. Hmm...Alek never speaks Russian when he's really, really wanting to make a point to someone who doesn't understand it."

Talia's long blond hair flew out as she turned to Elspeth, one finger raised. "He wants the Tallchiefs to see him coming. He's being very careful with the Tallchiefs, so they understand his exact motives and feelings for you, Elspeth. He wants to make certain that you do not misunderstand anything that he is intending to do, or anything about his feelings. Trust me, of all the Petrovnas, he can be the most...secretive—an element that isn't typical of any of us. Devious, yes. Secretive, no. I called Mother and told her that Alek had been a bad boy—that he wanted you and that he engineered that whole Denver contract business to be alone with you. I told her that he'd found Una's shawl and that he wouldn't let you have it. She's incensed. I almost feel sorry for him when my parents come...they'll be here before the baby is born.''

Elspeth thought of Alek, and her heart shifted into high gear. She remembered their lovemaking all down the mountain and in the old Kostya place throughout the night. He had taken exquisite care arranging her upon the old bed in the guest room, smoothing her hair across the old pillow decorated with embroidered flowers. Elspeth could sense when he wanted her, desire lurching within her, only to find his eyes dark and hungry. She'd cut his hair, trimmed the heavy, curling mane and fussed with it until she was pleased and he'd tugged her upon his lap. Sunday loving, he'd called her once, tickling her as they went down in the old barn filled with cows they'd just milked.

"Do you want the shawl?" he'd asked again, poised above her. Somehow she'd managed the truth, dying for him.

"No, I want you, Petrovna."

She'd learned that Alek Petrovna's law—always finish what you start—also referred to lovemaking. He had wonderful stories of other lands, outrageous ones about his family. The Petrovnas could ignite at any minute, shouting and throwing up their hands. Their mother, Serene, had ancestors that dated back in Texas history to the Alamo. She fought for what she believed in, a tiny, calm woman devoted to her family, all of whom towered over her. Alek Petrovna, Sr., a tough, raw-boned Texan, melted when he looked at her.

But Elspeth had had her measure, too, listening to the humming of his desire, the way he said her name. Her Alek. *I love you.* The words rang softly in her heart. Could she trust herself? Could she trust him?

They had met just exactly five years ago this month; she'd had her life torn from her, and now he was giving it back. *I love you.*

There were quiet times, too. Like the moment Alek came up behind her, holding her in his arms as they overlooked the Kostya fields. It was good standing with him, the late-June breeze playing with her hair and Alek, solid and warm at her back.

He'd left her at her doorstep on Monday morning with a mind-stopping kiss and gently pushed her inside her door. She'd gone to sleep well-loved, aching, exhausted, smoothing her mother's quilt and with the taste of that kiss and the look in his eyes.

She had drifted through Monday in a golden fog. She'd thought about surprising Alek, and a quick glance proved he wasn't home. At six o'clock that evening, she'd grinned at the light rap on her back door, and then Alek swept her out to his Chevy, burgers at the drive-in, a cruise down Main Street and back again. Alek had kept her hand on his thigh, firmly locked in his fingers, which he had kissed and suckled intermittently. Necking in his back seat left the windows fogged, Elspeth breathless and Alek playful and full of himself...until he pushed her into her house, alone and yearning for him. Sometimes old-fashioned males just didn't cut it, Elspeth decided, and when you took Alek apart, he ranged right in the old-fashioned-male depot with her brothers.

Elspeth frowned slightly and traced the lip of her glass of white wine. His look—she couldn't mistake that closed-in, level look at her—suggested he'd made a promise and that he'd be moving quickly upon it. *I love you....*

She wouldn't be pushed.

I love you....

Why did he leave her breathless and aching at her door? What game was he up to now?

She didn't trust him; Alek had skimmed his hand down her shoulder, to her wrist, then to her hip and thigh as if promising to make good his need for a longer contract— as if he'd be coming for her and wanted her to know it.

She sensed that about Alek. That he was coming for her very quickly— Elspeth frowned. She'd take her time deciding what was right for her. After a lifetime of the Tallchief brothers, she wouldn't be pushed.

A concession—no, a loving—on Tallchief Mountain, at the farm, in the barn, on the meadow—the back of her van would never seem the same again—a concession was all she was making at the time.

Alek had that look. He'd made up his mind to it, locked his teeth into it, and he'd gnaw at it until he got his way.

Elspeth glanced at Sybil, who had been too quiet all evening. "Are you feeling all right?"

Sybil studied Elspeth. "You should know. You usually know when something is brewing with the Tallchiefs...when Calum brought Talia home the first time... when Duncan—"

Elspeth caught a quick image of Sybil, rounded and glowing. "You're pregnant!" Elspeth exclaimed, delighted.

"Yep. Again. Three months gone." She lifted her wineglass, filled with lemonade. "A small concession I've been making for three months, right here, every Tuesday night. Duncan knew immediately, almost as soon as when we—" She stopped and blushed. "When we..."

"But you like a glass of white wine—" Elspeth stared at Sybil, just realizing that she'd missed the entire event.

"Elle, old girl, you're losing it. Even I thought she was pregnant," Lacey crowed, propping her work boots up on the table. "When he wasn't worrying about you, Duncan wore this goofy grin—nobody grins goofier than the Tallchief males. Calum—you can't tell much about Calum these days—he's always grinning. That idiot Birk actually picked me up and kissed me. One of those lip-sucking, mind-blowing Tallchief kisses. The ones he uses on his harem. I dumped a gallon of paint on him, and he stood there, sputtering and grinning. 'Lacey, I think I'm going to be an uncle again. Don't I deserve it? Don't I just?'"

Lacey wiped her mouth as if wiping off his kiss. "Jeez, give those guys babies, and they turn into a pile of daisies."

"Don't look so shocked, Elspeth," Talia murmured with a grin. "I'd say you've been so…busy that your seer and shaman abilities have been shafted."

"A real demolition derby," Sybil added, her topaz eyes sparkling.

"Poleaxed." Talia's grin widened. "Didn't know what hit her."

Lacey smirked. "Yeah. Poleaxed. I'd say that suits her about now."

"Calum has another Tallchief cradle hidden away. Sybil has the original, but Tallchief made several others and sold them. Calum is so proud of himself that I couldn't bear to tell him I found it." Talia beamed at Elspeth. "You Tallchiefs are so easy. You've got all these dark storm clouds swirling around you, and you're pushovers."

Sybil gave her a long, cool look. "You're a Tallchief, Talia."

Talia smoothed her tummy. "Yeah. And happy of it."

"Calum found another cradle?" Elspeth shook her head to clear it. She remembered thinking that Calum would soon be finding another cradle.

"Has the Celtic circle and the Tallchief feather markings. It's beautiful. The guys are at the house now. They're probably glowing with how they've kept Calum's secret." Talia's eyes misted. "I love that guy."

"They didn't totally keep it," Sybil murmured, her eyes lighting.

"No! Duncan told you, didn't he?"

Sybil smoothed her coppery chignon and smiled. "Darling, what do you think I was after, the night I got pregnant?"

Elspeth stared at her splayed fingers, locked to Maddy's scarred table. She usually saw everything, images moving through her, and Alek had shattered those visions and replaced them with ones of him. "I think...I think I am going to have to be very careful."

"Very careful," Talia and Sybil and Lacey repeated too seriously, and then began laughing outright.

"Should I tell her?" Sybil gasped.

"Do it." Talia smoothed her tummy again. "It's all right, baby. Auntie Elspeth may scream a little, but—"

"What?" Elspeth demanded, not certain she wanted to know.

"Today at oh...say...eleven o'clock, one tired Alek Petrovna gifted Duncan Tallchief—your eldest brother and therefore the one acting in your father's stead—with two horses and a flock of prize sheep. It was only two horses and a few sheep, Elspeth. I'd think you'd be worth more. Yes, after a day on Tallchief Mountain and a night at the Kostyas' farm place, Alek was definitely floating."

When her mind started clicking again, Elspeth groaned, placed her arms on the table and sank her head down to them. "Do you know how it feels to have an entire town know everything?"

"Details, Syb," Lacey demanded, setting down her beer mug.

Talia grinned. "I knew it. Junior is just as old-fashioned as Pop. Mom said she sometimes felt that Dad was a steamroller once he'd got it in his mind that she was the one for him. Of course, she gave him the idea in the first place. The horse and sheep are a version of the Petrovna bridal price. Tallchiefs aren't the only one with traditions."

Elspeth allowed herself another groan. She should have understood Alek's look; she should have stopped him.

Talia's laughter rippled over the room. "Syb, it's your decision. Alek is merely following our family tradition and showing that he wants you and that he'll take good care of you and that he sets your value at a few sheep and two horses."

Sybil rubbed Elspeth's shoulders and continued, her voice humming with laughter. "It was all very formal. Duncan stood there, tall and formidable, his arms crossed over his chest. By the way, darling, Duncan and Calum and Birk were all watching your progress up the mountain Sunday morning. It was a regular spy mission with phones ringing, regular reports and binoculars. I believe the words 'She nabbed him,' were used. He said, 'Didn't have a chance with her on his trail.' Birk said something about he and Fiona being the last of the mavericks. He sounded as if he were mourning the passing of an era."

Elspeth rubbed her aching temples. "Sybil, I love my brothers. But I could kill them."

"Don't worry about Birk. He'll be picking up another marriage prospect next week. He'd be all duded up and hot to trot," Lacey stated. "Get on with it. I'm all ears."

"So back to the High Noon of yesterday. There Duncan was shooting bullets with each stare and Alek leading the horses while herding the sheep. They're lovely sheep, Duncan said—"

"Sybil…" Lacey urged impatiently.

Elspeth sat up and lifted one finger. Maddy swooshed to her with another glass of white wine.

"It was really lovely and formal. A male-bonding thing. There wasn't an ounce of giving in Duncan or in Alek. I could barely keep Megan quiet, and then she launched herself at Alek and he cuddled her. He stood, combat boots locked to the porch, all tall and hard and tough and determined male, and cuddled Meggie on his hip.''

Sybil took a sip of lemonade before continuing. ''Duncan was weakening by then, but he leveled questions like a gunslinger at showdown time, and Alek answered them carefully, exactly. One of them was quite exact—'She cut your hair?' Alek said you did and at last Duncan nodded and said, 'Aye.' Then he added a threat about what would happen if Alek broke your heart. By that time, I was crying. After that, they both went to chop wood, just swinging axes away as if they wanted to brawl and knew they'd better not. Wood flew everywhere. It looked like a lumberjack contest. I found Duncan later, alone in the barn. His eyes were wet, he was hugging one of the sheep and he said he thought he was developing allergies and that there was too much hay dust in the barn.''

''Ha! Allergies, my foot!'' Lacey exclaimed. ''He cried because his baby Elspeth was leaving his nest.''

Sybil arched a brow. ''Don't you ever say anything like that around him, Lacey. He's delicate and needs protection, but especially now. He's been having morning sickness.''

Elspeth managed to speak. ''I believe that Mr. Alek Petrovna has a lesson to learn. He should have discussed this with me first—what exactly did Alek want, Sybil?''

''Your hand in marriage. He wanted permission to court you, and sure enough there you were cruising in his Chevy last night.''

''You're absolutely right. He should have asked you to marry him first...didn't he?'' Talia clearly was not happy with her brother.

''He did not. He's pushy, Sybil. I haven't decided whether I like the man or not. At the moment, I do not believe I want anything to do with Alek. Other than to teach him a lesson.''

Sybil leveled a look at Elspeth. ''There's a big difference

between *love* and *like*. I always love Duncan, but sometimes I really don't like him.''

Lacey licked the beer foam off her upper lip. ''Birk dumped poor Chelsey Lang. I have no idea why. She's such a sweet, old-fashioned, homey-type girl, too. Looks fertile…massive mammaries and big hips, just like what you'd think a Tallchief would want—no offense, Syb…Talia. Yep, I'd have thought Birk would have wanted that one. Instead he dumped her. Men.''

Lacey's tone put the male species in a box with cockroaches. The four women shot Maddy a dark look that sent him scurrying toward Miss Loretta. When he realized how close he was to her proximity, he reeled back, knocked over two liquor bottles and caught them. He kept a wary eye on Loretta as he wiped his bar.

While Elspeth dealt with just how much Alek had invaded her life and embarrassed her, Alek tossed a beer to Duncan. Alek almost felt sorry for Duncan, a man called ''Mother'' by the law; he'd risked his life to rescue kidnapped children and now he felt he was losing his sister. With Emily baby-sitting Megan and doing her homework at Duncan's, the three brothers sprawled on Calum's candlelit porch, wrapped in the citronella scent. Olaf and Thorn lay in the front yard, watching the Tuesday-night traffic of one truck, two bicycles and three cars in the space of one hour.

Calum propped his boots beside the other three sets on the railing. ''I added the horses and the sheep to Elspeth's portion of Tallchief cattle.''

''I'll keep them until Elspeth decides what she's going to do with you, Alek. She knows Una's legend concerning the shawl. She'll tell you when she's ready, Alek,'' Duncan said.

Alek didn't want the legend coming to him from anyone

but Elspeth and when she was ready; a man had to have some pride. Whatever the Marrying Moon was to the legend, it was his right to know. It had been five years since he'd first heard Elspeth sigh the words, and he could wait a little longer.

"She's keeping her secrets to herself. You Tallchiefs are a secretive lot," Alek noted, toying with a baby rattle. It nettled him that the woman he loved, who he wanted to marry him and who had given herself to him several times, could hold him at a distance when she wanted. Elspeth could have collected the shawl at any time and walked away with it, yet she hadn't.

He ran his thumb over the cool, damp aluminum beer can. He didn't intend to fail Elspeth a third time. Scotland and the damned Denver undertaking had been pure stupidity.

"I think ladies' night at Maddy's should be outlawed." Birk cuddled a teddy bear while Duncan arranged the tiny plastic horses around the crib mobile he'd been assembling. "Uh-uh. Trouble."

Alek, Duncan, Calum and Birk looked down the tree-lined street, past Mrs. Monroe's yard of roses, past the teenagers smooching on the Joneses' porch swing, to the four women storming toward them.

"Aye. Trouble," Duncan and Calum stated together. Calum reached for Birk's teddy bear and the mobile and placed them inside the house. The men propped the backs of their chairs against the wall, rocking on them as they crossed their boots on the railing.

"Alek, did you check with Elspeth about courting her?" Duncan asked carefully. "Did you talk to her before you talked to me? Ask her to marry you *before* bringing those horses and the sheep to me?"

Alek watched Elspeth steam toward him, the streetlight outlining her taut, curved body; her hair flew out from her shoulders, rippling in her passing. Desire shot straight down to his loins and pounded there. "Haven't had time. Brad Klein got sick, and I stepped in at the paper. Went out to cover the new plant nursery outside of town and helped pull a calf from the Stevenson's guernsey. I meant to call, but my truck broke down four miles out of town. By the time I got home, Elspeth was already barricaded at Maddy's."

Calum, Birk and Duncan stared at Alek. "We owe you. That's an outraged female posse coming."

"They're after Alek," Calum said finally. "We'll have to keep you here if you try to run. We can't have them taking out your lack of manners on us."

"Save yourselves, sweethearts." Just looking at Elspeth caused Alek to suck in air, steadying his light head. She looked better than the last time he'd seen her—which was when she'd tried to drag him into her house the previous night, after hours of necking. "I'm a saint," he murmured, and damned his righteous idea that the next time they made love, he'd have Duncan's permission to ask her to marry him. "A real saint."

Birk guffawed at that, spewing out his last sip of beer.

Elspeth, dressed in an emerald green sweater and jeans, marched up the steps to the porch, followed by the other women. While Elspeth stood beside Alek's chair, hands on hips, staring down at him, Talia placed a hand on Calum's shoulder to stay him. Sybil did the same to Duncan, and Lacey placed the tip of a broom handle on Birk's chest.

Elspeth's lips opened and closed, fascinating Alek.

"Yes?" he invited in a drawl. He floundered, went dizzy at the sight of her outlined in the street lamps and flickering candlelight.

Duncan, Calum and Birk slashed him a dark look. All four women acted at once: Elspeth reached for a bag of potting soil, ripped it open and shook it over Alek. Talia poured beer over Calum's head, and Sybil did the same to Duncan's lap. Lacey swept her foot beneath the back legs of Birk's chair, and he went down cursing. Then Sybil reached for another bag of potting soil and shook it over Duncan's head; Talia took it from Sybil and shook it over Calum's and Lacey dribbled beer straight down into Birk's face.

Elspeth lifted a watering can. "What's in this, Talia?"

"Water. Plant nutrients. Do it." She stood back, dusting her hands as Elspeth quickly doused Alek and dribbled the rest over her brothers.

The women shook hands. "Good job, Elspeth."

Duncan blew a clump of potting soil from his hair and slid Alek a dark look. "You should have—"

Alek swiped away the mud and ran his hand up the back of Elspeth's taut leg to pat her bottom. "I know."

He wanted to pack her over his shoulder and run with her. She swatted at his hand and lifted her nose. "This debris stinks. I'm going back to Maddy's."

"Uh…honey, precious, Talia…don't you think you've had enough activity for tonight?" Calum tried a hopeful smile.

"This gives me an idea for a play. I'm going back to Maddy's to sketch it out on a napkin, big boy."

"Sybil, you're coming home with me," Duncan stated, struggling out of his chair.

Alek studied the shape of Elspeth's firmly pressed lips and went lightheaded as he remembered them prowling down his chest. "You're a fine-looking woman," he said, meaning it.

"Jeez, Junior. Your fangs are showing. You're drooling," Talia muttered. "How dumb can you be? You're in real deep manure here, boy."

Elspeth inhaled slowly, as if tethering her temper. "Someday, Petrovna, someone is going to knock you off that overstuffed ego and grind you into the ground. The next time you get an idea that you and my brothers will settle my life, I'd appreciate a little notice.''

He lifted his eyebrows. ''I believe I've served adequate notice that I'm interested.''

''Interested? You're on thin ice here, Petrovna.''

''Home, Sybil,'' Duncan insisted, trying to hold his own on the porch.

''Nope. I'm not,'' Sybil returned lightly, and placed a firm finger in the middle of his broad chest. ''See you in the morning.''

Duncan glared at Alek. ''He's an ill-manned oaf.''

Olaf bounded up the stairs, certain that his name had been mentioned. Thorn joined him to sip the beer wasted on the porch. Talia's kitten and puppy romped across Birk's flat stomach on their way to play with Olaf and Thorn. The sheriff came by, sopranos at full blast. ''Maddy wanted to know if you men are okay, and if you'd keep your women here.''

''Tell him we're on our way back,'' Elspeth called, looping her arm with Sybil's as they began to walk back to Maddy's.

''Well, hell,'' Alek muttered, surging to his feet. None of this was going the way he had planned.

''I wouldn't—'' Calum said behind him.

Alek began singing ''You Are My Sunshine'' loudly, strolling after the women with his hands in his back pockets.

Elspeth pivoted and leveled a finger at him. ''You're pushing me, Petrovna.''

''That I am, darlin'. That I am,'' he admitted, undaunted.

The sheriff cruised by and Alek motioned him over. He took the loudspeaker microphone from the sheriff and lifted it.

Panic rippled across Elspeth's pale face. "Alek, don't you dare—"

"Elspeth Tallchief, I've made mistakes, but I'll learn. I'm here to stay and I'm nuts about you," Alek broadcast to the people lining the streets. She'd have to learn about Petrovna capers, Alek decided and grinned. Petrovnas could be wild, excitable, unpredictable. He didn't intend to give his love anything but the real Alek. The one she'd made love her.

She began to mutter amid the other three women, who were laughing. Birk had rolled off the porch onto the lawn, holding his sides and laughing. Calum was loping toward Talia, and Duncan was walking down Main Street, sighted on Sybil and twirling his lasso. An expert at cowboy rope tricks, Duncan stepped into the rope's circle, hopped out again and back in. He looked at Alek, who nodded and took the rope, performing the trick.

Calum walked by with Talia snuggled in his arms, clearly on his way to a making-up event. Birk and Lacey glowered at each other, then both crossed their arms across their chests and looked away.

Faced with determined women, Duncan and Alek passed the rope back several times, each matching the other for tricks. Sybil cursed darkly. "He knows that Will Rogers stuff gets to me. I turn into putty when he does it."

Elspeth couldn't take any more. She marched up to Alek, grabbed the rope from his hands and tossed it into the bushes. "There. You're finished," she said, placing her hands on her waist.

Glorious, he thought. Wild and glorious. Soft and sweet, delectable...his lifetime love, because he'd never love another, she'd taken him too hard and too deep.

He caught her to him, bent her over his arm and fused his mouth to hers. She was caught by surprise, and her gasp went into Alek's mouth, followed by the flick of her tongue, tasting him. Then her hands streaked to his hair, keeping his lips on her hungry ones. "Ah, you're a passionate one, Elspeth-mine. And you love me. Admit it," Alek managed to say when he had to come up for air and took her lips again, this time lifting her feet off the ground.

When he set her toes back to earth again, when his heart was racing with need of more than a kiss from his love, when he decided he'd better leave her or he'd shock Amen Flats then and there, Alek released her. He held her arm as she balanced, eyes glazed, mouth juicy and ripe with his kisses and hair gleaming like satin under the streetlights.

Then he managed to stroll away, though his knees weren't too steady.

Elspeth's voice shot at him from the sheriff's loudspeaker, "Wait!"

Alek inhaled and stopped. She had her pride; he had his. She'd have to come to him this time. He turned slowly to see Elspeth sauntering down the street. Alek jammed his fingers into his back pockets. He placed his boot on the curb and waited. "She's going to destroy whatever I've got remaining in the way of pride," he muttered, meaning it.

Elspeth sauntered down the street, long legs outlined in the streetlight, her hair swaying at her hips. She stopped in front of him. "We don't have a thing in common, Petrovna."

Alek steeled himself, suddenly cold in the June night air. He stared down at her and didn't trust himself for one heartbeat. "You're what I want."

"Why?" There wasn't an ounce of yielding in her, and he respected that.

Why? Because he needed her as he needed air. Because his heart raced at the sight of her; his pulses kicked into high gear with just a scent of her. Because he saw her in his dreams and in his future. Because he'd be a shell of a man without her. "I'm here, Elspeth. I'm staying in Amen Flats. I'm dependable and I'll be here when you need me."

"You can't gather me up like you gather bits of other people's lives to you." She traced the scar on his lip with her fingertip. "I don't like being pushed and currently I'm more than embarrassed…I'm good and mad."

"You're afraid I'll leave you…that I'll hurt you again. I won't. You've lost your parents. Let me give you mine. We had something then and we have it now." So much for pride, thought Alek. With Elspeth, he had none. "It's in my nature to push. Waiting for you to make up your mind is damn hard."

"Poor Alek." She served him with a soft, taunting smile.

His temper flared at that. "I could show you poor Alek pretty quickly without this audience, darlin'."

"You talk big, Mr. Petrovna." There it was, that flashing, dangerous, enchanting grin. Then she placed her arms around his neck, leaned against him and gave him the famed Tallchief kiss. It challenged, pushed him to the limit, moved into his body, ignited it and traveled up to cloud his brain. Hormones, he tried to think, keep the hormones on a level— Oh, hell…he sank into the kiss, hands locked in his back pockets because he knew he'd grab her and make off with her to the closest private spot. From there, he couldn't trust himself at all.

Her assault left him in a boneless, drooling, hormonal heap. When he could think again, Alek congratulated himself for not taking his hands out of his pockets.

Twelve

"**P**ushing," Elspeth decided as she opened her kitchen door. Tiny heather plants quivered in the early-morning light, resting on the doorstep, right next to Alek's boot.

He didn't look sweet or in love. Shadows ran under his narrowed eyes; a muscle clenched in his cheek, and the taut skin covering his cheekbones gleamed in the sunlight. "You're a hard woman, Elspeth Tallchief," he shot at her, and slanted a hot look down her body. "These are for you."

Unable to resist, she swooped to run her hand across the tiny plants, each with a cluster of tiny purple-pink feathers. "They're lovely, Alek. You shouldn't have."

"I should have." He looked as if he'd like to take her mouth, devour it.

She'd been weaving without her bra, losing herself in her circular creation—smooth colors and textures beginning, blending, curving and ending as they had begun. She'd been thinking of Alek and sipping herbal tea to calm herself. Now with Alek in reaching distance, calm slipped out into the morning sunshine. He bent to kiss her hard and hungry, leaving her shaking, dragging air into her lungs.

"Heather won't grow here, Petrovna," she managed to yell at him over the sound of his revving pickup.

He grinned back at her. "I know. They're for your parents, up on the mountain. It reminded Una of Scotland, and maybe they will grow."

Elspeth washed her hands over her face and closed the door to lean against it. Life with Alek wouldn't be calm or sensible. She should just take the heather and run Alek down and give it back to him.

She eased open the door to the tiny plants. They probably would flower best in the full sunlight next to her parents' graves. She couldn't wait to plant them and hurried to dress.

"Not much time for weaving anymore, huh?" Duncan asked as he held Delight and handed the bag with the heather seedlings up to Elspeth.

"I'm managing," she returned, not ready to admit anything to Duncan. She'd been working on one design in which a man and a woman stood close together walking through the circle of natural colors. She'd woven an arrow straight through the piece, as if it carried them into the universe for all time. That was how she saw Una and Tall-chief, loving for all time.

Duncan angled a wary look down at her. "Still mad at me?"

She didn't answer, but held up her scarred thumb and smiled. How could she stay mad at Duncan when he wanted the best for her?

She spent the day on the mountain, planting heather. When she returned after dark she was too exhausted to do anything but fall into bed.

The next morning, she heard Alek's boots on her front porch. He looked tough, angry and worn. She wanted to hold him.

"That damn mountain is dangerous," he shot at her, his tone shredding any tenderness instantly.

Hold him? She wanted to throw something at him. "I go where I want."

His smile was pure evil promise. "Things will have to change, Elspeth darlin'. Anything could happen to you, and I don't like having my guts tied in knots. Next time you want to go, I'll ride with you. We'll make it a couple thing."

"Says who?" she shot back, still pretty proud of the way she'd planted a Tallchief kiss on him in the street.

His hot, hungry kiss told her exactly who and what and why. When she was well into floating, Alek inhaled, gripped her arms to set her back a pace from him and plopped a large pink-wrapped box in her trembling hands. "I'd say we have plenty in common. You're not a failure, Elspeth-mine, because of the baby. The failure was mine in not keeping and tending you. I won't make that mistake again."

She shivered and wondered how she kept from dragging him into her house and having him on the kitchen floor. No man had the right to look that edible in the morning or to understand one of her darkest secrets. Now she saw she'd hurt him, excluding him from sharing the planting of the heather, his gift to her.

I love you....

Elspeth didn't wait to examine her wavering emotions as she usually did. She simply reached out and grabbed his worn work shirt. She returned his hot, eager kiss and, gripping her present firmly, stepped back to slam the screen door between them.

Hot eyed, he stared at her through the mesh screen and

looked as if he could tear it from its hinges. "Well, what's it going to be? Will you come to my house for dinner tonight? Or are we going upstairs right now?"

"I don't know if I can love you, Alek Petrovna, Jr." Elspeth went in the direction of her thoughts and not his questions.

"It's your call. It doesn't stop how I feel, heart of my heart," he answered, head at an arrogant angle, not bending an inch. "Dinner at six."

How could he deliver such a sweet sentiment and look hard as nails? When he had gone, Elspeth plopped into her kitchen chair and opened the package. The antique Celtic broach, a circle with a pin through it, was perfect for her tartan. Una's shawl was neatly folded beneath it.

She wiped away the hot tears brimming to her lids and knew that if ever a man hunted for the soft spots in her heart, Alek was a deadly shot. The heather seedlings just might grow on the mountain that had reminded Una of Scotland; they were beautiful, perfect little flowers catching the sunlight.

Now Una's shawl shimmered beneath Elspeth's trembling fingers; the legend whispered through the shadows, circling her.

When the Marrying Moon is high, a scarred warrior will rise from the mists to claim his lady huntress. He will wrap her in the shawl and carry her to the Bridal Tepee and his heart. Their love will last longer than the stars....

Vegetable lasagna was not as easy as the *Men Who Know They Can't Cook Cookbook* boasted. Alek should have tried something easier for his first at-home, courting-Elspeth dinner. He ached from riding, digging new fence-post holes at the Kostyas', from the butt of a playful young bull and from clearing out an overgrown garden perfect for Elspeth's herbs. Meanwhile, he kept up the telephone war to get a hot tub at the Kostyas'.

Alek carefully picked away a crust of the burned lasagna. Being an impatient man playing a patient, thorough game for keeps wasn't easy.

He hadn't a clue how to settle down, how to make a relationship work.

He'd realized during the day that he'd never had to try— Elspeth was a trying woman. He'd never had to work to make Melissa trust him, believe in him when he told her he loved her. He did love her, but in a tender way that a man loves a woman he's grown used to, an easy, uncomplicated loving.

When Melissa died, Alek knew that he'd never love again. That there wasn't enough of him left to give another woman. Yet he had loved Elspeth from the moment he met her, eyes flashing, hair gleaming in the bonfire, balancing a village child on her hip.

She wasn't an easy woman. Elspeth had been hurt early in life. He'd hurt her again. He wasn't geared to slow paces and wary women, but he'd learn for Elspeth.

Alek braced himself against the counter and muttered in Russian, venting his dark mood. The light touch on his shoulder caused him to jerk around to face Elspeth. "Alek?"

"Elspeth, I love you. I always have." He looked over his shoulder to where she stood, elegant in a short, dark red dress. He admired the lean, soft line of her, the length of her legs down into the strappy little sandals, then back up to the tiny gold beads in her ears. There. That was that. "You can chew on that, spit it out if you want, but it doesn't change things. I love you. Unless you tell me to stop, I'm going to keep on telling you, until you believe and trust in me.''

He'd expected her withdrawal, the shifting of her expression, drawing it in, hiding her emotions from him. Tallchiefs held their emotions to themselves, plowing slowly through them to reach an ultimate decision about exactly how they felt. They'd learned how to do that early in life, to protect the family that could have been torn apart at any time. Pride kept him from asking how she felt about him, about a relationship—hell, a life with him. He plunged on recklessly, letting his bottled thoughts fly at her. ''This is serious, Elspeth. For keeps. We've come full circle. How I feel about you isn't going to change. I intend to bring you flowers and heather and broaches and anything else I want.''

He tugged her into his arms and held her; she wasn't going anywhere, not just yet. He counted every heartbeat she did not move from his arms.

''You jump,'' she finally whispered against his throat.

''Jump?''

''Pounce. Sometimes I feel as though I'm in the walking wheel—a huge spinning wheel—rather than walking to and from it. I'm in the walking wheel, spinning around with no idea of what hit me.''

The wisp of a smile lurking on her lips sent his hopes soaring. Alek picked her up, kissed her hard because he had to and, when she nodded, he carried her up the stairs to the grand old four-poster bed he'd purchased from the Wheelers. It was a lovely old thing, sitting under a blanket in the barn, and Alek had lost his heart immediately.

Then Elspeth's lips burned, igniting him. Her body feverishly answered his, in tune to his needs and her own.

By the middle of July, Elspeth gave up weaving and began her first vacation, much to Mark's distress. ''What?

You're quilting? What's quilts have to do with anything? A vacation? Honey, we've got clients screaming for your work.... Remember that tiny piece, the one you made on an old pitchfork? It sold to a millionaire. And the breast-plate design with feathers? There's a rich buyer circling it. Come on. Now's the time to jump into the fire and run with sales."

Elspeth thought about the fire in her lately and how she'd changed. She swung a Navajo drop spindle from a length of thread, watching it go around. "It's my first vacation, Mark."

He hesitated, clearly balancing income against her needs. "Okay. Give me a call when you're ready. If I've learned one thing about working with artists, it's that they have to have time to focus."

The problem was that Elspeth's focus had changed, and the work flowing beneath her hands was traditional, what her mother had taught her, and her thoughts were filled with Alek. In the quiet moments, she began piecing together designs for a quilt she'd always wanted to make, one her mother had begun and hadn't finished.

Alek had moved to the farm, renovating it. He kept himself there, holed up and away from her, until she had to come after him. Or until he drove his Chevy up her drive-way. He stood outside her house, leaning against the car and looking tough and unreasonable.

Alek wanted a home. He wanted her.

Because she enjoyed him, liked working with him on the ranch, Elspeth found herself in his arms at night, not want-ing to leave him. She needed the comfortable loving, the feeling of freedom with Alek, to push back, testing herself.

Alek liked to hold hands, slow dance and push her into dark corners. He'd look at her, and she'd feel his leaping hunger, that lazy, warm slide of nerves and cords locking in her body. Alek delighted in teasing her and kissing her senseless. Tormented to the fullest, Elspeth had sailed a kitchen plate at him. She'd actually dumped a salad over his head, when she'd just dumped a bucket of milk over it the day before.

He liked homemade bread, devoured it and then turned to consume her, the flash fire running so fast it took her breath away.

The tender moments left her reeling, when Alek took her in his arms, slowly, purposefully as though nothing could deter him from loving her. He contained his urge to push her, to commit to him, though it simmered beneath the surface.

The Tallchiefs accepted Alek in Elspeth's life, and she met the Petrovnas. "This is her, Mom," he'd said at the farm, holding Elspeth's hand securely.

"Tall," Serene Petrovna had said, walking around Elspeth to inspect her.

"A match," Alek Petrovna, Sr., had stated, reaching out to snag Elspeth and to kiss her cheeks thoroughly. He guffawed at her surprise and thrust her back to Alek's arms. "We'll be your neighbors until Talia has her baby. Mom wouldn't be anyplace else, and we're camping at Alek's house. Sort of fun, just having the basics. Serene and me still fit into the same sleeping—"

He rubbed the spot where Serene's elbow had caught him and winked at Alek. "You're not getting any younger, Junior. And you're getting a hell of a lot slower than what I remember— Ah!" he exclaimed as Serene's elbow connected again with his ribs.

"I'm home, Dad," Alek had said in a quiet, old-fashioned way that brought tears to his mother's eyes. He wrapped Elspeth's hand in his and brought it to his lips.

"You always get what you go after, son. Just like all those war stories."

"I'm playing for keeps, and sometimes the story takes a

bit more patience to get the right finish,'' Alek had returned, looking at Elspeth.

Patience. The minute Alek and Elspeth were alone, he forgot patience and had her behind the bales of hay. Then, when she could think again, Elspeth pushed him down and reminded him that she wasn't an easy taking. She ripped a button from his shirt, which Mrs. Petrovna noticed immediately. Elspeth wished she could rip off Alek's silly grin and her blush as easily when Mr. Petrovna laughed and eyed Mrs. Petrovna. After a cruise to the ice-cream parlor in Alek's Chevy, the retired Texas sheriff began doing rope tricks for his bride.

''Did you grow up like this?'' Elspeth asked Alek as Mrs. Petrovna strolled into the house with Mr. Petrovna right behind her.

''I was lucky. You were lucky, too, having a family who loved you.'' His eyes told her that he knew she'd been damaged and that he'd try to make it up to her.

''I was afraid, Alek. Horribly afraid I'd fail to do something and that it would separate the entire family. Fiona was only ten, and my brothers were taking more responsibility than they should have. I never wanted to do anything but weave. I've always loved it. I liked being able to sell what I'd made and people enjoying what Mom had taught me.'' She leaned against him, his arm around her. Alek was comfortable, when he wanted, holding her hand.

''They handled it. You all did.'' Alek leaned down to give her a friendly, understanding kiss.

Elspeth let him hold her against him, rocking her, right in daylight, right on the sidewalk. ''Don't you dare ask me anything about the Marrying Moon. I get the feeling I'm a story and not—''

His kiss was not tender, but demanding and hungry. Alek left her in no doubt about his intentions.

There were moments when Alek waited for her to say

something, for something to pass between them, but she couldn't release her heart, not yet. She'd loved her parents deeply and lost them; then that Scottish night had lingered in her thoughts. Alek would sense her turning from him immediately, and his expression would cloud.

By September, Talia seemed ready to burst. While she took her condition with a grin, Calum the cool was the typical nervous papa-to-be. The Petrovnas treated Elspeth as if she were their daughter; Alek's and her relationship settled into an easy simmer, punctuated by long, passionate nights when they could manage to be alone.

"Me, a Petrovna?" became familiar to Elspeth, as did the sight of Mr. Petrovna caught in a passionate argument with his son. In the end, after all the yelling, there were the hugs. Alek Sr. kissed his son and laughed at the arm wrestling and shoulder-butting between them. There were moments when both men watched Elspeth with the same intent, black-eyed, closed-in look as though waiting for her....
"You love her, Alek," Mr. Petrovna said when he thought she wasn't listening.

Alek's reply had come back instantly, firmly as his gaze drifted to her. "I do."

"Good. She's a strong woman, son, and not too certain of you."

Elspeth had sucked in air, not wanting to listen further. Before she could move, Alek had spoken to his father. "I made a mistake with her. I won't again."

She'd been a mistake. Elspeth felt the floor drop out from under her. She stood, icy cold, ready to run—then Alek surged to his feet and tugged her to him fiercely. There was no denying the hunger of his kiss or that he needed her. He had locked her to him. "Now get this, Tallchief. I love you. Got it?"

Elspeth cried that night, uncertain of her emotions when Alek was so committed to his. She tasted the words on her lips, tried them in the silence of her bedroom and let fear take her. She couldn't trust herself, not just yet.

From Mrs. Petrovna, Elspeth learned how Alek had always been an impetuous rascal, but no more than his brother and sisters. Elspeth could see him as a little boy, filling his sisters' pockets with worms and then, in his tamed moments, braiding their hair, as he had done Elspeth's. Of all the Petrovna children, Alek seemed the most lonely, the one always seeking what happened beyond the hill and wanting the truth of it.

The truth of it. Alek had moved into her life, her heart. When he placed her hands on his face and bent into them, giving himself to her, she went weak and the thought frightened her. Sharing her life, her thoughts, with another person who'd grown to understand her so well, frightened Elspeth. She'd grown up shielding her fears to protect her family.

When she wavered, not trusting the visions within her, the moments of Alek laughing at her or an older Alek, faced with taming an unruly brood that could ignite at any minute.

She didn't trust the image of Alek lying in bed with her, a ring on his finger.

Or the image of her wrapped in the shawl, the Marrying Moon round and high in the sky and Alek walking toward her…

A keen sense of panic slid into Elspeth, soon to be noted by Alek. If he couldn't torment and tease her out of the moment, he became grim and aloof, a cool outrage that terrified her.

When he saw a child, there was no mistaking the poignant longing in Alek's expression. There was no mistaking the love he had for the children he'd fostered and supported in other lands. He shared their accomplishments, their growth with Elspeth and hoarded the letters with his pictures of them.

Alek loved. He simply loved people and life and nurturing, growing gardens, planting trees, raising sheep and cattle. Baby, a motherless calf that Alek bottle-fed, followed him around the ranch, and he tucked her in each night. Then Abby, Jules, Rommie and Lincoln arrived, calves bawling for his attention. Alek collected animals like he had collected children, fitting perfectly into the former Kostya farm. Fadey had gone with the Kostyas, leaving a pup—Sergio—with Alek. Sergio promised to be a better sheepdog than his parent and clearly loved Alek.

Elspeth borrowed scrapbooks filled with his stories from the Petrovnas. She cried at his printed images, the horrors he'd seen and shared with the world. Alek caught her in her weaving room, the scrapbooks opened on the floor in front of her.

"Hey! What's this?" he asked urgently, sitting on the floor to draw her into his lap.

She pushed at him, raw with the fresh discovery of what he'd seen. "Leave me alone."

"What? So you can make more walls, keep me out? Me, a Petrovna?" he demanded, outrage hissing through his low, dangerous tone.

"You want too much, Alek. I don't know that I can give you what you want," she burst out, tears streaming down her face. She flailed at him, and he caught her wrists, kissing them. She resented him; he did this to her, making the tears come. Since she'd met him, she'd been nothing but uncertain. She'd changed, and he'd been the cause.

"Oh, baby. Don't cry. You're wonderful. Just seeing you, loving you, makes me happy."

She let him comfort her, because she could do little else. But in the end, she knew that one day she'd come to a dangerous edge. As she stroked the shawl, she knew that whatever edge waited for her, Una had pondered the same decisions, picking her way carefully.

Maybe it was that premonition that caused her to weave a Tallchief tartan, to think of Alek while she worked, at home in her shadows and peace. The explosive Petrovnas consumed quiet, and Elspeth often surprised herself by forgetting everything but a passionate exchange on a simple matter.

They were on her porch swing, holding hands and watching the September evening dust the streets. Fall came quickly; it scented the air and touched the leaves. She held her breath when she gave him the parcel, wrapped in brown paper and twine.

He swallowed, clearly delighted. "You made this for me?"

"You've been giving me enough presents. The heather made it through this year, and I adore it. Open it."

His fingers trembled when he tore away the wrappings and held up the plaid. He turned to her, one fist gripping the plaid and the other hand reaching for her. Alek jerked her to him and buried his face in her hair, his body trembling. "I'll wear it. Thank you."

"Not on your suit at my next showing, Petrovna." Already she saw him, a fine bit of swagger to his walk, hair wild around his angular face, touching the tartan resting on his broad shoulders.

He held it up to the sunlight, admiring it. "I'll wear it and the kilts you'll make me to go with it."

She had to laugh. "You're pushing and full of yourself, Petrovna."

But the kilts were already dancing on her fingertips, waiting to be made....

"Look in the box again, Alek. You've missed something."

"Mmm. More," Alek exclaimed with the delight of a little boy approaching a chocolate cake. He picked through the wrapping and smoothed the swatches of Tallchief plaid.

"For my kids overseas," he murmured, running his fingertips over them as though the wool were polished gold, handcrafted and glowing. "They'll like these."

"They're only bits—" He'd humbled her, so thankful for so little.

Alek's finger on her lips stopped her. "You've given them and me something special, Elspeth-mine. You're wonderful."

He told her with his lips that he adored her, which only frightened her more.

The second week of September brought a cold wind from the mountains; the aspens now shimmered in brilliant orange shades. Elspeth finished two fresh designs for Mark, who rejoiced that Alek hadn't totally killed her creative urge. Using a triangular frame, she created Tallchief Mountain, surging out of the rest of the design, and dusted it with heather.

Oh, she had urges, all right. Big ones, where Alek was concerned. Elspeth frowned at the roses blooming in the September sun. She'd stayed home to take a call from Fiona before going to the rodeo. With October approaching, Fiona called home more often, reminded of their parents' deaths.

Delight waited, tethered to Elspeth's back porch by Birk—just in case she wanted to ride, showing off for the Tallchiefs. She planned to ride to the rodeo, but not the showy trick riding or barrel racing she'd done growing up; she wanted to show off Delight, representing Tallchief Cattle Ranch.

As usual, Fiona was late and in trouble with an attorney's son, a regular nerd-boy, she called him. It had all started as a protest on the steps of his father's offices—a man who was in favor of wiping out an entire colony of endangered reptiles to build an industrial park. Fiona had padded herself to look heavily pregnant and, when the newspapers

arrived, managed to look like the had-and-deserted by the
attorney's son.   Following his kidnapping of her, nerd-
boy had actually had the nerve to kiss her; he'd actually
had the nerve to tell her she was beautiful pregnant and
should reconsider her old-maid state. He'd eyed her appreciatively and told her she looked fertile and he wanted
healthy children.... Fiona had hit him over the head with a
chair, knocked him unconscious and then was faced with
guilt and nerd-boy's outraged fiancée. She missed home
suddenly, and Elspeth smiled, sensing that Fiona would
soon arrive in Amen Flats and not alone.

"Aye," Elspeth said with Fiona, no need for goodbyes
between them.

Mad Matt skidded his bike tires on Elspeth's driveway
and called through her open screen door, "Miss Tallchief,
you better hurry up. Alek is going to ride after the next two
guys. Talia said you'd want to see him ride Diablo."

Elspeth stopped on her way to the door, heart pounding.
Alek was a good rider—they'd raced horses, and she was
faster, lighter in the saddle. Amen Flats's rodeo wasn't for
an average rider. The westerners in Amen Flats had been
brought up on saddles and bucking horses. Diablo was a
mad-tempered horse, formerly owned by a man who'd
abused him; Diablo had broken bones of the men who tried
to ride him. The horse was what the old-timers called a
"killer". He knew how to jump on all fours, bend his back
and come down twisting. He knew how to ram against a
fence, catching a cowboy's leg, and once he got a cowboy
in the arena alone—

Elspeth let out the breath she'd been holding, caught by
the terror on the last cowboy's face. She didn't think; she
just grabbed the shawl she'd been holding, sensing a dangerous edge just as Una had long ago. Elspeth wanted the
safety of the past wrapped around her, because Alek needed
her protection.

"Go ahead, Matt. I'll be there in a minute."

The boy leapt on his bike, spewing dust on his way out of her driveway. "You'll have to hurry if you want to see him."

"I'll be there." Elspeth grimly strapped on her chaps over her jeans. With Delight under her, she'd be at the rodeo before Alek rode, and could save his neck. She slid into the saddle, stuffed the shawl into the saddlebags and bent low in the saddle.

Alek wrapped his glove in the rope, preparing to ride Diablo. He gently lowered himself. The horse was good and mean, just what Alek wanted. After this rodeo, Diablo was his; the horse had been maltreated, and Alek would give him a home. The horse already liked him in a mean-evil way, a case of mutual respect of man and beast. In a way, Diablo reminded Alek of Elspeth, hard clear through and breaking before bending.

He loved her, damn it. Loved her with every bit of his heart, his dreams.

She gave him only so much, and then the doors closed. He had dreams of her walking to him in that shawl, with the moon big and bright in the night sky. Of the Bridal Tepee behind her...of their life in front of them.

Being patient had just about ripped him to shreds. But he could do it, letting off steam once in a while, and right now Diablo seemed just mean enough to suit Alek's dark mood.

From the rough grandstands, Alek caught his mother's fears, the grim pride of his father and Talia's hesitant smile, Calum at her side. Everyone had someone, and Elspeth wasn't giving in easily.

He focused on the horse and lifted his hat to see if Talia's good-luck satin ribbon was still in place; Elspeth's swatch was in his pocket. He'd carried it through wars and he'd been safe enough. Then Alek lowered himself gingerly, firmly, onto the saddle, and Diablo bucked in the stall, edging around to try to crush his rider.

"Easy, boy." Alek gentled the horse as he had earlier. "When this is over, you're going home with me. You watch your side of the fence, and I'll watch mine. You'll have plenty to eat and maybe a few girlfriends along the way. But you won't have to worry about being hurt. Elspeth will have you eating out of her hand in no time, just like me."

Diablo reared again as another horse streaked by, the rider wearing a flash of red and gold. Elspeth stood on the saddle, her arms raised high and the shawl flapping behind her, drawing the audience's attention.

She dropped, and Alek almost lost his grip on the riding rope, quickly reclaiming it. His heart wasn't so easy to retrieve. Elspeth appeared low on the other side of Delight, supported by a stirrup and her grasp on the running horse's mane.

The audience stood to its feet, screaming, cheering as Delight rounded the arena in an easy gallop. Alek, worried about Elspeth, eased off Diablo and up onto the stall; relieved of his rider, Diablo settled down immediately. "What is that woman doing?" Alek asked Duncan hoarsely when he could speak.

"Saving your neck." Grim lines bracketed Duncan's mouth. "Taking the pressure off you. They've been waiting for her to ride for over five years, and now they have what they want. They won't care if you ride Diablo or not. She's giving you a way out, to save your pride." Duncan jumped down into the arena, followed by his brothers and Alek.

"Is that so? She's going to feel some pressure when my hand hits her backside. She could get hurt." Alek's heart plummeted to his boots when Elspeth edged up into the saddle and stood on the back of the horse, standing as i circled the arena. Just as suddenly, she dropped from sight and appeared at the other side, her moccasins skimming the earth, and then she swung up again.

"Don't distract her, Alek," Calum said quietly.

"She's out of shape. She almost didn't haul herself up in time. One hoof on that shawl, and her neck could be broken." Birk's face was as taut as his brothers'.

Elspeth quickly balled the shawl into her saddlebags as though recognizing the danger. Then she began the series of swings to the ground and back up into the saddle, pitting herself against the animal, concentrating on every trick.

"She's giving it everything she's got, just like she always did," Duncan noted. "But even a rider who practices every day shouldn't try that routine. She learned it from Mom."

The brothers shot Alek disgusted, threatening looks.

Wrapped in sheer terror that Elspeth could fall, that a hoof could kill her, Alek could not move. His boots were rooted to the arena floor, and he felt the blood drain from him. If she fell, he'd be there; if she didn't, he wanted her to know she'd purely raked the heart right out of him.

When Elspeth was seated on the saddle firmly, the shawl withdrawn from the saddlebags and now around her shoulders, Delight circled the arena in an easy canter. Alek walked out into the middle of the ring, slapping his hat along his thigh every step. She circled him slowly, the shawl flaming in the sun, as richly colored as the aspens on the mountains.

The dyes should have faded in Una's shawl, yet the colors remained strong, just as his love would remain for Elspeth. The shawl had been well loved and taken care of, just as he planned to do with Elspeth...if she didn't break her neck first.

"You're in for it," Alek snapped, meaning it. He slapped his hat against his chaps. Riding the edge of fear had set him off. "I can't find one bit of patience in me right now, lady. You'd better get off that horse now. You're an evil-hearted—"

"Save the sweet talk, Petrovna," she shot back, her eyes flashing steel at him. "You ride that killer horse and—"

"You would say that to me, a Petrovna? I finish what I start." Alek's leather glove shot out to grab Delight's reins; he glared up at Elspeth, not shielding her from his anger or his need. "Say you love me. Come out and say it. Say you were afraid what happened to me, just like that day you came running to save me from Duncan. You loved me then and you love me now. We've loved each other since this all began...we're a part of each other, lady, and you know it."

Delight pranced, sidestepping as the shawl fluttered around Elspeth's rigid body. "You're a hard ride," she said finally, employing a western term that meant he wasn't an easy man.

"I won't leave you. You won't wake up some morning and find that I'm off to cover a war. I won't hurt you. I'll love you all the days of my life and then some. I'll give you children, if you want, and I'll be by your side when you need me. You might not like hearing the truth, but I'll always give it to you. I'll be your best friend, if you'll let me, and ready to love you with my body in a heartbeat. You're moving in with me, and the next time you decide you're going to try something like this—" He fought the cold ripple of fear skidding along his skin, not wanting to think about the next time.

Tears shimmered in her eyes, dropping to the shawl. Fear rasped in her voice, her face pale with terror. "Promise me you won't ride Diablo. Promise."

Alek took a long look at the woman he loved. It would cost him a measure of pride to walk away from the horse. But with fear riding Elspeth, his pride meant nothing. She'd een through so much, and he hadn't been there for her. But he was now, in every heartbeat.

Alek reached up, grabbed the shawl and hauled her down or his kiss. He had to know that she was all right, that she asted the same, smelled the same, looked at him with that ame dark, mysterious, heavy-lidded stare after he kissed her.

"It will cost you," he said finally when her lips were ipe from his. "And you'll promise me that you'll never ide like that again, not until we've—a together 'we'—have alked about it."

She blinked and glanced at the pink bow tied neatly in his hair. Alek didn't want to explain Talia's good-luck charm. He slapped on his hat, walked back to a fence and swung up on it.

Elspeth followed on Delight. "Alek! Where are you going?"

He took off his hat and lifted it to the silent, watching crowd. Spellbound, they'd seen him grovel and break Perovna's law. They knew he loved Elspeth and that she'd come around. But right now, none of that helped, not while he was wearing a big jagged hole for his heart. "Ladies and gentleman. I am going fishing. And hell yes, I like to wear pink ribbons in my hair. Hell yes, I love stubborn, muley Elspeth Tallchief. If she rides like that again, I'm holding the whole damn town accountable."

He hopped off the fence and walked away, still caught by the terror of seeing Elspeth swing from her horse. Alek dashed away a tear with his leather glove and let his Russian curses roll over the sound of the cheering crowd. He'd lick his wounds in peace; he'd done it before.

So much for his patience. So much for his pride.

Thirteen

"*What do you mean, Alek is a champion rodeo rider?*"
Elspeth demanded that evening as her brothers sprawled on
her front porch. Talia, Sybil, Emily, Megan and the Petrovnas—minus one Alek Petrovna—were stuffed with
burgers and potato salad and awaiting the freshly churned
ice cream to ripen in the wooden bucket. The ice cream
would be topped with Talia's double-rich, super-chocolate-
frosted cake.

At almost seven months into her pregnancy, Sybil had
eaten her cake before her bean burger and potato salad. At
the baby-finish line, Talia picked at her food.

The hair on Elspeth's nape lifted as she rounded on her
brothers—the rangy, raw-boned, hard-minded, untamed
Tallchiefs wearing smirks. She pivoted back to Mr. Petrovna. She began again more quietly, spacing her words.
"Is Alek a rodeo champion?"

"My son is a born-and-bred Texan, no matter what foreign countries he's been in," stated Mr. Petrovna proudly.

'When he was just a pup, he started hiring out to ranches during the summers.''

"He can outride any man around," Duncan, an expert on the subject, offered. "Not the fancy trick-riding stuff, just good old bull and bronc riding."

Elspeth pivoted to him. "He's not much in a race."

Birk snickered; Elspeth shoved his plate of chocolate cake up into his face. Lacey burst out laughing, and Birk, in turn, pushed her mouth into the cake. She licked her lips and grinned through the circle of chocolate covering her face. "That was worth it, bub."

Calum cleared his throat. "I believe Alek prefers to ride behind you, Elspeth. There's…ah…certain advantages in that. And when he's feeling abused, he likes to pit himself against a real challenge, not one he wants to kiss. I'd say Diablo was what Alek needed at the moment. We had a hard enough time unloading that horse at Alek's after the rodeo."

"My boy will have that bronc eating out of his hand in no time." Mr. Petrovna licked the frosting-covered finger Megan held up to him. "I haven't set up a tepee in years. When I figured he'd be needing something to hole up in until he wanted to…until he calmed down, Duncan told me to borrow yours from his barn. Yep. That was something here at the lake…Junior looking hard as iron and twice as mean as that killer bronc."

Mr. Petrovna didn't know about the tepee, about how the Tallchiefs had started bringing their brides to it, reviving Una's legends. First there was Duncan and then Calum, and Elspeth had always known Birk would be the next to find his true love. She glanced at Duncan and Calum and found them looking at her, kneading the same thought. To Mr. Petrovna, the tepee served as whimsy, a family toying with their birthright, nothing more. Later they'd tell him, but not now, while Elspeth picked through her relationship with Alek.

She'd wounded Alek, torn the heart from him once, and time had passed, smoothing the edges for both of them.

She resented his damn contract, and he'd pay for that when they argued...because Alek Petrovna purely savored a good argument and Elspeth intended to let him sharpen his teeth on the bones she tossed at him.

Her mother had always said that the making up was worth the fight and that arguments cleared the fog between lovers. Elspeth smiled; Alek had torn her castle walls down, and he deserved a nip or two.

Elspeth looked straight at Sybil, nestled against Duncan, then at Talia, a tall, cool blonde in the midst of the Tallchief clan. Elspeth's brothers had pushed away the shadows; they'd found love, fought for it.

Images of other children danced by her, and she turned to Birk. He'd be finding love soon, because the rogue of the lot, he'd been searching longer, plowing through likely women with a charm that didn't give them a chance. One day he'd find a woman who didn't care for his charm and wouldn't have him on a platter, and then his hackles would lift—because if the Tallchiefs liked anything, it was a hard ride. He'd find Una's rocking chair and the woman to go with the legend, and then he'd be at peace.

Elspeth's gaze drifted to Lacey, and she corrected the thought. Birk would be blissfully happy, because the woman he chose was not likely to be a peaceful one; she would have her own shadows.

Fiona would come tripping to Amen Flats, tired from battling the world. And then she'd hunt Una's sewing chest, with its tatting shuttles, shoe button hooks and doilies and bits of her life. The buyer had wanted the tiny chest intact with its lovely feminine clutter, and Una—to save Tallchief land—had given her heart in the lacy heap. But still she'd loved the chest, as would Fiona.

"It cost Alek not to finish that ride," Birk stated. "Any man who'd walk away from something he'd started in front of a rodeo crowd has it bad."

Mrs. Petrovna stroked Elspeth's hair. She tugged Elspeth to a stool in front of her and began to braid her hair. "You see, honey, Alek has all sorts of rodeo belts and medals. You only saw his journalism scrapbooks. I kept all of his other things separate."

"They were a good match—that horse and my son. He's been feeling evil lately," Mr. Petrovna said.

Elspeth took in a long, steadying breath, and let Mrs. Petrovna finish her hair. Edges, she thought. Just like Una's edges—when she'd made her decision based on love and the man who had placed himself in her care. Elspeth smiled to herself. Tallchiefs weren't easy to capture, and she'd given Alek a good run, while she wound through her shadows to come full circle. Nothing had changed since that night in Scotland when he'd strolled toward her, wearing a grin that would knock the senses from under any reasonable woman. A second go-'round, and Alek had stepped into her shadows, tearing her from them. He'd taken away the distance she'd placed on her life, replacing it with himself. She'd tasted his dreams and found them true, and still she'd hovered in her shadows, until he made her so greedy for him that she'd stepped out.

Then the horrible, heart-stopping, icy fear when she knew Alek would ride Diablo. She'd hesitated outside the arena, sitting on Delight. Then Alek—his face hard and grim—had lowered himself onto Diablo. With Alek in danger, she had had no choice but to show her love. He'd given her everything, his dreams and hopes and his aching past; she couldn't imagine life without him—and she'd given him nothing, not a crumb.

The image of Alek lurched into Elspeth's mind—Alek slapping his hat along his chaps and stalking toward her looking twice as mean as the horse he chose to ride.

But now the time had come to claim him well and good. She intended to run Alek Petrovna down and—

She stood when Mrs. Petrovna said, "Come here, Talia. It's been so long since I've braided your hair."

Elspeth remembered the pink bow glistening in Alek's curls. "What about the bow?"

Talia smiled tightly and eased herself onto the stool. "It's my good-luck charm. He always wore my bows and usually won."

Elspeth stood still, remembering Alek in the arena, how firmly he spoke his vows—vows, she decided. Alek had made his vows to her right there in the September sunshine with a crowd of people straining to hear. *I'll be your best friend...I'll love you all the days of my life and then some....*

She'd come to the same edge as Una, to a moment when the awakening changed, deepened, ripened and clung.

She quite simply loved Alek Petrovna. He was hers; he'd always been from the first moment. Images flashed through her as she rode toward her love—Alek, laughing outright. Alek, impetuous, burying her in a mound of wildflowers. Alek, playing with her—her friend. Alek, telling her how much he ached for the war-torn countries. Alek, her tender lover...her love...her future.

Her mind racing forward to the moment when she faced Alek, Elspeth walked to Delight, tethered and grazing in a wild field near her house.

Watching her from the porch, Duncan shook his head. "I don't know if I can make it through all this."

Sybil patted his hand. "Darling, you're just emotional now. In another two months, you'll be just fine."

"She's hunting what she wants. She just needed time. It

will all come together." Calum spoke from experience; he'd placed his shadows aside with his wife's help. He took Talia's hand and drew it to his lips. "Honey, are you okay?"

Talia pressed her lips together, her knuckles white as she gripped Calum's hand. "I want my black boots...now!"

He plucked her up from the stool in a heartbeat and stood holding her in his arms. He looked as if he wanted to carry her off to keep her safe and wasn't certain which direction to take. Talia kissed him and grinned. "Hi, Pops. Just see that I get my boots and don't let the doctor bully you into taking them off— Ohhhh!"

"Boy. Don't you dare faint. Not while you're holding my daughter," boomed Mr. Petrovna.

"She's having the baby now. Here." Mrs. Petrovna, who had been keeping her hand on Talia's stomach, beamed. "I knew it. They're coming two minutes apart. Talia is unpredictable. I knew she wouldn't give us proper notice and that she'd pick a time when the doctor was out of town. This baby is on its way...fast."

"For once, this isn't my fault. It's Calum's. I thought it was the excitement and the hot dog at the arena.... *I want my boots!*"

Birk placed one hand on the porch railing and used it to swing down to the lawn. He landed at a run, heading straight for Calum's house.

Duncan turned to Sybil as if seeing her potential danger for the first time. "You wouldn't do this, would you?"

"Darling. I'm predictable as rain. The Petrovnas are another matter." She grinned at him over her shoulder, just enough to make him question what she'd just said.

Mrs. Petrovna and Lacey helped Calum carry Talia into Elspeth's house and bed. Mrs. Petrovna hummed between giving orders. Talia tugged Calum down on the bed beside her and started cursing him in Swahili. By the time another pain hit, Mr. Petrovna started the Russian music blaring. "To help my little girl. She always loved this music," he explained.

Birk arrived with the boots, and Calum placed them on Talia's feet. "Man, I can't wait to wear these things again, Tallchief. You'd better make good with your promise to wear those leather pants while we're dancing to that music. Look at him, Mom. Isn't he cute? Right now, he's trying to remember everything in all the books he read—the methodical stuff, steps one through—"

Then she screamed, bearing down. Calum went white and took her hand. Talia gasped, grinned weakly at him, and said, "Well, I've got my boots on. Let's get this gig on the road. Mom has done this before. She's an experienced midwife. Calum, don't you dare pass out."

Emily, almost sixteen, took Talia's other hand. "I'm going to be a doctor. Or a vet."

"Now is a good time to learn," Talia said, gritting her teeth. "You'll take care of Calum for me, won't you? When he passes out?"

"You bet. Hey, I like the boots."

"Aren't they fine? We'll get you a pair— Ohh! Calum, you are a low-down—"

When the Marrying Moon is high, a scarred warrior will rise from the mists to claim his lady huntress. He will wrap her in the shawl and carry her to the Bridal Tepee and his heart. Their song will last longer than the stars....

Elspeth dismounted and tied Delight to a tree. The mare whinnied as Elspeth hugged her for reassurance. She took the shawl from her saddlebags and wondered how the treasure, so fragile and light, had stood the poor use of the past months.

Yet it shimmered magically in her hands, just as it must have done in Una's when she'd claimed Tallchief. The shawl was a part of Elspeth's life, what had happened and what would grow deeper.

The words in Una's journals attested to how much she loved Tallchief, how the legend was a blend of their lives and how it had come true.

Elspeth didn't need her tracking skills to find Alek this time. The tepee shone in the moonlight, gleaming in the shadows of the trees. On Tallchief Lake, mist hovered over the black waves and whispered of other loves; on a moonlit night, it floated and curled around the reeds, swaying in the restless wind.

Elspeth braced herself against what Alek might say. He'd been hurt today, a passionate man wanting more from her than she'd given. She moved from the shadows of the pines into the moonlight lying on the mist; the cool, damp layer curled around her, whimsically choosing its path.

Suddenly Alek stood before her, his legs spread, arms crossed over his chest, and not an ounce of tenderness showing on his face. "Dad didn't know that the tepee had a special meaning. Duncan and your brothers did."

"I didn't come about the tepee."

The mist clung to his hair, making it even more unruly as she continued to walk toward him. His head tipped at an arrogant angle. "I meant what I said today in the arena. I'll be here when you need me. I've changed, Elspeth. I've found what I want with you. I'll be writing assignment stories, but I'm staying right here."

Fear ripped through her again, but she pushed it away, determined to let him know her mind...and her heart. "I love you, Alek Petrovna."

She gripped the shawl with aching fingers as he stared down at her, eyes narrowed. "Uh-huh."

"You're not going to make this easy, are you?" She

should have known Alek wouldn't make anything easy for her. She tossed away the image of him running to her, kissing her wildly and bearing her off to the tepee. This was Alek, hard down to the core, nasty, tender, sweet, passionate—

"Hell no. You ripped the heart out of me today, riding as though your life didn't matter. It does matter. To me. There you were, standing on that damn horse, that shawl flapping around your neck—"

She placed her hand on his, needing to anchor her tumbling world, share it with Alek. His fingers slowly wrapped around hers, and she sucked in air, just realizing that she'd been waiting for him to show that he hadn't stopped caring. "But my life does matter now, every color and every shred of it, since you've come into it. The weave has deepened, heated, come alive with you. I thought I was happy, living in Amen Flats with people I've known all my life. I thought I was happy when Duncan and Calum found their loves."

"Thought?" he shot at her, making her come all the way. Alek's fingers laced with hers, giving her support in a difficult passage. "And?"

Elspeth tossed away the need to shield emotions. She'd learn to share more easily with Alek in time. "And then you came, and I discovered that I needed more. I needed you."

"Did you?" The challenge was there, making her take that last step.

She moved close to him, so that he could see her face and know that she had no doubt about her love or her future with him. "Marry me, Alek. Give me your heart—I won't tear it. I'll be there when you wake up and when you go to sleep. I'll keep you warm in the hard, cold times and hold you when you ache. You ache, Alek. It rides just beneath the surface, what you've seen, what you'd like to change. I will help you—if you want to travel, I'll leave

Amen Flats to be at your side. Give me your children—I'll love and tend them and then love you more.''

"You love me," he repeated, his Texas drawl uneven. "Would you say that meant you were greedy for me? Really deep down, nasty greedy for me? Or just the innocent, temporary kind of greed?"

She'd hurt him, and his uncertainty had reared and his pride needed tending. She gave him that, because now it mattered; healing hearts wasn't easy, but was a blend of give and take. Elspeth placed her hand on his scars, smoothing them. "I'd say I'm on the high end of greed with you. You've walked into my life, turned it upside down, and I've lost most of my ability to see things clearly…no thanks to you. I used to sense things before they happened. Now I'm too busy with thoughts of you. Before you swaggered back into my life, I didn't let people too close to me, not even my family. Now I'm in a bog of people and loving every minute. I go a little lightheaded at the thought of you. I wonder how quickly I can corral you. Yes…I'd say I'm good and greedy for you.''

She lifted on tiptoe to kiss his lips, to caress the smooth, hard feel of them until they softened to her touch. "There's no reason I should, of course. You're arrogant, demonstrative, and you scared me badly today. I didn't know what I'd do if anything happened to you a second time. I didn't want to care, Alek, but I do and you're the cause, the only cause…I love you.''

"Say it again," he demanded, taking her hand to his lips and kissing her palm.

She leaned against him, this solid man who was a part of her life and a part of herself. "I love you, Alek Petrovna. I know we'll fight—I've grown to like a bit of spice in my life, thanks to you. You can set me off, and I'll set you off and then we'll make up. But there will be the quiet times, when I tell you what was in my heart back then, when we were struggling to stay together. I'll tell you what's in my heart for you.''

"Mmm. Sounds like a good story. I suppose I'll pay for that contract. You're getting good at pushing, if that horse-riding event was any indication.'' Alek placed his lips on hers, promising that the good times would be there, over-shadowing life's hardships. He'd always be there for her, and she'd return the favor.

"Let's say that it will be useful to drag up when we argue. This time is for keeps, Alek. Isn't it?'' Elspeth couldn't help giving way to the last of her doubts.

"For keeps.'' He looked up to the big, round silver moon. It had filled the night sky that way so long ago in Scotland, when they'd first met. "Looks like a perfect night after a long, hard day.''

He wanted to know about the Marrying Moon, about what she'd said on that night long ago. But Elspeth wanted to give him that present at a moment of her own choosing....

She chose now and whispered, "See that moon? How big and bright it is, hovering over us? The legend says that 'when the Marrying Moon is high, a scarred warrior will rise from the mists to claim his lady huntress. He will wrap her in the shawl and carry her to the Bridal Tepee and his heart.'''

Alek placed his face in the shelter of her throat and shoulder, giving himself into her care, the gesture filling her with love for him. "Thank you, Elspeth.''

She kissed his damp, curling lashes, and he kissed away the tears flowing on her cheeks. Then, with a flourish, Alek wrapped the shawl around her. He stood looking at her in the moonlight for a moment.

Pleasure rode his expression, pleasing her in turn. "You're unpredictable, Petrovna.''

"I'm in love for the last time, honey. Give me a moment

to enjoy my treasure, one that I'll always cherish.'' Then he bent to lift her in his arms. ''Tell me the rest of the legend. I can tell by your smirk that you're holding back.''

''I do not smirk.'' She wouldn't be easy, not with Alek Petrovna, who enjoyed a good battle. Elspeth trailed her fingertip over his lips, traced the scar and kissed it. ''Submit, Alek Petrovna. You're my love, my heart and dreams. Let me give you the best part of me, the part that's always been yours.''

Later, after Alek had carried her to the Bridal Tepee, after they had pledged their love again and tenderly dined upon each other, unwrapping and sharing each other's hearts, they began again in a searing heat that made them one.

This time, Alek rose above her, straining to leash his body, his hands wound in her hair. ''Tell me.''

Elspeth fought the pleasure washing over her, strained to think—to give Alek what he needed—past the desires of their bodies ready to shatter in a heartbeat. ''I love you, my heart, my love, my Alek.''

His lips attacked hers, hungry for her, their bodies fused together as he took them over the edge.

'' 'Their song will last longer than the stars,' '' she whispered later, wrapped in his arms as the Marrying Moon hovered in the sky.

Alek lifted her chin with the tip of his finger. ''I love you, Elspeth-mine.''

''Mmm.'' Elspeth gave herself to his kiss and dived into the images there of Alek, proud of his present, another Tallchief cradle. The baby would have Alek's black, curling hair and the Tallchiefs gray eyes—Una's inheritance. A girl this time, the baby would look fragile in Alek's hands, devastating him with the miracle of her birth. There would be a boy next, replacing another and astounding Alek, who would hold his one-year-old daughter close against him in one arm and his newborn son in the other arm. Tears would shimmer in his black eyes as he looked at Elspeth, and then he would tell her again that he loved her.

When the babies slept, Alek would come to Elspeth in the Kostyas' renovated farmhouse bedroom.

They'd come full circle, and there would be more circles, weaving their lives and love closer.

Alek smiled in the dim light. "Someday, you'll have to tell me when the images come and share them with me. From your expression, I'd say it was a good one."

"A very good one."

She could have throttled Alek, a pushy man set on a quick wedding. "What? You would ask me, a Petrovna, to wait months?"

She hadn't asked; she'd told him. So much for a logical discussion in the Bridal Tepee the next morning. After a night of making love, dozing and making love again, Elspeth had awakened to Alek packing his gear. He'd bundled her off to the farmhouse and immediately started making telephone calls to arrange their wedding.

No amount of arguing could stop him, but Elspeth dived into the flaming arguments, delighting in them, in the passion flaring in Alek's eyes when she did. Oh, she'd meet him on a level he understood and not on any nice, polite, shadowy, wishy-washy level, either. She'd chosen to stand and fight, and Alek would have to reap what he had sown....

Now, a full week later—that was all the time he gave her to prepare everything for a horde of relatives and friends, including the Petrovnas' Texas relations—Elspeth rode Delight down Amen Flats's Main Street. Ribbons and flowers decked the horse, and she pranced, showing off. Leading the horse, Emily—Sybil's daughter—would one day find her love.

Her hair loose and flowing around her, Elspeth wore LaBelle's diamond stud earrings; Elizabeth's long, lacy veil, topped with a tiny braided coronet from Elizabeth's mother, fluttered in the fall air. Elspeth wore the garter her mother had given her years ago, decked with ribbons. On the lace high on her throat, Elspeth wore her mother's favorite cameo; as a judge, Pauline had sentenced Matthew to jail wearing that cameo. A long-legged, tough Tallchief, Matthew had burst into her courtroom and called her a hard-hearted, evil woman who made him love her. Pauline had him hauled off to jail when she ordered quiet and Matthew had continued "contempt of court." Later, in his jail cell, she'd admitted her love for him, and the cameo had always remained precious to her. Una's shawl fluttered from the saddle horn, a fiery blaze amid the yards of pristine bridal gown.

Elspeth smoothed the gown, remembering how Talia, Sybil, Mrs. Petrovna, Lacey and a revolving sea of loving hands had fashioned the gown.

At the end of the street, waiting with a crowd of people she loved, waited her husband-to-be, dressed in a Tallchief kilt.

She wasn't happy. Alek had pushed and shoved, and if she hadn't wanted the same so much and as soon, she would have pushed back so hard she'd get that swoon out of him yet.

Alek had insisted she wear a long bridal gown and veil. She knew he still thought of how he'd taken her years ago, and it was a small thing to concede. But managing the whole affair on top of Delight's saddle was another matter. Then, because Megan wanted to ride the horse—Duncan was already making a horsewoman out of her—Elspeth held the toddler in her arms, her wedding bouquet of roses tied to the saddle horn with satin ribbons. She needed Megan's soft, chubby body against her for support.

There Alek stood in the street, legs spread—he was wearing proper hose and brogans, unlike her brothers, who wore their western boots with their kilts. Of the lot, there was nothing tamed in the men wearing kilts, despite their ruffled shirts and tartans with broaches, Alek's contribution. Into the broaches were tucked Mr. Petrovna's orchids, looking extremely fragile against the blue-and-green plaid.

Duncan stood next to him, then Calum with his new daughter sleeping in his arms. Then Birk… *Ah, Birk, love is coming to you sooner than you think,* Elspeth thought, wishing that his road would be smooth. But when he finally found love, it would be strong and lasting.

Oh, she loved Alek Petrovna, Jr., more with each heartbeat, though at times in the past week, she hadn't liked him at all. If only he hadn't held her, rested his face in the vulnerable part of her, her throat and shoulder and told her, "I want us to be married as soon as possible. I'm dying for you, Elspeth."

She'd gone down too easily, loving him, letting him have his way, because it was what she wanted. The moment she'd agreed, he'd tossed her over his shoulder and strolled over to the Petrovnas next door, despite the names she'd called him. Alek had told his mother and father that Elspeth had agreed to marry him within the week, right while Elspeth was hanging upside down on his backside. She bit him, of course, on a place she hadn't nibbled before.

She could feast upon him now—a big, darkly tanned man with untamed black curls drifting in the September wind. Alek wore LaBelle's earring and looked as unyielding as Tallchief Mountain. Megan sat perfectly still, pacified, now that she was riding a horse with her aunt Elspeth. Elspeth bent to the toddler. "Isn't he pretty, Meggie? Isn't he just?"

The quickening stirred within her as Duncan took Megan and Birk helped her down from the saddle. Alek, dark and somber, didn't move, wouldn't touch her now. She caught the image of Alek, standing behind her in the mirror, his ruffled shirt opened at the throat. In the mirror, his hands trembled when he placed his grandmother's pearls around Elspeth's neck and then slowly, carefully began to undress her for their first night as man and wife.

The entire audience watched as Alek strode to the horse and worked free Una's shawl. He carried it to Elspeth and gently placed it around her.

Talia's soft sob carried through the silence, and Calum reached out a hand to draw her near. They stood there—Calum and Talia and baby Kira, Duncan and Sybil and Emily and Megan. Birk, the Petrovnas and Lacey stood on the other side.

Circles, thought Elspeth, her heart full where once shadows roamed. Love for each other had seen them through, and now Alek added another dimension to the Tallchiefs.

She caught the fire in his look, the promise of what he would do later to claim her as his wife. There was tenderness roaming his face, softening the scars, and hope and dreams coming true.

She slanted him a look that promised what she would do to him in return. Then she moved to his side, admiring him, this man she loved more desperately each day.

Epilogue

Elspeth knelt by the mountain heather, leaves killed by October's freezing descent. She dusted leaves from her parents' stone and placed her cheek against Alek's hand, resting on her shoulder.

Though they'd only been married a month, she didn't have to tell him the images moving through her; Alek knew. Her safe world had been torn apart by two bullets, taking her parents, and she'd struggled to tend her family. Now she had Alek, a part of her heart and soul, to share her life.

He'd come to her out of the darkness he felt, revenge in his heart. But love had grown and captured them, despite the wounding of another time.

She'd brought him here, her husband, to meet her parents.

"I think the heather will come back," he said, drawing her to her feet. "If it doesn't, we'll plant more. They should have it in the summer."

Oh, honey, I'm so happy for you, Elspeth's mother seemed to say.

He'll cherish you all the days of his life, just like I did your mother, her father whispered in the wind.

Then Alek took Elspeth in his arms and kissed her, because he understood.

She clung to him and knew that she had crossed from one world to another. Their month of marriage had been sheer joy and promised more. The Marrying Moon was theirs to keep, a huge silver disk made for them alone.

The Bridal Tepee would be used again throughout their lives, as it had been the first week of their marriage.

Alek held her tightly, as though nothing could tear her away, and placed his rugged face within the hollow of her neck. "I like the name 'Heather Pauline,' do you?"

Elspeth held very still as Alek's lips drifted to her ear and nipped it. "Or Matthew. That's a good, solid name for a boy."

He cupped her face and drew it up to him. He grinned, the October wind sweeping through his curls. "Why, Elspeth-love. You're shocked. You actually have no idea, do you?"

She saw the images again, a black, curly-headed girl with gray eyes, a baby boy and Alek...Alek, forever her love.

"The legend of the shawl is true, Alek. How I love you...."

The wind slid through the pine boughs above them.

When the Marrying Moon is high, a scarred warrior will rise from the mists to claim his lady huntress. He will wrap her in the shawl and carry her to the Bridal

Tepee and his heart. Their song will last longer than the stars....

"Aye," Elspeth murmured before she sought her true love's kiss.

* * * * *

*Do you crave more irresistible
love stories from Cait London?
Look for Gabriel's Gift, Silhouette Desire,
on sale April 2001, part of her
FREEDOM VALLEY miniseries—and
featuring a MAN OF THE MONTH!*

#1 *New York Times* bestselling author

NORA ROBERTS

brings you more of the loyal and loving,
tempestuous and tantalizing Stanislaski family.

Coming in February 2001

The Stanislaski Sisters

Natasha and Rachel

Though raised in the Old World traditions of their
family, fiery Natasha Stanislaski and cool, classy
Rachel Stanislaski are ready for a *new* world of love....

*And also available in February 2001 from
Silhouette Special Edition, the newest book in the
heartwarming Stanislaski saga*

CONSIDERING KATE

Natasha and Spencer Kimball's daughter Kate turns her
back on old dreams and returns to her hometown, where
she finds the *man* of her dreams.

Available at your favorite retail outlet.

Where love comes alive™

January 2001
TALL, DARK & WESTERN
#1339 by Anne Marie Winston

February 2001
THE WAY TO A RANCHER'S HEART
#1345 by Peggy Moreland

March 2001
MILLIONAIRE HUSBAND
#1352 by Leanne Banks
Million-Dollar Men

April 2001
GABRIEL'S GIFT
#1357 by Cait London
Freedom Valley

May 2001
THE TEMPTATION OF
RORY MONAHAN
#1363 by Elizabeth Bevarly

June 2001
A LADY FOR LINCOLN CADE
#1369 by BJ James
Men of Belle Terre

MAN OF THE MONTH

For twenty years Silhouette has been giving you the ultimate in romantic reads. Come join the celebration as some of your favorite authors help celebrate our anniversary with the most sensual, emotional love stories ever!

Available at your favorite retail outlet.

Silhouette®

Where love comes alive™

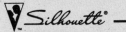

Silhouette ®

where love comes alive—online...

eHARLEQUIN.com

your romantic
books

♥ **Shop online!** Visit Shop eHarlequin and discover a wide selection of new releases and classic favorites at great discounted prices.

♥ **Read our daily and weekly Internet exclusive serials,** and participate in our interactive novel in the reading room.

♥ **Ever dreamed of being a writer?** Enter your chapter for a chance to become a featured author in our Writing Round Robin novel.

• • • • • • •

your romantic
life

♥ **Check out our feature articles** on dating, flirting and other important romance topics and get your daily love dose with tips on how to keep the romance alive every day.

• • • • • •

your
community

♥ **Have a Heart-to-Heart** with other members about the latest books and meet your favorite authors.

♥ **Discuss your romantic dilemma** in the Tales from the Heart message board.

your romantic
escapes

♥ **Learn what the stars have** in store for you with our daily Passionscopes and weekly Erotiscopes.

♥ **Get the latest scoop on** your favorite royals in Royal Romance.

SINTA1

Silhouette®

Desire®

proudly presents the exciting miniseries

MILLION DOLLAR MEN

by bestselling author

LEANNE BANKS

These super-wealthy bachelors form a secret Millionaires' Club to make others' dreams come true...and find the women of *their* dreams in return!

EXPECTING THE BOSS'S BABY—
on sale December 2000

MILLIONAIRE HUSBAND—
on sale March 2001

THE MILLIONAIRE'S SECRET WISH—
on sale June 2001

Available at your favorite retail outlet.

Silhouette®

Where love comes alive™

If you enjoyed what you just read,
then we've got an offer you can't resist!

Take 2
bestselling novels FREE!
Plus get a FREE surprise gift!

Clip this page and mail it to The Best of the Best™

IN U.S.A.	IN CANADA
3010 Walden Ave.	P.O. Box 609
P.O. Box 1867	Fort Erie, Ontario
Buffalo, N.Y. 14240-1867	L2A 5X3

YES! Please send me 2 free Best of the Best™ novels and my free surprise gift. Then send me 4 brand-new novels every month, which I will receive before they're available in stores. In the U.S.A., bill me at the bargain price of $4.24 plus 25¢ delivery per book and applicable sales tax, if any*. In Canada, bill me at the bargain price of $4.74 plus 25¢ delivery per book and applicable taxes**. That's the complete price and a savings of over 15% off the cover prices—what a great deal! I understand that accepting the 2 free books and gift places me under no obligation ever to buy any books. I can always return a shipment and cancel at any time. Even if I never buy another book from The Best of the Best™, the 2 free books and gift are mine to keep forever. So why not take us up on our invitation. You'll be glad you did!

185 MEN C229
385 MEN C23A

Name	(PLEASE PRINT)
Address	Apt.#
City	State/Prov.	Zip/Postal Code

* Terms and prices subject to change without notice. Sales tax applicable in N.Y.
** Canadian residents will be charged applicable provincial taxes and GST.
   All orders subject to approval. Offer limited to one per household.
   ® are registered trademarks of Harlequin Enterprises Limited.

BOB00   ©1998 Harlequin Enterprises Limited

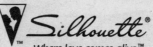